Within the Fetterlock

Within the Fetterlock

Brian Wainwright

Trivium Publishing, LLC

Library of Congress Control Number: 2003114672

ISBN: 0-9722091-1-5

First printing, February 2004

Published by Trivium Publishing LLC
PO Box 1831
Lake Charles, LA 70602
U.S.A.

Web Address: www.triviumpublishing.com

INTRODUCTION AND ACKNOWLEDGEMENTS

My interest in Constance of York, alias Constance Despenser, was awakened by a passing reference in a history book. That led to more years of research than I care to remember, taking in not only Constance and her circle, but also the places where she lived, the local and national politics of the time, and many varied aspects of medieval culture. It is a journey I have greatly enjoyed, and I have Constance and her family to thank for it.

I should like to acknowledge the support, encouragement and advice of many friends during the writing of this novel, especially Gillian Cook, Rania Melhem and Barbara Zuchegna for their special contributions, and Tamara Mazzei my helpful, patient and enthusiastic publisher. I must also include a special word of thanks to my wife, Christine Helen Wainwright, for putting up with the 'other woman' in my life for so long.

PRINCIPAL CHARACTERS (As in 1396)

Medieval English parents were exceptionally conservative when choosing names for their children, especially the boys, but I have deliberately refrained from re-christening anyone, and have tried to differentiate between characters by other means, particularly the use of titles. If in doubt, please refer back to this list. The upper nobility were intensively intermarried at this period, leading to some complexities—for example, Joanne Holland, the King's niece of the half-blood, became the King's aunt by her marriage to the Duke of York.

Royal House of Plantagenet

King Richard II, grandson of King Edward III, and son of Edward, the Black Prince and Joan of Kent.
Isabelle of France, his second wife.

House of Lancaster

John of Gaunt, Duke of Lancaster, eldest surviving uncle of the King.
Katherine Swynford, his third wife, formerly his mistress.
Henry (Harry) of Bolingbroke, Earl of Derby, his eldest and only legitimate son (by his first wife Blanche of Lancaster, the heiress who brought the bulk of the Lancastrian lands to his father).
Elizabeth (Beth) of Lancaster, Countess of Huntingdon, his daughter.
Sir John Beaufort, later Earl of Somerset and Marquis of Dorset. Gaunt's eldest son by Katherine Swynford.
Henry Beaufort, later Bishop of Lincoln and then Bishop of Winchester. Gaunt's second son by Katherine Swynford.

House of York

Edmund of Langley, Duke of York, uncle of the King.
Joanne Holland, his second wife, daughter of the Earl of Kent.
Edward of York, Earl of Rutland, York's elder son. Later Duke of Aumale, eventually second Duke of York.
Constance of York, Lady le Despenser, York's daughter. Married to Thomas le Despenser.
Richard of Conisbrough (Dickon), York's younger son.
(York's children were born to his first wife Isabel, whose sister Constance married John of Gaunt as his second wife.)

House of Gloucester

Thomas of Woodstock, Duke of Gloucester, youngest uncle of the King.
Humphrey of Gloucester, his son.
Anne of Gloucester, his daughter. Later Countess of Stafford.
Isabel of Gloucester, his daughter, a nun of the Minories.
(Gloucester's wife was the sister of Bolingbroke's first wife, Mary de Bohun.)

The Mortimers
Roger Mortimer, Earl of March and Ulster, the King's heir.*
Alianore Holland, his wife, eldest daughter of the Earl of Kent.
Sir Edmund Mortimer, his brother.*
Philippa Mortimer, Countess of Arundel, his sister.*
Sir Thomas Mortimer, his illegitimate uncle.
Hugh Mortimer, Thomas's son. A retainer of the Despensers.
(*Descended through their mother from Lionel, Duke of Clarence, elder brother of John of Gaunt, Edmund of Langley and Thomas of Woodstock.)

The Hollands
Thomas Holland, Earl of Kent, eldest son of the King's mother, Joan of Kent, by her first husband.
Alice, Countess of Kent, his wife. Sister to Richard, Earl of Arundel.
John Holland, Earl of Huntingdon, his brother. Later Duke of Exeter. Married to Elizabeth of Lancaster.
Thomas Holland the younger, his elder son. Later Duke of Surrey.
Edmund Holland (Mun), his younger son. Later Earl of Kent.

The Despensers
Thomas Despenser, Lord le Despenser of Glamorgan and Morgannwg. Later Earl of Gloucester.
Elisabeth de Burghersh, Dowager Lady Despenser, his mother.
Sir Hugh Despenser, his cousin.
Henry Despenser, Bishop of Norwich, his uncle.

The Despenser Affinity & Supporters
Sir Andrew Hake, a Scot in the English allegiance.
Blanche, Lady Bradeston, his wife, of Winterbourne, Gloucestershire.
Sir John Norreys, of Penllyn, Glamorgan.
Sir John Russell of Strensham, Worcestershire, Master of Horse to King Richard II. Married to Thomas Despenser's niece, Margaret Hastings.
Sir John St. John, of Fonmon, Glamorgan.
Agnes St. John, his niece.
Sir William Stradling of St. Donats, Glamorgan.
Hugh Tyldesley, of Tyldesley, Lancashire.

Others
Thomas Beauchamp, Earl of Warwick.
Richard Beauchamp, his son. Later Earl of Warwick.
Sir Thomas Erpingham.
Richard Fitzalan, Earl of Arundel.
Thomas Fitzalan, his son. Later Earl of Arundel.
Thomas Arundel, Archbishop of Canterbury, the Earl of Arundel's brother.

Sir John Golafre, of King Richard's household.
Philippa, his wife, cousin to the Despensers. Formerly Lady Fitzwalter.
Thomas Mowbray, the Earl Marshal.
Owain ap Gruffudd Fychan (Owain Glyn Dwr), esquire, of Wales.
Henry Percy, Earl of Northumberland.
Sir Henry Percy (Hotspur), his son.
Sir Hugh Waterton.

1

The court of England was on the move. It straggled for miles along the frozen, rutted high road like a disordered army in confused retreat. Royal sergeants-at-arms led the main body, clearing the way for their betters. Next marched a hundred of the King's favoured Cheshire Archers, professional soldiers such as England had never seen before, uniformed in scarlet and white, filling the width of the road with their swelling chests. Then rode the kings-at-arms and heralds, bright in their heraldic tabards, clarions resting on their hips.

Following closely was the King himself, Richard of Bordeaux, his handsome, rounded face reddened by the chill, January wind that swept across the wolds. He rode between his uncle, Edmund of Langley, the Duke of York, and his cousin, Harry Bolingbroke, Lancaster's heir. York, on Richard's right, was taciturn, his mind concentrated by the pain rising from his fused vertebrae and arthritic legs into the essential business of keeping his horse in its proper station, half a neck behind the King's. The agony was increasing as the journey progressed, and the Duke sat upright and very stiff in his saddle, his lips set. The King and Bolingbroke had given up trying to draw him into their talk, but their own discussion continued without a break, as if they feared that a minute of silence between them might renew their old antagonism, strip away the thin layers of their laboured friendship. Neither trusted the other out of his sight.

Flanking them were the knights and gentlemen of the King's household, some in full armour, all with Richard's white hart livery badge at their throats. The Master of the Horse led the King's favourite destrier as a symbol of his office. The richly caparisoned animal was an enormously expensive fighting-platform, not a mere means of transport, and would not be required today, or for the foreseeable future. Richard had established peace with France and Scotland, and very rarely chose to take part in tournaments.

Then followed the temporal peers and the bishops, the position of each lord marked by his own stiff banner and the distinctive livery of his discrete retinue. They jostled for place and precedence, each hoping for the summons that would take him forward for half an hour at the King's ear.

After these came the lumbering, wheeled carriages and swaying litters of great ladies, and of the occasional gouty old prelate. And beyond them the sumpter-carts, carrying everything from the King's bed to his greyhounds, from the court prostitutes to the chapel furniture, and trudging with them the lesser servants, clerks, musicians and priests. Next the local gentry and their families, hoping for an audience with the King, or at least a sight of him and the chance to bribe a courtier to convey a petition to his hand. Last of all, like the fish that swim securely in a shark's mouth, a tangle of ordinary travellers and petitioners, defended in so great a company from all the casual hazards of the high road.

***

There was only one topic of conversation in the Duchess of York's carriage, and Constance of York, Lady le Despenser, was heartily sick of it. To escape she closed her eyes and pretended to be asleep. Real sleep was, of course, impossible. The carriage, for all the expensive glory of its gilding, was in essence nothing better than an unsprung cart fitted with a hooped covering of painted canvas. It lurched crazily from one pothole to the next, shuddered over large stones, sometimes seemed to be on the very point of tipping onto its side. Constance alternated between bouncing up and down on her cushions and shuttling sideways between the carriage wall to her right and the shoulders of her immediate neighbour, the Countess of Arundel, to her left.

Such discomforts were nothing new to Constance, who had spent a large proportion of her twenty years trailing around England in court progresses. Her father had always spent at least as much time under his nephew the King's roof as he did under his own, and usually kept his family with him. It was cheaper to live so, and that was important, for the Duke of York's titles were far more impressive than his revenues.

A particularly violent jolt clapped her teeth together, and she hurriedly opened her eyes, convinced that an axle had broken. But the carriage continued its turbulent motion and the other ladies went on with their conversation, oblivious to all else.

'I blame the King,' Lady Arundel said bitterly. 'Even Lancaster, arrogant as he is, would never have dared to do it without Richard's permission. Richard takes pleasure in humiliating us all, that's the root of it.'

Constance contemplated the depth of her dislike for Philippa Arundel. The Countess was close to her in age, one of her endless multitude of cousins, granddaughter to York's long-dead and much elder brother, Lionel of Clarence and a sister of Roger Mortimer, Earl of March, who somehow contrived to be at once heir to the throne and the most self-effacing of men. Lady Arundel resembled him in complexion—like all the Mortimers she was dark to point of swarthiness, a hint of their distant Welsh ancestry—but not at all in manner. Enormously rich in her own right, enjoying a fat jointure as Pembroke's widow as well as generous provision from her present husband; she had far too high a regard for her own high birth and lineage. Arundel's excessive devotion to his young wife was a standing joke at court—he had even gone so far as to rename one of his castles in her honour—but Philippa was no less devoted in her own way. She had even adopted her lord's way of speech—harsh, hectoring and crude.

Constance emphasised a sigh, but her companions ignored her, still engrossed in their outrage.

The carriage had no windows as such, but there was an opening in the canvas next to her that was designed to serve as one. For the present it was covered by a flap that folded down sufficiently to exclude a proportion of the wind. She enlarged the gap with her long fingers, and looked out.

Another of her cousins, Elizabeth of Lancaster, the Countess of Huntingdon, was astride her jennet only a few yards away, more or less in line with the carriage. Elizabeth was revealing a most inappropriate amount of leg, with apparent unconcern. She was engaged in so deep a talk with Sir John Cornwall that from time to time it proved necessary for him to nudge his horse close to her so that he might touch the displayed leg, kiss her hand, or even extend his arm around her waist, as if he had thoughts of plucking her from the saddle.

It was Elizabeth's father rather than Elizabeth herself who was at the centre of the current scandal. John of Gaunt, Duke of Lancaster, King Richard's eldest surviving uncle and most senior adviser, had suddenly ridden off to Lincolnshire and married his mistress. The ladies of the court were infuriated, almost to a woman. Few of them took kindly to the thought of conceding precedence to Katherine Swynford, formerly the governess of the Duke's children, the daughter of one obscure knight and the widow of another. A creature who had spent well over twenty years living with Gaunt in the most shameful and open adultery, the mother of his four grown-up bastards, the Beauforts.

'I have already told York that I shall never receive that wretched paramour, much less give place to her,' said Constance's stepmother. The sixteen-year-old Duchess of York, who had been in a state of sulky rebellion ever since the news had broken, was scarcely profiting from Lady Arundel's counsel. Constance suspected that the Countess's objective in travelling with them had been to stir up as much trouble as possible.

The other passenger in the carriage was Philippa Golafre, a cousin of Constance's husband. Lady Golafre was by some way the eldest of the four, and the least well dressed. Sir John Golafre was neither generous nor indulgent, and his wife's cloak was thin and threadbare, poor protection from the cold.

'My mother says that she has heard of nothing more outrageous in all her days,' she said sympathetically, her long, red-freckled face assuming a suitable expression of concern.

'Certainly, I have never heard, or read, of ladies of our birth and rank anywhere, even in Turkey, let alone in a Christian land, having to defer to a common whore,' Lady Arundel asserted. 'It is the most shameful thing imaginable.'

'Surely,' said Constance, 'it is not *quite* so shameful as some as your own lord's deeds, Countess. For a beginning, not so shameful as to make war upon the King, or to use a treacherous Parliament to murder his friends and steal their property.'

Lady Arundel paused for a moment; it was as if she could not quite believe what she had heard.

'My lord did not act alone,' she pointed out. 'Not by any means. You would do well to remember that, my Lady Despenser.'

'I *do* remember.' Constance had had enough of the Countess's nonsense. Her temper was up and caution was flying to the winds. 'I was a child, but not so much a child as that. I remember them all, the so-called Appellants and their lackeys. I remember what they did. I remember what they *were*. Traitors, thieves and murderers.'

'Constance,' said the Duchess Joanne uncomfortably, 'this is not courteous.'

'Courteous enough, madame, after what has gone before! It may please you to listen to this spiteful bitch all the way to Nottingham, but I have heard quite enough.'

Pushing the canvas curtain aside, she leaned her head out of the carriage and beckoned to the page nearest to them. This happened to be Edmund Holland, Joanne's brother. She could not resist giving him a smile. He was a handsome stripling, bursting out of a Yorkist livery that he had outgrown in all directions a good six months earlier, awkward as a young colt.

'Mun,' she called, 'find me one of my lord's men. Have him bring my horse up for me. I need air. I'll ride with Lady Huntingdon from here.'

Young Holland, looking pleased to be of service, wheeled away. Within minutes he was back with a suitable animal. Instead of wasting time searching the length of the procession for Despenser livery he had simply commandeered one of the Duchess of York's jennets. It was a quieter mount than Constance would have had by choice, but suitable for her purpose.

He remained at hand to help Constance mount up.

'Thank you, Mun,' she said, awarding him another brief smile. She nodded towards the Duchess, a greater courtesy than she felt Joanne deserved, and nudged the horse forward in search of her cousin.

Elizabeth Huntingdon had sent her admirer on his way by the time Constance caught up with her.

'I must be careful,' she explained, 'or word will reach my brother. I've already had one long sermon from him, back at Leicester. He's no liking for John Cornwall. He lives like a stone saint himself, and expects the rest of us to follow his ways. That's what gives him so sour a face.'

'Harry must still be sorrowing over his wife,' Constance suggested.

Elizabeth's snorting laugh was explosive enough to startle her mare, which pricked its ears and sidled awkwardly until a decisive tug on the reins brought it back under control. 'Aye, no doubt. But when he had Mary he was never happier than when he was away from her, fighting in some fool war, trailing to

Jerusalem on pilgrimage, or showing off in tournaments. Even when he was in England he never bided with her longer than it took to fill her belly with another child. He was in Peterborough with the monks, or at Fotheringhay with your family as often as he was in her company. Christ forbid I should ever be burdened with such a man as that. Huntingdon and I fight like cat and dog, but at least he doesn't avoid my bed.'

Constance smiled awkwardly. In Elizabeth's place she would have been more than content to have her bed avoided.

King Richard had two half brothers, the product of his mother's first, undistinguished marriage to Sir Thomas Holland. Huntingdon was the younger of the pair, a reckless, violent man with at least two outright murders to his credit, one of them accompanied by torture. There was no denying that he was a fine jouster, but in all other matters he was thoroughly despicable. It was rumoured that he had raped Elizabeth before their marriage; certainly there had been a scandal, a pregnancy, and a hurried detachment of Elizabeth from her promised husband so that she could marry the father of her child. The elder Holland brother, Kent, Joanne's father, was as dull as ditch water but a much better man.

One of the Cheshire Archers had paused by the side of the road to void his bladder, taking care to soil a newly washed sheet that a cottager had spread over her boundary hedge.

'A stout fellow that,' Lady Huntingdon remarked, her eyes appreciative. 'Small wonder Cousin Richard sleeps sounder in his bed these days, with such men to guard him. Mind you, they're more trouble than they're worth. Everywhere they go they leave grievances behind them.'

'There are always grievances,' Constance objected.

'Yes; but some are more justified than others.'

'Most of the men of Cheshire have no trade but fighting. The King keeps them in livery so that they'll not turn outlaw and plague innocent folk. You know that as well as I do, Beth.'

Her cousin smiled tolerantly. She had a large gap between her front teeth, the mark of a lusty woman. 'I know that you'll hear no word said against Richard,' she sighed.

Constance shrugged, and changed the subject as tactfully as she could, conscious of the ill temper that had made her tongue sharp. Elizabeth had her faults, but she was not malicious, and there was no call for another quarrel.

'How far have we to go?' she asked.

'Too far for comfort, unless your arse is better padded than mine! I was beginning to envy you, out of this wind, sprawled on all those cushions. Mind you, I didn't envy you your company. I didn't like Joanne when she was my niece, and I like her even less now she's my aunt.'

'I'll like her better when she learns some sense.'

'You could have a long wait. None of the Hollands has a grain of it. Huntingdon certainly never had, and he's not improved with age. He'd still ride off a cliff if he were challenged to do it. They're a bad breed, Constance. Sprung up from nowhere like mushrooms. And yes, before you say it, I married one, and of my own choice. I was young, and easily tempted. They've nothing but wax between the ears, but a great deal between the legs. I dare say that's what your father saw in Joanne. That, or her dowry, or both. Console yourself with the thought that at least he had more courtesy than to marry your governess.'

***

Nottingham Castle towered on a rock above the town it had been designed to dominate, its whitewashed, rendered walls visible for miles. The court slid into its nooks and crannies like a snake returning to an old and unsatisfactory skin. By evening, with the Duke of Lancaster and his huge retinue newly-arrived from Lincoln, it was scarcely possible to find a spare tile to stand upon.

The chamber that Constance and her husband had been allocated was displeasingly small, its two narrow windows filled with translucent horn which excluded some of the draughts and much of the natural light, its paved floor worn and uneven. There was a fireplace, newly inserted by the look of it, and a cramped garderobe. Constance pondered on whether such accommodation was an affront to her dignity, whether Thomas Despenser ought to have complained to the Controller of the Household at the first sight of it. Instead he had gone off in search of the Master of the Horse, to ask his advice about a new destrier he had it in mind to buy.

All that could be said for the room was that it was close to her father's modest suite of apartments. So close, indeed, that the Duke could be heard shouting at his young wife, sometimes in the old-fashioned, elaborate Norman-French that he and his generation preferred, sometimes in the plain, abrupt English that came more naturally to her. The Duchess's replies were pitched too softly for them to be discerned, but it was clear that she was making them, and it could be inferred that they were by no means submissive.

Constance frowned, more concerned for her father's loss of dignity than anything else, but did her utmost to ignore the rising sounds of battle, to concentrate on her preparations for the evening. She was conscious of the subtle tang of horse-sweat that still clung to her despite a rapid change of clothing and a thorough application of rose water. A warm bath would have helped, but for the time being that could be no more than a delightful fantasy. There was no hot water to be had, even if the tub and its elaborate tentings could somehow be extracted from its sumpter cart and carried in through the crowds that thronged every stair. It was miracle enough that the bed was set up. At least it gave her somewhere to sit while her damosels, climbing over one another in the limited space, worked on her hair. There were three of them, near to her in age and gentlewomen by birth, companions as well as servants. They had grown up with Constance, always as close as lice, a symbol of her rank.

Agnes St. John, the eldest, completed the dressing by lowering a closely fitted jewelled caul onto Constance's tightly coiled hair, which it completely concealed. The caul was a newish fashion, and Constance was not sure that she favoured it. She carefully studied her reflection in the small, crystal looking glass that Katherine Mallory held up for her. An anonymous court lady stared back, devoid of emotion and individuality, her powdered face, shaven forehead and reddened cheeks and lips almost as daunting a defence as a knight's armour.

'It is unjust, fair Sister!'

Edward of York's voice had a familiar, mocking tone. Constance half-turned in her place, and saw that he was lolling in the entrance to the room, his hand still clutched on the curtain that divided it from the public staircase. He crossed the floor with a few unhurried steps, raised her hand to his lips and kissed it in elaborate and exaggerated homage.

'It is unjust,' he repeated. 'A spoilt brat with the wits of a demented sheep is Duchess of York. The widow of a paltry knight from the darkest ditch of Lincolnshire is Duchess of Lancaster. One of our cousins is Queen of Castile. Another, Queen of Portugal. And what are you?'

Constance raised the area of her face where her eyebrows would have been if fashion had not required her to pluck them out. 'I am the Dame le Despenser,' she said calmly. 'And content to be so.'

'Content? You are the granddaughter of two kings, and the cousin of a third—'

'And I brought my lord nothing save my quarterings,' she reminded him, reaching for the jewel coffer that Maud Mohun was presenting to her, and beginning to rummage through it.

'Your family connections are worth more than any amount of gold. Or they would be to a man who had the intelligence to make proper use of them. Despenser is a fool if he doesn't know that.'

'He's worth ten such as you, Rutland!'

Irritation always made Constance more formal. Two of the tail of richly dressed but penniless parasites her brother kept in his service had been bold enough to follow him into her room. They were already trying out their clumsy seduction techniques on her damosels.

'Perhaps you're right,' Edward conceded. The corners of his mouth twitched, threatening a smile. He was almost exactly three years her elder, their long bones and golden hair a common inheritance from their father. 'If I wanted a lance shattering I could call on no better man than Thomas Despenser to do it. But he lacks judgement. Always has. Forgets who his friends are, and which of them he has most cause to please. It's your duty as a good wife to offer him better counsel.'

Constance selected a ring, and discarded it again. It clinked as it dropped among her other pieces. 'You presume that I have influence.'

His eyes ran over her appraisingly, and the smile widened. 'I know that you do,' he said. 'You should make more use of it. To our common profit. As matters stand, I can't rely on your husband to support me as a brother should.'

'Perhaps that's your fault rather than his. You insist on quarrelling with his friends.'

'I never seek a quarrel.'

'You quarrelled with March.'

'March is in Ireland.'

'And you are content that he stays there, while you go on sharing his wife's bed.'

Edward's eyes flicked towards her damosels. 'Constance—' he began.

'Do you imagine it's a secret?'

He shrugged. 'There's always idle gossip about the court. I didn't think that you were one to repeat it.'

'Gossip? Alianore told me of it with her own mouth.'

'Did she? That was perhaps—unwise. To be so careless of her good name…'

'The fool loves you. You know that?'

The smile broadened again. 'I have my suspicions.'

'Are there not enough whores for your pleasure? There's no honour in leading a lady of noble blood into mortal sin.'

'Who spoke of leading? It was more a matter of following! Since you force me to speak of it, the lady seeks revenge against her husband, and why should she not? From what I can gather he's populated half the Welsh borders with his bastards. Nor is that the worst of his faults. I deem it my knightly duty to comfort her to the limit of my power. Besides, she may be of use to us.'

'To us?'

'To the King's Grace, and those who would see him keep his throne. She knows all March's secrets, or, at least, more of them than she admits. His secrets, and his ambitions. His tendency to dabble in treason with his brother-in-law, Arundel. Come, Sister, this is no surprise to you. You're not a fool. You know as well as I do that Arundel is led firmly by the cock these days, and who guides his charming wife if it's not her brother?'

'March has scarcely the wit to guide his feet to an alehouse.'

'Or so he would have the world believe. He's a great lord, with more lands and revenues than anyone except our uncle of Lancaster. If he were to gather a few powerful supporters around him he'd be more than dangerous. Despenser is his friend; you've said so yourself. Add to that the links between Thomas and Arundel.'

'What links?'

He took a step towards the door. 'Have you forgotten? He was brought up with March in Arundel's household. How else did they become friends? What's more it was Arundel who dubbed Thomas a knight.'

She adjusted the insignia of the Garter that circled her left arm above the elbow. The band of light-blue silk was perfectly placed without her intervention, but the task gave her a moment to think, to compose herself sufficiently to restrain her anger. 'It was a reward for my lord's courage!' she said fiercely. 'A knighthood earned at fifteen years old, fighting the French, is worth more than the one tossed at you as reward for being born the King's cousin.'

He shrugged. 'Yet such things bind men together. Perhaps sufficiently for misunderstandings to arise. There are ways for Thomas to dispel such doubts, and I'm anxious to help him do it. I count him as my brother and I want his friendship. March can do nothing for him, now or in the future. I can do much. Persuade him to see that.'

**

The great hall, lit by so many torches and candles that it was almost as bright as day, was loud with music and the hum of conversation.

Constance, making her way back from one of the overflowing garderobes, had gathered the spare folds of her sideless surcote in the crook of her arm to save it from further punishment. Every time she had allowed it to spread over the floor it had been used as a carpet by uncaring feet, and its train had swept up an assortment of liquid and solid filth that it was better not to analyse.

She glanced around for her damosels, but her mind was still troubled by what Edward had told her. When the girls gathered around her she found herself impatient with their intruding conversation, much of which was centred on the steward of her household, Sir John Norreys, Agnes' betrothed, the shape of his legs, and how well he could, or could not, dance. She retired into the impenetrable fortress of her own thoughts.

Her eyes focused on the far end of the huge room, where King Richard, stiff in cloth-of-gold fabric, burdened with a dazzle of jewellery, was sitting on his throne on the raised dais. A few feet away from him stood her father, drinking persistently from an enamelled goblet, trying to dull his pain with wine, his heavy frame stooped beneath its splendid clothing. Joanne looked tiny beside him, and utterly miserable, defeated, her eyes cast down. Constance was almost tempted to make her way forward to offer her stepmother some encouraging words, but knew there would be no profit for either of them in such a transaction. Besides, she was not at all in the mood for curtseying to Joanne and showing her all the rest of the deference that was mandatory while they were on public display.

Even nearer to Richard was her uncle, Lancaster. John of Gaunt, lord of more than thirty castles, of lands far greater than those of the King, and of wealth beyond measure. He gazed unflinchingly at the lesser mortals around him, self-assured to the point of complacency, an eagle among hawks, buzzards and crows, and stood as close to the throne as it was possible to do without actually sitting on its arm. His new duchess, elegant and fine-boned, was more honoured still. She was sitting next to Richard, placed as though she were the Queen of England, and the King was giving her all his attention, treating her with no less courtesy than would have been due to the greatest princess in Europe.

'Richard has a taste for the low-born,' someone sneered, not far from where Constance was standing. It was Lady Arundel again, posing in her finery, her chin held so high by the weight of her twin-horned headdress so that her natural arrogance was exaggerated. 'I wonder that he does not fetch a common harlot from the stews of Nottingham to share his table and partner him in the dance.'

She was addressing her husband, but her voice was pitched loud enough to travel well beyond him and the little group of friends around them. Arundel did not reprove her for her bold speech, but grunted his sullen agreement. He was in his middle forties, snub-nosed and powerfully built, and wore his customary contemptuous expression, as if he thought that the whole world, apart from himself, had run mad. Not ill-looking in his starkly masculine way, but dressed, shaved and barbered with a studied lack of care, as if he deemed undue attention to such matters to be beneath his manhood.

'As if the stink of these Cheshire peasants he keeps around him is not enough!' he added, gesturing towards the massive soldier guarding the stairs that led up to the King's private apartments.

'It's only a matter of time before Calais is sold to the French,' snorted Arundel's other neighbour. Constance saw it was Thomas Beauchamp, Earl of Warwick. Warwick was older and thinner than Arundel, his face yellow with ill health and marked with battle scars. 'Christ knows, Richard and Lancaster have already given away almost everything else that was ours across the Channel.'

Arundel nodded his agreement. 'And why must Richard marry this French child, this Isabelle of Valois?' he asked rhetorically, his voice a reckless, bellowing roar that might have betokened acute drunkenness in another man. 'I'll tell you why, it's because Lancaster still has hopes of the throne for himself. Why else has he retained half the knights and gentleman in England? For the joy of seeing them in his livery? No. Every month of delay makes it less likely that Richard'll father a son to succeed him. He'll not make old bones, that's for sure. He spends more on doctors' fees and medicines in a year than I have in a lifetime. If he dies, Lancaster will make himself king. Who shall stop him? March? He's young, with little following beyond his own household. Besides, he's in Ireland, and likely to stay there. Gloucester? He may be as much Richard's uncle as Lancaster, but he's neither power nor influence, or there'd be no talk of peace until the French were beaten and forced to terms. York? The thought's enough to make a pig laugh!'

It was certainly enough to amuse Warwick. He added some suitably witty comment of his own, his voice too low for the words to carry.

Constance took a step forward, with the idea of defending her father's name from insult, but they were already moving away, quite unaware of her presence, and before she could follow a firm hand clamped on her wrist.

'Well, Niece,' said a hearty voice, 'do I find you deserted?'

It was Thomas's uncle, Henry Despenser, the Bishop of Norwich. As perhaps befitted a man who had received his appointment from the Pope for services rendered as a mercenary on the battlefields of Italy, there was little about him that was remotely episcopal, his rich, secular clothing and forthright manner suggesting rather that he was a prosperous country knight with a taste for the pleasures of life.

She made him a small curtsey, out of deference to his age and office, and kissed the ring on his extended hand. 'My lord is not far away,' she answered, inclining her head in the direction of Thomas, who was in the midst of the little coterie that had attached itself to him. For the present he was talking to Sir John Montagu, the nephew and heir of the old Earl of Salisbury.

The Bishop's face darkened. 'I dislike his choice of company. I hope he doesn't bring that accursed heretic over here.'

'Heretic?' Constance repeated. 'I know Montagu writes poetry, but I didn't realise there was heresy in it.'

'His poetry is of no account. Merely the usual dross of lust and adultery wrapped in pretty words. It's his other writings that concern me. He's an avowed Lollard; one of the worst. I can forgive ignorant country hinds who wander into error. After all, they're little more than children, easily misled by a lying hedge-priest or a false friar. Montagu's wickedness has no such excuse. He's a man of great learning who understands exactly what it is that he's preaching. He should be sent to the stake as an example to others.'

Constance's mouth tightened. She thought it harsh justice that a man should be burned alive merely for holding foolish notions, but she was reluctant to express her opinion to the Bishop.

He interpreted her expression nevertheless. 'It is better for one man to suffer, here on earth, than for thousands to burn in hell for all eternity because of his false teaching. I wish I could persuade the King to accept my advice but, like you, he is tender-hearted. He says that Montagu is his friend. Well, he may be, but he's not mine, and if he approaches us I shall be forced to leave you. That would be a pity. There's little enough congenial company to be found this evening, and still less among the ladies.'

She nodded. 'There's been some grouching, but it counts for little. Nothing can harm the King as long as he can keep the support of my Uncle Lancaster and my lord father.'

The Bishop frowned. 'That's true enough, as far as it goes. But use your wits, child. Lancaster grows old. Older than his years, and small wonder. He's whored his way through life, may God pardon him. Look at him. There's pain in that face, as well as pride and satisfaction. What will befall, do you think, when he's called from us and his power passes to Harry Bolingbroke?'

Constance's eyes found Bolingbroke in the crowd near the dais. His face revealed little, but she was sure it could not please him that his half-brothers and sister, the Beauforts, were to be legitimated, established as his equals. He was wearing a black velvet houppelande, embroidered with gold, with trailing sleeves that almost reached the floor. She decided that the colour might be significant, and the thought pleased her.

Bolingbroke was chatting quite amiably with her brother, Edward, and with Thomas Mowbray, the Earl Marshal. About his neck was the largest and most richly bejewelled white hart cognizance in the room.

'Cousin Harry pretends to be as loyal as any of us these days,' she answered quietly.

The Bishop snorted. 'Because he must, to please his father. The last time Bolingbroke had freedom of action he proved himself false. Can the leopard change his spots or the Ethiopian his skin? Others may be deceived, but I am not.'

The King had led the Duchess of Lancaster down from the dais, and they were dancing in the space that had opened up to accommodate them, smiling and conversing like lovers.

Constance was still watching Edward's face. There was something in his expression that she did not quite trust, a light of calculation in his eye. It struck her that Bolingbroke might do well to be wary.

'I wonder who is deceiving whom,' she said quietly.

***

Naked except for the linen cap that protected her braided hair, Constance lay awake in her great bed, sorely tired but hopelessly restless. On the floor a few feet away her damosels dreamed on their straw pallets, Maud grunting a conversation in her sleep, Agnes snoring in approximate tune with the hail that was lashing against the shutters. Despenser's duty squire lay across the threshold, wrapped in a blanket, a token protection against intruders.

Next to her Thomas Despenser slept on his side, turned towards her, his breath heavy with wine fumes. He had been very late in bed, and it was his arrival that had disturbed her. He had been with the King. Since his wife's death, it had become Richard's way to keep late hours, withdrawn into his private rooms with a selection of those of his friends who were highest in favour, talking, drinking and gambling with them until well after midnight.

There was no way of knowing the time, and she was not even sure whether she had dozed for a while. The engulfing, chilly darkness was absolute and she could not even see her fingers as they idly traced the shapes of the embroidered cognizances that they had once worked into the curtains. She had been fifteen then, still a maiden in her father's care, and the task had absorbed most of the last autumn and winter she had spent at Fotheringhay. Thomas had been away fighting in Prussia, helping the Teutonic Knights in their endless crusade against the heathens of Lithuania.

She recalled every stitch, every small twist of gold thread. The beasts flinched away from the pressure of her fingertips. The proud griffin of the Despensers. The twin-tailed Burghersh lion that belonged to Thomas's mother, the heiress of her family. Her own mother's Castilian lions and castles. Most prominent of all the falcon and fetterlock of York, the device chosen by her father to symbolise the fact that he and his family were forever shut out from any hope of the crown. The falcon might have ambitions, but it was so tightly confined by the enclosing fetterlock that it could not do so much as spread its wings.

That turned her thoughts to her brother, Edward. He had always dreamed of opening the fetterlock. It was a foolish, impractical dream, yet he had power enough to damage others in pursuit of his folly, and he would drag March down if he could. There was obvious profit for him in such a transaction, for the Mortimer lands were vast, and if they were forfeited for treason he could be sure that a substantial share would come his way. The Countess Alianore would also be his for the taking, if he wanted her, or for the scorning if he did not.

Edward had warned her, in effect, that he would not allow Thomas Despenser to stand in his way. It was her clear duty to pass the warning on, and yet she was wary of doing so, for she could guess her husband's reaction to it. Nothing inflamed him more than a threat; nothing was more likely to turn him into her brother's irreconcilable enemy. She had long dreaded that she would eventually be forced to choose between them, and her policy had always been to postpone the day of decision. No one was more keenly aware than she of her brother's legion of faults, and yet she could not but love him. He had cared for, guided and protected her all through their childhood, and asked nothing in return except for her unquestioning loyalty.

Now he thought he could rule Thomas through her. He was mistaken in that, sorely mistaken. Despenser was no longer the naive young warrior who had come home to her from Prussia, inexperienced in all but fighting. He had been pliable in those days, easy to guide, but now he knew his own mind, and that mind was both surprisingly ambitious and infuriatingly stubborn.

Her restlessness had disturbed Thomas. She first became aware of this when he began to caress her thigh. It began as a gesture of affection, but when he came to realise that she too was awake, it changed into something more persuasive. His mouth closed on hers.

Constance was too weary to enjoy these attentions, but she gave way without fuss. It was a sin to deny her husband without good cause, and a lack of sleep was not one of the exceptions the Church recognised.

Thomas was strong, and she was hardly aware of his weight on top of her as he enjoyed her. It did not take long; certainly not long enough to do more than begin to arouse her. He rested for a moment, then rolled off her; awarded her a final kiss.

'I've agreed a price with Montagu for the horse,' he said unexpectedly. 'Russell says it'd be the next thing to a gift at twice the cost. Far better than anything I could get from the Warwick stud.'

'Your uncle says that Montagu is a heretic,' she told him.

Thomas snorted contemptuously. 'I dare say that his horse's religion will be orthodox enough. Uncle Henry's an idiot. Like my wife, he is all too apt to offer his opinions to the whole world.' He paused for a moment, and continued more gently. 'The Duchess of York said that you gave her and Lady Arundel the rough side of your tongue this afternoon. She bade me mend your manners.'

She sat up sharply in the bed. 'Manners? Joanne should look to her own! And choose better companions for her journeys.'

'I wish I'd been there,' Thomas admitted. 'It would've been an interesting sight, you and Philippa Arundel at each other's throats. I presume you had the best of it, or the Duchess wouldn't have complained. As for my uncle, I can't believe that he used to be accounted a warrior. He's more like a frightened old woman who sees a conspiracy or a heresy in every shadow. He's been troubling your father with all manner of dangerous talk.'

'My father?' Constance repeated, temporarily bemused. She was well able to imagine York's reaction to such an approach. He hated talk of politics at the best of times, and if the Bishop had expressed his suspicions of Bolingbroke it would have made matters worse. Bolingbroke was York's favourite nephew by some way, valued at least as highly as her two brothers.

'Yes. The Duke asked my counsel. Before we left Leicester. What could I say, but admit that my uncle reads so many books that he's half out of his senses?'

'He fears what may happen should any harm come to my Cousin Richard. He's not alone in that. I've heard others say as much.'

'If other people are fools it doesn't mean that we need to join them. Why should any harm come to the King? It's almost treason to imagine that it will. He's barely thirty and the wars with France are over for good. In five years or so Isabelle will be old enough to give him a son, and all will be settled.'

Constance sighed. His words were an unintentional reproach, and brought another and more personal concern to the front of her mind. It was strange that the four swift years that had passed since the consummation of their marriage had produced only the one child, their daughter Bess. Bess was two years old now, secluded in the care of her grandmother at Tewkesbury. Thomas's heiress, at least for the present. He had need of a son to succeed him, and even more so if he won the earldom he coveted. Her mother-in-law was always harping on the subject, as if the cause of the problem was a want of trying.

'Sons are not always so easy to produce,' she said quietly. 'I wish I could give you one. Perhaps a pilgrimage would help. Perhaps there's some fault for which we're being punished.'

Thomas shrugged in the darkness. The hail beat against the shutters with renewed ferocity.

'We'll have sons enough,' he said casually. 'There's plenty of time.'

'How can you be sure of that?'

'How can you be sure that I have not just got you with child?' He seemed amused by the thought.

'Perhaps in the summer,' she persisted.

'Perhaps. But there's work for us in Gloucestershire when we leave the court. The county must learn that I rule there now. I've the King's backing in that—I shall name the next sheriff—but Berkeley has had complete control of the patronage ever since my father died, and he'll not yield it without a struggle.'

Constance took her lower lip between her teeth for a moment. She knew that her part of the task would be to court the ladies of the two counties, to persuade them to accept her social leadership, and to charm as many of their husbands as possible. It was not work that she relished, for she liked few things less than the exchange of empty flattery and meaningless small talk, but it was her duty to help Thomas in every way that she could.

'Then the King will expect us back to attend him to his wedding,' Thomas went on. 'We'll need to purvey new clothes for ourselves and our retinue, and suitable presents for the little Queen. There'll not be much time to idle on pilgrimage.'

'I suppose you're right.' She took a breath and changed the subject. 'Thomas, I would like to know something. How closely are you tied to March, now that he is out of Richard's favour?'

'I still count him my friend, if that's what you mean. Besides, I'm not so sure that he *is* out of favour. Who says that he is?'

'My brother. He said it's because he's grown too friendly with Arundel.'

'That's nonsense! Your dear brother invents these tales because he's trying to turn the King against Roger. I'll not speak ill of a lady, but you know the reason for that as well as I do.'

He turned onto his side, his back to her, to signal an end to the discussion.

'You have heard from him lately?' she persisted.

'From Roger? Only through his men of business. You know that I've a claim to some of his lands, but we're close to a settlement. He's too busy in Ireland to write letters to me about nothing. He's a war on his hands, more or less, in Ulster. Now can we sleep?'

Constance paused for a moment to think over what had been said, but the answer to her next question was nothing more than a grunting snore. The few seconds had given Thomas time enough to escape into the refuge of deep sleep.

She remained awake for a time, frustrated in more ways than one. At last, she curled her knees beneath his buttocks for warmth and comfort, and drifted away into her own world of troubled dreams.

2

The portrait had been brought all the way to the city of York from the other side of the Alps, sealed within a black velvet cloth and carried by a liveried gentleman who wore the serpent cognizance of the Visconti family on his sleeve. It was small and exquisite, as was its subject. It stood on the top of a clothes press, propped up against the wall hangings, concealing part of an Argonaut's woven leg.

Lucia Visconti had been sixteen when Harry Bolingbroke had first seen her. He had been on his way home from his pilgrimage to Jerusalem, an honoured guest of her cousin, the Duke of Milan, who had murdered her father and married her sister. The painting suggested that she had changed but little during the three intervening years.

Harry rubbed his forked auburn beard between his thumb and his index finger, as he often did when in thoughtful mood. He was not sure that his taste ran to slight, dark women, nor to those who offered themselves before they were asked. There had been an embarrassing moment in Milan when Lucia made the extravagant, public declaration that her heart belonged to him and she was ready to wait all her life to marry him, even if she died three days after the wedding. He had been forced to explain that he already had a wife at home in England. Mary de Bohun.

He sighed over the remembrance. Mary had brought him a half share of her family's estates, worth in excess of a thousand pounds a year. The lands were his to retain for life. She had also given him seven children, all of whom had survived except for the eldest, born when Mary was twelve and Harry himself only fourteen. No man could ask more of a wife than that. She had died at twenty-four, quite worn out, about nine months after his return from the Holy Land. It pained him to think of her as she had been in those last weeks, pained him more to realise that he could no longer quite recall the colour of her eyes or the details of her face.

Now Lucia was offered again, this time by her cousin as well as herself. A healthy and beautiful girl who claimed to love him. Her dowry was not specified in detail, but the Duke's emissary had made it clear that his master was prepared to be generous, that eight or nine thousand pounds in gold was not too much to ask.

However, nothing could ever be so simple. It was not enough for King Richard to make peace with the French. Now he sought to appear as France's ally, and there was serious talk in the Council of sending an English expeditionary force to assist the French in their quarrel with Milan. No matter what the financial incentives, any thought of a marriage with Lucia would have to be put aside for the time being, lest it should seem to contradict Richard's policy.

Harry frowned. He could not afford that. His father frequently reminded him that he would be unwise to give even the smallest indication of discontent. He glanced down to the white hart at his throat, the constant symbol of his loyalty, like the collar of livery on a dog. Anything to persuade the world that he was Richard's man.

It was his own fault, of course, that the King distrusted him. Back in 1387, during his father's absence from England, he had joined his uncle, Gloucester, and the rest of the Lords Appellant in their campaign because he had thought Richard ill-advised and in need of better counsel. He had been largely responsible for the defeat of the King's army at Radcot Bridge, but it had never been his intention to harm Richard personally, much less to depose him. He had been young then, nineteen, inexperienced and easily outmanoeuvred by his elders. He and Thomas Mowbray had managed to stop Gloucester from taking the crown for himself, but that had been all the restraint they had been able to apply to their bloodthirsty colleagues.

Richard had never forgiven him. He claimed that he had, of course. Harry had a pardon, with the royal seal hanging from it. There had been other signs of favour too; but not enough of them to deceive him, and for each one a small snub to keep it company. When the King had campaigned in Ireland, Bolingbroke found himself left at home, serving on the Council with the old men and the clerks.

Yet I am the best soldier he has! thought Harry, who was rarely troubled by false modesty.

Below the window two armed knights were locked in friendly combat, fighting afoot with swords on a narrow and muddy patch of grass, part of the garden of St. Mary's Abbey where the King was lodged. The sound of their steel drew his attention, so that he looked out, screwing up his eyes as he sought to focus on them, for he was short of sight. Despite their open basinets Harry found the liveries their followers wore easier to recognise than the details of their faces. One was Thomas Mowbray, the other Thomas Despenser.

Bolingbroke himself had fought Mowbray in sport often enough to know how skilled he was. On horse or off it, with any weapon, the Earl Marshal was equally formidable. Despenser was younger, less experienced, and it was not surprising to see him on the defensive, forced backwards. He was holding his own, though, only slightly out of his depth. Then, with sudden swiftness, he reversed his grip on his sword, so he held its blade in his armoured hand, and thrust the hilt to threaten his opponent's unprotected face. Mowbray took a step backwards to save himself, lost his footing, and went down.

Harry suddenly became aware of a presence beside him, and turned his face towards it.

'My brother Despenser fights well,' Edward of York said in a conversational tone. 'He has the gift for it, and only one weakness.'

Bolingbroke's expression asked for further explanation.

Edward sprawled himself comfortably on the seat next to him. 'If I found myself alone, facing two hundred enemies, I'd run away. If I couldn't do that, I'd yield and offer myself for ransom. Tom would put his back to a wall, or to a tree, and fight. He'd fight all two hundred until he was killed, or until they knocked him senseless.'

'Some might find that admirable in a man, rather than a fault.'

'Some might, Harry. Neither you nor I would be among them.'

Bolingbroke said nothing for the moment. The sparring of the two knights was ended, and they stood together, helmets removed, exchanging friendly banter, their faces glowing with the sweat their exercise had provoked. Mowbray's hand rested amiably on Despenser's arm as if to confirm that there was no resentment for his defeat. The spectators drew closer, now that they were safe from accidental contact with one of the swords. His cousin, Constance, was among them. She picked her way through the mud as gracefully as she could, her clear laugh rising.

He turned away from the window, his throat tightening. When he had fought in the great tournament at St. Ingelvert, he had carried Mary's colours on his lance, and triumphed against the best knights in all Europe. He could still remember the warmth of her pride in his achievement. She had loved him quietly, unobtrusively, content to remain in the background of his life and yet always there when she was needed.

Now he had nothing. A score of houses and castles but no real home. He avoided the places he had shared with Mary because the memories were still too raw. His children were scattered across the country in the care of relatives and retainers because he could scarcely bear to look at them.

He could not even joust as he once had. His eyesight had deteriorated to the point where he had lost some of the essential accuracy. He practised almost as regularly as ever, but he could no longer be quite sure of taking the ring on his lance, or of hitting the quintain with absolute precision. Few were aware of this new weakness, and he was determined that no more should learn of it. He rarely fought in public now, exercising within the privacy of his own household, with men he could trust.

'Perhaps you are right, Cousin,' he said, 'but courage is always a virtue, and caution can so easily be mistaken for cowardice.'

Edward swept a persistent fly from his sleeve. 'No one doubts your courage, but you'd not be fool enough to fight where there was no hope of winning. We are alike in that. So alike that it would be ridiculous for us to quarrel when we could so easily agree an accommodation.'

'An accommodation? Have we need of one?'

'I think so, Harry. For the avoidance of doubt. So that no misunderstandings arise between us to spoil our friendship.'

'What is it you suggest? A bond—an alliance?'

'Nothing so crude. It might be better to call it an agreement to guard each other's interests. A private understanding between the two of us. We are bound by ties of blood and honour that mean more than a blob of heated wax on a strip of parchment.' Edward followed the line of his companion's gaze. 'Unfortunately I don't have a second sister to give you in token of our unity.'

Bolingbroke flinched as if a red-hot iron had brushed against his face. 'I need no such pledge,' he said. 'Your word is enough, or if it's not then all England would be insufficient surety, let alone a woman's body.'

Edward smiled. 'I can offer you something more reassuring than my mere word,' he said disarmingly. 'We have a common enemy, our cousin, Roger of March. Our remote cousin, whom some would like to set in Richard's place. We must not rest, Harry, until he is brought low.'

***

The greyhound Math, almost pure white save for the blue patches around his eyes, lay on his back on the King's great bed, eagerly presenting his pink belly to be stroked. He was the swiftest dog at court, and the most privileged, brought from Ireland by the Earl of Kent as a gift for his half-brother. A valuable gift, and one that was much appreciated.

The King sat next to Math, his hand moving automatically over the animal's thin coat.

Bolingbroke was surprised by the King's apparent calm. Their uncle, the Duke of Gloucester, had been talking for a long time now without saying much that was new. Richard was not usually so patient.

Gloucester paced about as he spoke. He was the youngest of Edward III's legion of children, only eleven years Richard's elder.

'It's one thing to have peace with France,' he said, 'but another to make common cause with them against those who could be our future allies if the war is ever renewed. It demeans us. Makes us little better than hired mercenaries. Vassals of Charles of Valois, a madman who thinks that he's made of glass!'

Richard stirred. He sat a little more upright on the bed. 'I'm no man's vassal,' he said placidly. 'I am the entire emperor of my realm, and owe allegiance only to God.'

'That may be, but you'll need money to pay for this expedition to Milan, and the Commons won't find it. They'll expect to pay less in tax, not more, now that there's peace. I don't blame them. So where will the money come from? Will you use your wife's dowry to fight her father's battles for him? You'd be wiser to pay off some of your debts.'

'Perhaps I would,' Richard agreed amiably. 'After all, your father left me plenty of them. He wasted hundreds of thousands of pounds on his futile dream of conquering France, and no one questioned him. My demands are far more modest. A pittance by comparison, and better spent to our advantage.'

Gloucester could not have looked more outraged if he had been punched in the mouth by one of his own serfs.

'Your grandfather did not count the cost of pursuing his rights in France,' he spluttered. 'He was a king and a great knight, not some grasping merchant. He was driven by honour and glory, not mere profit.'

'As well that he was,' remarked the King, 'since no profit accrued.'

He grinned, and his eyes flickered around the room, inviting the rest of the company to join in his amusement. Huntingdon brayed a coarse laugh, and Sir John Golafre snorted. Sir Edmund Mortimer relaxed his troubled expression sufficiently to display a couple of teeth. Harry Bolingbroke bowed his head almost imperceptibly and wet his lips with the tip of his tongue. Math lashed his long, whip-like tail.

'Your Grace is pleased to forget the glory of Crecy and Poitiers,' the Duke objected. 'King Edward was the greatest sovereign this land has known, and I'm proud that his blood runs in my veins, even if others are less so.'

'That blood is common currency.' Richard snorted. 'Even my clerk shares it.'

Richard Maudelyn stepped out of the shadows at the mention of his office. He bowed low before the King, and then more modestly in the general direction of Gloucester, who pointedly ignored him.

'As for Poitiers,' the King continued, 'that was my father's victory, and forty years ago. How many victories since? Tell me, Uncle. How many?'

'Not as many as there might have been if Your Grace had chosen better counsel.'

'Your counsel, for example? Well, I've always been prepared to give you a hearing—sometimes you've given me little choice—and I've also given you your titles, which is more than my sainted grandsire was prepared to do. Precious little I've had in return.'

'I've supported you in the matter of this peace—'

'Grudgingly, and at a price. My other uncles do not have to be asked for their loyalty. They give it without question. And you wonder why I favour them above you? Be grateful, sir, that you have a pardon for your past misdeeds, because you no longer command here, neither you nor your friends. If I decide to make war upon Milan, then I shall. But perhaps I shall not.' He turned a mischievous smile upon Bolingbroke. 'What did the Duke of Milan have to say in his letter to you, Harry? Do you intend to accept the offer of his cousin's hand in marriage? I hear that you sleep with a painting of her under your pillow.'

Bolingbroke took one step forward, bowing even more deeply than Maudelyn had done, his knee brushing the tiled floor. 'I shall not marry the Lady Lucia without your consent, Sire,' he said, his voice level.

'A wise decision,' Richard said approvingly. 'I'd prefer you to take a French wife. Perhaps you can make a choice when we go to collect the Princess Isabelle from her father. Not that there's any haste. You must show me the painting of your Lucia. I'm told that it's very beautiful. A most generous gift. The Duke of Milan is your friend, of course. Did you not meet him on your travels? You have so many friends and admirers, in so many foreign courts. I've heard he's a tyrant who poisons his enemies. Perhaps it's as well that I have my food tasted.'

'He's eager to be your friend, Sire, as well as mine.'

'And you appear to be eager to be his ambassador,' Richard said. There was a faint chill below his easy smile. 'Unfortunately, our alliance with France is more important, and your marriage can be used to strengthen it.'

Bolingbroke bowed again. Expressionless, he tried to weigh how much threat and how much promise there had been his cousin's words. A little too much of both, he decided. Well, he would not marry at Richard's behest, nor at any man's but his own, and certainly he would not take the French child, Isabelle's younger sister, that Richard had in mind.

The King turned to Edmund Mortimer, the Earl of March's twenty-year-old brother. Sir Edmund had arrived at York the previous evening, direct from Ireland, and had travelled in some haste. One of his eyes was covered with a patch of black velvet, the result of a dispute with the branch of a tree while galloping his horse. The velvet was almost as dark as his straight, shoulder-length hair.

'I have read the letter you brought from your brother,' Richard said. 'His justification does not interest me. He forgets that he is *my* Lieutenant of Ireland. He's there to maintain my peace, not to indulge in petty, personal quarrels.'

Math jumped from the bed with a loud thud; ignoring Gloucester completely he padded over to Bolingbroke and began to sniff around his legs.

Mortimer, distracted for a moment, was slow to offer the defence he had prepared. 'Sire—' he began.

'Do you question that?'

'No, Sire. But—'

'I led an army into Ireland at great cost to end the fighting and establish peace. Not to prepare the ground for my Cousin March to start another war. You will go back to him, Edmund. Is he at Trim? Wherever he is! He's to come to terms at once, and settle the country in peace, without further excuses. Either that, or I shall appoint a new Lieutenant, one who *will* obey me. I've others of my blood who would be glad of the advancement. Men who are perhaps more deserving of it.'

Bolingbroke concentrated on caressing Math's long, sleek back. He was fond of dogs, and it was no coincidence that he had chosen a greyhound as his personal cognizance. Certainly, he preferred Math's company to that of Math's master. He picked a wafer from a plate on the King's desk and slipped it into the animal's eager mouth.

'At least the *dog* doesn't bite,' Huntingdon said to him in an undertone.

Harry did not answer. He had never quite forgiven Huntingdon for debauching his sister, and often found himself fighting his long-held inclination to close his fingers around his corpulent neck.

'None of you begin to understand what I am trying to achieve,' Richard said, overriding the start of a new protest from Gloucester. 'The Great Turk has sworn that he will feed his horse from the altar of St. Peter's in Rome before going on to Paris. Shall we wait until he comes marching up the road from Dover? No. It's our plain duty to unite with France against him. To drive the Turks back beyond Jerusalem.'

Harry shuddered even as he crossed himself at the sacred name of the Holy City. He had once met a seer who had told him that he would die in Jerusalem. He had tempted fate by going there on pilgrimage, and been a little surprised to come home alive.

'We have the finest archers in the world,' the King continued, warming to his theme, 'and the bravest knights, but the French have ten men for every one of ours, and we need them to swell our numbers. Together we shall be invincible. Yet before we can do any of this we must have peace here in England. A settled kingdom, where my word is obeyed. Those who disrupt this realm are not only traitors to me. By delaying God's clear purpose, they also make themselves traitors to Him.'

There would have been more of this if Huntingdon had not had the initiative to announce that his belly was rumbling, and remind his half-brother that it was almost time to prepare for dinner.

'An interesting theory,' remarked Gloucester, as he and Bolingbroke backed from the room. 'Disagree with Richard about the colour of your hose, and you disagree with God. No wonder he thinks that the laws of England are born in his mouth.'

Harry himself had heard the King say as much about the source of laws, but had taken it as no more than a vain, empty assertion. Richard never meant half that he said, especially when he was in a grandiloquent mood. The skill lay in knowing which half to take seriously.

'In my opinion,' his uncle continued, 'it's not only Charles of Valois whose mind has been broken by responsibility. We're led by a lunatic who is incapable of taming the wild Irish, and yet dreams of conquering Jerusalem. It cannot go on.'

'It is only a dream,' Bolingbroke murmured. 'Nothing will come of it.'

'Dreams can be dangerous,' Gloucester retorted.

Harry shrugged. He knew what Gloucester was trying to persuade him to do, but he would not be drawn down that road again.

The Duke turned towards Edmund Mortimer, who had allowed them to go before him from the room out of respect for Gloucester's rank.

'I can't believe that your brother has broken the peace in Ireland for the mere pleasure of it,' he said.

Mortimer shook his head. 'It's a pity the King does not agree with you, Your Grace,' he said evenly. 'Though in all truth I suspect that his mind was made up on the matter before he even opened my brother's letter, and certainly before he read the explanation. It seems that Roger has powerful enemies here; fortunately he also has powerful friends.'

'Of whom I am one,' said Gloucester. 'I should like to know a lot more about what is going on in Ireland, for I'm damned if I can fathom Richard's purpose there. You'll sup with me tonight in my lodgings and we shall talk.'

Mortimer shuffled uncomfortably. 'I am most grateful for the invitation, sir,' he explained, 'but I have much business elsewhere and must be away at dawn.'

The Duke turned an icy stare upon him as if he had uttered an outrageous impertinence. 'It was not an invitation, young man. It was a command,' he said abruptly.

***

Constance stood motionless in her place among the ladies of the court in the abbot's hall as the King presented the Mayor of York with the city's new charter. Richard dominated the great room, his voice, high-pitched and melodic, carrying effortlessly to its most remote corners. He was at his amiable best, as he had cause to be. York had paid generously for the confirmation and extension of its privileges, and, unlike London, had never once questioned his authority or sided with his enemies. He handed over his sword, to be used in future as a symbol of the Mayor's authority, and made it seem the spontaneous gesture it was not.

The ceremony of mutual admiration continued, and although Constance contrived to maintain her pose, her attention began to drift. She felt distinctly queasy, and wanted nothing more than to rush out to the nearest garderobe to part with her breakfast. She blamed the previous evening's herring. She had forced herself to eat it, though the mere aroma of the fish had churned her stomach. Now she suspected that its covering of rich sauce had been designed more to conceal its decay than enhance its flavour.

She put her hand very briefly to her mouth, and swallowed hard, containing the crisis for a little longer. The interminable formality had to end soon. Surely there was little more that could be said about either the city's loyalty and importance or the King's wisdom and generosity.

Constance had begun to weary of the court, to yearn for her own roof, for the opportunity to stay settled in one place for more than a fortnight, and the sight of her daughter. Thomas kept speaking of going home, to Hanley Castle in Worcestershire, or to Cardiff in Glamorgan, or perhaps to beautiful Caversham, just across the Thames from Reading; but he seemed to be in no immediate haste to turn this proposal into action. The truth was that he was contented where he was, surrounded by friends and blessed by the King's favour, free to spend his days hunting, jousting, and discussing the points of fine horses. It was strange to think that it had once taken all her powers of persuasion to bring him within ten miles of the court. When he had first come back from Prussia he had wanted to do no more than live quietly in the country between crusades, devoid of all ambition save his desire to be respected as a knight. It was she who had educated his taste, but he had learned his lesson a little too well for her comfort.

Her eyes rose from the floor, and for an instant met those of Gloucester, who was standing next to the King's chair. He was the only one of Richard's uncles still in attendance. Constance's father and Joanne would be at Fotheringhay by now, for they had left almost before the Easter festivities were over. (She all but wished herself with them, until she remembered Joanne in greater detail.) Lancaster and his Duchess had not even travelled to York, turning back at Pontefract to spend Easter among their own people at Leicester.

Gloucester could have been a handsome man, she decided, if he had ever allowed himself to smile. Even when in a good mood he looked as if he was suffering from a particularly unpleasant toothache, and today he was not so light of manner. The men of York, however rich, however amiable, were not such company as pleased him. Shortly before the ceremony she had heard his loud voice complaining about the undue honour the King was bestowing upon mere provincial riffraff, tradesmen and moneylenders. He had little time for anyone who was not at least an armiger.

There was no denying, though, that Gloucester was popular with many of the knights and squires of England, perhaps even the majority. Those who believed that a renewal of fighting with France was their only hope for advancement or glory especially admired him. The Duke was outwardly reconciled to the King's policy of peace, but many of the warmongers still had high hopes of him, suspected they knew what was really in his heart. It was certain that he did not approve of the King's marriage to Isabelle of Valois; his own daughter, Anne, had been his candidate for Richard's hand.

The ceremony drew unhurriedly to a close. The King stepped down from the dais, and gestured the Mayor in the direction of the inner apartments, where there was wine and scope for informal conversation. The tableau of courtiers began to dissolve, some trailing in the King's wake, others, less

favoured, lingering to entertain the less senior of the guests, others still turning to converse with one another.

Constance cast around for her damosels, but they were lost somewhere in the
tangled crowd. There was no time to search for them, indeed little time for anything but to pick her way through such space as was available for manoeuvre, not
daring to pause. The route to the nearest garderobe was hopelessly blocked, so
she darted for the dark, insignificant entrance to the stair that twisted down to
the abbey garden. The steps were narrow and uneven, not designed for the use of
a court lady in an impractical gown, and certainly not one who was in a hurry. She
staggered, almost lost her footing, all but fell out into the open air. The grass was
damp beneath her thin leather soles, but there was no time to think of that. She
took three long steps and vomited into the bushes.

She staggered uncertainly to a turf seat and, though well aware that it was
damp and likely to stain her gown, all but collapsed onto it, wiping her mouth on
her sleeve for want of anything better. She had still not completely recovered herself when she realised that Edmund Mortimer had followed her into the garden.

She saw his eye-patch at once. 'Edmund!' she cried, forgetting her own discomfort, 'what has befallen you? Are you blinded?'

He grinned at her. 'I've sworn to wear until my lady shows me more kindness,' he explained, raising her hand to his lips.

Constance was used to such currency from Mortimer. Almost exactly her
own age, he had grown up in her father's household and, like most of York's
young esquires and pages, he had made great pretence of loving her, forever
seeking to drink her bath water, kiss her shadow, or steal small articles of her
clothing to wear as tokens. Such trophies had given the boys the justification
they needed to fight one another, but it had all been a game, and understood as
such. Edmund was the only one she had ever suspected of misinterpreting the
rules, of having a true ambition. He had never advanced his touch beyond her
fingers, but even at fifteen she had sensed that the least encouragement would
prompt him to hoist her skirts and throw her on her back. He was all Mortimer,
dark, fierce and unpredictable, and now he was a grown man with a way of
standing a foot closer to her than was suitably respectful.

'You'll soon grow tired of walking into walls,' she said lightly.

'I already am!' he laughed. 'Ah, it's nothing that won't heal. I thought of claiming it as a war wound, but I'll admit to you that I got it three days ago, running
away from outlaws on the road from Chester to Vale Royal. Our Cousin Richard
hasn't yet taken *all* the rogues of Cheshire into his service.'

'There must have been a host of them to make you turn tail.'

He smiled grimly. 'There were enough. Three with swords are no match for
ten or twelve hidden in thick covert and armed with bows. If I ride that way
again, it'll be in harness, with a score of men at my back. Arundel said that the

road was not safe, but Arundel says much that I choose not to hear. I admit he had the right of it this time.'

She nodded, remembering that Arundel had a castle at Holt, not far from Chester; presumably Mortimer had made a diversion in his journey in order to visit his sister.

'I've only just arrived here,' he went on. 'Roger sent me with messages for the King. I've a letter for your husband as well, but I can't get close enough to him to deliver it. He seems to have become a very great lord. Not as I remember him when he came back from Prussia, with a head full of lice and scarcely a shirt fit to be worn in decent company.'

'He lost most of his baggage at sea on the way home,' Constance said defensively.

'And very nearly his life. I know. There was a part of me so envious of his good fortune as to wish him overboard with his goods.'

'Edmund!'

'I'll not deny it was an unworthy thought, and I've more or less repented of it since. He's been a good friend to Roger, one of the few worthy of the name. I owe him my thanks for that at least.'

'There are those who have advised him to make less of the friendship,' she admitted, 'but of course he will not. It's not his way. He'll be pleased to see you, and to have word of your brother. You must sup with us tonight.'

He sighed. 'Would that I could. Gloucester has bidden me to *his* board, and made it clear he will brook no refusal. God knows why. He may be my kinsman, but I doubt whether I've exchanged more than forty words with him in my life.'

Constance frowned. 'I should have thought his reason obvious enough. Your brother is heir to the throne.'

'Is he? I've heard that questioned of late.' He snorted explosively. 'Roger wouldn't be troubled either way, you know, but no one will believe that of him. They think he's like themselves. Like me, if it comes to that. But he isn't. All he wants is to be left in peace. *All*, did I say? A man in his position might as well ask for the moon and the stars, he'd be more likely to get them.'

'He's fortunate to have such a brother as you, who cares for him.'

He shrugged. 'The truth is I can do little enough to help. I've just discovered how insignificant I am. I tried to explain to the King about the troubles that Roger is facing in Ireland, but he'd not heed a word of it. I should have found a way to make him listen, but I didn't dare to open my mouth again. I must own myself a coward.'

Constance shook her head. She knew well that he was no such thing. She recalled to him the occasion at Fotheringhay when he, clad in complete armour, had lowered himself on a rope from the battlements of the highest tower to the courtyard, just to prove he could do it.

He seemed pleased that she remembered the deed. 'A boy's folly,' he said dismissively.

'It took courage, nonetheless. As for Cousin Richard, it may be better to speak to him when he's in a different mood. He changes by the day, and always has. If you stay with the court for a few weeks, the chance will arise. You know that Thomas and I will do what we can to help.'

Mortimer nodded. 'My brother should come home himself, instead of leaving the burden upon others,' he said thoughtfully. 'There was a time when Roger was high in Richard's favour. It could be so again, but not until he's here to speak on his own behalf. I've tried to persuade him to it, but he's obsessed with securing our lands in Ulster. He will not see what that could cost him, though it could be everything he has.'

***

Heavy rain had sweetened the streets of York. Much of the thick compound of excrement and household refuse that covered them had been swilled away down the natural slopes that fed into the river. Here and there the underlying paving could be discerned, and the habitual stink of the city was much reduced, to the point where only the most fastidious of noses remained conscious of it.

The Despensers were lodged in a merchant's house, tucked away in a dark close near to the Minster. It was there, during the following afternoon, that Edmund Mortimer sought them out, to hand over the letter he carried to Thomas.

The three of them sat together at the high table in the cramped little hall of the house and drank spiced ale, Mortimer claiming that he had too great a thirst for it to be settled by French wine. He told them more of the difficulties that faced his brother. The truth was that Roger could not even hold what portion he had of his hereditary lands unless he fought for them, much less restore that rule of all Ulster that was his by right of inheritance.

The letter for Lord Despenser was lengthy and Constance could scarcely restrain her impatience as her husband spread it out on the table before him and began to read. His face suggested there was much in it that pleased him, and yet she could not imagine what good news could emerge from Ireland. Mortimer's detailed description of his reception by the King had only served to add to her unease.

Thomas took her hand. At last he was ready with the explanation. 'You remember my claim to some of March's lands? Roger has agreed to buy out my interest to settle the matter for good. But he suggests something more. A marriage between Bess and his eldest son.'

Constance was speechless with astonishment for a moment. She could not believe the offer, and still less that Thomas could be foolish enough to accept it. Such an agreement would bind him to March's uncertain fortunes almost irretrievably.

'Bess is very young for so firm a commitment to be made,' she suggested.

'Not so much younger than you were when we were married. We're not likely to find a better match for her, my lady. Can you suggest one?'

Constance could have suggested a dozen that were more prudent, but that was not the question. She shook her head, reluctant to be so discourteous as to question her lord's sanity in the presence of a third party.

There was an uneasy silence for a moment. It was Edmund who broke it.

'You have my cousin, Hugh Mortimer, in your service, do you not?' he asked.

'Yes,' nodded Thomas, 'though he's not with us at the moment.'

'Then you know his father? Sir Thomas?'

'A little. He was Arundel's steward when I was in that household—but it was your brother who recommended Hugh to me, and I'm grateful for it. I couldn't ask for a better man of law.'

'But was it ever explained to you why Hugh chose to quit the Mortimer livery and wear yours? Did you never think it strange? Well, the truth is that he and his father could not bear to sit together at the same table. My uncle has great influence over Roger, far more than I have. You might think him nobly born, and not the ditch-gotten bastard that he is. Since we have been in Ireland, his influence has grown even stronger, and the counsel more dangerous.'

'And is this offer made on your uncle's advice?'

'If it is, then it is not to your profit! As you say, he was Arundel's chief steward, and he is still Arundel's friend. It was he who made the marriage between Arundel and my sister Philippa, and carried it through so that neither my brother nor the King knew anything about the matter until it was concluded. Arundel owes him much for that. Her dower lands are almost as valuable as a second earldom. What I did *not* know, until last night, was that my uncle has another important friend. My lord the Duke of Gloucester.'

'The Duke has many friends.'

'Too many,' said Constance sharply. 'He's still a malcontent, and so is Richard Arundel. They'd take up arms again tomorrow if they thought they could win. How can you doubt it?'

Edmund sighed. 'All I can say is that in the short time I've been back in England both Arundel and Gloucester have sat me at their tables and made much of their fondness for the entire Mortimer family, a fondness which I have to say is news to me. My lady is right; they are discontented with the King's rule, and seek to change it. By whatever means. In my opinion, they hope to draw Roger into their fold, and perhaps you with him. Such an alliance of power would be formidable, and others would be quick to join it.'

Thomas shook his head. 'Your brother has his faults, but he would never lend himself to such madness!'

Edmund Mortimer was quiet again for a moment. He took a long, thoughtful draught of his York ale. 'You have more faith in his wisdom than I do,' he said at last.

3

Hanley Castle was hidden in the thickly wooded fringes of Malvern Chase, raised a little above the flood plain to the west of the River Severn. It was not the largest of castles, more hunting lodge than serious fortification, but it was delightfully remote, a pleasant refuge after the crowds and stinks of Nottingham and York. Apart from the castle and its surrounding park, the settlement at Hanley was no more than a hamlet, perhaps a dozen houses, clustered around a small, stone church and a couple of pottery kilns.

It belonged to Elisabeth, Lady Despenser, by right of dower; but Elisabeth had little use for such a place. She rarely stirred from her manor of Tewkesbury, some seven miles down river, where she was close to the abbey that housed her husband's tomb. Almost as soon as her son brought his wife home, and before he had possession of his lands, she had allowed them the use of Hanley for themselves, and when he came into his inheritance the simple loan turned into a formal lease. Her visits since then had been exceptional occasions, and her present one had been quite unexpected. Almost as unexpected as the guests she had brought with her in her barge.

Thomas walked with his mother along the narrow, gravel path that led through the herber into the pleasure ground beyond. His father had had these luxuries laid out beneath the castle walls, one of the many fruits from the profit he had made in the French wars. The herb beds had been neglected for years, and were still slightly ragged and unkempt, but order was slowly returning to them. Constance had surprised him by her interest in such things; but then Constance hated disorder above all else, and could never look at it without trying to mend it. His expression lightened as he thought of his wife, and of the good news she had lately confirmed. Neither of them had any doubt that it would be a son this time, the Duke of York's first grandson. Or at least his first *acknowledged* grandson. Thomas suspected that his brother-in-law Edward might well be responsible for a few of the other kind.

Elisabeth halted abruptly in her tracks, almost as if she had walked into an invisible wall. She was a slender woman of unexceptional height, dressed simply in a woollen gown of good quality but considerable age, its original stark black long faded to a dull charcoal. Her white coif and veilings enclosed her head so thoroughly that only the part of her face between eyebrows and lower lip was visible. Her piercing grey eyes turned upon her son.

'I wish you would explain to me why it is that Warwick has become your enemy. To the point where you go out of your way to threaten him. He was your father's brother-in-arms, and has shown me much kindness. I still count him among my friends. What has he done that makes you hate him so?'

Thomas answered promptly. 'His misrule is tearing Worcestershire apart, and I am the only man with sufficient power to resist him. I have instructions from the King.'

'From the King *and* from his cousin no doubt.'

'My lady has nothing to do with it,' he said impatiently.

'Nothing? Thomas, you have no idea how much you've changed. Has she nothing to do with that either? I do not know why you set such a value on her. She brought you not so much as a single coin, and she has taken her time about giving you a son.'

'I value her because she is a princess of the King's blood, as well as the lady of my heart.'

Elisabeth sniffed significantly. 'Warwick's son has made a more profitable match,' she remarked. Unhurriedly, she moved forward again, the gravel crunching beneath the wooden pattens she wore to protect her thin shoes from the mud.

Richard Beauchamp, the Earl of Warwick's heir, was a fourteen-year-old boy with a nose like a hawk's beak and an habitually solemn expression. His wife, Elizabeth Berkeley, was younger still, a lean, quiet girl with dark eyes and an uneasy smile. They were pacing together a few yards ahead of Thomas and Elisabeth, arm-in-arm and almost in silence, their every gesture a calculated imitation of maturity.

Thomas frowned. 'I wonder that you thought fit to bring them here, my lady mother.'

'He is my godson. Should I have turned him from my door? It's a great pity that *you* could not marry that girl. She will inherit her father's lands, and join them to the Warwick estates. They'll dominate both Gloucestershire and Worcestershire when that day comes. How will you prevent it? Already there is griping against you, talk that you will place outsiders in the Gloucester offices. It's notorious you've few men from these parts in your livery. Scarcely any among your Council.'

'Mother, what would you have me do? When I came into my inheritance most of the men of substance hereabouts looked either to Thomas Berkeley or to Warwick. I had to give my livery to such as would wear it. Lesser men. Men who married into these counties instead of being born here. Men who served me loyally when I was of no account. I'll not discard them just because their betters now deign to come crawling to me for favours.'

'Yet you may need these greater men. They're too powerful to be ignored if you are really to have the rule of Gloucestershire. The King's word alone is not enough, though you seem to think it is. You need the support of the county families, or at least the better part of them.'

'I'm sure that I shall have it. If not, and there are disorders, I'll have a special commission of judges sent down here to sit on the troublemakers. A commission with authority enough to hang Berkeley himself, let alone lesser men. I've only to ask for it.'

'Is it so? You put great faith in the King's favour. What if you lose it?'

'I shall not.'

A burst of laughter drifted to them from the direction of the pleasance. Elisabeth frowned. She was not in the mood for levity, nor for a meeting with those who were out of sight around the corner. There were a surprising number of visitors at Hanley; more, in truth, than Elisabeth liked or thought appropriate. It was almost as if Thomas and his wife were trying to create a small court of their own, largely made up of people who were not worth spit.

She let out a little sigh. She did not like to admit that she was disappointed in her last-born and only surviving son and found him difficult to understand. She had watched him grow into a promising young knight, and done all in her power to aid his development. Somehow, though, he had not grown into the kind of man she had expected. His resemblance to his father, so apparent to the casual eye, was actually quite superficial. Edward Despenser's warm heart had had little interest in local politics, still less in those of the King's court, and he had always been surrounded by friends. True friends, not like the leeches that hung on Thomas. Men were wary of her son, respectful of his power and influence, and they sometimes spoke well of his prowess as a knight, but very few seemed to go so far as to like him.

Elisabeth was convinced that Constance's influence was to blame. She had tried very hard to develop affection for her son's wife, to accept her as a daughter, but could not force herself into such a composition with her conscience. The girl's unsuitable interest in politics was pernicious, even dangerous, and the extent of her rule over Thomas was intolerable.

This matter of Warwick was a good example. It was certainly Constance who had encouraged Thomas to side with John Russell in his quarrel with the Earl. She had also arranged Russell's marriage to Thomas's niece, Margaret Hastings, Elisabeth's own granddaughter, to seal the alliance. Not because she held Russell in particular esteem, or cared about his innocent tenants having their barns put to the torch, but chiefly because Warwick had been one of those responsible for the defeat of her beloved Cousin Richard's army at Radcot Bridge. The King could do no wrong in Constance's eyes, and she had led Thomas to think in the same way.

Russell was one of those gathered in the circle of flatterers around Constance. He stood with one arm draped around his young wife, his twin tufts of white hair sticking out from beneath his tall, blue velvet hat. He was a troublemaker if Elisabeth had ever met one, a born malcontent. She recalled that he had been Warwick's retained man until ambition had led him to defect to the King's livery. That, indeed, was the root of his quarrel with the Earl.

'Perhaps,' she suggested, 'if Constance and I were to go to Lady Warwick, some understanding could be negotiated. It is the business of ladies to make peace, not to encourage disputes.'

Her son grunted. 'I don't doubt that you'd receive fair words; but it would change nothing.'

'It is surely worth the attempt. As an alternative to setting three counties alight, for which the King may not thank you. I don't place as much faith in his friendship as you do, Thomas. In truth, there are but few around you that I would care to trust.'

'I might almost say the same of you, madame,' he said tartly. 'As for my lady, I will not have her subjected to the humiliation of waiting upon Lady Warwick. Indeed, it would be more fitting for Lady Warwick to wait upon *her*.'

'Lady Warwick is much her elder, and a countess.'

'And my lady is the King's cousin. I will not allow it.'

'You mean that *she* will not allow it.'

'I mean exactly what I say.'

'Thomas, I think you should consider more carefully. Do you think it a matter of chance that my godson has come to visit me? It's a gesture, a clear sign that Warwick seeks an accommodation with you. Would it be so difficult to settle your differences?'

'What is Warwick's word worth, Mother? I doubt whether he's even in control of his retainers any more. He seems to give his ragged staff to any rogue who asks for it. John Russell will tell you what they have done to his tenants; of his servants, beaten to a pulp in the streets of Pershore; how he himself has been threatened with death for daring to be so bold as to use the King's highway. I can't even get justice for my own causes in Worcestershire, and lesser men have no hope. How can it be otherwise when Warwick himself is hereditary high sheriff, and his under-sheriff is always the strongest thief in the county? They pack every jury with liars and criminals; intimidate every witness who dares to speak against one of their gang. It's a waste of time and breath trying to negotiate with such men. Only force persuades them.'

Elisabeth frowned with concern; she had forgotten how stubborn her son could be, and had not appreciated how little he was persuaded by her advice. To talk to him of the danger she foresaw for him would only make matters worse. It might even spur him on to greater folly. His father had been like that, too proud to retreat even when it was sensible to do so. Such men were lucky if, like her husband, they survived to die in their beds.

She left him, avoiding any meeting with his obnoxious friends, and withdrew to the chapel for spiritual reinforcement. She knelt for a long time before the small, gilded statue of the Virgin that Edward Despenser had looted from some French *chateau*, but no voice spoke in her ear, nor did the image show its favour (as images sometimes did) by smiling or nodding its head. There was no answer to her prayers.

***

Edmund Mortimer had taken the precaution of bearing one of Despenser's goshawks on his fist. No one thought it at all strange that a gentleman at leisure might want to ride out in pursuit of a little sport, whereas one who merely wanted to be alone with his thoughts might well be considered eccentric. He had no real intention of flying the borrowed bird. However, at the very last minute, just as he was about to steer his horse through the gate, young Richard Beauchamp asked for permission to accompany him, and he felt bound by courtesy to linger long enough for the boy to catch him up.

This meant that the bird had to be flown after all, even though the country was rather more densely wooded than was ideal, and there were too many leaves on the trees for comfort, increasing the chance that the hawk might be lost. It was late in the season for the sport. In a few weeks at most every hawk and falcon would be at moult, and that would be the end of it until autumn.

After a while they entered slightly more open country, along the banks of the great river, and the noise of their approach flushed out a heron. That was far too large and wily a prey for a goshawk. A peregrine falcon at the least was needed, or preferably a cast of two peregrines. Even then there would be a long chase, with no certainty of success at the end of it.

Edmund rode on slowly for about another hundred and fifty paces, then unhooded the hawk and released it. The bird climbed rapidly, taking advantage of the thermal currents in the air. It would wait on, circling, until some more suitable quarry emerged. There was a good chance of taking a coney, if nothing better.

Mortimer's eyes followed the hawk, but his mind was on other matters. He had still not decided whether he ought to return to Ireland, or whether he could serve his brother better by remaining within reach of the court. He had held several further discussions with the King, formal and informal. He had found himself bribing a number of the King's senior clerks to gain the benefit of their advice and good will, and he had also gone before Richard's Council to explain the difficulties that faced the Lieutenant of Ireland. He felt he had made some progress during the long weeks of negotiation and petitioning, and there was talk of a new and more explicit commission for Roger that would give him clear authority to defend his possessions. Yet it was all very fragile, and the King's mistrust remained clear.

Edmund had not found as much relaxation at Hanley Castle as he had expected when he accepted Despenser's invitation to visit. The place was not as tranquil as it seemed on the surface; among the undercurrents were competing factions, just as at court. He himself had been considered worthy of cultivation, most notably by John Russell, who had filled his ears with a litany of complaints about Warwick. The Despensers themselves were friendly enough, and generous hosts, but Thomas was much occupied by the demands of local politics, endlessly pestered by petitioners and complainants, and Constance's company, though undeniably pleasant, was also ultimately frustrating. She was simply not accessible, and he had need of a woman, not merely an icon. He was not a hero in a book of poetry. He knew himself well enough to acknowledge that he would settle for second-best, and gladly. He would even settle for tenth-best, if it would spread its legs for him.

'She's on to something!' cried Richard Beauchamp, pointing.

Startled by this sudden break in a long silence, Edmund focused his attention on the business in hand. The hawk was swooping low over the long grass at the edge of the woods, and as they moved towards it he caught sight of something hurrying towards cover.

'Cock pheasant,' Beauchamp said with an air of satisfaction. 'She's got it!'

The hawk sat on its quarry as they rode up, but when Edmund whistled it obediently returned to his glove and accepted its reward of a small piece of meat. Young Beauchamp dismounted and secured the pheasant, and Mortimer hooded the hawk.

Beauchamp held up the kill. 'Almost worthy of the high table, I think,' he said dismissively. 'Will you fly her again?'

'In a while. After she's rested.'

'You should have brought the austringer to carry her for you.'

'I didn't want to trouble him—he's work enough.'

Beauchamp's eyes hooded for a moment, but he mounted up again, tying the pheasant to his saddle. 'I hear that March is coming home from Ireland,' he said.

It seemed a casual comment, but Edmund reacted with suspicion. 'Who has told you that?'

'Lady Bradeston was talking about it. At mass this morning.'

Mortimer snorted abruptly. 'Chivalry requires us to protect and revere ladies. Not to pay any heed to what they tell us.'

'So it is not true?'

'Did I say that? Certainly he will come home; but it will be in his own time. Lady Bradeston may talk as much as she likes, but she knows no more about it than your hood.'

They rode on for a little way in what Edmund considered to be a very proper silence. They had drawn close enough to the Severn to see the effect of the sun sparkling on the water, and he felt much inclined to enjoy the peaceful beauty of the place. Richard Beauchamp had other ideas.

'There are many who will be pleased to see him back to England,' he said.

'Are there? I can't imagine why. When he does return it will be to look to his own affairs, not to involve himself in other people's quarrels.'

'Not even in the quarrels of Despenser's making?'

Edmund's lips tightened for a moment. 'My brother March and Despenser are in perfect accord. I'd scarcely be here if it were otherwise.'

'You must know that there'd be no disagreement between my father and Despenser if it were not for John Russell. The man is half mad. He blames my father for every cow that strays through a hedge, every quarrel between drunken servants, every cottage that catches alight because the goodwife has not watched her fire.'

'From what I gather Russell is not the only one with grievances. You'll not ask me to believe that Lord Warwick's men are all saints?'

'Of course they are not! But we've no dispute with the Despensers. Lady Elisabeth bore me to the font, and her husband and my father were as close as brothers. It's Russell who has stirred the trouble, and he's the King's man. It may be that what he does is by the King's orders.'

'If that's true Lord Warwick would do well to seek an accommodation before matters grow any worse. But I don't know why you tell me of this. I've no influence over the King, or even over John Russell.'

Young Beauchamp paused for a thoughtful moment. 'Perhaps you've other influence,' he murmured. 'I've heard my father say that the Earl of March is England's only hope.'

Edmund shrugged impatiently, and touched his horse's flanks with his heels to quicken its pace a little. He found the boy's unrelieved seriousness unsettling.

'England is not in so desperate a state as that,' he said.

**

The tub, though disguised by its richly embroidered tentings and cloth lining, was nothing more than an old cask, sawn across and fitted with a crude wooden seat. Every time Constance entered it she was troubled with thoughts of her Cousin Richard's tiled bathroom at Westminster, with its hot and cold water supplied through pipes, or of the still more splendid facility that her Uncle Lancaster enjoyed at Kenilworth. She had tried to persuade Thomas to invest in a similar luxury, but he saw the proposal as a wild extravagance. He had money enough, and more, but he preferred to use it to mount four large guns on the walls of Cardiff Castle to improve its defences.

Constance shuffled on the seat as she became conscious of a splinter that had pierced the protective cloth beneath her buttocks. Those guns were the true extravagance. They would never be fired in anger. How could they be? Peace with France had been established for all time, and the Welsh had not stirred a finger in over a hundred years. Did he suppose that the Turks were likely to arrive in South Wales?

She suppressed the rebellious thought and relaxed as her damosels began to wash her down with scented oils. Katherine Mallory, Maud Mohun and young Mary Russell, Sir John's daughter, did most of the work; Agnes, conscious of her new dignity as Lady Norreys, was more inclined to supervise.

Agnes was newly returned from her husband's principal manor, Penllyn in Glamorgan, and was full of pointed tales of the decrepitude she had found there. John Norreys had not lived at home since childhood, except for the briefest of supervisory visits, and several roofs were on the very point of falling down. Norreys spent so much time on his lord's business, Agnes said accusingly, that he had none left for his own affairs.

Constance pondered on this. Thomas had already made a very substantial contribution to Agnes' dowry, for her father had left her nothing but five pounds and a couple of cheap rings, while her uncle, Sir John St. John, with children of his own to provide for, had not offered more than bare duty required. Still, there was timber enough on the Despenser demesne lands in Glamorgan to rebuild a hundred manors from the ground, and her lord would not begrudge a friend an oak or two, or the labour to cut and shape them. She would have to speak to him about it, for John Norreys would never ask for himself. He was too proud and too honourable to make the most of his position. In that he was exceptional. An honest, reliable steward was as rare as snow in August, and worth a small investment if it served to retain his good will.

'Hake tells me that your ladyship will move to Cardiff before the summer ends. Is it really so?'

The speaker rose from the window-seat, and moved unhurriedly towards Constance, a picture of languid elegance. Blanche Bradeston was one of the Gloucestershire ladies who had deemed it profitable to pay her respects at Hanley Castle. She was dressed more splendidly than either her rank or the occasion required, in a gown of rich, figured emerald silk, as if she anticipated an imminent visit from the King.

'If nothing prevents it.'

'Ah! Then it is not certain?'

'Nothing is certain, but I intend to lie-in there,' Constance said.

'Truly? Your ladyship astonishes me! To lie-in at the edge of the world! Would she not be easier here? When Hake told me, I thought he had misunderstood. He often does, I find.'

Sir Andrew Hake was Blanche's husband, a good-looking but impecunious Scot who had by some doubtful means transferred himself to the English allegiance and the King's livery. (Her previous husband had been a man of greater importance, so she had, of course, retained his name.)

'Glamorgan is my lord's most important holding, and Cardiff its principal castle,' Constance explained. 'Where else should I bear his son?'

'But your ladyship will be so far from the court! I hope that she has not forgotten the small request that we discussed?'

'I have forgotten nothing, Lady Bradeston, I assure you.'

If Norreys was easy enough to accommodate, Blanche Bradeston was less so, for she wanted a place in the new Queen's household. Constance knew that the competition for such a prize would be far fiercer than Blanche realised, especially as some of the appointments were bound to be reserved for the French. She was not altogether confident that her influence was strong enough to assure success, but she had promised to do her best. It was a promise she had every intention of keeping. If it were established that she could place her friends into influential and profitable positions in the Queen's household, it would greatly enhance her own status as patroness of Gloucestershire society.

She spared a moment to consider her tactics. A direct approach to the King would be best, but it was always important to catch Richard in the right frame of mind, and that judgement could only be made on the spot. Unfortunately, the places in Isabelle's household would be long filled by the time she returned to court. The answer might be to put the request in writing, and ask Edward to choose the right moment to deliver it; although the difficulty with that was that he might well want something for his trouble.

Her thoughts were interrupted by her mother-in-law's unexpected arrival in the room.

'I need to speak with you, my daughter,' Elisabeth said in her abrupt fashion. She had brought no attendant with her save for the solitary, elderly gentlewoman who acted as her companion. Despite her wealth and status Elisabeth kept no great state, preferring to devote much of her revenue to the Church.

Constance half stood in the bath for a moment in a gesture of respect for her elder. 'As you will, madame,' she said.

Elisabeth seated herself, and surveyed the room, sparing Blanche Bradeston nothing more than a cold and momentary glance of recognition. She had a low opinion of any woman who married for a second time; such conduct implied too great an interest in matters of the flesh, and not enough concern for the soul. Lady Bradeston, without even the hot blood of youth to excuse her, had gone well beyond that. She had used her wealth to buy a husband she could dominate, which was against nature. And such a husband! Elisabeth barely acknowledged Hake's existence. A courageous enemy could be respected, even honoured, but a renegade was contemptible. Edward Despenser would not have allowed a man of that kind through his gate. Yet both Thomas and Constance treated Sir Andrew as a welcome guest, and frequently encouraged him to play the expensive lute that his wife's money had bought him, and which he carried everywhere, disturbing the peace with his frivolous tunes and lewd songs.

Elisabeth's eyes returned to the bath and its colourful drapery. Her expression was faintly contemptuous. She judged bathing to be a dangerous indulgence of the flesh, an unnecessary luxury, and particularly hazardous for a pregnant woman, who must surely run the risk of drowning her baby in the womb. However, she was so gratified to find herself in reasonable privacy with her son's wife that she kept her opinions on the matter to herself. Instead she explained her proposal that she and Constance should visit the Countess of Warwick.

Constance nodded. 'It's an excellent idea, madame. Such a gesture would put us more clearly in the right, and Warwick more clearly in the wrong, if there is more trouble. But, as I understand you, my lord does not agree. I can't go to Warwick without his permission, much less against his will.'

Elisabeth flicked her hand dismissively. 'Of course you cannot. But I doubt whether his mind is so firmly set against it that you could not persuade him to reconsider.'

Constance shook her head. 'Not when he has already rejected your ladyship's counsel. He'd not heed me. In such a matter I could as soon move this castle as move him.'

'Will you not try? There's no advantage in maintaining a quarrel with our most powerful neighbour when we could have his friendship for the asking.'

Constance rose from her seat, and stepped out of the tub; the damosels, needing no instruction, began to towel her dry, keeping their silence. 'I fear that Warwick's friendship would be of no benefit to us. Quite the reverse. The King has never forgiven him for Radcot Bridge.'

Elisabeth averted her gaze, looking through the open casements to the distant prospect of the Malvern Hills. She found something vaguely disquieting in her daughter-in-law's ample, flaunting nakedness. Thomas was ruled by his lust for that young, white body, a fatal sin that might well lead him to destruction. Her mouth felt suddenly dry. She remembered with shame and regrets her own youth, her heedless sins and fleshy desires, now long banished by fasting, denial and prayer. God demanded repayments of his debts with heavy interest; she had watched helplessly as her other sons died, one by one, some in their cradles, some in the early morning of boyhood, the penalty for her former wickedness. Only Thomas was left to her, and he was in danger because he was too weak to resist a woman's wiles.

'If the King had been more fitted to his office there would have been no Radcot Bridge,' she said bluntly. 'A man such as Warwick does not take up arms against his liege lord without good cause.'

'A man such as Warwick?' Constance repeated disbelievingly. She paused as the damosels eased her into her shift, and then continued, her voice icy. 'A man who sets his brutes to burn houses and beat and murder helpless people, for no better reason than that he has a grudge against their master. By what right does he dare to judge his anointed King? His head would have been on a spike these six years, and others with it, but for the King's mercy.'

'All he seeks now is peace. He's an old man, Constance.'

'As was Sir Simon Burley! Do you remember him, madame? I do. He was kind and harmless. The King's old tutor. His only real fault was that he had lands that my Uncle Gloucester wanted for himself. The Queen begged on her knees for his life, my father pleaded for him in Parliament, and all they had in return were foul insults and threats to their own lives. The charges against Burley were enough to make a cat laugh, everyone knew that he was innocent, but they still butchered him. Where was your precious Warwick then? Did he offer mercy? Where was he when they murdered his own cousin, Beauchamp of Holt? Another old man, but one who dared be so bold as to be loyal to his King. Splendour of God, you expect *me* to speak for Warwick! I'll not stir my smallest finger for him or any other traitor.'

'You would sooner see your husband dead,' said Elisabeth. Her voice was low, almost to the point of being inaudible. 'You fool, do you not see? It's not Warwick I seek to protect. It's Thomas!'

***

Constance sat her horse at the very edge of the park, beneath the shade of a great oak and close to the ditch and palings that kept the deer from escaping into the freedom of Malvern Chase. The castle poked its towers through the trees in the distance, the Despenser colours on its highest point scarcely stirred by the breeze. The wall walks were manned by archers, the gates and drawbridges guarded by liveried soldiers armed with bills, and outside, next to the tilt yard, a small village of pavilions had been erected to house those retainers who could not be crammed into the castle. Nor was that the end of the defensive measures. There were more archers protecting John Russell's manor at Strensham, and others still guarding the bridges at Upton and Defford.

The presence of large numbers of idle, armed men was already stirring trouble. John Norreys had more than once been conscripted to soothe disputes over stolen chickens and straying daughters, leaving her to manage the household without his aid. That was no sinecure, with so many extra mouths to feed and supplies uncertain. Outlaws from the Forest of Dean were plaguing the barges that came up the Severn from Gloucester and Bristol, and her stocks had grown depleted as a result, particularly fish and wine. They were struggling to brew enough ale to meet demand, and although there was plenty of cider available it was a somewhat dangerous substitute in the circumstances, especially when given to those not familiar with its lethal strength.

Two weeks had gone by since Elisabeth had stormed out of the castle, taking the young Beauchamps with her back to Tewkesbury. Yet still Warwick had made no hostile move against the Despensers, and the relentless persecution of John Russell and his tenants had come to an abrupt end. The Earl's followers in the two counties, if not exactly lying low, were certainly not offering any provocation. The peace was uneasy, but it was holding, and it had been brought about by nothing more than an elaborate show of force.

Constance was somewhat puzzled by this turn of events. Warwick was a proud man, a warrior, and she had not expected him to draw back so comprehensively from the threat of conflict. Perhaps he was shrewd enough to realise that Thomas had the King's authority behind him, with all that that implied. Or perhaps it was simply that he was waiting upon events. So many soldiers could not be kept in idleness forever. Her household accounts were already dominated by the cost of their food, drink and wages, and eventually the majority of them would have to be sent home.

Sir John Golafre, newly arrived at Hanley with his wife, Philippa, had brought another explanation with him. It seemed that Thomas Mowbray, the Earl Marshal had brought a suit against Warwick to the court of King's Bench, laying claim to the lordship of Gower. Gower, which bordered on Glamorgan to the west, had been disputed between the Mowbray and Beauchamp families for almost seventy-five years, but the Beauchamps had never been so far removed from royal favour as they were now, and Thomas Mowbray, traitor though he had been in his youth, was now very much Richard's friend.

Although the verdict would not be known for many months, the case would give Warwick something to think about other than his petty quarrels in Worcestershire. Gower was his single most valuable property, providing him with at least a quarter of his income. From what Golafre said, the judges already knew the King's mind on the matter and Warwick had every reason for apprehension.

Such a loss of money and prestige might even be sufficient to drive Warwick to revolt, Constance thought. It occurred to her that perhaps that was the intention, to provide the excuse the King needed to destroy one of his old enemies.

She nudged the jennet into a quarter turn, and headed back towards the rest of the company. John Norreys had arranged for food and drink to be brought out of the castle so that they could dine in the shade of the trees, a rare escape from ceremony. Though, in truth, there was still ceremony enough, with white cloths laid out on the ground, plenty of gold plate and crystal on display, and a good dozen liveried esquires, yeomen and pages to act as waiters. The honour of the household demanded that guests should be suitably impressed.

It was Edmund Mortimer who stepped forward to help her down.

'This reminds me of Fotheringhay,' he said quietly.

She nodded. There had been many long days such as this in the park at home; it was her father's favourite form of hospitality, and even those who wanted to talk about business or politics were often forced to do so while standing on grass. *Home?* She checked herself sharply. Fotheringhay was no longer her home, and never would be again. This was home now, this or Cardiff or Caversham, or one of Thomas's other manors.

'It's a long time since we were there,' she answered. 'The world is different.'

'Very different. It's strange to think of Joanne Holland in your mother's place. I never knew my own mother, you know. The Duchess was the nearest I ever had to one. I pray for her often. She was a good woman.'

Constance smiled in courteous agreement, though she judged the assessment generous. Such love as she herself had known in her childhood had come from her father, her brothers, and her cousin the King. Isabel of Castile, always a lover of male company in all its forms, had made little secret of her preference for her sons, particularly her last-born, Richard of Conisbrough. Dickon, as the family knew him, was eleven years old now, and lately attached to the Despenser household as page because Joanne did not want him under her feet. He was among those waiting to serve the food, a slight, solemn, unobtrusive boy who did not resemble his siblings in the least.

Constance could not help but worry a little about Dickon, another responsibility thrust upon her. He was too quiet for his age and gender, far too obedient. So far neither she nor Thomas had had to do so much as reiterate an instruction. It was not natural.

Edmund was talking again, explaining something about the need for him to travel to Usk to see his sister-in-law, Alianore, the Countess of March.

'But before I go,' he went on, 'there is something I must ask you. Do you think it possible that I might find your brother there?'

She was momentarily startled. 'Edward? Why should he be?'

'My sister writes that he is. That he has put it about that he has gone to St. David's on pilgrimage, but that the truth is otherwise.'

Constance assumed the sister in question was the Countess of Arundel. A man wearing Arundel livery had called briefly at the castle the previous afternoon, bearing a letter for Edmund.

'I've not heard from Ned in weeks,' she admitted. 'He was at Easthampsted, with Cousin Richard, and as far as I know he's still with the court.'

Breath escaped through Edmund's teeth. 'Then you know less than I do. I don't blame Alianore, you understand. Roger's never shown any interest in her, and they've always been happier apart. My sister makes no allowance for that. She never did like Alianore. She babbled about it at Holt, but I thought it was just that. Spite and babble.'

'What does she suggest you do about it?'

He looked awkward for a moment. 'She seems to think I'm likely to catch them in bed together. Or at least that they'll be the common talk of the town of Usk. She says Roger must be told, and that I must do the telling, since he'll not believe *her*. She seems to think it will bring him back from Ireland. To kill your brother and shut Alianore in a convent. *After* he's beaten her senseless, of course.'

Constance became aware of Philippa Golafre's speculative gaze upon them, and began to move towards her other guests.

'It is—difficult,' she ventured.

'Difficult? Bones of Christ!' For a moment Mortimer's impatience and frustration broke through the walls of courtesy. 'I think it's more than bloody difficult!'

'What will you do?'

'What can I do? Hope and pray that he isn't there, I suppose. Hearsay is one thing; it's another to see it with my own eyes.'

Constance nodded. 'Then perhaps you'd be better not to go to Usk. Not yet at least.'

He shrugged. 'As I said, I can't find it in myself to blame Alianore; but I wish she'd chosen someone less dangerous. Not her husband's worst enemy. I thought she had more sense.'

'Love rarely has much to do with sense.'

'You think it love?'

'On her side at least. I'll not vouch for my brother.'

Andrew Hake had begun to improvise a tune on his lute, and now he began to add the words of a song, his voice deeper than seemed to fit his spare frame. The lyrics drifted over to them.

> *Your womanly beauty delicious*
> *Hath me all bent unto its chain;*
> *But grant to me your love gracious*
> *My heart will melt as snow in rain.*
>
> *And though ye be of high renown,*
> *Let mercy rule your heart so free;*
> *From you lady, this is my boon,*
> *To grant me grace in some degree.*

The words were Edward's, written a year or so earlier for some woman he had hungered for, perhaps even for Alianore. Constance recognised them at once, and it seemed that Edmund Mortimer did as well, for she felt him flinch.

'It'd not be right for me to stay here much longer,' he said.

'We're moving to Cardiff soon. Usk is on the way. Come with us.'

'I'm not sure I should.'

'I'll send a harbinger ahead of us. Alianore will have plenty of warning.'

She dismissed the matter from her mind. Thomas was talking to John Golafre, or at least exchanging an occasional grunt. Golafre was tall, and very lean save for his potbelly. He dressed like a man of twenty, regardless of how ridiculous it made him look, his gown cut absurdly short to emphasise his legs and his bulging manhood, his sleeves trailing in the dust.

Thomas did not much like his cousin's husband, and it showed on his face, almost to the point of contempt. Constance did not care for Golafre herself, but he had influence, and could prove useful to them. There was little sense in alienating him. She moved swiftly towards them, rested her hand affectionately on her husband's arm, and gave Golafre an apologetic smile before reminding Thomas that their guests were growing hungry.

∗∗∗

Dame Golafre had Bess perched on her knee, firmly held as the carriage jolted along the twisting, rutted road. For several minutes they had been quite absorbed in each other.

'She is such a lovely child,' Philippa said at length, 'and growing quickly. You must be very proud of her.'

Constance glanced briefly in the direction of her travelling-companion. Philippa had powdered her face so thoroughly that her extensive freckles were almost hidden; but not quite sufficiently to disguise her blackened eye and slightly swollen upper lip. The unfortunate woman had a way of walking into doors, or so she claimed.

'The child is well enough,' she agreed.

'It's her fortune that she favours you rather than Cousin Thomas. Not that there's anything wrong with Tom, of course. But he's very much a man; his looks wouldn't sit well on a girl.'

Constance weighed the comment for a moment, then nodded dismissively and looked out, attempting to judge the time by the position of the sun. They had paused at Monmouth Castle to give the horses some respite, and to ease and feed themselves, taking advantage of the hospitality of Harry Bolingbroke's Constable. (Bolingbroke himself was elsewhere.) It was hot enough to put most of the party in the mood for a second quart of ale, and quell any haste to set off again in the full heat of the June day. By the time they were out of the town and beyond the fortified bridge over the Monnow the afternoon was half gone.

They were still a good three hours away from Usk even if they maintained their present pace, roughly equivalent to a moderate walk. The deeper into Wales the sketchier the roads and the steeper the ascents. They would certainly not be in time to eat supper at the normal, civilised hour of five in the afternoon. It would have to be a rere-supper, however much that inconvenienced the Countess of March and her household.

Constance's carriage was smaller and less grand than the Duchess of York's, but it was every bit as uncomfortable. However it was undeniably the sensible way to travel while she was pregnant, and as the unrelenting climb continued she could only watch with envy as Thomas, John Golafre and Edmund Mortimer took advantage of the freedom their horses gave them. They were following a narrow track, some twenty feet above the main road, on the pretext that it gave them a better vantage of the way ahead, though in truth it did nothing more than remove them above the haze of rising dust and small, irritating flies. From time to time they added to her discontent by pausing to wave at her from the ridge.

John Golafre had interests in Oxfordshire that he hoped Thomas would help him to advance, as well as a yearning to join Lord Despenser's council, or at least to collect the rich fees that would flow from such an appointment. That was presumably his reason for joining them on this journey, and for making it clear that he intended to leave his wife in Constance's care once they reached Cardiff. He himself was expected back at court, and had pointedly suggested that Thomas might do well to accompany him.

As for Edmund Mortimer, he had scarcely spoken to her on the whole journey from Hanley Castle. It was as if she had done something to offend him, though she was at a loss to imagine what it might be. She wondered if he knew of and resented her persistent attempts to persuade Thomas not to agree to March's proposals for Bess. But that made little sense. At York Edmund had made it clear enough that he shared her misgivings.

Her efforts had borne some fruit. Thomas still favoured the idea, but he had conceded that it could be put on one side for a time, at least until March returned to England. He had also agreed to seek her father's advice on the matter. Constance had little enough faith in the Duke of York's counsel, but he was usually cautious, and she suspected that he would incline towards delay. That was better than nothing.

'All I ever wanted was a child,' Philippa went on. 'I was very young when I married my first husband, and he was quite old, and always away, fighting. His wounds killed him in the end, you know. So it wasn't a surprise that nothing happened. Then my mother made me marry Sir John. Well, I suppose I *could* have refused, but I was still in awe of her, and she talked me into it. The one thing I liked about Sir John was that he wanted children—the more the merrier. As matters stand his nephew will inherit all, and he hates young Jack, even though they're alike enough to be brothers. That's why he thinks me so useless. I *am* useless, really. It's not that I haven't tried to do something about it. I've prayed and prayed, until my knees ached. Four years ago I walked barefoot from Norwich to Walsingham, and made ever so large an offering to Our Blessed Lady. But it did no good. I've given up hoping now. I tell myself that there are other things in life, that God must have some other purpose for me. But it still hurts when I let my mind dwell on it. Sometimes it feels as if I've been cut open, and a part of me ripped out.'

'Perhaps there's still time,' Constance said consolingly. She often felt the need to console Philippa, and that was how Lady Golafre had come by the gown she was wearing. It was a good three years old, and its dark crimson did not really sit well with its new owner's colouring, but it was far better than anything else she possessed, and had scarcely been off her back since its donation.

Philippa laughed, just for an instant. 'I'm close to thirty,' she pointed out, 'and I've never had cause to hope for a single day. I don't deny that miracles are possible, but they are rare. At least I've kept my figure.'

Constance nodded. That at least was true. Lady Golafre was as slender as any young girl, and the bone structure of her face was all but perfect. A decent gown had helped. All she needed now was a respectable surcote and cloak, a few more trinkets, and a kinder husband. She considered whether a discreet word in John Golafre's ear would be helpful, or more likely to make matters worse. He was not the sort who took counsel easily, still less when it came from a woman. Certainly he was not advancing his cause with Thomas by abusing Thomas's cousin, and if he possessed any subtlety at all he must surely have noticed the distinct chill in Despenser's hospitality.

'Sir John says that I may stay with you until after your lying-in,' Philippa went on. 'After all, Connie, you should have some member of the family with you, since Elisabeth will not trouble herself. Tom tells me that Cardiff is beautiful—I look forward to seeing it. I've never been to Wales before. According to Sir John the Welsh are barelegged savages. Is it really so? Edmund Mortimer's servant is Welsh, and he seems a proper man.'

It took Constance a moment to recover from the abbreviation of her name. Then she had to think about Glamorgan. She had been there before, of course, but the truth was that she knew little of it beyond the inside of its castles. The gentlefolk, English and Welsh, seemed much alike to her. They all wore clothes that were fifty years out of fashion, and spoke with a similar accent, whether in English or French. Even their names did not distinguish them, for there was intermarriage between the races, and even the pure-bred English sometimes called their children Morgan or Gwenllian. The ordinary people she did not know at all save as anonymous faces in a crowd.

'Edmund Mortimer speaks the language,' said Philippa. 'Did you know that? I heard him talking to his man in it. Though the man speaks perfectly good English. Perhaps it's a way of keeping secrets. I think Sir Edmund has a few of those. He's a strange man. He broods. Have you not noticed?'

'He has his brother's troubles on his shoulders as well as his own. Enough to give any man cause to brood. And if Edmund speaks Welsh to his servant it will be out of kindness rather than for any other cause. I've known him for years, and he has a generous heart.'

Philippa snorted her deprecation. 'I still think it strange. I can't imagine my cousin Tom talking in Welsh to accommodate some peasant's feelings!'

'Some of our people understand nothing else.'

'Or so they claim, eh? A good way to avoid answering questions when you're caught with a couple of stolen conies at your belt! If there's one thing I know about it's the tricks of lazy serfs. My Fitzwalter manors are full of them. Not even Sir John can make them pay what they should, and no one could accuse *him* of being an easy master.'

'I'm surprised that he has agreed to leave you at Cardiff for so many months. Does he not want you with him when he goes to France for the King's wedding? I've no choice, but it seems hard that you should miss so great a ceremony for my sake.'

Philippa considered that for a few moments. 'Sir John wouldn't take me to France in any event,' she said at last. 'He'd begrudge the cost of my clothing, of a jewel or two to wear at my throat. I'd sooner be with you than left alone at home.'

***

Alianore, the Countess of March rode out to meet her guests a mile from the gates of Usk, which was a very great courtesy on her part, for her rank more than entitled her to wait in her solar for them to arrive or, at the very utmost, to greet them on the courtyard steps. Though no soft-featured beauty like her sister the Duchess of York, she was still a very handsome young woman.

'Roger's letter reached me,' she said, treating her guests to an engaging smile, 'but I grew weary of waiting for Edmund to follow it. I began to wonder whether you were keeping him at Hanley against his will.'

Edmund shrugged. 'There seemed no sense in making a journey alone when I could have the benefit of good company. The last time I made haste it almost cost me an eye.'

Constance was already preparing to descend from her carriage.

'Do not stir from there!' Lady March cried, dismounting from her horse so swiftly that her esquire scarcely had time to hold her stirrup. 'If one of your women will make way for me, I shall travel with you back to Usk.'

'I think I can manage the horse,' Philippa volunteered, 'though I'd prefer it to be led. Sir John says I am not a good rider, and the road looks steep.'

She passed Bess over to Agnes Norreys, who promptly lifted the child over to her nurse at the back of the carriage.

The Earl of Kent had a favourite castle no more than a day's comfortable ride from Fotheringhay, and he and York, united by a common interest in hawking and hunting, had always made good use of each other's parks for their sport. Their families had been apt to keep close company, both at court and in the country. So Constance had known Kent's eldest daughters, Alianore and Joanne, for many years; long before Joanne's marriage to the Duke of York.

'I'm glad you're here at last,' Alianore said when she had settled into the space that Philippa had vacated. 'Now I can start negotiations with Thomas, and you can see my Eddie, what a fine boy he has become.'

'Negotiations?'

'Roger's letter gave me authority to begin them. Did you not know?'

The carriage lurched forward, giving Constance some cover for her discomposure.

'No. I thought it would have to wait until your husband came home.'

'And so it will, I expect, as far as the final agreement is concerned; but we can make much progress.'

'They are both very young, Alianore. I see no need for any haste.'

The Countess snorted. 'You begin to sound like Edmund! Of course, that should not surprise me. You've always admired each other. He more than admires, I think. For my part I should like matters settled. If Thomas will only give up the claim he has to some of the Mortimer lands, we'll be more than glad to balance that by accepting a very small dowry with Bess, little more than a token. It would settle our families in friendship for another generation.'

That, Constance had to concede, would be an achievement. There was a history of bad blood between the Mortimers and the Despensers, almost into living memory. The first Earl of March, lover of Queen Isabella, Constance's great-grandmother, had arranged for Thomas's great-grandfather to be hanged from a forty-foot gibbet. There had been other, earlier clashes, back to the days of King John.

'Much can happen before they grow up,' she said.

'Nothing can be binding, of course, while they are so young. But I thought you would be more pleased.'

'Whether I am pleased or not is of no force. Thomas will make the final decision.'

'Not without consulting you, I think.'

Constance was forced to admit that was true. The trouble was Alianore seemed to expect that she would give her automatic support to the match, when all her instincts were to reject it.

'Have you spoken of this to Ned?' she asked.

'No. Why should I?'

'Secrets have a way of being exchanged in bed.'

Lady March flushed. She had the kind of complexion that reddened very easily, and more conscience than she would ever have admitted. 'You know, then, that he is at Usk?' she asked.

'Do you mean that he is here, *now*?'

'Yes. But it's only by chance. He's on pilgrimage to St. David's.'

'Oh, *Alianore*! I don't believe you, and neither will anyone else. Why do you think I was so careful to send word ahead of our coming? Thomas will keep his tongue still, but Edmund has a duty to his brother. He's not a fool, you know. What will he tell March? You should take more care. At least try to be discreet.'

Alianore's lip quivered. 'I've not seen him for months. Do you blame me for taking the one chance that's offered?'

'It's not a matter of blame. I'm not your confessor. As your friend I do but fear for you. I love my brother, but I know he can never be trusted, and in some matters less than in others. Be careful that you do not tell him too much. Especially about this matter of our children. He'd move heaven and earth to block such a marriage; there's nothing he wants less than for Thomas to grow any closer to Roger. It'd please him better if he could find some way to set them at odds.'

Lady March paused, a fractional hesitation. 'Then I'll keep the secret from him. Though I think you misjudge him.'

'It might also be better to hold back from breaking the matter to Thomas, at least until there are fewer people about to hear. It would be safer so.'

'Perhaps you could speak of it to him. When you are private.'

Constance nodded thoughtfully. She had no intention of doing any such thing.

4

Lady March stood by the oriel window of her chamber and watched as the summer storm blasted across the hills that rose above Usk. The virtual darkness of the room and the muttering discomfort of her women contrasted with the vivid flashes that lit the peaks and the drumming of the teeming rain against the roofs and walls of the castle. The Despensers had arrived just in time. Another five minutes of delay and the whole party would have been soaked to the skin, and not merely the struggling squires and yeomen of both liveries, squelching their ways around the courtyard as they led horses and dogs in one direction, carried baggage in another, and manhandled carts and carriages into shelter.

She had learned to love the fierce beauty of Wales and to prefer Usk to her lord's other great castles. To remote Wigmore in particular, since it was there that March kept his favourite mistress and her train of bastards. Alianore knew little of this creature save that she was Welsh and the sister of a bard, a relationship sufficient to qualify her as a gentlewoman in the eyes of her own people.

Roger had other women as well, of course. Doubtless there was one in Ireland. He was generous with them, open-handed, as he was with all his companions. As he was, indeed, with every friar that found his way into his path, with every beggar he passed in the street. Even with Alianore herself, as far as money was concerned. Nothing that gold would buy was denied her; but she could not be bought so easily as his whores.

She started as Edmund Mortimer's polite cough announced his arrival in the room. He was still wearing his travelling clothes, and in the limited light bore a closer resemblance to her husband than she found pleasing.

'I've never seen such a storm!' she said awkwardly.

'I find that hard to believe,' he said, bowing over her extended hand. 'You've lived enough years in Wales to have seen as much and worse before now, Alianore.'

She nodded briefly. 'I'm glad that you're here, Edmund. You're welcome to stay for as long as you wish. I can't tell you how lonely I've been.'

'Lonely?' Edmund repeated, as a peal of thunder crashed around them, loud as any siege gun. 'That's not what's said of you.'

She flinched. 'Then what is said?'

'Enough. More than enough. Of you and Edward of York. More than I truly believed until I came here and found him standing in your solar as if he owned the castle. As if he owned you! You must see it's dangerous, for you and for your children. Would you have it said that they are *his*?'

'I only wish they were!' The words burst from her, filled with bitterness. 'I can't bear the thought of the nights spent in Roger's bed, conceiving the four of them! It's even worse now that I know what it is to have a man's love. To have a man who doesn't think it necessary to get drunk first!'

She turned back to the window. The cool, damp, fresh air was sweeping in, relieving the stifling heat of the day.

He advanced until he stood next to her. 'I'm your friend in this,' he said quietly, 'for you know you're dearer to me than the sisters of my blood. Besides, I understand what it is to love; to love a woman more than my own soul, and to have no hope, no hope *at all* of winning her. But you *must* give him up, for your own sake. He's worse for you than any poison. There are other men in the world.'

'Other men? As there are other women for you?'

He nodded abruptly, troubled by the thought of the girl he had had at Hanley. She was one who had driven a flock of geese to the castle kitchens, flaxen-haired, rounded, earthy and very willing. She had been mortally offended when he had offered payment, but had taken his coin in the end, persuaded that it was but a gift. The more he reflected on it the more squalid the transaction appeared, a momentary satisfaction of lust among the straw of the Despensers' stable with one who was probably the village trull, who might even now be enjoying the favours of some ditcher or swineherd.

'Then you do not love as I do. Or at all. Perhaps I should not be surprised. You're like your brother, ready to mate with any bitch that will stand for you.'

'And you suppose that Edward of York is better than either of us? Because I assure you that he is not! No, he's worse. He *uses* you, as one more way of attacking Roger, whose head he'd like to see adorning London Bridge. Can you not see the truth of it?'

'You waste words.'

'Yes. I fear I do, and I shall waste no more. But think on it, Alianore, I beg you, before it's too late.' The storm was easing now, and as his eyes turned back to the hills he saw a crown of sunlight perching on the peaks. He sighed and said, 'I always forget how much of my heart is in this country—until I return to it.'

'It is beautiful,' she agreed. 'And profitable.'

He nodded. Perhaps a little too much so, he thought. The value of English land had fallen since the great plague of fifty years earlier, and wages had soared, despite all statutes to the contrary. Wales, though, could always be squeezed that little bit harder, and squeezed it was. The marcher lords were sovereigns in their petty kingdoms, save that in matters of finance they had more power than King Richard dreamed about. Even the Welsh on the Mortimer estates were growing restive, though the Earl of March had the advantage of being descended in blood from Llywelyn Fawr, which soothed their discontent somewhat.

'From what you wrote to me from Hanley I gather you know what was in your brother's letter,' Alianore said.

'I know what he told me. No more.'

'And you don't favour the marriage. That's clear.'

He shrugged. 'I told Roger as much when we were still in Ireland. A betrothal of babies? Of course I don't favour it! What does it gain us? Nothing.'

'Yet your brother disagrees with you. And so do I. It'll be much to our profit to bind the Despensers closer. Especially as the girl is their heiress.'

'For the present. You know that will soon change.'

'Even so, their alliance is worth the having. Thomas is the most reliable friend we have.'

'Oh, we've friends aplenty,' Edmund snorted. 'Ever since I came back from Ireland they've been throwing themselves at my feet; my sister's husband, Arundel, for one, and those who think as he does. They seek to use Roger as a weapon against the King. My uncle, Thomas Mortimer, is hand-in-glove with Arundel, and it was he who counselled my brother to make this marriage. Either they hope to draw Thomas Despenser into their conspiracy, or they think to keep him neutral, seeing what his daughter will stand to gain.'

Lady March shook her head. It made no sense to her at all. Her husband was not in the least ambitious—that, in her eyes, was his gravest fault, far worse than any small matter of adultery. He was like to run a mile from the offer of a crown, or from the hint of conspiracy. As for Despenser, all knew him as one of the small, trusted group close to the King.

'I think you must have misunderstood what people have said to you, dear Edmund,' she said indulgently.

'I didn't say I thought they were likely to succeed. They're desperate men, out of the King's favour and with no hope in hell of regaining it. My brother is their best hope, and he's fool enough to listen to them—or at least to my uncle, which amounts to the same thing. They're playing into the hands of their enemies, and we must do nothing, *nothing*, that will make matters worse.'

'But surely our alliance with the Despensers would be a sign that we are loyal to the King.'

He snorted. 'It might be represented so, by those who bear Roger good will. There are other ways of looking at it. Thomas is an ambitious man. It might please him to see his daughter as Princess of Wales. Even as Queen, one day. *That* might be called treachery. Not by me, Alianore. By the King. It could ruin the Despensers as well as ourselves.'

***

Lady March's principal guests settled down for a rere-supper in the splendour of Great Chamber, beneath a priceless tapestry that told the story of Tristan and Iseult. Wax candles were lit even though it was not yet fully dark, and the food and drink were borne in by formal processions of liveried gentleman and yeomen, with little less ceremony than for a feast, while Alianore's troupe of musicians stood in their gallery, playing lively tunes that stirred the feet. Edward led such conversation as there was, assisted by the Golafres, who shared his understanding of court gossip, and by an unreasonably cheerful Alianore.

Constance knew her brother too well to be surprised by his complacency. She was less prepared for his open admission that he had no intention of going anywhere near St. David's. It was, he said, merely a tale he had put about the court to cloak his true intent from those who bore him ill will.

'The truth is that I'm here at the King's bidding,' Edward went on. 'I brought news to Lady March. Good news, about her lord. I expected to find you here with her, Cousin Edmund. I'd no idea that you'd been detained so long at Hanley Castle.'

Constance heard the growl of fury rising in Edmund's throat, and hurriedly laid her hand on his arm, silently pleading with him to keep his temper.

'News so important that you had to bring it yourself?' Thomas asked incredulously.

'My cousin the King thought so. Far be it from me to dispute the matter with him. March has been granted a new commission. As Edmund so wisely requested. There's no longer any question of his being summoned home, or deprived of the lieutenancy. I had an idea that you might be pleased. Perhaps even grateful for my intercession. Did I not explain that the commission was issued by my advice?'

Thomas had little to say after that, beyond responding, usually with more courtesy than depth, to the occasional remark that Lady March directed towards him. It was only when the Despensers retired to the relative privacy of their bed that he became more voluble.

'Your brother is a lying bastard, *treschere*,' he said. 'What's even worse, he's a lying bastard who thinks we are all fools. He expects us to believe that the King uses him to carry messages? That's work for a sergeant-at-arms or a clerk, not the heir of York. He's as much piety about him as my horse's arse, but even the pretence of a pilgrimage was more believable.'

Constance stirred uneasily in the impenetrable darkness of the bed. Outside somewhere an owl hooted its challenge. 'I know. But he could scarcely admit his real reason for being here.'

'Though it is obvious to all! He might as well have his herald proclaim it at Paul's Cross! Has he no thought at all for Alianore? For her honour and good name? God's truth, she's a single heartbeat away from waking as Queen of England! Rutland mocks us all, and I can't tell you how much I longed to ram his lies down his throat, but what could I do without harming her? What could Edmund do?'

Constance paused for thought. 'On the other hand,' she ventured, 'you've won a great victory, and it's small wonder that Ned is trying to make light of it.'

'Victory?' he repeated impatiently. 'What victory?'

'You told me yourself that he was trying to turn the King against March. Well, he's failed. He's found that it's beyond his power, and he's no choice now but to pretend that this new commission he talks of was granted at his behest. Though it's clear that it wasn't. It *must* strengthen March's position, or Edmund wouldn't have asked for it in the first place.'

The room grew very quiet for a few minutes as Thomas considered the suggestion.

'It may even be,' she persisted, 'that he has found he has other enemies, more dangerous to him than March. And that he has remembered you are his brother, and a useful ally against them.'

'Whatever you say, I still don't trust him.'

'Nor do I. Or at least, not in all things. Yet I think that, in his way, he means us well. That he would be glad of your friendship.'

Despenser snorted. 'To do him justice, I think he has some care for you. I give him credit for that at least. As for me, he has never thought me worthy of your hand. He made that clear long ago, before ever I went to Prussia. He'd have been far happier if my bones had been shipped home in a box.'

'Is that what he said?' Constance was horrified; the more so because it had the authentic ring of Edward about it. She recalled his remarks on the subject at Nottingham.

'Not in plain words, but he let me know what he thought, nonetheless. I don't think it would much trouble him if I were to come to an ill end, provided that you were protected from harm.'

She reached out towards him. 'It may have been so once. Surely not now. I know he respects you. Perhaps more than he allows you to see. Why should you be at odds with him, now this matter of March is settled?'

'Because it isn't settled, Constance. As you well know. It may be that it's been put on one side, but that's all.'

'Even a truce is better than open war. And I think you should consider your own interests as well as Roger Mortimer's.'

'What you mean is you would like me on better terms with your brother. Even if that entails doing as he bids me. Perhaps you would have me wear his livery?'

'Thomas! You know well that I meant no such thing!'

His tone softened. 'I don't blame you for loving Edward, *treschere*. It's only natural that you should. I promise I'll not go out of my way to quarrel with him, but if he seeks my trust he'll have to earn it. It's a man's deeds that count with me, not his words. And so far he has never troubled to put me in his debt.'

***

Constance woke with the first blackbird, disturbed by a full bladder and then, as soon as she had got back into bed, by lustful thoughts. It was excessively tempting to wake Thomas, for she knew from long experience that it took little more than a smile to arouse him, and that, if anything, he was more eager at the start of the day than at its end. Yet it was sinful while she was pregnant, and they had already sinned enough in that respect. A woman who led her husband into such a fault was much more to be condemned than one who merely submitted. Moreover, God might punish her by deforming the child in her womb, or even killing it. Her confessor had told her as much, though he was a worldly and understanding old man and his penances were uncomfortably lenient. (They kept him as much for his politics as his doctrine, for he was a Grey Friar as well as a priest, as hot for King Richard as the rest of his order.)

It was better to remove herself from temptation. She rose from the bed, drew on her chamber-robe and moved to the nearest window to open first the shutters and then the casement. The fresh air carried the hint of dew on grass to her nose, drove away the staleness of the room. The castle was like an island rising from a sea of transient mist that shrouded the surrounding town of Usk and merged into the river. She judged that it would be a warm day. Too warm for comfort, perhaps.

She stirred young Mary Russell with her foot and bade the girl help her to wash and dress, working in silence so as not to disturb the rest. She had it in mind, for once, to attend the first mass of the day.

The chapel was old and surprisingly modest in size, the congregation largely consisting of Alianore's lesser servants, those with a full day's work ahead of them and most cause for early rising. It took Constance a moment or two to realise that Philippa Golafre was standing among them, and as she looked she saw that Edward, half hidden by an intruding pillar, was standing next to her.

Constance's astonishment at seeing her brother out of bed at such an hour of the morning was such that it quite eclipsed the lesser wonder that he should be deep in conversation with the vacuous Dame Golafre. They were sufficiently absorbed other in each to be unaware of her arrival until she drew up next to them.

'Of course, it was Sir John who saw them. Not I,' chuckled Philippa, concluding her anecdote.

Constance saw that Edward had noticed her arrival. He wiped the amusement from his face, offered a slight bow, and made room for her to stand between him and his now silent companion.

'It seems,' he said wryly, 'that Lady Golafre and I were not the only ones who had trouble sleeping. I swear my belly is not settled from last night. I think I swilled too much of March's claret. In truth, he spares no cost as far as his wine cellar is concerned. I must remember to thank him for his generous hospitality when next I see him.'

'Do you mean to accept much more of it?' Constance asked abruptly.

'I thought perhaps I might travel with you to see how you and Despenser treat a guest at Cardiff. I presume you won't be leaving today. No one can think of travelling on a Sunday and, besides, I'm sure you've much to discuss with Alianore. Another day or two would make no difference. I'm in no haste.'

Constance was surprised to find him so ready to leave Usk, still more by his wish to visit Cardiff. However, her speculations were cut short by the arrival of Alianore's sleepy old chaplain, a Welshman by the accent in which he spoke his Latin. She gave her attention to the mass, though aware, more than once, that her brother and Philippa were exchanging inexplicable grins around her back, as if they shared some wonderful secret from which she was excluded.

No sooner was the service ended than Dame Golafre hurried away, mumbling something about her sleeping husband and her need to be back before he woke.

'I think I could grow to dislike John Golafre,' Edward said unexpectedly.

They moved off, conscious that the rest of the congregation were holding back, allowing them precedence. Philippa had been at fault in that, Constance thought, and with far less excuse than men with hours of hard work before them.

'He uses his wife abominably,' she agreed. 'I know that Thomas thinks the less of him for it.'

'And has told him so?'

'My lord doesn't need to tell a man what he thinks of him. It shows in his manner. Or even in a glance. Whether Golafre has the wit to see it I do not know, for unless I'm much mistaken he's a fool as well as a brute. I wonder that our Cousin Richard holds him in such regard.'

Edward gave her a wry smile. 'He's always been loyal. He never wavered, not even when the Appellants had all in their hands, and threatened him with death. Richard values such faithfulness above all else, and so he should, for it's a lot more rare than gold. Besides, Golafre is not one to ask questions. Such men are useful tools for a king. You don't shift dung with a silver fork.'

They had found their way out into Alianore's garden. It was quite empty but for themselves and Mary Russell, who was keeping herself at a discreet distance. White roses were in bloom on every arbour, their perfume hanging in the air like an invisible web. Constance was compelled to touch one, to draw it closer and feel the fresh dew on her fingers.

'Nor,' she said, 'do you order your own cousin to carry a simple message. Ned, it would have been better if you had not been here. If you had to be, you might at least have had the courtesy to think of some better explanation.'

'You know the explanation.'

'You have scarcely left room for doubt! Has it not occurred to you that even a wittol like March may be driven too far? Or that, even if he lacks the means to harm you, he may take his revenge on Alianore?'

'What would you have me do? Give her up?'

'It might be better for her if you did. You don't love her. You could at the least be more cautious—more discreet.'

He shrugged, took an undecided step away from her, and turned back. 'You know less than you think, Constance,' he said.

'I know that you need a wife. A wife of your own, I mean, someone who can give you a lawful son. Alianore can never do that.'

'Not while March lives.' Edward's voice was suddenly very chill. He put his hand to one of the Mortimer roses and snapped it off, tearing the stem into a jagged wound.

Constance said nothing for a moment. It seemed to her that it might be good policy to allow him to reflect upon his folly. She walked on beneath the tunnel of the arbour, leaving him a step or two behind. At the end there was a bench, and she settled herself on it. It was as private a place as could be found in a great castle, and if he wished to continue to spout nonsense there was at least the consolation that he would not be overheard.

'You are right,' he said at last, approaching her. 'I should be more careful. It's not the time to renew my quarrel with March.'

'After what you said last night, I thought you'd given it up.'

He shrugged. 'Say rather that I've decided there are other matters that are more important. You may even say that I've been persuaded by your husband's arguments. I've need of his friendship, and am ready to pay for it.'

'I think you'll find that Thomas is not so easily won.'

'I know; but you can help me in this. I've need of a brother. A brother grown to manhood that is, not a boy like Dickon.'

Constance took her lower lip between her teeth for a moment. She wanted very much to have faith in him, to take him at his word, but she was not at all sure that she dared to do so.

'It's a pity you did not tell him that four years ago,' she said tartly.

'I've always wished him well. It's only this matter of March that has come between us. You know that.'

She did not, but allowed it to pass. 'And now you need him?'

He shrugged. 'Cousin Richard has not given up his idea of sending an army to help the French attack Milan. He speaks of giving me command of it. Not because I'm worthy of it, you understand, but there's no one else of fit rank whom he trusts. Mowbray is to command under me, but Richard doesn't even trust *him*.'

'So you want Thomas to go with you?'

'No. I want him in England, to guard my interests. He's the only one *I* trust. You know well enough that our father cares for nothing but hunting deer and rogering his fool of a wife. I daren't leave anything in his hands. There's some cause to think that dear Uncle Gloucester and his friends are having fresh thoughts of treason. It may come to nothing, but it's better to be sure, to know that there will be someone at home to lead the York retainers, and mine.'

Constance nodded grimly. 'Sooner or later the reckoning must come,' she said. 'Richard cannot truly be King while they have power to threaten him.'

'Nor while they still breathe,' he amended.

She swallowed, taken aback by his stark logic.

'Think of the good men *they* killed, when they had power in their hands,' he continued, his voice calm, free of emotion. 'Think what they would do to *us*, if they had the chance. Their hearts haven't changed; they're what they've always been. When the time comes, we must make an end.'

'Gloucester is our uncle...'

'Yes. So loving an uncle that he'd gladly murder Thomas and me and arrange for you to spend the rest of your life in the Minories. It wouldn't cost him an hour's sleep or a single grey hair. He'd do worse than that if it gained him the crown. Do you doubt it?'

Constance found that her lips were very dry. For a moment she was twelve years old again, a frightened child hiding herself in an obscure corner of the Tower of London as hordes of filthy, arrogant, unruly armed men threatened and mocked the King she loved as dearly as a brother, and dragged his friends and servants away to imprisonment and death. She saw old Beauchamp of Holt, Steward of the King's Household, his head pouring blood after it had hit the wall when they kicked his legs from under him. She saw again the triumphant hatred on the faces of Gloucester, Arundel and Warwick, the amused satisfaction of Thomas Mowbray and Harry Bolingbroke as they revelled in their victory. It was Bolingbroke who had winkled her out of her refuge and carried her off under his steel-clad arm to the protection of her terrified mother. She had never quite been able to forget that humiliation, and had hated him for years with every corner of her heart. Yet Bolingbroke and Mowbray were Richard's allies now—or were for the time being.

'No,' she said, 'I do not doubt it. I know that what you say is true.'

***

Something resembling a large gallows had been erected at the top of the Great Tower of Cardiff, and from it a system of ropes and pulleys descended to the courtyard. The first attempt to haul the gun barrel to the top had ended in failure when one of the ropes snapped and several hundred pounds of iron, after hanging precariously in its sling for a moment or two, had slid from its last restraints and come crashing to earth. The great barrel still waited where it had fallen, while additional ropes, pulleys and labourers were procured from the town.

Constance watched from the comfort of the solar, glad of the cooling breeze drifting in from the estuary. It was possibly the hottest day of the year so far, the sky absolutely cloudless.

'It's a miracle that the goddamned thing didn't shatter in pieces,' said Sir William Stradling with a snort that somehow managed to convey amusement, contempt and disappointment all at the same time. 'Bloody fools! Mind you, after a drop like that it'll probably blow itself apart the first time it's fired.'

It irritated Constance that a man she had disliked at first sight and detested at second should mirror her own private thoughts on the matter so precisely.

'I suppose you could do better?' Sir John St. John enquired icily. He was an older, plumper man than Stradling, and, as sheriff of Glamorgan, more surely established in Despenser favour.

'Anyone could see that it needed more ropes,' said Stradling. He shook his head in despair, stirring the long hair beneath his feathered cap. His forked beard was curled in the best imitation of court fashion that a Glamorgan barber could achieve.

'*I* couldn't. I don't know anything about ropes, or about hauling guns up walls. I'm a knight, not an engineer.'

'Some knight!' sniffed Stradling, turning away from him.

'*What* did you say?'

'I said that some knights know more about it than others. Just as some knights know how to line their purses with other people's money.'

'I'm not sure I like the way you said that, Stradling!'

'If the cap fits!'

Constance stirred reluctantly in her place. 'They should have sent to Llandaff for masons,' she said calmly. 'Masons know how to lift great weights up the side of tall buildings. It's a part of their trade; they do it every day of their lives.'

The two men stopped quarrelling at once, and exchanged glances.

'Perhaps for a few priests as well,' added Philippa Golafre. 'Prayers might help.'

'Prayers?' repeated John St. John.

'You might care to suggest it to my lord, Sir William,' Constance said. 'He might take it better from you than from me.'

Stradling nodded, appearing to find the suggestion quite reasonable. He made an elaborate bow and withdrew.

Philippa gave Constance a small, appreciative smile. 'Good riddance, too. I don't like him *at all*.'

'Hmm,' grunted John St. John. 'He's an ambitious man, Stradling. Resents me, you know. Thinks *he* should be sheriff.'

'Well, perhaps he will be, one day,' said Constance levelly, 'but I can think of many reasons why he should not be. The ones you showed us when we arrived here.'

The castle treasury was stacked to the ceiling with barrels of coin, almost all of it raised from the people of Glamorgan in fines and customary fees. The sheriff was responsible for the administration of the lordship, and his proud boast was that it had never been so profitable in all the three hundred years since its conquest. Constance, brought up on her father's debts, had been greatly impressed; she had not realised, until that moment, the extent of the wealth Despenser had at his disposal.

St. John allowed himself a smug smile, and stroked his beard. 'Of course,' he explained, 'there was a great levy when my Lord Despenser entered Glamorgan for the first time. That'll not be repeated until his son inherits. But if your daughter is to be married, my lady, we can raise a feudal aid on the strength of it. *Pour marier sa fille.* That should fetch in a fair sum, though we may have to allow some of them time to pay. Of course, we can charge them for that grace as well.'

'My daughter is not likely to be married yet,' said Constance pointedly.

'But I understood—' St. John broke off for a moment before plunging on. 'I understood that certain arrangements had been agreed. Obviously there can be no true marriage for many years yet, but the celebration of the sacrament will be enough to justify the aid. There's ample precedent for it. My lord told us that the dowry would be no more than a token, and so there will be a clear profit.'

'*Us?*'

'His council. Those of us who were assembled here. Surely, my lady, you know of this? I gathered that you did.'

'I knew of it, Sir John. What I did *not* know was that my lord had chosen to open the matter to half the household.'

Constance stood up. She was furious with Thomas, and furious with Alianore into the bargain. Clearly they had found time at Usk to negotiate together behind her back, despite all the advice she and Edmund Mortimer had given them, advice they had clearly ignored.

'Scarcely that, my lady. To half a dozen of us at most, and we his most trusted advisers.'

Constance shook her head. She did not trust any one of them to keep his mouth shut. Norreys would certainly break the news to Agnes, and Agnes could no more keep a secret than she could fly. She began to pace about.

'Such a marriage,' she said, 'will require the King's consent, and that has not yet been sought. It should not be spoken of as settled until the King's pleasure is known. Better if it is not spoken of *at all.*'

St. John nodded. 'It's true enough that nothing can be settled until Lord March returns from Ireland, but the terms the Countess has proposed are very favourable. If her husband confirms them it will be most profitable for your daughter, and I'm sure the King will have no objection to the arrangement. Especially as it will put an end to an old dispute between two loyal families.'

She frowned. Though he wore the King's livery badge he obviously did not know Richard's suspicious mind as well as she did, or at all. Nor did he appreciate the fragility of the precious new accord between her husband and her elder brother. How hard and tedious it was to build security; how easy to shatter it with a single, careless blow.

'I am sure you're right,' she said, in her normal, calm voice, 'but I'd still prefer the matter to be kept close.'

'Look at Edward!' shrieked a delighted Philippa, pointing out of the window.

Edward, wearing only shirt and hose, was tugging on one of the ropes, encouraging his team of labourers to greater efforts with a barrage of crude but amiable abuse. The men were grinning and pulling with a will, and the great barrel was rising again, slowly but with an impressive air of security.

'Perhaps the masons will not be needed after all,' John St. John said triumphantly, rushing away in the hope of being in time to share in the success.

'He looks even more handsome, somehow,' Philippa observed.

'John St. John?' Constance was deliberately obtuse.

'I mean your brother—Edward. How clever of him, to encourage them so!'

Constance surveyed the scene for a moment or two. 'He's doing no more than your husband.'

Sir John Golafre had attached himself to one of the other ropes in an effort to show willing, though his enthusiasm for the work was less evident than Edward's.

Philippa snorted. 'Golafre will make little difference! He wouldn't know how to persuade a river to run downhill except by kicking it. Besides, he's not even trying. I expect he thinks it's not fit work for one of the King's knights. See, your other brother is helping him. I don't suppose *he* makes much difference either, but at least he's trying his best.'

It was true. Young Dickon's face was a mixture of concentration and delight, and there was no doubt that he was thoroughly enjoying himself, though it was equally obvious that the contribution of his modest body weight was very marginal to the process.

'I dare say they're all looking forward to seeing it fired,' Constance said coldly, her eyes turning to Thomas, who was standing a little way back, supervising the work. She could see by his restless bearing that he too was itching to get hold of a rope.

'And you are not? Oh, Connie, how grim you are at times! It'll be wonderful. I wish I could set it off myself, perhaps put a hole in one of the ships in your harbour. I wonder if we could buy an old one to sink? We could pretend it was full of French pirates. Wouldn't you enjoy seeing that? Tom would do it for you, I know he would.'

Of course he would, thought Constance, as he would grant any trivial request of mine. He'd not turn a hair. It's only in matters of substance where he is less accommodating. He listens, perhaps, but he does not heed, and he sees what he wishes to see, and no more. The trouble is there is nothing I can do now that will not make matters worse.

'I'm not interested in the gun,' she said. 'It's a useless thing, and complete waste of good money that would be better spent on the poor. I'm going…'

She broke off. She had thought of visiting the chapel, where she could pray and think at the same time, but that would not serve. Philippa would insist on going with her, and so would the rest of her women. Their babbling company was the last thing she wanted.

'I'm going to write a letter,' she concluded.

'A letter?' repeated Philippa. 'Then shall I send for your clerk?'

'I need no clerk. I'm perfectly capable of holding a pen, Cousin, if I am left in peace.'

Lady Golafre stared at her for a moment, absorbing the hint. Then she rose, and moved towards the door, saying something about taking a closer look at what the men were doing.

Constance sat at the small desk that Thomas used for his administrative work, swept a petition from the men of Cowbridge onto the floor, selected a clean piece of parchment, and began to write, in the old-fashioned Norman-French her father expected and preferred:

'To the high and mighty prince, Edmund, Duke of York and Earl of Cambridge, Lord of Tyndale, etc., be this delivered in haste.

'Most excellent and honourable Father, I recommend me to you as lowly as I may, seeking your daily blessing. Please you to know that a marriage is lately agreed between your granddaughter Elizabeth and the eldest son of my cousin, March.

'It is said by some here at Cardiff that the King is wroth with the Earl of March, for one cause and another, and that this marriage will displease him; which I should not do for this world. Whether this be a false rumour or not, I do not know. Therefore, honoured Father, I beg that you will advise my lord according to the truth when he returns to you, and before he breaks the matter to the King. For if there is doubt, I think it better that the matter be delayed.

'By your humble daughter, Constance, the Dame le Despenser.'

She dusted it down, watched as the ink dried, and pondered on whether to send it. Might it not be better to speak to Thomas first? No, for he had already made it clear what value he set on her counsel. There was just a chance, a slim chance, that he would heed the Duke where he would not heed her.

Her mind made up, she folded and sealed the parchment, then rang the bell that summoned the duty esquire. She handed him the letter, with instructions that it was to be sent at once, and did not rest again until she had seen the liveried messenger riding towards the castle gates.

5

'I think the French bastards are trying to poison me,' complained Sir John Golafre, clutching at his middle. 'I've never felt so ill in my life.'

Thomas snorted. 'Why should they bother?' he asked impatiently. 'I should look closer to home if I were you.'

Golafre guffawed. It was astonishing, Despenser reflected, just how many insults the man was prepared to interpret as humour. As long as they came from his betters, of course. He had a different way with his underlings, or with anyone he could threaten or bully.

Thomas had almost given up trying to get rid of the fellow. Golafre clung like moss to a rock, stubbornly impervious to slights and cold shoulders, offered confidences as though they were the dearest pair of friends in the world, made it seem that he needed Despenser's advice and guidance before he could do so much as pass water.

'He *does* look ill, though,' commented Huntingdon, without undue concern.

They were standing together in one of the enormous canvas palaces that had been set up near Ardres to house the English court, waiting for something to happen. There had been a great deal of that, with so many great personages to accommodate, so much detail of protocol to be agreed in touchy, last minute discussions with the French.

Despenser gave Golafre another brief glance. The man's colour was certainly less than healthy, and profuse sweat was standing on his brow. Perhaps he needed fresh air. The huge tent was packed with stale, overdressed, befurred humanity, all more or less standing on top of one another.

'He's not the only one, of course,' Huntingdon went on. 'Gloucester looks like he's got a pain in *his* belly too. I know he hates these French, but he might at least have the courtesy to hide it. Especially when they've done nothing but load him with one present after another, trying to buy his good will. Christ's bones, I wish they'd bid as high for mine! My brother the King has been bribing him as well, but the man is never satisfied. Nothing will ever serve but that he shall have all his own way.'

'What has the King offered him?' asked Thomas, for this was news to him.

'More than he can afford to pay. Much more than Gloucester can possibly expect to receive if he has any notion of the state of the Exchequer.'

'The Queen's dowry, of course,' Golafre suggested, mopping his brow with the back of his trailing sleeve.

Huntingdon made a disparaging noise. 'What the hell do you think is paying for all this?' he asked, with a comprehensive gesture that took in the tent, the guests, the rich cloth they stood on and all the splendours that lay outside. 'By the time she's been crowned at Westminster there won't be enough left to hire a boat to ferry you across the Thames, let alone to keep Gloucester happy.'

'Then...?'

'Then he's going to be *unhappy*, isn't he?' Huntingdon broke into snorting laughter, as if he had provided them with a brilliant witticism. 'Almost as unhappy as his Duchess is now, with her face fit to turn milk. Mind you, I don't much wonder at it. My Beth is easy natured enough, but even she doesn't much like having to give place to the Swynford woman. I dare say, Thomas, that your wife feels the same about it. Where is she? Keeping out of the way?'

'At Cardiff, close to her time,' Despenser said quietly.

'Ah, I see. Well, I dare say she blesses you for that. A lot less painful for her than being here. Hoping for a son this time I expect? I had her mother once, you know. More than once, to tell the truth. She was a warm woman; such as I'll never forget. If the daughter is half as hot you can count yourself a fortunate man.'

Thomas glowered at him. 'I'll thank you to consider your words more carefully when you speak of my lady,' he said quietly. 'Unless, of course, you wish to discuss the matter somewhere less crowded, and with a sword in your hand.'

'You're in a touchy mood, Despenser. I said you were a fortunate man. Surely you find no insult in that?'

'I'm sure that no disrespect was intended to Lady Despenser,' said Golafre anxiously.

Thomas looked him up and down as though he had just emerged from a pond. 'Do you imagine I care what *you* think?' he asked brutally. He pushed roughly past the man, leaving him and Huntingdon to gobble their astonishment at one another.

The mention of Constance had struck a raw nerve, for he was worried by her recent strange behaviour. During his last few days at Cardiff she had treated him with a polite coolness that was far more troubling to him than her usual brief outburst of anger. At the time he had presumed it related to her disapproval of the time and money he had spent on installing the castle guns, and been annoyed in his turn by the disproportionate nature of her response to his project. It had taken Edward—of all people—to draw him aside and remind him that pregnant women were subject to strange fancies and unaccountable swings of mood, and that such things were not to be taken to heart.

But that was not the end of it, because as soon as he had returned to the court at Windsor the Duke of York summoned him to his presence. York, in no amiable mood, drew him into the most private corner of his suite of apartments, locked the door behind them, and then more or less accused him of treason. This, coming from one whom Thomas had grown to love as a father, hit hard. Harder still when it turned out that a letter from Constance was at the root of the Duke's complaint, a letter about which he, Thomas, had known nothing at all. He hastened to explain that there was no question of concluding the marriage alliance with the Mortimers without the King's consent, and that he had been about to seek York's advice on that very point, but his father-in-law was not convinced, and waved Constance's letter about in his hand as though the parchment was afire.

'Your wife says the marriage is *agreed*,' he pointed out. 'If it was your intent to ask my advice, why did she go so far out of her way to ask me to give it?'

Thomas tried very hard to hide his exasperation. 'I don't know. It is *not* agreed—I've negotiated a draft of terms with Lady March, but that's all. Nothing is binding on either side.'

York shifted on his chair to ease his discomfort, his hand clutching at the adjoining table for assistance. 'Thomas, I've thought you many things, but never a fool. Is it possible that you do not know how much the King mistrusts March? Would you have him doubt you too? Will you have him doubt *me*? For you may be sure that he'll suspect that I've encouraged you in this. He knows I regard you as a son.'

'Sir, you know as well as I that there is no earthly cause for any man to mistrust March, and least of all the King's Grace.'

'On the contrary, there's word out of Ireland that the whoremongering young idiot is involved in a conspiracy with his brother-in-law, Arundel. Are you a part of that? I'm told that one of Arundel's men visited you at Hanley Castle.'

'*Told*? Told by whom?'

'You do not deny it?'

Thomas snorted. 'Does Your Grace seek to hold me accountable for every person who spends an hour under my roof? I don't begrudge food or shelter to any man who behaves peaceably, no matter whom his master may be. I can swear, and *do*, that I've had no dealings with Arundel since I left his household. Nor do I seek any.'

'Arundel is the world's greatest lunatic,' York remarked. 'The King was not enemy enough for him, so he's made another of my brother, Lancaster. There can only be one ending after that, especially as he keeps adding fresh provocations to all those that have gone before. And now, as I tell you, he conspires with March.'

'Who says that he does?'

'Who do you think? The King's loyal servants in Ireland.'

'I take it, sir, that you speak of spies? Bought creatures, not honourable men.'

'Call them what you will. It's enough that their word is believed. Must I say more?'

Thomas shook his head in some bewilderment. 'I understood that March had been granted a new commission—that the King was assured of his loyalty.'

'Yes, yes, there were many who wished him well and spoke for him. I did myself. As did Edward, out of a desire to please you. Or so he told me, before he went into Wales. The commission was issued and sent, and then, within a week or two, this new report arrived. The King was furious, of course, and we who had advised him were not spared the length of his tongue. Edward did well to be away from court and out of sight. I wish to God I had been with him! March is summoned home to explain himself, and he's fortunate it's no worse than that. There was some talk that he should be arraigned before Parliament.'

'I'm sure he'll be able to prove that he's innocent of any ill intent.' Thomas said uncomfortably.

'He may. He may not. Either way, this is no time to seek an alliance with his family. I think you would be wise to let the matter drop.'

The Duke's tone upgraded the suggestion into something very close to an outright command, and Despenser had not debated the point. He had reflected on this conversation several times since coming to France, and although he was forced to concede that Constance and her father had some justification for their caution, he still could not make sense of Edward's behaviour. There was something contrived about his sudden support for March, and the explanation for it that Constance had put forward was not altogether convincing. It was probably, Thomas thought, exactly what her brother had told her to say to him.

Realising that he was wandering aimlessly through the crowd, like a mindless drunk, Thomas paused momentarily to collect himself, and then walked on towards the nearest exit. Beyond that, at least, there would be fresh air. He nodded curtly to those who greeted him, and was quite unaware of the grimness of his own expression.

Outside a group of horses were being assembled. He was surprised to see his squire holding the bridle of his own favourite palfrey, and other of his retainers standing around in expectation, including Hugh Tyldesley, who was carrying his banner.

'Ah, there you are, my lord!' exclaimed the bluff, bulky Tyldesley. 'Forget, did you?'

Before Thomas could answer Edward of York emerged from around the corner of the tent, already mounted up.

'Good morning, Thomas,' he said amiably. 'I've had my men and yours scouring the whole camp for you, and through half of Ardres and Calais besides. I was beginning to think you were still in bed with some French whore. Come on, we mustn't keep Burgundy waiting any longer. He'll think it's a deliberate snub.'

Despenser climbed into the saddle automatically, without a word. The courtesy visit to the Duke of Burgundy, arranged in some confusion the previous evening, had almost entirely slipped his mind. He had somehow gained the impression they were to go across much later in the day.

'I wonder that you needed to seek for me,' he said as they moved forward. 'You had your man watching at my side as usual.'

'What man?'

'Golafre. He's your man, isn't he?'

'He's the King's man. I think Richard sent him to you at first to see how you were dealing with Warwick. You disappointed him by not coming to blows. I don't think it would have troubled him much if you had burnt one or two of Warwick's manors, or taught his retainers some better manners.'

Thomas shook his head. 'I thought I did well to keep the peace. Was that not my duty?'

'You need not have kept it so thoroughly. As for Golafre, I dare say he also hopes for your good lordship, some place about you or the like. I know he's your kinsman by marriage, but I'd not retain him if I were you. You've far too many of Richard's men about you as it is. Russell. St. John. Even that damned Scot.' He gestured in the general direction of Sir Andrew Hake, who had attached himself to Despenser's retinue. 'A man can't serve two masters, and I'll have none that are like to choose my cousin above me.'

Thomas started. 'That's strange counsel,' he said. 'Do you think I'm like to turn against the King?'

Edward shrugged. 'I can't read the future. Certainly you may not always agree with him, or he with you. All I say is that you should be sure you can depend on your friends, the men you will need to call upon if times grow hard. You'll be stronger so, and I need your strength.'

It was the first time he had ever admitted such a need, and Despenser was unsure whether to be pleased or merely suspicious.

'You presume, then, that we shall always agree with each other?' he asked.

'Why should we not? We are brothers.'

'We are when it suits your convenience.'

'Tom, I've no wish to quarrel, but you are unjust. I've served your interests with the King more times than you will ever know, and never waited to be asked. I don't seek your gratitude, but at least have the courtesy to own that I am not your enemy. I can never be that, because I know there's no way for me to harm you without hurting my sister. Besides, as I said, I need you. You're the only man in England that I trust, and while I'm away in Italy all my interests will be in your hands.'

This was flattery indeed, and Thomas was not impervious to it, no matter what doubts he retained.

'Then I may ask a service of you?' he enquired.

'Anything you will.'

'Will you get Golafre out of my sight?'

Edward smiled. 'I'll advise the King to send him on some mission beyond the seas. It will be a kindness to his wife, as well as to you. I think your cousin has suffered enough at his hands.'

Despenser nodded his agreement. 'She has. What's more, if he lays another hand on her I swear I'll kill the bastard, no matter what the King thinks of him.'

Edward was strangely quiet for a moment. 'You forget my rank, Thomas,' he said at length, his eyes staring into the distance, to a point some miles beyond the sprawling town of French tents. 'I have precedence.'

***

The castle of Calais had never been so crowded since the glorious celebrations that had followed Edward III's conquest of it. The English had Isabelle in their hands now, cared for by their ill-assorted duchesses and a flock of other great ladies, the French having handed her over at the boundary, their princes unwilling to enter a city that they still claimed as theirs by right.

The sight of King Richard standing next to his tiny new Queen was either charming or ludicrous, depending on the viewpoint of the observer.

Thomas Despenser had his doubts. When he had considered Isabelle in abstract it had seemed to him she would soon be an adult, and the mother of a string of sons. Yet to see her in person, still a small child, was to realise that she had a lot of growing to do. Who knew what could happen in the meantime? It seemed to him there was ample cause to pray for Richard's continued good health, for if harm came to him while there was still no undoubted heir it was likely that the issue of succession would be settled by civil war.

Constance and his Uncle Henry of Norwich had seen this before he had. He had an uncomfortable memory of scoffing at their fears. Now he shared, or at least understood, the concern. The King is still young, he repeated to himself, seeking reassurance. He will live long enough to breed heirs, and the danger will recede. There's no real cause to worry.

As the celebrations proceeded he took an opportunity to approach the Duke of Gloucester about the activities of the outlaws from the Forest of Dean. The outlaws were seriously damaging the trade that flowed up and down the River Severn, and the men of Tewkesbury and Upton were full of complaints about it. It was Gloucester's business to take action, for, among other things, he was the King's Warden of Dean.

The Duke was surprisingly accommodating. He promised to do all that he could to reduce the nuisance. It was impossible to stop it altogether, he said, short of sending an army into the Forest, an army he did not possess.

'Your father was as fine a man as I have met,' he went on unexpectedly. 'A most noble knight. You have his looks, you know, and you've proved yourself his equal as a warrior. What do you think he would say about this day's work?'

Despenser shook his head. 'I do not know, Your Grace. I was very young when he died. I think I can remember him lifting me on his shoulders, but we never discussed political issues.'

Gloucester seemed impervious to irony. 'You have seen for yourself that the French still dine off gold and silver,' he said. 'It's a rich country. I think we have been in too much haste to make peace, to throw away all the sacrifices that were made in years of fighting. We haven't even a struck a good bargain. What have *they* conceded? Precious little it seems to me.'

'Peace is surely worth something. At least the people of England will have less tax to pay.'

'Really? I think you know as well as I do that my nephew the King has an insatiable desire for money. There'll always be a new jewel to buy, or a castle to rebuild. Besides, it isn't even a peace as such. Just a long truce. Twenty-eight years, by the end of which most of us are like to be dead; but it settles nothing. The root of the quarrel is still there, still unresolved. All that's changed is our admission that we lack the stomach for a fight. Peace? You can call it that if you like. But don't be surprised that you have outlaws in Dean, when every shire in England is plagued with discharged soldiers. All men must eat, after all.'

***

'I was surprised, Harry, that you did not choose to take part in the jousting. It was remarked upon.'

Bolingbroke met his father's gaze with equanimity. 'I'm sure, sir, that if I *had* jousted then *that* would have been remarked upon. It's the way of the world. At least, the way of the world as it stands.'

They stood on the quay at Calais by the side of the King's great ship, waiting for Richard to precede them aboard. The wind was in the right direction for England, strong enough for a swift crossing, and the sailors were anxious to be gone. Richard, however, was taking his time. Huntingdon had already informed the Duke that there would be a delay. Sir John Golafre had fallen very ill, and the King had gone to visit him.

'A world you would like to change, no doubt,' Lancaster said, his tired eyes looking out to sea. He drew his cloak a little closer around him, for the wind was icy cold when it blew its strongest.

'Not the whole world. Only a small part of it.'

The Duke snorted. 'You're too downcast, Harry, for a man of your years. You need something to cheer you. Something, or someone. It's more than two years since Mary died, and it's unnatural to live as you do. What you need, my son, is a woman.'

Bolingbroke grimaced. That was his father's prescribed remedy for every ill, a woman, taken twice a day.

'The Duke of Orleans suggested that I should open negotiations for a marriage to Lucia of Milan,' he said. 'As you know, sir, she is his lady's cousin, and she has been offered to me before. I've met her. She's very beautiful, and will bring a great dowry. It is, I suppose, a possibility to be considered.'

'I do not speak of marriage! I speak of a woman. Take some pleasure from your life, before it grows too late. You'll have responsibility enough when I am gone. It's useless to think of Lucia of Milan. Must I remind you that the King is about to go to war with her uncle? Why not do as Richard suggests, and marry Queen Isabelle's sister?'

Harry did not reply. There was no need. His expression contained all the answer that was required.

The Duke was thoughtful for a few moments. 'It would be unwise to give the impression that you are against this peace,' he suggested. 'Especially as almost everyone accepts it.'

'Sir, I am not against it. It is your policy, as well as Richard's.'

'Yet I think it would not be yours? It is much to your benefit, Harry. It will be a long time before this new Queen of ours is old enough to produce a son. As long as you remain loyal to your cousin, you have a hope of succeeding him.'

Bolingbroke shrugged. 'Many would say that March is the rightful heir.'

'The son of my brother's daughter? Are we not nearer in blood?'

'The son of your *elder* brother's daughter. If the Lancastrian inheritance can come to me from my mother, why then should not the crown come to Roger Mortimer from his? Some would certainly see it so. Perhaps sufficient to make a war of it, a war we might not win.' He paused, considering. ' It may even be that the war has already started.'

***

Sir John Golafre was carried from Dover to Eltham in a litter, the griping pain in his belly seeming to grow worse with every step, as if some monster was trying to chew its way out of his bowels. King Richard's own physicians had fussed over him, examined his water and the position of the planets, then poured their foul potions and powdered jewels down his throat. As the pain had grown worse they had given him poppy juice, and when that eased him but little they began to shake their heads. Though they kept trying new and more expensive mixtures of filth, they also allowed the King's chaplain to confess their patient. Golafre was left in no doubt that he was dying.

At Eltham they found him a cramped, dark chamber, close to the King's apartments, almost unfurnished except for his small, comfortless bed. Later Richard sent word that he wished Golafre to be buried in Westminster Abbey rather than at home in Oxfordshire. It was intended as an honour, a reward for undoubted loyalty, but the knight was past caring now.

Golafre ordered a servant to ask Thomas Despenser to come to him.

'I know you've never much liked me,' he said, as soon as Thomas poked his head through the curtain that partitioned his deathbed from the rest of the world. 'I regret that, but it's too late to do anything about it.'

'I will pray for you,' Thomas said uncomfortably. 'Whatever our disagreements, you are my kinsman.'

'You can see how matters stand with me. I swear I have been poisoned. My guts burn and I cannot last long.'

'What do the doctors say?'

Golafre could feel the pain growing stronger. He shook his head, almost in tears as he struggled to fight it off. 'The doctors are bloody fools! I tell you I have been poisoned! I think I know the reason, but I cannot prove it. I'll not damn my soul accusing a man who may be innocent. Better to leave him to God. I don't want you to avenge me, but I do ask for one last kindness.'

'I'll not refuse that.'

'I know. That's why I ask it. I want you to take care of my wife, your cousin, when I am gone. She'll need protection, assistance in claiming her dower rights. My nephew will steal the clothes from her back if he can. She may be a fool, she may even be worse, but I'll not have her robbed.'

'You could have spared yourself the trouble of asking. As you say, Lady Golafre is my cousin. That is enough.'

Golafre gave him a feeble smile. 'Thank you. I know she could not be better placed, not if she had ten brothers, than with such a kinsman as you are. Ask her to forgive me if she can. I've not been kind to her. It was not intended. It just—became so. In return there may be one service I can still do for you. At least I can offer a simple word of warning. Nothing passes in your household but Edward of York knows of it. Nothing. Beware of him, for I think he is not your friend.'

6

The Duke of York's town house in London, the *Old Inne*, stood in Thames Street, but its principal rooms overlooked the river. This was pleasant enough in summer; but in January the bitter chill rising from the water made the opening of windows unthinkable on even the brightest of days, and there was no view through the opaque glass. Constance's idle hand occupied itself by scratching at the internal frost with her wedding ring, but not with any expectation of being able to see what was going on outside.

'The King expected you both to be at the Queen's coronation,' her father said. He paused to cough as pungent smoke from the sea-coal blazing in the great hearth near his chair billowed up into his face. Defeated for the moment, he passed Richard Despenser over to the Duchess, who at least knew how to hold a baby the right way up. 'He asked me where you were, and I knew not what to answer.'

'My lady was in no condition to travel,' Thomas answered, his eyes flickering to Constance, 'and most certainly she was not strong enough to stand for hours in Westminster Abbey.'

'Is this so, Constance?' York asked, irritated by the fact that his daughter did not appear to be hanging on his words. 'Have you truly become such a weakling?'

'I was not churched until after Epiphany, Father,' she pointed out, pausing to smile at Joanne's brother, Mun Holland, who had appeared in front of her to offer a large goblet of mulled wine. It was exactly what she needed to drive the icy chill from her bones. 'Even if we had set out at once, with wings to fly, it would have made no difference. My lord got me with child at an unfortunate time, but Cousin Richard is not so unreasonable that he will hold us to account for that!'

The Duke frowned at her. There was an edge of levity, even of insolence, in her voice, which he disliked. It reminded him of her brother, Edward. He wondered, not for the first time, how he had contrived to father two such children, so sure of themselves, and with a quick answer to everything. He had never possessed such limitless confidence in himself.

'I should have thought your husband capable of finding his way to London without you, madame,' he said abruptly. 'I think he indulges your whims too much; allows you too much slack rein.' He turned back to Thomas. 'As soon as the Parliament has ended I'll take myself off to Fotheringhay,' he grunted. 'There are too many rogues at court for any honest man's comfort, and the greatest rogue of all is my own heir, God amend him! I begin to think Richard would believe that the moon was made of green cheese, and that it hung from the sky by a string, if Edward told him it was so.'

'Edward has great influence,' Thomas said levelly, 'and could, I think, make better use of it. I wish you would stay with the court, sir, for he can only benefit from your counsel.'

The Duke snorted. 'Do you suppose he heeds it? My brother Gloucester and his friends talk all manner of nonsense among themselves, I don't deny it, but that's all it is. Talk! The trouble is that Edward seeks to make it more. Fills Richard's head with tales of treason. He and that damned rogue, Mowbray. It's as well for us all that they are both going off to war. That is, of course, if the Commons will find the money to pay for the venture, and the word is that they won't.'

'So our treaty with the French is already as good as broken,' Thomas said grimly.

The Duchess moved to sit next to Constance, passing the baby back to her with a certain reluctance.

'My lord the Duke is in an ill mood,' she said confidentially. 'The cold troubles his old wounds. I doubt he meant to snap at you; he was delighted when word came from Despenser that you were safe, and had a son.'

Constance nodded. She was well aware that her father was sharper of tongue when he was in pain, and had no need of Joanne to confirm it. She did not doubt her father's love. He had sent a basket of expensive oranges all the way to Cardiff for her pleasure, a well-intended gift that had eased some of the tedium of waiting. He had no need to know that Philippa Golafre had eaten most of the fruit.

**

Lady Arundel was in full flood.

'Well, Brother,' she sneered, 'are you the Earl of March and Ulster, the heir to England's throne, or are you a pauper and a coward? How much longer will you allow these humiliations to be heaped upon you? How much more will you stomach? As God sees me, I grow weary of inventing excuses to explain your timidity.'

March sighed, and consulted the shadows in the room. He judged it was no more than three o'clock. In London the days seemed to last forever. It seemed unlikely that his sister would be in any hurry to leave. His need for another swallow of his favourite claret was becoming oppressive. Sitting up, he poured a very generous measure into his crystal goblet from the large jug standing on the press, and drank deeply. Philippa Arundel sniffed disapprovingly, although she was forced to admit that Roger was still a long way from being drunk. His capacity was immense.

'Where is she?' she demanded, giving up hope of an answer to her tirade.

'Who?'

'Who do you think? Your so-called Countess.'

'My lady is with the Queen.'

'So she says.'

'She has a place there.'

'For every hour that God sends? Is that French brat's conversation so utterly absorbing?'

For the first time he smiled, albeit thinly. 'I do not lack for company, Sister,' he said—and just stopped himself from winking.

'That is not the point!'

'Then tell me what is the point,' he yawned.

She snorted with contempt. 'The point,' she spat out, 'as you well know, is that your sweet wife is having herself serviced by your worst enemy.'

He glanced up at her. 'Would it be better if she had chosen a friend?' he enquired.

Lady Arundel ignored his comment. 'If you cannot beat decency into her,' she went on, 'you should lock her away. In Our Blessed Lady's name, you have castles enough for the purpose! Aye, and nunneries under your patronage. A few months spent scrubbing cloister floors would cool my lady's blood for her. If you care nothing for your own honour, you should at least consider that of your family.'

'It would be more than unkind to use Alianore so. She didn't ask to marry me any more than I asked to marry her. We had to do as our elders bade us. We've had our children together, as duty required, and now we go our own ways. That's all there is to it.'

'*All?*' repeated his sister.

'I've no wish to make her unhappy. What good would that do me?'

She shrugged and gave up the unequal struggle, defeated by his sheer stolidity. She was convinced that the jibes she had thrown at him would have stirred any remotely normal man into a passion of fury, and had been quite prepared to accept a blow or two from him in a good cause. She wondered whether he would be as easy to stir up into rebellion as her husband supposed.

'My lord and I are going down to Reigate once the Parliament is over,' she announced. 'We look to spend a few weeks there. Why do you not come with us? I can promise you good entertainment. The park hasn't been hunted for a twelvemonth, we've a new cook who knows his business, and no one has ever found fault with our wine cellar. There'll be good company, too. Your spirits need cheering, Roger. You look sick at heart.'

He accepted her invitation, although with misgivings, because it seemed the only way to be rid of her.

'I'll follow you when I can,' he said, hurriedly. 'I've business to settle first. With the King, and with Thomas Despenser.'

'You'll get nothing from Richard,' Lady Arundel said bluntly. 'He despises you, as he does all honest men. You shouldn't trust Despenser, either. He's the King's man beyond doubt, and that wife of his and her damned brother are as thick as thieves. It's better to put your faith in your own family.'

**

'I cannot tell your ladyship how much I am in debt to her for this appointment,' bubbled Blanche Bradeston. 'It's a scarcely believable honour for me to be a member of the Queen's household. It's entirely due to your ladyship's intercession for me. The King himself as good as told me so.'

Constance shrugged dismissively, though she was quietly pleased by the extent of her own influence. It had taken nothing more than a word to Edward, backed by a suitable letter to the King.

'I am your servant forever,' Blanche went on, 'and you may call on me for anything. I only wish that I could have attended you at Cardiff, but with my new duties it was quite impossible.'

'You must not trouble yourself, Lady Bradeston. I had far more attendance than I required.'

That was true enough. For the weeks of her confinement half the gentlewomen in Glamorgan had competed to cram themselves into her chamber, nominally to wait upon her, but in practice to exchange gossip, admire or criticise one another's clothes and jewellery, complain about their husbands and arrange marriages between their children. Blanche's presence would certainly have been superfluous.

'However,' Constance went on, 'I shall always appreciate news of the Queen's welfare. You understand me, of course?'

Blanche did so. She nodded like a bird pecking at a crumb.

Together they entered the Queen's chamber. Constance made a profound curtsey, and Blanche, six feet behind her, simply knelt. Constance advanced, made a second curtsey, advanced again…

King Richard had his little wife sitting on his knee, holding her with the affection of a kindly father for a favourite daughter. He himself presented his cousin to Isabelle.

Constance rose from the third and final curtsey that etiquette required. The new Queen of England stood about four feet tall in her delicate little slippers, a pretty child with dimple cheeks, who wore an outlandish gown of stiff bejewelled velvet. There was a collar of diamonds about her neck, and she had rings jostling for position on each of her tiny fingers. It was clearly intended that she should grow up as quickly as possible, imprisoned by her status and surrounded by adult women.

As soon as Constance had been named to her, Isabelle began to ask numerous questions. Reclining on the King's lap, with every sign of assurance, she spoke in torrenting French or stumbling English as the mood took her, and it was not long before the conversation became utterly tangled. Was it true that Madame Despenser had just borne a son? That he was named for the King? Where was he? When was he going to be brought to court so that the Queen might see him? What was the colour of his eyes? Did the Lady Constance know that she would soon be the Queen's sister by marriage, as well as her cousin? That little Jeanne would be coming to England to keep Isabelle company and to marry my lord of Rutland?

Constance struggled to keep pace, handicapped by the language difficulties and the broad grins worn by all the other adults in the room. Her Cousin Richard seemed particularly amused.

She was a good deal more grateful than she cared to admit when the King broke into the discussion to say that enough was enough and that his Queen must now return to her schoolroom. Isabelle wrinkled her nose at that, but obediently allowed the Countess of March and Lady Bradeston to lead her away.

'She is truly a jewel,' Richard said softly, when the door had closed. 'I hope, dear Cousin, that you will help me to protect her from the evil that is around us. Our Uncle Gloucester sees that sweet child as an enemy. He would stop at nothing to renew the war, and claims that the peace is dishonourable, that I am badly advised, and that far too much has been yielded to the French. He is already conspiring against me, I am told. Just as before. Except that, on this occasion, we are better prepared.'

Constance looked into her cousin's eyes. There was something more than concern there. Something that was close akin to fear, if not terror.

She swallowed. 'My lord Father and my Uncle Lancaster will never allow any harm to come to you, Sire, or to the Queen.'

'So they say.' Richard was brisk, almost dismissive. 'Oh, my Uncle York means well, I know, but there's no strength in him. And Lancaster grows old, and feeble. Will Harry Bolingbroke fight Gloucester for my sake? He might, but I have my doubts. That's why I'm so pleased to see you back at court, fair Cousin. I need every friend that I can muster.'

He had drawn her into a windowed alcove, overlooking the grim, grey Thames. After a moment he seated himself, and with a casual flick of his wrist indicated that she might follow suit. A book, richly bound in red leather, was lying next to the window, where it had been left by one of the Queen's women. He opened it, idly flicking through the thick parchment pages as if looking for inspiration in the poetry it contained.

'A woman's friendship can be of but little value to you in the face of such dangers, Cousin Richard,' she suggested.

'While you are his wife, Despenser will be loyal,' he answered, bluntly. 'I know that. And God knows how I need his loyalty, for he is about the only lord in the Welsh Marches whom I can trust.'

'Surely, Roger Mortimer—' she began.

He interrupted her immediately. 'Our Cousin March has large ambitions,' he answered sharply, 'and he keeps ill company. Small wonder, when he married his sister to that evil man, Richard Arundel.'

Constance knew it was useless to point out to the King that the Arundel marriage had been made against Roger's wishes. She could guess what manner of welcome March had received when he returned to court, and from what she knew of him he was not the kind of man who would patiently strive to rebuild his relationship with the King. It was far more likely that he had retreated into a sulky world of drinking and whoring, in order to escape the realities.

'Cousin Richard, are you sure that March intends you harm?' she asked, carefully keeping her voice mild. She knew that, when he was under stress, the King's temper was uncertain, to say the least.

'Of course I am sure,' he snapped. 'Do you think me a fool? Do you imagine that I allow so dangerous a man to go unwatched? His uncle, Thomas Mortimer, keeps me informed of his treachery, do not doubt it.'

'Thomas Mortimer? But was he not—'

'A traitor?' Unexpectedly, Richard laughed. 'Yes. In his day he was. And now he seeks to be loyal. Such men have their uses, Cousin. At least for the time being.'

***

Unquestionably, when Thomas had arranged for his lady's portrait to be painted, his only intention had been to please her. Yet had he wished to inflict a subtle but severe punishment upon her he could not have chosen a more satisfactory method by which to achieve his purpose. Constance had never been very good at keeping still, and to sit without moving for hours at a time and for days on end was remarkably close to her personal conception of purgatory. Often during those long hours she sighed audibly, and only her innate sense of dignity prevented her from protesting more forcibly.

The young Flemish artist Despenser had commissioned for the task also sighed more than once before his work was completed. Apart from the obvious difficulties entailed in painting such a restless subject, he was troubled by the feeling that he had merely depicted the features and the clothes, with very little of the interesting character concealed beneath them. At a more practical level, his limited patience was constantly tested by a freckle-faced lady, dressed in shabby mourning—presumably some obscure Despenser dependant—who frequently insisted on watching over his shoulder while he worked, offering comments and advice, and urging him towards completion. He had some cause to be glad when it *was* finished.

'It really is quite good,' said Freckles, with the air of an experienced critic. 'Come, Cousin, and see for yourself.'

The artist said something very abrupt in his native tongue, which, fortunately, the ladies did not understand.

Constance rose to her feet, rather stiffly, and moved forward at the sedate pace dictated by her heavy, trailing dress to inspect the painting. On the wooden panel was a representation of her sitting upright on her high-backed chair, the background dominated by a small shield bearing the arms of Despenser and a lozenge of the arms of York.

She nodded, and spoke a few words of courteous, approving French to the young artist before despatching him in the company of one of her pages to receive the reward for his labour.

'Ah, me, Connie,' sighed Philippa Golafre, 'what a comfort this limning will be if ever you should lose your looks!'

She smiled, revealing her very large white teeth, and, infected by her companion's merry humour, Constance chuckled. Philippa had blossomed now that she was free of John Golafre's meanness, cruelty and petty suspicions, and become a surprisingly amusing companion.

'At least it will prove that I was fashionable,' Constance said, with an amiable grin. She was wearing the latest style of gown, called the houppelande and based on the male garment of the same name, though longer, of course, and very high-waisted so as to emphasise the breasts. (In Constance's case the emphasis was scarcely necessary—it had been provided by nature.)

Lady Golafre sighed again, with emphasised wistfulness, as she struggled to conceal her envy. The embroidery of Constance's gown alone had cost over twenty pounds, enough to retain a knight for a year. Despenser griffins, and Yorkist falcons and fetterlocks, worked in gold thread, jostled for space on the rich, red brocaded silk. 'If I only had other clothes fit to be worn in the King's presence, I should burn this accursed mourning within the hour,' she declared, speaking with apparent flippancy. 'As if I do not look hideous enough, without being swathed in black like a nun.'

Constance had one of her generous impulses. 'If it is only a matter of clothing, we shall find you something,' she assured her companion. 'Ah, but I must have a look at the children now. It'll soon be time to make ready to go to Westminster.'

Philippa followed her up the tight stair that led to the nursery. Here was another source of envy, and the more so in that Constance seemed to have little more than a dutiful interest in her two healthy children. Bess was particularly neglected now, her seven-month-old brother having become the centre of attention. Philippa picked the little girl up in her arms, kissing her plump cheek, and feeling a familiar ache in her own heart.

Constance had taken her son from his nurse. 'I am sending them to Caversham at the end of the week,' she said. 'Now that it is summer, there is too much pestilence in the air here in London for babes to be safe. They'd have gone earlier, if I could have persuaded my lord to agree. He likes to have them with us.'

Her mouth tightened. The connection she had made in her mind between her husband and the children had reminded her unerringly of his plans for their daughter's future. March had visited them upon his return from Reigate, and over supper it had emerged that he and Thomas were now firmly agreed on the marriage between Bess and March's elder son.

She would have been less concerned if March had not seemed curiously abstracted, even while he was discussing the issue over their meal. A few days later he had departed abruptly for Ireland, without consulting the Despensers, and apparently without seeking the King's leave. A letter sent from Ludlow, supposedly in explanation, was barely intelligible. Constance suspected that March had been blind drunk when he had dictated it. It seemed folly to seek alliance with someone who was so wildly irresponsible.

She had reminded Thomas of all the old arguments against the marriage, and added what she had learned of the King's regard for Roger Mortimer, but Thomas had been incredibly stubborn, and impatient with her arguments, suspecting her, she felt, of representing Edward's interests.

'Will your brother be at the banquet tonight?' Philippa asked suddenly, breaking into her thoughts.

Constance nodded, and said, rather absently, that she expected so. Had she been less preoccupied she might have asked herself why it was that Philippa was interesting herself in Edward's doings.

Her brother had been abroad since February. Instead of war he had gone on a diplomatic mission, first to France and then to Germany, with the Earl Marshal in his company. Part of their business, it was whispered, had been to bribe the Electors of the Holy Roman Empire into the selection of King Richard as heir to their present Emperor, Wenceslas of Bohemia.

It hurt her that Edward had not found time to visit her and give her his news at first hand. There had been only a brief note, announcing his return to England, and a few empty courtesies from the mouth of the squire who had carried it. Of the outcome of his mission she knew only what Thomas had chosen to convey to her, and that was little enough.

∗∗∗

Alianore Mortimer, Countess of March and Ulster, still flushed from a recent and fairly heated demarcation dispute with the Queen's governess, was in no mood to deal patiently with petitioners. Giving up the attempt to ignore the fool who was tugging at her sleeve to attract her attention, she span angrily upon him, only to find Edward of York grinning at her.

'Have you taken a liking to my sleeve, my lord?' she demanded sharply.

'It is,' Edward admitted, 'a most tasteful sleeve. Its colour matches your complexion most excellently, Aunt Alianore.'

The sleeve was a very rich scarlet, and, as it was accounted a deadly insult to describe a court lady's skin as anything other than the shade of pure milk, the compliment was of limited value. Even so, a smile began to play around the edges of the Countess's lips.

'I am no aunt of yours, Rutland,' she said impishly.

'Only in the most formal sense. For which I own myself grateful. I don't much care for incest.'

'Your wit has risen early today, it seems.'

'And not only that,' he grinned, bending his neck to kiss her with more warmth than courtesy. After the briefest moment of hesitation, her arms went about his neck, and she responded with a ferocity that surprised herself, let alone Edward.

'I'm greatly honoured,' she said with deliberate lightness, skirting around a core of hurt. 'Months have gone by since you last deigned to speak to me. Longer since you seemed inclined to drag me into dark corners.'

'Not by my choice, I swear it. You know that I've been abroad on the King's business. There were preparations to be made before it, and since my return I have spent almost every waking hour with Richard or his Council.'

'Ah, yes, the great Earl of Rutland, the Lord Admiral, burdened down with all his many offices. I hear that one of your duties was to conclude terms for your marriage to the Queen's sister. I suppose that it is fitting, since the King already calls you his brother!'

Edward smiled thinly. It was true that as often as not Richard addressed him by that title, and for some time now he had even been accorded the style in official documents. It was comforting that the King held him in such high regard, but even so there was something vaguely risible in this need to elevate him to the status of a sibling.

'I have no intention of marrying Jeanne of France,' he said bluntly. 'Now or ever. Nor have I any intention of making that fact clear to my cousin. I do but wait for the hour to pass.' He offered his hand in courtly gesture, and they made their way along the gaunt and echoing vaulted passage, Edward carefully adjusting his impatient step to Alianore's statelier pace. 'Have you had any word of your husband?' he asked, suddenly.

'You would speak to me of March, Ned?' A brief laugh burst from her.

'It would be interesting to know why he was in such haste to leave us all. Even his beloved wife. Why he became so anxious to hurry back to his Irish bogs.'

'Why do you hate him so?'

'Do I?'

'It shows in every word you speak about him.'

'Then it may be that I covet his property.' He stared directly into her eyes, pointing his meaning. 'Or perhaps it is simply that I know he's a traitor. I can't prove it. Not yet. But the proof will come. What a fool he is, to go seeking Arundel's friendship! He has been taking too much of the counsel of that old wretch his uncle, Thomas Mortimer, who has ever been the King's enemy.'

She shook her head firmly. 'Roger is no traitor. A fool, perhaps. He's no wish to be king. None. He wants nothing more than his wine cup and his whores.'

'He would make such a king, then, as would be pleasing to many. One who would do Uncle Gloucester's bidding willingly, if only to be left in peace. Alianore, be wary. My enemies are thick on the ground. They are seeking to ruin me, and the King, and all those who are loyal to him, to break the peace with France and destroy all that we have built. When in peril, I grow vicious.'

She turned on him abruptly. 'Do you call it love, to threaten me?'

Edward drew her closer, his blue eyes twinkling persuadingly. 'I do not threaten you, my sweeting. I will do all in my power to protect you from harm. To that end, I will even risk my own position. But you must help me.'

'As a spy in my lord's bed? Is that what you would have me?' She shuddered, and would have left him if he had not kept her sleeve tightly gripped in his hand.

'No,' he said, very quietly. 'No, not that, Alianore. I would have you Queen of England. Not Roger's Queen. Mine.'

***

In his own Glamorgan, Thomas Despenser ranked next to God; he cut less of a figure at Westminster, where he rated no higher than an important baron, and for the King's great feast had to be satisfied with a relatively modest place. His wife, however, was allowed the precedence due to her father's daughter, and thus a place at one of the highest tables, between Harry Bolingbroke and Thomas Mowbray.

The chance of numbers had arranged for her to share a plate with Harry, but it was Mowbray who had most to say to her, much to the displeasure of his other neighbour, Anne of Gloucester. She tried to steer him onto the topic of his visit to Germany, but he seemed to imagine that talk of such matters would bore her, and that she required a diet of empty flattery, mixed with an element of assiduous praise for her brother, Edward.

'I hope I shall soon have the honour of visiting you at Cardiff, my lady,' he said, preening himself, 'for I am to be a neighbour of yours in Wales. My right to Gower has at last been confirmed, and Warwick has been ordered to yield it to me. I think it fair to say that my good cousin, Edward, did much to smooth my path.'

Constance looked up sharply from her wine, for this was news indeed. The case had been going on for so long that she had quite forgotten it. Somehow one did not expect a conclusion to such matters.

Bolingbroke, courteously attentive, was offering her a piece of richly spiced veal, but Constance shook her head, having already had enough of that particular dish. Her cousin swallowed it himself, a little of the sauce dribbling down his forked beard.

'You'll be a neighbour of mine, also,' he pointed out to Mowbray. 'My Brecon lordship marches with Gower, as well as with Glamorgan. A useful gain for you, Cousin. I wonder what price you will be expected to pay for it.'

The Earl Marshal did not answer Harry, except with a grunt, and then had his attention diverted by Anne of Gloucester, who had somehow managed to knock over her glass of wine, brim full. It soaked both of them, with Mowbray getting the worst of it. Confusion reigned.

Bolingbroke smiled thinly at Constance. 'It seems that you are rescued from tedium,' he said, his eyes flickering towards the adjoining chaos. Three yeomen of the Crown and one of Gloucester's squires were already falling over each other as they sought to repair the damage, and Mowbray was on his feet, cursing their clumsiness as well as Anne's.

Constance fought back a burst of laughter as Mowbray, aiming a blow at one of the yeomen, misjudged his aim and stumbled into the hangings behind them, cursing volubly.

'A richly rewarded jester,' Harry said. 'I do wonder at your brother Edward's taste in friends.'

'I thought Mowbray was your friend also,' Constance returned, swiftly on the defensive.

'He's been every man's friend at one time or another. He is apt to shift his loyalty rather abruptly. No doubt but that he will do the same again, if he sees a profit for himself.'

'No one could possibly say the same of you,' Constance said. 'The very perfect, gentle knight.'

To her surprise, he smiled at her irony. 'What a harsh tongue you have, my dear Cousin. How have I offended you? I've long made my peace with Cousin Richard, and have almost as much of his favour as he grants to Mowbray. Your brother and I have become good friends. What more would you have of me?'

'You could carry my favour on a very long crusade,' she answered, refusing to soften.

'Preferably one from which I did not return?' He seemed amused. 'You may one day have your wish. I've sworn that I shall return to Jerusalem, and not as a peaceful visitor, but with harness on my back. But not yet, I think. There's work to be done in England first. A treaty of peace between us, for one thing. I am sure your lord would agree that he'd sooner have me a friend than an enemy.'

'That sounds rather like a threat, Cousin.'

'I do not threaten ladies, Constance. As a knight I deem it my duty to shield them from all risk of danger. When one rides close to the edge of a cliff, my instinct is to call out a warning to her. Even to seize her horse's reins, if I can reach them, rather than see her fall into the pit. My lands all but surround Glamorgan. Is it not to your lord's profit to have my good will?'

Constance swallowed, wondering for a moment whether her ears had deceived her. She was still struggling for an answer when a more serious and much louder dispute broke out at the centre of the table. Her uncle, Gloucester, was on his feet, shouting at the King, and Richard, no less angry, was shouting back.

With the French wars now concluded, Richard had recently evacuated the English garrison from Brest, and indeed the men concerned were present in the hall, sharing in the banquet. This had been in strict accordance with a treaty with the Duke of Brittany, but Gloucester saw it as a betrayal of England's interests, as cowardice and weakness and folly. He had now seen fit to make a public declaration of his opinions, and in no measured terms.

'Sire,' he concluded, audible to every person in that vast room now that the lesser conversations had stilled, 'you ought first to hazard your life in conquering a city from the enemy before you give away what Englishmen have won with their blood.'

The King roared back. Was Gloucester daring to accuse him of cowardice? There was a stir as Richard's other uncles made their way to his side, anxious to keep the quarrel within bounds. Already it was calming, Gaunt all but forcing his youngest brother back into his place, while York sought to soothe the King's ruffled feathers.

'The man is insane,' Mowbray hooted. He had given up all attempts to dry himself, and was sprawled in his place, his back turned towards Anne of Gloucester.

'We followed him once, Thomas,' Bolingbroke said, matter-of-factly.

Mowbray did not seem to appreciate the reminder. His swarthy face reddened. 'And now?' he enquired sharply, almost aggressively. 'Will you follow him now?'

Harry stared back at him, his eyes hard. Then he exchanged a glance with Constance, and treated her to a small, enigmatic smile. Lifting his goblet, he rose to his feet, and bowed gravely in Richard's direction. 'God save the King's Grace!' he boomed, leading the company in loyalty.

7

Constance sat by the open window in Lady Huntingdon's solar, grateful for the cool evening air floating in from the Thames. Huntingdon's house, Coldharbour, was a glorious palace, but London, in the heat of July, stank to high heaven. You could grow more or less accustomed to the stench, given time, but there was always the risk of disease. Plague had flared up not three streets away from the Despensers' own house near the Minories, and it was small wonder, when meat grew rancid almost as soon as it was bought, and idle citizens threw their filth and offal into the highway. Small wonder, either, that city families were counted fortunate if one child in five survived to adulthood.

Her own children were safe, at Caversham. She had not seen them in many weeks. Thomas had been asked—more than asked—to remain with the court, settled at Westminster since the end of May. The men of her household had been preparing for war for weeks, and the letters that would summon the Despenser retainers were already written, requiring only the insertion of a date and a rendezvous to make them effective.

Constance dreaded the thought of fighting, but did not see how it could be avoided. Edward had told her privately there was no doubt that Gloucester and his allies were brewing fresh treason against the King, and added that the unreliable Thomas Mortimer was not the only source of information. The only question was how many others were involved in the conspiracy. Gloucester, Arundel and Warwick had repeatedly refused to attend the King's Council, either making excuses or, in Arundel's case, maintaining a stark silence. All three had been invited to tonight's banquet, but only Warwick had made an appearance.

Elizabeth Huntingdon had arranged suitable entertainment for her guests and it was unfortunate that not all of them were present in the solar to appreciate it. King Richard's arrival had been marked by an immediate announcement that an impromptu meeting of his Council was necessary. The assembled company had promptly split into two groups, with only the women, and such male guests as were not included among the King's advisers, left to hear Master Chaucer recite some portion of his famous rhyming tales of the Canterbury pilgrims. The old poet, stooped so deeply over his lectern that his eyes were practically touching the paper, was still more than capable of holding the attention of an audience, even though few of those present were hearing the tale for the first time. His voice, low and caressing, dominated the room. Only the occasional coarse shout rising from a waterman on the river below served to break into the magic.

Constance's back was leaning against Edmund Mortimer. She could feel the tension in him, as if he were straining not to move even closer. Sometimes his head turned towards her, and she felt his hot breath in the small of her neck. What troubled her most was that she found inexplicable comfort in his proximity, and was glad of the excuse of the crowded room, which kept her from moving away from him. She had the Duchess of York pressed up equally close on her other hand, and at her feet, sitting on the cold, painted tiles, were the Duchess's brother, Mun Holland, and her own younger brother, Dickon. She could not rise from her place without disturbing all of these, at the least, and in any case there was nowhere else to sit, except on the floor.

Suddenly feeling that someone was staring at her, she looked up, and met the unperturbed, speculative gaze of Philippa Golafre who was seated on a cushion, next to the daybed on which Lady Huntingdon and John Cornwall were sprawling. There had been a subtle change in Philippa's manner recently, though it was hard to define. If she was not insolent, she was certainly less deferential. She spoke with greater confidence, and acted with greater independence. It helped, of course, that she had now secured her life share of Golafre's property, her nephew's wrangling having crumbled dramatically in the face of the formidable forces ranged against it. Young Golafre had a place at court, and good hopes of succeeding to his uncle's sphere of influence in Oxfordshire. He was wise enough to know when to give way.

Geoffrey Chaucer's melodic voice died away in mid-stanza interrupted by a notable clamour of voices on the stairs leading up from the great hall. It was clear that the King's Council had broken up.

Within a minute the door was thrown open, somewhat roughly, by one of the Cheshire Archers, who then hurriedly stood back to make room for his master. Richard stood framed in the doorway for a moment, a blinding vision of jewels and cloth-of-gold, while the assembled guests made what obeisances they could in the restricted space that was available to them. As she rose from her curtsey, Constance saw enough of her cousin's face to be aware that he was in no merry mood.

Richard walked slowly across the room to where Lady Huntingdon was standing. Elizabeth curtsied again, but this time the King took her hand, and bowed low over it with gracious courtesy.

'Beth,' he said pleasantly, 'I have a need to borrow your solar for a few minutes. Perhaps you would lead your guests down to supper? We shall join you very shortly.' As Elizabeth moved away from him, he turned towards the window, adopting a very different tone. 'You stay, Mortimer,' he rapped out.

Constance threw a sympathetic glance at her companion, who had suddenly turned quite white. It was obvious that he had incurred Richard's wrath, and that the interview which lay ahead would not be amusing. She gathered her skirts in her hands, and prepared to follow her stepmother, but, before she could take her first step, the King nodded in her direction.

'You will stay with us also, Cousin,' he instructed, only slightly more gently.

Constance did not like the sound of that, but she had no choice but to do as she was told. She watched as the departing guests trailed out, and sought to convey by her expression that she was the most puzzled of them all. It was not, after all, so very far from the truth.

After the last of them had gone, Thomas followed the King into the room. Constance took in the grim, controlled expression on his face. There was serious trouble brewing here, and she racked her brain as she sought an explanation for her own involvement.

Richard walked to the lectern, idly scratching at one of the illustrations on the manuscript that Chaucer had left behind.

'Edmund,' he said, coldly, without looking up, 'we have just had cause to arrest the Earl of Warwick, who is now on his way to a safe prison. We now know why your brother returned to Ireland so abruptly. It seems that he was involved in discussions with my uncle of Gloucester, and your sister's husband, Arundel, who had the insolence to elect him to my throne!' He brought his fist down on the lectern with a dramatic thud. 'What part had you in this treachery? Your uncle, Thomas Mortimer, already lies chained in the Tower. He thought that he could run with the deer and hunt with the hounds. Well, by St. John the Baptist, he has found otherwise! Are you another of his stamp? Do you dare to say that you know nothing of this?'

Edmund, horrified, had already fallen to his knees. 'Sire, I must say so, since it is the plain truth. I am no traitor, and nor is my brother. That I swear.'

'Your Grace,' Thomas put in, 'it is obvious enough that March would not have taken himself off to Ireland in such haste if he had wished to have any part in any plot against you. Nor would he have remained there. He'd be on his lands in Wales, mustering his thousands to fight.'

The King snorted. 'You said enough of this in the Council. Spare me the repetition. March could have proved his loyalty by bringing me the tale of this treason. As was his simple duty. Do you deny it?'

'It would have been an act of wisdom, Sire. Roger is not always wise.'

'His folly put my life at risk,' Richard pointed out angrily. 'If March is not a traitor, he is at least a coward. What other name shall be given to a man who deserts his sovereign lord in the face of danger?'

'Cousin,' Constance put in warily, 'March has not been in England for months. Whatever he has said or done, he is not one of the men threatening you now. Is it not so?'

Richard did not answer for a few moments. The silence hung icily over the four of them.

'There is some truth in what my cousin says,' he acknowledged, after suitable thought. 'March cannot do me harm from Ireland, whatever his intentions. The others are somewhat closer—and stand to be dealt with first! Get to your feet, Mortimer. You shall have ample opportunity to prove your loyalty. As will others. For now, we may as well enjoy our supper.'

That appeared to be the end of it, and Constance found herself wondering why she had been brought into the meeting, while at the same time discovering room to congratulate herself on a successful defusing exercise. Gloucester, Warwick and Arundel were going to face the King's wrath, and richly deserved to do so, but her husband, Edmund Mortimer and March were safe from it, at least for the time being.

Just as he reached the door, however, Richard turned again.

'Thomas,' he said, with a charm that was as careful as it was casual, 'you will, of course, write to March, to make it quite clear that there can be no question of any marriage between your children. You know I have a right to be consulted on these matters. It does not please me to learn of them indirectly, through our family connections. Do not make the same mistake again, my friend.'

With a smile that was chiefly directed at Constance, he left them, Edmund Mortimer trailing closely in his wake.

'You would not see your daughter married to March's son, and so you carried the tale to the King. That's the measure of the loyalty I can expect from my wife, is it?' Thomas scarcely raised his voice, but the naked anger in his eyes made her flinch.

'How can you think such a thing?' she protested.

'You intervened before, when you wrote to your father. This time you thought it better to go to the King, even though I made a point of asking you to keep the matter to yourself.'

'Yes, and I did exactly as you told me!'

'Do not lie, lady! It ill befits you. How else did the King learn of what was settled between us? I didn't tell him, and I'm bloody sure March didn't. I was careful, because Golafre, when he was dying, warned me that I had a spy in my household. I little thought that you were the one betraying my trust!'

Constance's own anger was beginning to rise. She faced him squarely. 'March is close to ruin and mixed in treason. If I'd found the means to stop you binding yourself closer to him, I'd be very pleased with myself.' She paused for breath. 'How Cousin Richard came to hear of your plans I don't know, but it was not through any work of mine. If he's angry with you, my lord, you've only yourself to blame.'

Thomas struck the lectern with the full force of his right hand, so that it toppled and the poet's manuscript scattered across the tiled floor.

'I don't want to hear anything more about it, Constance,' he said coldly. 'Not tonight, and not ever. I don't trust myself. I think it might be better for us both, and safer for you, if you joined the children at Caversham.'

Before she could answer, he had walked abruptly from the room.

***

That same night, moving by torchlight, the King led an army out of London. It was a mixed force, hurriedly assembled, made up of courtiers, the retainers of loyal lords, men of the King's household, and armed citizens of London, led by their Mayor, Richard Whittington. Only a small minority of those involved knew where they were going, or the name of the potential enemy.

As dawn broke they arrived at Pleshey Castle in Essex. The gates opened for the King, and an astonished Duke of Gloucester, still with sleep in his eyes, came out to meet his sovereign. With him were his Duchess and three chaplains.

Edward sidled his horse over to stand next to his brother-in-law.

'It seems my uncle did not expect us,' he remarked, grinning.

'I expect he's not as well informed as you are,' Thomas said. 'After all, you take greater trouble than most of us, have your agents well placed.'

'I don't know what you mean.'

'I think you do. John Golafre told me much about your dealings, though not quite all.'

'Golafre? What had Golafre to do with me?'

Gloucester and his companions were kneeling on the stones of the court-yard. The King leaned forward in the saddle to address the Duke.

'You would not come to Us, Uncle,' he said coldly, 'and so We have come to you.'

Thomas continued his conversation. 'A great deal, by his account. Though he didn't go so far as to tell me that you had placed one of your spies in my bed. I suppose I should have guessed that for myself. After all, half what she says to me has its beginnings in your mouth.'

Edward threw him an impatient glance. 'Tom, this is no time or place to dispute the matter, but you are mistaken. Just about as mistaken as a man can be. Constance would let me burn in hell for eternity rather than do anything to harm you. If you know a lady who loves you better, or is more loyal to your interests, I suggest you go to her.'

Gloucester was arrested and removed to imprisonment at Calais, in the care of Thomas Mowbray. Arundel prepared Reigate for siege, but within days, following persuasion from his brother, the Archbishop of Canterbury, he surrendered and joined Warwick in the Tower. The King had moved against them so swiftly, so unexpectedly, and with such force, that there was no possibility of sane resistance.

The court went on progress to Nottingham. There, in the great hall, amid due ceremony, eight of the King's closest friends and firmest supporters, including Edward of York, Thomas Despenser, and Thomas Mowbray, formally accused the three prisoners of high treason, and demanded that they be tried by Parliament.

**

When the King returned to Westminster, a personal bodyguard of over three hundred Cheshire Archers protected him, further security provided by the enormous armed forces his noble supporters had been licensed to bring with them. Since Westminster Hall was being rebuilt, Parliament would necessarily have to meet in a temporary, wooden structure. Richard watched with satisfaction as the carpenters knocked it together—they were building a scaffold for his enemies.

The King's Council had been forced to accept that it would be too difficult to prove fresh charges of treason against the accused. Revoking the pardons granted to Gloucester, Warwick and Arundel for their crimes as Lords Appellant, committed ten years earlier, solved the legal problem.

Richard cared little for the legalities, as long as he had his revenge. Almost alone, he went at the break of day into Westminster Abbey, there to offer grateful thanks for his victory at the shrine of Edward the Confessor. Then he walked to the newly completed tomb that one day he would occupy. He and his beloved Queen Anne already lay on it in effigy.

The representation of Anne was so lifelike as to bring a tear to the back of his eye. He stroked the cheek of the effigy with his fingers, almost expecting it to grow warm beneath his touch. Dear Anne, who had died of plague, an extraordinary plague that had killed no one else. Not Richard himself, who had held her in his arms only hours before. Not Edward of York, Thomas Despenser or John Holland, who had spent her last evening dancing with her and sharing in her games of cards. Not Constance Despenser or the Countess of March, who had helped her undress on that last night, long after midnight, even as she began the horrid process of dying painfully in her own filth. His own private belief, impossible of proof and kept from all but Edward, was that the Duke of Gloucester had poisoned her so as to make room for his own daughter, whom he had been quick to offer as a potential replacement.

Arundel and his haughty wife had been late for the Queen's funeral, and then had the audacity to ask to be allowed to leave early. It had been a deliberate insult. Richard remembered with satisfaction how he had struck the Earl to the floor, how the man's blood had run out in streams, polluting the abbey and forcing its reconsecration. Because of that, the ceremonies for Anne had not been completed until the middle of the night.

Richard felt the tears flowing over his cheeks, soaking into his beard. 'You are avenged now, my love,' he said.

**

The Lords Appellant had been so named because of the novel way in which they had 'appealed' their enemies in Parliament, a procedure that left the accused with little chance of defending themselves. Now this weapon was turned on the men who had invented it. Into the assembly strode seven of the new appellants, dressed in houppelande of red and white, the King's livery colours. One by one they pointed their fingers at Arundel, the first to be tried, and accused him of treason. Only Thomas Mowbray was missing.

Harry Bolingbroke had agreed to act as a witness.

'You are a traitor, Arundel!' he shouted, above the growing hubbub. 'I remember when we all met at Haringey, the first thing you said was that we must seize the King's person and bend him to our will.'

'You lie at your soul's peril!' cried Arundel. 'Never was I a traitor! What's more, I have a pardon, granted to me by the King of his own free will.'

The Duke of Lancaster was sitting as judge. 'The pardon is recalled,' he said coldly. 'But you say you were never a traitor? Why then did you seek a pardon.'

'To close the mouths of my enemies,' cried Arundel, in a last burst of defiance, 'of whom you are one! You, John, are in greater need of a pardon for treason than I have ever been.'

The King leaned forward in his place to speak for the first time. 'I told you that my knight, Simon Burley, was innocent of any crime. Yet you and your fellows treacherously slew him. You shall have the same mercy that he had.'

Arundel fell silent, and Lancaster took pleasure in sentencing him to death and forfeiture. The Earl was at once escorted to the block.

Warwick made a rambling confession of guilt, on his knees before the King, and thereby saved his life—though not his lands or his liberty. Gloucester was not brought to trial. It was announced that he had died of illness in Calais, though not before leaving a full confession behind him. His lands were forfeited.

The Commons now proved their loyalty by impeaching the Archbishop of Canterbury, Lord Cobham, and Sir Thomas Mortimer. Archbishop Arundel was banished, and old Cobham sent to prison for the rest of his life. The reckoning for Mortimer was postponed. There was to be a further session of the Parliament, at Shrewsbury, to which March would be summoned to give his advice as to the fate of his uncle.

And so it was concluded, quickly, relatively cleanly, and with a reasonable element of mercy. Of course, what really mattered was that there were now many thousands of acres of good English land available for redistribution.

A few days passed before a rumour began to spread that the Duke of Gloucester had been smothered with pillows at a Calais inn by murderers acting under the direction of Thomas Mowbray, Earl Marshal of England.

***

The Countess of March had an unexpected visitor. Sir Thomas Mortimer. He crouched like a black dragon in a chair in the corner of her solar.

'They've released you?' she asked, more than surprised.

'Released?' His laugh was bitter. 'No, lady, I escaped. Bribed my way out. That's why I'm here. I've nothing left. I need a change of clothes, a horse, and enough money to get me passage to Ireland. I'll be safe there. Your husband will hide me.'

Alianore had never liked him, but he was Roger's uncle, and in need of help. She could not find it in her heart to betray him.

'They'll look for you here,' she objected.

'Will they? I doubt it! They're too busy celebrating their victory, the King and his cronies. I'm a very small fish, and with luck they'll not even notice that I've slipped the net until morning. I'll be away as soon as it grows light, if you'll provide the means for my journey.'

March's house in Aldgate was massive, as befitted his rank, and Alianore's household occupied only a small part of it. Sir Thomas was bestowed in a remote cranny where food and drink were brought to him. Alianore and her women then began the task of sorting out some old clothes for him to wear. A servant's livery would be most suitable, Alianore decided.

The light was fading fast when Edward of York arrived. He walked straight into her solar and found her still absorbed in her preparations.

'I must have private words with you, my lady,' he grated. 'Now.'

Lady March's mouth moved in wordless protest for a moment before she gave in and dismissed her attendants. 'You have no right to shame me so,' she told him sharply, after the curtain had tweaked closed behind the last of them.

'I am not here for pleasure, madame,' he retorted. 'Thomas Mortimer has won free from the Tower.'

She laughed, not very convincingly. 'And what has that to do with me?'

'Is he here?'

'Of course not.'

'You are sure?'

'Quite sure.'

'Sure enough to allow my men to search this house?'

She swallowed uncomfortably, and then launched a bold counterattack. 'Is this what your vows of love amount to, Edward? Is my word not good enough? May I remind you that I am the King's close kinswoman—aye, and that I am but a single life away from being Queen of England! Do you dare to suggest that I am a liar?'

Edward treated her to one of his cynical smiles. 'If you ever become Queen, my lady,' he said, calmly, 'you will find that an ability to lie convincingly is all but indispensable. Fortunately, I don't think that your present marriage will cause you to be burdened with such weighty responsibilities. Roger's head is in great peril. Thomas Mortimer knows quite enough to ensure that it is spiked on

London Bridge. You could easily find yourself free to become my wife before many more months are out.'

To his surprise tears appeared in her eyes. 'God forbid!' she sniffed, winning the struggle within herself, 'God forbid that I should ever be so vile as to soil my soul with my lord's murder, or so great a fool as to place the rest of my life in your hands. God knows how ever I came to love you.'

'Doubtless it was my ineffable charm,' he replied, raising a challenging eyebrow.

She ignored the naked invitation to banter and, wiping the tears away with the back of her hand said, in a quiet, hurt voice, 'It is certain that you never cared for me; that from the beginning you did but seek to use me as a weapon against my husband.'

He shrugged. 'You are right, of course.'

'Edward!'

'Why else should I waste so much time on a woman who cares nothing for me?'

'Ned,' she whispered, 'you do not mean it.'

He had not raised his voice, and that, strangely, was what frightened Alianore more than anything.

He turned an icy stare on her. 'I came here to put your loyalty to the test—now I know where it lies.'

'Why, Edward, I am the King's own niece! How can you question where my loyalty is given?'

Suddenly, violently, he seized her by the shoulders. 'Damn Richard! For all I care, you may make a wax image of him, and stick pins in it! I speak of your loyalty to me. If you loved me, you would put all your trust in me, no matter what. No one else would matter. No one!'

'You expect me to help you kill my husband and disinherit my sons?' She shook her head. 'It is you who do not love, for if you did you would not ask for such a thing. It would not even enter your thoughts.'

'We could have sons together. Fine sons. Better than any of March's getting. The heirs of York. Help me, help me, and I swear, on my mother's soul, by Our Blessed Lady and all the saints, by my own salvation, that I shall not rest until I have made you the greatest lady in England.'

'And damned us both,' she answered quietly.

'What is March to you? In God's sweet name, Alianore, you were but two children brought together because your father bought the marriage and dreamed that he might live to see you reigning as Queen. Admit the truth, which is that you'd not spit to save your precious lord from thirst.'

'Can you not be content with what we have? Is it not enough?' She smiled at him artfully, put her arms about his neck and kissed him for the first time that night. It was a long, deep kiss, and it only ended when he dragged himself away from her.

'It seems that it will have to be,' he snorted. Without warning, and as swift as a striking snake, he put his hand into the neck of her gown and wrenched downwards, tearing the delicate fabric like paper. Knocking the breath out of her, he threw her onto the bed, slapping her hard across the mouth.

'Edward!' The name burst from her lips like a scream of disbelief. She stared up at him in horror, terrified by the expression on his face. She had never seen its like, but she recognised pure, unqualified hatred.

The moment passed. He took a step backwards, shaking his head. 'Don't be afraid, lady,' he said, 'I'm not going to waste any more of my seed on you. You're not worthy of it. I'll go to Westminster, and seek out an honest whore.'

Alianore lay where she was, panting like a trapped animal. Tasting her own blood, her lips moving wordlessly, she listened as his footsteps receded into the dark.

***

On Saturday, 29th September 1397, Edward of York was created Duke of Aumale by the King in Parliament, and was endowed with a generous grant of forfeited lands. On that same day four other dukedoms, one marquisate, and four earldoms were also bestowed. Thomas Mowbray, suspected murderer or not, became Duke of Norfolk. Thomas Holland, the elder of Alianore's brothers, who had succeeded his father as Earl of Kent only a few months earlier, was made Duke of Surrey, while his uncle, John Holland, was created Duke of Exeter. Bolingbroke's evidence against Arundel was rewarded with the dukedom of Hereford, while his halfbrother, the erstwhile bastard, John Beaufort, became Marquis of Dorset.

Thomas Despenser naturally received his long-desired earldom. With it came several manors that, as he had asked, were to be held in jointure with Constance, the constableship of the royal castles of Gloucester and St. Briavels, and the wardenship of the Forest of Dean.

He did not linger at the celebrations for an hour longer than was necessary. Even while the King and the Duke of Lancaster were still inspecting a great parade of the London militia, he was spurring west. He rode through the night by torchlight, and then all through Sunday, pausing only once to hear a mass and twice to rest the horses and take food. Even so, it was after midnight before he reached Caversham.

His wife had already been in bed for two hours. She woke uncertainly from her dreams. The room was very dark; she had left the shutters open, but there was scarcely any moon.

'Thomas? Why did you not send word ahead? There's nothing prepared.'

'I'm my own harbinger,' he answered, 'and my needs are simple. I trust you've no objections?'

'You're still angry with me,' she said bleakly. She cursed her own pride. It would have been better, when Despenser had accused her of betraying his secrets to the King, if she had thrown herself to her knees, wept, and begged forgiveness. It was certain that his anger would not have survived such an assault. But she had balked at owning a sin, which she had not committed. She had argued with him instead, and found herself banished to Caversham. And still peace had not been made between them. 'Let me at least get you something to eat,' she went on. 'And what of your men? They must want something.'

'My men can look to themselves. John Norreys has all in hand, never fear.'

'He's cared for me well in your absence. I've been so useless, worrying about you, worrying about what you thought of me.'

She slipped on her chamber-robe, and moved to the table on which stood the regular night livery of bread, beef and wine, provided so that the lord and lady could break their fast at any time they chose. She could feel his eyes on her as she struggled in the darkness to cut up the food and pour out wine for him.

'Are the children well?' he enquired.

'Very well. Bess has been asking for you all this week.'

'You had no cause for fear,' he said. 'I didn't even have to draw my sword.'

She placed the simple meal on the lid of the chest next to his chair. 'I was not to know. I thought there was going to be a battle, or some fighting at least. I've heard nothing but rumours. Is it true that Arundel is headed?'

'Yes.'

'And that my uncle has been murdered?'

He shrugged. 'Perhaps,' he admitted, 'but if he was, it was not by my hand, nor with my consent. Has your conscience suddenly grown tender, my lady? Gloucester deserved death. He more than deserved it. He all but asked for it.'

'He did not deserve to be murdered. It makes a martyr of him, as an open trial would not have done.'

'A martyr? God save us! He was an arrogant, greedy, rapacious traitor. You know that.'

'What does my father say to it? And my uncle of Lancaster? Their brother, murdered!'

He shook his head, unable to understand. 'In all our days together, until this hour, I have never heard you say a good word for him.'

'I do not say one now. He was all you called him, and worse.'

'Well, then—'

'I can't believe that my Cousin Richard ordered such a thing. It must be that Mowbray took the deed upon himself, thinking to gain favour.'

He nibbled briefly on one of the pieces of bread. 'You must ask your brother. Edward sent men of his to Calais, and I doubt whether it was to buy cloth at the market.'

Constance felt her blood run cold. 'Are you saying that *Ned* had my uncle killed?'

'I'm saying nothing of the kind. I don't know, and to be truthful I don't much care. I'm too tired, too weary of it all. If a man's to die, do you think it much matters to him whether he has his head struck off in London or is smothered in Calais? I dare say he was given time enough to make his peace with God, and there's no doubt of his guilt. He confessed it before a judge, in the presence of witnesses. He's dead, and I've been given his title. I'm the Earl of Gloucester now.'

She swallowed. 'I didn't know.'

'So you are a countess,' he went on. He reached out, placed his hands on her buttocks, and drew her closer to him. Her chamber-robe had opened, and she could feel his hot breath against her belly. 'I've never had a countess before. I wonder what it will be like?'

He nuzzled her skin, very gently, and her hands buried themselves in his hair.

'Does this mean you have forgiven me?' she asked, her breath catching.

'Is there anything to forgive? It's common knowledge that women are not very good at keeping secrets. Any fool knows that. Why did I think you any different to the rest?'

'Thomas—'

'There's no need to explain, *treschere*. The fault was not yours, but mine. You are my wife, and in future I shall treat you as such, with love and courtesy. You shall know all of my business that you need to know, but I'll not burden you with my other cares, matters that do not concern you.'

His hands had moved to her breasts, were working there with such quiet, effective persistence that she was scarcely aware of the import of his words, nor yet of the robe beginning to slide from her shoulders.

'It's not food I want,' he said, 'nor wine.'

After a while she bent down until her mouth was able to close on his, while her fingers worked at the untrussing of the lacings that confined his manhood. By the time this intricate task was complete she was more than ready to lower herself slowly upon him.

'This is sinful,' she said breathlessly.

'Is it?'

'You know it is. It's not for *me* to mount *you*.'

He laughed with pure pleasure. 'I dare say God will forgive us. We'll go on pilgrimage, next spring, by way of penance. We already owe thanks for our son; and I certainly owe thanks for *this*.'

She moved gently upon him, seeing no immediate cause for haste. 'It's been a long parting, my lord. Perhaps you'll think twice before sending me away again.'

8

Constance tore Alianore's letter across, and threw it onto the back of the fire. She did not dare to show it to Thomas for fear of the consequences. Instead, when he emerged from his morning meeting with his council of advisers, she told him only that Lady March had written from Ludlow, from where she meant to go on to Chester, taking ship there for Ireland.

Thomas was puzzled. 'What has brought Alianore to this change of heart? From what I understood, she and March were agreed that they were better apart.'

'She's quarrelled with Edward. A bitter quarrel from the sound of it.'

'Ah,' said Thomas, and sprawled himself on the cushioned window-seat, satisfied by the explanation. He was quite able to understand how anyone might find scope to quarrel with his brother-in-law. 'Perhaps it's for the better. I always said she was a fool to let him into her bed in the first place. No good could come of it.'

Constance moved to stand next to him, following his gaze through the open window. The gardens at Caversham were particularly beautiful, sweeping down to the Thames, and ending at their private landing stage. Nearby a stone bridge carried the road from Oxford to Reading over the river; the towers and spires of Reading Abbey, and of the other churches of the town dominated the view to the south. The abbey was no more than a mile away. She had made the journey on foot several times during his absence, to pray for his welfare, and twice, barefoot, since his return.

'Will you explain to me about Thomas Mortimer?' she asked. 'I don't understand why he was accused with the others. Cousin Richard himself told me that the man was his servant, working to his orders. Was it not so?'

Despenser shrugged. 'Mortimer was trying to ride two horses at once. So Edward said.'

'Edward? He arranged for Mortimer to be accused?'

'He and Mowbray—Norfolk as he now is—arranged everything between them. Under the King. The rest of us did as we were told.'

Constance considered this. 'Edward, and Mowbray,' she repeated thoughtfully.

'But, of course, Thomas Mortimer managed to escape.'

'Yes. I wonder how that was contrived? From the Tower?'

He chuckled. 'Coins have a way of speaking persuasively in men's ears. Doubtless someone was bribed. By Alianore, perhaps? Was that the reason for the quarrel?'

Constance began to pace. 'Thomas,' she said at last, 'you said that Mortimer was playing a double game. What if he still is? What if Edward is using him for his own ends? I think you should write to March. Today. Have the letter carried by a sure man; Tyldesley perhaps, or Hugh Mortimer. Warn him not to receive his uncle. If he does, it could be taken as proof of treason.'

He stared at her. 'You seem very sure. What makes you fear such a thing?'

'I know my brother's ways. He's Constable of the Tower now, among other things. No man could be better placed to order Thomas Mortimer's escape. I wonder what limits there are to his wickedness.'

'All this because he quarrelled with Alianore?'

'That's part of it. Only part.' She fell quiet for a moment then, plucking at one of the embroidered fetterlocks that decorated her skirt, asked him if he remembered the meaning of the cognizance.

Thomas nodded. He knew it as well as she did.

'What if Ned thinks he has found a way to open the fetterlock?' she asked. 'He told Alianore that he would make her his queen. If she helped him to bring about March's ruin.'

'She wrote that in the letter?'

'That's why I burnt it. Such a thing, in writing, is not safe.'

'Not safe?' he repeated explosively. 'God's truth, woman, you held your brother's life in your hands. It touches Richard as closely as it touches March. Does Alianore realise the blow she could strike, if she so chose?'

Constance shook her head. 'The word of a woman, a discarded mistress, against that of the Lord High Constable of England? Ned would deny it, and Richard would laugh at it. Or, if he did not, his anger would fall on Alianore for revealing his secret intentions. Who would Richard wish to succeed him? You know how little he trusts Roger Mortimer, and he hates Harry Bolingbroke still more. But Edward he loves as a brother.'

'Do you think it possible?' he asked. 'It may be no more than Alianore's spite against him, or something he said thinking to win her to his purpose. The King would surely not name your brother as his heir.'

She did not answer. Her eye had been caught by a movement on the river, a large barge coming into sight from the east, its liveried rowers easing their pace and then raising their oars from the water as the vessel drifted towards the mooring. She recognised the yellow and green colours at once.

'Salisbury,' she said, mildly surprised. 'I suppose he expects to dine with us.'

John Norreys and such of the other household officers who were at hand were already on their way down the garden to receive the guest. The Despensers went out together to add to the welcome.

Salisbury was the Sir John Montagu of former days, the Lollard poet; he had now inherited the earldom from his uncle. He was almost fifty, and inclined to be portly, but his eyes were as lively as a youth's, and his smile was as warming as the sunlight. Constance noticed with some surprise that he had brought his wife with him; Lady Salisbury was rarely seen at court, indeed was somewhat reclusive.

Their purpose at Caversham seemed to be nothing more than a social visit, an excuse for a pleasant row upriver from their home at Bisham. It was taken for granted that they would wish to stay for a day or two, of course. Dinner suffered a mild delay while it was restructured at short notice; for the interim they lingered in the garden, walking along the long, gravel paths beneath the arbours that protected the ladies' complexions from the sun.

Constance found that Lady Salisbury had a lot to say to her; rather too much, Constance thought. Maud was excessively proud of her lord's poetry, and insisted on sitting on one of the benches and reading a sheaf of it aloud, while the men walked further and further away, strolling along the edge of the river towards the bridge, absorbed in their talk.

When she had run out of poetry, Maud called over a slim, pimpled youth who bowed low before Constance, but remained courteously silent.

'This is my eldest son, Alan de Buxhull,' Lady Salisbury said proudly. 'My second husband's boy. Salisbury's my third, you know. I was widowed twice before I was eighteen. Adam's father was kindly enough, and everyone liked him, but he hadn't an idea in his head, and certainly no poetry. Salisbury's the cleverest man I know. Too clever for his own good, some say. And he has such *ideas*. Do you know, we were no sooner married than he had all the statues of saints thrown out of my church at Shenley. He says they're contrary to God's law.'

'A strange fancy. I take it you do not agree?'

Maud shrugged. 'He's my husband. How should I not agree with him on such a matter? I've not read the Scriptures, as he has.'

It was clear to Constance that if Salisbury had read the Scriptures he had certainly not understood them. 'Such questions are beyond me,' she shrugged. 'I'm content to follow the advice of my confessor. As is my lord.'

'Oh, I think Salisbury just enjoys arguing with priests, friars and the like,' Maud said. 'I don't think he'll be talking of such matters to Despenser—to Gloucester, I mean. Oh, dear, I find all these new titles very confusing. I've scarcely got used to my own. I was Dame Montagu for so long, I still think of myself as such. I never thought he'd live long enough to inherit, you know. The uncle hadn't set a foot out of Bisham these ten years, was nigh as old as the hills, but showed no signs of dying until the day he went. Miserable old fellow! Sold off half his land so that John shouldn't have it. Mind you, my lord has sold more, including some of my inheritance. He's always short of money, always spending it on new things. If he sees a book he wants, he doesn't care if it costs him fifty pounds, and I've known him give a common musician ten pounds for an evening's work.'

The Countess of Salisbury had been born plain Maud Francis, daughter of a citizen of London. Constance supposed that explained her failure to understand the principle of largesse, the open-handed generosity that was a cornerstone of knightly culture. An English earl could not live like some cheese-paring scribe. Only merchants were base enough to use their money to make even more money. 'It little profits a lord's reputation to be thought ungenerous,' she said.

'It profits it still less to be thought penniless,' Alan de Buxhull remarked sullenly, 'which is what he'll be before long.'

'Be quiet, Alan!' Maud snapped, as if addressing a particularly stupid dog.

'It's true, Mother. He's already worked his way through most of your property. He'll be selling Bisham next. Where are we to live? In one of his fancy French manuscripts?'

'That is not a matter for discussion here. My lady of Gloucester will think you ill bred. Kindly apologise.'

Young Alan bowed again, his face sullen. 'I apologise to you, madame,' he said to Constance, 'if I have given you any offence.'

Constance shrugged the matter off, and suggested that it might be pleasant to walk by the river for a time. However, it proved that Lady Salisbury had an urgent need to make use of a privy, and so instead they went inside, leaving Alan de Buxhull to join his stepfather and Thomas at the edge of the water.

It was well after dinner before Constance had a chance to exchange a private word with her husband, to ask him what it was that Salisbury wanted. She had the distinct feeling that it might be a loan.

Thomas laughed at the very idea. 'Salisbury has a claim of sorts to March's lordship of Denbigh,' he explained. 'He wants to compound with him for it, and, as he doesn't know Roger as well as I do, he's asked me to intercede on his behalf. He's prepared to sell out cheaply rather than waste time and expense going to law. I'll send Hugh Mortimer to his cousin. He can mention the other matter at the same time.'

Constance was not convinced by the explanation; she was still less convinced when, after supper, Thomas and Salisbury locked themselves away in an inner chamber, excluding their advisers as well as their womenfolk. She was left to entertain Lady Salisbury and Master de Buxhull and, even with Philippa Golafre and the Norreyses to assist, this was no light task. It helped that one of Dame Golafre's elder sisters was the widow of Salisbury's uncle, giving Philippa a chance to exchange some family reminiscences with Maud. After that a great deal more of Salisbury's poetry was recited; his lady seemed to have brought an entire library of it in her baggage.

The evening ended with music, Salisbury and Despenser emerging from their conference just in time to take part. Salisbury led the singing, treating them to several of his own compositions. He had, Constance acknowledged, a very fine voice, though the concentration she found she needed to play her cithar to a reasonable standard prevented her from thinking about very much else. They concluded by dancing several rondes together, Salisbury again leading the proceedings on merit. It was so enjoyable that Constance almost forgot her earlier irritation.

She knew her husband well enough to know that he was keeping information from her, but she was also aware that pressing him too hard would only serve to make him stubborn. She tried to persuade herself that the secret was something insignificant—the purchase of another horse, perhaps—but could not quite succeed.

In the morning their guests visited the chapel with them, ate breakfast, gave thanks for hospitality and took their leave, Despenser very graciously handing Maud into the barge.

'We are invited to Bisham,' Thomas said, as the barge pushed out into the channel.

***

The crowbar squeaked in protest as it was applied to the tomb, settled reluctantly into the gap between the stone slab and its neighbour. The sexton sweated with a mixture of fear and effort as he applied the requisite leverage. It was dead of night in the church of the Austin Friars in Broad Street, London. The friars, disturbed from sleep, clustered together in the shadows.

Beside the tomb, their drawn faces lit by torchlight, several of the leading lords of the King's Council stood in a semi circle. At the centre was the Duke of Lancaster; arranged around him in some approximate order of precedence were Edward of York, Thomas Mowbray, Thomas Holland, Duke of Surrey, Northumberland, Salisbury and Thomas Despenser. A host of lesser men filled the rest of the building.

There had been tales of miracles at Arundel's grave. It was said that his head and his body had joined themselves together. These stories had found their way into King Richard's dreams, troubling his sleep. There was only one way to disprove them.

The dislodged stone was swung noisily across the pavement. Beneath it, wrapped in cerecloth, Arundel's body was dimly visible.

'Open it!' snapped Lancaster. 'Let's all see this wonder for ourselves.'

Two of the friars stepped from the shadows to perform the noisome task. Working by the uncertain light of the torches they cut and tugged at the stitching of the shroud until the cloth parted and the Earl's corpse slowly emerged from its wrappings. It was in one piece, the head reunited with the neck... In the background someone retched.

'Jesus save us!' Mowbray exclaimed.

Edward stared intently at the body, holding his torch close to it so that all could see what he had noticed. 'The angels who performed this miracle used a needle and thread,' he said contemptuously.

Lancaster took one look and stepped back, away from the stench of decay. He pointed at one of friars. 'You! Unpick the stitches.'

It was gruesome work. Thomas drew back as far as his duty as an official witness allowed, his stomach churning. He had no doubt at all that Arundel had deserved execution, but this seemed gratuitous. Was it so important that the head should remain severed? The man was dead. Only a fool would believe him capable of working miracles, and the opinion of fools was surely not significant.

The head was separated from the body at last, and placed, at Lancaster's order, a good two yards from the trunk. Then the friars were made to process repeatedly over the pavement between the two, so as to emphasise the point.

'By order of the King's Grace, all those involved in this deception are banished from the realm,' Edward announced, his voice cold and formal. 'They have ten days to leave England, never to return, on pain of death. The attainted traitor, Richard Fitzalan, late Earl of Arundel, is to be re-buried in an unmarked place beneath the pavement of this church. God save the King—and may all his enemies rot in the ground!'

It was too late to go to bed. Thomas went with Salisbury, the Duke of Surrey, Sir John Russell and Sir William Bagot to Salisbury's house in Oldnes Lane, where they shut themselves in the parlour with what was left of the fire and warmed themselves with spiced wine.

'I think Lancaster enjoyed that task,' Salisbury said. 'It gave him another chance to spit on his enemy.'

Thomas watched his companions in silence, savouring the wine, glad of the warmth of the fire. Salisbury was composed and at his ease, and Surrey, equally relaxed, was leaning back in his place, his long legs stretching out across the floor as he talked. Russell was quiet, almost to the point where Thomas suspected he was drifting into sleep. Russell's young wife, Thomas's niece, had died in childbed during the summer, a blow that seemed to have aged the Master of Horse by ten years. Or perhaps it was the ruination of his old enemy, Warwick, which had removed the driving force from his life. Bagot, by contrast, was distinctly restless, as if sitting on a thorn, and having obvious difficulty in keeping silent. Thomas did not much care for Bagot, instinctively disliked the sly, calculating look in the man's eyes, and wondered why Salisbury had included him in the invitation. He doubted whether the two of them were friends.

Salisbury was speaking again. 'It seems to be forgotten that Bolingbroke was just as much a traitor as Arundel, that he and Mowbray fought against the King at Radcot Bridge.'

Surrey yawned and stretched himself. 'We've said all this before. Lancaster is too powerful to be touched. He has the King's favour, and we've just been looking at the last man who dared to stand up to him.'

Thomas stirred at that, flexing his back against a cushion. 'You're close to saying that it was a mistake to kill Arundel.'

'Not a mistake—but it was a good day's work for Lancaster. That's why Harry Bolingbroke spoke out in Parliament—he and his father wanted Arundel dead, at least as much as the King did. It's too late for regrets now, there's nothing we can do about it.'

'He needs a son,' Russell grunted, as if speaking in his sleep. 'The King I mean. A son would settle all. He should never have wedded himself to that child.'

Salisbury took a deep breath. 'Sir William, you must tell these lords what you told me.'

Bagot stood up, glanced from face to face, and wiped his mouth with the back of his hand, setting up a jangle from the folly-bells that decorated his wide sleeves.

'Some months ago,' he said, his head low, 'before he married the Queen that now is, the King spoke to me of giving up the throne. He said that once his enemies were brought low, and the power of the crown restored, he would abdicate.'

Thomas laughed, unable to contain himself.

'It is no jest,' Salisbury said quietly.

Surrey put his wine down with a resounding thud. 'Then it's a lie. Why should my uncle the King think of giving up the throne? If he did, would he not speak to me, for one, before the likes of this fellow?'

'What do I gain by lying, my lord?' Bagot asked, his brusque voice rising a little in anger. His eyes narrowed. 'This touches me as much as it does you. More. I'm the King's man, and he's shown me great favour. Whoever sits on the throne, you'll still be a great lord. I have no such assurance. Without the King's favour, I am *nothing*.'

Surrey addressed himself to the others. 'I think Lancaster has put this tale in his mouth, to see how many of us would be willing to accept Bolingbroke as king. Bagot wore Lancaster's livery for years. The chances are that he's still nothing more than his puppet.'

'It's true I was once in Lancaster's service,' Bagot said angrily, 'and little reward I had for my trouble. He treated me worse than a dog, and I swear before God that I'll give my life before I'll see him or his precious son on King Richard's throne. That's why I spoke to Lord Salisbury.'

Salisbury raised his hand before anything more could be said. 'And that is why I asked him here to meet us, so that you, my lords, might hear the tale.'

'Do I understand this aright?' Thomas asked. 'Do you say, Bagot, that the King has chosen Lancaster as his heir?'

The knight shrugged his broad shoulders, and hesitated for a moment as if giving the question thought. 'The King said nothing of that. But you know as well as I do, my lord, that Lancaster would not allow any other man to stand in his way. It must not be so. We must find a way to prevent it, whatever the cost.'

'It may be something the King said when he was in an ill mood,' Thomas suggested. He was desperate to believe that, to put off the crisis. 'Nothing more than a passing whim. The only way to be sure is to ask the King, and I doubt whether that would be wise.'

The others, apart from Bagot, chuckled at the understatement. Then there was a long silence.

'All we can do is wait upon events,' said Salisbury. 'In time the truth will become clear. We are the King's men, and there are others who think as we do and are ready to join us. If we stand together, I think we can deal with any who think to put themselves in Richard's place.'

Bagot shook his head and sat down by the fire. After a while picked up a poker and began to prod at the coals with a vigour that suggested he was thinking of Lancaster's heart.

'Waiting will not serve,' he said at last. 'It is time to act, my lords. If you do not wish to soil your hands, then I'll do what must be done without your aid.'

***

The court was gathered at Coventry for Christmas, centred on the cathedral priory, a vast complex of buildings that provided more than sufficient accommodation for the formal celebrations, both religious and secular—though the King's guests were lodged all over the city, even as far away as Sir William Bagot's castle at nearby Baginton.

The Despensers had travelled by way of Bisham, where they had met not only the Earl and Countess of Salisbury but also the Duke and Duchess of Surrey, and William le Scrope, Earl of Wiltshire and Treasurer of England. The pretext of the gathering had been the betrothal of Salisbury's eldest son to Surrey's last unmarried sister, Eleanor, but the seal had been set on an alliance much wider than that. They had arrived at Coventry as a single great procession.

Constance was still not sure that she had her husband's full confidence, or that all had been explained, but she gathered that the new faction was established for mutual defence against those who resented the downfall of the King's opponents. She could not deny that Surrey was a useful ally. He had been granted Warwick Castle, and most of the Beauchamp lands in Warwickshire and Worcestershire that had not been given to the Despensers themselves. With his support they were supreme in the lower Severn valley, with only Lord Berkeley a potential rival in Gloucestershire. Thomas had already sent Hugh Tyldesley and fifty archers into the Forest of Dean to acquaint the troublesome outlaws with the new order of government.

'Constance,' said the King, draping his arm across her shoulders, 'I hope that if you ever seek an astrologer you will be a better judge of the breed than is your brother. I can't tell you how highly he spoke of this wretch he found for me. And then all the fellow could do was babble that I should beware of toads! That a toad should be my bane!'

He ended in an explosion of laughter.

'Edward should know better than to waste Your Grace's time,' she said, shaking her head.

'He tells me he relies on the man himself—has never known him to be wrong. Imagine, after defeating all my enemies, I shall be brought low by a toad! Do you think it likely?'

Constance did not. 'I think it nonsense. Of course, the man may have been too much in awe of you to speak sense,' she suggested.

Richard nodded, finding the explanation reasonable. Then, abruptly, he was off on another tack. 'I've noticed that you and Edward seem to be at odds. Am I mistaken?'

'No.'

'How has he offended you?'

'By his falseness.'

'I see. You don't wish to say more?'

She bowed her head. It was difficult to go further without revealing some of the secrets Alianore had confided to her, matters she had not even discussed with Thomas.

'I don't wish this quarrel to continue,' Richard said. He spoke lightly, almost playfully, but there was an underlying note of command. 'It pains me to see you at odds. Ned will ask your pardon, and you will grant it. Will you not, my dear Cousin?'

Constance curtsied submissively. She knew there was no point in further discussion. 'As Your Grace pleases.'

Her tone was flat, but the King seemed satisfied. He beckoned to Richard Maudelyn who, as usual, was within call. 'Fetch the Duke of Aumale here. We have need of his counsel.'

Edward was actually within sight, talking to Philippa's mother, Lady Mohun; but in so crowded a room he was well beyond earshot. Maudelyn had almost reached them when Constance's attention was drawn to the entrance of the hall. The crowd was parting, making way for important new arrivals. As the first obeisances were made she saw that it was her uncle, Lancaster, and with him, a step behind, his son, Harry Bolingbroke.

'It seems we must postpone the reconciliation,' Richard said quietly. 'I did not expect us to be so honoured today.'

He made a gesture to the musicians in the gallery to halt their playing, and, as Lancaster knelt stiffly before him, stepped forward more than the two or three places that courtesy required, removing his hood as an additional sign of respect for his elder.

The Duke rose with difficulty, evidently glad of the hand that the King had extended to him. 'Sire,' he announced, 'my son has important information for Your Grace's ear.'

Bolingbroke rose to his feet, his expression solemn but composed. Constance saw him gaze around, as if trying to make sure that everyone was listening.

'Your Grace,' he said, in a voice that carried to the rafters, 'it is my duty to tell you that Thomas Mowbray, Duke of Norfolk, questions your royal clemency. I met him by chance on the road near Brentford, and he warned me that our lives were in danger, that we had cause to take measures to defend ourselves. When I asked him for what cause, he said: "Because of Radcot Bridge." When I mentioned your recent gracious pardon, freely granted to us, confirmed by Parliament, and covering all our former offences, he laughed, calling me a fool for thinking it of any worth. Sire, it seemed to me that these words were slanderous and an offence to your royal dignity, and that as your loyal subject I was bound to acquaint you with Mowbray's contempt for your word.'

'Where is Norfolk?' Richard asked, the quiet question ringing in the stillness of the hall.

Mowbray was already pushing his way to the front of the crowd. 'I said no such words!' he shouted. 'No such words, Sire, nor anything like them. This bastard lies!'

Constance felt her arm gently squeezed. Somehow, Edward had worked his way around the back of the King to join her. 'What witnesses were there to this conversation?' he asked.

'We'd drawn apart from our retinues,' Harry answered impatiently. 'There were no witnesses.'

Edward smiled, and turned to the King, shrugging. 'Then, Cousin, there can be no proof, one way or the other. Sire, I suggest that you order our two kinsmen to bury their differences. Let this be called a misunderstanding.'

'*Misunderstanding?*' Harry repeated. 'This rat has called me a liar and a bastard, here, before all. An insult such as that cannot be smoothed over. Especially when it comes from the mouth of a murderer.'

'I shall decide how this quarrel is settled,' Richard said. 'You will swallow an insult if I so order it.'

'Sire, it is well known among your people, even if it is not known to you, that this man murdered your uncle and mine, the Duke of Gloucester, and prevented his proper trial before Parliament. He has stolen money intended for the payment of the Calais garrison, which makes him a thief, and by doing so has jeopardised Your Grace's possession of Calais, which amounts to treason. All this I will maintain with my body, if so required.'

'And I will defend myself with my sword, if these slanders are not withdrawn,' Mowbray shouted back. 'You are the traitor, Bolingbroke! You are the one who covets the throne, not I!'

The King did not respond. He seemed to be staring thoughtfully at Harry Bolingbroke. Constance, following his gaze, suddenly understood the reason for Richard's abstraction. The sleeves of Harry's brown and gold houppelande were covered with embroidered toads.

'This is a matter for Parliament to determine,' Richard said. 'You shall be judged by your peers, and until then you shall both be kept in ward.'

'Your Grace,' Edward murmured, 'I am willing to be bound as a surety for Harry. There's no need for him to be confined.'

Lancaster threw him a grateful glance. 'I am also ready to stand surety for my son, in whatever sum Your Grace deems proper.'

Richard thought for a moment, and then nodded abruptly. There were other pledges for Harry, but none for the man he had accused. Mowbray was arrested, Edward taking charge, and led away to confinement.

Almost before the commotion had died down, Constance found Bolingbroke at her side. 'You see, Cousin, how loyal I have become,' he said quietly. 'Even to the extent of reporting those who slander the King's Grace.'

She took a step away. 'There may be a price to be paid. We shall all have to be careful when we speak to you in the future. Now that you are turned informer.'

Harry forced a smile. 'I thought you might be pleased, to see me so anxious to defend Cousin Richard's good name against Mowbray's lies.'

Constance did not answer directly. Instead she touched his sleeve, running the tips of her fingers over one of the gold embroidered toads. 'Beautiful work,' she said. 'Do you know, it seemed to me that Cousin Richard could scarcely take his eyes from it. I think, Harry, you have at least one thing in common with my brother, Edward. One thing at least, unless I am much mistaken. You share the same embroiderer.'

9

It was the afternoon of Twelfth Night. Constance had spent three hours since dinner in the company of the Duchess of York, a duty rather than a pleasure, and was grateful for the chance to escape to her own lodgings on the pretext of needing to make herself ready for the evening.

The lodgings, though, were occupied. Constance guessed as much when she saw a group of the Duke of Aumale's liveried followers lounging around at the foot of the staircase, and all doubt was removed when she found Edward warming himself by the fire, Philippa Golafre in the process of handing him a cup of wine. She had a fleeting impression that her entry had caused them both to start, but Edward was rapidly on his feet, smiling and self-confident.

'I am told,' he said, 'that I am to ask your pardon.' He seemed to find the idea amusing. 'For what it is that I am to be pardoned, God knows, not I. Even so, I ask it, for the sake of family peace at Christmas.'

Constance drew closer to the fire. She hated this time of year, with its chills, draughts and short days. The short walk across the courtyard from the Duchess's rooms had reddened her cheeks and turned her fingers stiff with cold. She signalled to Mary Russell to help her discard her cloak.

'I told you what would befall if ever you hurt Alianore,' she said, 'that I would never forgive you. You hurt her more cruelly than I imagined possible.'

Edward nodded, sat down again, and stroked the head of the young greyhound, Paris, who was lying on the rug. The animal was one of Constance's Christmas gifts from the King, a son of Math, no less. 'A fine dog this,' he remarked. 'You should have some rare sport with him next season. If he does well, we could put him to that fawn bitch of mine, the one I brought back with me from Ireland. She's as fast as any I've seen, save Math himself. When old Math did a job of work instead of lazing on the King's bed.'

'Are you truly as cold and callous as you seem?' she demanded. 'Or is it but another of your pretences? You ask for forgiveness? Should you not at least mouth some words of regret? Even if they mean nothing!'

He looked up at her. 'I understood that you had been told to make your peace with me. I have apologised for any action of mine that has offended you. Why waste words? Is it not better to look to the future? To consider the advantages of friendship?'

'Or of how I may profit from being the sister of the next King of England?'

She had the satisfaction of seeing his expression darken. That, at least, had nudged the target. 'I do not aim so high,' he grunted.

'No? Alianore seems to think otherwise.'

'You place too much weight on Alianore's opinions. She's as capable of lying as anyone else. It's Harry Bolingbroke who thinks he should be in Richard's place. His quarrel with Mowbray is part of his design, as he expects to win, and be made stronger thereby. I've been watching him for some time.'

'Hence your trick with the toads?'

He smiled his surprise. 'You perceived it?'

'It was not difficult. Knowing what your astrologer had told Cousin Richard.'

'Ah! I must learn to be more subtle. Fortunately not all are as keen-witted as my little sister. Most will remember only that I was the first to stand surety for Harry, even before his own father. I felt Richard had need of a warning. That it should come to him on that particular evening was more than I could contrive. It was truly an act of God.'

Constance settled herself on the chair opposite him. 'I thought Harry had become your friend, but you seem to take pleasure in betrayal.'

He shook his head in disbelief. 'You've always hated Bolingbroke. I can remember when he used to come to Fotheringhay to hunt with us. You'd never go out on those days. As often as not you'd find some excuse to go to your room and stay there until he left. You used to say he was as bad as Arundel, but less worthy of forgiveness, being closer to Richard in blood. What has changed?'

She stared into the fire. 'Nothing. I know well what they did, Ned. You reminded me of it yourself when we were at Usk. With his father in Spain, Harry had the whole power of Lancaster in his hands. He was the one man who could have stopped it all, if it had pleased him to do so.'

'Then?'

'I've never pretended to be his friend. He knows exactly what I think of him.'

'And you think that an advantage? Constance, I wonder at you! How many years have you lived at court? Have you still not learned that the way to survive is to keep our enemies guessing? Do that, and stand together as a family, and we have some chance.'

'You keep your family guessing as well as your enemies, Ned. We can't stand together while we mistrust one another, and you've given Thomas too much cause to doubt you.'

'Then I must find a way to change his mind. Do you think it might help if I were to tell him that I intend to marry his cousin?'

She was puzzled. 'His cousin? What cousin?'

Edward smiled, obviously well pleased with himself. 'Lady Golafre has kindly agreed to accept me as her next husband. We count ourselves betrothed.'

Philippa had withdrawn to the far side of the room, but now advanced again, stood by his chair and put her arm around his shoulders, as if to demonstrate the union. 'I am sure Tom will be delighted,' she said. 'He has been so anxious for my welfare since Sir John died, so kind and protective. And we shall be sisters, Connie, able to share all our secrets.'

Constance felt her mouth moving wordlessly, became aware of a cold trickle of sweat running between her breasts. 'Philippa,' she got out at last, 'I pray you, tell me that my brother hasn't tricked you into his bed with his lies. Not while you are under our protection. God help us all, Thomas will surely kill him if he has! He can't make you his wife, no matter what he has promised. He's to marry the Queen's sister. He has no choice in the matter.'

'You're mistaken, Sister,' Edward said, 'as well as insulting. I've never had the least intention of marrying that little child. I've need of a wife, not a daughter. Richard knows of my decision, and has no objection.'

'You truly intend—'

'I intend to marry the Earl of Gloucester's cousin,' he interrupted. 'I trust that we shall have his approval, though we do not require it. Still less do we require yours.'

'It's only natural that your sister is shocked, Ned,' Philippa said gently, a thin, complacent smile spreading over her face. 'It's only to be expected; she had no reason to imagine that you intended to honour me in this way. I think you should have broken the news more gently. Now she needs a little time to accustom herself to the idea. That's all. Isn't it, Connie?'

Constance locked her gaze on her, stared at her down her long nose until Dame Golafre gave way. 'A love-match is it, dear Cousin?' she asked. 'I suppose it must be, since you are all but ten years his elder, and far below him in rank. If it were truly so I could find it in my heart to be happy for you. There's little enough love in the world to grudge it where it arises. Unfortunately, Philippa, my brother is incapable of love. He doesn't even begin to understand what the word means. Your dower lands must be far richer than I imagined. Still, Edward is right. It's none of my concern.'

She rose, walked unhurriedly from the room. When Mary Russell tried to attend her she ordered the girl back, her voice harsh as a blow from a crop. She descended to the darkening courtyard, where Richard of Conisbrough was engaged in a desultory game of football with one of Beth Holland's sons and a couple of the priory's schoolboys. She watched them for a moment, and then called to Dickon to escort her.

'Where are we going?' he asked. 'Where are your women?

'I don't need them, and I don't need you to ask questions. I'm only taking you because Thomas wouldn't like me to walk about in the dark on my own.'

'Aren't you cold? Shall I run up and get your cloak?'

Constance only became aware of its lack as he spoke. 'No—yes. But hurry. Find a plain one.'

She waited impatiently, worried that Edward would emerge; it was bad enough that his idling followers were watching her from the shadows, their bored voices seeming to bounce from the cobbles, occasionally loud when they reached the highlights of their discussion. The boys' ball thudded against the wall, rolled lazily towards her. One of them ran over, picked it up, apologised. Then Dickon was back.

'You don't look well,' he said.

She snatched the cloak from him. It was a very plain one, belonging to Agnes Norreys. She fastened it about her, pulled the hood over her head. 'I'm perfectly well,' she said. 'Come on.'

It was only then she realised that she hadn't the least idea where she was going. She just kept walking, until she found herself at one of the doors of the great Cathedral.

Inside the service of Nones was reaching its end, the monks chanting in their stalls.

She saw it all now with dreadful clarity. It was Philippa who had been spying on them, passing their secrets to Edward. It was obvious! How could she have been so blind? She remembered them together in the chapel at Usk, their hushed conversation, and their air of amused conspiracy.

Philippa had been present on the evening of March's visit, a discreet waiting-woman in the background, never speaking, never drawing attention to herself. Constance had not suspected her for a moment. She was Thomas's own cousin, sheltering in the safety of his household, and had shown every sign of gratitude for their protection. She had been with them for over a year, dogging Constance's steps, rarely out of hearing.

Constance stumbled on a worn tile. The vast, dark, Norman nave was almost empty. Two or three of the Coventry merchants were agreeing the details of a business deal, and, next to a knight's tomb, an enterprising trader was selling cheap relics and pilgrim badges, while another was offering cold pies from a tiny, portable table. No one paid her the least heed. Concealed in Agnes' modest cloak, even her face largely hidden, attended only by a solitary boy, she had the rare privilege of anonymity, might well pass as one of her own gentlewomen.

Thomas's faith in her loyalty to him had been absolute. They had had few secrets, had from the first discussed politics together, and debated his plans and aspirations for the future. Often he had gone so far as to seek her advice, and she had never feared to offer it. That was all lost because Edward and Philippa, slowly and methodically, had undermined the foundations of his confidence in her. Because of them he thought her false, incapable of holding her tongue.

She retained his love, but even that was threatened. How long could a man continue to love a wife he did not trust? They would surely begin to resent one another as the suspicions festered. She could not bear to be shut out, as Maud Salisbury was by her husband, treated as a child or an untrustworthy fool. It was intolerable.

'Do you not need to make ready for the King's feast?' Dickon asked tentatively.

Constance nodded. There was little enough time in truth, but she needed a chance to think in silence. 'I am going to pray for a little while,' she said. She gestured towards the nearest side chapel. 'In there. You can walk around for a while if you like. I'll be all right on my own.'

The chapel was empty, silent, and almost completely dark but for the light of the candles burning before the image of St. Osburg, a virgin saint of local importance. Constance knelt in prayer for a few moments, grateful for the solitude, and began to feel her calmness return. Edward was right. It was foolish to reveal too much of one's feelings. Better by far to conceal them and await an opportunity for revenge. Strangely it was Philippa's treachery that hurt the most. She had expected nothing better from her brother.

***

'I had an idea that Edward was interested in her,' said Thomas Despenser, talking across the large dish that he and his lady were sharing. He had to raise his voice a little so that she could hear him above the babble of competing conversations and the lively accompaniment provided by the King's musicians. Politely he cut a manageable piece of eel, dripping in sauce, and placed it in front of her.

They were so crowded on the bench that there was no option but to sit close together, their heads almost touching. Constance took the proffered morsel in her fingers, and cautiously transferred it to her mouth. Cinnamon burst on her taste buds, the rich sauce almost disguising the taste of the fish, but unfortunately not quite succeeding.

'I didn't think that it was marriage he had in mind,' Thomas went on. 'Though she's not without property, of course. Her Fitzwalter dower lands might bring in two hundred and fifty marks a year, perhaps more; and Golafre's settlement probably adds half as much again. But they are only dower lands, for her lifetime. They can't be inherited, and I know for certain her mother has sold the reversion of the Mohun lands, so there's nothing to come there. Edward surprises me. I thought he had more ambition. He must truly love her.'

'Truly? I think he truly loves no one but himself.'

'Of course, he makes much of her being my cousin. Perhaps you were right, *treschere*, when you said he wanted my friendship. Though I think you were wrong about him aspiring to greater things. No one could imagine Philippa as Queen of England!'

Constance snorted. No one could imagine Philippa as Duchess of York, and yet she would be, one day. 'I dare say she'll still expect me to carry her train,' she said coldly.

'She's carried yours often enough. Ah, that's what you dislike about it, I suppose? Well, I can understand that, but there's nothing we can do about it. Edward's his own master.'

She did not answer. Her fingers reached automatically for another small slice of eel. They had scarcely reduced the edible mountain that had been set before them. The various dishes added up to far more than the pair of them could possibly wish to consume for a whole meal, let alone a course. More than sufficient, indeed, to serve as a portion for those, lower down the hall, who were eating four or six to a mess. This feast would produce cartloads of surplus food that could be given away to the poor at the gate, a symbol of the King's wealth and generosity.

'Has my father given his consent?' she asked.

'I don't believe he's been consulted. Anyway, he's no more power to stop it than we have. The only person that Edward would listen to is the King, and he says he has the King's agreement.'

Constance took a sip of her malvoisie, its sticky sweetness contrasting sharply with the bite of the cinnamon. 'I think I might ask my cousin later tonight exactly what it is he thinks he has agreed,' she said. 'Ned has a way with his words, a way of twisting his meaning.'

Despenser shook his head. 'This marriage cannot harm us. It *does* bind him closer to me, there's no denying it. And they are not likely to have any children.'

She stared at him, surprised. 'You mean—'

'I mean they're not likely to have any children. Fitzwalter bred out of his first wife, and I can't believe that Golafre was incapable—she must be barren. And your brother Dickon is only twelve years old. He's growing to do yet before he can even think of siring heirs. In time it could all be to our son's profit.'

Constance considered that. She decided not to quibble about the fact that the dukedom of York and most of its lands were entailed on the male heir, and not transmissible through her. It would be time to worry about that when the situation arose, a day which neither of them might see. 'We should not wish it,' she said.

'Of course not. But there have been less likely inheritances. All I say is that it could be so, and Ned has made it more likely.'

'I don't understand what he's about.'

'I still think love is the most likely explanation. I remember something he said while we were in France. It angered him as much as me that John Golafre used to beat her.'

'I begin to think that Golafre had his reasons. God knows how long she has been Ned's whore.'

Thomas put his goblet down abruptly. 'Constance,' he said reprovingly, 'she is my cousin.'

'I don't care if she's your sister!' Her eyes turned hard and cold, and he was suddenly reminded of her cousin the King in an evil mood. 'Surely you can see what she has been about for this last year and more? Do you still wonder that Edward knows all your business?'

It was clear from Thomas's expression that this explanation had not occurred to him. 'She may, I suppose, have picked up things that were said between us,' he admitted, 'but I doubt she had the wit to understand the half of it.'

'Or so she would have you believe. I grant you, I thought her a fool myself. But she isn't, is she? Ned wouldn't be marrying her if she were. We're the ones who have been fools.'

He nodded solemnly. 'Perhaps. But we'd be greater fools to let them see that they have hurt us. Better, I think, to take your brother at his word, to pretend that his marriage to Philippa pleases us above all things. We are armed against them now.'

Constance took a breath to calm herself. 'I dare say he has already found someone else to spy on us.'

'*Treschere*, I am sorry. That I accused you. It's just that I know how much you love your brother.'

'*Did* love him,' she corrected. 'Thomas, he didn't care what harm he did us, whether you thought ill of me or not. Oh, if you so wish I shall smile at him, and even call Philippa my dearest sister, but I have a long memory, and I shan't forget. They damaged your standing with the King, and set us at odds with each other. Even now you don't trust me as you did. How can you? The doubt will always be in your mind.'

'Perhaps you misjudge me now,' he said, taking her hand.

* * *

The tables had been cleared away, and the rest of the night's entertainment began. The Duke of York's troupe of players acted out the story of the Epiphany, the three Kings arriving from afar to bring their gifts to the Christ child. On the dais, the King and Queen of England wore their crowns to mark the solemnity of the occasion, little Isabelle proudly resisting sleep, stubbornly holding her head high despite the weight pressing down on it. Her governess, the Dame de Courcy, stood immediately behind her, available to offer support if it was required.

After the brief play was over, dancing began. Thomas, in accordance with his policy, went off at once to ask Philippa to be his first partner, saying that he thought it proper to offer his congratulations. Constance stayed where she was, and after a few minutes Blanche Bradeston appeared at her side.

'I have had word today that one of my tenants at Winterbourne has had his house burnt to the ground, and all his animals driven off,' she said. 'I hope your ladyship will be gracious enough to speak to the Earl on my behalf. Hake and I cannot afford many such losses; we need protection.'

Constance frowned momentarily. 'Protection from whom?'

'From Lord Berkeley, of course.'

'You mean that Berkeley has attacked your property?'

'Your ladyship misunderstands me. Berkeley is far too wise to take part in such work—but he maintains those who persecute us. Much more of this and Hake and I will be ruined.'

Blanche looked very far from ruin. Her gown was as rich as Constance's own, and the blue garter on her arm was a new mark of the King's favour. Of course, Constance reflected, it was obligatory to keep up appearances at court, and Blanche's extravagance in matters of clothing and jewellery might well be financed by credit rather than income.

'My lord will have a word with Berkeley on your behalf, I'm sure,' Constance said.

'And I am sure that that will be enough. I am most grateful to your ladyship. Berkeley had the rule of Gloucestershire for years. It sticks in his craw that the Earl is master there now; and, of course, there are those about us who resent Hake and always have. It would be bad enough if he were from Somerset or Devon, marrying me and taking a part in the business of the shire. That he's a Scot is more than they can bear. It's not difficult for Berkeley to stir them up against us.'

Constance shook her head. She found the men of Gloucestershire infuriatingly insular, resenting the least influence that was gained in the county by any man born outside it. With Warwick far away, imprisoned on the Isle of Man, Berkeley was at the head of those who opposed Thomas's domination of the shire. So far the faction had done little but grumble. They had, for example, resented Hugh Mortimer representing them in Parliament, making much of the fact that all his landed property was across the border in Herefordshire. Now, it seemed, they were doing more than just grumble. They were attacking a weak link. Andrew Hake was unpopular even among those who sided with the Despensers. As Blanche had said, there were many who simply could not forgive him for being born a Scot.

'There is another matter on which I should value your ladyship's advice,' Blanche continued. 'I am very troubled by the behaviour of the Dame de Courcy. Since the Countess of March left to join her husband in Ireland there has been no one to keep the wretched woman in check. I cannot begin to describe her arrogance. One might almost think her to be the Queen herself. She is actually building her own chapel at Windsor, for herself and the rest of the French persons in the Household. A very extravagant one, I might add. I do not know where the money is coming from, though I believe that one may venture a fair guess. I am almost tempted to speak to the King about it, but it is scarcely for me to do so. I cannot but think that it might be better for an English governess to be appointed. A great lady such as yourself, perhaps, close to the King's blood.'

Constance had no desire for such a post. 'Allowances must be made for the Dame de Courcy,' she said. 'She's in a strange land, and must find it difficult to understand our ways. I think you were right not to trouble the King about it. Watch her by all means. Advise her if she will heed you. If matters go too far, you may come to me again. I'll speak to the King myself if there's good cause.'

***

Lord Berkeley's face seemed to grow redder with every minute.

'I had nothing to do with this attack on Hake and his wife, and I resent the implication!' he snapped, thumping the table before him.

The court had moved on to Shrewsbury, and Berkeley was one of many who had travelled there to attend the reconvened Parliament. It had been obvious from the first that he was suspicious about his summons to the Despensers' lodgings, and now he was positively hostile. No doubt, Constance reflected, it displeased him to be held to account by a man who was his junior in all but rank.

'There is nothing to resent,' Thomas said briskly. 'I accept your word as a knight that you had no part in it.'

Berkeley's eyes bulged beneath his iron-grey hair. He was dressed in unrelieved, country-tailored black broadcloth, a continued mourning for his long-dead wife. 'It's no marvel to me that Hake is disliked by his neighbours,' he said. 'What do you expect? He rides about the county in the King's livery, giving himself airs and interfering with other people's business. And what is he? A damned, penniless Scot, made by his marriage to that simpering Bradeston bitch. God alone knows who his parents were, or what blood he has in him. Anyway, my lord *Earl*, we're told you have the governing of the county now. You head the Commission of the Peace, and so it's your business to keep order, not mine.'

'I require your assistance.'

'You do?'

'You have great influence, Berkeley. Men respect your opinions.'

'You've done all you can to destroy my influence! You've left me with no say at all in county affairs.'

'On the contrary, I'm more than ready to listen to your advice.'

'Provided I accept your authority.'

'Naturally so. My authority is given me by the King. You are the King's subject.'

'The King's perhaps. Not yours.'

'So you refuse to assist me? In suppressing disorder?'

Berkeley shook his head abruptly and stood up. 'I'll look to my own affairs. Guard my own boundaries. You wanted the rule of the shire. Well, now you have it, and you must manage it as best you may.'

He left without saying much more, quite unreconciled.

'Was I unreasonable?' Thomas asked his wife.

Constance set aside the needlework she had used as a pretence of occupation. 'No. I was surprised by your patience. But perhaps there was no point in being conciliatory. I don't dislike Berkeley. I think he's honest enough in his way. The trouble is that nothing will satisfy him short of being the greatest man in Gloucestershire, and he can never be that again while you live. Two dogs with the same bone. Only one can have it. The stronger of the two.'

'Dogs fight,' Thomas said.

'Yes, and I dare say he will fight, one way or another. But he can't win. You're a greater lord than he, and you have the King's favour.'

'I like to think so,' he said, with a shrug. 'Ah, Constance, I wish I had your certainty. I sometimes think that you are the stronger of us. All I see around me is more and more trouble. It's as if—as if all the walls are moving towards me. To be truthful, there's a part of me that wants to run away. Go on another crusade, perhaps.'

She was momentarily amused. 'You think that would be a refuge from danger?'

'At least all my enemies would be in front of me, and I'd know how to deal with them. It's easier so, I swear it.'

She rose and moved towards him, troubled by the tone of his voice. It was not like Thomas to despair.

'It is not that you doubt the King's good will?' she asked, placing her arm around his shoulders, caressing them.

He shrugged. 'I don't even know what he wants any more. He seems to change from day to day. Sometimes he seems ready to conquer the world. Then the next morning—well, it's wrong of me to say it, but it seems to me that he'd welcome death.'

'His moods have never lasted long. I've never known him either angry or happy for more than three hours at a time.'

'Yes, but it's growing worse. More extreme. *Treschere*, I would say this to no other than you, but I begin to fear for his reason.'

Constance shook her head impatiently. 'My cousin is *not* mad. Thomas, you must not even think such a thing.'

'I didn't say he was mad. I said I feared for his reason. Is it possible, do you suppose, that he regrets your uncle and Arundel? That they weigh on his conscience? Remember how he had us dig Arundel out of his grave? They say it was because his dreams were troubled, that he used to wake screaming, shouting that Arundel's blood was all over the bed.'

'*Who* says these things? Traitors and liars! Arundel deserved death as few men have. You know that. You'd not have been one of those who accused him otherwise.'

'Of course he deserved death. But where has it brought us? Is the King better loved? Are we safer than we were? Now it begins again, with Bolingbroke and Mowbray, and who knows where that will end?' He halted, kept silence for long enough for her to think the conversation was over, and then began again. 'You have not heard the worst, Constance. William Bagot has been plotting to murder Lancaster.'

Constance first wondered whether she had misheard him, and then, seeing from his face that she had not, tried to say that it was impossible. The words stuck in her throat, and would not form.

'You must speak of this to no one,' he went on, 'least of all to your father. Bagot must be half mad to think of such a thing. We did not think him serious at first.'

'We?'

'Salisbury and Surrey and myself. We thought it no more than wild talk.'

'But *why*, Thomas? Bagot was my uncle's own man at one time. Why should he wish to kill him?'

'Perhaps for that very reason? For some old grudge? He *says* that Lancaster and Bolingbroke have their eyes on the throne, that they will steal it if they can. He thought to act first, before they did.'

Constance still found it incredible. It was true that Bagot was a very powerful man in his own Warwickshire, and a favoured member of the King's Council, one of the small group in Richard's confidence. But compared to Gaunt he was of no account at all. It almost beggared belief that he should make such an attempt.

'You have prevented it?' she asked.

'My cousin Salisbury did that. When he found that Bagot was serious about it, he went straight to the King.' He hesitated for another moment. 'It's been kept as quiet as possible, but Bagot now knows the King's mind. He's been bound in a great sum, and threatened with death if does harm to Lancaster or his family. He's also been sent from the court for a while, at least while this quarrel of Bolingbroke's is settled.'

She was appalled. 'You know that such a thing cannot be kept secret, Thomas. There are no secrets at court, only pretences. My uncle is certain to hear of it before long.'

'The chances are that he already knows. It may even be what lies behind Bolingbroke's accusation of Mowbray. If they think Mowbray stands behind Bagot.'

'But does he?' she asked, frowning as she struggled to make sense of it. 'What would he gain from it?'

Thomas gave her a cynical smile. 'We should all gain from it, *treschere*. You know your uncle is the richest and most powerful man in the land. There'd be pickings for all, from the King downwards. I do not say that Mowbray has any part in it; only that Lancaster and Bolingbroke might think it so. And Mowbray and Bagot are the King's men, and do his will. There lies the danger.'

10

It was Sunday morning, 27th January 1398. The burgesses of Shrewsbury, made uneasy by the large number of armed men in their midst, walked cautiously home from church across a thin veneer of snow that covered expanses of frozen mud.

A herald's braying clarion broke the stillness of the morning at the approaches to the Welsh Bridge. In the centre of the town the clatter of hooves was no more than a murmur at first, but then it grew louder as the cavalcade advanced up the hill from the river, advancing through the narrow, deserted streets at something more than a brisk walk. A merchant's clerk opened the shutters to investigate the noise, rubbed his eyes against the sudden light, and recognised the blue-and-white livery of the approaching riders, and the starched banners at the head of the cavalcade.

'It's March!' he cried, in a voice loud enough to disturb the neighbours on both sides of the street. He was an elderly man, born in Wigmore and devoted to the Mortimers. 'God bless you, my lord!'

Roger swept off his hat and smiled in acknowledgement. Next to him was his brother, Sir Edmund, and behind them five hundred men, no less, every one a liveried warrior. A few dozen knights, squires and other armigers, but for the most part archers, recruited from Wales and from the English borderlands. Some of the company had returned with their lord from Ireland, but the majority had simply put aside their private business at his call, and hurried to Wigmore to attend him. There were even those who had not needed to be asked.

The people of Shrewsbury began to turn out of their houses, and to lean from windows. Roger saw the joy in their eyes, heard their cheers, and was at a loss to understand why he was so popular.

'It's simple enough,' said Edmund dryly. 'They don't know you. You're young. You've a kind face, and you throw your money about. They think you'd make a better king than the one they've got. Perhaps one day they'll have the chance to change their minds.'

His brother made a face at him. 'I pray they will not,' he said.

'You'll not give way to Bolingbroke?'

'No. Of course I won't. I just hope that the matter does not arise; that Richard lives to be eighty and fathers a dozen sons on his little French girl. To be

Earl of March and Ulster is more than enough for any man. You'd know that if you had the responsibility of it bearing down on your shoulders.'

It was Edmund's turn to make a face. Responsibility was not the word that first came to his mind when he thought of his brother. Roger had a way of running from it, of putting awkward decisions to one side. He had a way of looking splendid, always wearing the richest and most fashionable of clothes, charmed people with effortless ease, and was so generous that he could not pass a beggar without spinning a coin in his direction. But there was no substance beneath. He was so lazy that more often than not he didn't even bother to get out of bed to go to morning mass. He had no stomach for work, or for matters of routine. No passion to put his stamp upon the world, save through the faces of his bastards. He was likely to be an indifferent king, clay in the hands of those around him. Of whom Edmund intended to be the principal. As Duke of Clarence, perhaps.

For the present Edmund had little but his ambition, apart from the lands in the far south west of Wales that his brother had lately gifted him. They were worth four hundred marks a year, enough to make him a rich knight by any standards, but not sufficient to give him real power where it mattered. In effect, he was nothing more than Roger's servant—though a slightly more influential servant since their uncle had fallen into disgrace. Thomas Mortimer had applied to Roger for aid and shelter, and Roger had been inclined to grant it until the message from Thomas Despenser had been received. Then the scales had fallen from his eyes, although only, Edmund was sure, because the allegation came from Despenser rather than from himself. Had the decision been his own, he would have sent Thomas Mortimer back to England in chains to face the King's justice, or at least to be exposed for what he was. Roger, more sentimental, had merely refused to assist their uncle in any way, though later he had made pretence of trying to hunt him down.

Perhaps this had been enough. For it seemed that they were back in the King's favour. In the last few weeks Roger had received three personal letters from Richard, each warmer than the last. There were clear indications in them that the Earl of March would be welcome back at court, that his regular presence at the council table would be agreeable; besides this, more than a hint that Ireland perhaps required a lieutenant with different skills. The trouble was that Roger did not really welcome this change. He had no trust at all in the King, and told Edmund that he felt safer in Ireland, however savage his enemies there, than he did in Richard's presence. There was also the little matter of the significant Mortimer lands in Ulster, not yet properly secured, and far more vulnerable than his Welsh and English property.

So it seemed to Edmund that it would be for him, once again, to uphold the Mortimer interests at home, and he had persuaded his brother that there was no cause for him to return with him to Ireland at the end of the Parliament. He had business of his own in England that could no longer be delayed now that he was duly established with an independent livelihood. He needed to cast around for a wife with whom to breed his heirs. A lady with an inheritance of her own, if such was available. Or perhaps a wealthy and youthful widow. Property apart, her family connections would require careful consideration. It occurred to him that Constance would be well placed to advise him as to his options. There might well be a suitable candidate among her circle of relatives and acquaintances. Thomas certainly had a number of nieces and cousins who might be eligible, and Constance was sure to know all about their status and availability. There was no one whose judgement he trusted more.

***

King Richard stiffened his back, sat a little more erect in his chair. To calm himself he stretched out his hand, ran it over Math's smooth, streamlined head.

'It is not a proper subject for discussion, either in Parliament or elsewhere,' he said. 'I am young, and I intend to have heirs of my own body.'

The Duke of Lancaster took another small step towards him. 'You are past thirty, and not in the best of health. In truth, there are times when you seem weary of life. Your wife is seven years old. Do you wonder that men discuss it?'

The King's eyes narrowed beneath their hooded lids. 'I wonder at their motives. Most especially when they claim to be my loyal subjects.'

'Loyalty, if I may remind you, cuts both ways.'

The Duke's voice, a little raised, seemed to thunder from the high vaulted ceiling of the Abbot of Shrewsbury's great chamber. Richard glanced around, to see who had heard. They were by no means alone, although their attendants had withdrawn to the far fringes of the room, stood clustered together in uncertain groups.

'Perhaps you would care to explain exactly what you mean by that remark,' he said icily.

'I mean, Richard, that I have heard rumours of your intentions towards me and mine. Or rather, I should say, the intentions of those you keep about you. The opinion of some of them is that I have lived too long in this world, and that my days would be better shortened. I've spent the last twenty years as your loyal servant, and asked nothing in return but reasonable reward and your trust in my good faith. I put it to your conscience. When have I betrayed you?'

When you fathered Harry Bolingbroke, Richard thought. Aloud he said, 'When did I accuse you of betrayal? You've little enough cause to think me ungrateful for your services. All the world knows you have as many titles as I have myself, and a greater livelihood.'

'There are those who think I have too much of both. Who begrudge me each breath I draw. Men you call your friends.'

Richard shook his head in a display of bewilderment. 'Are you not my friend, Uncle? I had the impression that you were. Now I begin to wonder. First you make it clear that you expect your son to succeed me. Next you accuse me of seeking your death.'

'I speak of those about you. Not of yourself. God forbid!'

'Yet you seem to imagine that I might heed such evil counsel. Or perhaps you think that I am weak and foolish. In the hands of those I cannot control. Who are these men you fear?'

'Fear? I fear none!'

'Then you scarcely require my protection from them, do you?'

'I don't ask it. My only request is that you silence those who slander me, who tell you that I intend you harm. What better way to demonstrate your faith in me than by naming my son your heir? There is no one closer to you in blood than Harry, and he has proved his loyalty.'

'By denouncing Mowbray? You consider that an act of loyalty, I suppose?'

'I do. Mowbray was once his friend.'

'I remember exactly *when* they were friends—at that time neither was a friend of mine! Well, we have yet to examine Harry's motives. Who knows? Perhaps he made an accusation before he could be accused himself.'

'How can you believe that? Mowbray is a piece of filth! You know he is.'

Richard smiled, a thin, assured smile. 'I can't prejudge the case. You are well aware of that, dear Uncle. To do so would be a desertion of my duty. But never fear. I've little doubt that Harry will be able to prove the truth of what he has alleged. Were it otherwise, I'm sure you would not have advised him to speak. He shall have a fair hearing, before his peers, and justice after it. I promise you.'

***

Thomas Despenser was well pleased with himself. His petition to the Parliament, seeking reversal of the forfeitures imposed upon his ancestors, Edward II's favourites, had been granted without fuss, though with reservations to protect the interests of the Duke of Lancaster. He had removed a blot from his family's name that neither his father nor his great-uncle, his predecessors in the title, had been able to expunge. Nor was that the end of his cause for satisfaction.

'The King will progress through Worcestershire and Gloucestershire before Easter,' he announced. 'He's promised to lodge with us at Hanley Castle.'

Constance was torn between pleasure and concern. She knew what preparation would be necessary for such a visit, and Hanley, for all its beauty, was a modest housing for the royal court. They would probably have to move out under canvas themselves to make room.

'That will give Berkeley and his friends something to think about,' she remarked.

'It should keep them very quiet. I doubt whether Andrew Hake will be troubled during the next few months. Or anyone else. Surrey has been having some trouble with Warwick's old retained men, you know. In a way that's no surprise.

He's as much a stranger to Warwickshire as if he were a Frenchman. Has no following there at all. We're better placed than that.'

She nodded, though she was inclined to think that he was simplifying the true position. Their take-over of the Warwick lands along the border between Gloucestershire and Worcestershire, manors such as the Combertons and Elmley Castle, could scarcely be said to have been uneventful, or popular with the Warwick tenants, while such Beauchamp officials as had been left in place were not, in her opinion, to be relied upon in a crisis. She would have preferred a clean sweep, the immediate replacement of them all with men she could trust, but Thomas's policy was to be as conciliatory as possible, at least in the beginning. All men deserved a chance, he said. Besides, he was not so well supplied with reliable officers that he could afford to spread them more thinly than they were already.

'March is back in favour,' he went on, still congratulating himself. 'I'm almost tempted to open the question of Bess's marriage again.'

Constance sniffed, moved to warm her hands at the small charcoal brazier that heated the room. Her silence was of the sort that made her opinion clear to her husband.

'Not that I shall,' he added reassuringly. 'Better to wait a while, I think.'

She nodded her agreement. 'I think that's wise. Though there may be another way to tie ourselves to the Mortimers by marriage, if you think fit. Edmund is looking for a wife. He asked my advice.'

The request had come to her as a great surprise, and she had spent a long time thinking about it. She was still not sure whether she found the task a pleasing one.

'Has he really? You don't suggest that we should offer him Bess?'

She frowned, briefly irritated by his levity. 'Of course I do not! He needs a wife his own age; someone who can give him children. Your cousin, Sir Hugh, has a daughter. How old is she?'

Thomas shrugged. It was not something to which he had given thought. 'Anne? I'm not sure. She's perhaps a little young, and she won't bring much of a dowry.'

'I can break the matter to Sir Hugh, if you agree. Or there's your niece, your sister Margaret's girl.'

'Younger still, I think, and sickly.'

'I can still make the suggestion. It'll take time to come to any conclusion, and Edmund is not likely to settle for the first he sees.'

'I'll leave it to you, since he puts such value on your judgement. I'd certainly not object to having him in the family. He's ambitious, and well placed to climb higher. Though it's you he really wants, of course.'

'Thomas! How can you say such a thing?'

'Because it's true. I'm not blind, *treschere*. I see how he looks at you.'

She paused, took a breath. 'And you don't resent it?'

He smiled. 'Not as long as he does no more than look. Why should I? I trust you to tell me if he attempts anything more, and I know that you'd never betray me. Not in that way. It'd be beneath your pride.'

Constance had not thought him so perceptive, to recognise so clearly something that she barely admitted to herself, Edmund's hopeless desire for her. Nor had she appreciated the extent, the boundless depth, of Thomas's faith in her, his utter lack of jealousy or doubt. It left her temporarily deprived of speech, her hand reaching out towards him. He took it, kissed her fingers, his soft beard running along them.

'It is almost time,' she reminded him.

Time, that was, to make their way to the great feast the King was holding to mark the end of the Parliament. It had been a much shorter session than expected, generous with taxes but awkward in other ways. Richard had denied a petition from the clergy to introduce the death penalty for heresy, and there had been no progress at all in settling the quarrel between Bolingbroke and Mowbray. Both had been cited to appear before the King at Oswestry on 23rd February, a strangely remote place for such an event. Some muttered that it had been chosen because it was close to the Cheshire border, where Richard's most trusted followers were readily available.

Constance wondered how her cousin the King could hope to settle such a quarrel, where there was no evidence beyond one man's word against another's. But the thought passed swiftly from her mind. She was sure that it would all blow over in the end.

***

The King's harbinger rode into Hanley Castle at so early an hour that Constance was scarcely dressed. Bowing low, almost to the floor, his face bright red from riding through an icy March night, he announced that his master would spend the next day, Sunday, at Worcester with the Bishop, and arrive at Hanley at some time on Monday. He would stay for one night, or two at most.

Constance ordered the man fed, and warmed, and shown to a bed. He was gone before she remembered that she had not thought to ask him the outcome of the proceedings at Oswestry.

Well, Thomas would tell her, soon enough. He was with the King, having left the court only for sufficient time to escort her home and spend a few days relaxing with her before heading back north. She sorely missed his company, his conversation, the security and contentment she felt in his presence, and the mere thought of seeing him again brought a smile to her face, a light to her eye and a certain familiar itch of desire to her body. She detested the compulsory chastity of Lent even more than the monotonous diet of fish.

When the harbinger woke it was still short of noon. He toured the castle with John Norreys and Constance, enquiring as to what accommodation was available, and rubbing his chin when he discovered how restricted it was. Pavilions had already been brought out of store and erected in the park to accommodate some of the overflow, and the harbinger confirmed that more tents were on their way from Worcester in carts, sent on in advance of the King. It was as well, he said. While it was true that the Earl of March had returned to Wigmore, and gone on from there back to Ireland, the King's uncles were still with the court and Lancaster's retinue was almost as numerous as the King's own. Where were they all to be housed? As for the stables, they were grossly inadequate. Sumpter horses and the like might be tied in lines in the park, but the nights were chill, and the lords and ladies of the court would expect their highly-bred animals to be lodged under cover. The harbinger drew air through his teeth, and cast his eyes towards the village. What about the nave of the church? Might that be used as a temporary stable?

Constance thought that it could, but felt that some negotiation with the parish priest might be appropriate, especially as Elisabeth, rather than Thomas, was his patron, and so she did not have the hold over him that she would have liked. After some further discussion she left Norreys and the harbinger to wander around the castle chalking symbols on doors to signify room allocations, and rode the short way to the village, taking her brother Dickon and Mary Russell as escort. A smaller retinue than suited her dignity, but adequate to the purpose.

The priest, a short, rotund, red-cheeked man, was leaning on the gate of his house. His Lenten fasting seemed to have had very little impact on his waist, which bulged formidably against his substantial leather girdle. He pointed out that such a use of the church would be particularly unfitting at so holy a season, when villagers were more than usually inclined to worship.

Constance, addressing him from her horse's back, drew his attention to the fact that the King did not visit every day. She added a reminder that she was lady of the manor, and, of the two of them, the more likely to entertain his bishop at table. He spoke of a necessary repair to the roof and a statue of the Virgin that needed a lick of paint and an element of gilding. Constance mentioned the possibility of gold finding its way from her purse to his hand, and added that there was no need of any strict accounting of the sort that a bishop might order if certain parochial matters were drawn to his attention. Notably the priest's excessive charity towards certain fatherless children in the district, subsidised, it seemed, by the neglect of the chancel roof and of holy images.

The priest maintained his objections for a while, evidently enjoying the pastime of debate under the eye of those members of his flock who were resting their weight on the alehouse bench across the green. A good ten minutes went by before Constance's eloquence and the first of her coins persuaded him that expensive horses were a part of God's creation, whose presence in a church was no less appropriate than the frequent use of the nave as a venue for bride-ales, church-ales and similar drunken carousing.

The conclusion of the negotiation was interrupted by the arrival of a group of riders who rounded the bend of the road between the wattle-and-daub cottages and drew to a halt on the green. Constance glanced across and saw that their leader was Sir John Russell, and made an abrupt end to her discussion with the priest by exchanging a further coin for a blessing. The priest bowed low, and made a cautious progress across the green, giving the various horses a wide berth as he hastened to minister to the alehouse customers.

Sir John dismounted, and scuttled across to bow before Constance and kiss her extended hand.

'God's greeting, my lady!' he said enthusiastically, his scarlet liripipe hat clutched in his fist. 'This is indeed a fortunate chance. I hoped that I might have a private word with you.'

She nodded, suddenly aware of the unexpected presence of two women in his company. The elder of them, dressed in the sombre garb of a widow, a handsome lady of perhaps forty years, nudged her horse forward, smiling submissively.

'I believe your ladyship knows my Lady Clinton,' Sir John prompted, just as Constance was wondering how best to conceal her lapse of memory. She had, in fact, met Elizabeth Clinton before, but she was not at all sure of the occasion, or whether they had exchanged words.

Lady Clinton mumbled a respectful greeting, and then fell into a silence that rapidly started to become awkward.

'You are most welcome to Hanley Castle,' Constance said uncertainly. 'I suppose you have come from Strensham, Sir John?'

'Yes, my lady. I've been there for some weeks.' He coughed, suspecting an unspoken criticism where none had been intended. 'I know that I ought to have waited on you before this. Forgive me.'

'There is nothing to forgive.' She glanced towards his daughter. 'You will be glad to see Mary, of course. She is very valuable to me, but if you'd like her at home for a little time, I shall understand. After all, you've seen little of her of late.'

Sir John spared the girl a moment of his attention. 'I'm glad that she is of some use to your ladyship. She has certainly benefited from your care.' He paused for a moment as if the matter required consideration. 'I think her much better with you than sitting idly at home. She's still young, with much to learn.'

Constance was unsure where all this was leading. 'Then I suppose you're both here to attend upon the King? We don't expect him before Monday, but there's work enough to keep us all busy, and I'll be glad of your help.'

Russell nodded assent, but still seemed to have unfinished business. He reached out, and secured Lady Clinton's hand with his own.

'We have,' he said solemnly, 'a great favour to ask of your ladyship.'

***

Elisabeth Despenser had arrived at Hanley Castle very early on Monday morning, having begun her journey before dawn. She had not wished to spend more time there than was necessary and, of course, travel on Sunday was, for her, quite beyond consideration.

The thought of seeing her grandchildren was much more pleasing to her than any prospect of meeting the King. He had come to Tewkesbury two years earlier, but thankfully he had chosen to lodge with the abbot, and Elisabeth had kept herself out of his way. Hopefully he would not pay her any great attention among the throng of people who had gathered to receive him. Many of them were old friends of hers, like Thomas Berkeley, discontented with Richard's rule and yet forced to truckle to it. It appalled her that her son—her dear Edward's son—should be the local agent of the King's tyranny, and yet he was, there was no denying it. Men grumbled about it even when they sat at her table. Perhaps they thought she had influence where she had none.

She glared at Constance, who was close to the King, talking more or less into his ear. It was *she* who had the influence, unfortunately. Elisabeth whispered a swift prayer, certain that she sinned by wishing ill to befall the mother of her own grandchildren. But what a creature she was! No one would think it Lent, seeing her standing there, dripping in crimson silk and costly jewellery, her face a painted mask that must have cost an hour's work, time that probably kept her from mass.

Thomas stood next to his wife, listening to what she and the King had to say to one another, beaming his approval as if it pleased him that she should speak for him under his own roof. One hand rested easily on the hilt of his arming-sword, the other, gentle as a leaf, protectively curved around Constance's waist.

On the other side of the King were John Russell, grinning like an unruly skull, and Lady Clinton, their intended marriage indulgently announced by the King himself, as though it were a matter of state. Elisabeth was shocked to the core. She, unlike Constance, had been present at Margaret Russell's fatal childbed. Her poor young granddaughter was forgotten so quickly, casually replaced with the evident approval of her son and his wife. It was a wonder to her that Lent had been allowed to delay the wedding ceremony itself.

'My lady,' said a respectful voice in her ear. It was Lord Berkeley, his eyes a lot brighter than his expression. With him was his son-in-law, her godson Richard Beauchamp.

Elisabeth inclined her head towards them. 'Cousin, I am glad to see you, though surprised that you are here.'

'We were both *summoned*.' He shrugged. 'I suppose it completes your son's triumph, to have us here in our proper place. Or perhaps Russell or Hake had a word to say to the King. My son Beauchamp and I are of no account these days, must be content to stand quietly among the serfs, hood in hand.'

Elisabeth turned towards her godson. 'Richard. Have you had any word from your parents?'

The hawk-nosed youth made a solemn bow. 'One single letter, my lady. They are as well as you might expect, but my mother says they have not had the money promised for their upkeep. Fortunately, in that barren place, their needs are small.'

'Remember me to them when you write again. Say I will do what I can for them.'

But that would be precious little, Elisabeth admitted to herself, burning with humiliation. Warwick had been her husband's comrade in-arms and trusted friend, a valued support in the early years of her widowhood, and she was powerless to do more than pray for his welfare.

She excused herself and moved away from them, suddenly uncomfortable in their presence, anxious for escape. But there was no escape. The castle was packed to the doors, and most of those present were either strangers to her or courteously indifferent, while there were others she was anxious to avoid. In dodging the Duke of York, she stumbled blindly into her cousin, Philippa, the Duchess of Aumale.

'Good morning, Cousin,' said Philippa. Her eyes were as bright as the chain of emeralds about her neck. 'Forgive me, I've only just noticed you, hiding at the back.'

'I've no wish to push myself forward,' said Elisabeth.

'Ah, it's as well we are not all so restrained. Otherwise I should not be Duchess of Aumale! That now, and Duchess of York in a few years. Who would have thought it?' She stroked her sleeve, rich summer green velvet of the best quality, trimmed with ermine, as if to emphasise the point.

'I thought you might have mourned your husband longer.'

'Golafre? Saints, what a fool you are, Elisabeth!' Philippa leaned back and laughed. 'Do you really think I was going to wait to be asked twice? I'd have lost him for sure. My Ned. The greatest man in the realm, after the King and Lancaster. He's already Duke of York in all but name, and more important than old York has ever been.'

'I wonder how you won him,' said Elisabeth, chillingly. 'Or, should I say, I do not. I don't wonder at all. It's as obvious as my hand before me.'

'I don't care to be insulted, Cousin.'

'It would be an impossibility to insult you. You and *her brother* are perfectly matched.'

Philippa smiled at her, a contented, evil little smile. 'You are right. We are. And between us, we are going to rule England.'

11

York rearranged his cushions, for the greater ease of his bones, realising as he did so that his attention had been drifting and that his guest was waiting for an answer.

'Move closer, John,' he grunted, 'I can scarcely hear a word you say.'

His elder brother, who was in the matching chair on the opposite side of the fireplace, leaned forward and raised his voice. 'I said that I have spent the last twenty years in Richard's service, propping his throne with all my strength, and *this* is my reward; that he suffers my son and heir to do battle for a thing of naught.'

York frowned. He hated disturbances to the comfortable pattern of his life. 'Harry should have kept his mouth shut,' he objected.

The line of Lancaster's mouth hardened. 'Harry acted on my advice. Mowbray's words were close to treason, and to conceal his discontent from Richard would have been dangerous.'

'It's all folly. God knows I am tired of hearing about it. First at the Shrewsbury Parliament. Then at Oswestry. Then at Bristol, with the Committee of Parliament. Then with the Court of Chivalry at Windsor. I could repeat every word, backwards, and I still don't know which one of them is lying. Small wonder that the King can't decide between them. Lacking witnesses how else can it be settled but by combat?'

'You do not prefer my son's word to Mowbray's?'

'I didn't say that,' York protested, although he had. 'You know that I've always thought well of Harry. What I said, what I *meant*, was that you can't expect Richard to show favour, one way or the other. Lacking proof. That's all.'

'Do you know what Richard said to me? That if Harry is vanquished he will see him hanged from a gibbet. Yes, and that I was not to wonder at it, since if I were in like case I'd be treated no better! This to me, Lancaster!'

'What would you have him say? That if Mowbray fails he dies, but Harry shall be safe whatever befalls? Would Harry have it so? I think him a better man than that. I don't see the cause for worry. I doubt not he will slay Mowbray within the first ten minutes, perhaps even at the first pass.'

'Mowbray is a better man of his weapons than some judge him. I remember him finishing off that Scots fellow, Mar, a few years back. Mar was no easy opponent for any man. Harry hasn't fought seriously in years. If my son makes some slight misjudgement, if his horse slips—'

'*If!*'

'The point is it should not have come to this.' Lancaster's anger was scarcely controlled. 'Richard should have smoothed over the quarrel as soon as it began. Or found some other way than this. Something has changed in him, these last few months. I thought that he and Harry had begun to trust one another, even to work together. Now it's as bad as ever it was. He looks at Harry in a way that chills my blood.'

York tutted. He could offer his elder brother no comfort. He still held to his view that Bolingbroke had made a serious mistake by provoking the quarrel in the first place. The result was that hares were running off in all directions. It was never difficult to arouse Richard's suspicions and Harry, in particular by bringing up the issue of Gloucester's death, had not only trodden on dangerous ground but jumped up and down on it in heavy boots. Any fool could see that if Mowbray had murdered his prisoner he had not done so without authorisation. Accusing Mowbray of murder was as good as accusing the King himself.

York really did not want to think about it. If trouble was coming he had no wish to be involved. He cursed the hot-headed truculence of Harry Bolingbroke and the long and unforgiving memory of Richard Plantagenet in equal measure.

***

Constance, the table before her laden with account rolls, was presiding over a meeting of her household officers at Hanley Castle. They had answered all her questions, and were waiting, more or less patiently, as she sat with her head over another long sheet of parchment. The still, summer afternoon had barely opened, and there was scarcely a breath of air in the room. Occasionally, through the open window, some nearby trees could be heard stirring and rustling in the light breeze. One of the men reached out to serve himself a cup of ale, and the chink of the pewter pot broke into the silence like a small explosion.

Constance looked up from the document. 'I can find no fault at all,' she announced, smiling. 'It would appear that not a single penny has gone astray. The few small doubts I had, you have resolved. Even the charges paid seem quite reasonable. Long ago, when I was managing my father's household, there were certain gentlemen about me who imagined that in my youth and ignorance I would not know the reasonable price of a quarter of wheat.'

She paused. They had all begun to relax, some even to smile their contentment.

'So why is it,' she went on, her tone hardening, 'that I cannot walk out of the chapel without having the like of *this* thrust into my hand?' She produced a folded piece of parchment from beneath the folds of her gown and dropped it onto the table, where it landed with a satisfying thud. 'A petition, gentleman, from half the community of Gloucester, reminding me that they have not received payment for meat, fish, wine, cloth and God knows what else supplied to this household during the last six months.'

The smiles disappeared. Norreys suddenly sat up bolt upright.

'Madame,' he said quietly, 'you should not have been so troubled. It would have been proper for them to come to me. Or to Stradling, as chamberlain.'

William Stradling hawked, and spat into the fireplace. 'Your ladyship should not pay too much attention to the whining of townsfolk,' he grunted. 'Most of them are richer than any of us around this table, and can stand a little bleeding. They profit greatly from the trade you give them, one way and another. I expect most of them have been paid, and seek now to gull you into paying twice. They're full of such tricks. What do you expect? The majority of them are nothing more than upjumped villeins.'

Constance tried very hard not to frown at him. Despite her distaste for him, and his for her, they had to try to work together.

'You may be quite correct, Sir William,' she agreed, summoning up a further smile from somewhere, 'but if you are—*if*, I say—it is better that they be paid twice than that my lord's reputation be dragged through every gutter in Gloucester.'

'If your ladyship wishes to be taken for a fool—so be it.'

'Better a fool than a thief!' She rose abruptly, conscious that she was losing control of herself. She knew what Stradling was, and she despised him. It sickened her that such a creature had the right to wear a Despenser livery. God alone knew what other wickedness he did under the cover of it. 'Norreys—see to it! I want all settled, within the week.'

With that she swept from the room, but not before she had time to see the look in Stradling's eye, an undiluted hatred that shocked her to the core. She knew that she had made an enemy there.

Thomas was with his cousin, Sir Hugh Despenser, so she could not break the matter at once.

'There shall be no forcing,' Sir Hugh was saying. 'If my Anne does not care for him, I'll not insist, earl's brother or none.'

He might have passed for Thomas's elder brother, though he was stockier in build, almost short.

'Of course there must be no forcing,' Constance said, by way of announcing herself. 'Neither my lord nor I would wish that. Nor is there any great need for haste. She's very young, after all. Younger than I thought.'

'Ready for marriage, though,' said Hugh's wife, Dame Sybil, belatedly rising from her place by the solar window. 'I think it would be an excellent marriage for her. March's brother? It's far better than we hoped. Besides, he could be more than that one day. We'd be fools to miss the chance to make him our son.'

'We'd all like to see it concluded,' Thomas agreed. 'If I'd a daughter of my own of the right age, or a younger sister, I'd think Edmund a fit husband for her. But Anne may not like the look of him; for that matter, he may not like the look of her. We must all be patient. Give them time. They've only just met one another.'

'Where are they?' Constance asked.

'Out in the pleasance,' said Thomas. 'It seemed the best way to give them a chance to talk to one another.'

'Anne has my woman with her,' Sybil added hurriedly.

'She will be perfectly safe with Edmund,' Constance said sharply. She was surprised by her own tartness.

'I'm sure she will,' said Sybil, nonplussed for a moment by the hardness she saw in her hostess's blue eyes. 'I meant no offence. Only that I thought it seemly. In the circumstances.'

'I think it might be time to take a walk ourselves,' Thomas suggested. He did not wait for debate, but offered Sybil his hand. That left Constance with Sir Hugh, a good-natured enough companion but one who did not seem to know what to say. She sensed that he was slightly in awe of her.

'I wish that you and your wife would visit us more often,' she said encouragingly. 'It surely isn't so very far from Solihull, and you'll always be very welcome. It's not as if you don't know us. You used to come to Fotheringhay often enough when I was a girl. My father always counted you his friend, and you used to go hunting with us in our park. You must remember all that?'

Sir Hugh did. 'They were good days,' he agreed, and for a moment his eyes took on a distant cast, as if he was dwelling on happy memories. 'I don't spend as much time at Collyweston now. Sybil prefers Solihull, though I don't know why. There's more trouble in Warwickshire than I like. I'd be a liar if I said otherwise. Surrey doesn't help. The man's a fool, in my opinion.'

'The Duke of Surrey is our friend. Also the Duchess of York's brother.'

Hugh shook his head sadly. 'I'm well aware of that. I'm sorry, lady, I don't wish to give you offence, but the truth is he's not well served in Warwickshire, and that's the kindest way I can put it. He's stuck a statue of a hind above the gate of Warwick Castle, to show that he owns it, and that's about all he's done. He's scarcely set foot in the shire, and he's done nothing to conciliate Warwick's old followers, nor yet has he put his own people properly in place, apart from a couple of outsiders. William Bagot is more or less ruling the county, and you know what men say about him!'

'I do not.'

'Well, let's say he's not much liked. He takes up arms as a first resort, not the last, and God help anyone who crosses him.'

They had reached her herber, and Constance paused to look around her, remembering what it had been like when Thomas had first walked her along this path. Elisabeth had allowed all to go to ruin. The herb beds had been eighteen inches deep in grass, and the very paths had been invaded by intruding weeds. Now all was ordered again, the herbs confined to their respective beds, even the side paths clear and neatly bordered with timber edgings. She had undertaken some of the work with her own hands; she had directed all.

Her cousin, King Richard, had found England in an equally sorry state. Burdened with mountains of debt, torn by dissention, fighting an endless, unprofitable, and unwinnable war. Slowly, despite all opposition, against all odds, he had restored the authority of the Crown, established peace at home and abroad, and filled his coffers. And yet there were those, even loyal men like Sir Hugh who wore the King's own livery collar, who disliked the implications of the changes. Who thought, for example, that because the Beauchamps had dominated Warwickshire and Worcestershire for centuries they should be excused their treason, allowed to continue their wretched oppressions and petty tyranny. Elisabeth Despenser clung to much the same opinion. Well, no doubt there were those who preferred the sight of long grass to profitable herbs. Donkeys, for example.

They walked on, into the pleasance, where Edmund was walking with Anne between the arbours. It was hard to say which of them looked the less comfortable. Certainly neither was at ease.

'You have beautiful grounds, Thomas,' Mortimer said awkwardly. 'As I've been saying to your cousin here, I've nothing to match them in Wales.'

'I'm sure that you will find means to have something as good of your own,' Sybil protested.

He nodded. 'Perhaps. But when a man has seen perfection, it's difficult for him to be excited by an inferior imitation.'

'At least you will have the advantage of starting with an untouched piece of ground. One which you may mould as you will, instead of having to amend something that another man has put in place before you.'

'Better anyway,' said Hugh, 'to have something of your own than whine for something you can never possess. This garden is beautiful, it's true; but you can have one that is equally fine, if you're prepared to put the effort into it.'

'Perhaps,' Edmund said again. He glanced briefly at Constance, then towards the castle, and, at last, towards the Malvern Hills to the west. 'There's much to discuss, Sir Hugh. Let's all be sure that the decision we take is the right one. No need for haste. Your daughter still has growing to do, I think. Who knows? Perhaps some time in the Countess's household would profit her. Allow her to judge whether there is a face in the world she finds more pleasing than mine.'

'When you say the Countess...'

'I mean my lady of Gloucester, her kinswoman, naturally. I doubt whether she would gain much from being with my sister-in-law in Ireland. Though they are coming home, you know. The King has decided that Surrey shall be Lieutenant in my brother's place.'

This was news to them all, even to Thomas.

'I thought that March was determined to stay in Ireland,' he said.

'So he was; but the King has other ideas, and who may gainsay the King? Roger is going to be where the heir should be, at Richard's right hand.'

'And you will be a greater man in consequence,' Hugh said gruffly, thinking he could discern a reason for Edmund's inclination to delay.

Mortimer shrugged. 'I am what I have always been,' he said. 'My brother's brother. No more, no less. As Roger thinks it fitting to marry his eldest son to the Earl of Gloucester's daughter—as I know he still does—I'd be a fool indeed to account myself too great to accept the hand of the Earl of Gloucester's cousin. If it so befalls.'

Before anyone could answer, they were interrupted. Sir William Stradling came striding around the corner, a stripling at his heels. Constance drew herself erect, conscious of the possibility that Stradling's purpose was to appeal to Thomas against her authority.

'My lord,' he said breathlessly, 'there's one here who says he comes from the Countess of March. He claims his message is urgent. That it can't wait.'

The boy stepped forward, kneeling courteously to hand over the letter he carried. It did not occur to them to wonder why he was dressed in black.

Thomas broke the seal and scanned the contents, and Constance watched as the disbelief and horror spread over his face, like spilled water across a floor. Wordlessly, he passed the letter over to Edmund.

Roger Mortimer, Earl of March and Ulster, was dead.

***

It was St. Lambert's Eve, Sunday 15th September 1398. The morning would see Bolingbroke and Mowbray striving to hack each other in pieces. It was not surprising, therefore, that a certain air of restraint, not unlike a state of mourning, had settled over the court, though it was a restraint tinged with more than a streak of excitement.

Constance was standing in the great hall of Baginton Castle, the home of Sir William Bagot that stood just outside the walls of Coventry. Next to her was her father, who was engaged in a long conversation with the Chancellor, Bishop Stafford of Exeter. It was already some ten minutes since York had found anything new to say to the Bishop. In essence he kept repeating his opinion that it was a very ill business indeed.

Constance found herself thinking of Roger Mortimer, not for the first time since that day at Hanley Castle. There was more than an element of mystery about his death, one report holding that his own men had killed him, having somehow mistaken him for an enemy. The certainty was that he had died uselessly, in an obscure skirmish in the wilds of Ireland. The vultures had been quick to swoop, with the wardship of his lands shared out between Surrey, William le Scrope, Earl of Wiltshire, and Edward of York.

The Chancellor, who was not only very polite but also very patient, at last found an excuse to be gone, and York, deprived of his audience, turned to his daughter.

'Where is that brother of yours?' he asked irritably.

'At Gosford, my lord, seeing the lists prepared,' she answered, containing her own impatience. She was sure that her father was perfectly aware that this was Edward's duty as Lord Constable.

'Ah, yes, to be sure, I had forgot,' the Duke grunted. 'I see that damned wife of his is here though, giving herself airs.'

Philippa, magnificently gowned, was talking to the King. She seemed entirely at ease, as if she had been brought up as Richard's sister, and the success of the conversation was obvious from the number of amiable smiles she was generating.

'The woman is barren apart from anything else,' York went on.

Constance looked at him, taken aback by the note of despair in his voice. 'Her other husbands were rather old,' she ventured.

'Not that damned old!' he snapped back. 'I don't know what in hell he was thinking about. He'll have no son to follow him, that's sure.'

'Philippa can't be that much more than thirty, my lord.'

'I know how old she is, girl! Old enough for it to take a miracle to get her in whelp, as you know better than I do.'

'Even if you are right, sir, you have my brother Richard to succeed you. Your line will not come to an end.'

York looked away from her, his eyes fixed on the cloth-of-estate above the King's head. 'Were it possible, I'd sooner my estates and titles came to you,' he said stiffly.

Constance opened her mouth, and then closed it again. She had stumbled onto difficult ground. There was something about young Dickon that the Duke did not like. It was never fully explained, but from time to time the issue rose to the surface. She thought she knew the reason, but she could by no means question her father on the issue.

A stirring near the entrance of the hall made her turn to see who had arrived. It was Bolingbroke, not in armour but in courtly garb, come to take formal leave of the King. He was not alone. At least a dozen knights and esquires in Lancastrian blue-and-white followed at his heels, as if in demonstration of his power.

Constance watched as her cousins embraced and exchanged what seemed to be amiable words. She wondered at the subject of their conversation, for surely both were at the undefined boundary between courtesy and hypocrisy, concealing their mutual hatred beneath a thin veneer of politeness.

It was at this moment that the Duchess of Aumale arrived at her father-in-law's side. 'Ah, there you are, my lord Duke!' she said briskly, as if York had spent the last hour hiding under a table. 'I've been looking for you. I swear you've been avoiding me. You're almost as wicked as my husband, and just as handsome.'

York coughed uncomfortably. He had too much courtesy bred in him to shake off the bejewelled hand that had been laid familiarly on his arm. However, he could not quite trust himself to speak.

'My father and I were just talking of Edward,' Constance said, anxious to break the silence. 'We think he must still be at Gosford. Will he be staying there all night?'

'I hope not, Sister,' Philippa answered. 'If he does, it'll be his first night out of my bed since we were married. It may be that he'll spare me at least an hour or two from his other duties.' Her smile grew into an open laugh. She had not released York's arm, and now with her other hand she touched the collar of emeralds about her neck, as if to check it had not been stolen.

One of the circulating servants offered a tray of comfits. Constance took one of the spiced cakes and held it thoughtfully in her fingers. It was better, she decided, to say as little as possible to Philippa. After all, if she lost her temper, she would lose her dignity with it. She was still making a task of eating the comfit when Harry Bolingbroke joined their little group.

'I hope, my lord Uncle, that I have your blessing,' he said to York, kneeling in expectation of it. This development both surprised and embarrassed the Duke, but he rose to the occasion.

'I could not wish you better if you were my own son,' he said quietly. 'You're a fool, boy, but I believe you honest. May God and His saints protect you.'

Harry rose with his usual easy grace and smiled at them, pleased that the formality was over. 'Perhaps my cousin will be kind enough to grant me the favour she once promised me,' he suggested. 'Tomorrow sees me engaged in a crusade of sorts. Against evil; against one who is both a murderer and a traitor.'

Constance recovered from her surprise at the length and detail of his memory. 'I will pray that you receive justice, Cousin, as you deserve,' she said, 'but I think the day too serious for the giving of favours.'

'Your cousin faces his death,' York pointed out, his eyes hard. 'What he asks of you is little enough.'

Bolingbroke shook his head. 'No, perhaps it is too solemn an occasion for such fripperies. I am content with my cousin's prayers, provided that she thinks me a more honest man than Mowbray.'

Constance flinched, for that comment had struck home. However much she disliked her cousin, she could not deny that she had a certain wary respect for him. Norfolk, on the other hand, was simply a rogue, ready to change sides with every breeze. What was more, until recently, he had been one of her brother

- 136 -

Edward's closest associates. Since Edward had so clearly marked Bolingbroke as the enemy, was it likely that he would allow the outcome to be a matter of chance?

Philippa tore a piece of veiling from her headdress.

'Take this, Cousin,' she said, with extraordinary graciousness. 'I at least am on your side. Others may think what they will.'

***

St. Lambert's Day had not quite dawned. Subdued voices, rising from the courtyard of Baginton Castle, spoke of early mass and breakfast and the preparation of horses. Distantly, the assorted bells of Coventry's churches and religious houses were stirring into life, one by one, competing to disturb the faithful from their slumber.

Constance had opened the shutters, and, from the high window of her lodging, watched Thomas Mowbray ride in through the gatehouse, for it was his turn, now, to take formal leave of the King. Plainly clad as a duke could be, in a short black gown and black hose, he was followed by a single squire who bore his banner. She had a brief view of his face as he dismounted, and saw that it was grim.

She had gone to the trouble of dressing herself, and it was some indication of the time that had elapsed since she had left the bed that this task was almost complete. Only her headdress remained to be put on, and she was in the process of combing out her hair, ready for it to be braided and bound up. She had not called her women to aid her, this eccentric behaviour on her part being justified by her need to think without distraction.

Thomas yawned himself into wakefulness. 'You are up betimes, my love,' he said, shaking the sleep out of his eyes.

'I could not sleep.'

Hugging his knees, he anxiously inspected her, taking in at once her drawn expression, the unusual dullness of her eyes. 'You are not well,' he stated, stretching out a hand towards her.

'It is but lack of sleep.'

'Is it, *treschere*? You are sure?'

She nodded. 'It's not my body that troubles me, so much as my mind. I *know* that Ned intends some wickedness. I can feel it in my bones, and I think I can see it in his face, but what it is...' She sighed wearily. 'There'll be thousands there today, watching every blow that's struck. If any deceit is used it will be obvious to all, and he's too cautious to risk that. And yet...'

'You think he cares whether Bolingbroke or Mowbray dies? One of them must, and they both have broad, rich lands, from which he may claim his choice. You've been troubling yourself for nothing. There's no need for treachery. Whatever happens, Ned will profit thereby. He has only to sit back, watch and enjoy himself.'

Long before the Despensers had completed their dressing, Edward of York, riding his favourite grey palfrey, was busy with the final inspection of the lists that had been erected under his direction at Gosford Green, just outside the walls of Coventry. Already the happy holiday crowds had begun to arrive, anxious to see such rare entertainment as was to be provided. There would inevitably be some stimulating bloodshed, and there was the exciting possibility that the day would end with the beheading of a duke, for that was what would befall the combatant who was defeated, but not killed outright. The purpose of the very stout wooden barriers that had been put up around the field became evident as the people pressed six deep against them, and began to push and threaten one another for possession of the best vantage points.

To accommodate the great, and keep the delicate, milk-white complexions of the ladies out of the sun, a large wooden stand had been constructed on the southern side of the lists. In the exact centre of this structure, at a level calculated to give the best possible view of proceedings, two large thrones had been placed for the King and Queen. Another three chairs that were almost as impressive awaited the two royal uncles and the most important of several foreign guests, the Count of St. Pol, emissary from King Charles, and widower of Richard's half-sister, Maud Holland. On either side of this central position were long rows of cloth-covered, backless benching for the less exalted members of the court.

The Despensers had been allocated an excellent vantage point, close to the centre of the stand, and once Constance had settled herself on the cushions Agnes Norreys and Mary Russell had brought for her comfort, she began to make a study of her surroundings. Edward, on his grey, caught her eye as he continued his tour, his golden hair exposed to the light breeze and a friendly smile on his face as he threw jokes and small coins into the crowd. The people seemed unimpressed. If they had a hero at all, that hero was Harry Bolingbroke, still reckoned the foremost knight in Europe and judged by most to be the man in the right in this quarrel. There was precious little hope that caps would be thrown into the air for anyone else.

Bolingbroke was already waiting at the eastern end of the lists, an undeniably magnificent figure in costly Italian armour. This harness had been procured from his friend, the Duke of Milan, who had sent the pick of his own armoury from Milan, and with it a whole team of skilled armourers to make any necessary adjustments. Harry's bearing revealed no hint of impatience or nervousness; on the contrary, he seemed to be enjoying a relaxed chat with his entourage as he rested on the large chair that had been provided for him.

Philippa was nearby. She gave Constance a nudge. 'Jesu, Connie, is this not exciting? Look at Aumale! Is he not magnificent? The others are nothing next to him! Surrey's little more than a boy, and as for Bolingbroke! God's truth, some say he's handsome, but he's a head too short for a start, and little better than a monkey compared to my Ned.'

Constance frowned. 'I've never liked Harry,' she said. 'He was as much a rebel as my Uncle Gloucester, Arundel, or any of them.'

'A damned traitor!' hissed Philippa, who had apparently forgotten where she had bestowed her favour.

'Perhaps even that. But today, madame, he is facing something your husband would never find the courage to face, not even if he lived to be a thousand years old. I give him credit for that.'

Philippa rocked back, as if struck in the mouth by a fist. But she was relieved of the need to reply by the arrival, amid due ceremony, of the King and his little wife. Richard and Isabelle were resplendent in cloth-of-gold and white respectively, and wore their crowns in honour of the occasion, the Queen's being a simple, light circlet, suitable for a child's head and worn over unbound hair. A few deferential paces behind them were the King's uncles, both looking grave. The lounging occupants of the stand rose to their feet and made their cramped obeisances, and all around people knelt in the mud.

Once Richard was in his place it was time for the defendant, Thomas Mowbray, to make his appearance. Mowbray had armour, horses and attendants that were every whit as fine as his opponent's, and yet it seemed to Constance that he failed to impress the eye as Harry did. Perhaps it was simply that he lacked the aura of popular support. Even his destrier looked uncomfortable, seemed to be taking every chance to dance sideways.

Edward and Surrey, who was acting as marshal, had the combatants brought before the King. There was a formal measuring of weapons and reading of rules, and then the mounted Bolingbroke and Mowbray reaffirmed their determination to fight, swore to use no treachery or foul blows, and retired to opposite ends of the great field to await the signal that would begin the trial. Constance saw that Harry was wearing Philippa's favour, not on his arm as a knight was normally inclined to do, but at the tip of his lance, where it was more likely to confuse his opponent.

She glanced in the King's direction, and won a brief, preoccupied smile from her father for her trouble. York was calming himself by chewing on some dubious confection. Richard looked no less worried, was twisting a gold tipped baton in his long, nervous fingers. He did not seem to be paying attention to the proceedings, but was exchanging quiet words with the Count of St. Pol.

Edward made his way to the special place reserved for him as Constable, close to the King's feet, Surrey gave the vital signal of command and, to a blare of trumpets, the two powerful destriers were released simultaneously.

A second passed, perhaps two, and then Edward was on his feet again, shouting and making frantic gestures to his assistants. These men ran forward in two groups, waving their arms and struggling to seize the reins of the charging, frantic destriers. It was dangerous work, but by some miracle no one was hurt as the frightened and bewildered animals were dragged to a halt with about ten yards to spare. A howl of puzzlement, frustration and plain anger rose from the crowd, and in the stand men and women shot to their feet in a witless, futile attempt to gain a better view. Constance saw that the baton the King had been holding was now lying in the centre of the lists, a few yards from where her flustered brother was standing, still issuing his instructions. She was not at all clear what this meant.

Thomas answered her unspoken question. 'The King has taken the quarrel back into his own hands. It's within his rights. It looks as if there will be no combat after all.'

Richard paused to exchange a word with Edward, and then strode off in the direction of his own great pavilion. An immediate meeting of the Council was announced, and its members, exchanging shrugs, extracted themselves from the stand and followed their sovereign.

For everyone else there was a long and tedious wait, with little to do but speculate about the King's intentions. Mowbray and Bolingbroke retired to their chairs at opposite ends of the lists, and were left to glower at each other, and swelter in their heavy armour as the sun rose higher in the sky.

After about two hours, some of the King's advisers returned to their places. Richard himself did not appear, and nor did his uncles or Edward.

Thomas whispered in his wife's ear as he sat down. 'There is to be no fighting this day. Both are banished.'

'Banished? Both?' Constance could not make sense of it. 'How can they both be guilty?'

He shrugged. 'The King has judged them so. Though not equally. Harry Bolingbroke goes for ten years. Mowbray for life.'

'And it has taken all this time, to settle it so?'

Thomas rewarded her with one of his wry smiles. 'The King asked for advice. It took time for some of us to realise what advice he wanted to hear. Your brother is well pleased with himself, though he's at pains to hide it from us all. If I didn't know better, I'd swear all this was ordered in advance, and by his counsel. Which would mean that all this has been no more than play-acting. With the King and Edward using us all as their puppets.'

Constance frowned as she struggled to make sense of the judgement. 'It was the only way he could be sure that Harry would not win,' she said at last. 'Ned feared that, above all. I thought that some treachery might be used, but this, this is much more clever.'

Thomas sighed. It made sense. Rather too much so for his comfort. 'I suppose,' he said dryly, 'that an honest fight and a clear victory was too much to hope for. That would be far too straightforward, would it not, *treschere*?'

12

Constance rose carefully from her knees, and smoothed down the flowing black folds of her gown. She had not been excessively attached to her uncle, John of Gaunt, Duke of Lancaster, while the Duke, for his part, had shown precious little interest in her existence, but it was proper that she should wear mourning for him and offer prayers for his soul, and she accepted the duty unquestioningly.

She paused for a moment, grateful for the silence in the chapel, and the opportunity for a moment or two of peaceful reflection. Then she emerged into the chaos of the crowded anteroom. Some of those waiting to see her were genuine petitioners. Others were Despenser officials, looking to her for instructions in her lord's absence. But many, she suspected, were there because they had nothing better to do but stand out of the wind. It being Lent, there were numerous pilgrims to St. Anne's Well, Caversham's most famous attraction, and although only a small minority of them had travelled very far so early in the year, there were quite a few who had arrived on bare feet, having walked five, ten or twenty miles over icy, rutted roads. The likes of these were grateful for whatever hospitality they could find, and were apt to linger when they found it. They had to be fed and sheltered, however roughly, and certainly could not be turned away from the door.

A somewhat decrepit knight pushed his way towards her. Bowing as low as his stiff joints would permit, he opened with a string of compliments, from which, eventually, emerged a request for support for his ambition to be the next sheriff of Oxfordshire. A Despenser tenant explained, in graphic detail, about the plague that had destroyed his cattle, and with them the ability to pay his rent. If the distraint against him were carried through, it would be his utter undoing, and that of his wife and eleven children. A young priest, who had apparently walked all the way from Oxford, enquired with more hope than expectation about the possibility of being granted a living. The nervous widow of a yeoman thrust her spindly son forward, asking if my lady could possibly find him a place in her household—perhaps in the stables, for the lad was good with horses. John Snede, the Despenser receiver in Oxfordshire, sought to explain an inconvenient deficiency in his accounts, which a recent audit had highlighted. And so it went on.

Constance heard them all out, with such good humour as she could muster. The yeoman's son she sent off joyfully to find a Despenser livery, for it chanced there was a vacancy, and he seemed to her a deserving lad. For the rest, she promised to intercede for them with her husband, when he returned from court. She told Snede, however, that it would be wise for him to put his case into writing for Thomas's consideration, since some of the points he had made were beyond her simple understanding. Snede looked at her keenly when she said that, but promised to follow her advice.

The young man in black, with the greyhound badge on his chest, waited until all the others had been dealt with, and longer still, until it had been made quite clear to the assembled pilgrims that they were welcome to partake of dinner in the great hall before going on their way. Only then did he step forward, to kneel and present a cloth-wrapped package and a folded letter.

Constance had been watching him out of the corner of her eye for some time. She had wondered what business a servant of Harry Bolingbroke could have at Caversham. Now she had her answer.

'You, sir, must have travelled far,' she remarked.

'From Paris, my lady.'

'You are welcome to take your rest here. Until you are ready to return.'

The boy shook his head. 'I must be away after dinner, my lady. I have other letters to deliver. To your brother, my lord the Duke of Aumale. I expect he will be with the King?'

She nodded, struggling with renewed surprise. 'It is likely,' she agreed.

'Also to the Earl of Northumberland, who is likely to be in his own country. And to my lord the Marquis of Dorset. So, my lady, I have much riding to do, and cannot linger here. Though, in all truth, I wish I could. It's sweet to be back in England, and I'm in no haste to set foot on a ship again.' He ended with an expansive smile, which would have softened a much harder heart than Constance's.

Returning to her solar, she unwrapped the cloth package. Inside was a gilt greyhound, with a forget-me-not clutched between its fore paws, two of Harry's cognizances combined in one. The letter was brief.

> 'Madame,
>
> 'I recommend me to you, and to my lord your husband. I ask you to accept the unworthy gift sent by the bearer, that it might prompt you on occasion to recall me in your prayers. My lord father, whom God pardon, asked me to remain in France, but now that he is sped it is my purpose, once my English affairs are set in order, to bear my sword once more against the enemies of Christ as you suggested I should. It may be that I shall not live to return to England, in which case I hope that will think more kindly of me.
>
> 'By your cousin,
> Henry, Duke of Lancaster.'

'Ill news, my lady?' asked Agnes Norreys, who always liked to be well in-formed.

Constance shook her head. 'My cousin of Lancaster has decided to make good use of his ten years abroad. He goes to fight the Saracens, and asks for my prayers.'

She walked slowly to the window, and looked out over the Thames. There was more than an even chance that Bolingbroke would never come home. And in his absence her brother would rule England, under the King. With Lancaster and March both gone, there was no one strong enough to stand in his way. At one time she would have thought that a triumph but now the prospect filled her with dread. Edward was not fit to possess such power. He was likely to destroy them all.

'Agnes, why is nothing ever simple any more?' she asked.

'My lady?'

'It doesn't matter.' She extended her left arm. 'This sleeve is soiled.'

'No wonder, when you suffer half the scum of Oxfordshire and Berkshire to pull on it! God knows, most of them stink like pigs, so they are like to have filth on their hands.'

'Have some charity, Agnes. They have a right to come, and I have a duty to hear them. Change me this sleeve, before the dirt carries elsewhere.'

The flowing sleeve of Constance's houppelande was detachable, by means of fine pins. The removal was a fiddling job, and Lady Norreys tutted over it, strug-gling with the pins. At last it parted, and Agnes laid the sleeve aside, none too rev-erently, before going off in something of a huff to rummage for its substitute.

Agnes ranked beyond dispute as the first of Constance's women nowadays. Maud Mohun and Katherine Mallory were long gone, to households and hus-bands of their own, and their replacements could not possibly compete with Lady Norreys in status or long service. Yet they were not close, scarcely friends. Constance had never felt able to confide in Agnes, and Agnes resented it. Sigh-ing, Constance picked up the black, discarded sleeve, and twisted it in her hands as she considered the problem. It was tempting to find an excuse to be rid of Agnes, but that would make a difficulty with John Norreys, the best officer they had, who thought his wife was a saint. Nothing, indeed, was ever simple.

Agnes bustled back into the room, carrying the clean sleeve and trailing young Mary Russell and Anne Despenser in her wake, determined to make the process as much a ceremony as was possible. Constance submitted patiently, keeping her eyes on the river and her mind as far away from the tedium of Caversham as she could.

'Agnes,' she said at length, when the task was more or less completed, 'send to see whether my cousin of Lancaster's esquire is still in the hall. I wish to speak to him again.'

Lady Norreys made no reply, apart from a movement of her body that a generous soul might have interpreted as a curtsey. As she left the room to seek out a page to run the errand she did, however, allow herself an audible snort of irritation.

When the young esquire knelt before her again, Constance handed him the soiled sleeve. 'Give this to your master, as my token,' she said, 'and tell him that, as a Christian, I am bound to pray for his safety among the infidels. Say I know that he will return to England as no less loyal a subject of the King's Grace than when he left.'

She was rather pleased with the subtlety of that last comment. Bolingbroke, she knew, would appreciate it.

***

John Bushey's elegant, lawyer's voice droned on. He had been speaking for almost a full half hour, and, although no one was actually asleep, there were those around the council table whose attention had wandered, to say the least. Bushey, prominent member of the King's household, trusted legal adviser, and late Speaker of the Commons, was not markedly popular, even in his present company.

Thomas Despenser stared at the King's ornate, empty chair. It was by no means unusual for Richard to absent himself when there was only routine business to be discussed. On such occasions, however, it was customary for most of the great lords to stay away as well, because few of them had the stomach for administrative detail. Today, however, the attendance was notably aristocratic, with the Duke of York close to the head of the table. Even the Earl of Northumberland, who spent much of his time in the far North, had made one of his infrequent appearances. Despenser was not naive enough to suppose that this was a mere matter of chance. Even the King's proposed new campaign in Ireland, important though it was, did not seem to justify such interest.

Bushey was, finally, reaching the point of his argument. The Shrewsbury Parliament, he said, had given this Council, acting as a Committee of Parliament, complete power to determine all matters moved before it. The Council was, therefore, more than competent to deal with the great matter that stood to be considered.

Bishop Stafford of Exeter, the Chancellor, took up the tale. 'The King has grown concerned about the sentence passed at Gosford Green on the Duke of Hereford and the Duke of Norfolk. Legal opinion has been sought on the matter.' He coughed briskly, and leafed through his papers. 'In effect, my lords, the sentence declared them both to be guilty of high treason. I need not remind this Council that the lands and goods of traitors are forfeit to the Crown. Yet, by inadvertence, such forfeiture was not put into effect. Moreover, both the offenders were granted royal licences enabling them to enter into possession of such estates as might pass to them by inheritance. These licences were granted because of inadequate and mistaken advice, and are contrary to law. It follows that they are void. If we were to accept the principle that adjudged traitors may not only retain their lands, but may also continue to receive inheritances, the statute against treason would be seriously undermined. I am sure all will agree that this cannot be allowed. It is for this Council, my lords, to regularise the position.'

'What are you saying, man?' York demanded irritably. 'It all sounds like a damned lawyer's quibble to me. Are we to annul the sentences? Recall them to England?'

'Indeed not, Your Grace,' the Bishop answered. 'It is proposed rather that the banishment of Bolingbroke be extended to cover the term of his life. And that his lands, and those of Thomas Mowbray, be declared forfeit.'

'The King himself gave a solemn promise that my nephew of Lancaster would be allowed to enter into his inheritance,' York returned, concern furrowing his brow. 'To take back such a promise, for the sake of some—some petty point of law...' He paused, shaking his head. 'It is not well done, my lords. If it is not dishonourable, then it is close to it. Too damned close for my taste.'

'His Grace the Duke of York forgets that we are dealing with the safety of the Throne, not merely with our own personal conceptions of honour,' Bushey said. 'To allow Harry Bolingbroke, a man of questionable loyalty, if not worse, to enter into possession of lands far more extensive than those of the King himself would be an act of folly. Madness. Indeed, were we to consent to such a course we would be little short of traitors ourselves.'

William le Scrope, Earl of Wiltshire and Treasurer of England, coughed. 'The forfeitures will do much to fill the King's coffers,' he said, 'and avoid the need for further forced loans to finance the King's necessary campaign in Ireland.'

Northumberland's chair scraped back. A spare, elderly but unstooping figure, he stood in his place. 'So,' he said, 'it is not, after all, a matter of law. It's a matter of expedience. If men are to be disinherited on such a basis then not one of us is safe, my lords. Not even you, my lord Bishop of Exeter. For the Church has great lands that might be thought likely to serve the King's purpose better than they do God's. I will not stay to take part in such dealings.'

Bishop Stafford shook his head. 'You must do as best accords with your conscience, my lord,' he murmured, spreading his hands.

'The rest of us,' sneered Bushey, 'will remember that we are assembled here as servants of the King, to act in his interests, and not those of the traitor Harry Bolingbroke.'

Northumberland stared at him. The Earl was genuinely too shocked to speak. He simply could not believe that he, Henry Percy, could be addressed in such terms by a mere esquire.

'My lord of Northumberland's loyalty has never been questioned,' York said, 'and it ought not to be questioned, unless by one who is at least his equal. You should mind your tongue, Bushey, lest it run away with your head.'

'Even so, Your Grace, and by your leave,' Bushey continued, 'the choice for the members of this Council is clear. They may serve the King, or they may serve Bolingbroke. Not both. That applies to all. No matter how humble. No matter how—elevated.'

'God's truth!' roared York. 'Do you now seek to instruct me in my duty?'

Bushey actually smiled. 'Of course not, Your Grace,' he answered, bowing his head. 'I do no more than most humbly draw this Council's attention to the evident facts of the matter.'

Thomas wondered what contribution his brother-in-law would have made to this debate; but Edward was conveniently absent, on the northern border, where he was helping to investigate violations of the truce with the Scots. That perhaps explained Northumberland's presence here, because the haughty Earl would certainly not relish playing second fiddle to Aumale in such diplomacy.

The door closed behind Northumberland, its slam echoing across the lofty room.

'If there are no other objections we can perhaps proceed to the next business,' suggested Bishop Stafford.

Thomas opened his mouth to speak, but then recollected himself. He was bought and sold like the rest of them, laden with promises. He had the honour of being appointed to command the rearguard of the King's army in Ireland. He had been in the minority often enough over March, and it was not a comfortable position. There were others there, of higher rank than he, who were well content to keep silent. John Holland, for example, whose lady was Bolingbroke's sister, and John Beaufort, Marquis of Dorset, Harry's half-brother. If such as these did not object, why should he?

York cleared his throat uncomfortably, but no one spoke. Some, in truth, were already counting their gains. The forfeitures hung in the air for a moment, and then were implemented without a further word as the Council turned unthinkingly to the next item on its agenda.

**

It was a chill, bright morning when they set off from Caversham. Looking back for a moment as they made their way slowly against the steep slope of the Oxford road, Constance was surprised by the cold sparkle of the river, the clarity of the view over the water meadows to Reading, and the dominant towers and pinnacles of the great abbey. She had rarely seen it so beautiful.

Their pilgrimage, so often deferred, was begun at last. She and Thomas, dressed in the oldest and most undistinguished clothes they could find, and pilgrims' hats of woven straw, were completely alone together, an astonishing experience in itself. For the present they were walking, because they were sharing a saddle horse, a mediocre rouncey that was not strong enough to carry both of them, and their belongings, up such a sharp ascent. Thomas had proposed to lead the animal while she rode, but it was far too early in the day for her pride to allow her to accept such a concession. If he walked, so would she.

'I meant to tell you something,' he said, 'but there was little chance last night, and less this morning. Lady March is back at court, in the Queen's household.'

'Alianore? You've seen her?'

'Oh, yes. Just briefly, before I left Windsor. She had to buy March's body back from the Irish rebels. Bought a chalice for a church in exchange for him. God's truth, I hope you don't have to do the same for me!'

Constance was silent for a moment. She wished he were not going to Ireland, especially as he had signed a contract for a whole year's military service, but there was no point in saying that. He was looking forward to the fighting.

'We're going at the wrong time of year,' he went on. 'The leaves will be on the trees, and that'll suit our enemies. They like to skulk in forests, where the archers can't see them. I'm surprised the King's in such haste, but the fact is that he burns to avenge Roger's death. Strange that, when not so long ago he'd have been glad of it.'

'Yes, and if Roger had survived for just a few more weeks, he'd have been safely home in England, and high in Richard's favour. God's will, I suppose. How has Alianore taken the loss?'

'Well enough, I think. If she's shed any tears, they're long dried. She's the richest widow in England, of course, and something of a prize. I dare say your brother is regretting that he didn't wait a little longer.'

'There was a time when I almost believed he loved her; of course, I should have been wiser than that.'

'He would have dearly loved her dower lands; the wardship of her sons. That's certain! He must be cursing himself. As it is, some other man will reap the benefit.'

'You think she'll take another husband?'

'Why should she not? She might even be wise to choose for herself before someone decides to choose for her.'

At the top of the climb Thomas mounted up, and aided her onto the pillion behind him. The rouncey moved on unhurriedly, its pace steady and not particularly smooth as they picked their way down the narrow way that forked off to the right and led to the ancient road below the ridge, a chalk scar that ran eastward through the woodlands, bounded by low earth banks.

Before long they caught up with a middle-aged man and his young son who were riding in the same general direction. They were wool merchants, the elder man explained, on their way to Missenden to discuss business with the abbot. It might be well to bear company, he suggested, since there was always a hazard from outlaws.

'I have my sword,' said Despenser, 'but you're welcome to ride with us if you will.'

Constance was aware of the merchant's eyes running over them both, as if he was trying to put a price on them.

'You and your lady are travelling far, Sir Knight?' he asked, having made his assessment. He had perhaps noticed Thomas's gold spurs.

'To Walsingham.'

The merchant crossed himself devoutly. 'A blessed place. I beg that you remember me in your prayers. I, alas, have no leisure for such holy work. I need to agree a price for the wool from the abbey's flock; the abbot says he's no longer bound by our old agreement, that it's his duty to sell to the higher bidder he says he's found. He could be lying, of course, but I can't take the chance. It's too important a contract, and there's already too much that is uncertain. Who knows what demands the King will make of us all? These blank charters of his are hard to swallow. No man can be sure what he may have to pay.'

The King had required all the leading men of all the counties he judged to have sided with the Appellants to seal blank charters on behalf of their communities. The threat was obvious.

'I've heard it said that the King will make no use of them, so long as the country remains peaceful,' Thomas said. He himself had his doubts about the charters; holding a knife to a man's throat was as likely to provoke resistance as submission.

'I say nothing against the King. God forbid that I should! It's those around him. Wiltshire, Bushey, Bagot and the rest. You may be right, sir, and I pray that you are. But it puts questions in men's minds, makes them uneasy for the future. Then there are other rumours. A friar told me that the King intends to rule from outside the realm. From Chester, perhaps, or even from Ireland.'

'I don't know how anyone can believe such nonsense!' snapped Constance, unable to restrain herself. 'If you were king, would you choose to live in Ireland? Where would his profit be?'

'I don't say it's true, my lady,' the merchant answered stiffly, 'but it's what the friar told me. Why should a holy man lie? He must have had it from somewhere, and you know what friars are. In and out of the houses of great men, picking up all the gossip.'

'It's probably a misunderstanding,' said Thomas. 'Of course the King is leading an army to Ireland, against the rebels who oppose him, but he'll be back in England as soon as order is restored. I know because I'm going with him myself.'

'Then I wish you good fortune,' the merchant said, but he looked at them a little askance, as if he was unsure whether he had said too much. 'Whom do you serve, Sir Knight, if I may ask?'

'The Earl of Gloucester.'

'I hear he is none so ill a master to those he favours.'

'I have no complaints against him.'

'Save that he is too apt to tolerate fools,' Constance added sharply.

'Ah, there are worse faults in a great lord than that, my lady,' the merchant sighed. 'Not that I would think of speaking ill of such, of course; far be it from me to judge my betters. As long as I can buy and sell my wool in peace, and pay no more tax than is just, I have no complaint. The Earl has some land at Burford that I should like to lease, to run my sheep upon, though I doubt he knows the value of it. I know his man, John Snede, well enough to hope that he might say a word for me. Though of course it may cost me a supper or two. You will know Master Snede I expect, sir, being in the same meinie.'

'I believe I've met the man,' said Thomas.

'Then you'll know that he's not averse to allowing a few coins to influence his mind where matters of business are concerned. Not that I blame him. Christ knows, there's little point in holding an office if you can't make a profit from it. Of course, Snede is a great man in Oxfordshire. Gathers all Lord Gloucester's rents, among other things. It's a heavy responsibility, with auditors breathing down his neck all the time. I'd not do it for nothing, and I don't suppose you would, either.'

'Not unless they were my own lands.'

The man hooted with laughter, throwing back his head. 'God's truth! You'd have cause to rejoice if they were! I wish they were mine; I could make twenty times what your lord earns from them in rent. I'd clear the tenants out, every man jack of them, and especially the serfs, who are more trouble than they're worth. Then I'd put sheep on the land, thousands of 'em. If I couldn't be bothered to manage it myself, I'd lease it out to those who were. But of course I wouldn't charge the same rents that were being paid fifty years ago, and let my tenant have all the profit, which is what's happening at the moment. Small wonder Snede is growing rich!'

They spent the night at the priory at Notley, and, with the genders segregated into separate dormitories, Constance at least had some relief from the merchant's tedious tongue, though it was at the price of sharing a straw mattress with an elderly, toothless widow who was almost equally garrulous. When she arose, she found that the fleas of the bed had risen with her. Much of the morning's journey was spent scratching, the consolation being that they were alone again, for the merchant and his son were on another road.

'It's a long time since I've been this way,' said Thomas, 'but we should reach Dunstable well before dark. We'll lodge with the Black Canons there. It's a richer house than Notley, and should be more comfortable.'

'If you're not sure of the direction, we should perhaps hire a guide,' she suggested.

'A guide? This isn't the Prussian wilderness, treschere. I think I can find our way well enough.'

He sounded hurt, and Constance held her tongue on the subject. A steady rain had begun to fall, driven into their faces by an icy wind, and she was grateful of the protection provided by his back.

In one of the villages they passed through an old woman was sitting misera-bly on the step of the charred ruin that was evidently her cottage, with a group of people gathered around a cask of ale they had set up on a trestle table at the edge of the road. Most of them were drinking from coarse, earthenware vessels, and they eyed the arrival of the Despensers with hostile, silent suspicion. With-out exception they were thin, ragged and dirty.

Thomas halted the horse. 'Will this road take us to Dunstable?' he asked.

One of the older men stepped forward, belatedly remembering to touch the edge of his hood in salute. His face was disfigured by a hairy, swollen growth below one eye. 'It will, if you take the right fork in a little way. You pilgrims?'

'Yes.'

'You can do a little charity here if you like. Old Goody there has lost her house, and just about everything in it, so we're having a help-ale, to raise some-thing for her. Two pence a cup—for a gentleman.'

'My lady and I will have a cup apiece,' Thomas said, drawing out a clutch of small coins without bothering to count them.

The man bowed, almost mockingly, smiling to reveal his brown and broken teeth. 'Hey, Giles, fetch the lord and his lady their ale. Hurry, you young bastard!'

Constance saw that some of the tension had gone out of the villagers, and she breathed more easily. She had not been afraid, not with Thomas to protect her, but she had been uncomfortably conscious of their hostility.

The ale, when it came, was thin and disgusting, not worth a farthing, the cups cracked and dirty. She would have preferred to drink water from a horse trough.

'Will your lord not help her?' Thomas asked.

The man laughed aloud. 'That's a rich jest! We don't even know who our lord is any more. It *used* to be the Duke of Lancaster. Not that he came here much, you understand. Can't say I much blame him. *I'd* not come to this hole if I were the King's uncle. Anyway, he's dead, and his son's banished, and God alone knows who our lord is now. I dare say we'll find out when the rents are due, or when someone decides that there's money to be made from holding a manor court. Whoever the new man is, I don't suppose he'll much care whether old Madge has a roof over her head or not. He's more likely to fine her for being clumsy with her fire.'

The Despensers finished their ale, and then rode on.

'What a place!' Constance said. 'Have you ever seen so ill-managed a manor? Half the houses looked as if they were ready to fall down, and those people were as ragged as scarecrows. Do you think my uncle really was their lord?'

'Why should they lie?'

'My father has no such village on his estates. He'd think it a disgrace!'

Thomas snorted. 'Have you visited all your father's manors, *treschere*? Or mine? There are plenty of people who live as ill as that, or worse.'

'Not at Fotheringhay there aren't!'

'No, not at Fotheringhay. But elsewhere? I'd not wonder at it.'

'Something should be done for that woman.'

'I dare say her kin will take her in. Anyway, whoever their new lord is, you know it isn't me.'

That at least was true. Thomas had not petitioned for a share of the Lancastrian lands, and the King had not seen fit to press a share of the spoils upon him.

The rain eased for half an hour, almost to the point of clearing, then suddenly began to fall in torrents. Within minutes they were no longer merely wet, but soaked to the very skin.

'I hope it's not far to Dunstable,' Constance ventured, reluctant to complain.

Thomas looked about him, his eyes narrowing in the driving, icy rain.

'I think it is,' he admitted, 'and I doubt we'll reach it today. We'd better seek shelter.'

But there was no shelter in sight, unless a tree or a bush could be counted as such. Slowly, reluctantly, they pressed on, cold and miserable. It took an hour or more before they reached a crossroads, and found an inn of sorts, a low, straggling building of wattle and daub covered by a roof of long-neglected thatch.

Constance dripped by the fire in the centre of the hall, while Despenser lodged the horse in the inn's crude stable and tended to its needs, rubbing it down and seeing that it was fed and watered.

'It's a good man who cares for his horse before himself,' remarked the alewife, a small, rounded woman of uncertain age, placing a beaker of warm, spiced ale into Constance's hands. The ale was drinkable, infinitely superior to that they had bought back at the village. What was more, its heat drove some of the chill from her bones. 'Have you travelled far, Mistress?'

'From Notley Priory today. Is it far from here to Dunstable?'

The woman rubbed her chin to assist her thoughts. 'You've come out of your way. It's a good four hours' walk; but with this rain, the road will be as good as a quagmire. I doubt you'll reach there before dark.'

'Can we lodge here?'

'You can if you don't mind sleeping on the floor, before the fire. Or there's the hayloft if you prefer. As for food, you're welcome to what's in the pot.'

After due discussion, the Despensers decided to stay where they were. There was no luxury available at the inn, assuredly, but at least they were out of the rain, and the woman's broth, though thin and apparently made from a mixture of cabbage and sundry root vegetables, was at least warming, and served well enough to fill the stomach. They could hope for better weather in the morning.

'I suppose it's a little early in the year for such a journey,' Thomas said, 'though we couldn't have left it much longer, if we're to be at Windsor by the middle of next month. Perhaps we'd have been wiser to go with the King to Canterbury. Still a pilgrimage, but I swear your cousin will not be sitting in a stinking hole like this, nor eating such swill. I care not for myself. I've had worse on campaign, and I'll do well to fare so well in Ireland. But I don't like to see you so, *treschere*, or think of you having to lie all night on a dirty floor.'

'There's always the hayloft,' she pointed out, lightly. 'At least we should be private there. Many would think it as good as a bridal bed.'

'It might be warmer near the fire.'

'I don't think we'll be cold. Do you?' She leaned against him, as close as their large-brimmed hats would allow.

The light of understanding appeared in his eyes at last. 'No,' he conceded, 'I dare say we'll find ways to be warm enough.'

13

Harry Bolingbroke threw the letter down with a frown and looked out through the open window of the Hotel Clisson to the Seine.

'I don't know what man I may trust,' he said gloomily. 'Fair words from Northumberland. Fair words from my cousin, Edward of York. But to what do they amount? Richard will not heed them, and they'll not risk their necks for me.'

'It is a sin to despair, my son.' Archbishop Arundel had drawn back the hood of the monkish robe that had served as his disguise for his journey to Paris. He was grizzled and heavily jowelled, resembling a badger that had run to fat. 'There is hope. Every cause for hope. The great injustice that has been done to you has offended almost every man of property in England; even some of those who are close to Richard have their doubts. Your uncle, the Duke of York, for example, is known to have quarrelled with the King and withdrawn to his estates.'

'So it is said. I don't believe it.'

The Archbishop sniffed. 'I have many agents in England. Men who still regard me as the rightful primate. They cannot all be liars.'

A flicker of amusement lit Harry's eyes. He had no great liking for interfering, politically minded priests, and he knew well enough what Thomas Arundel was doing in Paris. Deprived of Canterbury, he had been nominally translated to a See outside the obedience of the Pope of Rome, and Richard had appointed Roger Walden, one time soldier and the son of a butcher, in his room. It was not Harry's restoration that motivated the Archbishop; it was his own.

'Thomas Despenser, the Earl of Gloucester, has refused any portion of your lands, and gone on pilgrimage. No man knows where.' The Archbishop sniffed again, and cleared his throat. 'It may, of course, be significant that he is York's son-in-law.'

'I'm well aware of that,' said Harry.

'Nevertheless, the point is worth making. I believe that if you were to make a landing in England there would be few willing to oppose you. No one can trust Richard's word, as we both have good cause to know. He burdens the people with taxes and tallages, and he doesn't uphold the law. The land is all but overrun by outlaws, and by the Cheshire rogues he keeps about him. I believe you have a duty before God to put an end to his misrule.'

'A duty to rebel?'

'Against a tyrant? Yes! Certainly it's a duty. The clear duty of all honest men. Richard is concerned only with his own profit, not the common good of the realm. Such a king is an abomination in the eyes of the Lord. Anyway, what is your alternative? To sit here and rot on the charity of the French?'

'I can do nothing more for the moment. The Duke of Burgundy commands all here, and he is Richard's ally. Why should he allow me to mount an invasion of England? I've no hope of persuading him to support me.'

'France has more strings to her bow than Burgundy!'

'You mean Orleans? We're on good terms, it's true, but he doesn't have the power to help me.'

'Not yet, perhaps. But I hear that Burgundy intends to leave Paris in the summer, to go to his own lands in Flanders. That will be Orleans' chance. And yours! We must begin to prepare for that moment. We have, perhaps, three months. By which time Richard, and all those willing to fight for him, will be in Ireland. Do you not see how clearly God's purpose is revealed?'

Harry was silent for a moment. 'Richard should have been more patient,' he said at last. 'If he'd but waited, I'd have been in Rhodes by now, fighting the infidel. I might even have been dead. I'd prepared myself to give up my life in a holy cause.'

'This *is* a holy cause!' the Archbishop hissed. 'You will be fighting for freedom and justice, and doing God's will. Later, when England is saved, you may take up the banner of a crusader if that is your wish. God understands the necessities which cause delay, and He sees the good intent in your heart, just as clearly as if the deed were already performed.'

Bolingbroke took up Edward's letter again, held it closer so that the words were clearer. So much sympathy, so little commitment, was contained in its cautious, friendly phrases. The one piece of information that intrigued him was that his estates had not been irrevocably alienated. According to Edward they had been placed in the custody of the grantees—of whom Edward was one—with the saving formula: 'until Henry, Duke of Lancaster, shall sue for the same.'

Richard had banished him for life, and yet he had left that small hint that the sentence was not irreversible. It did not make sense. But then again, thought Bolingbroke, so much of what Richard does fails to make sense. Perhaps that is his strength. He keeps us all guessing at his intent, hoping against hope that we may yet win his favour.

'I must consult my friends,' he said dismissively. 'Here—and in England.'

***

The Despensers walked the last mile into Walsingham barefoot, as did even the least devout of pilgrims. Spring was stirring in Norfolk, noticeable new warmth in the air. The occasional flint cutting unexpectedly into her sole was not trouble enough to daunt Constance's contentment.

'I shall be sorry to go back,' she said quietly.

Thomas nodded. He looked serious for a moment as he calculated the days. 'We've little more than a fortnight to get to the tournament at Windsor,' he told her. 'We have to be there, it's expected, and I'd like a day or two to practice beforehand. We've idled too long on the road.'

'Do you regret it?'

'Regret time with you, *treschere*? Of course not! But we have our duty. If we don't fulfil it, we've no right to claim the bread we eat.'

'We shall be apart for a whole year.'

'Yes.'

'Is that not duty enough? Must I long for it to begin?'

'Perhaps you'll find I've left you something to remind you of me,' he suggested, his eyes bright. 'I'd expect it, after that hayloft.'

Constance did not meet his gaze, but smiled in complacent satisfaction. There was reason in what he said. All knew that a woman was more likely to conceive if she received pleasure, and that night in the hay had been one to remember. They had taken each other to new heights, and in the most unlikely of places, with their damp underclothes still clinging to them, and with no bed but the prickly stalks of the fodder. It had been ecstatic, and certainly sinful, for they had not been out of Lent then. Well, they were in a good place to ask forgiveness, and indeed the Virgin might grant her petition for another child. It was almost two and a half years since their son's birth. High time he had a brother.

They were no longer walking alone, but as part of a swelling crowd. Though a majority of the people spoke with the rich, flat burr of Norfolk, there were many from further afield, including a good number whose English was so strangely accented as to make it unintelligible, probably northerners or Scots, an old man and his wife who spoke Spanish to one other, and several pilgrims who conversed in French. Every type of clothing could be seen from tailored silks to sackcloth, from religious habits to beggars' rags, and the pace of the procession was slowed by the many who hobbled on sticks and crutches, or were carried along by their friends on pallets or in litters. Our Lady of Walsingham was credited with numerous miracles, and many of the pilgrims were hoping for a cure of one kind or another, from barrenness, perhaps, or blindness, or deformity. They might, after all, be the one person in a hundred, or a thousand, who was blessed.

At last they arrived in the little town, to find the market place so crammed with people that it was almost impossible to move, except with patience and persistence and the occasional exasperated shove. The market stalls seemed evenly divided between those selling basic necessities such as bread, ale and cloth, and those seeking to attract the pilgrims. The latter offered lead medals crudely stamped with a representation of the Virgin's statue, crucifixes and rosaries of every imaginable quality, pieces of bone or tattered cloth that alleg-edly belonged to one saint or another, and small, cheap images of Our Lady, carved in wood or bone. There was even a man in clerical dress selling pardons that he claimed were direct from Rome, and personally signed by the Pope.

'I wish the Pope were here,' Thomas said wryly, examining one of the parch-ments, 'for I doubt he'd recognise his own hand or seal.'

'It seems we have a Lollard here, good people!' shouted the vendor, over-hearing. 'One of those who mocks your piety.'

Despenser took him gently by the throat. 'If I were not on pilgrimage, I'd break your bloody neck for that insult. As it is, my uncle is the Bishop of Nor-wich, and he shall hear of your doings.'

Released from the iron grip, the man staggered back, rubbing at his bruised flesh. Constance pressed her husband's arm, concerned that he might yet take the matter further and perhaps start a riot in the crowd. But Thomas had full control of himself. He smiled at her, and they walked on, the pardoner's curses following them.

As they approached the shrine their progress became still slower, and the Black Canons of Walsingham regulated the flow of pilgrims by offering relics to be kissed and seeking appropriate contributions in return. More than an hour passed before it was their turn, among a small group of other pilgrims, to enter the tiny chapel where the jewel-encrusted statue of the enthroned Virgin and Child stood, lit only by the burning forest of votive candles that rose before it. They knelt in silent prayer for a time, until the canon in charge of the shrine took over, telling the story of how, long ago, the lady of the manor had been honoured by a vision of the Virgin, and told to build a replica of the Holy Mother's house in Nazareth. Using a long stick, he pointed to several of the larger jewels, naming their donors, and speaking of the great miracles that had been wrought by means of the Virgin's intercession.

Constance was surprised by the extent of her own awe. There was a special holiness about the place, one that almost reached out and touched the soul, and made you forget the stink of humanity crowded around, or the venality of such low wretches as the pardoner in the market place. Silently she promised to amend her ways in future, to spend more time in prayer and contemplation, to follow Elisabeth's example and be more generous to the poor, more humble in her devotions...

On the way out, those who still had money to spend were allowed to kiss a miraculous phial of the Blessed Virgin's milk. The size of Thomas's donation surprised the canon so much that he almost dropped it. The milk made a pal-pable movement within the phial, and the witnesses gasped audibly.

'Your petition has been heard by Our Lady, my son,' the canon announced, with deep solemnity. 'You are truly blessed. Go in peace.'

He raised his hand in a sketch of benediction above their bowed heads. The moment passed, and the Despensers found themselves outside, surrounded by smiling, congratulating fellow-pilgrims who seemed to think that they had shared in the Virgin's favour.

Constance discovered that her legs were so weak that she could scarcely walk, and leaned on her husband for support. Their sins had been forgiven, and their prayers answered. Never in her life had she felt so secure.

***

Henry Despenser, Bishop of Norwich, kept a fine table. After weeks of plain fare, Constance found the sheer amount of food set before her excessive, the rich spices overpowering, and the wine too sweet. She barely touched the meal, though she saw that Thomas was troubled by no such lack of appetite.

The Bishop frowned his concern. 'You are not ill, dear Niece? I've seen a sparrow eat more.'

'I'm perfectly well, Uncle, but not very hungry.'

'Hmm,' said the Bishop, raising a speculative eyebrow. 'Perhaps you should both rest here for a few days. You know that I welcome your company. I see little enough of my family. Your sisters, Thomas, only write to me when they want something.'

'A few days, perhaps,' Thomas agreed. 'We're expected at Windsor, and there are other matters requiring my attention before I go to Ireland.'

'Ireland,' the Bishop repeated thoughtfully. 'I wonder that the King goes there at this time.'

'Since March's death the country is in chaos.'

'Bolingbroke is only just across the water, and if he returned to claim his inheritance there'd be many who'd rise in his support. As you know, I've had my quarrels with Lancaster's men hereabouts in the past. Erpingham and his gang of thieves. Lollards, most of them, at least in their hearts. Of course, it was old Gaunt who first gave succour to the wretch Wycliffe, the founder of their pestilential creed. He changed his mind quickly enough when Wycliffe went too far, but not all his friends were so wise.' He paused, tutting, impatient with himself. 'That's beside the point. What matters is that the whole pack of them are beginning to stir. Meeting together. Preparing their men as if for war.'

'I thought that Erpingham had gone abroad with Bolingbroke.'

'He has, but his steward has been riding around Norfolk, visiting his master's friends. It's very suspicious, and I can't believe it's a matter of chance. With Mowbray in exile, and Oxford too feeble to climb out of his bed, there's no one in East Anglia with power enough to stop them. I'll do what I can, of course, but it'll not be much. I might be able to stop some of the preachers who are wandering about, claiming that the King intends to sell Calais, that he plans to reduce all men to serfdom, and God knows what else. I've already half a dozen of that sort in my prison, along with the usual crop of heretic priests. I think the King would be well advised to put England in a state of defence.'

'Against Bolingbroke? The French will not aid him. Anyway, what power can he muster? I doubt he has two hundred men with him, and nothing much to pay them, or to hire shipping.'

'Yes, but he has many friends and well-wishers in England. That's what signifies. Men who think he's been ill-used. As perhaps he has, if you discount his past treasons. It may well be that Ireland is in chaos, but let it stay in the same state for a year or two, and keep England secure. That would be my advice, if the King asked it.'

'My father will have all in his care, as Keeper of the Realm,' Constance pointed out. 'We shall not be defenceless.'

The Bishop did not meet her eye. Instead he took a slow sip of his wine. 'The Duke of York is a good man,' he said, after some thought, 'and I've no doubt that he'll do all in his power; but he's no match for Harry Bolingbroke. Not even if he can bring himself to resist him.'

Constance stirred at that. 'You think that he would fail in his duty to his King?'

Thomas recognised the look in her eye, the backward tilt of her head, the slight but significant change in her voice. 'Constance,' he said soothingly, 'my uncle intended no insult.'

Henry Despenser shook his head. 'It's only natural that a good daughter is loyal to her father. I mean no disrespect, my dearest child, when I say that the Duke loves his nephew Bolingbroke. Do you deny it? Well then, if it comes to a fight, do you suppose his heart will be in it? He should not be put to such a test. The King is taking a wild risk, and for no worthwhile cause that I can see. Ireland! Is it worth keeping? What riches are there in such a place?'

Thomas sighed. 'It's useless to talk to the King. He has his mind set on this campaign, to avenge March's death and restore his authority in Ireland. At least this way he will have an army in the field. It can be carried back to England swiftly enough if necessary, though I still doubt that Bolingbroke has the means to make war upon us. He's sworn to go on crusade, and I think it more likely that he'll fulfil his vow.'

'I pray he does,' said the Bishop, 'but I doubt it. He's waited all his life to inherit his father's power, and he's bound to try to recover it. So I believe, and I shall keep such men as I have at my disposal prepared for war. I've fought rebels before—aye, and hanged them. Old as I am, I'll do it again if I must.'

***

The Duchess of Aumale rose languidly from her chair, and took a single step towards her visitor.

'This is an unexpected delight, my dear Sister,' she said. 'Of course, I had heard that you and Tom had arrived, but I scarcely expected to see you so soon.'

Constance nodded abruptly, and paced away towards the oriel window. Philippa's apartment was notably splendid, as good as the Queen's own, her large, richly-hung bed dominating the room.

'I thought that the Duke my father would be here at Windsor,' she said, almost making it a question.

'So did I, Connie! So did—others. But he and Joanne are still at Fotheringhay, for all that I know. I'm surprised you didn't take the opportunity to visit them, on your way back from Norfolk.'

Constance frowned momentarily at the reminder. The simple pleasures of the pilgrimage were almost forgotten now, and she was troubled by a vague sense of unease. She had not quite succeeded in banishing Bishop Despenser's concerns, and added to that was the disappointment of discovering, while they were still at Norwich, that her hopes of a child were premature.

'It would have taken us out of our way,' she explained.

Philippa smiled. 'I dare say that you didn't much care to be seen there in your pilgrim gear!'

She drifted towards Constance, her green velvet skirts rustling across the tiled floor. 'My own dear lord is not here either. He should be on the road back from Scotland by now, unless he's found some other occupation in the North. His last letter came from Berwick. Ah, but I expect I need not tell you this, for you and he have always been close. No doubt you have a letter of your own?'

'I'm afraid that your husband's doings are of scant interest to me, madame,' said Constance, giving her a freezing look.

Philippa indicated a tray of nuts and dried fruit. 'Would you care for one of these? No?' She put one of the fruits in her own mouth and sucked it pleasurably. 'Ned would be so hurt to hear that you wish no news of him. He loves you dearly, Connie.'

'My given name, if you insist on using it, is Constance.'

'My beloved Sister, you seem to have come back from your pilgrimage in a very ill mood! Perhaps you've seen too much of the sun. I believe it's reddened your nose. Indeed, you are quite brown. One might think you'd been working in the fields. Anyway, what I said is perfectly true. He never mentions you, or Tom, without it's to talk of some service he might do you. Ned's grown very powerful now. The greatest man in England, after the King. One day we may be able to say more.'

Constance took a step away, turning her back firmly on her sister-in-law and staring out of the window.

'Will you not sit down?' asked Philippa. 'There's no need of ceremony, between us.'

'You have had no word of my father?'

'Nothing. Not a word. I presume he's still flying his hawks. Or spending his days in bed with Joanne. The King is not at all pleased with him. *I* have had to intercede.'

'I scarcely think that the Duke of York requires your intercession.' Constance turned on her, furious. Only her sense of dignity prevented her from striking the wretched upstart.

Philippa gave her a complacent smile. 'I find that Cousin Richard is very accommodating to my wishes. It's my duty to use my influence for the benefit of my family, and I intend to do so, irrespective of your opinions. I am here to serve my husband's interests. In his absence, I speak for him.'

Constance looked her up and down. 'Then I suggest you learn to speak more wisely. For both your sakes.'

She began to move towards the door, but Philippa insisted on having the last word.

'Has it occurred to you, dearest Sister, that in Joanne's absence I am the ranking lady at court? After the Queen, of course. Who would have thought it?'

***

The tournament began with the customary procession, headed by the officers-of-arms. The defending team, challenging all comers, was made up of a dozen knights, all of whom wore the King's white hart badge, and had their horses barded in his red and white livery colours. At the head of the column, riding side-saddle on a fine grey jennet was Philippa, Duchess of Aumale, leading her chosen knight, Sir Thomas Percy, Earl of Worcester, with a golden chain. Worcester, Northumberland's younger brother, had no wife of his own, still less a lady to whom he was devoted, and so the arrangement was mutually convenient. Fully armed, he walked on foot, behind the tail of Philippa's horse, the nominal prisoner of love. Following came one of his squires, riding his destrier and carrying his lance, shield and tournament helm. Then a succession of similar trios. Elizabeth of Lancaster, Duchess of Exeter, with Sir John Cornwall. Margaret Holland, Marchioness of Dorset, with her husband, John Beaufort, on the golden leash. Constance of York, Countess of Gloucester, with Thomas Despenser. So it went on, in order of the precedence of the ladies, down to Blanche Bradeston and Sir Andrew Hake.

The King was not fighting today, but he came down graciously from his place in the stands to receive Philippa and help her down from her horse. Then he escorted her to her place next to him, set only a little lower than that of Queen Isabelle on his other side.

Constance settled herself next to the Countess of March, who had not taken part in the procession, being still in mourning, at least as far as matters of ceremony were concerned.

'There are fewer here than I thought there would be,' Alianore remarked. 'Not many challengers, and a very thin crowd. I believe Richard's archers out-number the people.'

'I wish your sister were here—Joanne.'

'You do?' Lady March looked puzzled. 'I didn't think you were particular friends.'

'Her absence enables my brother's wife to flaunt herself like the fool she is. Oh, Alianore, I wish you were in her place! How could Ned turn from you to *that*?'

Alianore said nothing to this. Instead she pointed across the lists. 'Do you see my brother? Mun? He's squiring my Uncle Exeter today. Exeter's own lad is sick, but Mun's more than happy to take his place. Look at the size of him! Barely sixteen and still growing. Six foot if he's an inch, and itching to fight in Ireland. He's going to join my brother Surrey's contingent.'

Constance was not at all interested in Mun Holland. Her eyes went to Thomas, seated outside the tents at the far end of the lists with the other members of his team. Their shields were hung up, waiting for challenges to be issued, the butt of the challenger's lance being used to strike the shield for a friendly joust, or the point of the lance for an *à outrance* bout with sharpened weapons. The latter, ob-viously much more dangerous, was usually chosen only by hostile foreigners or hot-headed youngsters.

'It seems there are no challengers,' said Blanche Bradeston, who was sitting in the row behind. 'Perhaps no one *dares*. I thought Berkeley might be here, but it seems that his bravery stops with sending his paid ruffians to burn my ten-ants out of their homes.'

'Those men are in prison, Lady Bradeston. My lord did that for you, and they'll not be released until Berkeley, or some other friend, finds surety for them. Which should take some time.'

'I am all gratitude for your ladyship's kindness. Though there's another mat-ter your ladyship should hear of. Something here at court.'

'Really?'

'Your ladyship particularly asked me to keep an eye on the matter, if she recalls. The Queen's governess. The Dame de Courcy. I believe the woman has gone quite mad. I told your ladyship of the chapel the creature is building for herself and the other French parasites. Well, it's even larger than I thought at first. The next thing to a cathedral, and almost as costly, I should think. She's also keeping more horses than the Queen herself. It's all paid for out of the Queen's revenues, and I can prove it. Lady March can confirm my words.'

'I know of the chapel,' Alianore nodded. 'The walls are already half built, and I believe it's being done under colour of the Queen's authority. The King knows nothing of it, I'm sure of that. As to the horses, it's true she rides nothing but the best, and I very much doubt that the cost comes from her own purse.

I've already told the Queen's chamberlain that it's his business to tell the King, but of course he's a Frenchman. All he does is shrug.'

'Quite!' snorted Blanche.

'You should have told the King yourself, Alianore.'

'My uncle has only just arrived at Windsor. There's been no chance. Besides, he's closer to you, more likely to take your word on the matter.'

By this, of course, Alianore meant that she did not relish the task herself, and wished to pass it on.

Constance nodded decisively. 'I'll speak to Cousin Richard as soon as I can. You shall come with me, Lady Bradeston. Such a scandal can't be allowed to continue.'

The blast of a herald's clarion announced the arrival of the first of the challengers, who was riding a light-boned bay, trapped out in red and gold bardings. On his shield were the bear and staff of Warwick.

'Richard de Beauchamp, Esquire, of Salwarp, requests permission to make a challenge,' announced the herald.

The King absently waved consent, returning at once to his huddled conference with Philippa and the Queen.

'Is he allowed to fight?' Blanche asked irritably. 'The son of an attainted traitor? Not yet even a knight?'

Constance nodded. 'At least he shows spirit. He can't be much more than seventeen. Anyway, if the King says he can take part, he needs no other authority.'

Beauchamp rode towards the row of potential opponents, riding the length of it, his lance raised. At last he halted before Sir John Russell, and lowered the lance, not only touching Russell's shield with the point, but knocking it roughly from its peg.

'Good God!' hissed Blanche. 'This is beyond all!'

'It's perfectly within the rules,' said Alianore, 'though scarcely wise.'

Constance said nothing, but she was feeling more than a tinge of concern. John Russell was a superb horseman, but he was no great master of weapons, and certainly not of the finer points of jousting. This was no simple contest of sport, but a grudge match that could easily end in death. Sharp spears left little margin of error for the incompetent.

'The King should stop this before someone gets killed.' It was Edmund Mortimer who spoke. He had moved from somewhere at the rear of the stand to take the vacant place next to Blanche. 'I've been watching young Beauchamp at practice, and I'd not much care to cross a lance with him in anger. I doubt whether Russell knows what he's up against. He probably thinks he's dealing with a silly boy.'

'I thought you'd be jousting yourself, Edmund,' Alianore smiled.

'I fight when I have to, not for the joy of it. Not that there's any pleasure in jousting *à outrance*, unless you're a damned fool. Constance, Alianore, go to the

Queen. Ask her to order that they fight *à plaisance*. That's within the province of the ladies. It's one of the things you're here for.'

Constance was already on her feet, and after a momentary hesitation Alianore followed suit. There were little more than two steps and a curtsey to where Isabelle was sitting.

'Madame,' cried Constance, 'we beg that you do not allow this to proceed. Not with sharp weapons. There's bad blood between Beauchamp and Russell, and it could end in a death. That would spoil the day.'

The little Queen look pleased to have an appeal directed to her, but she immediately looked towards her husband for guidance. However, it was the Duchess of Aumale who spoke.

'There's always risk, even with blunted weapons,' she remarked. 'Everyone knows that. I think men have the right to prove themselves. There'll be much more danger in Ireland.'

'I do not think English knights lack the courage to fight *à outrance*,' said the Dame de Courcy, from her place behind Isabelle. 'We should admire their valour, not discourage them with our fears.'

'Courage is better saved for battle,' Alianore objected, 'and sharp spears for our enemies.'

'The Dame de Courcy,' Constance added, 'would do better if she advised the Queen's Grace that this is a day for friendly sport, not deadly quarrels.'

'Oh, really, this grows tedious,' Philippa yawned. She stretched out a hand and laid it gently on the King's arm. 'If they do have a grudge against one another this will surely settle it. Besides, Richard, you don't want a reputation as one who is always stopping combats. You'll have people thinking that you're afraid of the sight of blood.'

Richard nodded absently, and waved a careless hand. 'Let them fight. If young Beauchamp seeks an early grave, I see no reason to stand in his way.'

There was no gainsaying the King, and Constance and Alianore could only return to their seats, Edmund Mortimer shaking his head in solemn despair. John Russell and Richard Beauchamp had already taken up their positions, at opposite ends of the lists. As the marshal signalled, the heralds yelled '*laissez aller!*' and the opponents spurred towards one another.

It was all over at the first pass. Russell's lance missed its target completely, but Beauchamp hit his opponent fairly and squarely, and though the lance broke with a resounding crack that seemed to echo around the lists and bounce back from the castle walls, Sir John was still knocked clean out of his saddle, sprawling backwards on the ground. The head of Beauchamp's lance was embedded in his right shoulder, where it had pierced the relatively weak protection of mail at the joint the steel plate encasing his arm and his trunk.

'Fool!' hissed Mortimer, almost contemptuously. 'What did he think his shield was for? A quintain would have given Beauchamp more trouble!'

'The man is badly wounded,' Alianore objected.

'As much through his own folly as anything.'

Russell was being carried towards his tent, quite motionless. Constance beckoned her brother, Dickon, and told him to find out how the unfortunate knight was faring.

Beauchamp had ridden over to the stand, and lowered the stub of his lance in salute to the King.

'With your permission, Sire, I shall offer another challenge,' he said through his open visor.

Richard hesitated, torn between his anger at the damage done to his friend Russell and his desire to see this impudent boy humbled. It was doubtful whether any one of Beauchamp's potential opponents was as lacking in technique as the Master of Horse had proved himself to be. 'Very well,' he said at last. 'Do so, and be damned. I doubt you'll be so fortunate again.'

Beauchamp dipped again the lance and nudged his destrier into a walk. There was stark silence as everyone waited to see who the next choice would be, and no particular surprise when it turned out to be Thomas Despenser. The significant difference was that this time the shield was touched with the butt of the lance.

'This boy is no fool,' Edmund mused, 'he knows exactly how far to go, how to judge his risks. That little victory over Russell hasn't made him reckless.'

A breathless Richard of Conisbrough had returned, having run both ways. 'The surgeon says that Sir John Russell will live,' he reported, 'provided the wound doesn't fester. But it's a sore wound, Sister. The blood's still pouring out. I saw the tip of the lance, covered in it.'

'William Willoughby is here,' Edmund interrupted, gesturing in the general direction of a new challenger who was approaching the list. 'Lancaster's man, from Lincolnshire. I wonder if more of the same kind are on their way. If so, it will make this interesting. I may yet have to fight myself. Perhaps take Russell's place in the mêlée.'

Constance turned to him. 'Do you mean that these challenges are being made on behalf of Bolingbroke?'

He shook his head. 'I'm not sure, but I begin to wonder. When did you last see Willoughby at court?'

It occurred to Constance that the tournament would also provide excellent cover for any faction that wished to gather together to conspire against the King. However, she did not reply, her concentration centred on the progress of her husband, ready at his end of the list with her favour of crimson silk about his arm and his coronel-tipped lance in his hand. She had no real fears for Thomas, not in a joust *à plaisance* against a mere stripling, but there was always the element of chance to bring a dryness to the mouth.

Her confidence was justified. Thomas and Beauchamp simply shattered their spears against each other's shields, their poise in the saddle scarcely disturbed, almost an exhibition of technique. A second pass with new lances was little different, and it was only on the third attempt that Thomas took a chance by switching his aim to his opponent's helm, setting it spinning backwards on its laces. It was a victory, but by no means an overwhelming one.

'The boy's horse stumbled, or he might have held his own,' Edmund grunted, reluctantly admiring.

A whole queue of challengers had built up by now; though some of them, it was true, there for the pleasure of the sport rather than for any political purpose. Yet it could not be denied that there was a sizeable coterie of Lancastrian retainers and sympathisers, and while these were by no means all as skilled as Beauchamp, with many, indeed, no more significantly talented than John Russell, there were certainly enough to give each member of the defending team at least two or three contests. There were obvious possibilities of attrition.

Constance's thoughts were interrupted by the blare of a herald's clarion nearby, followed by a loud announcement. 'Sir Edward Charlton of Powys craves a gage of my lady the Countess of March.'

The newly arrived challenger's lance was extending towards them, and Alianore rose, tearing off a piece of veiling from her headdress and attaching it to the weapon. Her expression was a strange mixture of embarrassment and pleasure.

'Well, he at least is here for you, not for Bolingbroke,' Edmund said, casting a speculative eye over his sister-in-law.

'I could scarcely refuse,' protested Alianore, making some business of adjusting herself on the cushions.

Her words were not true, for it was open to any lady to give or withhold a favour as she saw fit, but it was the defensiveness of her tone that caught Constance's attention.

'I see,' she said.

Charlton picked out Andrew Hake for a friendly joust, and succeeded in unhorsing his opponent after two passages, though without any real harm other than to Hake's dignity. The loudest cheer of the day so far rose from the crowd. Hake, as the King's man and a Scot, was doubly unpopular.

So it went on, with victories for both challengers and defenders, until the Queen and the Duchess of Aumale began to show signs of restlessness, whereupon the marshal of the lists, at the King's order, announced an end to the individual jousts. There was to be an intermission for refreshment, followed by the mêlée.

There were relatively few injuries among the various competitors, John Russell's skewered shoulder being by far the worse, though there was plenty of bruising, a few dislocations, flesh wounds and minor broken bones and the odd shattered tooth. The young Earl of Stafford, who had made the mistake of challenging the highly experienced and ruthless John Holland, was said to be coughing blood. However, the defending team was proportionately more damaged, individuals having fought more contests, while the more numerous challengers were in a position to select an opposing team from among themselves that was made up of those with trivial injuries or none.

The Queen and the Duchess of Aumale had withdrawn from the stand, presumably to attend to their personal needs, but King Richard remained in his place, attended by several squires who served him wine and sundry delicacies on bended knee. Edmund Mortimer approached him to ask permission to take part in the mêlée and this being readily granted, hurried away to prepare.

Constance was very much surprised when her cousin half turned towards her and beckoned. She rose, advanced and, as soon as there was space enough, sank into a curtsey of acknowledgement.

'Sit there,' Richard directed, pointing to Philippa's chair. As soon as she had settled, he went on, 'I should have listened to you before, Cousin. They tell me that Russell will be in no state to go with me to Ireland. It's not just his wound. He's taken a knock to his head and is gibbering nonsense. Even more than usual, that is.'

'It's to be hoped that Your Grace will lose no more of his best knights.'

'Well, we can't cancel the mêlée now. Though it's tempting.'

He paused for a moment, and then let out a sigh that came from the heart.

'Why do you sigh, Cousin Richard?' she asked.

'Constance, this campaign in Ireland troubles my mind. I've no choice but to defend what's mine from rebels, and yet I fear it will not turn out well. Apart from that, here at home my people are malcontent, and I know not whom I may trust.'

He produced a crumpled and torn piece of parchment, and handed it to her. It contained part of a poem.

> *For where was ever any Christian*
> *King that you ever knew that held*
> *Such a household by the half*
> *As Richard in this realm*
> *Men might as well have hunted a hare with a*
> *Tabor, as asked for any amends...*

'A traitor wrote this,' she objected fiercely.

'Yes; but there are many such. I can't hang them all. Do you wonder that I sigh, when I am fated to so many unavoidable evils?'

She shook her head. 'What I must tell you may give you fresh cause to sigh,' she said.

'You may ask what you will, dear Cousin, without fear. We've been through much together. You were in the Tower with me all those years ago, when the

Appellants shamed me. You know what they did. You were with me when Anne died, that awful night at Sheen when I was half out of my mind. You and Alianore risked your lives caring for her, or you thought you did. It wasn't plague you know, it couldn't have been or we'd have all died that were there, or most of us. She was poisoned, because Gloucester wanted her place for his daughter. The bitch that's married to Stafford now. It's not forgotten, not any of it.'

Constance was almost too astonished to speak. Her mouth moved silently for a moment or two, thinking of a way to question his version of events without going so far as to contradict him. It was impossible, so she gave up trying, and turned to the matter of the Dame de Courcy's corruptions.

His anger flared at once, and he stuttered out questions that Constance could not answer, so that an awed Blanche Bradeston had to be brought into play. Blanche did not fail, however. She not only gave details of the chapel and the horses, but also added a number of direct quotations from the Dame de Courcy concerning the barbaric English and their sovereign, and how easily they were gulled.

'I realised that the woman was a fool, but not that she was stealing the Queen's revenues to pay for her follies,' the King said at last, his face pale with fury. 'She shall be dismissed at once, and an English lady set in her place. It is, in any case, more fitting. The fewer French we have about us, the better our people will like it. An appointment for you, perhaps, my dear Cousin?'

'With your permission, Cousin, I shall decline the honour. I've a wife's duties to perform. It's more a task for a widow, I think.'

'My niece, Alianore, then,' Richard said decisively, flicking a hand in the general direction of the Countess of March. 'You may tell her, when you go back to your place.'

Constance rose and curtsied again, recognising dismissal. She had no particular desire to linger, lest she be forced to be seen yielding her seat to the Duchess of Aumale.

Sir Edward Charlton had taken Edmund Mortimer's place. He was no longer in armour and evidently had no intention of participating in the mêlée. He was the younger brother of the Lord of Powys, and Constance did not know him particularly well, but it soon became clear that Lady March knew him very well indeed. She was making a great deal of fuss about a mild scrape he had suffered to his forearm, though it was nothing more than a child might sustain by falling from a wall, and seemed inclined to use her returned favour to bind it up, though binding was scarcely necessary.

The mêlée had almost begun before Constance found a break in their conversation that was long enough for her to insert the news of Alianore's appointment into it. Lady March was far more delighted than her friend had anticipated, and hurried away to thank the King for so great an honour.

'I take it that your wound is keeping you from the mêlée, Sir Edward?' Constance enquired lightly.

He shook his head, and treated her to a grin of surprising warmth. 'I decided, my lady, that I'd be among better company up here,' he said. 'I took part for the sport of it, not to make a point.' He gestured towards the assembling challengers. 'I'd not want the King to think me a part of that.'

The mêlée began much as the individual jousts had done, save that there were twelve knights on each side, and their horses and battle cries made proportionately more noise, while the crash of their meeting seemed to shake the whole stand, and was sufficient to shock Alianore into crying out, and Edward Charlton into laying a consoling hand on her arm.

'Edmund is down!' Alianore cried, horrified. It was true enough, but Mortimer was by no means the only one to have been knocked from the saddle. Apart from the damage done by some of the lances, there had been a significant collision of horses in the centre of the line, and four men had been dismounted in the chaos, Thomas Despenser among them. Among the challengers William Willoughby lay pinned beneath his struggling destrier, its leg and his both broken.

Constance watched her husband climb to his feet, and satisfied herself that he was not hurt. Given that he was not much disadvantaged by his fall, for the rules decreed that all would fight on foot after the initial clash, the only permitted weapon being the blunted sword, using the flat of the blade, with the point encased, for better security, in a tip of lead. Men protected by an armour that was almost all of plate could batter at each other all day on such terms without much risk of mortal damage, and it was now as much a contest of strength and stamina as skill.

Thomas had scarcely settled himself before he came under a fierce attack from Lord Morley. Morley was one of his brothers-in-law, but they were not on good terms, and there was no holding back on either side.

The fighting went on for a good half hour, the number of knights gradually being reduced as men were backed against the fence of the list (they were disqualified as soon as they touched it), were disarmed, or simply reached the point where their strength and skill failed and they had to concede defeat.

At last there were only four of the defending team still in the game, John Holland, Thomas Despenser, Edmund Mortimer, and Andrew Hake. They were facing six challengers, two of whom had the luxury of resting while they waited for an opponent to become available.

Hake had fought as though for his life, and proved that he was far more capable with a sword than with a lance, but he made the mistake of misjudging his position, and backed into the fence. That left three against six.

The King had had enough. He made an impatient gesture, the heralds blew on their clarions, and the marshal of the lists and his staff, shouting and gesturing with their wooden rods of office, put an end to the tournament. The mêlée was declared a draw.

***

It fell to the ladies to decide what prizes should be awarded. Nominally the Queen was in the chair for their meeting, but it was the Duchess of Aumale who led the debate. The Dame de Courcy was a notable absentee. She was already packing her boxes.

They were in the Queen's great chamber, thankfully clutching warming glasses of hot, spiced wine. A stiff breeze had risen during the mêlée, a blessing for those taking part, but less welcome to those in the stands, for it had driven straight into their faces.

'I think we are agreed,' said Philippa, 'that the prize for the best knight among the defenders should go to the Duke of Exeter?'

It was reasonable enough. John Holland had fought well, and he was the King's half-brother, which had to be taken into account. Constance privately considered that her own husband had done just as much, but she could scarcely say so. She consoled herself with the thought that she had the power to bestow a reward on him that he would esteem better than a bejewelled ring that looked too small for a man's finger and was presumably intended to be passed on to his lady.

'What of the challengers?' asked Philippa.

That was more of a problem. The wrong choice here might well displease the King, and the most successful of the challengers were those he would least want to see honoured.

'Richard Beauchamp,' suggested Anne of Gloucester, the Countess of Stafford. Her eyes cast around them, defying dissent, and the cast of her head, the expression of earnest assurance, gave Constance a chilling reminder of her late uncle, Anne's father.

'Richard Beauchamp!' cried Lady Clinton. 'That witless boy? How dare you suggest such a thing? He almost killed my husband by his wantonness. The last thing that is needed is for us to puff up his pride.'

No one had ever heard John Russell's wife say so much at once, and it had a powerful effect, even Lady Stafford looking abashed.

'If we give Beauchamp the prize it might encourage others to fight à outrance against their fellow Englishmen,' Alianore pronounced carefully. 'I think it our duty to do all we can to keep our men from such folly.'

'The obvious choice is Sir Edward Charlton,' Constance said suddenly, the words flowing out of her almost before she had had the thought.

'Why?' Philippa demanded. 'I think he only jousted once, against that Scotsman, and he didn't even take part in the mêlée. It's hard to think of anyone who deserves it *less*.'

'He was the only challenger with the courtesy to ask a lady for a token. We should encourage that behaviour by rewarding it. He's also the King's man.'

'And for that, rather than his courtesy, he should have the prize,' the Duchess of Exeter said wryly. 'As for tokens, given to knights, I set little store on those. I hear that you, Constance, bestow them in some very strange places. Strange and unexpected.'

Constance swallowed. She had more or less forgotten about the favour she had sent to Bolingbroke, but it was clear that Beth had somehow heard of it. She did not look forward to explaining her impulse to the King, if ever word of it reached Richard's ear.

14

Constance sat silently on her horse, her eyes focused on the far distance. Here at Birdlip, where the road descended with sudden sharpness from the Cotswold uplands to the fertile plain of Gloucestershire, there was plenty of scope for such gazing. To the north, the straggling village of Cheltenham lay spread out far below, and to the west it was possible to make out the towers of Gloucester, shrouded in the heat haze. Closer to hand, sitting under the limited shade provided by a stunted tree, were two archers in the livery of the Duke of Exeter. They were Essex men by their accents, and as if to confirm this they were discussing some argument one of them had had over the purchase of a pig at Colchester market.

'We'd better not stand here much longer, or the King will be catching up with us,' Alianore said. It was her way of announcing that she had seen quite enough of the Cotswolds for one day. She was looking forward to reaching Gloucester and the comfort of a bath. Constance smiled. She did not point out, as she might have done, that her Cousin Richard was a full twelve hours journey behind them, and in no particular haste. It was three days now since they had left Windsor. The tournament there, in retrospect, had had a false and brittle atmosphere, like an episode in a dream. Intended to demonstrate the King's strength, it had served rather to remind people of the events of Gosford Green and emphasise the absence of England's foremost knight.

She hurriedly put the gloomy thoughts out of her mind, and turned her head towards Lady March. 'The truth is,' she said, 'you don't care to waste time here that could be spent in bed with your new husband.'

Edward Charlton had won not only the fine falcon that was the prescribed prize for the best of the challengers, but also Alianore's hand in marriage, swiftly granted with the King's full approval.

Alianore threw a warm glance in Charlton's direction. He was but a few yards away, talking with Thomas. And beyond them, riding in Lady March's carriage with their nurses, the Mortimer and Despenser children squabbled together in happy unity.

'At least he comes to it sober,' she said, 'which is more than could be said for Roger.' She paused, sighing. 'Constance, does it not seem strange to you that the King is going to Ireland to avenge Roger's death? And to go at such a time, when there's so much ill-feeling against him, and Harry Bolingbroke may well come in arms to claim his own.'

Before Constance could answer, Edward Charlton nudged his horse forward. 'Come on, my ladies,' he interjected, his ready smile spreading over his face, 'there are more miles between me and my supper than I care to think about. Let's move on before my rumbling belly deafens us all.'

He led the way over the crest without a further word, setting a fair pace, and his new wife urged her jennet forward to catch him.

'Truly,' said Despenser, nudging his horse forward and grinning wryly at his lady, 'they seem well smitten with each other. Though Charlton has good cause to be smitten. It's a fat dower she's brought to him.'

Constance nodded. 'I like Edward Charlton. I dare say he's moved by her dower, but I don't think that's the end of it. Not by the look of them. Alianore deserves some happiness, for she's had little enough so far.'

'Hmmm. I hope, *treschere*, that you will not find such easy consolation if I come to an ill end in Ireland.'

She grinned back at him, declining the bait as too obvious. 'It would certainly not be easy,' she murmured, 'not with so much choice. I'm not sure whether I'd have them draw lots from a hat or make them fight it out. Three days of jousting at Cardiff might provide some entertainment.'

Thomas grunted his amusement, and they walked their horses forward after the Charltons. The road descended steeply now, and as it curved downwards it entered the cover of trees. A team of men and oxen were edging one of the King's great guns very cautiously down the hill, the wheels being constantly braked by wedges of wood. Alianore laughed at something her husband had said, and the sound seemed to echo back from the tunnel of leaves, a challenge to the stifling silence. Constance opened her mouth to speak, and found that she could not. Her common sense told her there was nothing to fear, but another sense gave warning of danger, running a cold finger down her spine.

'THOMAS!' The word broke from her with explosive force. He turned questioningly towards her, and as he did so the arrow skimmed his cheek and buried itself deep in the bole of an oak some five yards beyond. Despenser did not hesitate. He turned his horse's head in the direction of the skulking archer and charged, not even bothering to draw his sword, intending simply to ride the man down before he could fit another shaft. It would have been an effective tactic in open country, but here the space between the trees was thick with undergrowth, and the ground rose sharp and uneven from the road. It was difficult for Thomas to make progress, impossible for him to make speed. He was swift to recognise his predicament, and, careless of knightly dignity, he kicked his stirrups aside and threw himself down among the bushes. Even as he did so another arrow flew past, somewhat closer to him than was comfortable.

By this time Hugh Tyldesley had ridden up, summoning urgent reinforcements with shouts and gestures. Constance found herself surrounded by a throng of men in the red, white and yellow colours of her husband's livery, while as she looked further down the track she saw Edward Charlton hurrying back. Thomas had drawn his short sword and was advancing cautiously, using the cover of the trees. 'Come on,' he shouted at his men, 'hurry, before the rogue escapes us. It's only one man, you fools.'

Constance saw that the mountainous Tyldesley, standing next to her, was making no step forward. Instead he was calmly stringing the bow he used for hunting. He notched an arrow, drew the string back to his ear, considered for what seemed an age, and then loosed.

The lone archer had turned to flee. The arrow hit him squarely in the upper back, burying itself almost to the feathers, and he fell forward among the bushes.

'I wanted him *alive*!' Thomas shouted.

'I wanted *you* alive, my lord,' Tyldesley answered. 'Better safe than sorry.'

The body was retrieved from the undergrowth, borne back up to the road. A black-bearded young man whose features, in other circumstances, Constance might have considered handsome.

'I know this rogue,' said Tyldesley. 'He's one of those, my lord, we took for his part in the attack on Hake's place at Winterbourne. God knows his name, but I don't forget a face. Someone must have broken him out of the gaol at Gloucester—or bought him out, more likely.'

John Norreys added his agreement. 'I recognise him too. It explains his reason for trying to kill you—he had a grudge.'

'This is one of Berkeley's men?' enquired Constance, seizing the implication.

'You may be sure he is, my lady, for all that he wears no livery.'

'Surely Berkeley would not—'

'That's why I wanted him alive,' Thomas interrupted, 'so that I could know what caused him to loose a shaft at me.' He kicked the body. 'This piece of filth—a discharged soldier, I expect—may have taken it into his own head to murder me, or he could have been doing his master's bidding. Now nothing can be proved. Tyldesley, pick half a dozen of the men to ride with you. Take this carrion to Berkeley Castle, and throw it down outside the gate. If Berkeley objects, tell him where he can come for redress.'

They journeyed on in silence. The joy had gone out of the day.

***

'I hear that English ships are gathering at Boulogne,' said the Duke of Orleans, his hands toying with the small, ivory statue of a saint that he had plucked from the adjoining dresser.

Bolingbroke leaned back in his seat, screwing up his eyes against the glare of the May sun that was streaming through the open window. He suspected that Orleans had deliberately settled him where he was at a disadvantage.

He considered Orleans' features; his long, ugly Valois nose, his cold, deep set eyes, and his mean, cruel little mouth. A man who was commonly reputed to cuckold his own brother, though that brother was also his sovereign. That the French King was insane was undeniable, but the fact made the betrayal worse. He wondered if a woman might think Orleans' face attractive. Queen Isabeau presumably did.

It was unfortunate that he needed Orleans' good will; but it was a political necessity. In effect, while Burgundy remained in Flanders, this man was the ruler of France. Not by any official appointment, of course. The French were not like that. They simply recognised the realities.

He must do so too, for the present. A man could not always have the luxury of choosing his friends. As often as not they were chosen for him by his enemies. The current battle lines were clear. Orleans, the Duke of Milan and himself on one side; Richard and Burgundy on the other. Orleans was married to the Duke's daughter, Valentina; a witch if Burgundy and his friends were to be believed. A witch who was guilty of casting a spell on their King and driving him to madness. Bolingbroke had met her, and found her charming, though perhaps a little grave. The old proposal that he should marry her cousin, Lucia of Milan, had been revived, though there was an alternative candidate for his hand, Orleans' own cousin, Marie de Berri.

Harry was not sure that either was the wife he wanted. Fortunately, Orleans was not likely to press him on the matter while his future remained so uncertain. They both knew his head could be lodged on a spike on London Bridge before the summer was out.

'Is there any objection to the presence of our ships?' he asked. 'In time of truce?'

Orleans shrugged expansively. 'I am merely surprised that the ships are available. Has King Richard not requisitioned everything that can float, to sail his army to Ireland?'

'Evidently not. We English have a great number of ships. We find them invaluable, living, as we do, on an island.'

'There is a reason for my concern. My uncle of Burgundy has many sources of information, and he is much closer to Boulogne than we are. His agents will be crawling all over the town, like maggots on a corpse. He will prevent your enterprise if he can, he and his lapdog, St.Pol. Burgundy's whole policy has been built upon his alliance with your King—though it has been of great disadvantage to us. You, my Cousin, are not the only one to discover that the promises of Richard of England are worthless.'

'Obviously, we are doing all we can to keep our intentions secret, and our enemies guessing. I have given out that I am going into Spain, to visit my sister, the Queen of Castile.'

Harry paused for a moment, suddenly struck by a clear recollection of Catherine of Lancaster. Catalina as the Spanish called her. His half-sister, the daughter of Gaunt's second wife, Constance of Castile. It was all of fourteen years since he had seen her, and, though they had corresponded since, it pained him to realise that they would probably never meet again.

Orleans coughed to regain his attention. 'I see. You think that Burgundy will swallow such a tale?'

'Is there any reason why he should not? It's obvious to all the world that I've no army about me. Merely my retinue. Less than three hundred men in all, and only fifteen armigers, including myself. Why should anyone imagine that we are in any case to invade England?'

'It is certainly a great risk. The Duke of York, with his authority as Regent, will be able to muster a much larger force to oppose you.'

'Of course. But the Duke of York has no notion of where I intend to land, and my intention is to do all I can to keep him in doubt. What's more, I have those about him who are my good friends.'

'I see. Then your uncle may be influenced?'

'I think it possible. There are many in England who weary of Richard's follies, hate the parasites around him, and wish me well. My uncle has always been kind to me, as good as a second father. He will at least—hesitate.'

Yet it troubled Harry that he had had no reply to the letter he had sent to the Duke. Not a line. York had always stood with the King, through thick and thin. Why should he change now? He would fight York if he had to, but he dreaded the thought of it.

Orleans nodded. 'When you are established in your rightful place at the head of King Richard's Council I trust, my dear Cousin, that we shall be the most perfect friends.'

I doubt it, thought Harry. You've ambitions in Gascony that neither Richard nor I would ever tolerate. Do you imagine I am so stupid that I do not know of them?

'I suggest we sign a private treaty to that effect,' he said, 'pledging ourselves to oppose our common enemies.'

Orleans seemed pleased.

'There will have to be exclusions, of course,' Harry pointed out. 'Naturally. I should not be so foolish as to expect you to take up arms against King Charles on my behalf. Our sovereigns must certainly be excluded, and my uncle, the Keeper of England.'

'I shall have my chancellor and staff work on a first draft for your consideration. It's an excellent idea, my good Cousin. A symbol of our future understanding.'

Harry nodded amiably, and took a swallow of the wine that had been set before him. It was far too dry for his taste, but it warmed the throat. Orleans was welcome to the bond if it made him happy. There would be more exclusions than inclusions by the time he himself was finished with it. For a beginning, all his relatives and all his tenants and retainers. That would cover most of the English.

***

'I see my mistake now,' said Thomas Despenser. 'I've tried to be moderate in my dealings with Berkeley, not to push matters too far. The trouble is he and his friends don't see that as justice. They think I'm weak, or too much of a coward to seek an accounting. Well, they shall discover their error.'

Constance said nothing, simply settled herself on the edge of the bed for want of any better seat. Her husband's voice was quiet, his anger tightly controlled, and when he was in this dark mood there was no counselling him. She found that her lips had grown unaccountably dry, and ran her tongue over them.

'I have given the sheriff his orders,' he went on. 'In my absence, he is to obey you.'

She nodded briefly to indicate that she understood what he had said. The sheriff of Gloucestershire, John Brouning, was one of their retainers, and she anticipated no difficulty in managing him.

'I shall also leave Tyldesley with you. He's the best man I have for the sort of work that may be necessary. If there's any trouble, from Berkeley or anyone else, don't hesitate to use him and Brouning as you see fit. They'll not debate with you. I suggest that you lodge yourself at Hanley, put the castle in a state of defence, and be ready to act against our enemies.'

The suggestion was, of course, an instruction. She understood it as such.

'I have written to my cousin, Hugh, asking him to bring his household down from Solihull to join you,' Thomas continued. 'John Russell will be at Strensham, recovering from his wounds, and Edward Charlton and Alianore will be at Usk. There's also my mother to advise you. You'll not lack for friends if you need them.'

She was by no means enchanted by the thought of entertaining Hugh and Sybil Despenser for anything up to a year, and her head tilted back. 'What of Glamorgan?' she asked. 'I thought I was going with you as far as Cardiff, and I had it in mind to stay there for at least part of the summer.'

'Of course you shall come with me to Cardiff,' Thomas answered impatiently. 'The King will expect to find you there to receive him. But there's no call for you to stay there. I don't expect any trouble in Glamorgan, and John St. John and William Stradling will take care of our interests.'

'Those two will not work together.'

He frowned. 'I know you don't like Stradling. I don't much care for him myself, but he's a powerful man, and close kin to most of the important families in Glamorgan, Brecon and Gower. Welsh and English alike. I can't risk discarding him, not at a time like this. I just have to hope that I've bought his loyalty by making him our chamberlain.'

Constance repressed a sigh. She didn't trust Stradling as far as she could throw him, and Sir St. John was not much better, a cautious man who always put his own interests first. Well, there was nothing to be done about it, as she could not be in two places at once, and Thomas had obviously decided that Berkeley was the one who needed to be watched.

Her women had gathered for her undressing ritual. It was growing late, close to midnight, and there was a distinct chill in the room, a suspicion of damp. The castle at Gloucester was old, and not in good repair; the hangings Norreys had had set up to cover the walls merely served to disguise the truth from the eye, without making the faults good.

Agnes was mumbling some complaint about the permanent staff of the castle, claiming that they were being uncooperative even over such minor matters as the provision of hot water. They were still, of course, the people installed by Constance's uncle, the Duke of Gloucester, during his tenancy, and presumably they resented the necessary change of allegiance. It was a matter that would have to receive attention, but it was scarcely pressing when so many other issues needed to be resolved. Fortunately, the King intended to lodge at the abbey, where the hospitality would be less questionable. Constance was beginning to wish that she and Thomas had decided to do they same, instead of taking the opportunity to assert their new authority over the castle.

Richard, of course, would be visiting the tomb of their great-grandfather, King Edward II, whom he venerated. Indeed he had gone so far as to ask the Pope to canonise the murdered King, but so far neither gold nor persuasion had achieved the necessary transfiguration, and King Edward had to be satisfied with a local cult, and a small name for working minor miracles.

Constance shuddered involuntarily as she recalled the tale of her great-grandfather's death, passed on to her by her father long ago, his knowledge coming from men and women he had known who had been alive at the time of the event. The deposed King had been kept in a filthy vault below Berkeley Castle, in the hope that the sheer stench and corruption would kill him. When that had failed, his wife, Queen Isabel, and her lover, the first Earl of March, had ordered him murdered. So as to leave no visible mark on him, a red-hot iron stake had been pushed into his body through his anus. The local country folk claimed that from time to time his agonised cries could still be heard around Berkeley Castle.

So easily might a man, even a powerful King, fall from his glory. Fortune's Wheel was always liable to take an unexpected turn, to topple those who least expected it. Richard had almost lost his throne when the Appellants had risen against him. Now, despite all the blows they had taken, his enemies were stirring again, and if Bolingbroke did not come back to fight for his inheritance this summer he would surely renew the struggle one day. It was true that the King had Harry's children as hostages, but anyone who knew Richard knew that no consideration on earth would persuade him to harm a hair of a child's head. That the worst he would do would be to sicken them with too many sweetmeats. Bolingbroke would have no fears on that score.

Constance had difficulty in sleeping that night, her senses preternaturally alert, and each time she woke her eyes were drawn to a particular corner of the room, where it seemed to her there was a threatening shadow, some kind of hostile entity that was almost tangible. Her whispered prayers seemed to have little effect, and no holy water was available to dispel it.

It vanished as dawn approached, became a mere trick of her imagination, too absurd to be mentioned. Once she had heard mass her spirits were quite recovered, and she ate a hearty breakfast in preparation for the journey, the light and cheerful chatter of Alianore and Edward Charlton banishing all dark thoughts. Only Thomas remained solemn. He swallowed a little food and drink in hasty silence, then withdrew to confer briefly with John Norreys and Hugh Mortimer before calling for one of the clerks. There were letters to be dictated before they left Gloucester.

**

The guns of Cardiff coughed in uncertain salute, their intermittent thunderous blasts followed by dense, acrid clouds of blue-grey smoke. King Richard was approaching at the head of his army, Edward of York, Duke of Aumale at his right hand, Exeter, Surrey and Salisbury following closely. Behind them the straggling tail of men stretched back for miles, men of all ranks, mounted and on foot, supply carts, some drawn by horses, others by oxen, and artillery of various dimensions, ranging from the great bombards that were intended for use against castle walls to light pieces that would be deployed in the field against enemy troops. The Tower had been denuded of such weapons, for this was a full-scale campaign, no mere punitive raid. Less well-equipped English armies had been sent against the French in King Edward III's day.

Constance watched as the head of this great procession emerged from the portal of the gatehouse, standing with Thomas on the stairs that led up into the castle apartments. She was appalled to see that there was a woman at Richard's left side, none other than the Duchess of Aumale, side-saddle on the same grey she had ridden into the lists at Windsor. Since Philippa was most unlikely to be travelling on to Ireland, she presumably intended to settle as an uninvited guest at Cardiff. Constance could only wonder at her impudence.

Responding to the gentle pressure of Thomas's hand on hers, she descended the steps with him to the courtyard, where they made profound obeisances of welcome to the King.

'As you can see, we came across your brother on the road, and brought him to see you,' Richard said cheerfully. 'I was beginning to worry that he'd decided to turn Scot.'

'He would never do anything so unprofitable,' said Constance, provoking a general laughter.

Aumale grunted. 'I've already explained the cause of the delay, Cousin,' he said, slightly peevishly. 'The Scots are a people who take delight in negotiation. If I'd not cut them short I'd still be among 'em. God knows, there are no pleasures to detain a man north of Trent. Just the Percys and the Nevilles and the damned Scots, and I don't know which of the three are the most trouble.'

'The Nevilles, beyond doubt,' said the Earl of Worcester, with a snort of amusement. As a Percy himself he was fully entitled to resent Edward's comment, but seemed utterly disinclined to do so.

'Your brother Northumberland would certainly prefer a Scot or a Neville's company to mine,' Edward added, his tone equally light. 'That was made clear enough.'

Richard was clearly growing impatient with this, and moved towards the stairs leading into the castle. 'I see that you've been building since I was last here, Thomas,' he said conversationally. 'You must let me see what you've changed. It'll be more interesting than standing here listening to your lady's brother talking about the many hardships he has suffered in my service. Ned, kiss your sister, and let's go inside.'

It was all very light, and spoken with a smile, but Constance sensed an unexpected tension beneath the words.

'Have you quarrelled with our cousin?' she asked Edward, once the King and Thomas had moved out of hearing.

His eyebrows lifted a little. 'Why should you think that?'

'Because I've known you both all my life.'

Philippa appeared at his other hand. 'Your father has not helped the situation. Dawdling at Fotheringhay until the very last moment, arriving at Windsor almost as we left the place. Then speaking up for Bolingbroke!'

'What?'

'So Ned has had to smooth matters over, and it's not been easy. One would think it was *his* fault that he was delayed in the North.'

Aumale grunted. 'Let be, my dear. Not everyone is deaf. Yes, Constance, it's true. I don't know exactly what was said, but it seems our honoured parent made some kind of speech at Windsor, dwelling on all the wrongs that poor Harry has endured, and begging Richard to call him home and restore his lands. Our cousin seems to think—though God knows why—that this has become our family policy, and that I've been busy trying to persuade Northumberland and Westmorland to side with us. Need I say that I have not? That I'd as soon wake in bed with the devil as see Harry Bolingbroke back in England?'

They began to ascend the stairs.

'I can't understand why York cares so much for Bolingbroke,' Philippa said. 'It's almost as if he prefers him to his own sons.'

'You must remember that he and old Gaunt were a good deal closer than most brothers,' her husband explained, 'and, besides, when Harry used to live at Wansford with his wife he probably spent as much time with us at Fotheringhay as he did at home. Constance will tell you that we used to get sick of the sight of him. At times it was almost as if he was another brother, and the heir at that. Even so, I didn't think my father would be fool enough to make such a plea. It's bad enough that he's been sulking in Northamptonshire all these weeks, and God knows what he thinks *that* achieved.'

The King had paused to make a fuss of his godson, Richard Despenser, and of the boy's sister, Bess, and the procession that had formed behind him had no choice but to stop and wait until he was done with them. Constance noticed with satisfaction that although her children were on their best behaviour, they were by no means in awe of her cousin, and trustingly put their hands in his, agreeing to lead him on a tour of the castle.

'You'll have to be careful, my lady, or he'll be taking your boy to Ireland with us,' Worcester said, drawing to a halt behind them. 'We've already had to recruit nursemaids for Bolingbroke's boy, and your cousin, Humphrey of Gloucester.'

As Constance turned she saw that the two boys were standing together. Hal of Monmouth, Harry's eldest, was twelve years old, solemn-featured, with nut brown hair and an ugly nose. It was his eyes that were striking, large and grey and unwavering. They reminded her of someone long dead—his mother, Mary de Bohun. Humphrey was a few years Hal's elder, a handsome youth with a bitter expression who spat on a friendly dog that approached him. She would have to welcome them, as a duty of kinship, but she did not relish the task of dealing with the openly resentful Humphrey, and decided it was a task that could reasonably be postponed for the present.

'Hostages,' Worcester added, in an undertone.

'Are they hell!' snorted Edward. 'You have to be prepared to kill hostages. He's trying to win them over, and I tell you this, he's succeeding with young Hal. The boy already worships him as though he were a plaster saint.'

'Faith,' sniffed Worcester, 'you sound like you fear for your own position, Ned. Perhaps you should. That boy could be Duke of Lancaster one day. A useful alliance for the King to forge. I doubt he'll win over Humphrey so easily. That one hates him. Hates you as well, by the way. Seems to think you killed his father.'

'I don't much care what the stupid bastard thinks. If he's very fortunate Richard might allow him his mother's inheritance eventually, but you know the sentence that lies on him. He'll never be received in Council or in Parliament. He'll have to learn to swallow his grievances, and if he's wise he'll not speak slander of me.'

It was much later before Constance had another chance to speak to her elder brother. Cardiff had rarely been so crowded, and it took time to have a word with all the important guests, while still keeping an eye on the arrangements made for their hospitality. Nominally the King's officers were in charge now, but it didn't work that way in practice. Worcester, the Steward of the King's Household, spent the evening lounging next to Edward and getting increasingly drunk, waving away any subordinate who approached him for instructions. The time flew by, and it was well after midnight before she was able to think about bed. The Despensers' normal sleeping quarters had had to be given up to the King, and so there was a trek to be made into the old keep, where there was a less desirable but still relatively spacious chamber available. Unfortunately, the pressure of numbers meant that it would have to be shared with Edward and Philippa, and the floor carpeted with the pallets of their attendants.

She looked out from the narrow, unglazed window to the scores of camp-fires burning around the castle and lighting the night. There would undoubtedly be a few missing hurdles and outhouses in the morning, and very likely an unofficial depletion in the local livestock. Such thievery was inevitable, and there was nothing to be done about it, except perhaps to offer some limited compensation to those who grumbled loudest. Hopefully there would be no worse damage done.

'There are a good five thousand out there,' said Edward, suddenly standing next to her. 'What's more, there's ample money to pay for more, if they're needed.'

'You think they may be?'

'Not against the Irish rebels. My guess is that they'll submit, without much fuss, and wait for us to go home again. That's what I'd do, in their place. Such expeditions as this can't be mounted every year. It's not as if we can expect any worthwhile ransoms or plunder to offset the cost. No, it's the defence of England I have in mind. Harry Bolingbroke has many friends in the North. More than I realised until I ventured up there. There's a danger that they'll begin to stir on his behalf.'

'Have you said as much to Richard?'

'That and more. I've urged him to abandon this campaign and go on progress to the North, to draw any rebels out into the open. Needless to say, he will not heed me, thinks that our father and the Council are well capable of dealing with any trouble that may arise. Well, he may be right, but we're taking a chance. I've kept in touch with Cousin Harry, you know. Done all I can to persuade him that he will have an evil reception if he comes home.'

'You've written to Bolingbroke?' Constance was astonished.

'Of course I have, many times. Which reminds me of something. A strange tale I heard, of someone sending a token to him, her sleeve, no less. I truly wondered that the lady concerned should do such a thing, unless, perhaps, she was constrained by her husband. But that also seems unlikely, unless that lord is a great deal more subtle than I ever imagined.'

'Ned, you know the matter was different! He told me that he was going on crusade, that he was likely to die fighting Christ's enemies. His lands had not been forfeited, he'd not been declared traitor.'

'I'm not angry with you, fair Sister. Merely surprised. I always thought you hated Harry, but one thing and another has led me to think you hold him in a certain regard. I remember Philippa telling me what you said about him at Gosford. I thought the comparison rather harsh, my dear. I'm many things, but I'm no coward. I'll fight if I must, for what's mine. But not by the rules that others have set. I'll fight on my own terms, or none.'

15

The weeks slipped by peacefully at Hanley Castle, May turning into June, and June into July. The woods and meadows around the castle turned to a richer green, and the white and red roses in the pleasance bloomed and filled the soft breeze with a perfume so sweet that it was almost sickly. Smoke from the village pottery kilns rose almost vertically, and to the east the River Severn sparkled its endless way past the landing stage, while the road from Upton to Worcester was a narrow strip of light grey dust that emerged briefly into view between the encroaching trees.

Along that road a solitary man was hastening from the direction of Worcester, his horse kicking up a cloud behind him. He turned from the high road, past the kilns and through the village, spurring through the park as if pursued by more than dust. Frustrated, he stood calling at the edge of the moat until the gatekeepers recognised his Despenser livery, and the drawbridge creaked its leisurely way down into position.

He hurried across it into the castle, and was surprised when the bridge was immediately raised again behind him. Perhaps the news has already reached here, he thought, that they take such precautions.

'Where is the Countess?' he demanded of those who hurried out to take his horse.

Constance was sitting on the window-seat in the solar, combing her daughter's hair. The hair was not really in need of attention, for Bess's nurse was thoroughly efficient, but the task gave her pleasure and occupied her idle hands.

'Master Throckmorton,' she said in acknowledgement of the new arrival.

Throckmorton knelt before her, a little surprised that she had remembered his name. He doubted that they had met more than twice in the two years he had worn her lord's livery.

'There's trouble in Warwick, my lady,' he announced, his face grim. 'A riot of sorts, though it's worse than that. They've taken the castle. Cast Surrey's device down from the gate.'

'They?'

Throckmorton shook his head. 'The Beauchamp retainers. Those that were such, I mean. Led by Robert Hugford. John Mountford's there. Thomas de Crewe. All of them.' He swallowed uneasily. He had been Warwick's man himself up until the Earl's disgrace, and was one of the minority who had transferred his allegiance to the Despensers. Hardly anyone had taken Surrey's livery.

Constance frowned. It was the first she had heard of any disorder. 'It's a matter for the sheriff of Warwickshire, not for me,' she observed.

'My lady, you don't understand. It's not so simple. It's rumoured that the Duke of Lancaster has landed in the North Country. That's what's made these men so bold. Who knows what else may befall? What if they decide to take Elmley Castle next?'

She saw his point. Elmley, just a few miles away towards Evesham, was one of the former Beauchamp properties that had been granted to Thomas and her. Its defences were far less formidable than those of Warwick Castle, and such garrison as it possessed was small and by no means certain in its loyalty.

'Elmley is not of such significance as Warwick,' she said, hurriedly assessing the situation and reassuring herself. 'I doubt these gentlemen will wish to spread themselves too thinly, and if they do they'll be easy to defeat. You say they have done this because they think Bolingbroke has landed in the north?'

'Yes, my lady. In Yorkshire it's said. Though whether it be true or not is more than I know.'

'My cousin was in France. What manner of fool would set out from France, and land in Yorkshire? It makes little sense.'

Constance summoned such advisers as she had immediately available. Sir Hugh Despenser and Hugh Tyldesley. The Duchess of Aumale, although not summoned, was not to be excluded, her freckles stark on her pale face and her expression already one of mild panic.

'It grieves me that there should be such disorder in Warwickshire,' Sir Hugh said, shaking his head, 'but I doubt these fellows will trouble us at Hanley. I think my own duty's clear enough. I must leave my wife and children here, where they'll be safe, and return to Solihull. God knows what other scores are being settled in the county. I must protect what is mine, and, as the King's knight, and a Justice, do what I may to restore the peace. As for you, Cousin, I don't believe you're in any danger, and certainly not within the walls of this castle. You've men enough to defend it against anything short of an army, and I know you're well supplied with provisions.'

'Bolingbroke's *got* an army,' Philippa objected. 'He wouldn't be in Yorkshire without one, would he? Or perhaps you think he's there on his own? How dare you think of leaving us, Sir Hugh! You belong here, to organise the defence. Or to escort us back to Cardiff. That might be better. Safer. We could go as we came, by water.'

'It's not even certain that Bolingbroke is in England, my lady Duchess,' Throckmorton pointed out. 'It's only what some say. Yorkshire's a long way off.'

Tyldesley grunted. 'It'd take him a week at least to get here. More like ten days or a fortnight. Even if he was so minded, which I doubt.'

Constance was silent for a few moments. 'Cousin,' she said to Sir Hugh, 'I think you're right. That you should be at Solihull. There's no disorder here, and you may better serve the King in Warwickshire. You can send us word of what's happening, and, if necessary, you may always return here. Tyldesley, we must know more. Choose good men, and send them, out of livery, to all the towns around us, to gather what news they can. You and I will go to see Sir John Russell at Strensham. He's of the King's Council, and may have word from my lord father. As, for you, Sister, you may stay here, with Dame Sybil and the children. Tyldesley and I will not be away for long.'

This programme seemed to satisfy them all, though Philippa's mouth opened and closed again, as if she had considered a protest.

Constance made the journey to Strensham on horseback, with Agnes Norreys as attendant and Hugh Tyldesley and half a dozen of the yeomen of the household as escort, the men armed to the teeth at Tyldesley's insistence. There was, however, no sign that anything unusual was in the air. Upton-on-Severn was busy in its usual, modest way. A train of packhorses, carrying salt from Droitwich, was halted in the street while its leader exchanged words with a girl who was driving a flock of geese into the town. The girl had a toddling, raven-haired child by the hand, and the child was prodding one of the geese with a long stalk of grass. The parish priest, leaning on his church wall, looked on with such interest as he could spare from his pot of perry, as he gave nominal supervision to the men who were re-thatching the church roof. A glance from the bridge revealed the usual small huddle of trading boats, a few in the process of unloading, but most simply standing there in idleness while their crews sought out refreshment.

John Russell's arm was still in a sling as a result of the wound he had received at Windsor. When Constance arrived he was pacing up and down his hall in pointless agitation, his wife Lady Clinton following him around, flapping her arms as she tried to calm him. Behind them a small gang of workmen was busily engaged in laying new floor tiles.

'Thank God you're here, Countess!' he cried. 'You've saved me a journey. I was about to go to you, to give you the news. Your father's man has just left. Henry of Bolingbroke has landed in Sussex. He's taken Pevensey Castle, and I'm summoned to London to join the rest of the Council. Look at me! Look at this arm! It's not strong enough to lift a pen, let alone a sword.'

'You say that they've landed in Sussex? We've heard that they're in Yorkshire.'

'You may read the Duke's letter for yourself!' he snapped, thrusting it at her and continuing to pace around, nervously chewing his left hand and occasionally pausing to kick the furniture, the workmen, or the walls.

York's letter was a formal one, devoid of any hint of emotion or concern, and Constance was confident that only the seal and signature were truly her father's. It confirmed that Bolingbroke had captured Pevensey, and added that the sheriffs of all counties south of Trent had been ordered to call out the *posse comitatus* to resist the rebels. Sir William Bagot had been despatched to South Wales, there to take ship for Ireland to warn the King.

She had visited Pevensey with her parents many years earlier, when the castle had belonged to her Uncle Lancaster. She tried to recall the details of the place, but remembered only its remote location, on the edge of a marsh near the sea, with nothing for miles but shingle and rough pasture. An unwelcoming place to land, but it made much more sense than a descent on Yorkshire. From Pevensey it would not take more than three or four days to march to London.

'What are you going to do?' she asked.

Russell viciously booted one of the workmen out of his path. 'Do? What d'you think I'm going to do? I'm going to get out of Worcestershire before Warwick's friends come calling here. Your father's going to have to fight. D'you understand? There's going to be a bloody war, and I'm useless for anything beyond talking. All our enemies will come crawling out of the woodwork at once, every rogue who has half a grudge against us, and we'll be lucky to get out with our lives, let alone our property.'

'Sir John—,' Lady Clinton began, in a soothing tone.

'Shut up, woman! What do you know? Countess, do me a service and take her back to Hanley with you. I can't leave her here, and I'm damned if she's going to London. The silly bitch is neither use nor ornament.'

Constance was astonished. She had never seen Russell in such a mood, so utterly out of control. It had not occurred to her that he would panic.

'In God's name, Sir John,' she said coldly, 'calm yourself.'

'Calm myself? It's well for you to say that! I don't suppose your cousin, Bolingbroke, will do much to you, even if he lays his hands on you. My case is a damned sight different. He's likely to take my head off.'

He turned his back on them and stalked off in the direction of his solar.

'Forgive my husband,' pleaded Lady Clinton. 'He's not himself. I don't know what to say. That he should speak to you in such a way...'

Constance shrugged. 'I can see this news has hit him hard, and his wound will not help his temper.'

'It's not healing as it should,' Lady Clinton said, tears forming in the corner of her eyes. 'He's no strength in the arm, so he's defenceless. He fought all those years against Warwick and his affinity, and thought he'd won, and now it all begins again.'

Constance called to Agnes. 'Stay here with Lady Clinton. Help her ready herself to go with us to Hanley. We'll call here to collect you on our way back.'

'My lady, where would you go?' asked Tyldesley. 'It grows late in the day.'

'There's hours of daylight yet. What troubles you, Hugh? Do you fear you might miss your supper? I want to be sure that all is calm at Elmley Castle. It shouldn't take long.'

'I could easily do that for you, my lady. No need for you to trouble yourself.'

'Call for the horses, if you will.'

Tyldesley took in the set of her lips, and did not dispute the matter further.

They crossed the Avon at Defford, and worked around the back of Bredon Hill, through wooded country and rich pastures. The sun was well beyond its zenith now, and in the dappled shadow of the trees it was almost cold. A silence hung over the land, broken only by the regular tread of their horses' hooves and the occasional distant bleating of a goat.

The village of Elmley Castle appeared deserted, its long, single street empty except for a few rooting pigs and scratching chickens. The castle itself stood at the end of the street, perched on the edge of the hill, its drawbridge down and its gates open wide. They passed through the dark tunnel of the gate house, and emerged into the bailey, the hooves loud on the paved surface. No one emerged to greet them.

'Are they all dead?' Tyldesley asked, his voice loud. 'Or drunk? Fools, dogs, where are you? Your lady the Countess of Gloucester is here! Show yourselves!'

No answered returned. Constance had the distinct feeling that they were being watched, but made an effort to keep calm. Her jennet was already stirring beneath her, sidling nervously as if her own doubts had somehow transmitted themselves to the animal. She leaned forward in the saddle and stroked its neck.

'Gerard,' Tyldesley said to the closest of his men, 'get you down and see if you can stir some rogue from his slumbers. Take care.'

Gerard nodded, climbed from his horse and drew his long knife. Cautiously he walked towards the nearest of the doors, closely watched by the others, and not least by Tyldesley, who was preparing a crossbow. He raised it as the door swung open, just before Gerard could lay his hand to its ring.

The stout, balding fellow who emerged was dressed in ragged red hose and a white shirt, over which he wore a protective leather jack. His face was shaven, though it looked as if it had not seen a razor for a week, and his expression was one of stupefied surprise, as if he had just woken to find himself in an alternative universe.

'Who in Christ's name are you?' asked Tyldesley.

The man bowed awkwardly. 'Sir, I'm Matthew of Comberton, the gateward. You weren't expected.' He bowed again, deeply. 'My lady.'

'We can see we weren't expected,' Tyldesley said. 'Where's the Constable?'

'Don't rightly know, sir.'

Tyldesley climbed down from his horse with unexpected speed, and closed the distance between himself and the gateward in three great steps, before giving the man a brutal kick between the legs that set him rolling and howling on the floor.

'Get him up!' he ordered Gerard. 'Now, pig, let's try again, shall we?' He held the crossbow about an inch from the gateward's face, and eased his finger onto the trigger.

'Enough!' said Constance angrily. 'Give him a chance to speak. Can you not see that he's terrified?'

Tyldesley lowered the crossbow. 'He *ought* to be terrified, my lady. Clear neglect of duty. Drunkenness—he stinks of cider! Surprised you can't smell it from there. He's not even wearing his livery. I don't suppose that he turns down your wages, though. Dare say he takes those happily enough. Where's the rest of them, that's what I'd like to know. Three blind nuns and a moon-kissed pot boy could take this castle, guarded as it is.'

'They've gone to Warwick,' the gateward gasped, still retching for breath. 'All of 'em but me. Word came that we were wanted there. Don't know who sent it, but all the Earl's men are to gather there.'

'The Earl of Warwick's men, you mean,' Constance interjected angrily.

'Yes. I'm sorry, my lady, but it's true. I'd have gone myself, but I was too drunk to get out of bed 'till now.'

'You're lucky,' said Tyldesley. 'Very lucky. Drunks get away with a beating. Rebels hang. Thought about that, have you? Stinking bastard, I ought to cut your throat. I would, if my lady the Countess were not here to see it.'

'Leave him, Tyldesley,' Constance snapped. 'He's not worth it. Let's get out of here.'

Tyldesley signed to Gerard to release the gateward, and mounted up.

'Close the gates behind us,' he commanded the drunkard, 'lift the drawbridge, and don't let anyone in unless I'm here to order it. Disobey, and I'll make you pray for death.'

Matthew of Comberton knuckled his forehead. 'Aye, sir. I'll shut it all up, tight as a drum.'

'You'd better!'

As they emerged from the gatehouse, they found that many of the houses had opened their doors, and men and women were standing around in sulky groups, some clutching scythes, axes and other farm implements, a few even going so far as to be in the process of stringing their bows.

'Swords!' cried Tyldesley, and drew out his own blade. The other men followed suit, greased steel rasping against the leather scabbards as the weapons emerged.

'Take care,' said Constance quietly. 'The last thing that's wanted is a massacre. Deal gently with them.'

'Gently? My lady, do you imagine I'm a coward, that I'm going to allow these scum to threaten *you*?'

'No one is calling you a coward. There's no threat. They're wary of us. Defending their homes. Look at them! Most of the men are greybeards, or little boys. The others must have gone to Warwick with the castle garrison. Use the flats of your swords if you must, but don't strike the first blow.'

They moved off cautiously, but no one made any attempt to stand in their way. Indeed some of those closest to them drew back, unwilling to risk contact with the drawn swords. The hostility was one of silence, broken only by the creak of chains as the drawbridge was raised behind them.

***

Harry Bolingbroke watched solemnly as the last of the brief summer cloud-burst poured in torrents from the roofs of the houses at the other side of Doncaster marketplace. Everywhere he looked were armed men, mostly wearing his livery, though a few were masterless rogues who emerged from forests and wastes to attach themselves to his fortunes and take the opportunity to steal, rape and burn under the cover of his quarrel.

Many of his father's Yorkshire retainers and tenants had gathered around his banner almost as soon as he had landed at Ravenspur. They had advanced to his castle at Pickering, which had surrendered at the first summons, and there had received the adherence of the local peer, Lord Roos of Helmsley. Skirting well to the north of the city of York, they had gone on to Knaresborough, where some fighting had been necessary before the castle yielded. Then on to Pontefract, the strongest of all the Lancastrian fortresses in the north, where the gates had been thrown open to him and he had been joined by knights, squires and gentlemen from all the southern parts of Yorkshire, as well as many from Lancashire. The majority being Lancastrian retainers, but by no means all. He was under no illusions. They were attracted to his success like bees to flowers but the least setback could as readily set them scuttling home.

Now he was on the road to London, and more reinforcements were expected. His brother-in-law, Ralph Neville, Earl of Westmorland, had sent a letter of support and a promise of five hundred men. And Henry Percy, Earl of Northumberland, was also reported to be approaching, an armed force at his back that was reckoned to be the equal of Harry's own. Northumberland presumably intended to join him, but it could not be taken entirely for granted. He was a shrewd fox, and no particular friend of the House of Lancaster, a veteran of numerous quarrels with Harry's father. Though it was also true that he had a grievance of his own to settle. The profitable wardenship of the West March had been taken from him and given to Aumale. That might tip the balance.

Idly, Harry picked up the rough draft of the letter that had been sent out in his name to the lords of England, to all other great men, and to the significant towns. Clerks had bent over the task of copying for hours, even Archbishop Arundel himself lending a hand. Men needed a justification to rebel, and this manifesto was an attempt to provide it. It claimed that Richard intended to sell Calais and Guienne to the French; that he intended to impose unprecedented and intolerable taxes and tallages; that he would subject the villeins to harsher bondage, and execute the chief magistrates of every town; even that he would bring in his French allies to crush his own people's resistance. It ended thus:

> '...when the aforesaid matters came to my
> knowledge, I came over as soon as I could to
> inform, succour and comfort you to the
> utmost of my power; for I am one of the
> nearest to the crown of England, and am
> beholden to love and support the realm as
> much, or more than any man alive, for thus
> have my predecessors done. And so, my
> friends, may God preserve you. Be well
> advised and ponder well that which I write
> to you.
>
> 'Your good and faithful friend, Henry of
> Lancaster.'

Could sane men read such a document and not laugh? Selfless Harry, returning home at great trouble and expense to right a nation's wrongs, including several that were utterly imaginary. Well, the Archbishop seemed to think it struck the right notes, and so did the rest of his advisers. He seemed to be the only one with doubts about the exaggerations.

'Northumberland is here!'

'Northumberland!'

He heard the shouts long before Sir Hugh Waterton came running in with the news. Already on his feet, he was half way across the room before Waterton has finished speaking, the Archbishop and the Archbishop's nephew, Thomas Fitzalan, at his elbows, almost like constables taking a prisoner before the magistrates. Did they remember, he wondered, that he had given evidence against the man who had been the brother of one and the father of the other? Perhaps they preferred to forget, or to persuade themselves that he had acted as he had out of fear of Richard's displeasure. It was remarkable that he, of all men, should find himself their champion. He and his father had been as glad as anyone to see Richard Arundel's head struck off.

There was cheering as he emerged into the open. Northumberland was already dismounting, and with him his son, Harry Hotspur, a man of Bolingbroke's own age, and much regarded as a warrior, though the only significant battle he had fought had ended in defeat and capture by the Scots. It was a mark of the Percys that they talked of Otterburn as if it had been an English victory.

'Welcome, cousins,' Bolingbroke said, bowing and removing his hat out of respect for Northumberland's age.

'My dear cousin of Lancaster,' Northumberland responded, equally polite. 'It's a joy to see you back on English soil, and already in possession of part of your rightful inheritance.'

'I hope, with your aid, and that of my other friends, to recover the rest.'

'We're with you in that,' jerked Hotspur. He had an abrupt way of speaking, almost as if he found it hard not to be aggressive. 'Yet we need assurances from you, my lord of Lancaster.'

'Assurances? Of my gratitude? Do you doubt it?'

'Assurances that you do not seek to lead us in treason. Many hold back from you because they question your intentions.'

'Do they?'

'They do.'

Northumberland nodded. 'My son is a lover of plain words. He might have been more circumspect. We are confident that all men standing here, including yourself, fair Cousin, are loyal subjects of King Richard. We seek, as you do, to ensure that he receives better counsel, and to establish justice in the land. Nothing more.'

'Then we are not at odds,' said Harry calmly, 'for that is exactly my intent.'

'My lord of Lancaster!' the Archbishop protested. 'This is not the place for debate. Perhaps these matters would be better discussed indoors, when the Earl and his son have received refreshment and eased their bones.'

'Are you prepared to swear?' demanded Hotspur. 'To swear that you come only for your inheritance? Not for the crown?'

Bolingbroke controlled the anger swelling within him. It was all he could do not to hurl himself at Hotspur for daring to make such a demand.

'I will gladly swear to it,' he said, 'if it will comfort men's minds.'

'It is quite unnecessary,' protested the Archbishop. 'Your word suffices. The word of the Duke of Lancaster. Who dares ask more?'

'We do,' said Hotspur, bluntly. 'We'll serve in an honest cause, and gladly, but we'll not be called traitors.'

'Let the Sacrament be brought!' Harry snapped. 'I'll swear what you will.'

There was a long wait while a pyx was brought from the nearest church. Bolingbroke knelt reverently, and laid his hand upon it.

'I, Harry of Lancaster, swear that I am returned to England to recover the estates of my inheritance, and those of my late wife, whom God pardon, and for no other cause.' He stared directly at Hotspur. 'I further swear that it is my whole intent that my sovereign lord, King Richard, shall reign to the end of his life, advised by a Council of the lords of this realm, spiritual and temporal. So help me God!'

The square had fallen silent. Bolingbroke's eyes were still fixed on Hotspur, holding them until Percy looked away.

Northumberland nodded his approval. 'It's well done,' he said thoughtfully. 'No man of honour will oppose you now.'

***

The Duke of York had abandoned London. He had not needed Mayor Whittington's advice that the majority of the citizens were sympathetic to Harry of Lancaster. He had seen it in their faces, interpreted it from their desultory response to their call for arms.

He had assembled an army of three thousand men, but all his efforts could not persuade it to grow any larger. It was not that the Treasury was short of money; indeed there were ample funds to pay men in advance, and pay them well. The Treasurer, Scrope, Earl of Wiltshire, was ready to authorise double the normal rate. The truth was that the greater part of the knights and squires of England were not prepared to shed their blood to keep Bolingbroke out of his inheritance.

The most important noble who had answered his summons was John Beaufort, Marquis of Dorset, Bolingbroke's own half-brother. The other leading recruits were the Earl of Suffolk, the Bishop of Norwich, and Lord Ferrers of Chartley, who was one of Thomas Despenser's brothers-in-law. None of these men inspired York with much confidence, and only the Bishop seemed keen to fight.

The Council, meanwhile, was panicking. Bishop Stafford, the Chancellor, was sound enough, but most of the others seemed to be on the edge of flight. Wiltshire, John Bushey, Henry Green and John Russell, had been loud in their advice that the government should quit Westminster, but they were no happier at St. Albans, and seemed to have made no great effort to unpack their bags. When York suggested that the Queen needed to be moved from Windsor to Wallingford Castle, which was more defensible, these four were quick to volunteer for a task that would take them further away from Bolingbroke. Meanwhile he led his army, such as it was, northwards, as far as Bedford, his intent being to confront the rebels somewhere in the midlands.

But at Bedford new reports came in, the most important from two squires he had despatched to Bolingbroke to demand his purpose in returning to England without the King's leave. The reply these men brought was equivocal, but their tale of the numbers with Bolingbroke forced a review of strategy.

York called his advisers together. They met in the friary of the town, sitting in candlelight because it was well after midnight. 'My nephew of Lancaster has been joined by the earls of Northumberland and Westmorland,' he announced gravely. 'Also by Lord Willoughby from Lincolnshire. Their combined numbers are put at ten thousand. We cannot fight them.'

'Cannot? Or will not?' demanded the Bishop.

'Cannot, Bishop. We've less than a third as many men, and although we counted on reinforcement there's little coming in to us. You must also remember the landing at Pevensey.'

'A feint.'

'Perhaps. But for all I know it could be the beginning of a French invasion. Certainly we can't be sure how many men there are in Sussex, or what they're planning. We could be trapped between two hostile forces.'

'So what does Your Grace propose? Surrender?'

The Bishop's voice was as contemptuous as his expression. The others merely looked awkward.

'I propose to do the only thing I can do,' York answered, his voice hard. 'March to the West. By now the King should have received the letter we sent to him by Bagot, and he'll surely waste no time in coming home with all the forces at his command. When he lands, we'll be there to join him.'

'Meanwhile Bolingbroke will be in London. For all practical purposes, England will be in his hands.'

'My uncle of York is right,' ventured John Beaufort. 'We're in no condition to defend London, and still less can we fight at odds of three to one. We've no choice but to try to join with the King.'

'It makes sense to concentrate our strength,' Ferrers agreed. 'What's more, there's hope of reinforcement in the West. Lancaster has little influence in Worcestershire or Gloucestershire; certainly far less than he has in the Midlands. If we have to fight him, let's fight him where he's weakest.'

Despite the Bishop's protest, they decided that their next move would be westward, to Oxford. From there Wiltshire and the other absent members of the Council, who were presumably with the Queen at Wallingford, would be summoned to join them.

There was nothing now between Harry Bolingbroke and London, if he chose to march that way.

16

The news from Glamorgan was not good. Sir John St. John's letter said that Bolingbroke's tenants in Brecon and Ogmore were arrayed in arms; because of that, he had ordered the men of Glamorgan to prepare to defend themselves. He doubted whether they would do anything more than that, and he strongly advised against trying to use some of them in England, bearing in mind that the most trustworthy warriors had already gone away with Thomas, leaving the Lordship severely weakened. There had already been minor incursions, and he feared that matters could grow worse. Sir William Stradling, he added, had friends and relatives in Brecon, and would need to be watched.

From Stradling himself there was no word at all.

Constance put the letter down, having found no more satisfaction in it than at first reading. Then she began to pace, her lower lip secure between her teeth. There was no doubt that matters were beginning to look grim. It was clear no help could be expected from Glamorgan, and that meant they would have to manage more or less as they were. She had summoned together such Despenser retainers as were still in the country, but their response had been mixed. Hugh Mortimer, for example, had made it clear that he was ready to offer advice, and to defend her person if it became necessary, but beyond that he would not go. Others had simply ignored her call altogether.

Paris, sensing her mood, padded across and laid his long head on her lap. He was panting from the heat, and slavering over her clothes, but she was too preoccupied to be concerned, and comforted herself, as much as him, by absently stroking his velvet ears.

Philippa was in the chapel, where of late she had spent the greater part of each day. Her prayers were for Edward's rapid return, which she seemed to think would be the complete solution to all their difficulties. Constance had her doubts even about that. Civil war seemed inevitable, and there was no certainty that they would end on the winning side. The consequences of defeat were too terrible for contemplation.

Constance was surprised by the change wrought in her sister-in-law, yet at the same time understood her sense of helplessness. There was nothing they could do to take the fight to the enemy, and, what was more, their security at Hanley Castle was largely illusory. The defences were modest enough, certainly nothing to compare to those at Warwick. The Beauchamp affinity, Berkeley, or both, could move against them at any time, and if they did she and Philippa would, at best, be shut up in the castle, deprived of any contact with the outside world. They might not even be able to hold the place against a determined attack.

It was tempting to withdraw to Usk, which Alianore and Edward Charlton were reportedly fortifying against potential attack, or even to do as Philippa had suggested, and retreat all the way to Cardiff, a place of still greater security. But Thomas had wanted her at Hanley, and she was reluctant to leave unless absolutely forced to do so. While she remained where she was and kept her people in arms they still kept a tenuous hold on Gloucestershire and southern Worcestershire. If she left, then all the waverers in the district would desert at once to the other side.

Richard of Conisbrough had been sent to the top of the adjacent tower to watch out for any sign of trouble, as a way of keeping him occupied. Now he came running down the tight spiral stairs.

'Someone is coming along the road from Upton,' he said urgently. 'I've counted at least half a dozen horses, but I think there are more. Armed men, riding at the trot. They're still quite a way off.'

Constance wet her lips with her tongue.

'What are the livery colours?' she asked.

'That's what I can't understand. Some of them are ours.'

'Ours?'

'York. Murrey and blue. But it *can't* be our father. Why would he come here? It's even less likely to be the Duchess. She'll be at Fotheringhay.'

Constance was puzzled. There was certainly no call for the Duke of York, or men in his livery, to be in Worcestershire. They would surely be fully occupied with the defence of London. Yet Dickon seemed very sure, and although he was only fourteen years old she knew that he was keen-sighted and far from a fool.

'And the other colours?' she prompted.

'I'm not sure. The sun's too bright.'

'Go and have another look.'

He hurried off and Constance, having fretted for a moment or two, forsook her dignity sufficiently to follow him.

The tower gave a good view of the surrounding countryside, although with the trees in full leaf and the effect of heat haze it was not as commanding as it might have been. She took a moment to orientate herself, her eyes caught by the sparkle of the sun on the Severn as it snaked its sluggish way down to Upton, Tewkesbury and Gloucester.

Dickon pointed as the cavalcade emerged from a tunnel of trees and began to turn from the main road and into the park. There was no doubt about the predominant livery. It was indeed that of the Duke of York. Then banners began to appear between the trees, and the sun reflected from the polished armour of the men riding beneath them.

'It *is* our father!' Dickon gasped, shaking his head. 'I don't understand. It doesn't make sense.'

Constance didn't understand either. She spoke with confident authority, the better to disguise her bewilderment. 'Tell Tyldesley to have the gates opened. Then get our sister Philippa from the chapel.'

He ran off without a word to do her bidding. Constance continued to watch, as more and more men came into sight, many on foot, straggling along at the edges of the road as if they had walked for many miles in the summer heat. They had the look of defeat about them, and yet it was impossible that there had been a battle. The latest word she had from the agents she had placed in the surrounding towns was that Bolingbroke was still several days away, in the area of Leicester, and presumably moving on towards London.

She made a somewhat cautious descent of the stairs. It was only on the way down that she realised how dark they were, how easy it would have been to slip on the narrow treads.

In the solar Agnes Norreys and Sybil Despenser were hugging each other in delight, as though they thought that all danger was gone, and Anne, Sybil's daughter, was dancing with Elizabeth Clinton and Mary Russell. Constance's arrival stilled them all, and they formed up as if in preparation for a procession, but the joy remained spread across their faces.

'The Duke must have won a splendid victory!' cried Agnes. Constance had rarely known her to be so enthusiastic.

'Calm yourself, Agnes,' she said. 'It's true that my father is here, but I don't know the cause of it. We must go down at once to greet him.'

'Is my husband with him?' asked Lady Clinton.

Constance shook her head. 'I didn't see his banner,' she said. Only now did it strike her that that was strange. She would have expected Russell to keep close to his commander-in-chief, especially as he was in no condition to do more than offer advice. 'I suppose he could be one of those in charge of the rear. It's a great host that's coming. I dare say some of them are still beyond the bridge at Upton.'

They went out together to receive the Duke, but by the time they reached the flight of stone stairs leading down the inner courtyard he was already emerging from the gatehouse, bareheaded but otherwise in complete armour, with John Beaufort, Bishop Despenser, and Suffolk clustered around him, and Robert Ferrers only a little behind. There was no sign of John Russell, but John Brouning, the sheriff of Gloucestershire, had somehow attached himself. Presumably the force he had raised from the county in support of the Duke was somewhere in the column behind them.

Constance frowned slightly as she tried to remember when she had last seen her father in armour. She had a vague memory of him riding out from

Conisbrough to fight the Scots, in the same year that her brother Dickon had been born, but she doubted he had worn harness since. She certainly could not recall him practising his fighting skills, as Thomas often did, much less taking part in tournaments; though she supposed he had done so in his youth.

She curtsied deeply. 'You are welcome, my dear lord Father,' she said. 'I fear you find us unprepared for such an honour, but what we have is at your disposal.'

'Good day, Daughter,' York grunted, already struggling down from his horse. Sundry squires hastened to assist, but it was difficult work for him, and from the expression on his face it was evidently a painful process. 'I need food and drink for all — we've been marching since before dawn. That, and a private room with a table in it. There's much to be considered, and I must take advice.'

Philippa came rushing up, her skirts tucked up in both hands. 'Father! We are so glad to see you! This is the answer to our prayers. More than we dared hope. Does this mean that you've beaten the rebels?'

The Duke stared at her with scarcely concealed disgust. 'Beaten them? We've not even seen them. You'd do well to go back to your prayers, madame.'

Constance greatly regretted the absence of John Norreys, who was in Ireland with Thomas. She had no officer at hand who was remotely his equal when it came to the management of the household. So there was no choice but to take on his responsibilities herself, to ensure that accommodation was allocated in accordance with rank, that the kitchens swung into action to prepare at least some of the necessary food. That wine and ale were brought up from the cellars and men were sent out into the park to ensure that it was not entirely destroyed by her father's motley collection of soldiers. All of which she could have trusted Norreys to do on his own initiative. It was inevitable that her stores would be severely depleted, but if care were not taken to prevent it there'd be trees cut down and palings smashed for cooking fires, and the deer would be used for target practice.

She was not invited to share in York's counsels. He and his principal lieutenants were shut away behind a closed door, their refreshments carried to them by their own squires. The debate was long, and at times it was loud, voices carrying into the adjoining rooms and out through the open windows into the close summer air.

'I expect your father's legs are paining him,' Philippa said. She paused, reaching out to pluck a sweetmeat from the tray on the press next to her chair. 'I know he suffers from old wounds, and that long journeys are not something he enjoys. Even so, there was no need to address me as he did, in the hearing of so many inferior persons. I think he sometimes forgets that I am the wife of his heir, and as much a Duchess as he is a Duke.'

Constance threw her a freezing glance, but said nothing, not trusting herself. Instead she walked to the squint that gave a view of the hall below. It was a scene of confusion. Some men were disarming, others arguing, others still squatting on the floor, drinking their ale and dicing, or tossing coins against the wall and gambling on which one would bounce back the furthest. Many were lying listlessly on the rushes, too exhausted to move, or too apathetic.

The council chamber her father was using was at the other end of the hall, raised above ground level like the solar and reached by a flight of stone stairs. As she watched Henry Despenser emerged from the portal leading to these stairs, and began to cross the hall, pushing aside those who got in his way. He stalked out through the main entrance, fury written all over his face.

Constance hurried to the spiral stairs again, but this time instead of going up to the tower she went down to the courtyard, and slipped out of the small door at ground level, her mind set on intercepting the Bishop. He was half way to the chapel before she managed to catch him, and such was his pace that she had to almost run to keep up with him.

For a moment the Bishop did not seem to recognise her. His eyes were blank, as if he had just suffered the worst shock of his life. His harness of plate had been removed for the sake of ease, and he stood in the quilted, protective garments that were worn beneath. After a long hot day dressed in armour, the stink of his sweat was pervasive, even in the open air.

'Constance,' he said numbly. 'I think I need to go to sit in your garden for a time. Guide me to it, will you?'

She was astonished. 'Honoured Uncle, tell me what is wrong.'

'Everything,' he said sadly. He took her arm, and they walked together towards the herber, his pace suddenly reduced to little more than a shuffle, as if his earlier haste had burned away his energy.

He halted as soon as they reached the first arbour, and settled down on the turf seat, gesturing for her to sit next to him. 'This has always been a fair manor,' he said gently, 'and you have made it still fairer.' He paused, and there was a long silence as his eyes surveyed the Malvern Hills in the distance. She was almost taken aback when he continued.

'Constance, if there is one thing I have regretted about being a priest, it's that I've not been able to have children of my own. Yes, I know there are many lewd men in orders who sin in that particular. Some in high places. But when I entered Christ's service I swore that, however unworthy and sinful I might be in other matters, I should at least remain chaste of my body. I've often looked at you, and at my other dear nieces, and thought how much, in especial, I'd have loved a daughter of my own. Now I thank God that I've neither wife nor child. The thought of them might turn me from my duty. As matters stand, life is not so very precious to me that I must cling hold of it even at the cost of my honour.'

'Tell me,' she said, 'tell me what has happened.'

He shrugged. 'It began at Oxford, where Wiltshire, Bushey, Green, and your friend John Russell were supposed to meet us. Your father sent to them at Wallingford, and they made their excuses. They proposed that we fortify Bristol, and await the King there. The Duke didn't agree, but he didn't actually forbid it, either. And so they went. Trembling, gutless cravens, in fear of their lives. Well, after that others began to desert us. It's no great wonder. Take men to war, and they expect leadership, not uncertainty. Some, I think, have put the King's money in their purses and gone home. The chances are that the rest have run off to Bolingbroke, bearing with them the tale of our weakness. This army has grown smaller by the hour. Some have joined us, it's true, but nowhere near enough to make up for the losses.'

'My cousin the King will be back from Ireland before long. That will change everything.'

The Bishop shook his head, 'He should already be in Wales by now. We've heard nothing from him. Nothing, not a single word! Your father intended to march through Worcester, and then into Wales to meet him, but now he's unnerved. We thought Bolingbroke would go to London, but he's said to be at Kenilworth, his advance guard already at Warwick. Worcester was thought too close to him, so we've turned away, and now we'll turn again, march on this side of the Severn down to Gloucester. Then on to Bristol, to hide within the walls with the other cowards and hope for the best. Anything, rather than risk a fight with the rebels. Well, I shall fight, if it comes to it, even if I fight alone. I swear it by Christ's own precious blood! No one shall say that Henry Despenser failed to strike a blow for his King. I'd sooner lie buried in a ditch than yield to rebels.'

'My cousin of Lancaster says that he is here only for what is his own. Perhaps there may yet be some accommodation.' She was trying to convince herself as much as him.

'Do you believe his lies?' He stood up, rigid with fury. 'God's truth, I thought you had more sense! Rebellion can never be accommodated. It's the most grievous of sins. As bad as heresy. Our whole society is based on subordination and example. If Bolingbroke has the right to flout his king, then why should the servant obey his lord, or the wife her husband, or the child its parents? Why should mankind submit to God's holy law? The alternative to proper subordination isn't freedom. It's chaos, the rule of brute force, a world where no man will know what's his own, where the weak become slaves and there's neither faith nor justice. Don't speak to me of accommodation, child. You can't offer terms of peace to Satan. It's better to resolve to die.'

***

Bolingbroke was riding out of Warwick, his tall, furred hat in his hand as he acknowledged the cheers of the crowd gathered around the approaches to the bridge over the Avon. He was not wearing armour, but simple, black mourning in honour of his father. There was no prospect of imminent fighting, and he saw no reason to suffer unnecessary discomfort. With ten thousand armed men surrounding him he could allow himself the luxury of civilian clothing. Its rich simplicity made him all the more striking to the eye.

'I doubt that any man has ever been more warmly welcomed,' the Archbishop said to him. 'They rejoice that you are here to save them from ruin.'

Harry shrugged, and restored his hat to his head. 'I dare say they'd cheer as loudly for Richard, if he were here with his army. They'd cheer if I were on my way to the gallows. The people are like that.'

'The voice of the people is the voice of God.'

Bolingbroke snorted. 'Do you truly believe that, Archbishop?'

'At a time like this I do. England wants you, and needs you. That foolish oath at Doncaster—you must not be bound by it.'

'I *am* bound by it. If my word can't be trusted then I'm no better than Richard. Surely you see that?'

'I see what will happen, unless you take the throne. Richard will accept any terms you offer. Then he'll begin to build again, slowly, patiently, until he's strong enough to destroy you. You and all who have served you. Do you imagine that you can rule England without making enemies? I say you've no choice. You'll never be safe while Richard wears the crown. You *must* be King.'

'I shall be—in all but name.'

'It's the name that signifies. Even if you care nothing for your own neck, you should think of these men around you, men who are risking everything in your quarrel. Think of them, and think of your sons. What will happen to those boys if you fail?'

Harry was quiet for a few moments.

'At least consider it!' the Archbishop urged. 'If Richard isn't fit to rule, then neither is he fit to reign. Is any man more fitted to his place than you are? If it's Northumberland that worries you, I tell you he's a man who can be bought. Give him the wardenship of the West March, just that, and he'll gladly kneel and kiss your hand and call you his sovereign lord.'

'And my Uncle York? What do you think he will say?'

'All the signs are that his men are deserting him in droves. What can he say? More to the point, what can he do? Few are willing to fight to keep you out of your lawful inheritance. That's already been made clear, thanks be to God. I doubt whether York can find the means to oppose you even if he wishes to do so.'

'I need to speak to him. I need to know...'

'To know what, my son?'

'To know he approves of my actions. I need his blessing. Do you understand that?'

The Archbishop pursed his lips. 'No,' he said slowly, 'I do not understand. Perhaps you can explain your reasons.'

'In many ways he was more a father to me than my own father. I can't bear to think of him as my enemy. My conscience won't be clear until we're reconciled.'

'You've no cause to feel any guilt. We are embarked together on a just cause. To rid England of tyranny.'

'Then let us keep our cause just,' said Harry abruptly. 'I'm here for what is mine—no more.'

'There are other injustices that must be remedied.'

'They shall be.'

'Injustices,' stressed the Archbishop, 'that can only be remedied by the King of England.'

***

Early in the morning of Wednesday 23rd July 1399, York's small army began its retreat towards Bristol. From Hanley Castle they moved through Upton, and along the dusty lanes on the western side of the Severn, keeping the great river between themselves and the threat of the enemy. Between Upton and Gloucester there was no bridge, only various ferries, notably the one at Tewkesbury. In effect, the river was impassable to Bolingbroke.

Although York had decided not to go into Wales, he had sent messengers off in that direction, in the hope of making contact with the King. These men carried a substantial sum in gold with them, for which Richard might find good use. There was no shortage of funds, whatever else.

The latest rumours said that Bolingbroke was approaching Evesham, which placed him no more than a day's march away, perilously close to being in a position to intercept them at Gloucester. For there the river would have to be crossed, if they were to reach Bristol.

Constance rode close to her father, being reluctant to share a carriage with the Duchess of Aumale. York's insistence that they should evacuate Hanley Castle had astonished her, but he had been implacable on the matter, standing on his authority as the King's Regent. He had decided that no men capable of fighting could be spared to protect the castle, and nor could women and children be left at the mercy of an advancing enemy. They must, therefore, go with him to Bristol. Hanley had been left to the care of a skeleton garrison, most of whom were ancient or infirm, and Constance had felt bound to authorise them to surrender if that was demanded.

The Bishop of Norwich was some way behind, in command of the rearguard, which also included Hugh Tyldesley and most of the men of the Despenser household. The Bishop was still in an angry mood, making no effort to conceal his doubts about York's strategy. The other principal leaders were grouped around the Duke, but only Robert Ferrers had made any attempt to talk to her, and that had been nothing more than a brief exchange of courtesies. She had to make do with the conversation provided by her brother, Dickon.

'Is that the tower of Tewkesbury Abbey over there?' he asked, pointing through a gap in the trees.

Constance glanced to the left for a moment. 'What else do you think it is?'

'Lady Elisabeth will still be there. Do you think we should ask Father to send some men across the ferry to rescue her?'

His sister shook her head. 'She'll be perfectly safe. Half of our enemies are her friends. You can be sure that her godson, Richard Beauchamp, will take care of her.'

'Constance, the Bishop says that we should be marching into Wales. What do you think?'

'I think the Bishop is right; but my opinion is of small account. I'm not even suffered to stay under my own roof. I wish now that I'd listened to Philippa. We'd have been better placed at Cardiff. I only refused her advice because I thought her a coward.'

'She *is* a coward.'

'Perhaps. But she was right this time.'

The boy thought for a moment. 'We could still go there.'

'Not without an escort. Father will not spare us one.'

'Have you asked him?'

Constance shook her head. 'There's no need to ask. He'd not leave me the men of my own household to hold Hanley, so why would he allow me to take them to Cardiff? I just hope that when we reach Gloucester there'll be some news of our cousin, the King. If it's known that he's landed in Wales, it may just be that Father will see the sense of going into Glamorgan.'

'I think he'll go anywhere rather than fight.'

Her eyes flashed at him. 'Richard! Remember that you speak of our father.'

'He thinks that Harry Bolingbroke is in the right. I heard him say it. No one argued with him, except the Bishop.'

'Such things are better not repeated.'

'I know, and I'll not tell anyone else. But that doesn't make it untrue.'

Constance fell silent. She remembered what the Bishop had said all those weeks ago at Norwich about her father and his attachment to Bolingbroke. There was truth in it, and that was why it had angered her so much. She had never thought that Bolingbroke would return, had deemed it impossible, and so the Bishop's fears had seemed to her to be an impertinent irrelevance. Now it was clear they were justified, and York's loyalty to the King was sorely strained by the dilemma he faced.

Gloucester did not close its gates against them, but nor were they received with any show of rejoicing. The long march from Hanley Castle exhausted all those who had made the journey on foot, and the city gates had to be kept open until the last stragglers tottered through them, round about midnight.

York himself, after almost four whole days on horseback, encased in armour, was almost prostrated with pain. His back and legs tortured him at every step, the alternatives of sitting, lying or standing merely providing a source of variety in his agony.

'My dear Father,' Philippa said solicitously, 'you'd be wise if tomorrow you rode in my carriage. I don't see how you can ride when you can scarcely stand.'

The Duke eyed her balefully. 'You are insulting, madame,' he grunted, through clenched teeth. 'I'm not quite ready for my tomb, and I can still manage a horse.'

'My lord Father,' Constance said, 'if your strength fails, then all is lost. Gloucester is a defensible town, and it controls a road into Wales. Is there need for us to go further?'

York turned on her. 'Nor am I so old that I need to be taught strategy by my own daughter! The matter is decided. We march to Bristol, and I shall ride at the head of my men. We'll leave here as soon as it's light. Instead of fussing over me, you'd do better to look to the children's comfort.'

'He cannot go on,' Philippa whispered, as she and Constance left the room.

Constance did not whisper. 'I know that. Your folly has ensured that he will go on, nevertheless. If you'd held your tongue I might have been able to persuade him to hold Gloucester instead.'

***

Constance knew that she had been unfair, but could not bring herself to apologise to her sister-in-law. They, the children, and the other women spent the night together on pallets and dirty rushes in the same, airless room in one of the oldest parts of the castle, the walls unrelieved by hangings and stinking of mould. No one slept much, and Constance perhaps least of all.

York had to be more or less hauled onto his horse, but no sooner was he mounted than their departure was interrupted by the arrival of one of the city officers, with news that an armed force had been sighted approaching from the direction of Wales.

Henry Despenser broke out into a beaming smile. 'It must be the King!' he said to Constance, who was sitting her horse next to him. 'We're saved, dear Niece, thanks be to God!'

Constance looked around, and saw the relief flooding over the faces of the other men as responsibility and fear of defeat lifted from them. York himself suddenly looked ten years younger than his true age, instead of twenty years older. Philippa was positively glowing.

'It looks like we'll be staying at Gloucester after all,' she said. 'All will be well, now Ned's here. He'll know what to do. Bolingbroke's head should look good on a spike, don't you think?'

The rejoicing was both brief and premature. The new arrivals turned out to be Bolingbroke's own tenants from the Lordship of Brecon, in search of their lord and his army. There were around five hundred of them, and although Bishop Henry was for giving them battle at once, no one else thought it a good idea, since Bolingbroke could arrive at any time with his main force, and if he did then they would be trapped. The Bishop rejoined that Bolingbroke was very probably still at Evesham, and that the defeat of his Welsh reinforcements would be a blow to him and a boost to their own spirits. He wasted his breath. They continued the retreat and, as they left, Gloucester opened its gates to the men of Brecon.

Constance had Hugh Tyldesley riding with her now.

'I've been asking a few questions, my lady,' he said suddenly, 'and I don't like the answers. You probably haven't noticed, but there are a lot less of us than there were yesterday. I don't just mean the other retinues, either. Hugh Mortimer seems to have found business to keep him in Gloucester. As for Brouning's fellows, a good half of them have already gone home. Even Brouning himself hasn't got much to say. This array is melting away faster than ice in the sun, and if you want my opinion we won't have a chance in any kind of fight. The last straw was when we turned our backs on that handful of Welshmen. That's taken the heart out of everyone.'

'My father expects reinforcements at Bristol.'

'If we get that far! Lady, where on earth is the King? Has nothing been heard? Some say he must be dead.'

'There's sure to be news at Bristol. It may be there'll be ships there, come from Ireland. Perhaps even some part of the King's army. I don't know.'

Tyldesley's face set into an expressive grimace. 'No one seems to know anything, my lady. That's the trouble. Oh, I'll not fail you. There's nothing waiting for me at home in Lancashire. But I'm only one man, and your father is too great a lord to pay heed to a squire's counsel.'

They rode on into the heat of the day, through clouds of dust thrown up by the hooves and carried on the brisk wind that was blowing in from the Severn estuary. As the sun rose to its highest point York slumped lower and lower in his saddle, until John Beaufort, suddenly appreciating his uncle's frailty, called for help. The Duke was on the point of falling from the saddle, but still made feeble protests as Beaufort, Ferrers and various lesser men first supported him and then lifted him from his horse. They lowered him onto the grass, removed his helmet, and put a cup of thin ale to his lips. York's mouth moved, but no audible words emerged.

'Christ pity us, I think he's dying!' Beaufort cried. 'Get the rest of his armour off! The heat must be too much.'

Constance rode up just in time to hear this declaration. She immediately jumped from her horse and ran to where the Duke lay propped up on the grassy bank at the side of the road.

'Just tired. Just very tired,' he mouthed.

'Get a litter!' Constance snapped at Robert Ferrers. 'Will you leave my lord father lying at the side of the road like a dog? An hour or less will take us to Berkeley Castle, where there'll be a bed for him, and a physician. Make haste!'

'You think that Berkeley will admit us?' asked Beaufort. 'He's no friend of your husband, Cousin, or so I hear.'

'He'll admit my father, and I don't give a damn about the rest of you.' She knelt down in the dust, and took York's hand. 'Father, we'll take you to Berkeley. You need rest. Just a few hours. My cousin here will manage all until you are well again.'

York made a grunt that sounded as if it might be assent. They stripped off his armour and lay him in the litter that Ferrers had purloined from Philippa's waiting-women. In that state he travelled the last few miles to Berkeley.

17

Lord Berkeley was far more hospitable than John Beaufort had suspected he would be, though Constance noted a certain glint in his eye that spoke quietly of triumph and satisfaction. He had York placed in his own great bed, where the Duke, after being tended by the household physician, fell into a sound sleep. His numerous liveried servants bustled around, bringing generous quantities of food and drink to their unexpected noble guests, and York's army, what was left of it, lounged in the shade of trees in the park, comforted by cart loads of bread and ale from Berkeley's cellars.

Berkeley was long a widower, and it was his daughter, Richard Beauchamp's young wife, who showed Constance and Philippa into a comfortable room with windows that overlooked the park. The Duchess of Aumale spread herself on the bed, and showed every sign of staying there for the rest of the day. Constance, having made sure that her father was in good hands, and that her children were settled and fed in the small, adjoining alcove with their nurses, rested her weight on the window-seat and shared a simple meal of frumenty and venison with Agnes Norreys and Sybil Despenser.

Elizabeth Berkeley returned at length to satisfy herself that all was well, and, when this was established, asked Constance if she would go with her into the garden, where Lord Berkeley was already waiting for them.

Constance was sufficiently intrigued to agree, and followed the girl along various passages and down winding back stairs until at last they emerged on a terrace that overlooked a dry ditch on the southern side of the castle. It was a surprisingly peaceful place, with a long, wooden tunnel covered in roses and ivy. Through this a gravel path led to a large arbour, where Berkeley was sitting on a backless wooden bench. He rose as they approached, and bowed low to Constance, uncovering his head.

'Forgive me, my lady,' he said, 'that I should so far forget myself as to summon you here, instead of seeking permission to attend you in your own chamber. However, I know of no other place in the castle where we may speak privately. I wish to do so.'

Constance nodded. 'I am too grateful for your kindness in receiving us, Lord Berkeley, to stand on any ceremony. You have no particular cause to be generous to me.'

He shrugged, and indicated the bench, inviting her to sit down. 'I don't deny that I've had my disagreements with the Earl, your husband. However, I don't extend my quarrels to women. Certainly not to ladies. No honourable knight should do so. Moreover, I have the greatest respect for my lord the Duke, your father. I don't forget that he is the last of King Edward's sons.'

She settled herself. 'That is something, Lord Berkeley, that others seem all too ready to forget.'

'I am told that he needs a day or two of rest, nothing more. That's not a difficulty in itself but, as you know, matters are not so simple.'

He pulled a large piece of folded parchment from the lining of his hat, opened it out, and placed it gently in her lap. It was a letter, signed by Harry Bolingbroke and dated at Kenilworth. A letter of moderate tone, speaking of justice, the restoration of the Lancastrian inheritance, and the better governance of the kingdom.

'Your cousin of Lancaster may be here tomorrow, or the next day,' he said thoughtfully. 'God knows how many men he has with him. Eight thousand? Twelve thousand? Twenty thousand? Who can say? Most of them northerners, tough-skinned fellows used to fighting the Scots and hungry for plunder in these rich shires. I've no intention of resisting them. Your cousin wants only what's due to him, and it's hard to deny that his cause is just. Do you deny it yourself, in your heart?'

Constance met his gaze. 'My opinion is of little consequence, Lord Berkeley.'

'It's of great consequence. You're your father's daughter. You can persuade him to come to terms, instead of trying to fight a battle he can't possibly win. This pitiable rabble about him—how many of them do you think will strike a blow? Young Beaufort won't, that's certain. Not against his own brother. Suffolk's not worth a straw, and Ferrers isn't much better. If your father agrees we can send an officer-at-arms to Lancaster at once, offer a truce while talks are held. Let's not waste men's lives.'

'The King himself could be here within days,' she pointed out.

'He could be, but it isn't very likely. Has the Duke had word from him? No, and nor have I. I can't think that he's any nearer than the furthest edge of Wales, that is if he's not still in Ireland. Bolingbroke will be here first.'

'So you would have me urge my father to surrender? To betray the trust the King has placed in him?'

'I spoke of negotiation—talk. Between uncle and nephew. Rather than a useless shedding of blood.'

'Is it not the same thing?'

'If you insist upon the word, my lady. For my part, I see no need to describe it in such terms. The Duke may reasonably act as mediator between his nephews, and bring all to a peaceful conclusion, to the benefit of the whole realm. That will be to his honour. To fight would be a futile gesture, when there's no possibility of victory. Surely you see that?'

She did not answer, but simply looked out across the gardens to the west, where the sun was now low in the sky, barely above the trees. It was not possible to see the Severn, because of the woodlands, but it was there. And somewhere beyond that wide river were the hills of Wales, and Richard's army, marching towards them. Thousands of men, but too distant to be of any immediate assistance. Perhaps still in the far west. What would Thomas want her to do in the circumstances? She could picture his face very easily, but not what was in his mind.

'I shall leave you to consider the matter,' Berkeley said, rising. 'Elizabeth will attend you, if you so wish.'

Constance did not require anyone's presence, but it seemed discourteous to say so. She wrestled with her conscience for what seemed an age. It was true that she and Thomas had felt some sympathy for Bolingbroke when he had been banished, and that they had felt still more when he had been deprived of his lands. They had spoken of it, and agreed that it was a great injustice, one, they suspected, that Edward had engineered for his own profit. Certainly the King had been badly advised. Yet that did not, could not, justify Bolingbroke landing in England and leading an armed revolt. Even if his intentions were as modest as those set out in his letter to Berkeley, he was still a rebel against his anointed Sovereign. Indeed it could be argued that this fresh treason had vindicated the King's suspicions of him.

She remembered what the Bishop had said at Hanley. Richard, for all his faults, ruled because God had willed it so. A subject who made war upon him, no matter on what grounds, was no better than a heretic, an enemy of God and the natural order. That was what she herself had been brought up to believe.

'My husband is with the Duke of Lancaster,' Elizabeth said, breaking the silence.

Constance gave her a brief, searching glance. 'I never doubted that he would be.'

'My father is right, my lady. If this quarrel could be settled peacefully, it would be to the profit of us all.'

Constance shook her head. 'It would, if it were possible, but it's not. I know my cousins, you see. Richard will never forgive this rebellion, or anyone who has taken part in it, until the day he dies. Harry Bolingbroke must realise that, and it follows that he dare not trust the King. Neither can feel safe now until the other one is dead. Oh, we may avoid bloodshed tomorrow, or the next day, but let's not be fools enough to think that that will give us peace. The war, I'm afraid, is only just beginning.'

***

Constance was woken by the sound of hammering. She had slept far more deeply than she had expected, and it took her several moments to recall where she was, to understand what she was doing at Berkeley Castle, sharing a bed with Sybil Despenser and a still-snoring Duchess of Aumale. Then the recollection flooded over her, and she slid her feet onto the floor, narrowly missing Agnes' head and momentarily trapping Paris's thin tail. The dog growled his brief protest, and promptly went back to sleep.

She retrieved her chamber robe, picked her way through the rest of the sleeping women and girls, and threw open the shutters. It was already full light, and the men in the park had found a new occupation. They were cutting down small trees, and branches from larger ones, and from this timber they were fashioning stakes about six or eight feet in length. These were sharpened at both ends, and then driven into the ground at an angle of about forty-five degrees. It was a defence against cavalry, behind which archers could bend their bows in relative safety.

Bishop Despenser was riding from one group to another, obviously giving orders, and trying to encourage the men. To some extent this was working, but the line of stakes was far from complete, and only a minority seemed to be assisting in the task, mostly those who wore the Bishop's own livery colours.

Suddenly Philippa appeared at her side. 'Jesu, but I'm hungry!' the Duchess informed her. 'Has anyone thought to bring us something to eat?' She glanced out of the window, taking in the scene. 'It looks like there's going to be a battle,' she commented. 'Ah, well, we shall have a good view from here.'

Constance glared at her. 'Does it not trouble you, what may befall in such a battle?'

'Why, whatever happens, no one will touch us. We're under Berkeley's protection.'

'And my father? Do you not care what befalls him?'

Philippa shrugged. 'Of course I care. But what can I do about it? It's the way of men to fight. I wish you'd met my first husband, Fitzwalter. He talked of nothing else but how many Frenchmen he killed or forced to yield. Why, he *enjoyed* fighting. Men do, mostly. It's one of the things that makes 'em men. I don't suppose the Duke's any different to the common run of them. He's always talking about the fighting he used to do in France and Spain when he was younger. I dare say he's looking forward to showing them all what he can still do.'

'Splendour of God, Philippa, he can barely walk! It'll be more like a massacre than a battle. The men of my household are out there, nearly all of them. I say "men," though half of them are more or less boys. Do you think I want them killed? Those most skilled in arms are with Thomas, not here.'

'The Bishop says that God is on our side. That we shall prevail.'

'I can't believe that and my father and his advisers don't believe it either, or they'd have stood and given battle long before this, and saved themselves the labour of days of marching. They've halted because they can't drag themselves any further, not because they wish to fight.'

Constance began dressing herself as quickly as she could, indeed with a speed that Thomas Despenser would have thought quite impossible of achievement. She had gone to sleep confused and uncertain, but now she knew exactly what she had to do. She had to speak to the Duke of York.

There was a certain bustle around the entrance of the Duke's chamber, men standing around in small groups, talking quietly and looking serious. Her cousin, John Beaufort, was among them, and she approached him and asked whether her father was yet awake.

'He still sleeps, Cousin,' Beaufort said. His heavy hooded eyes reminded her of King Richard, but his nose was unusual for a Plantagenet, unduly stubby and turned up at the end. He gazed at her with a certain bewilderment, as if he had never seen her walking about with nothing on her head but a plain linen coif. 'They dosed him well you know, Berkeley's people. Probably a good thing. They need looking after, these old men, don't they?'

Constance did not think of her father as old; he was still in his fifties. However, it was no time to debate the issue.

'Then, as next in rank, you take command, do you not, Cousin?' she asked.

'I don't know about that.'

'Of course you do. You're the King's cousin, and a marquis. Who else is in command if you're not? You've fought in battles, haven't you, Cousin?'

'Yes. But against heathens. Not against Englishmen. Not against my own brother. There's a world of difference.'

'I was hoping that you were going to order us all to continue the retreat towards Bristol. Everyone's rested now. Rested and fed, thanks to Lord Berkeley. My father can go in a litter if he must. Please, John, while there's still time.'

'I can't,' he said bluntly.

'Why not?'

'Because no one will go another step. We're all exhausted, not just your father, and stragglers are lying at the side of the road all the way back to Gloucester. At least here we're in some kind of battle order, not spread out in a column.'

'You mean to fight your brother? Here?'

'I don't mean to fight him at all unless I'm forced to it. Our best hope is that he won't pursue us; that he'll go off into Wales to confront the King. I don't think he will. *I* wouldn't. But we all have to have something to pray for, and I've been lighting candles in the chapel that Harry will go to Monmouth next, and Brecon. It's what he's done so far. Taken possession of the main Lancastrian lands. First the ones in Yorkshire, then Kenilworth and the other estates in the Midlands, and now, if we're very lucky, he'll remember what lies beyond the Severn.'

'Berkeley thinks that we should send a herald to your brother, and try to negotiate.'

'He does, does he? We'll, it's sound enough advice. The truth is that there's scarcely a man in this whole company who's willing to do so much as loose a single arrow at Harry. He's come for his own, and it's hard to blame him. What's more, we're in no condition to resist him even if we wanted to.'

'So you agree with Berkeley?'

He chewed his knuckle for a moment. 'I don't think there's an alternative, is there? Not if Harry decides to come this way, as I'm more or less sure he will. At a guess he'll have at least four or five times our numbers by now. We can't hope to defeat him, and we can't even run away. What is there to do but talk?'

Before she could answer, Berkeley's physician bustled into the antechamber. He was a tall and painfully thin Dominican friar, who brought with him an air of importance and a small boy to carry his box of potions and implements.

'I am here to attend my patient,' he informed the world in general. 'Pray have me announced.'

One of the squires passed through the curtain into the inner chamber, and the friar promptly went in after him, pausing on the threshold only to raise his hand in blessing.

'*Pax Vobiscum!*' he intoned with due gravity.

His boy followed him closely, and after a moment of hesitation, John Beaufort and Constance followed the boy.

The Duke's room was very dark, almost as if light had been deliberately excluded as part of his cure. Such light as there was came from the three or four candles that were burning. It was also uncomfortably close, filled with the earthy stinks of humanity and of illness. The friar, Constance noted, did not help in this respect. He was evidently one of those religious persons who believed that too much cleanliness was a surrender to evil.

York, having been shaken awake, wanted to know where he was.

'Your Grace is in Berkeley Castle,' said the friar, assuming an air of authority. 'Your humours are quite out of balance, and must be duly restored.'

His young assistant, in response to a snap of his fingers, poured a dark liquid from a phial into a small, earthenware cup. The friar took the cup, and placed it to the Duke's lips.

'Phew!' snorted the Duke, striking the man's hand away. 'What are you about, fellow? Trying to poison us? It stinks like a rotting corpse.'

'It is necessary medicine,' objected the friar, advancing the cup again.

'Nonsense!' said York, putting his feet to the floor. 'Think you that I have time to loll in bed in the middle of a campaign? Get from my sight, you damnable quack salver! Give me my shirt!'

'Father, you are recovered?' asked Constance, greatly surprised.

York rubbed his head against his hands. 'Of course I'm recovered! All I needed was a sleep. Open the shutters! Let some air into this stinking pit!'

'I can take no responsibility,' said the friar, with awesome solemnity.

'No one is asking you to take any, fellow. Constance, why are you here? I need to dress, and arm, and I'm not accustomed to doing so in a room full of women.'

'With such an obvious superfluity of the choleric humour he is certain to collapse within minutes,' said the friar. 'It wouldn't surprise me if his heart burst. There's an urgent need for him to be bled, and certainly he must not get out of bed.'

'Get out before I have you carried out!' York snapped. 'Bleed me, would you? By Our Lady's precious soul, I'll bleed you first, and in a way you'll not like! Have me as weak as a newborn kitten would you? That's close to treason, as matters stand. Nephew, arrest this rogue and put him in chains. Any blood I shed will be lost in battle.'

Beaufort seemed uncertain what to do. 'Most honoured Uncle,' he said, 'we all feared for your life. This physician cared for you when you were insensible. I'm sure he means you well.'

'My lord Father,' said Constance, drawing closer, 'the friar may be wrong. You may not need to stay in your bed, or to lose blood. But you've been ill, and you must take care not to make matters worse.'

He turned to glare at her. 'You want me to lie here and let you spoon pap into my mouth, I suppose?'

'I think we should go on to Bristol, as you planned. Provided that Your Grace is pleased to allow himself to be carried in a litter; for your strength must be conserved, Father.'

York snorted his disgust. 'Litters are for women and cripples. I am neither.'

He gestured for the shirt that one of his squires was holding out for him, and pulled it over his head. Then he put his foot to the floor, tried to rise, staggered, and fell back. Stubborn determination kept him sitting upright on the edge of the bed.

'Lord Berkeley thinks that you should send a herald to my cousin of Lancaster,' said Constance. 'If you can't go on to Bristol, then it seems to me that there's little choice.'

York glared at her. 'When I require your counsel, Daughter, I will surely ask for it. Nephew, show your cousin out of here. Kick that fool of a friar through the door while you're about it. We're not beaten yet.'

He grimaced with pain and determination, and raised himself to his feet.

***

By early afternoon, Bolingbroke's advanced scouts were to be seen, almost within arrow shot. The defensive line of stakes had progressed somewhat, but only a minority of York's men appeared to be making preparations for the battle. Most still lay about indolently under the trees, stirring for a few minutes if someone in authority bothered to shout at them, but rapidly returning to their idleness.

The small group around the Bishop of Norwich looked the most enthusiastic for battle. The Bishop himself was mounted and armed, and clutching his war hammer, while his friend from Norfolk, Sir William Elmham, had taken up a lance. Their retainers, apart from a couple of mounted gentlemen, were mostly spearmen. These soldiers were lined up in orderly ranks, under the Bishop's banner, awaiting only the order to advance. Such archers as he had were stringing their bows, ready for action.

Constance's high vantage point enabled her to see the rebels approaching from a long way off. They were marching in what seemed to be an endless column, a black, glinting mass of men and horses with numerous rigid banners and standards above them, still too far away to be recognised. Relatively small groups of lightly armed horsemen advanced on either side of the main body, protecting its flanks.

'There must be a hundred thousand of them,' gasped Philippa, her calculation based on her inability to think of a larger number. Her eyes had grown large with horror as she realised the true enormity of their situation for the first time.

'There are certainly a lot more of them than there are of us,' Constance said, trying to keep calm for the sake of the others.

'I can't understand why our men aren't inside the castle, instead of out there.'

'Because Berkeley won't allow it, that's why,' Constance answered impatiently. 'He told me himself that he won't lift a hand against Bolingbroke.'

A solitary rider emerged from the great mass in the distance, hurrying his horse forward at such a speed that within a very few minutes he was recognisable as a herald. He paused, about a hundred yards from the defensive line, raised his clarion to his lips, and blew the notes that signified a request for a parley. Then he advanced, obviously confident in his immunity. Behind him Bolingbroke's army began an unhurried deployment into divisions, the lead group forming up to the left of the road, a great host that clearly outnumbered the whole of York's army. Northumberland's banner was the principal among many.

Constance called Agnes to her, and they went down together to the great hall, arriving just as Bolingbroke's herald emerged from the screens that concealed the main entrance. York, John Beaufort, Suffolk and Ferrers stood on the dais, all fully armed, and with them Lord Berkeley in his rich but rather old-fashioned civilian clothing.

'What have you to say, my man?' York demanded of the herald. His abruptness reflected the pain etched across his face, and when he caught sight of his daughter his expression was enough to freeze her in her tracks, and persuade her to settle silently on the nearest window-seat.

'My master, the Duke of Lancaster, sends Your Grace the most humble of greetings,' the herald replied, bowing elaborately. 'I am to request that you will allow my master the honour of a personal hearing, that he may explain the reason for his presence here in arms. He wishes me to stress that he intends no harm to you or yours. Indeed, his only quarrel is with those who have acted contrary to the common profit of the realm.'

'Your master must be well aware,' York said, 'that I am the King's officer, and can by no means enter into negotiations with rebels. If he comes alone, and unarmed, and submits himself to the King's mercy, *then* I may receive him, but not otherwise.'

'The Duke of Lancaster is in such danger from the malicious counsellors around the person of the King's Grace that he has no choice but to take up arms, with the assistance of his friends, to ensure his own security. There is no other way for him to approach the King with a petition of his grievances.' The herald paused for effect. 'Your Grace's position may be correct, but it is unrealistic. It is also untenable.'

'I take it then,' York said, 'that I am one of those whose malice your master fears.'

The herald bowed again. 'I have obviously failed to make myself clear to Your Grace. The Duke does not regard you as his enemy, but as his most honoured uncle. He is most anxious to avoid any possibility of misunderstanding.'

'Let us at least hear what my brother has to offer,' said John Beaufort. 'We have no right to ask men to die, unless there is no alternative.'

'The church would be an appropriate meeting place,' Berkeley suggested quickly. He meant the one that stood just outside the castle gate. 'Permit me to go with the herald, and I shall make all the necessary arrangements.'

'No!' York said. He hammered his armoured fist on Berkeley's table. 'No! I shall fight. I have no choice. The King has placed his trust in me, and I cannot fail him.'

'I beg Your Grace to reconsider,' said the herald, unabashed. 'No harm is intended to the King, nor to anyone here. In the circumstances, there's little justification for useless bloodshed. As the Marquis of Dorset has said, it is surely reasonable to parley with my master and consider whether there is any way by which battle may be avoided. Nothing will be lost to you except a little time.'

'In God's name!' Ferrers burst out impatiently. 'What harm is there in talking? We're in no condition to fight.'

Constance knew her father well enough to be aware that he was standing on his pride. His bodily weakness and the hopelessness of his military situation made it all the more difficult for him to compound with his conscience. There was no one in the room less anxious than he to fight Bolingbroke, but his self-respect did not allow him to admit the fact.

She rose from her place and moved forward, still uncertain of what to say, allowing instinct to rule her. She knelt before her father, as if for his blessing.

'Sir, as you love me, and as you love your grandchildren, I beg that you do not fight without first hearing what it is that my cousin has to say to you.'

York's expression was furious, but she held his eyes and saw it crumble, become first confused and then controlled.

'You see how we are burdened with women and children,' he said to the herald. 'If we were not, I'd not contemplate a parley with a rebel, not for an instant. Berkeley, go with him, tell my nephew I shall meet him in the church. A truce for the time being, to be observed by both sides.' He turned back to Constance. 'Get to your feet, girl! Go to the chapel if you feel the urge to kneel, and keep that silly bitch, your brother's wife, out of my sight. There are matters to discuss which do not concern you.'

***

The Bishop of Norwich broke the truce. He and the closest of his followers suddenly charged into the Lancastrian line, shouting their defiance. The fighting did not last long, and had an air of unreality about it. The Bishop and his men seemed somehow to be absorbed by the superior numbers that closed around them, and within minutes it was almost as if nothing had happened.

Constance watched in horror as the Bishop's banner vanished from view. She had no doubt that Henry Despenser was dead, and all his men with him. He had followed his conscience to the end, and she had not.

'Blessed Mother of God, help us all,' said Philippa. Her voice was barely audible, little more than a whisper. After such a provocation, the massacre of the rest of York's army would surely follow. Anything could happen after that. Who could possibly control such numbers as Bolingbroke had with him? Berkeley certainly could not.

They were still in the chamber in which they had spent the night, with its excellent view of the approaches to the castle. Sybil Despenser sat silent, a little apart from the others. She had seen her husband's banner, very close to that of Bolingbroke himself. He had obviously changed sides, and the fact made her uncomfortable in her present company, especially after what they had just witnessed. Henry Despenser was Hugh's uncle as much as he was Thomas's, and she had always been fond of him. It was useless, at the moment, to make that point. She did not dare to look at Constance, let alone speak to her.

Surprisingly, there was no counterattack. After a while Constance saw a group of men riding forward under a forest of banners, and recognised Bolingbroke at the front, on his way to the church to meet her father. He had Northumberland with him, his brother-in-law, Ralph Neville, the Earl of Westmorland, and Archbishop Arundel. Richard Beauchamp was there as well, riding with his wife's father, Berkeley.

They rode close to York's men. So close, in fact, that one flight of arrows would probably have accounted for them all. But no arrows materialised. Instead the soldiers took off their hats and helmets, raised their weapons in salute, and cheered with the joy of men who were reprieved from the very teeth of death.

There was a long wait after that. The armies settled down as though they were all part of one large force, men mingling together inextricably and with no hint of hostility. The defensive stakes were already being cast down as redundant obstructions to friendship.

Eventually the door opened, and Bolingbroke himself stood there, his hat in his hand. His presence inside the castle made it clear that a settlement had been reached. His only companion was Sir Thomas Erpingham, a barrel-shaped Norfolk knight high in his favour. Erpingham's face bore an ugly scar on the right cheek, a souvenir from one of Bolingbroke's crusades.

Harry made them a deep bow. 'My ladies,' he said, 'I am truly sorry for the inconvenience you have suffered. Had I been aware of your presence, I would have sent to my uncle before this, offering you safe conduct. However, there is no cause for you to be in the least concerned. My uncle and I have spoken together, and are in perfect accord.'

Philippa stood up, and smiled at him. 'Dear Cousin,' she simpered, 'you are most welcome. Though my husband has done all in his power to have you restored to your rightful place, we did not hope to see you in England so soon. Now that you are, I'm sure that all will be well, and no man will be a better friend to you than my dear Aumale.'

Harry inclined his head, but did not answer. Instead he advanced towards Constance until he could see her face more clearly. 'Cousin,' he went on, 'I am given to understand that I owe you a great debt of gratitude. Berkeley tells me that it was by reason of your pleading that my uncle agreed to meet me in parley. You have saved many lives, and helped me achieve a peaceful agreement with your father. I thank you for it.'

Constance was still sitting on the cushioned window-seat. 'I don't seek your gratitude,' she answered ungraciously, 'for it was not done for your sake. I ask only one thing of you, and that reluctantly.'

Harry's expression hardened. 'Name it, Cousin. I shall deny you nothing that is reasonable.'

'Then I require of you the Bishop of Norwich's body, for honourable burial. I shall take him to the monks at Tewkesbury.'

She was bewildered and angered by the toothy grin that spread over Erpingham's damaged face.

'That you will not!' Bolingbroke paused, allowing himself a dry laugh. 'The Bishop is alive. He and his friend, Elmham, are prisoners, but no harm will come to them. They'll be released as soon as their tempers are cooled. They lost some of their men, but it was through their own folly. I'd no wish for any bloodshed.'

'You have a strange way of expressing your wishes,' Constance said chillingly. 'You think to avoid bloodshed by taking up arms against your King? By leading his subjects in rebellion and treason?'

'Those are hard words, Cousin. Unwarranted words. I'm here for what is my own, the Lancaster inheritance, which was taken from me against all law and reason. That's all I seek, that and the Bohun lands that came to me from my wife. If it's treason and rebellion to claim my own rightful property, then I say it's justified, and it seems that most of England agrees with me. Including your father!'

'Constance, what is wrong with you?' Philippa demanded. 'You heard what Harry said. Your uncle is safe, and no one of any importance has come to harm. Is that not more than we dared to hope for this morning? Harry's cause *is* just; everyone says it is. Now your father and Ned will intercede with the King, and all will be well. It doesn't help to make more of this than it is, a family quarrel, a misunderstanding that can be put to rights.'

Bolingbroke nodded his agreement. 'Exactly so,' he said briskly. 'A misunderstanding, nothing more. Richard and I need only meet, and we shall come to terms, and be perfect friends again.'

'I'm sure you will,' said Philippa.

'Lord Berkeley has ordered a great feast,' said Harry, 'to celebrate the peaceful accord that has been achieved today. I trust that all you ladies will condescend to honour it with your presence. You, my dear cousins, will sit on either side of me, in the places of greatest honour.'

'We shall,' said Philippa, her eyes gleaming. 'You must tell us of France, Cousin, and of all your doings since you landed in Yorkshire. I want to hear all your adventures.'

Constance was silent for a moment. She had not moved from her seat, and now she looked out of the window, to where a corpse in Henry Despenser's livery was being dragged across the grass towards the church.

'I do not sit at table with rebels and traitors,' she said abruptly.

18

Bolingbroke's army had reached Bristol. Heralds rode up to the closed gates to announce his peremptory terms, in his own name and that of the Duke of York. All those who came out of the city and surrendered would be spared; those who remained within the walls would lose their heads.

It was the purest bluff. Despite Harry's numbers, now further swelled by the addition of almost the whole of York's army, he had neither siege engines nor cannon, and the city's massive defences were strong enough to deter thoughts of taking the place by storm. Only starvation might work, and that would take time, time Bolingbroke did not possess.

Constance and Philippa sat their horses on a small knoll, only a few paces from where the leaders stood underneath their mass of colourful banners and standards, and just out of bowshot of the city's defenders.

'Look,' said the Duchess of Aumale, pointing with one heavily bejewelled hand and stifling a laugh with the other. 'People are climbing over the walls! Oh, how droll! See that great fat fellow! What a hole he'll make when he lands!'

Constance saw little cause for amusement. Citizens were escaping, some by simply lowering themselves as far as they could and then dropping, at the risk of broken bones, others scrambling down ropes, ladders and knotted sheets. There were whole families with children, richly-clad merchants in the liveries of their guilds, beggars in rags, priests, even nuns. Soon the walls were virtually invisible beneath the dark swarm of frightened humanity, until, with such guards as there were no longer able to hold back the crowd, the gates swung open, and the full flood of people burst out, stumbling and crushing in haste. As the pressure eased a little, the Mayor and Aldermen emerged in a relatively dignified procession, bearing a token set of keys. Bristol had yielded.

'None of these good people are to be harmed,' shouted Harry, 'for they are not our enemies, but friends. Fellow victims of the King's tyranny and extortion. I forbid any man, of whatever degree, to do them hurt, or touch their property. Everything we take, including our food and drink, is to be paid for in good coin. He that disobeys me in this shall hang.'

When the cheering had died down, he addressed Northumberland, a little more quietly. 'My lord, lead some of your men into the city, if you please, and demand the surrender of the castle. From what my uncle tells me, there are likely to be traitors within. Secure as prisoners those who have given the King false counsel. The lesser men may go where they will in peace, provided they don't resist us.'

The castle opened its gates almost before the heralds had time to blow their clarions in summons. After some short time Northumberland returned, his retinue leading four men at the end of ropes. Since the escort was mounted, and inclined to haste, the prisoners' progress was untidy, a mixture of running, slipping, and being dragged. The surrounding crowd, Bristol citizens and Bolingbroke's followers inextricably compounded together, closed in around the unfortunate men, spitting and cursing their contempt.

Constance guessed who the victims would be long before she could discern their faces. There was William le Scrope, Earl of Wiltshire, John Bushey, Henry Green and John Russell, his injured arm still in a sling. Dragged before Bolingbroke they stood, ashen with shock and bewilderment, until forced to their knees by kicks and prods. Russell made a strange whimpering sound, and then rolled on his back, his legs lashing in the air like those of a playful, submissive dog. Then he began to scream and roar with terror, regardless of the blows that Northumberland's men struck him with their bowstaves.

Harry glared at them through narrowed eyes. 'Your false counsel has divided the King from his natural advisers,' he said, 'and brought about dissension in the realm. You have burdened the people of England with unjust taxes, and urged the King to reduce his subjects to slavery. Tomorrow you shall face trial for high treason.'

Constance scarcely knew Bushey, except by his reputation as a clever lawyer, but Wiltshire was on the fringe of Thomas's circle of friends, and had been entertained under their roof. He was certainly no saint, but it was hard to see what he had done to deserve the axe. Henry Green's son, Ralph, was married to her former damosel, Katherine Mallory, and she was godmother to their daughter. Then there was John Russell...

She nudged her horse forward, until she was next to her father. 'Will you try a madman for his life?' she demanded loudly, indicating Russell. 'Can you not see that he's out of his wits?'

'He's just a bloody coward,' snorted Northumberland. 'No more mad than I am.'

Bolingbroke watched for a moment as Russell continued to roll around on the grass, howling, weeping and pleading incoherently for mercy. 'Either way, he's not worth killing,' he said decisively. 'My cousin has asked for his life, and I grant the petition. As for the others, tomorrow they shall answer to the Constable's court, in accordance with martial law. You, my lord of Northumberland, shall act as Constable. My brother of Westmorland shall act as Marshal.'

'It'll be a damned brief trial,' Northumberland snorted.

'A trial, nevertheless. Our first business of the morning.'

'A waste of time. You should head them here and now, if you ask me.'

'I don't.' Bolingbroke was short with him. 'Let justice be done, not murder. See to it, my lord.'

***

The block had already been set up, and was visible through the open window. The outcome of the trial was by no means in doubt.

Constance, looking out over the place of execution, spared a moment to say a silent prayer for the three men facing death, and for John Russell, driven to insanity and chained in a dungeon somewhere below her feet. It was certain that Richard would never forget this day's work. He would demand blood for blood.

She turned towards her father. They were quite alone in the innermost of the three substantial rooms the Duke had been allocated in Bristol Castle. His bed stood at the far end, away from the window, and he rested his weight in a heavy wooden chair close to the fireplace. His favourite set of hangings was deployed on the wall. Behind him, a faded and moth-eaten Greek army threw themselves into a frozen attack on the walls of Troy.

'I fear for you, sir,' she said, advancing towards him. 'How will you justify yourself to the King?'

'I don't know,' said York quietly.

'Can you not stop this trial? It's surely unlawful.'

He spread his hands, and shrugged. 'Let it be, Daughter.'

'You can at least make a protest.'

'To what end? Anyway, better that those rogues should die than their betters.'

'He dares to accuse them of treason, when he himself is the foulest traitor ever known in England.'

'Constance,' York said fiercely, forcing himself to sit upright, 'these are not words you should use of your cousin. You've already called him as much to his face, so I understand. Never let me hear you say the like again. Do you belong in Bedlam with your friend Russell?

She snorted. 'Perhaps Your Grace would prefer me to be more like my sister, Philippa. Fawning, simpering, dissembling, all but inviting Bolingbroke to bed!'

'I'd prefer you to remember that you are the granddaughter of two kings, and bear yourself with the dignity that befits a great lady, instead of opening your mind to the whole world, like a drunken slut in a market gutter.' He leaned forward, his hands gripping painfully on the arms of his chair. 'Do you imagine that I take pleasure in this state of affairs? My brothers' sons, tearing the country apart between them? How shall it profit me to call one a traitor and the other a tyrant? The only small hope I have is that somehow I can find peaceful means to reconcile them. You don't help me in my task by making your hatred so plain. Harry spared Russell's life at your request. You might at least have thanked him for that.'

'Thanked him? For sparing one innocent man while murdering another three, and implicating you in their deaths?'

'You may yet have to sue to him to spare your husband, and your brother. Have you thought of that?'

She looked at him down her nose. 'I may equally have to sue to King Richard for your life. Have you thought of that? As I said, I fear for you. The King still has a great army, a *loyal* army, and is likely to prevail in the end.'

'You yourself begged me to come to terms with Harry.'

'Only because there was no other choice. I didn't expect you to be so accommodating. To lend your authority to his enterprise. Now you're as good as committed to his cause.'

'I think you have said quite enough,' the Duke rapped. He struggled to his feet. 'You criticise my actions? How dare you? I'm not only your father, but also still the King's deputy in his absence. Amend your manner, and quickly, or I'll amend it for you. Splendour of God! What has your husband been about all these years? Do you speak to him so? I warrant you do, and that he's fool enough to suffer it. Well, I am not.'

She met his eyes without flinching. 'Perhaps it would be better, my lord Father, if you were to send me and the children back to Hanley Castle. I should not have left it in the first place.'

'You, and Edward's wife, are going to Fotheringhay. You will stay there with my Duchess until the land is restored to peace.'

'But—'

He raised his hand to interrupt before she could say more. 'It is not a matter for debate. The decision is made. Your cousin and I are in agreement that it is the best place for you.'

'It seems that I am a prisoner, then.'

'Of course you are not a prisoner!' York snapped impatiently. He stalked around, rubbing his knee to ease a momentary new ache.

'I am prevented from going peacefully with my children to our rightful home. What is Your Grace pleased to call it if not imprisonment?' Constance began to pace after him, and then halted abruptly as she became aware that one of her garters had worked loose, and was already beginning to descend her leg. For the moment it rested precariously on her knee-cap.

'Protection, girl! Have you no sense at all?'

'Protection from whom? Are you implying, my lord, that Bolingbroke cannot control this rabble he has gathered about him? That I, his own cousin, *your* daughter, am not safe on the roads, or under my own roof? I find that astonishing. God help England if that is to be the way of it. If I am not secure from harm, then what of my people? How much greater must their danger be!'

York grimaced. Standing or sitting, he could find no escape from the agony in his legs, neck and back. 'At Hanley Castle you'd as like as not find yourself caught between the two armies. Would Despenser wish that, for you or his children? I'm sure he would not, and I will not allow it.' He eased himself back into his chair. 'I've worries enough without fearing for you and your little ones. I want you where you are safe.'

Outside there was a sickening thud as the axe cut through the first neck, and embedded itself in the wooden block. A ragged cheer rose from the watching crowd. York and his daughter crossed themselves in unison.

'May God have mercy on us all,' the Duke said softly, his face etched with lines of pain.

Constance's garter had completed its descent to the floor. She took a pronounced side step, so that it emerged from beneath her skirts, and made her father a deep curtsey, recovering the accessory as she did so with a subtle sweep of her right hand.

'I had better make ready for my journey, Father,' she said, frowning slightly with concentration as she tried to remember which of her attendants had been responsible for her careless dressing. She found it impossible to recall.

'Yes,' York nodded, somewhat absently. 'Go with my blessing, child. Nothing is as it should be, but we must make the best of it.'

***

The King's army was camped outside the town of Carmarthen, and the banner of the lions and lilies hung over the castle, where Richard himself was lodged. It stood out clearly at a distance, even through the mist of morning drizzle.

Thomas Despenser was not relishing the prospect of his interview with the King. Sent into Glamorgan to secure reinforcements, the plain truth was that he was returning with fewer men than he had led away from Haverfordwest only a few days before.

'It doesn't look as if anyone has any intent of moving,' John Norreys observed quietly. 'This late in the day, I thought we might have met them advancing along the road, not stuck in camp.'

'I can only think that he's waiting for us,' Thomas said, 'and that's folly. Enough time has been thrown away already, by God! We must move swiftly now, as Bolingbroke surely will. Not loll around as though we were on a pilgrimage, with all day to walk to the next alehouse. I'll advise the King to march straight to Brecon, and lay it waste. That'll be a good start, and encourage our men with plunder. That's what's needed. Something to lift their spirits and lend them courage.'

On his way in to see the King, Thomas met his brother-in-law.

'Where are the men you promised?' Edward asked, his face drawn. 'Tom, tell me that they are following, that you have ridden ahead.'

'I have those who rode in with me, no more,' Despenser said. 'Bolingbroke's tenants in Brecon and Ogmore have risen, and there's scarcely a man in Glamorgan who's willing to leave his door undefended with that threat on our border.'

He did not add that Sir William Stradling had more or less laughed at the suggestion that they might, or that John St. John had shut himself up in his little castle at Fonmon, and scarcely been willing to emerge to discuss the matter.

Edward shook his head in evident despair. 'You heard the news from Bristol?'

'What news?'

'A friar came seeking Richard with it. He came across the Severn Sea by boat. Cousin Harry has taken the city.'

'Impossible! It'd take him weeks to capture it, even if he's managed to march so far. Has this friar been properly questioned?'

'Yes. He's not one of the breed of holy men that's half mad. He told a plain tale, and I believe it's the truth.'

'Then your father and his army must have been defeated.'

'It's worse than that.'

'Worse? Are you saying that...' Thomas halted, reluctant to complete the sentence. York must be dead. That would explain the dazed expression on Aumale's face.

'He's joined Bolingbroke. He and the whole of the army he raised. He ordered Bristol to open its gates. What the hell are we going to do?'

'Your father has joined Bolingbroke?' Thomas felt as if the world had shifted beneath him. The Duke of York had always been an unwavering example of loyalty, a King's man to the backbone.

'Yes! How many times must I say it? I knew the old fool felt sorry for him, but I didn't think he'd go as far as this. Tom, we need to talk, you and I. To consider all the circumstances. I think—I begin to think Richard blames me for what my father has done.'

Despenser used the adjacent wall for support. His thoughts went to Constance, who loved the King and her father in roughly equal measure. How would he ever find the means to comfort her? Whatever happened now, she would suffer a great loss. If only he could be with her, at Hanley Castle. It was not so very far away. A swift horse, ridden hard, would get him there within a week. Four days might be enough. If only he had left her at Cardiff, instead of telling her to go back into England. If only, for once, she had disobeyed him. They could have had at least a few hours together. It was torture now to think of it.

The young Duke of Surrey emerged from the King's apartments. He was obviously flustered. 'Thomas!' he cried, 'thank God that you are here! We had begun to think—well, never mind what it was. My uncle the King is waiting for your report. Come through to him.'

There was no denying such an invitation. Thomas exchanged a last grim glance with Aumale and followed Surrey into Richard's presence.

The King was pacing around the room, his face grim. With him were his half brother, John Holland, his secretary Maudelyn, and Thomas Merke, the Bishop of Carlisle. These three stood around the fireplace, looking distinctly uncomfortable. The King's greyhound, Math, lay on his back on the bed, the only one of them careless of the atmosphere.

Despenser knelt and sought to give an account of himself, but Richard did not seem interested.

'A few more men from Glamorgan would have made little difference,' he shrugged. 'My Uncle York's betrayal means that there is no one I can trust outside this room. Well, perhaps one or two others, but that's all. I can't fight Harry Bolingbroke knowing that half my army could turn against me at any minute.'

'I see no option, Sire,' Thomas said bluntly.

John Holland spoke. 'You forget, we still have Salisbury, up in the North. He's recruiting the men of Chester. *They'll* fight, we can be sure of that.'

Because of a shortage of shipping at Dublin, Salisbury had been sent ahead to North Wales with a token force; the bulk of the army had marched across country to Waterford, and sailed from there, though by no means all were gathered at Carmarthen. Some had been driven by storms onto other shores, and others had simply caught the smell of home in their nostrils and deserted.

'Then we march to join Salisbury?' Thomas was happier with that, though he knew it would not be an easy task to take a demoralised army across the grain of Wales, with mountains and estuaries in the way, and no assured supplies.

'Some of us will go to Salisbury,' Richard said mysteriously. 'Not all. Not those I can't trust. Will Worcester fight his brother, Northumberland? Will Edward fight his own father? No, of course they will not!'

'You doubt Aumale? Your Grace, he and I have not always agreed with each other, but I can't believe that he'd fail you.'

'It was he who advised the King to send Salisbury ahead, to divide the army,' Surrey pointed out.

'With good reason. You know we lacked the ships we needed. We all agreed to the plan.'

'He's been exchanging letters with Bolingbroke,' John Holland grunted. 'Besides, think about what he was doing just before we embarked for Ireland. Where was he? In the North. Conspiring with Northumberland and Westmorland, no doubt. It all fits together, do you not see? That, and much more.'

'I wonder at Ralph Neville,' Richard mused, 'for I made him what he is, believed him my man to the death. How could I be so mistaken? Even Northumberland, though we have not always agreed, I never thought a traitor. And my uncle, above all. How could he, Thomas? How is it possible?'

'We believe there's a conspiracy to take the King prisoner,' the Bishop said sombrely. 'There have been rumours. Many rumours. The army is discontented.'

Despenser began to wonder whether they had become mad in his absence, or whether he had. At Haverfordwest the King had been full of plans for marching across Wales and meeting Bolingbroke in battle. The only question had been over the best route to take, whether to aim for Shrewsbury, Worcester or Gloucester.

There had been no hint of defeatism. Now Richard seemed to have lost all his fighting spirit, to be all but ready to give up the struggle.

'The men need their spirits lifting, that's all,' he said. He was reluctant to teach his king his business, but he made himself go on. 'Sire, you should speak to them. Explain the justice of your cause. Tell them that those who wish to leave us may do so, with your good will. The great majority are loyal and will fight for you, I'm certain of it, if you're but ready to lead them. Let's go on into Brecon, and devastate Bolingbroke's lands. Remove that threat from their backs and the men of Glamorgan will join you, as sure as I stand here.'

'This has all been discussed,' said Surrey.

'The risk is too great,' said John Holland. 'As the Bishop explained, this army around us can't be trusted. Aumale's men and Worcester's form too great a part of it, and our own are starting to desert.'

'The King has decided to go north,' added the Bishop.

'We have but awaited your return, my lord of Gloucester,' the unctuous Maudelyn confided.

'We go under cover of darkness,' said the King. 'Tell no one, Thomas. No one. Not even your own squires. I'll send for you when the time is right. Let them think we are eating a supper together. By this time tomorrow we'll be safely within the walls of Llanbadarn.'

***

Thomas Percy, Earl of Worcester, Steward of the King's Household, held his staff of office in his hands for the last time. Tears streaming from his eyes, he bent and twisted the ends towards one another until the white-painted wood snapped like a dry twig under a man's foot. He allowed the pieces to fall from his grip, down into hiding places in the thick grass at his feet, grass still wet with the morning dew.

He glanced around at the circle of men who had witnessed his resignation. Soldiers in various liveries, armigers and common spearmen; cooks and scullions; squires and yeomen of the King's own chamber. Some, like him, were weeping openly. The majority simply stared at him, their expressions a mixture of confusion and anger.

'Go to your homes,' he said sorrowfully. 'The Household is dissolved. The army is dismissed. There's nothing more to be done.'

He ignored the swelling protests—most of them were very far from home, and incompletely paid—and retired into the pavilion behind him.

Inside, Edward of York, Duke of Aumale, was sitting at a table, in the act of helping himself to a cup of wine. Unlike Worcester, he had not bothered to encase himself in his armour, was dressed simply in pourpoint and hose.

'I've told them all to go home,' Worcester announced, the tears still stream-ing down his face. 'In God's name, Ned, that it should end so! Is there some of that left for me?'

In silence, Aumale poured the older man a generous drink.

'It's a rare moment in history,' he grunted. 'Common men have been desert-ing armies since armies were first called into being, but I've never heard of a king doing it before. Well, Richard always did like to take people by surprise.'

'They're looting his baggage.'

'What do you expect?'

'He's left almost everything behind. Even his chapel furnishings...'

'More to the point, he's left *us* behind, without so much as a word. He must be moon-kissed. Clean out of his mind. Someone has persuaded him that we are traitors. I suppose it's something to do with our family connections.'

Worcester gave him a wry grin. 'I take it that he no longer regards you as his successor?'

Edward shook his head in despair. 'He's only one possible successor now, and it isn't me. Well, if he doubts us so much, let's give him cause for doubt. I dare say that my father and your brother will welcome us warmly enough. Cousin Harry certainly will. We've no choice anyway, unless you've a fancy for taking a ship to France.'

'We could still rally this army.'

'You think so?'

'They're running around like lost sheep. Most of them would follow you, would be glad to follow any man bold enough to ask them. You're as much the King's cousin as Bolingbroke.'

Edward shook his head. 'If you mean what I think, you're as mad as Richard. We can't fight Cousin Harry, not now. I'm not even going to try. I've suddenly become his dearest friend in the world.'

Two other men came thrusting through the flap of the tent. Lord Lovel, and Sir John Stanley, the Controller of the Household.

'The men are fighting among themselves,' Lovel complained. His gnarled features revealed his shock and outrage. 'Someone must take charge. Aumale, you're Constable. It's your business.'

Aumale topped up his cup of wine. 'Worcester and I have just resigned our offices. We appear to lack the King's confidence, so we've retired into private life. Care for a drink, Lovel?'

'We're not safe ourselves,' Stanley pointed out. 'They could turn on us. Make prisoners of us, and sell us to the rebels. God help us all! My lord of Aumale, you are the only one here of the King's blood. They might listen to you.'

Edward shrugged. 'We've already told them to go home,' he said. 'I dare say they will, once they've plundered what there is to plunder, and got themselves blind drunk. For the present, they won't listen to me or to anyone else. Why should they? Like us, they've been betrayed.'

'Perhaps we should gather together such men as we can, and go after the King,' Lovel suggested.

Aumale gave him a look of pity. 'The King has already rejected our services, Lovel. Would you have us pursue him up and down the hills of Wales, like unwanted lovers chasing after an unwilling maid?' He shook his head. 'No. No one treats me so. Worcester and I are already agreed as to our purpose, and I hope that you'll both join with us. If King Richard has no use for us, we shall see whether King Henry is more accommodating.'

'King Henry?' Lovel repeated, bewildered.

'Do you think there can be any other outcome, after this? Men can be persuaded to fight for a tyrant. Even for a madman. Not, I think, for a coward.'

19

The Earl of Salisbury had done his best to gather together the King's supporters in Cheshire and North Wales, had even succeeded to a degree. But then a rumour had spread that Richard was dead, added to which was sure news that Bolingbroke was marching north with his huge army, approaching the borders of Richard's beloved Principality of Chester and threatening it with devastation. Salisbury's force had simply dissolved. Even the men he had brought from Ireland had gone, save for a handful of his most trusted retainers and household men.

Now, including the select group the King had brought with him from Carmarthen, there were less than thirty men in Conwy Castle. Food was in short supply, and, more to the point, there was no one present who was competent to cook it properly. They had to make do with bread and ale for the most part, and sleep on straw, or on the bare floor, rolled into blankets. The King lay on the same rug as his dog, Math.

Thomas Despenser was not much troubled by such minor hardships. He had suffered far worse in the Prussian marshes in his crusading days. Here at Conwy they at least had a roof over their heads, and the summer heat made the lack of fires an irrelevance. His concern was that the King refused to listen to reason.

Conwy was a formidable castle, built upon rock, and it defended a harbour. In that harbour there were ships, including several of a size more than adequate to convey the whole group of them back to Ireland. That was the obvious course of action, because Surrey's brother, Mun Holland, had been left at Dublin with sixteen hundred men and almost all the artillery. Even in his present straits, Richard had two dukes and two earls with him, as well as several knights and almost a convocation of bishops, not least among them Henry Beaufort, Bishop of Lincoln, Bolingbroke's half-brother. Their situation was desperate, but not beyond hope of recovery. Men who had started with far less in the way of resources had won crowns. All that was needed was decisive leadership.

Unfortunately that was just what Richard was unwilling or unable to provide. The King seemed stunned, as if he was still waking from some bizarre dream, constantly hesitated and prevaricated. The defection of York had hit him hard, undoubtedly, as had the consequential doubts about Edward's loyalty.

From the perpetual circle of discussion that was inevitable when an acknowledged leader declined to lead, a decision had eventually emerged, more or less by consensus. John Holland, Duke of Exeter, and his nephew Surrey had ridden off to Chester to confront Bolingbroke and ask what terms he would agree for a peaceful reconciliation. Richard had insisted only that remaining his supporters at Conwy should be indemnified, and with them, rather surprisingly, Edward of York.

Days had passed since then, and the two Hollands had not returned.

Thomas went up on to the wall walk to escape the King's alternating bouts of fury and despair. The view over the estuary was strikingly beautiful, with the sun glinting back from the broad sweep of water. Inland, the mountains of Snowdonia were clear of cloud for once, their towering peaks sharply defined. With a cooling breeze drifting in from the sea, it was near to idyllic, almost sufficient to make him forget the extent of his troubles.

'By now, Bolingbroke's host will be on its way here,' said a voice near his ear. It was Salisbury, his face distracted with worry.

'This isn't a castle he'll find easy to enter,' Despenser answered, without taking his eyes away from the vista they beheld.

'He'll starve us out in a week. Anyway, what shall we gain from being mewed up here, in the last place God made? We should take ship to France. I've friends there, Thomas, and I prefer to take my chances with them if the alternative is to fall into Bolingbroke's hands.'

'If you could persuade the King it would be well.'

'But I cannot, and nor can you; and we can't desert him.' He sighed in exasperation. 'I fear that Bolingbroke bears no more love for us than he had for Wiltshire, Bushey and Green. The King is safe, because he is the King. We can only say our prayers, and perhaps write our letters home.'

Thomas wondered whether Salisbury would recant his heresy before he died. 'We have bishops enough to confess us,' he said dryly.

The older man snorted his derision. 'God knows my sins; he knows how far I have regretted them. I don't fear death. Only the shame that may accompany it. The blessing of a lewd priest has no more virtue than the braying of an ass, and is of no more profit to a man's soul.'

'My belief is otherwise,' said Despenser bluntly.

'I know. May your belief comfort you, and may the Blessed Christ protect us both.'

Thomas did not answer. He could not imagine how Salisbury dared to detach himself from the universal Church, to be, in effect, his own Pope. It required an awesome leap of faith, a certainty in the self that he himself did not possess, and knew he could never acquire. His friend's argument made no sense to him. If a sinful priest had no authority, neither had a sinful knight, or a sinful king. All were sinners, except in heaven.

Something stirred in the shade of the trees beyond the broad river. Despenser doubted the evidence of his eyes for a moment, and then suspected that he had caught a fleeting glance of a deer, or perhaps even a wild boar. Then the whinny of a horse carried across the water, and a small party of men emerged from the woods and rode at a walk onto the shore. They were unarmed, and above their heads were carried the banner of the Earl of Northumberland, and a flag of truce.

***

In the great chamber of the castle, Northumberland presented Bolingbroke's terms. He stood erect, his steel-grey hair uncovered when he had removed his hood on entering Richard's presence. His rich blue houppelande was spangled with gold stars, and his neck was ornamented with a gold collar that bore his device of a blue lion rampant, worked in enamel and surrounded by rubies.

'The Duke of Lancaster,' he said, kneeling, 'wishes nothing more than to be Your Grace's loyal subject. He has but three requests. First, that the lands of his inheritance be restored to him.'

Richard was seated on the window embrasure, for there was no chair or other furnishing in the bare, stark room. He still wore the simple priest's robe that he had adopted as a disguise for his journey across Wales; almost all his finery had been left at Carmarthen in their haste. He detached his caressing hand from Math's head, and gestured impatiently. 'I freely agree to that.'

Northumberland nodded as he rose to his feet. 'I'm sure you do, Sire—now. Secondly, he requires the summoning of a Parliament, over which he shall preside in his capacity as Lord High Steward. Thirdly, the trial before that Parliament of the Duke of Exeter, the Duke of Surrey, the Earl of Salisbury, the Bishop of Carlisle, and Richard Maudelyn. For high treason.'

The King laughed bitterly. 'Treason? *You*, Northumberland, dare to accuse these—dare to accuse *any* man of treason?' He hurled his empty cup at the Earl. 'Get out! I decide who are the traitors in this land. I name you among them.'

Northumberland had not flinched as the cup flew past his ear. Now he made a deep bow. 'I am no traitor, Sire. I'm your dearest friend, and only wish that you'd recognise me as such.'

'Traitor! Liar! Pig! Get out!'

The Earl pursed his lips and withdrew in silence.

Richard was on his feet now, pacing about.

'Truly I swear to you,' he said to his companions, 'by St. John the Baptist I swear, whatever assurances I give him, he'll be put to a bitter death for this outrage he has done to us, he and Harry Bolingbroke his master. There'll be no Parliament at Westminster on this matter. I'll muster men from all over Wales. All I need is time. Just a little time.'

'Northumberland can't be trusted,' said Salisbury. 'Who knows if what he has delivered is all of Bolingbroke's intent? You must not put yourself in their power, Sire. Take ship to France.'

'To France? The French have betrayed me! Could Bolingbroke have prospered so well without their aid? I'll not go to France. I'll not give those traitors the satisfaction of seeing me run from them.'

Despenser sighed. This determination would have been admirable at Carmarthen, where Richard had possessed an army. Now it came too late, when the only sane option was to take to the ships.

'You sigh, Thomas?' asked the King. His voice was bitter. 'Why? You're not marked for trial. Not declared a traitor. Your family must have spoken for you. No doubt my Uncle York cherishes all his sons.'

Thomas flinched at the implied insult. 'Northumberland is a man of honour,' he said. 'No liar. The terms he brings are reasonable, bearing in mind that we're defenceless. Since Your Grace has already rejected the only possible alternative, there's no choice but to agree.'

'Man of honour? Northumberland?' Richard snorted. 'He's a stinking traitor! He and all those who have taken up arms against me. I am their King. God's anointed. Nothing they do or say can change that, and their resistance imperils their souls. I'll not rest until I've seen their heads on London Bridge.'

'For the present, it's necessary to be more subtle,' said the Bishop of Carlisle.

'Even to seem to submit,' added Henry Beaufort. His eyes, small, dark, and sunken in his plump face, glanced around them.

'Accept the terms, but first make Northumberland swear to them,' urged the Bishop of Carlisle.

Richard nodded vigorously. 'On the Host itself!' he cried, as if the solution to their problems lay in such an oath.

'Let him swear that my brother has no concealed intent,' Beaufort added.

'If he's forsworn, he'll condemn himself to hell. No man does that lightly, not even Northumberland. He *shall* swear, or we'll not make terms.'

So it was settled. A solemn mass was celebrated in the castle chapel. Misted in clouds of incense, the Earl placed his hand upon the pyx that contained the sacred Host, and before the King and all his company made a vow as solemn as that which Bolingbroke himself had taken at Doncaster. That the terms of settlement he had brought were honest; that no manner of deception was intended; that Richard would retain the crown. All this on the body of Christ.

Northumberland rode ahead of the King's company, to ensure, he said, that a meal would be waiting for them when they reached Rhuddlan Castle. Richard and his friends emerged from Conwy, crossed the estuary, and climbed the steep road that led eastward over the high ground, a narrow pathway through flowering gorse bushes. After a couple of hours the way grew so steep, as it passed over the headland of Penmaeurhos, that they were forced to dismount and lead the horses in single file, Richard at the head of the column.

They rested at the summit, and as they looked ahead their eyes detected the glint of the sun on armour, and on the tips of spears, saw the movement of banners and streamers. Northumberland had not gone on to Rhuddlan. He was waiting here for them, and his men were already pushing around the flanks of the headland to ensure that there could be no retreat to Conwy. The King and all those with him were his prisoners.

**

The new day was still considering its options in quietness. Fotheringhay Castle stood within the ring of its double moats, further protected by the broad defensive lake to the north, and the still River Nene to the south. Inside the castle its pale stone, grey in the uncertain light, was cold to the touch, cold enough to give the impression of dampness, chill as a forgotten tomb.

Constance was back in the lodging that had been hers before she had been handed over to Thomas. Just under the leads of the reconstructed keep, the great tower that was called the Fetterlock from its shape, the room was reached by many steps, remote from the chapel, the Duke's great chamber, the hall, or any other centre of activity. It also faced to the north and west, the colder and less desirable aspect.

It had been raining all night. The lake was black and lifeless and a thick, pernicious mist hung over the edges of Rockingham Forest so that, even from this high vantage point, it was impossible to see much beyond the village.

She had slept in late, after a disturbed night. She judged by the light that it was approaching seven of the clock, though the prevailing gloom made it hard to be sure. Her eyes still half closed, she allowed her women to fuss around her as they dressed her and prepared her for the day.

Mary Russell had started to weep again.

There had been a great deal of this, and Constance was growing impatient with it. She felt like weeping herself, and she suspected that Agnes Norreys, frantic for news of John, was in no better case. They could all collapse into tears, but it wouldn't solve anything.

'Dry your eyes, child!' she ordered sharply. 'I've told you. Your father's life is safe.'

'Only because you spoke for him, my lady,' Lady Clinton put in. 'No one in the world but you.'

Constance shook her head, disclaiming credit. Somehow she felt guilty for failing to save the other three from the murderer Bolingbroke. So she thought of him. *Rebel, traitor, murderer.* In view of her father's instructions, she tried very hard to keep this opinion to herself. She was not always successful in doing so.

A knock on the door preceded the entry of two of Joanne's gentlewomen. They curtsied, advanced to within six feet of Constance, and then curtsied again.

'My lady,' said the elder, 'Her Grace the Duchess of York asks whether you would care to attend her to mass? If so, we shall be honoured to escort you to her chamber. The Duchess particularly asked us to say that she would welcome your company.'

Life at Fotheringhay had always been more formal than it was at Hanley Castle, Caversham or Cardiff. Constance had rather forgotten this fact, but it seemed that Joanne was maintaining the traditions of the house, even in the face of crisis.

'I will very gladly wait upon the Duchess,' Constance said.

She was more or less ready. Once the final adjustments had been made, they formed up into a procession, Constance walking with the Duchess's gentlewomen on either side, a half pace behind her. Outside the door a group of the Duchess's officers were waiting to receive her. The steward of the household, Piers de Mohun, lent Constance his arm. In token of the solemnity of the ceremony he was wearing his sword and carrying his rod of office in his left hand.

She knew him well from the old days; indeed he seemed quite unchanged since her childhood. He was thin, ageless, and rather serious of manner. 'Is your cousin with the Duchess, Piers?' she asked him.

She referred to Philippa, who was Piers's cousin, though somewhat remotely.

'I believe that Her Grace of Aumale is ill, my lady. Too ill to leave her room, or indeed her bed.'

'Truly?'

'So we are given to understand. A messenger arrived for her, just before midnight. That might explain it.'

They descended the broad but spiralling staircase to the lower levels, passing the door of the room Philippa had been allocated. Constance had a brief thought of seeing for herself what manner of illness this might be, but quickly decided that etiquette required that the Duchess of York should not be kept waiting.

'This messenger came from my brother?' she asked.

Mohun shrugged. 'I think it probable he came from the Duke of Aumale, though he wore no livery.'

'He may have news of my lord, and of the King. I should like to question him.'

'I'm afraid that's not possible, my lady. He left the moment the gates were opened this morning.'

Constance gave him a glance that would have frozen a flame, but he did not allow it to disturb his composure, and she did not waste further words on him.

They paused at the entrance to the great chamber. Agnes relinquished Constance's train, which she had carried thus far, and carefully arranged it in the crook of her lady's arm, for only the highest ranking lady in any company was entitled to have her train carried by another woman. Due deference had to be shown to the Duchess of York.

Joanne was sitting on her bed, having not long finished her dressing. She had a flock of damosels and gentlewomen about her, but also an array of household men ready to form up into a procession to chapel, as well as two or three persons who ranked as guests, having taken shelter for the night. Even the addition of Constance's people was far from sufficient to fill the room, which she well recalled as the scene for far greater receptions.

Constance made a formal curtsey, and Joanne rose to receive her.

'My dearest daughter,' she said, with equal formality, 'I'm very glad to see you. Pray sit with me.'

They settled together on the edge of the bed, less than a foot between them. The others stood around, at a suitable distance.

'I've had a fearful night,' Joanne confided, 'full of horrid dreams. To think of my sweet brother Surrey, and your dear husband, as prisoners of that evil pig, Bolingbroke! I dread what the next news will be. I've tried to pray, but I can't. I never thought I'd hear myself say it, but I wish your father were here. Between us we could make him do something.'

'I'm sure my father is already doing what he can, Joanne.'

'I'm sure he isn't! He said all along that Bolingbroke should have his inheritance. He cares more for that traitorous dog than he does for my family or me. Or for you. How else is it that he allows his brother-in-law and his son-in-law to rot in dungeons, with the threat of the axe upon them? Tell me that!'

'I think we should wait for more certain news. It's dangerous to trust to idle rumours.'

'You must have ice in your veins, not blood,' Joanne said. Her desperate tone purged the words of insult. 'I am so frightened, Constance. I love my brother dearly; and I'm fond of Despenser as well, of course I am. I can't bear to think of them in such terrible danger. Or the King for that matter, my dear uncle. I feel so helpless. I'm the Duchess of York, but I might as well be a tapster for all the power I have to amend matters. You saw with your own eyes what was done to Wiltshire, Bushey and poor Henry Green. That was no rumour.'

'I understand that Philippa received word from my brother last night. If matters were as serious as you fear, she'd not have kept the tale of it from us.'

'She might. Out of spite. I *detest* the woman! How she gives herself airs, thinking she shall have my place one day. Well, she hasn't got it yet! I really don't understand what your brother saw in her. What is she? Near old enough to be his mother, the widow of a knight of no significance at all. My laundress is better bred.' She paused, and turned towards Piers Mohun. 'You say, Mohun, that the Duchess of Aumale is unwell?' she called. 'Has the physician gone to attend her?'

Mohun bowed. 'My understanding was that his services were not required, Your Grace.'

'Then it cannot be an illness of any moment. Send to her again. Say that I *require* her attendance. Her *immediate* attendance, to go with me to mass. We shall pray for her swift recovery.'

'Your Grace, if I may say—'

'You may not! Do as I command. Her ladyship needs to be reminded that *I* rule here, and no other.'

Philippa did not refuse the summons, though she made them wait for a very long time, appeared dressed as for court, even to the coronet on her head, and had her train carried almost all the way to Joanne's bed. Her curtsey of acknowledgement was little more than a brief flex of the knee muscles.

'We understand,' Joanne said coldly, 'that you have news from your husband. I think it a great discourtesy that you have not shared it, knowing, as you must, that he has not troubled himself to send word to us.'

Philippa sat down on the bed next to Constance. 'There is nothing to tell,' she spat out angrily, 'save that the wretch Bolingbroke has made the King take the Constableship from my lord, and has given it to that false traitor Northumberland.'

'A very poor reward for Aumale, after deserting his King,' Joanne said harshly.

'What are you talking about? Edward didn't desert the King, madame. The King deserted *him*! Ran away in the night from his own army, the coward, to hide in the hills like some Welsh cattle-thief. If anyone deserted the King it was *your* husband, not mine. After my sister here knelt in front of half the people in Berkeley Castle and begged him to surrender, because she couldn't stomach the sight of blood. Don't talk to me of betrayal. I'm proud of Aumale. He did what he had to do, to save our family.'

'To save himself, you mean,' sneered Joanne. 'We are not fools; we know that he brought all this about. He was part of Bolingbroke's conspiracy from the beginning, and that's why the King had to flee from Carmarthen. He uncovered the treachery that was planned against him.'

'Then why has Ned not been rewarded?' Philippa asked angrily. 'He's as much a prisoner as your brother, Joanne. Or as your husband, Constance. Bolingbroke says it's for their protection. I say he's a damned liar. He means to bring them all to trial.'

'Are they still at Chester?' Constance asked. She hoped that a civil question might have a calming effect. Though her blood was as roused as theirs, she saw little point in fighting among themselves, like cats in a sack.

Philippa shook her head. 'They've started on the road to London, from what Ned tells me. I expect we'll hear more before long.'

Joanne stood up abruptly, which meant that Philippa and Constance had to follow suit.

'We shall go to mass,' she said decisively. 'After that, I shall write a letter to my lord the Duke, reminding him that I am still alive. Constance, you may bear my train for me, if you please.'

***

Edmund Mortimer had ridden all through the morning, with his usual companions, his squire and his Welsh yeoman, the two he trusted above all others. The tree canopy of the forest showed the dense dark green of high summer, and the road seemed far longer than he remembered it from his boyhood. Then, quite suddenly, he emerged into a clearing, and saw the white rendered castle towers and walls soaring in the distance, dominating the flat country around them. His heart leapt with the memories that flooded over him. He had not counted on visiting Fotheringhay again.

He walked his horse along the village street, through the small market and past the ancient and rather neglected Saxon church, which York had so often talked of replacing, but somehow never touched. He just managed to reach the outer gate house of the castle in advance of a ponderous cart load of Barnack stone, on its way to contribute to the work being carried out on the chapel that served the household, extending it in every direction, including upwards, so that it might more fittingly serve as a college of priests, priests who would pray for the souls of York and his family.

The approach to the castle was a narrow causeway that ran between the outer moat and the lake, the entrance, a good hundred yards along this path, being through an enormous gate house, almost a castle in itself. His arrival had not gone undetected, and some of York's officers came out to receive him, though no one of importance, the modest size of his meinie having been given due weight.

'I bear a message for my lady, the Countess of Gloucester,' he said.

'You are very welcome, sir,' said the leading gentleman, a very young man who neither recognised Edmund nor was recognised by him. 'My lady of Gloucester is in the pleasure ground, so I believe. I hope you will accept the hospitality of the household, once your letter is delivered. I shall send a page to guide you.'

'No need,' said Edmund abruptly. 'I know this castle as well as you do. I'd be grateful, though, if you'd see that my men and the horses are refreshed.'

The route to the pleasure ground was relatively tortuous, and involved the transit of a narrow wooden footbridge over the inner moat, but Mortimer found his way without difficulty, and passed through the narrow gate that led into the gardens that he recalled so well. It was a place of arbours and latticed walkways, but there was also a large herber, and a considerable orchard. A small world in itself, where it was possible to hide if one wished, though the massive castle stood nearby, a stark reminder of reality.

He saw Constance almost at once, and for a happy moment thought her alone; but then he saw the child, Bess, laughing and throwing a ball towards her mother, and a little behind Bess walked Agnes Norreys and a plainly-dressed woman he took to be Bess's nurse. Constance caught the ball one-handed, and immediately pitched it at Agnes, a little far to the left for Lady Norreys to take it cleanly. Paris had it in his mouth in a moment, and was away into the bushes, pursued by a joyful Bess and a less joyful red-faced nurse.

Mortimer leaned against the trellis for a moment, his foot poised on the stone step that led out onto the grass. He had wanted Constance for as long as he could remember having such desires, and every sight of her was a strange mixture of delight and sorrow. Here at Fotheringhay, somehow, it was worse, for it reminded him of the days when he still retained slim, shameful, youthful hopes, mainly centred on the possibility of Thomas's death in Prussia. They had walked together in this very garden, even shared their confidences—though never all of them—and only the ever-presence of her attendant damosels had kept him from attempting that which was forbidden. That, and the fear of losing the small, precious consolation of her friendship. But all the women he had ever enjoyed, English, Welsh or Irish, highborn, serf or whore, had been mere substitutes for her, and he knew that all those he might have in the future would be no more fortunate.

She saw him at last, and began to walk towards him, smiling a welcome. She was, by her standards, very simply dressed, in a gown of good brown wool, and a linen coif held down by a plain circlet. There were grass stains on the skirt, where she'd been kneeling to play with the children. Young Richard Despenser was crawling around in the background, investigating some insect he had found among the flowers under the supervision of his uncle and namesake, Richard of Conisbrough.

He told himself that he had, in fact, seen her looking more beautiful; however, it was not easy to be precise about the occasion. She was not quite the girl of his old memories; more voluptuous now around bosom and hips, and none the worse for the change. He wondered what she would look like without her clothes, soft in his arms with her hair hanging about them…

To avoid the image he knelt and carried her hand to his lips, as though she were his sovereign. In a sense, she was.

'Edmund!' she cried impatiently. 'Have you brought news?'

He rose to his feet. 'Yes. Word from your husband.'

'He is well?' she interrupted.

'Yes—quite well. He's no men about him though, apart from Norreys. That's why he asked me if I would go to you. He gives you a choice. To stay here; to return to Hanley Castle; or to join him in London.'

'I will go to him, of course.' Her face had brightened with relief.

He snorted. 'If you were mine, I'd not have given the option.'

Constance smiled. 'Ah, but you would have been less certain of my preference, perhaps? Oh, Edmund, I've been so afraid for him. We heard he was Bolingbroke's prisoner.'

'He's a prisoner of sorts. They all are.'

'You are not?'

'I'm not important enough. Constance, you've no idea what it was like when the King abandoned us at Carmarthen. Chaos. The men ran wild, as if they were in a foreign land. They more or less sacked the town. I'll spare you the detail, but you can guess what it was like when all discipline and order broke down. I found I couldn't even control my own followers. They were mad with drink and fighting among themselves, Welsh against English. I thought to get to Alianore at Usk, but after I'd wandered about Wales for a while, and found trouble everywhere, I heard that the King was dead, and Bolingbroke in Hereford. So I went to Hereford and submitted. It seemed there was no other choice. He welcomed me like a brother, told me he had no quarrel with me or mine. I hate the man, Constance, but someone must rule this land, and there seems to be no one else. Everyone has yielded to him. Everyone. They say he means to be King, though he swore at first that it was not his intent. He's sent to all the monasteries in England for their chronicles, seeking precedents he may use to depose Richard.'

'Richard is King. Nothing can change that. Even if he were dead, Harry Bolingbroke is not his heir.'

He smiled bitterly. 'I need not you to tell me of my nephew's claim. Nor does Bolingbroke need to be reminded. He sent men to Usk; the boys are no longer in Alianore's care.'

'He has taken her children?' Constance was appalled.

'Only the boys. They are safe, so he says. Gone to Windsor, I believe. His own children are gathered there, save for the eldest.'

'Thomas has accepted this?'

'Thomas has submitted like the rest of us. He had no alternative. You'll find him changed.' He paused, looking for words, and finding none that were ideal. 'He's taken it very hard, all this. Before I left him, he was talking of exile. Of going to Rhodes to fight the Turks.'

20

Math the greyhound lay on Bolingbroke's bed now, in the royal apartments within the Tower. At Flint Castle, in front of several thousand men, he had left Richard's side, run across the courtyard and put his paws joyfully on Harry's shoulders. It had been the most astonishing defection of all, an unexpected reward for the small kindnesses that Bolingbroke had bestowed on the animal over the years. Harry had thought at first that the dog would soon weary of his company, and begin to pine for Richard—but Math showed no sign of pining. He was utterly content, utterly untroubled by his new Lancastrian livery collar. He asked for no reward but a soft bed, suitable food, and the occasional affectionate stroke of the ears.

Bolingbroke wished that his fellow men were so easily pleased as the dog. Those who had supported him felt that he had treated Richard's friends too gently, grumbled that no more seemed to be in danger of execution and forfeiture. Those who had favoured Richard hid their resentment at being displaced from power under a thin veneer of submission, but were doubtless already beginning to conspire against him. The elders of the City of London had petitioned him to execute Richard. Northumberland and his son, Hotspur, wanted Richard to keep his crown, though with restrictions and safeguards placed upon him, restrictions and safeguards that Richard would shatter within a year. The Duke of York wanted peace and order, but had little in the way of practical advice. Edward of York was full of advice, but could not be trusted—and seemed astonished and outraged that he was not the first in Harry's counsel. Even his own son, Hal, the putative Prince of Wales, newly brought home from Ireland, was proving incredibly awkward to handle. Somehow, in a few short months, Richard had become Hal's idol. In Hal's eyes, Bolingbroke was a contemptible traitor.

They brought William Bagot before him. The knight, dressed in a ragged shirt and filthy hose, was burdened with chains, and looked as if he had gone a year without either a wash or a shave. He had returned from Ireland by the same ship as young Hal, but with less promising prospects for his future.

Harry settled himself on his chair. 'There are those, Bagot, who say that I should have you drawn and hanged. However, you were once my father's man, and I am inclined to be merciful. Provided you tell the truth. Do you understand?'

'Yes, Your Grace.' The once-prosperous Bagot, the terror of Warwickshire until recently, was remarkably submissive.

'You might begin by explaining what lay behind your conspiracy to murder my father—whom God pardon. You are a little man, Bagot, of small account. Whose orders did you obey?'

'I sought to please the King, Your Grace.'

'And so did his bidding?'

'The King told me he intended to resign the crown. Once he had defeated all his enemies. He said that the Duke of Aumale should succeed him. I counselled him to the contrary, said that you were nearer to him in blood, and more favoured by the people.'

'I had no idea, Bagot, that you loved me so tenderly.'

Lord Grey de Ruthin, standing by Harry's side, snorted with derision. 'My lord, this dirty piece of shit will say anything to save himself. Why waste your time listening to such drivel? What he needs is a long swing at the end of a rope.'

'Thank you, Lord Grey,' Harry said abruptly, waving his hand. 'Bagot, what did the King say to your suggestion?'

'He said that you were the enemy of God. That you would plunder the Church to fund futile wars in France, because there was no other source for the money that would be required. He said that my lord your father favoured the Lollards because they wanted to disendow the Church, and that you were no better. After that I thought it would greatly please the King if I cleared a way for Aumale, and so I sought to bring about the Duke's death.'

'By the King's orders?'

'No, Your Grace. Forgive me, but it was my own folly, nothing more. I broached the matter to Lord Salisbury and others, but they would not hear of it. The King was furious when he learned what I was about. He made me apologise to your father, who, in his kindness, forgave me. This you must already know, my lord.'

Bolingbroke waved that away. 'Do you say Richard called *me* a Lollard?'

'Not in those words, my lord Duke. He meant it so, meant you were not fit to succeed him.'

'And even before he married the present Queen, he was willing to resign the crown?'

'Yes.'

'No doubt he is still willing to do so,' remarked Archbishop Arundel. 'His insufficiency for the high office he has held must be apparent even to himself. A voluntary abdication would be a great convenience.'

'Another matter,' Bolingbroke said, before the Archbishop could develop his point. 'I wish to know, Bagot, which of Richard's advisers counselled and undertook the murder of my uncle, the Duke of Gloucester. Think carefully before you speak, for this was a high crime, for which death will be the proper punishment. That Thomas Mowbray was involved is beyond doubt—but you must tell us whether he acted alone.'

Bagot's mouth trembled. He was uncertain what Harry wanted to hear.

'Speak!' commanded the Archbishop. 'If you were party to it, confess your guilt and beg for mercy.'

'I had no part in that deed!' The knight's chains rattled as he gestured defensively with his hands. 'It was done by the King's own command. Even Mowbray was reluctant to obey. He hesitated, but the Duke of Aumale sent men to Calais to complete the task. He—Aumale—said that there would be no peace in England while his uncle lived.'

'He said that? In front of witnesses?'

Bagot nodded vigorously.

'Christ forgive him! You are ready to testify to this? Before Parliament?'

Another nod. 'Yes, Your Grace. If you so order. I'll do whatever you bid me.'

'Aumale's head must fly for this evil crime!' cried an outraged Grey. 'Parliament will be satisfied with nothing less. He should be arrested straightaway.'

'It shall be one of my first deeds as your King to place him on trial,' Harry announced. 'That I promise you. But have no doubt. I alone shall decide his fate. Not the Council. Not Parliament. Not you, Grey. The Duke of Aumale is my cousin. He shares in King Edward's blood, and enough of that blood has already been shed. What's more, you must bear in mind that he was only obeying King Richard's orders. At least, that's what he will plead. '

'You will spare him? That double-dealing traitor? When you have proof that he murdered your uncle? Proof that he has designs on the throne itself?'

Bolingbroke fixed him with his stare. 'I shall do what I think necessary for the common profit of the realm,' he said.

When Bagot had been removed, taken back to his dungeon, and the others had gone about their business, Harry settled himself to read some of the numerous petitions of grievance that had been submitted to him. He had two trusted clerks with him, and with their assistance the pile of documentation was rapidly sorted into piles, some to receive immediate executive action, some to be referred to the Council, the great majority to be ignored.

After an hour or so of this, tiring of work that put a sore strain on his eyes, he stretched his legs, going into the outer chamber to speak to those who were waiting to see him. The most important of them was Thomas Despenser, and Harry went to him at once.

'I'm here to ask your permission to leave England,' Thomas said, without preamble.

Bolingbroke stared at him, screwing up his eyes. From the pale, expressionless look of Despenser's face he judged him to be ill, or at least to be suffering from a serious lack of sleep. 'There's no need for that. There's a place for you on my Council. I must restore the lands that Richard took from Warwick, Arundel and my uncle of Gloucester, but all else is assured to you. I thought I made it clear to you at Chester that there was no quarrel between us. That I'd be glad to have you in my service.'

'I'm determined to go to Rhodes, to fight the enemies of Christ.'

'A most noble intent.' Harry crossed himself devoutly. 'You are truly resolved to this?'

'Yes.'

'Then I'd be guilty of a great sin were I to stand in your way. But I beg you to consider carefully whether your decision is right.'

'I've done so.' Despenser's mouth set in a stubborn line.

Rhodes! thought Harry. The place I chose for my own exile when I was in despair. The most distant of Christian outposts, just a few miles from the Turkish mainland, and subject to endless attack. *A place from which a man of courage may well not return.*

'I must also ask that you extend your protection to my wife and children in my absence.'

There was a momentary pause. 'I shall, very willingly,' Bolingbroke said gravely. 'As though they were my own. Your passport shall be made out, Thomas, and you may go whenever you wish. I hope you will feel able to return to England, one day.'

***

Richard, it was said, had abdicated—but as his friends were not allowed to visit him the truth of this could not be tested. Some went so far as to claim that he had abdicated at Conwy, which he most certainly had not. In any event, the resignation was not deemed sufficient. Parliament resolved to depose him, and did so without hearing his defence.

In the Parliament House Harry Bolingbroke put his hand upon the arm of the empty throne.

'In the name of Father, Son, and Holy Ghost, I, Harry of Lancaster, claim this realm of England and the crown, being descended by the right line of blood coming from King Henry III,' he declaimed. 'God of his grace has sent me, with the help of my kin and friends, to recover the realm, which was on the point of being undone, for default of governance, and the undoing of the good laws.'

One of the absurdities he had allowed to be put about was that his descent through his mother from King Henry III was senior to that of either King Richard or the Mortimers. It was a plain lie, but too good a falsehood to be allowed to drop altogether. Some would be deceived, and the rest had no choice but to swallow it.

No one opposed his claim. No one dared. Not yet.

The Despensers took delivery of their coronation robes with scant pleasure.

'I don't know how I can stomach it,' Constance said. It took more than a free gift of twelve ells of scarlet cloth and a fur of miniver to win her over.

'It must be faced,' Thomas answered. He hung his head. 'God knows, you stomach worse. You have to share a bed with a man who has failed his King; a man who is not worthy to touch you. You sit at table with him. You have borne his children. Tell me, how can you stomach *that*?'

'You accuse yourself too much. You did what you could, and I can think of no man who did more.' She walked over to his chair, placed her hand on his shoulder in a gesture of comfort. There had been much of this since her arrival in London, strange black moods that seemed almost to sap his reason. It was as if something had broken inside him, some essential mechanism of his being, so that he was no longer Thomas Despenser but a stranger who resembled him, a wounded soul whose pain she could not find the means to ease.

'I'm ashamed to be alive,' he said quietly.

'You've much cause to live. For me; for our children; for all who depend on you and call you their lord. They need you. *I* need you. You are my husband. Do you imagine that your life is not precious to me? I don't know how you can even *think* of going to Rhodes! Your proper place is here in England.'

'I must redeem myself, give you cause to be proud of me again.'

'I *am* proud of you!'

'So you say, but it's your duty that speaks, not your heart. How can you possibly be proud of me, a man who has no honour? A man who despises himself!'

She drew back from him, began to pace around the room. It was a grim, dark afternoon, rain lashing against the windows. Smoke billowed from the fireplace, caught by an errant draught from the chimney, and filled her nose with the acrid scent of sea-coal.

It was useless to talk to Thomas while he was in this mood. She bustled out of the room, and sought out Norreys, finding him in the tiny closet he used as an office. Allowing for his desk, and storage space for his numerous account rolls, letters and memoranda, there was barely enough room to accommodate the pair of them. A small charcoal brazier burnt in a corner. He began to rise, but she immediately gestured him back to his stool, and propped her buttocks against the edge of the desk so that he would not feel uncomfortable sitting while she stood.

'The chimney in the parlour needs cleaning,' she said abruptly, an unintended sharpness in her voice. 'Before it makes me cough up my lungs.'

'I'll order it done, my lady.'

Constance paused to think, found occupation for her hands by adjusting the hang of her skirts to her satisfaction. 'Are we not friends, John, after all these years?' she asked.

He put down his pen and nodded, a little absently. 'I'd be honoured to think so.'

'Then I think you may use my given name, while we're alone.'

He struggled with that concept for a moment. His wry smile suggested that he thought her whim mildly ridiculous. 'As you will—Constance.'

'You're certainly my lord's friend. You've known him longer than anyone except his mother. You more or less lay in the same cradle. Can you remember Thomas ever being as he is now?'

'No,' he sighed. 'Troubled, sometimes, but not so completely downhearted.'

'He's told you of this plan he has of going to Rhodes?'

'Yes.'

'And asked you to go with him, I expect?'

'No—he's said he'll not take any of us. That he'll go alone.'

'*Alone?*' Constance repeated incredulously. This was getting worse and worse. 'How can the Earl of Gloucester possibly go to war alone?'

Norreys shrugged. 'It's what he intends.'

'I've never heard of anything so ridiculous in my life! What am I to do, John? He must be made to change his mind. Warwick and Berkeley will be at our throats in any event, but if he's out of England...'

'His following will dissolve,' Norreys predicted, his face grim. 'I need not tell you, men look to a lord to advance their interests at court and protect them from their enemies at home. His position in Gloucestershire and Worcestershire has never been easy; but with Warwick back from banishment and Berkeley in favour again, it'll all but collapse if he goes out of the country. When he returns he'll find he has no influence at all, and I doubt he'll have any way to regain it. As for Glamorgan, he's already neglected it too long. He can salvage something from the wreck, but only if he stays and works at the task.'

Constance thought for a moment. 'I must persuade him that it is more to his honour, and a more knightly deed, to stay in England and resist the malice of his enemies. I doubt whether he will listen to any other argument, though you and I know that it's simple folly for him to venture on a crusade at a time like this.'

A momentary frown clouded his face. 'If you truly seek my opinion, Constance, you'd do well not to press the matter too hard with him. You know that no man cares to admit that he's doing his wife's bidding, even when he believes her to be in the right. Let him have time to think, and encourage others to open their minds to him. Those he respects. Lord Salisbury, for example. You might ask His Grace, your father, to have a word. Perhaps also Sir Hugh Despenser. I'd suggest the Bishop of Norwich, but I doubt whether the Bishop's counsel would be very profitable. He might even approve of the crusade. I'll do what I can myself, but Thomas doesn't much care for my advice either at present, not on matters such as these.'

She nodded, and rose from her resting-place. 'Thank you, John. I'm glad to have you on my side.'

Norreys picked up his pen again, prepared to return to the letter he was writing. 'It's not a matter of sides. It's a matter of what's best for us all,' he said thoughtfully. 'The family and the affinity. It bears on many lives.'

Constance left him and went out into the passage, then up a short flight of steps and along the dark vaulted corridor that led first to a heavy door that marked the beginning of the precincts of the adjoining nunnery, and then into the chapel gallery. From this gallery, as a privilege of patronage, she, Thomas, and their household were entitled to hear the ceremony of the mass performed for the ladies of the Minories, and indeed to view all their services, if they so wished. She looked down into the body of the chapel, empty at this hour, and was grateful for the silence, the refreshing peace of the place. Yet her enjoyment of that peace was spoiled by the knowledge that only a few hundred yards away, within the depths of the Tower, her cousin, King Richard lay alone and neglected, a prisoner in some barren chamber, deprived of his crown and of all that was his except his knighthood, condemned to perpetual confinement. No less did it trouble her to think that within that same Tower her other cousin, Bolingbroke, profaned the royal apartments with his hateful presence, heard petitions, and commanded all from the throne he had usurped.

She prayed that Richard might be restored to his own, and that Bolingbroke might be plunged into the darkest pit of hell for all eternity. She found some consolation in this prayer, though very little, and when she looked up she discovered that she was no longer alone in the silence of the chapel. Down below, in the minoresses' stalls that faced her viewpoint, was a solitary figure, clad in the brown robes of the order. (Or an approximation thereof, because the robes in this case had a look of silk about them.) Suddenly the nun raised her eyes to the gallery, and fixed directly onto Constance's gaze, her face twisted with hatred and contempt.

It was her cousin, Isabel of Gloucester.

News had lately come from Ireland that Isabel's young brother, Humphrey, lay dead in Trim Castle. Some said he had been poisoned. Worse, some whispered that Thomas Despenser had poisoned him.

No one who knew Thomas even superficially could possibly believe such a thing, even setting aside the undoubted fact that he and Humphrey were many miles apart, and separated by the width of the Irish Sea, at the time of the latter's death. It was obviously a slander, perhaps provoked by the transfer of the Gloucester title from one family to the other. But Isabel cared nothing for that. She needed someone to hate far more than she needed to know the truth.

Constance rose quietly to her feet. The chapel was no longer a place of refuge, and in any event, it was nearly the hour for dinner. There was just sufficient time to draft a letter to the Countess of Salisbury, and think about what she must say to the Duke of York. Thomas needed all the friends that could be gathered about him.

***

In the yellow-grey light of early morning, the Duke of York's barge pushed away from the rivers steps of the *Old Inne*, its ranks of liveried oarsmen straining to take it out into midstream, their blades digging a sparkle of life into the dull, sluggish Thames. It was Bolingbroke's coronation day, Monday 13th October 1399. There was a slight dampness in the air that intensified when out on the water.

'If those bells do not stop soon, we shall all be deaf as posts,' the Duchess of Aumale grumbled. 'God knows, I can't even hear my own thoughts.'

Constance nodded, hoping that that answer would suffice. She was not in the mood for conversation with Philippa. They were seated together on cushions under the striped, blue and murrey awning of painted canvas that protected the aft part of the barge, at approximate right angles to the Duchess of York, who rested in solitary splendour on a gilded chair, raised on a small dais at the stern. All three were in their ceremonial robes, those of the two duchesses being slightly fuller and more trailing than Constance's, because they had been allowed more cloth in acknowledgement of their higher rank, Joanne's also being more heavily furred as a mark of her special seniority. They each wore a coronet over a bejewelled caul, and an heraldic mantle bearing the arms of their father and their husband. Their attendant gentlemen, ladies and damosels either stood or crouched on the carpeted deck, as they preferred.

The bells of London, Southwark and Westminster, of parish churches and houses of religion, had been sounding out for three days now, the campanologists refreshed by endless supplies of free ale. Hundreds of bells, pealing in simultaneous salute, intermittent cannon fire from the Tower, the cheers and carousing of drunken crowds of people, sick on the cheap wine that ran in the public conduits—even at this early hour, even out in midstream, the noise was all-pervading.

On the previous day, Sunday, Bolingbroke had ridden in a splendid procession from the Tower to Westminster accompanied by his four sons, by all the peers of the realm, by hundreds of knights and squires, and by the Mayor, livery companies, and religious orders of London. The ladies had not been required to take part, though they had of course been expected to watch, Constance having done so from the windows of the *Old Inne*, one of the many guests Joanne had gathered for the occasion. The Duchess of York's hospitality had been splendid, and she had extended it in all directions, even to some of the city wives. Though only, it had been noted, to those whose husbands were aldermen or officers of great guilds and were in addition part of the silent minority in the city that still adhered to King Richard.

Constance knew that her father would not be pleased by the detail of Joanne's guest list when he discovered it. If, as she strongly suspected, Surrey was hatching a conspiracy against the new government, he was deeply mistaken if he thought that he could use his sister to drag York into it. The Duke wanted peace and quiet above all, and would not lift a finger against Bolingbroke; certainly not once Harry had gained possession of the crown. He might defer to Joanne's wishes in small things, but in matters of politics he was as likely to listen to the Duchess's pet starling as to Joanne herself.

Constance had nothing against Surrey. He was pleasing to the eye, and he always treated her with the greatest courtesy; but he was also young and inexperienced, and she had no more faith in his judgement than in Joanne's. She gathered from some of the abstruse comments Lady Salisbury had made during the passage of the great procession that John Montagu was also involved. Salisbury was certainly older and more learned than Surrey, but she was not at all sure that he was any wiser.

She would have to keep an eye on the matter, lest Thomas be drawn into folly. Surrey and Salisbury were his friends, after all. She had hoped that Salisbury, at least, might be a calming influence, not a deviser of reckless schemes. Clearly, she had been mistaken in that hope.

They didn't even have the sense to plot in secrecy. Lady Salisbury was not normally taken into her husband's confidence on such matters, so presumably she had been given the role of helping to recruit Richard's London supporters, being, of course, a Londoner herself by origin. But Maud was scarcely discreet, or Constance herself would not have fathomed what was going on. If she had made the necessary deductions, she was sure the Duchess of Aumale would have done no less. God alone knew what Edward might do with the scent of intrigue in his nostrils. Anything was possible, from involvement to betrayal.

'Clumsy fools!' snapped Philippa, waving an angry hand in the general direction of the oarsmen. 'Look how they've splashed me!'

It was probable, Constance thought, that the rising wind had produced the offending minuscule blot on the Duchess of Aumale's robes, rather than any awkwardness with an oar.

'We're almost there,' she said, in an effort of consolation. The ugly assortment of buildings that constituted the Palace of Westminster were drawing close, so close that it was no longer possible to see more than the highest pinnacles of the abbey beyond.

'I hate goddamned boats!' Philippa grumbled, rubbing uselessly at the stain. 'I don't see why we couldn't have ridden. Is Joanne frightened of horses?'

'We'd never have got through the crowds. Nothing can move in the streets.'

They bumped decisively against the landing-stage, the discussion terminated by the need to gather themselves into the proper order required to step on shore, the Duchess of York leading the procession.

Since there was no Queen to be crowned, there was no active part for the ladies to play in the ceremony. They were merely privileged spectators, if it could be deemed a privilege to stand in the abbey, motionless and silent as statues, for the interminable duration of the proceedings.

Bolingbroke was anointed on head and body with an oil which, it was alleged, had been miraculously discovered in the Tower, an oil specially blessed by St. Thomas a' Becket and the Virgin Mary. A great convenience for a usurper who needed as many blessings as he could accrue. Constance noted with regret that it failed to smoke and sizzle on his flesh, and that the crown, lowered into place by the Archbishop of Canterbury, was significantly cooler than the temperature she thought proper for the occasion.

Her father was the second to pay homage, after the new Prince of Wales. He showed no sign of reluctance, any sorrow on his face being due entirely to the pain from his agonising joints. Immediately after him came Edward, whose expression suggested that this was the happiest day of his life.

Thomas's turn came rather later, towards the end of the earls. Constance had not had a chance to speak to him since Friday night, and that had been an exchange of few words. He had been dreading this ordeal, and she feared that he might balk at it, regardless of the consequences. Instead he knelt, bright-eyed, put his hands between Harry's, and spoke the words of homage in a loud, clear voice. It was almost possible for her to believe that he had recovered his spirits.

***

'They say that when the Archbishop dripped the oil onto Harry's head, it set lice running in all directions.'

Constance had grown unused to her brother's whispered confidences. It was a long time since he had last addressed her at such close quarters. Before his break with Alianore. She was momentarily reminded of bright, far-off days at Fotheringhay when they had exchanged their childish secrets, united in mutual trust and understanding. They were barely friends now, so far had they diverged in their ways.

'Who says?' she enquired.

'I had it from one of the clerks who assisted the Archbishop. One of the Mortimer men. He was close enough to see for himself.'

'Presumably the miraculous oil will cause the lice to miraculously disappear.'

He snorted. 'Perhaps they're happy in the Mole's fur.'

'The Mole?'

'Haven't you noticed how he screws his eyes up when he looks at you? Or how close he holds papers to his face? Anyway, that's what the Welsh call him. The Mole!'

'Moles are harmless creatures. Bolingbroke isn't.'

It was getting towards midnight, though no one at Westminster seemed to have any idea of going to bed. The great coronation banquet had been proceeding in Westminster Hall, under the new hammer beam roof, with its angels bearing the fresh-painted heraldic devices of King Richard II, since late afternoon. There were three courses, but each course involved a huge number of dishes, to say nothing of elaborate ceremonial, and between the courses there were extended rest periods, during which entertainment was provided, and a degree of socialising was permissible as a rest from the formality. Though strictly a breach of etiquette, even some temporary absence from the room was acceptable—indeed necessary, in light of the vast quantities of wine that had been consumed.

They stood together in a window embrasure that overlooked the Thames—though for the present all was blackness. They were some way from the hall, almost out of earshot, but still not in privacy. Every public room in the Palace was crammed with guests.

'Hotspur is not here,' Edward said.

She shrugged, not really caring whether Northumberland's son was present or not. She hadn't noticed. There were about three thousand people milling around in groups, and it was impossible to keep a tally.

'You must ask your friend Edmund Mortimer about it,' he went on. 'He knows Hotspur better than any of us. There's a rumour that the good Percy and his father are much aggrieved by today's work. Northumberland swore his soul away to get Richard out of Conwy. It seems he really believed that Harry would keep his hands off the crown, and considers himself duped. Well, he's either a fool or a liar.'

'They've not refused their rewards,' Constance sniffed. She drew her robes more closely about her, suddenly aware of the chill draught from the ill-fitting window.

'Of course they have not. But it's interesting. They'll not sit in peace with the Nevilles for too long, and Worcester is still Richard's man at heart.'

'And I thought you were Harry's.'

He smiled for a moment. 'I am. Are we not all? Newly sworn as such. You know that nothing is settled yet. I've already heard it said that some are seeking a way to restore our Cousin Richard to his rightful place. Perhaps you've heard the same?'

She shook her head, declining to reveal the suspicions she had picked up in the company of Joanne and Lady Salisbury.

He sighed. 'Ale takes its time to brew, Constance. Try to drink it too soon, and it's foul, worse than ditch water. A wise man allows time for it to settle in the cask, and mature a little. You take my meaning?'

He offered his hand, and they began to walk back towards the hall.

'I think you might find it more profitable to speak to the brewer.'

'Perhaps you have more influence in brewing circles at the moment than I do. The important thing is that we do not quarrel among ourselves.'

'Ourselves?'

'Those looking forward to the new brew. We've not always agreed in the past, but now we've enemies enough, my dear, without turning on each other.'

They entered the hall at the end close to the King's raised seat, their ears blasted by the celebratory music and the drone of conversation. The ceremony had begun in proper silence, but that discipline had eased now, and wine had taken the rein off men's tongues. Some of the individual voices were very loud, if not downright aggressive. The King's officers moved around, ceaselessly watching for any hint of violence. It was unlikely that anyone would be fool enough to draw steel in Harry's presence, but anything was possible when hatreds were warmed by drink.

'If you doubt me, look around you,' Edward said. 'Look at them! I can still see old Warwick grovelling before Richard for his life, weeping like a cowardly child. Do you think he'll have forgotten that humiliation? The only part he'll have forgotten is that Harry was one of those who brought it about! Look at the boy, Arundel, and his uncle, the Archbishop. They want blood for blood. Look at Grey de Ruthin, forever licking Harry's arse. Richard didn't like him, so he hopes to do better with a new master. It won't occur to him that no king has much use for an ignorant cutthroat with the brains of a sheep! The wolves are gathering, and seeking the courage to attack. Tomorrow perhaps, in Parliament, or the next day.'

He was interrupted by the arrival of a page. The King wished to have a word with the Countess of Gloucester.

Constance was mildly surprised. It was true that Harry had spent much of the intervals between courses in conversation with individual guests, but she had not expected to be selected for such a sign of favour. She followed the boy through the throng, and into the small amount of open space around the King's throne. There was just sufficient room to emerge from the crowd and make the requisite three curtsies as she approached him. Harry stood up, and offered his hand as she rose from the third, enabling her to kiss it before he made the gesture of assisting her to her feet.

'Fair Cousin,' he said, peering at her at close range, 'it gives me joy to see you here; and to have your husband in my service at last.'

'You seem to have gained everything you wanted, Cousin,' she answered coldly. 'Your father's lands. Richard's crown.'

'Not quite everything,' he said quietly. 'No man ever has all that he wants. Not even a king. However, it's fair to say that my fortunes have improved since we met at Berkeley. Remind me what you called me. Rebel, was it? Traitor? You would not sit at table with such. Well, it seems matters are amended now.'

'You have just been crowned as our King,' she said.

'You choose your words carefully.'

Constance stared at him for a moment, surprised that he was sharp enough to notice. It was a timely reminder that it was not only in the lists that Harry was a dangerous opponent.

'You were careful,' he prompted, '*not* to acknowledge that I am in fact your rightful King. Perhaps, Constance, you still retain some doubt in your mind?'

'My simple opinion on such a matter is below your consideration,' she said. 'My lord speaks for me, and he has vowed fealty to you. As you know, Cousin, any knight or gentleman holds sacred oaths to be inviolable. I believe that you have occasionally been bound by them yourself.'

To her annoyance he was not angered, but seemed to enjoy her comment. He turned away from her for a moment, picked something up. It was a piece of black cloth. No, it was more than that. The sleeve she had sent him from Caversham.

'Your token has brought me great fortune,' he said, placing it in her hands. 'Now I return it to you, with gratitude. You may bestow it on another crusader. I mean your husband, Cousin. I think it well that he should go to Rhodes, as he intends. It'll be much to his profit, in this world and the next. Don't try to dissuade him from his purpose. He may be in some danger fighting the Turks, but safer there, perhaps, than here.'

21

The first two days of the first Parliament of King Henry IV all but ended in a riot. William Bagot repeated his evidence against Edward of York, who angrily refuted all Bagot's charges against him and said Bagot himself was responsible for far greater crimes, including a conspiracy to murder the present King's father. Of which evidence, Edward said, could be found on the public record, since Bagot had been forced to bind himself in the sum of a thousand pounds that he would never attempt the like again.

Edward's defence was far from perfect, but it took the worst of the sting out of Bagot's accusations, and the atmosphere of the Parliament calmed a little. The neutral majority, recognising his high birth, were inclined to allow him the benefit of the doubt. But then one John Hall was produced, a former valet of the Duke of Norfolk, pale and thin from many weeks spent chained in a dungeon. He confessed that he had been present when the Duke of Gloucester was smothered to death at Calais, but stressed that two of Edward's squires had journeyed from England especially to take part in the deed. He had no doubt that the Duke of Aumale had ordered the murder.

After that it was almost as if a dam had burst. Half the peers gathered in Parliament angrily threw down their gages to challenge Edward to combat, including Lord Morley, Despenser's brother-in-law, and Lord Fitzwalter, Philippa's stepson. Edward, his anger roused, offered to fight them all, one after the other, and when Surrey and Salisbury threw down their hoods in his support they were challenged in turn by Morley and Fitzwalter, and by various others who clambered over the cloth covered benches to get to them. Bolingbroke sought to calm the atmosphere by having Hall summarily executed, but not even the prospect of stepping outside to see the unfortunate valet hanged, drawn and quartered was enough to turn the tide of hatred. The Parliament loudly demanded the trial of Edward, and the rest of Richard's advisers. All who had counselled the arrest and impeachment of Warwick, Arundel, and the Duke of Gloucester.

The King rose, promising to take the advice of his Council.

The Council met at once, if Council it could be called. It was an informal meeting of such of Harry's senior advisers who were most anxious to press their opinions on him, as well as bold enough to follow him into the depths of his private apartments.

'I will not have Aumale executed,' he told them abruptly. He sat, jerked a finger as an instruction for an esquire to put a glass of wine in his hand.

'You will not take our advice, Sire?' Archbishop Arundel enquired. 'As you have just promised your Parliament? It seems you are already falling into the errors that undid you predecessor.'

Harry checked his anger. 'You would have me execute the son and heir of my Uncle York? King Edward's grandson?'

'A treacherous murderer, and your enemy,' said Grey de Ruthin.

'I know who my enemies are! York is dear to me, and has served me well. Shall I repay him so? Turn his love to hate? Is that your idea of good policy? Is there not hate enough for you in this land? I suppose you'd also have me kill Exeter, my sister's husband?'

'He merits it!'

'Do none of you understand, damn you? Have you forgotten how I became Duke of Hereford?'

There was a moment of uncomfortable silence. They all remembered it very well, but thought it convenient to forget.

'You were constrained, Sire,' Ralph Neville pointed out. 'You had no choice but to do King Richard's bidding. I was in the same case.'

'As was Edward! As were they all, and so they will plead! Does anyone here *dare* suggest that Richard could constrain *me*, and yet not the others? Of all of them, I have least excuse, being the greatest lord. If anyone should have defied Richard, I should.'

'You acted unwillingly, my son,' said the Archbishop.

'Can you prove that *they* did not? Well?'

'They were Richard's friends, glad to do his bidding. They advised your banishment, *and* mine. Two great injustices. They agreed to the forfeiture of your lands, so that they might share your property among them. They deserve condign punishment.'

'You didn't send men to murder your uncle,' Grey de Ruthin added. 'You can be acquitted of that, Sire.'

'My uncle was in Mowbray's charge. There's no doubt of that. Mowbray has died in Italy—let him bear the blame. There's no worthwhile evidence against my Cousin Edward. Bagot is a rogue, and Hall was a confessed murderer. What they have said is of small account.'

There was a great deal of uncomfortable shuffling as his advisers digested that opinion. None of them agreed with it.

'Aumale and the rest belong in the Tower,' growled Sir Thomas Erpingham, fingering his scar.

'They do,' agreed Neville, 'if only for their own safety. The feeling against them is very high. It could lead to trouble.'

Harry glared at him. 'I'll have the head of any man who takes the law into his own hands. Mark it well, all of you. I did not take this crown lightly, without advice, without thought, without many hours of prayer. I took it because there was no other way to ensure the proper government of the realm. I'm no tyrant, and I'll not start my reign by bathing in the blood of my own relatives. Not when their chiefest fault has been that they have obeyed their sovereign too readily. These are able men, experienced in affairs of state, and I want to win their loyalty, make use of their talents. I'll not sacrifice them to satisfy the spite of hot-headed fools like Morley and Fitzwalter, men who don't come to court from one Parliament to the next, and are as fit to advise me on matters touching the good of England as a pair of woodcutters.'

'The former King's friends will not necessarily appreciate your clemency,' the Archbishop said. 'There's already talk...'

He left the word hanging significantly in the air.

'Talk of what?' Bolingbroke demanded. He was growing increasingly impatient with the stubbornness of his advisers.

'It's said that Salisbury is already conspiring against you.'

Harry's expression soured for a moment. If there was one man among Richard's coterie for whom he felt a strong personal dislike that man was Salisbury. Richard had sent John Montagu to France as an ambassador during Harry's period of exile, and Salisbury had been at pains to make life as difficult as possible for him.

'It's also said,' he grunted, 'that a child has been born in Hertfordshire with three heads. I don't believe that either. Salisbury is *nothing* without Richard's favour behind him. He may grumble to his heart's content. I don't count that as treason. If he does more than grumble I'll crush him like a fly against a wall, and he knows it.'

He sat back in his chair, waiting for further argument. None came, but he could sense from their expressions, from their very way of standing, that they were far from content. The silence was, in a way, more telling than anything they had said.

'Very well,' he conceded. 'Let them all be arrested. A few weeks of confinement will not harm them. They shall be examined as to their part in Richard's follies, and especially in regard to my uncle's murder. Some punishment may be necessary, to appease Parliament. But I'll not touch their lives, or the lands of their inheritance. Not unless they force me to it. That, my lords, is the end of the discussion on this matter.'

**

The storm had burst suddenly upon the Thames, stirring its murky depths and throwing up tiny splashing columns of water that rose above the sluggish ripples. The river was high at the dock of the *Old Inne*, almost as if it had ambitions to enter the house itself, most of the stairs already hidden beneath it.

York clambered awkwardly from his barge, shaking off the fussing attentions of his household officers in his anxiety to get out of the wet. The fiercely driving rain had pierced his heavy cloak and everything he wore beneath it, through to his skin. The barge's awning had offered more display of his cognizances than protection, and he was only marginally less soaked than his unfortunate oarsmen.

Within the house it was almost as dark as night, but in the parlour Joanne had had a fire made up and candles lit. In other circumstances it might have been thought a cosy refuge from the weather.

Constance was on the window seat, with her children and her brother, Dickon. Philippa had seated herself on a press, her back to the wall. She looked as if she had just been dragged from bed, had not even bothered the cover her hair, which hung about her in dull plaits. Joanne sat by the fire, in her own high-backed chair. They all rose to greet him, apart from his Duchess.

'Well?' she demanded, without preamble.

York stepped onto the rug that lay before the fire, cast off his cloak, and wiped the rain from his face with the back of his hand.

'Your brother and my son have been taken to Windsor,' he said. 'Despenser, Salisbury and Exeter are in the Tower. It's for their own safety.'

'Bolingbroke told you that, did he?'

'I've spoken to the King, madame, as I promised you I would.'

'What King?' Joanne stood up angrily. 'Harry of Lancaster is no lawful King, and never can be. He laughs at you, my lord.'

'It's scandalous!' Philippa burst out. 'How does he *dare* to arrest Ned? My lord has done nothing to deserve such treatment. *Nothing!* Is it because of those vile liars who accused him in Parliament? That man, Hall. What was he? An underling of Norfolk's. A *common valet.* Whoever heard of peer of the realm, let alone a duke, being arrested on the testimony of one of such mean rank? A person none of us would recognise if we fell over him. A rogue who has since been hanged for his crimes!'

'Your husband, lady, was very fortunate not to be hanged himself,' York said, trying very hard to keep calm. 'If you'd been in Parliament yesterday, and seen what was damned near to a riot, you'd be glad that he's safe and out of the reach of his enemies. The King intends no harm to him, or to any of them. They'll be tried, of course, but he has promised me that their lives and lands are secure.'

'How can you trust a word Bolingbroke says?' Joanne sneered. 'I never will! He swore on the Host that Richard would keep his crown. Why should he keep a mere promise, after so wicked a perjury? What shall be said of you? You've such influence that you can't even protect your wife's brother, your daughter's husband, or your own heir! Small incentive, then, for men to seek your patronage or look to you for advice. They may as well wear the livery of Jack the hog man as yours for all the good it will do them. When our marriage was arranged, my father—God pardon him—told me that he was giving me into the care of one of the greatest lords in the realm. He was mistaken and I'm *ashamed* to be your wife.'

'Madame, I think you forget yourself,' the Duke roared back. 'Whether you like it or not, Harry Bolingbroke is King now. Do you hear me? My King and your King. You had better get used to that fact. Don't think I don't know what you're about, you and that fool brother of yours, and that bloody heretic, Salisbury! It's fortunate for you that the King doesn't take them remotely seriously, that he knows they can do nothing to harm him. I'm interested in making sure that this family *survives*. Not in empty dreams and witless conspiracies.'

'Sir,' said Dickon, 'it seems to me that the King shows no great kindness to your family, using us in this way. Humbling us. Perhaps it's a taste of what we may expect in the future.'

Dickon had walked in the coronation procession, taking precedence of all the barons in token of his status as Harry's cousin. It was his first role as an adult, and had lent him a certain new confidence.

'It may be,' York answered tartly, 'if we are stupid enough to give him cause to suspect us of seeking his ruin. Be in no doubt. Richard's day is done. He's admitted his own insufficiency, and Parliament has deposed him. I've pledged my allegiance to King Harry, and will be his loyal subject. As shall you all, if you wish me to know you.'

'How can you side with that devil against your own son?' Philippa demanded. Having made sure that she was close enough, she sank back onto the cushioned press, as if her legs had given way. 'Unnatural man! One might think that *Bolingbroke* is your heir. I remember how you pleaded with King Richard on his account, caring nothing for the trouble that caused, angering Richard and making him doubt our loyalty. I tell you, if Ned comes to harm through your idleness, I will never speak to you again.'

'That,' said the Duke, struggling for patience, 'is yet another affliction I shall have to learn to endure. But I believe, madame, as I have already told you at least once, that your husband is in no danger, and will be back in your arms within a few weeks. Perhaps sooner. If you have any sense—which I doubt—you'll thank the King most heartily for saving his life. Which he could have cut like a thread, as easily as he did that of the fellow, Hall.'

Constance picked up her train and looped it over her arm, a preparatory of movement as manifest as that of a ship making sail. 'I am astonished,' she said, her voice level, 'that Harry Bolingbroke should treat you so, my lord Father. I am still more astonished that you accept his insults so lightly. Your brothers, I know, would never have stomached such an affront from King Richard, who had twenty times more right to command them. Never for a minute.'

York turned to her, and saw in her eyes something he had never seen directed at him before. Undisguised contempt. It shook him more than all the abuse that Joanne and Philippa had hurled at him, just as her quiet, icy anger made more impression on him than the others' querulous protests.

'I shall go to Bolingbroke myself,' she added, moving off across the tiled floor, 'offer my own petition.'

'You'll take your children on the river in this storm?' York objected. 'Impossible! I doubt you'll get the barge out of the dock. Anyway, the King will not receive you.'

'The children may stay here, with my lady the Duchess. I'll wait in the barge until the storm abates, or the tide turns, or whatever is necessary for me to get up to Westminster. And if my cousin will not receive me I'll sit down outside his door until he does.'

'It will avail you nothing. You cannot be so mad as to suppose that they'll be released on your pleading?'

She halted. 'I suppose no such thing. I intend to ask to be allowed to join my lord in the Tower, to be of what comfort I can to him. Since King Richard is there, and Salisbury, we shall be in good company. Certainly far better than I can find elsewhere.'

***

Within the Tower Sir William Bagot, still burdened with heavy chains, had been removed to a dry cell above ground, and mildly encouraged by some vague hints of future pardon. Sir Richard of Bordeaux, lately King, had been informed that it was King Harry's pleasure that he should be transferred to another place of confinement. Though he raged at them, and paced about his barren chamber like a caged lion, his gaolers would not disclose his destination, or even the exact time of his departure, lest he find means to pass on the information to those who might seek to aid him. John Holland, Duke of Exeter, drank endlessly in his thinly furnished lodgings, threatening the servants set to wait on him and calling down the wrath of God upon Harry of Lancaster and all his treacherous underlings. John Montagu, Earl of Salisbury, sought comfort from his Lollard Bible. Occasionally he broke off from reading to scribble a few lines of verse. His stepson, Alan de Buxhull, visited him regularly and conveyed his messages to the outside world. Sometimes Alan brought with him Ralph, Lord Lumley, a northerner who wore Northumberland's livery badge at his throat, or Sir Thomas Blount, a knight of Oxfordshire. They gathered together as far from the door as possible, spoke in low, hushed tones.

Thomas Despenser also received various guests, including his cousin, Sir Hugh, who brought him reassuring words from King Harry. Hugh was Bolingbroke's man now; drawing his hundred pounds a year at the Exchequer, and wearing his Lancastrian livery with the same contentment that he had once displayed the white hart. He was surprised when his cousin's wife did not enquire after the health of Dame Sybil and their children, puzzled when she withdrew herself to the furthest corner of the chamber and concentrated on some mending work she had in hand.

'My cousin means well,' Thomas said, after Hugh had gone. The note of reproof in his voice was mild, but noticeable.

Constance did not look up from the shirt she was repairing. 'Does he?'

'I think so. You can't blame him for submitting to Bolingbroke. We all did that.'

'Not as readily as he did.'

'We need such friends as we can find. You may have cause to be glad of them.'

'While you are away on your crusade?'

'If I'm allowed to go. Perhaps I shan't be.'

Her hand froze in the middle of a stitch, and she raised her eyes to look at him. 'Thomas?'

'We are much hated, *treschere*. So far your brother has had the worst of it, but he's as much King Edward's grandson as Harry Bolingbroke himself, and that still counts for something. Salisbury, the Hollands and I have no such protection, and the Parliament is hungry for blood. That man they hanged, Hall, was just a servant who did the bidding of his betters. How can they put such a one to death and leave alive those of us who had the King's ear, and knew his secret counsels?'

'My father was promised that your life and lands would be safe.' Constance fought to keep a tremor out of her voice. She had doubted that pledge, but kept her suspicions from him. It troubled her that he had come to the same conclusion without any external assistance.

'King Richard promised that he would not execute Arundel,' he reminded her. 'That's how the Archbishop came to persuade his brother to surrender. Some might see it as justice if Bolingbroke broke his word in the same way.'

'Arundel deserved to die. You cannot compare your case to his.'

'I dare say Lady Arundel thought *her* husband guiltless. She was not his judge, and nor will you be mine.'

Constance rose from her place and moved towards him, and he took her hand and pressed the back of it to his lips. It was strange, she reflected, that he seemed to be in better heart now than he had been when still at liberty, even though apparently contemplating the possibility of his own death.

'It may not be so bad, my love,' he said. 'We may find ourselves banished to the Isle of Man, as old Warwick was. Or perhaps your cousin will keep his word, and I shall go free after all. Hugh seemed to think all would be well, and it may be that he wasn't just trying to cheer me. You must pray for me. There's nothing else you can do.'

She nodded. She would indeed try to pray, though her faith had been severely shaken. It seemed to her that the patronage of a God who allowed an anointed King to be deposed and imprisoned was about as much to be relied upon as Harry Bolingbroke's good will.

***

Constance composed herself, bit colour into her lips, stood up and shook the creases out of her gown, as the sound of bustle on the stairs heralded her husband's return from his trial. Above all, she must not show weakness. Thomas had enough to face. She must support him, not burden him with her emotions.

The door opened, and then was closed behind him. He was angry, angry as even she had rarely seen him. It was one reaction she had not expected. Resignation perhaps. Even despair. Joy if their hopes of freedom were justified. But not anger.

He threw his gloves to the back of the fire, and she watched dumbly as the leather twisted and blackened. Then he plucked a precious glass goblet from their table and hurled it in the same direction, using all his great strength and shattering it into a hundred expensive fragments.

'*Thomas!*' The waste shocked her to the heart. So did the blind fury in his eyes.

'Do you know, madame, what your damned cousin, Bolingbroke, has done to me?' he demanded. 'That stinking traitor, who dares call himself King? He's shamed me! He's taken my earldom from me!'

Relieved, she put her hand on his arm, intending to reassure him. 'The earldom is nothing.'

'*Nothing?*' His fury turned upon her. 'You dare to say that it's *nothing*?'

'Next to your life it is nothing. Your life is what matters to me.'

'Oh, yes, he's spared me that!' He flung himself away from her and staggered around the room in his rage. 'Such a life as it will be! Life as the butt of men's jests! I prefer to die than live so. The others have suffered much the same. Your brother has lost his dukedom. We are all humiliated. Shamed!'

'Surely it is not so bad,' Constance said quietly, trying to calm him. 'What is lost can be regained.'

'It will be,' he promised, 'never doubt it. But you've not heard the half of it. Every petty rogue with a grievance against us is to be encouraged to come forward to have it redressed. What man is so low, so wicked, that his word will not be preferred to mine by this King's Council? We are forbidden to grant liveries, save to our household servants, so we shall have no influence in the shires. And if we make any move to aid Richard, to restore him to his rights, we are to be treated as traitors, without any trial. So, Bolingbroke may kill me whenever he chooses. He's only to dream of a conspiracy, and he can take my head and forfeit my lands.'

She was quiet for a few moments. 'So, what will you do?' she asked at last. 'Do you still mean to go on your crusade to Rhodes?'

He glared at her as if she had insulted him. 'Crusade be damned!' he roared. 'What do you think I am? There'll be fighting enough here in England. That I promise you.'

22

The rich red hangings of the great bed were decorated with embroidered blue garters and white ostrich feathers, the latter representing the plumes that Edward of Woodstock, the Black Prince, had taken from the body of the King of Bohemia after the battle of Crecy. It was more than fifty-three years since that famous victory, forty-three since Poitiers. Now, some said, with an acknowledged warrior on the English throne, the wars would begin again. The French were showing signs of hostility, shaken by King Richard's deposition, which not even Orleans had anticipated. The Scots, in clear breach of their truce with England, were already raiding across the border, doing great damage and taking prisoners for ransom.

Edward of York lay on his back in the bed, with his head resting on his clasped hands, deep in contemplation that did not touch on war or diplomacy. He had been thinking a great deal lately, in prison at Windsor and then in the somewhat slacker custody of the Abbot of Westminster. Now he was free again, or as free as a man could be who had so many statutory Damoclean swords hanging over his head; but he was still uncertain as to his future policy.

'What will you do?' asked Philippa suddenly.

'Do?'

'About *King* Bolingbroke. He has treated you *appallingly*.'

'He's just granted me the Isle of Wight and Carisbrooke Castle.'

She ran through her mental inventory of their property. 'You had those before, didn't you?'

'Yes. Richard gave them me two years ago. Under my sentence it was forfeited, but Harry has confirmed me in possession. I didn't even have to ask. I find that interesting. It's a sign of favour, a small change in the wind. He's also given me custody of the Channel Islands and appointed me to his Council.'

'It's nothing to what he's taken from you. Holderness. Clun.' Philippa's lips tightened with anger. 'Your dukedom!'

He grunted. 'Yes, I regret Holderness. The richest lordship in all England; but I was bound to lose it once the judgement on Uncle Gloucester was reversed. It's not really Harry's fault.'

'Not his *fault*? Whose fault is it then? Mine, perhaps? The Mayor of London's? The Pope's?'

He rested his hand on her heavily freckled thigh. It was still rather clammy from the heat generated by the love making they had both regarded as an appropriate celebration of his release.

'Patience, my dear,' he said gently. 'This is a time for cool heads. Let me put it this way. It's as if we've been very ill. We've been very thoroughly bled. We need to take the time to recover our strength.'

'The *dukedom*!' She squeezed the word through her large teeth, as if it gave her physical pain.

'It isn't important. In a little while I shall be Duke of York. My father's ailing, and he really can't last much longer. That wife of his has probably stolen ten years off his life! To be Duke of York is a far, far greater thing than to be Duke of Aumale. As the sun is greater than the moon. When I'm head of the family, I shall know how to make proper use of our power.'

Philippa's grey-green, contemplative eyes met his. 'The others will not wait so long,' she said.

'I know. You forget I was with them in the abbot's lodgings. It's fortunate that they don't trust me, or they'd have tried to drag me into their mad schemes. The abbot is with them. He's Richard's man. Small wonder, after all the money Richard poured into the place.'

'Do you know what they're planning to do?'

'No, but whatever it is, they can't hope to succeed. I wish I could keep Thomas out of it, for my sister's sake; but you know what he's like.'

'Pigheaded,' said Philippa. 'Pigheaded and proud. Have you spoken to Constance?'

'No. Not since the day of the coronation. How could I have done? She wasn't lodged with us at Westminster, you know.'

'She was with him in the Tower. Imagine that! How could she be so absurd? Anyway, she's the only person I know who might possibly change his mind. I'll talk to her if you wish.'

Edward glanced at her. 'I think I'd better do that myself,' he said. 'It may be difficult. It may even be that she's as crazed as the rest of them. You know how she hates Bolingbroke.'

Philippa snorted. 'She called him rebel and traitor to his face at Berkeley. I was surprised he took it from her.' She shifted her weight onto her side, and reached out to take a sugared fig from a gold plate standing on the adjoining dresser. She stuffed it into her ample mouth and chewed for a moment. 'Mind you, she doesn't hate him any more than I do myself. I can *never* forgive him for treating you as though you were no better than a common felon. Throwing you into prison for no good reason. You, his own cousin! The horrid little man!'

'Hatred clouds the mind. Leads us into folly. I didn't want Harry to be King, but now he is, and my business is to turn the situation to our advantage. I don't quite see how, as yet, but I will.'

'Ned,' Philippa began, frowning with the thought that had occurred to her, 'when you say you have no part in whatever it is that Surrey and Salisbury intend to do, I believe you. But will Bolingbroke believe you?'

He met her gaze. 'I'd not considered that,' he admitted. 'It's a shrewd thought, my love. A very shrewd thought. It would come down to my word, and he might not have any faith in my denials. And there are many around him who would be glad to see my head on the Bridge.'

'So you must persuade the others to give up their conspiracy. Or, if they will not, you must find a means to prove beyond doubt that you are loyal to him.'

He hesitated for a moment, digesting the implication in her words. Then he put his feet to the floor, and reached for his shirt. 'You are quite right, my dear,' he said, 'and I think it's time for me to set about the task.'

**

The Despenser household was moving to Caversham for Christmas. There was a great deal to arrange, the more so since its organisation had been severely disrupted by the events of recent months, with many of the officers and servants dispersed to their homes and in need of summoning back to their duty. The family's barges were lodged at Caversham, and needed bringing downstream to London, and there were horses and sumpter carts to be retrieved from Hanley Castle and Fotheringhay. There were even bits and pieces still at Berkeley. Food and other essentials needed to be gathered at Caversham for the twelve days of feasting, and invitations had to be sent to those who were to be entertained for all or part of the period. Thomas's list of people to be so honoured was remarkable for its exclusions as well as its inclusions. Sir Andrew Hake and Sir John St. John were to be summoned, and so was Sir Thomas Blount, who Constance scarcely knew from Adam. Hugh Mortimer, Sir William Stradling and Sir Hugh Despenser, on the other hand, were not under any account to be asked for their company. The Earl of Salisbury, Thomas said, would also be visiting them at some point, although in his case no formal bidding was necessary.

Constance was much occupied by the management of these evolutions, and though John Norreys was as reliable a support as ever, the general shortage of available officers meant that there was little time available for dwelling on politics, and still less for a proper investigation of her husband's intentions. Thomas showed no inclination to go into details with her, though the proportion of his time that he spent with Salisbury, Surrey and the rest was so great that she rarely saw him, except in bed. Even when he was at home he was constantly exercising with his weapons, as though preparing for an important tournament. He used his weeks of idleness in the Tower as an excuse for this, claiming that he had grown fat and sluggish.

Edward's pretext for his visit to his sister was that he wanted to report to her on the progress and welfare of their brother, Dickon, who had recently been recalled to their father's household. The Duke's decision had hurt Constance; indeed it had angered her. It implied that he did not trust her husband to keep the boy out of trouble. Perhaps even that he did not trust him at all. The fact that York had some justification for his prudence did not mollify her. If anything it added to her resentment.

The pretext was rapidly put aside. He sat down by the parlour fire, staring into the glowing coals. 'You know what Thomas and his friends are about?' he asked.

Constance looked at him, and then glanced around her. Her women were several feet away, engrossed in their work and their own quiet chatter. 'I know something,' she admitted, keeping her voice low, 'but not all.'

'In God's name, can you not keep him out of it?'

She shook her head. 'I don't believe I can.'

'Then you had better order your mourning,' he said brutally. 'Have they no sense at all? How many men can they muster in such a cause? Not nearly enough, that's for sure.'

She paced about for a moment. 'I know that Thomas dare not trust the half of his affinity. I am not sure of even some of those he thinks he *can* trust. It is asking much of men to put their lands and all they own at stake, as well as their lives. Even when the cause is good.'

'You think it a good cause, do you?'

'Of course I do! Do you not?'

He was silent for a moment. 'It'd give me joy to see Harry Bolingbroke's corpse rotting on a hearse; but the truth is that Richard no longer trusts me as he did, and I'm not sure what I'd gain from his restoration, except more trouble. Anyway, as I've told you, I'm sure the attempt will fail, good cause or not. When it does Bolingbroke is bound to take revenge on me, because he'll think I've had a hand in it, especially if you and Thomas are active in whatever it is that's planned.'

'So it's your own neck you fear for?'

His hand went to his chin. His red-golden beard, usually sleek and elaborately barbered, was ragged with neglect, a symptom of his weeks under arrest and the depth of his depression. 'Yes. I admit it; and why should I not have such fears? Harry is surrounded by men who hate me. The likes of Grey de Ruthin would be glad of any excuse to have me killed. But I don't want Thomas killed either. Or the rest of them. The time to fight is not now, but in the future, as I told you when we last spoke. We need more allies before we start a rebellion. Far more. Have they no wits that they cannot see it? No one even knows where Richard is lodged. For all we know his gaolers could have orders to kill him if there's any attempt at rescue. Have they thought of that?'

'You'll have to speak to Thomas.'

'I will—I hoped he would be here; but the truth is, dear Sister, that he's more likely to heed you than me. I think he doubts my honesty. I think they all do.'

'With you to aid them, Ned, they might have some hope of success. Perhaps you should think of that.'

He shrugged. 'If I were to join them they'd still have no hope. I've been stripped of half my livelihood and almost all my influence. I'm powerless, Constance, and must build anew from the ground.'

'You could surely bring some of our father's men into the quarrel—'

Edward interrupted her with a harsh, bitter laugh. 'You have been his daughter all these years, and still do not know him? He's Harry's man now, as much as ever he was Richard's. He'll not stir a finger, and he'll make sure that I don't stir one on his behalf. My advice is that you'll say nothing to him that you'd not wish him to repeat to Bolingbroke.'

'Ned, if they go ahead, and fail, and are put to death...' She closed her eyes for a moment, contemplating the horror she had conjured, then forced herself to go on. 'How can that be to your profit? What friends will you have to aid you in two or three years time when Harry is perhaps less favoured? And what if, by some miracle, they should succeed without your aid? Where would you stand with Richard then?'

He shook his head. 'I think there's little chance of that.' He paused, his eyes turned to the fire again as if he found inspiration there. 'I'll stay if you wish; try to talk sense into your husband. He should take you and the children to Cardiff. Keep you all as far removed from this insanity as possible.'

It was late in the afternoon before Thomas returned from his latest visit to the Earl of Salisbury. He seemed momentarily surprised by the presence of his brother-in-law under his roof, but he hid it well, and settled down to converse with him. After Constance had satisfied herself that they were peaceable together, she left them alone on the pretext of arranging for them to be supplied with food and drink. It seemed to her that Thomas would be far more likely to climb down if she were not there to see him do it.

***

'Your brother has agreed to join our enterprise,' Thomas said.

Constance started from sleep, woken by his words and by the touch of his hand on her waist, and before she could consider his words, or reprove him for his folly in bringing a lighted candle inside the bed-curtains, his lips closed on hers.

'What time is it?' she asked.

He shrugged. 'Late. Very late. Does it matter?'

'He's gone?'

'Ned? Yes. Only just now. I told him he was welcome to stay, that we could bed his men down in the hall; but he said he preferred to sleep in his wife's bed. For which I don't blame him.'

She sat up, shook herself into wakefulness. 'He told me that you had no hope of success. That he would not venture his life in such a cause, and that he would persuade you to withdraw from it.'

'He made the attempt,' he grinned. He paused for a moment, bent his neck and nuzzled gently at her breast, just brushing against the nipple with his lips. 'He argued for hours, but in the end, I persuaded *him*!' The note of triumph in his voice reached a new peak. '*Treschere*, I doubt Ned and I have ever been more agreed. We've concocted a plan between us, a plan that can't fail. I can't wait to bring Salisbury and the others into the secret. It's so much better than anything we've discussed before.'

Constance could not keep her eyes from the leaping candle flame. 'In God's name, Thomas, be careful, or you'll have us alight!'

'I'll buy new curtains for the bed when I'm Earl of Gloucester again,' he said. 'New everything. A fine coronet for you, set with the dearest jewels that can be bought. Whatever you want. I don't want to be in the dark. Not tonight. I want to see what's mine. Every inch of you. Take that coif off, and let down your hair.'

It was obvious that his negotiations with her brother had involved much lubrication of the throat.

'Is Ned as drunk as you are?' she asked.

He grinned. 'I'm not so drunk that I can't pay the marriage debt. Come; unbraid your hair. I want you, my wife.'

'Put the candle outside the curtain,' she insisted. 'I don't want hot wax dripping on me either. Are you sure about what Ned has said to you? He swore he'd have no part in it, said it was madness. Even that I should order my mourning if I couldn't persuade you to give up and take me to Glamorgan, away from the danger.'

He turned away from her and, sitting on the edge of the bed, put the candlestick on the adjacent stand, pushing aside their night-livery of bread and wine. 'Well, I must have put some spirit into his heart,' he said happily. 'Ned's very clever. There's to be jousting at Windsor on Twelfth Night. That's our chance. We can fetch all the armour and weapons we need, without rousing suspicion. We can fill whole carts with them. Bring our retinues as well. No one expects great lords to appear at a tournament unattended. We'll take Bolingbroke completely by surprise. Most of *his* supporters are going home for Christmas. Northumberland has already ridden north, and Ralph Neville will not be far behind him, with the Scots over the border. Once Bolingbroke is dead, Richard's friends will rise, all over England. Everything will be well, *treschere*. I know it in my heart.'

Constance's heart was full of doubts, for she sorely mistrusted her brother's sudden conversion to her husband's way of thinking. She put her arms about Thomas, pressed herself against his back. 'Ned cares for no one but himself. Do not trust him too far.'

'He can't betray us without betraying himself,' he said, pleased with himself. 'We shall sign and seal a bond, each of us, and every one of us shall have his own copy. There'll be no going back for Ned, or for anyone else.'

'It's so dangerous.'

'Of course it's dangerous! But we're not fools, Constance. We've weighed the risks, found a way that stands a good chance of success. What would you have me do?'

She shook her head. She wanted him, alive and safe, at any cost. She wanted him to live to see his son grow to manhood. All else was secondary to that. But she could not permit herself to tell him so. He needed her support, not the additional burden of her fears. Perhaps they stood some chance now, if her brother played his part. Ned was shrewd. He would find a way for them to triumph against the odds. So she hoped.

She unpinned her linen coif, allowed her yellow-gold hair to fall around her in its abundant folds, and unfastened the braids. None could say what the future would bring, or how long she would have this man who, for all his faults, she loved with her entire heart. They were safe for tonight, secure behind their heraldic curtains, and he was hers.

***

The circle of men gathered around the great table in the Abbot of Westminster's lodging passed the parchment bonds from one to another, each signing in turn and applying his signet to the blood-red wax next to his name. It was late in the afternoon of Wednesday, December 17th 1399. They had gathered for a leisurely dinner at noon, and the winter darkness was already closing around them, the only light provided by the red coals of the fire and the silver candelabra in the centre of the table, which reflected in their eyes, and sparkled on the jewels they wore on their hands and at their throats.

Edward of York sat next to the abbot. He seemed the most relaxed of them all, even to have a measure of amusement in his eyes, a host of silver folly bells jingling from his sleeves as he worked his quill. Claiming precedence of rank, he was the first to sign the bonds, writing his name with a bold flourish. About his neck was a large and heavily bejewelled livery badge of the white hart.

Thomas Despenser watched his brother-in-law closely, less sure of his honesty than he cared to admit even to himself. Edward's long but shapely Plantagenet nose reminded him of Constance, and their eyes were almost exactly the same shade of vivid sky blue; and yet in those eyes was a difference. You could look into Constance's eyes and see her soul; Edward kept his soul well concealed, protected by his outward show of amused good humour. Either that, or there was no longer a soul to conceal.

John Holland was next to Edward; he was indulging himself with the abbot's wine, but as yet was not outwardly affected by it, save perhaps to the extent of a slight slurring of his speech, and a gradual increase in its volume. His hard, leathery hand gripped the pen as if he was trying to crush it into submission, and his signature was little more than an untidy blotch. Next to him sat his nephew, Thomas Holland, Duke of Surrey, similar enough in features to be his son, but quieter, less forceful. He was several inches taller than Exeter, and sat slightly stooped as if he wanted to make up for this difference.

Thomas Merke, the Bishop of Carlisle, sat at Despenser's left. The bishop was even quieter than Surrey, his composed expression concealing his thoughts. Sometimes his lantern jaw moved a little, as if he was on the verge of saying something, but his comments were infrequent. Salisbury was on Despenser's other hand. His round, plump face wore an expression of deep contentment. He had enjoyed his dinner, and his eyes kept closing for a moment or two, as if he was drifting into sleep. The silver doublet he was wearing glowed in the candlelight, and matched the colour of the long, curling hair that emerged from beneath his hood.

Salisbury's stepson, Alan de Buxhull, stood by the fireplace next to Ralph, Lord Lumley. Thomas scarcely knew the northerner, even as a nodding acquaintance, and was by no means sure how he had become part of the conspiracy. He was Northumberland's man, even wore his livery. Though not today, Thomas noted. The presence of Thomas Blount from Oxfordshire was easier to explain—he was on close terms with Salisbury—and Sir Benedict Sely was the master of Exeter's household, as well as one of the knights King Richard had retained for life. The clerk Richard Maudelyn was there because of his physical resemblance to his former master. Until King Richard's whereabouts could be discovered, Maudelyn would serve as his double. The similarity, given royal robes and a crown, was close enough to deceive a casual onlooker. After all, people were not in the habit of staring at their sovereign.

Only the principals signed the bonds, and when the last line of ink had been sanded and dried, a service performed by the abbot himself, the copies were distributed so that each signatory had his own copy, and thus a hold upon the others. They were agreed to meet again at Kingston on Sunday, 4th January, save for Exeter, whose task it was to stay in London and secure the city in Richard's name once Bolingbroke was known to be dead.

Led by the abbot, they made their way in informal procession along cool, dark, vaulted passages and into the great abbey itself. In the majestic stillness even Edward and the mildly intoxicated Exeter grew solemn, and did not speak. Monks chanted in the choir as the conspirators walked between the tombs of kings and queens to the jewel-encrusted shrine of Edward the Confessor. There they knelt and solemnly swore, one by one, that they would keep faith with one another, and, no matter what the hazard to their lives and property, would not rest until King Richard had been restored to his throne.

***

Edward had not told Philippa of his decision; he thought it might cause complications to do so, and there were complications enough. They spent Christmas in London, with the Duke and Duchess of York, and it was not until the 3rd January, when they were actually on their way down to supper, that he broke the subject. Even then he broke it only so far as to inform her that he would be leaving early in the morning, riding to Windsor to take part in the jousting.

His wife was immediately suspicious. Edward was no jouster, and often remarked that he saw neither sport nor pleasure in it; indeed, although he filled his leisure hours with hawking, hunting, and the writing of poetry, he rarely exercised with arms at all unless he was about to take part in a campaign. Though a competent strategist and tactician, he had little subtlety in personal combat, relying on his size and strength rather than any outstanding skill.

'You've left me little time to prepare for the journey,' she protested.

'What journey? You're staying here, in London. There'll be no women at Windsor.'

Her lip trembled, and she almost lost her footing on the stairway they were descending. 'Then it must be a very strange kind of tournament! Do you think me a fool?'

'I do not, my dear.'

She halted abruptly, seemed to dig into the stairs like a dog fighting the leash. She made an elaborate task of arranging her skirts so that they cleared her feet by an inch or so, but still did not move. 'The presence of ladies is the whole point of a tournament,' she went on. 'Everyone knows that. I expect your sister will be there, won't she? Despenser won't leave *her* at home while he enjoys himself with whores.'

Edward snorted with impatience. 'My sister is capable of walking down stairs without falling over her own feet or showing her legs to the world,' he remarked, with massive irrelevance.

'How can you be so cruel, to shame me so? Other men at least have the decency to be circumspect in these matters.'

'You don't know what cruelty is! I tell you, there will be no women there, neither Constance nor anyone else.'

'I don't believe you!'

Almost before the words had finished emerging from her mouth Philippa flinched, realising what she had said. John Golafre would have punched her face, or kicked her down the stairs, if she had dared imply he was a liar. Edward had never laid an angry hand upon her, but then she had never questioned his veracity before. He was not like Golafre, of course. In some ways she found him more frightening.

He shrugged, and drew a piece of folded parchment from the leather purse that hung from his belt.

'Read this,' he said, 'and amend your belief.'

She opened the document, took in the array of seals and scrawled signatures, and then the short declaration of intent at the top, written in the clerkly hand of the Abbot of Westminster.

'Oh, Ned!' she gasped. 'How can you be part of this, after all you said? It could be your death.'

He gave her a reassuring kiss. 'I think not. I think it may make you a duchess again. Perhaps more.'

'More? More than a duchess?'

'No one knows where Richard is. My guess is that if he's not dead already, he'll be killed at the first whisper of trouble. Our friends should rid the world of Harry Bolingbroke. Once they are gone, who shall be best placed to be King?'

'Ned, it's a fearful danger...'

'A risk, I agree; but a smaller one than I imagined. The rewards are in proportion to the hazard. As my sister reminded me, if they succeed, and I am not part of it, it'll not be to my profit.'

'You told me they could *not* succeed.'

'I've been persuaded otherwise. I think they can, given luck. *We* can. They've adopted my plan; I'd not have trusted myself to any of their mad schemes.'

She lowered her head. 'I was a fool to doubt you. A jealous fool. Can you forgive me?'

'I believe I might,' he nodded, bending to kiss her. 'If, in return, I may have the garter, warm from your leg, to bear as your token for the jousts.'

He did not wait for her answer, but began to fumble for it, Philippa squealing in exaggerated protests, and their attendants grinning and drawing closer, enjoying what was obviously a piece of Christmas horseplay. The piece of parchment and it seals slipped from her fingers, brushed off the edge of her skirt, tumbled its way down two stairs.

Richard of Conisbrough, who had been waiting for them in the hall, chose this particular moment to climb the stairs to investigate the delay. He first saw his brother and Philippa tussling with each other, obviously in play, and then the piece of parchment lying near their feet. Meaning to be helpful, he stooped and picked it up.

Edward, having captured his prize, was smiling and flustered. He bowed to Philippa, then to the company that had gathered around them; then the smile vanished as he saw what Dickon had in his hand. Dickon was paying no attention to his brother. The seals had caught his attention, and he stared at them struggling to determine their significance.

'Give me that, damn you!' Edward snapped, snatching the parchment from the boy's grip. He was so rough about it that Dickon's hand went to his dagger's hilt. Not with any real intention of drawing, but as a matter of simple instinct.

Somewhere above them, a woman screamed. The Duke and Duchess of York were descending, accompanied by a whole procession of attendants. They had seen the interplay between the brothers, and Joanne had so far misjudged the situation as to think that blood was about to be shed.

York advanced, making his way through the gaudy crowd around Edward and Philippa, men and women stumbling over each other as they backed off, attempting to make obeisances as they did so.

'What is that?' the Duke asked.

Edward stood before him, his face sheepish, holding Philippa's garter in one hand and the all-important bond in the other. 'Nothing of significance, sir,' he said.

'Significant enough to quarrel with your brother about it, and upset my wife. Let me see.'

Philippa choked, and began to cry.

'A mercer's bill,' Edward explained with a shrug. 'Philippa is extravagant. I am sure Your Grace would not be interested, and I have arranged for the debt to be settled.'

York glanced at Philippa, and did not like what he saw. 'Show me,' he said remorselessly, holding out his hand. He was not the most intelligent man in England, but he knew that mercers did not weigh down their accounts with multiple noble seals, and he didn't care to be taken for a fool.

Edward shrugged in resignation, and handed over the bond. York scanned it, but scarcely read it—the seals and signatures were sufficient explanation of its purpose. For a moment he gaped in disbelief, and then he exploded. 'Fool! Madman! Cursed young idiot!' He tore the parchment across, threw it to the floor and trampled it. 'Can you not breathe for an hour without seeking mischief? Do you not know that Parliament has bound me as a surety for your good behaviour? Will you bring ruin on us all? I shall go at once to the King. I don't care if it costs you your head.'

Philippa screamed, and pretended to collapse, so that her women and Joanne hurried to fuss over her.

Her husband glanced at her, then at his father's impassive face, and carried on. 'The roads between here and Windsor are already blocked. There's no way through, sir. You'll be captured.'

'I'll find a way!' York snapped, and he stumbled away, shouting for a horse and an escort.

His heir hurried after him. 'You don't understand. I joined this conspiracy so that I could discover the depths of their treason. I meant to go to Cousin Harry myself, with the bond you have just destroyed. Evidence, sir, to prove me more than an idle bearer of tales.'

The Duke shook his head. 'You think to gull me,' he said miserably.

'I do not! If you want to know who is at the heart of this plot, it's Despenser and my sister. It's she who encouraged me to join it, and he who planned what was to be done. It is the truth, Father, as God is my judge.'

'Then why did you not come to me before? I could have put a stop to this before any harm was done. Now it's too late.'

'I expected you not to trust me. As you do not! But there is still time. We shall ride together to Windsor, Father. Warn the King of the great danger he faces.'

York shrugged. He was not deceived by Edward, just very, very tired. A hasty ride to Windsor through a cold, black night was the last thing he wanted, but there was no choice.

'Very well,' he conceded wearily. 'You are my son, despite all. I'll do what I can to save your life. Even pretend that I believe your lies.'

***

Out on the river it was as chill as ice. Constance was wearing her thickest cloak, but she still kept shuddering beneath its folds. Even the men rowing her barge looked uncomfortable, for despite the heat generated by their work their hands were almost frozen to the oars.

'We'd have been wiser to ride to Sonning,' Agnes Norreys said, her complaint forming a cloud of steam that drifted off towards the skeletal trees that lined the bank, carried by the thin breeze.

Constance shook her head. She had not wanted to attract attention by showing herself in Reading; had she done so the abbot, at least, might have expected a visit at this time of year, and that would have involved delay. Besides, the narrow, rutted tracks across the chalk from the town to Sonning would be made hazardous by expanses of thawing ice. At least by river they were certain of reaching their destination. Three miles at most, speeded by the current; their discomfort would be brief.

'Perhaps,' Agnes ventured, 'we should have sent a man ahead to inform them of your coming. They may not allow you to see the Queen.'

'There was no one to be spared. Besides, it will be more difficult to refuse me if I just arrive without warning.'

'I'm surprised that Tyldesley is left to us,' Agnes said tartly. 'I'd have thought he'd be more use at Windsor than here.'

Constance frowned momentarily. In a way it was strange that Thomas had selected Hugh Tyldesley to stay with her, for a less likely squire of dames was hard to imagine. She suspected that Tyldesley was not happy with his allocation of duty either, although it was difficult to be sure. He was not a man given to questioning his orders, or saying much at all, as long as he received his pay. Bright in the new red, white and yellow Despenser livery he had received at Christmas, he stood in the centre of the barge, just outside the protection of the cered canopy, his eyes constantly scanning the banks as if he anticipated an ambush.

'Norreys might have been a better choice,' Agnes went on. 'He certainly has better manners. I find it hard to believe that Tyldesley is a gentleman. Well, perhaps he is accounted one in Lancashire. God knows, they're as wild as Scots in the north parts.'

Tyldesley had won, by the lottery of finding a bean in a pudding, the traditional office of Lord of Misrule over Christmas. He had made good use of the powers conferred on him, among other things requiring Agnes to kiss the pig boy, and dance on the top table. This had not endeared him to her, especially as he had claimed to be punishing her miserable face, saying her expression was a sin against Christmas. Agnes did not consider herself to be at all miserable, and made no allowance either for the season of the year or the fact that they had all been very drunk.

Constance could be tart as well when it so pleased her. 'It is not for you to question my lord's decisions,' she said. 'You should be pleased that he wishes to keep your husband by him. He trusts no man more than he does John.'

'He has cause,' said Agnes, in no way abashed. 'John's been his right hand since the days when they were both sucking milk from the same tit.' Her narrow lips curved downwards into the deep arc that they found most comfortable. 'Jesu! I swear my feet are turned to stone for all the feeling that's in 'em. And your nose is glowing as red as a coal, my lady. We shall have to paint it before you go into the Queen. You cannot be seen like that! It's not fitting.'

The large house, or small palace, at Sonning emerged into view around the next bend of the river. It was a squat, elderly place, long disused except as a very occasional lodging on royal progresses. Within its low walls, more a boundary than a protection, an untidy collection of buildings reached back from the water's edge, many of them mere pentices of lath-and-plaster that hung like barnacles on the ancient stone core of the house. Thin plumes of smoke drifted from its chimneys and louvres, at a distance the only sign of occupation.

They landed at the small mooring and a party of the Queen's officers came out to receive them, the little procession headed by the diminutive Monsieur de Vache, the Queen's chamberlain, whom Constance recognised at once.

Tyldesley nodded to de Vache, and spoke abruptly, in his painfully laboured version of the French tongue. 'The high and mighty princess and lady, Constance of York, Dame le Despenser, to attend the Queen's Grace.'

Monsieur de Vache made an elaborate bow, and spoke directly to Constance. 'If you will permit me, madame, it will be the greatest honour to escort you into the presence of the Duchess of Ireland.'

Constance accepted his arm, though it was so low down that she almost had to stoop in order to walk with him, and she exchanged inconsequential chatter with him as they entered the building, passing between a small guard of archers. Not Richard's Cheshire Archers, disbanded now, but men of the old Lancastrian retinue put into royal livery.

De Vache's mention of the Duchess of Ireland gave her pause for thought. Philippa, Duchess of Ireland was yet another of her vast array of cousins, but one she had almost come to think of as dead, since in recent years the Duchess had never shown herself at Richard's court, preferring to live in seclusion. She was the child of King Edward's late daughter, Isabel, and her noble French husband, Enguerrand de Coucy, and had been the wife of Richard's friend, Robert de Vere, promoted by the King from Earl of Oxford to Duke of Ireland, but then driven by the Appellants into an exile that had lasted until his death in a boar hunt a few years later. While at the height of his powers de Vere had striven to divorce his Plantagenet wife so that he could marry the woman he loved, and King Richard had supported his petition to the Pope. The Duchess of Ireland had never forgiven Richard for that.

De Vache answered her unspoken question. '*Madame la Duchesse* has been placed in charge of the household of the Queen.'

'Then the Countess of March is not here?'

The little chamberlain made an encompassing gesture with his left hand and the rod of office he had clutched in it. 'Certainly the Countess is here. But as one of the Queen's ladies, that only.'

Constance told herself that she should not have been surprised by the change. Bolingbroke had no particular cause to trust Alianore; the Duchess of Ireland, from his point of view, was a much more reliable guardian for Queen Isabelle.

Robert de Vere's widow had once been a very handsome girl; unfortunately she had been struck by a particularly virulent attack of smallpox in her late teens, which had left her face scarred and pitted to the point of disfigurement. Even thick painting could disguise this only to a degree. Her wimple covered as much of her face as possible, but this tended to emphasise rather than mitigate the cruel damage to her features.

The Duchess was huddled in a chair by her well-stoked fire; a boy was serving her with a large goblet of mulled wine. Her women sat at a distance, in a row on the edge of her great bed, their hands tucked away in the folds of their gowns, their eyes fixed wistfully on their lady's fire, which they evidently did not dare to approach without invitation.

De Vache announced Constance and the Duchess turned stiffly towards them, moving her whole body.

'Ah,' she iterated briefly, though whether this was a communication or an expression of pain was not immediately clear.

'Cousin,' Constance said in greeting, choosing to accept the grunt as an acknowledgement of her arrival.

'You may go, Mowbray,' the Duchess sniffed, addressing the boy. Constance gathered, as much from his looks as from his name, that this was the son of the late Duke of Norfolk; she had heard that he was in the Queen's household. He was a stocky youth, with black, curling hair and an expression of sullen malice. After the door had closed behind him, the Duchess spoke again, in Constance's general direction. 'The Lady Isabelle of Valois is living in seclusion, under my care, and may not receive unauthorised visitors. What is your purpose here?'

'My purpose, madame, is to deliver a Christmas gift to the Queen. A reasonable purpose, I should have thought.'

'That is not for you to judge. I have authority here.'

'Then you should exercise it with some care, Cousin.' Constance's temper was beginning to rise; she took a sharp breath to control it, threw her head back, and advanced until she stood on the rug before the fire. She unfastened the cords of her cloak, and cast it down. 'I am quite prepared to wait here for your decision. My lord husband has gone to Windsor, to take part in the tournament there, and I am at leisure until he chooses to return to Caversham. That may not be for several days. Weeks, even. Ample time for you to seek new instructions, if you feel unable to make up your mind. I dare say that my aunt by marriage, the Countess of March, will be glad to house me in whatever corner you have been kind enough to leave to her use.'

The Duchess looked up at her, thought about standing, then realising it would give her no advantage, changed her mind. 'This gift,' she said irritably, 'let me see it.'

Constance indicated to Agnes Norreys, who came forward, eyes cast down, made a deep curtsey to the Duchess, and presented a richly enamelled box. Lying within this, set on a bed of blue silk, was a small crucifix of gold, lavishly ornamented with jewels.

The Duchess took the crucifix into her hands, examined it and the box as if she proposed to offer a price for them, even poking into the silk lining in case anything was concealed within.

'A lavish gift,' she said disapprovingly. 'I'm surprised, Cousin, that your husband can afford to be so extravagant, after disgorging so many of his ill-gotten gains.'

Constance tweaked an imaginary piece of fluff from her crimson velvet sleeve, her long fingers brushing against the broad ermine trim. 'The lands of the Despenser inheritance could bear a far more significant loss, and still support a great earldom,' she remarked casually. 'Others are less fortunate; possess fine titles without the means to maintain them, like a knight with two pounds a year of rent. An embarrassment to all, and most especially to themselves.'

This was a low blow. The earldom of Oxford was by a long way the worst endowed in England, and Robert de Vere's exile had cost all the augmentations that Richard had granted it. The Duchess, despite her rank, was only a moderately wealthy woman.

'De Vache,' the Duchess said coldly, 'be so good as to show *Lady Despenser* into Madame Isabelle's presence. I suppose it possible she may amuse the child.'

'Thank you, Cousin,' Constance nodded, retrieving her cloak and giving it to Mary Russell to carry. 'You are most gracious.'

'Once, that is, she has taken the oath.'

'What oath?'

'That no word shall be spoken to Madame Isabelle about Richard of Bordeaux. By the King's express command.'

Constance sighed briefly, took the Queen's gift from Agnes, held the crucifix in her hand. 'I so swear, on this cross.' She kissed the small figure of Christ.

'Go, then,' said the Duchess irritably, jerking her head, and with it the top
third of her body.

Constance was more than happy to go. De Vache led her across the dark
hall, with its shuttered windows and central, smoking fire, up a staircase and
into another suite of rooms, thinly furnished and hung with pieces of arras
that had seen better days. A few women and boys huddled around charcoal
braziers, chatting with each other in a desultory fashion, pausing occasionally
to blow on their hands or rub them on their clothes.

'Monsieur de Vache,' she said quietly, 'I think you are a good friend to the
Queen, are you not?'

He shrugged eloquently. 'She is the daughter of my master, the King of
France. It breaks my heart to see her in this vile place, desolate, a prisoner. Under the rule of *that woman*.'

'The Queen has many friends; some of them may be visiting her in the next
day. Bringing her better news than she has heard for many months. If there are
others here who are as loyal as yourself, it might be well to prepare them. To
secure the Queen's safety. I think you understand?'

A light sparkled in the little man's eye. 'Perfectly, madame! My God, I have
waited for this day! I began to fear that the English...' He halted abruptly, repeated his shrug. 'Do not fear. All shall be in readiness, and your friends will
enter this house without difficulty. On that, madame, you have my word. I
pray that King Richard may be among them.'

***

'I spared these men's lives,' Bolingbroke said, his voice bleak as the frost. 'Is this
how mercy is repaid?'

He sank back into his chair, the light of the fire reflecting in his unblinking
eyes.

York cleared his throat, shuffled his feet. 'Harry,' he began. 'Sire...'

'In God's sweet name sit down, Uncle. You've been riding all night. You must
be in agony. Edward, pour your father some wine.'

The wine, in a silver jug, stood on a low table, next to a chessboard. Harry
had been sharing a game with his eldest son, Hal, at ease for the first time in
months. He had thought to ride out later, simply for the pleasure of it, to meet
with some of his humble subjects, wish them a good Christmas, and distribute a few coins. Now, stupefied, he watched as his cousin hesitantly picked up
the jug and served the wine, noticed the slight but unmistakable shake in Edward's hand.

'What will you do?' asked York.

'Do?' Bolingbroke sat with his head in his hands, still trying to make sense of it all. There was silence for a full minute.

'By now they will be gathering at Kingston,' Edward reminded him. He leaned against the back of his father's chair, stared into the fire. 'They'll be here in a few hours, but there's time enough to make Windsor secure against them.'

'Time? You've left me precious little of it! Why did you not warn me before this?'

Edward had been practising his reply to this all the way from London. 'Because I feared they would have means to excuse themselves,' he answered, 'whereas now they are committed, risen in arms against you, and at your mercy. There can be no further deceptions. Now you are warned, they cannot hope to enter the castle by stealth, and they've not the numbers to storm it, nor any guns or siege engines. You are safe.'

Harry shook his head. 'Safe? Cut off from London? With my dear brother-in-law about to raise the city against me?' He snorted. 'Safe as a rat in a trap! I've hardly anyone about me but my own household. All my surest friends are back in the shires, and mostly in distant shires at that. My best hopes lie in London. The people there cheered themselves hoarse for me only a couple of months ago—they'll be loyal, once they know that I still live.'

'The men of London are no warriors,' York objected. 'They care for nothing but their moneybags. It'd be better to call out the *posse comitatus* of all the southern counties. Most of the knights and squires of England will fight for you, and gladly. I've some cause to be sure of it.'

'I'll summon every single loyal man within a hundred miles,' Bolingbroke said, coming briskly to his feet, 'and crush these rebels utterly. You will both ride with me to London, and you, Edward, you will lead the van of my army, the first thousand men that I can gather in arms.'

York forced himself to his feet, his determination compelling his stiff joints into reluctant submission. He put out a hand to rest on the wall hangings, needing the support of the stone that lay behind their flamboyant colours.

'Do not do that,' he urged breathlessly. 'Hold him in arrest until this trouble is behind us. He intended to betray you.'

'I know it, Uncle. I knew it as soon as I saw your face. What need had you to make such an arduous journey, if not to protect him?'

Edward knelt before him. 'Sire—Cousin. My sister and her husband led me astray with their persuasions. I repented of my mistake, and came here in good faith, to give you warning.'

Bolingbroke looked down on him for a moment, his eyes cold. 'Get up!' he said contemptuously. 'Get from my sight, and on to the road to London. Array such followers as you have in my cause. You may scatter the lesser men, but give no quarter to the leaders. I don't want to be troubled by prisoners; only to see a basket filled with their heads.'

23

Outside it was still full dark, and now snow had begun to fall.

Constance watched it for a few minutes, her concern growing as she realised it was no mere flurry but the beginning of a major storm. Then she closed the shutters, excluding the chill morning air from the room, and moved to the freshly lit fire to warm her hands. Save for her silk chamber-robe, furred at its edges, she was quite naked, and goose pimples were springing up all over her.

'You are up betimes,' protested the Countess of March, still luxuriating in the large bed they had shared. 'Getting dressed? I'm staying here until the room warms. No need for haste. We're not expected to attend the Queen when she rises, you know. There's no ceremony in the Household these days, or none to speak of. The Duchess shuts herself up in her room most of the time—complains that living near the river makes her bones ache. I do much as I like, though of course I have no authority any more.'

'I'm surprised that you want to be here, Alianore.'

The Countess shrugged. 'I'm fond of the Queen—I do what I can to comfort the child, though there's not much gratitude to be had for it. And I'm close to Windsor. My sons are there, and I hope I can persuade Bolingbroke to let me see them.'

Constance lit another candle from the one burning on the mantel above the fire, extending the brightness around them into the corners where their women and Alianore's daughters lay snuggled close together on their pallets. No one was stirring, although Alianore's senior chamberer, an elderly Welshwoman called Eluned, had not only started the fire but set a pan of water to warm on it, before hurrying off to the first mass of the day.

'Perhaps you will see your sons sooner than you think,' she said absently.

'What do you mean? Bolingbroke doesn't visit here. He hasn't the courage to face that child and tell her what he's done to her husband, whom she loves as a father if not as a man. Even if he did come, I don't suppose he'd bring my boys. Have I not told you? They're kept close, under lock and key.'

Constance sat on the edge of the bed, 'Matters may be otherwise,' she said quietly, 'in a day or two. I thought perhaps your brother Surrey might have told you something of what is in hand.'

Alianore yawned. 'I've never been as close to my brothers as you have to yours. I suppose it's because I had five sisters to talk to, and you had none.' She mused on that for a moment, dwelling on her own analysis. 'I don't know what you're talking about. Has Edmund asked him to help? Is that it?'

'Edmund? I've not seen him since the coronation, and even then only for a moment. He's not involved. I thought he'd gone into the country, to his own estates.'

'Not involved? What are you talking about? He and Charlton have been talking to half the lawyers in London, trying to win the custody of my sons. They're going to bring a case before the Common Pleas. Though I think they waste their time. If Richard is deposed, then my son March is the lawful King by true descent. Bolingbroke knows that.' She took in the troubled expression on Constance's face and promptly misinterpreted it. 'I take it you do not agree? Perhaps you favour your brother Edward's claim?'

'As far as I am concerned, Richard is still King,' Constance said bluntly, 'and after him, your son.'

'Do you think Richard is still alive?' Lady March asked, her voice a careful murmur. 'Some say that Bolingbroke has had him murdered. Our cousin the Duchess will not allow the matter to be discussed, but that makes people talk the more. There's even a rumour that Bolingbroke will make the Queen marry his son, Hal, to maintain the truce with France.'

'I believe we shall find Richard alive. Though where he is, I know no more than you.'

'Find him?' Alianore's voice was suddenly almost suspicious. 'What are you about, Constance? I know you're not here for my company, or you'd have come before this. You didn't even answer my letter when I told you about the new babe that is on its way.' She touched her swelling belly for a moment, almost unconsciously. 'I know you've had other matters to trouble you, but surely you could have spared a word of kindness for me, wished me well?'

'I'm sorry if I have failed you as a friend, but you're right, I've had other matters on my mind.' Constance stood up, paced about. 'To be plain with you, Bolingbroke should be dead by now, and Richard proclaimed King again. I have warned de Vache; he knows which of the men here he can rely upon to protect the Queen. Word should reach us before the end of the day.'

The words were not out of her mouth before shouts rose from the courtyard, and with them the muffled beat of hooves on snow. Many horses carrying many men.

Alianore wrapped her naked body in the coverlet, and somehow reached the window a fraction before her friend, throwing back the shutters once more.

'My brother Surrey is down there,' she said slowly, like one speaking in a trance. 'Could you not have told me? Do you think I'd have betrayed *him*?'

Constance shook her head. 'I don't understand. They're far too early, should still be at Windsor. Something is not as we planned.'

She glanced around the courtyard, trying to identify the men. A few of the pathfinders were carrying blazing torches, but in the morning darkness they were largely anonymous in their armour, even their heraldry mantled in veils of snow. She recognised Andrew Hake first, because he had taken off his helmet, and was shouting instructions in his distinctive Scottish voice. His accent was always stronger when he was excited. Thomas and Surrey were already off their horses, entering the building. There was no sign of any resistance developing. Salisbury was here now, beneath his yellow and green banner, leading in a second wave of men...

'Awake everyone!' Alianore shouted. Constance had never heard her so loud, or so abruptly commanding. 'Out of bed, you idle sluts! We must dress at once, all of us. Hurry!'

Constance had found John Norreys now. Seen Maudelyn disguised in his kingly robes, and the Bishop of Carlisle, close to him, like a guard. She had even identified Lumley in the crowd. But of Edward, her brother, there was no sign at all.

***

The household gathered in the Queen's chamber of presence, some of its members imperfectly dressed and none of them either washed or fed. Mercifully there had been no fighting, although some of the men, identified by Monsieur de Vache as untrustworthy, had been disarmed. The strong element of surprise, and the balance of numbers, had ensured compliance.

The Queen sat under her canopy, with her ladies, headed by the Duchess of Ireland, gathered about her, and the men of the household, led by de Vache, flanking them on both sides. At a nod from the chamberlain, the doors were opened, and the leaders of the revolt, bareheaded but otherwise fully armed, entered in formal procession, Alianore's brother leading the way, and having something of the bearing of a heron clad in steel.

'Your Grace,' Surrey announced, kneeling before the Queen, 'the traitor Harry of Lancaster has fled to London like a coward. King Richard is proclaimed at every village cross between here and Kingston, and he is marching to join us with a large army. You are no longer a prisoner.'

Isabelle stood up, clapping her hands with delight, her beaming smile reflected in Surrey's face as he rose to his feet. But Constance knew that something was severely amiss. Bolingbroke was supposed to be killed—evidently he had escaped, and escaped to London, where he was safe among the majority of citizens who idolised him. As for this talk of Richard and his army—that was a tale for children, not one that she believed for an instant. Her eyes sought out Thomas, standing some paces behind Surrey, and she saw in his face that her concern was justified. Indeed, it was worse than that. He looked desolated.

Isabelle was practically dancing. 'Off with the traitor's livery!' she cried. 'Off with it! Throw all his cognizances into the river! Into the cess-pit!'

De Vache was wearing a collar of Lancastrian esses. He tore it from his neck, and threw it down. Alianore followed suit with her livery-collar, made a point of treading it with her foot. The rest accepted the example, those with cloth badges using knives to cut the stitching away, those with collars tearing at the clasps. At last only the Duchess of Ireland was still wearing a collar. The Queen fixed a petulant look upon her, and weeping, her hands trembling, the Duchess removed the device.

Constance walked around the edge of this little ceremony, and joined her husband, close to the door that led out into the hall.

'Where is Edward?' she asked quietly.

Despenser took her upper arm in his gauntleted hand and guided her through the door into the hall. The room was crowded with men, but as they kept moving room was made for them, and when they progressed into one of the window embrasures it was promptly vacated by those who had established themselves there, Andrew Hake and a party of Welsh spearmen in the Despenser livery.

'He was not at Kingston, and not at Windsor,' Thomas said grimly. 'He's either captured, dead or turned traitor. Since Bolingbroke was warned of our intent, and had time to escape, the chances are that he has betrayed us.'

'No—no, he could not!' Constance did not want to believe it, preferred even to think that Edward might have been killed. 'The plan was his own! How could he betray it?'

'Who was better placed? *Treschere*, it's too early to be sure, too early to condemn him, but I myself have little doubt, and nor do the others.'

Neither did Constance, in her heart. She felt the tears welling up in her eyes, and somewhere within her, in some deep, untouchable place, was a searing agony where the love she felt for her brother had finally been torn away. A wound beyond mending.

'Do not weep, my love,' Thomas said reassuringly. 'The fault is not yours. You warned me not to trust him too far, and I was fool enough to do exactly that. I've doubted him before, God knows, but that night when he came to see us in London it was otherwise, and I had faith in him. It was as if, at last, we were truly brothers together. Well, whatever happens now, whoever wins, he is surely finished. No one will ever dream of trusting him again after this. No one, friend or enemy. He'll be an outcast, despised by all.' He had not been speaking loudly, but now he lowered his voice still further, spoke almost into her ear. 'You must go back to Caversham; pack what you must, and set off for Cardiff. Don't delay; I want you on the road by noon. The safest way is probably to ride to Bristol, and then take ship across the Severn Sea.'

She understood well enough what lay behind his words. 'Are matters so grim?'

He shrugged. 'Grim enough. We'll follow Bolingbroke to London; try to catch him before he has time to assemble enough men to counter us. We still have some benefit of surprise, and Exeter may have been able to do something. It's a hope—a thin one. It's either that or run away. If we fail, I'll do what I can to join you in Glamorgan. Cardiff is strong—put it in a state of defence, and we shall have a bargaining counter, at the least. Those guns may have a use at last.'

Her voice shook. 'I'd prefer to wait at Caversham.'

'There isn't time to argue, Constance. Get Tyldesley and the rest of your people together, and do as I ask. There's no need to take leave of the Queen, or of anyone else. Move quickly enough and you'll be in Bristol by tomorrow night, ahead of any news of our rising. Keep the ship at Cardiff if you can; we may have use for it.'

He took her in his arms, bruising her against his steel plated chest. They kissed, and then stood looking at each other, prolonging the moment, each knowing that they might well not meet again in this life.

***

Bolingbroke was secure at Westminster with his household around him, the men of London flocking to his banner and the gentry of the surrounding counties and their tenants already beginning to arrive in support. Of Exeter there was no sign. His wife, Beth, told her brother that he had slipped away by boat, heading east, presumably to his estates in Essex. John Holland, it seemed, had recognised the realities of the situation, and could be discounted. The same could be said of the small Ricardian faction in the City. Apart from the few who had fled, these men were either lying low or changing sides.

York had retired to his bed, partly because he was exhausted, but mainly because, sunk in despair, he no longer wished to live. He would barely speak to Joanne, and not at all to Edward or Philippa.

Edward had little time to dwell on all this. He was too busy organising his portion of Bolingbroke's army, a thousand men in all, an eclectic mixture. There were his own adherents and his father's and some members of the King's household, including Sir Hugh Waterton. But there was a high proportion of Londoners, some of them lightly armed, carrying only the weapons they had snatched from their walls in haste, but the majority well-equipped and eager for the fight, a formidable militia, organised by wards and led by their aldermen. The vanguard marched out under the banners of York, with drums beating and heralds' trumpets blasting the eardrums. King Harry was taking the field against his rebels.

***

The rebels had barricaded the lengthy, narrow bridge over the Thames at Maidenhead.

Edward had seen them turn back as he approached, but had not dared press them too hard for fear of ambush. Now they were in a strong defensive position, protected by upturned carts, and he paused for thought. For a great deal of thought.

'There's only a few of 'em,' said Sir Hugh Waterton. He was an abrupt, middle-aged northerner with a grizzled beard and hard, searching eyes. 'What are we waiting for?'

'Only a few that we can see,' Edward answered. 'There could be a lot more in the town beyond and, anyway, four determined men could hold that bridge against an army.'

'Not when our archers start to use them as butts!'

'They've archers too, man! Look at the length of the bridge before the barricade—there's no cover, and we'll have to go forward in column, trampling over our own dead.' He paused and looked for the position of the sun, found it low in the west and as red as a coal, glowing behind the defenders. 'The sun's already in our eyes, and in two hours it'll be full dark.'

Sir Hugh stared at him. 'You seem strangely reluctant to advance your banner, my lord of Rutland!' He turned his eyes to the bridge, taking in the colours hanging stiffly above the defenders. 'We seem to be facing your stepmother's brother and your sister's husband. Perhaps you'd feel more comfortable on the other side of the barricade?'

'By Christ, Waterton, you forget to whom you speak!' Edward rapped back. 'I command here, by authority of my cousin, the King. I intend to parley with them, to gain time. Meanwhile, we'll send half the men on, along the north bank of the river. They can cross at Marlow, and take the rebels from the rear.'

'Not tonight they won't! You've said yourself that it'll be dark in two hours. I reckon nearer three, but it'll take longer than that to reach Marlow, never mind to work their way back here. We must attack. The King would expect no less.'

Edward understood the underlying threat behind the words. 'Very well,' he conceded, 'have it your own way. Let's see a few of our men killed for no particular reason if it'll make you more sure of my loyalty. Archers first. *Elite* archers if we've got any, which I doubt. Pick off as many of the rebels as we can. Then, when the arrows are used up, you and I will go forward, on foot, with the knights and anyone else who's decently protected. Oh, and send someone to scour the banks. If we can find a boat or two, we might be able to land a few picked men on the far side; that'd give the enemy something to think about.'

He dismounted, sinking at once into a cloying mixture of snow and mud, and watched as the archers assembled into ranks. They were Londoners for the most part, ranging from mere striplings to men with the look of grandfathers, all of them accustomed to shooting at targets of Sunday, as the law required, but, by and large, with much less experience of shooting at their fellow Englishmen. A few had steel cuirasses and helmets, the majority no more protection than that provided by a leather jack and a cap. There was scarcely a pavise in sight.

'Aim high, lads,' Edward told them. 'Plunging shots. As if your mark was a cushion on the cobbles of the bridge, just behind that barrier. First volley on my order, then loose as you will.'

They shuffled into place, not only at the foot of the bridge, but along the riverbanks on both sides. As they drew back their bows, the first arrows flew from the other side, and here and there a man dropped.

'Loose!' Edward cried, and a black cloud of arrows, released almost simultaneously, arced towards the crowded centre of the bridge, descending on the rebels like a sudden lethal hailstorm. Cries and shouts rose up from the wounded, and one man staggered over the parapet and fell into the Thames, his half armour sufficient to drag him beneath the deep and rushing water.

The rebel archers, though fewer in number, were more practised. Despenser's Welshmen from Glamorgan were among the best in the whole kingdom, their rate of shooting so fast that they often had a second shaft in the air before the first had found its mark, and their accuracy exceptional. More and more of the London archers fell wounded, some mortally, and the rest gradually grew discouraged, and began to draw back, so as to be out of range.

'Now, my lord,' said Waterton, closing his visor. It was, Edward presumed, a suggestion, but it sounded very like an order. He lowered his own visor, and signalled with his war hammer, moving forward at the best pace he could muster, stepping over the occasional corpse and sliding on the frozen cobbles and congealing blood, his steel footwear uncomfortable on such a surface. Those around him were all knights and squires in full armour, though others, less well protected, advanced behind them. To some extent the press of numbers might decide the engagement.

Arrows showered upon them, mostly glancing off, but a few finding the weak places at neck and joints that were protected only by mail, or even passing clear through plate and the protective padding beneath. Edward, clad in the best steel that Milan could fashion, was more fortunate than most. A loud grunt alerted him to the fact that Hugh Waterton had been wounded at his side, but the knight merely staggered and pressed on, brushing the shaft of the arrow from his shoulder as if it were nothing more than a mild irritation, like a stinging insect.

The barricade of carts was suddenly before them; through Edward's narrow eye slits it looked as tall as a town wall, and just as incapable of being climbed. But the ranks behind were pressing forward, almost lifting him off his feet, and there was no time to stop and consider his tactics. The bridge was another confining factor, the men on either side of him so close that he could scarcely raise his arms sufficiently to strike a telling blow. He caught a glimpse of something swinging towards him, instinctively thrust the war-hammer up in a gesture of defence, and almost had it torn from his hands. Pressed against the barricade, he fought for his life, knowing his main salvation was that his enemies were almost equally constricted.

'Forward, forward!' Waterton was shouting. 'St. George and England! Kill the bastards! Kill them!'

Edward wondered how the man could find the breath; but then discovered that he too was shouting, though the words were nonsense, like something cried out in terror during a drunken dream. Thomas Despenser and Surrey were shouting too as they swung at him, half across their barrier as they struggled to reach him. He fought desperately, as he had never done in his life, against men he wished no harm, men who had to die so that he might live. Defensive, strenuous fighting, that seemed to go on for an eternity and stretched his strength to its limits.

Waterton was trying to mount the barricade, something that was all but impossible in the conditions. Despenser struck him, very hard, with his poleaxe, and the knight fell backwards onto the cobbles, a great gash in the steel plate protecting his chest. Someone stood over him, resisted the next blow, while others dragged the inert man away, his armour scraping along the cobbles.

'Back!' shouted Edward, daring to open his visor so that his voice would carry. 'Fall back and regroup!'

The enemy did not follow, but merely gave an ironic cheer and sent arrows after them, well directed arrows that seemed to home in on the least well armoured and select the weakest point of any harness.

It was too late for any renewal of the attack. The rebels waited for a while, as if they wanted to be sure that their opponents had given up, then set fire to their barricade, and withdrew into the darkness. Edward was far too astute to make any attempt to follow.

***

Cardiff emerged gradually from the mist, the dark bulk of the castle and the modest towers and spires of the churches and religious houses appearing first, like a mysterious kingdom floating above the water. The cog, *Katharine of Bristol*, was drawing closer now, entering the estuary of the Taf, and losing way as the wind dropped, drifting along with the rising tide.

Hugh Tyldesley stood by the rail, his hand close to the hilt of his sword. He was ill at ease, and could not explain the feeling, though he had given it a great deal of thought. There was something about the shipman and his crew that he did not like. It was partly that there were too many of them to work the vessel—that was obvious even to a layman, and Tyldesley was no fool. Since merchants were notoriously stingy about paying unnecessary wages, it followed that the surplus men were *not*, in fact, surplus to the ship's requirements. The most likely explanation was that the cog indulged in piracy, at least on a part-time basis. The truce with France and Scotland did not extend out of sight of land, whatever kings decreed.

The shipman padded towards him, a stocky man with lank hair and teeth that resembled a row of broken tombstones. He leaned his back against the rail, his leather jerkin making a protesting squeal against it.

'Half an hour should get us alongside the quay,' he said. 'Normally, I'd be out again on the next tide. You know it'll cost you to have my ship sitting at Cardiff? It means giving up another cargo I could have in Bristol, and, beside, idle hands get bored, cause trouble. They need money for drink, money for women, to keep them quiet.'

'You'll be paid,' Tyldesley grunted. 'Well paid for waiting, and for any voyage that's required.'

The shipman snorted, cleared his nose out over the side. 'Your lord's King Richard's man, isn't he? Not very popular in Bristol, King Richard. First taxing us left, right and centre, then holding the blank charters over our heads, then threatening to take away our liberties and more or less make us serfs. We weren't sorry to see the back of him. Dare say your lord thinks otherwise. Dare say it cost him plenty. Thinking of going on crusade, is he?'

'Not my business to know. Or to say.'

'That right?' The shipman raised an eyebrow. 'So he doesn't let you into his secrets? Keeps you and these other fellows just to guard his lady, eh? Pleasant work, I should think.'

Tyldesley's eyes fixed on him. 'Perhaps you think too much, friend. Say too much. Maybe you should keep your mind on handling this floating shit-house of yours.'

'Ha!' the man grinned, revealing the full glory of his shattered teeth, 'by Christ, I like a gentleman with a sense of humour! Ah, you take me wrong; I mean no discourtesy. I'd guard such a lady well myself, were she mine.'

The lady in question was standing by the opposite rail, with her children, her arms around their shoulders so that her cloak partially covered them and kept the worst of the wind from them. The children were very excited. Bess had begun to identify the church towers, and young Richard was full of questions about the swivel gun mounted on the rail next to them. He was disappointed by his mother's complete ignorance of its range, or its ability to sink enemy ships.

Constance was almost as excited as the children, although she would have found it difficult to explain the emotion. She had somehow persuaded herself that all would be well. She *knew* that Thomas was alive. Sensed it with her whole being. Perhaps Edward had not betrayed them, after all. Perhaps he had simply found another way to victory. Perhaps King Richard really had escaped. Perhaps he did have a great army with him. Perhaps the risings they had planned in various shires had been successful. There was enough hope to avoid despair.

***

The town of Cirencester was ablaze.

Thomas Despenser, woken abruptly from sleep by the smoke, shook John Norreys and Andrew Hake, who were sharing the narrow chamber with him, and dressed in haste. There was no time to arm, no time to do much more that snatch up such weapons as were to hand. Flames were already consuming the wooden staircase that led down into the body of the inn, and escape that way was quite impossible. Shouts, and screams of agony rose from the hall below.

Andrew Hake struggled with the shutters, smashed them open. 'We must away over the roof,' he stated. 'There's no other way down.'

'You first,' Thomas said decisively. 'Take care.'

Hake nodded, and put his legs out, then rested his buttocks on the tiles, through which smoke was already beginning to emerge. He eased himself across the steeply pitched roof, suddenly found himself sliding on the accumulated ice, lost control and vanished out of sight, crashing through the thatched roof of the barn that leaned onto the main structure of the building. He cursed, loud and long, and with a poet's eloquence.

'Hake, what's happened to you?' demanded Thomas.

'I'm up to ma neck in shite, and I think I've broken ma bloody leg. Other than that I'm just fine, man.'

Thomas and Norreys exchanged a glance and then, without a word, began to drag sheets from the beds and knot them into a crude rope. There was little time. Flames were licking around the edges of the door, and the room was pervaded with smoke. Even low down, next to the open window, it was barely possible to breath.

Norreys descended next, the sheets providing him with a useful handhold, and although he slid off the edge of the roof he came to no harm. Thomas shouted a warning, and threw their meagre collection of weapons after him; then he began his own descent, a cautious feeling of his way across the treacherous tiles until he reached the edge, then a twelve-foot drop into the snow-covered yard.

Norreys had gathered the weapons together, and was now helping Hake out of the barn. The Scot was covered in an eclectic mixture of snow, thatch, hay and animal excrement, and was favouring his right leg. The limb was not actually broken, but it was obviously very sore.

After the little battle at Maidenhead Bridge, a mere delaying tactic, the rebel army—if a force of no more than six hundred men could be so called—had ridden through the night and all the next day to reach Cirencester, pausing only to proclaim King Richard in every little town they entered, encouraging the impression that they were part of a greater and victorious force. The truth was that they were in flight, to Despenser's own Glamorgan, where they hoped the raise the country, garrison some or all of his castles, and make a fight of it. If all else failed, there was always the ship that Constance would by now have arranged to moor at Cardiff quay.

They had halted at Cirencester out of sheer exhaustion, having missed a night's sleep and covered about sixty miles in less than twenty-four hours. The usual proclamation had been made, and they had settled down to sleep, confident they were safe until morning; instead they had woken to chaos.

Thomas looked back at the inn, which by this time was simply a huge bonfire, scarcely distinguishable as a building. Somewhere in that inferno was their armour, most of their weapons, and all their money. To say nothing of a good dozen of his men, and some of Salisbury's. He could only hope that they had found another way out.

A figure emerged from the billowing smoke. It was young Robert Rous, one of his squires, coughing, eyes streaming, his face blackened with smoke.

'My lord!' he cried. 'Thank God you are alive! I swear I thought you were roast meat by now, all three of you.'

'What the hell's going on?' Hake demanded. 'It looks as if the whole street's burning.'

'Probably some drunken fool has been careless with a coal,' grunted Norreys.

'The townsfolk are rioting,' Rous coughed. 'Can you not hear them?'

Thomas slowly became aware of a roaring that had nothing to do with the flames and the crashing of blazing timbers. Somewhere beyond the burning structures, presumably in the market place, was a seething mass of angry humanity.

'They're probably gathered to fight the fires,' he said.

The young man shook his head. 'They're not bothering with the fires. They're busy on the other side of the market square, besieging the inn where my lords of Surrey and Salisbury are lodged. There's no fire there, but they were taking axes to the door, shooting arrows through the windows. There are hundreds of them. The whole town, risen in arms.'

'The stables are burning,' Norreys interrupted. 'We must save the horses.'

Despenser nodded. 'Come; let's get in there before matters grow worse. Turn the destriers loose. We've no need for them now. It's the riding horses that'll be of use.'

The stable was already permeated with dense smoke, the thatched roof blazing, and it was no easy task to extricate the terrified animals, least of all the destriers which were fierce as well as powerful, and apt to bite and kick without much discrimination. Fortunately, two of Despenser's Welsh archers had been sleeping in the stable, and had already woken and begun the work of turning the horses out. The surplus creatures were simply encouraged to run across the yard and find their way out through the open gates into the market place. Six of the remaining palfreys, selected more or less at random, were saddled and then led out through a kind of postern gate that opened onto a narrow back alley, fortunately one that led away from the flames and the trouble in the centre of the town. The horses balked and sidled, confused and frightened by the fires, noise, and lack of room for manoeuvre, and the men struggled with them, slipping on the icy, uneven cobblestones beneath their feet. The fire was a blessing in one way—without it they would have been in total darkness, groping their way forward. At last they emerged into a deserted side street, and Despenser was able to give the order for them to mount. They did so cautiously, reassuring their disconcerted horses.

'We'll rally some men—then attack the townsfolk,' Thomas said.

'Rally them?' Hake answered incredulously. 'How? When we can no see our hands in front of our faces?'

'Our men are scattered all over the town,' Norreys pointed out. 'All over the town, and in every barn and alehouse for five miles around. Those that haven't dropped by the way. Thomas, I don't know how to begin rallying them. There's hours to dawn, and until then all we can do is wander about in the dark, hoping for the best.'

'We should be away over the hills, to Tewkesbury,' Hake went on. 'God knows, I'm no afraid of a fight, but I'm half naked, and I've no weapon but this.' He held up a long bladed kidney dagger, its blade glistening in the light of the young moon.

Thomas assessed them as best he could in the dark. The two archers had slept fully clothed in the straw, and had their bow staves and a modest stock of arrows. He and the others were clad in hose, shirt, and quilted arming doublets, save for Hake, who had only his shirt. They were all bareheaded. He still had his sword, his weapon of last choice; Norreys had a sword and a poniard. Rous only a baselard. From what he could see of their faces, they had had enough. The Scot, the Welsh archers, the English gentlemen were united in that. Their utter defeat was obvious to them all, and it was time to go home.

'We must see if there's anything we can do for our friends,' he persisted. 'We can't just ride off and leave them. We have the cover of dark; it can work to our advantage, conceal how few of us there are. I ask it of you. This last thing.'

The men looked at each other, trying to find the courage to refuse, and failing. It was one of the archers who spoke.

'We are your men, my lord. We'll follow you.'

He was a man in his forties, his dark hair greying from nature as well the effects of snow, stocky, but with the broad shoulders and muscular arms that were the mark of his trade. Thomas recognised him as one who had served him well in Ireland, struggled momentarily for his name.

'Thank you, Adda. Come, let's find our way around these backs to the market place, see what's going on.'

What was going on was that every man, woman and child in Cirencester was gathered in the square, all armed with at least a club or a knife, their faces illuminated by the flames leaping high above their blazing homes. They had fallen silent now, and a little space had opened up around the entrance to the inn they had been besieging. Well-armed, mounted men wearing the livery of

Lord Berkeley policed the edge of this space. Berkeley himself stood within the circle of his followers, apparently speaking to the men trapped inside.

Thomas and the others sat their horses in the road, hidden by the darkness. As they watched the door of the inn slowly opened, and Surrey, Salisbury and Lumley emerged, casting down their swords.

'In the name of God!' Hake protested.

No sooner had he spoke than they were seen, and the nearest portion of the crowd began to surge towards them, shouting angry threats that merged into an incomprehensible roar. There was nothing to do but turn and kick their horses into a gallop, escaping into the darkness. As they fled, a shower of arrows whistled around them, and a deep groan emerged from Norreys, who had been hit. He slumped forward, clinging to his horse's neck, the animal keeping pace with the others out of instinct.

'Leave me! Leave me!' cried Norreys, his voice maddened by pain. The arrow was deeply embedded in his upper back, and blood was pouring out over his thick, quilted doublet, though the darkness hid the worst of the damage from his companions.

'We'll take you to the monks at Tewkesbury,' Thomas said briskly. 'There's no danger, not now we're away from the town. No need for haste. They'll never follow us in the dark. We could have a hundred archers for all they know, and no man goes seeking such company with a burning brand in his hand.'

'It's true enough,' said Hake, cheering at the thought, 'though it's a long ride to Tewkesbury. Let's take ourselves another mile or two along the road, and try to take a look at that wound.'

***

The wound was severe. They had been able to judge as much even by moonlight, but as the dawn began to break the extent of the loss of blood became obvious, and they stopped and made fresh but ineffective efforts to staunch it. Norreys was growing weaker by the mile. By the time they reached Tewkesbury it was mid morning, and the wounded man had been tied to his horse for safety, more or less unconscious.

The great abbey provided temporary sanctuary. Thomas, like the majority of his Despenser and de Clare ancestors, had been a generous patron, and, even in his present difficulties, there was no doubt about the warmth of his welcome. The monks carried John Norreys off to their infirmary, their faces grave.

Andrew Hake had come to a decision. 'By your leave, my lord, I'm going home to my wife.'

'Across Berkeley's lands?'

Hake shrugged. 'What choice do I have? With luck I'll be overlooked. I've no lands of my own to seize, and they can't well hang a Scot for treason against the English King. You're for France, I suppose?'

Thomas nodded, and shook the man's hand. Hake was no saint, never had been, but he couldn't help liking him. 'Good luck, Andrew. Keep out of Berkeley's way. You may have been born a Scot, but you're of the English allegiance now. Keep your head down for a while, and then buy a pardon. That's my advice.'

Hake nodded. There were tears springing in his eyes. He turned on his heels and walked away, saying nothing, his limping steps ringing on the abbey tiles.

Thomas knelt at the side of his father's tomb and prayed for a while, for the souls of the recent dead, for Norreys, for his captured allies. It was there that his mother found him.

'It's only a matter of time before Berkeley or Warwick seeks you here,' she said. 'Gloucestershire is not safe for you. You should already be across the ferry, not wasting time.'

He rose to his feet, finding a smile from somewhere. 'I never thought, Mother, that I'd live to hear you say that time spent in prayer is wasted.'

Elisabeth's face clouded. 'There is a season and a place for all things. How could you be such a fool? You've lost everything your father built, everything that his uncle achieved before him. Your life and lands in forfeit, because you've never listened to any counsel but pillow talk! That wretched girl, and that treacherous snake, her brother! They have led you to this. If it were not for them, you'd never have been involved in the filthy dealings of the court. Why could you never see it? Are all men blinded by their own lust?'

He laughed bitterly. 'Faith, Mother, how little you know of me! Do you seriously imagine I'd have been content to live in Berkeley's shadow? To wear Warwick's livery, perhaps? Constance has supported me in everything I have done, even against her own conscience, but the decisions have been mine, always mine. The responsibility also. You insult me when you suggest otherwise.'

Her expression indicated that she was not convinced, but nevertheless she pressed a purse of money into his hand. 'You'll need this. Go now, for your life's sake. You're the last of my sons, all that's left to me of your father. Go!'

'Not without John Norreys.'

She shook her head. 'I met the infirmarer on my way in—he was seeking you. Norreys is in no case to travel further. His wound is mortal.'

Thomas almost ran from her, into the monastic buildings and through to the Infirmary. Norreys was lodged in a curtained alcove, the abbot himself and the Infirmarer praying over him. The abbot looked up briefly as Thomas entered, shook his head, and continued his prayers.

Despenser clutched at the wall to support himself—it had somehow never entered his head that Norreys would need more than patching. But there Norreys lay, his oldest friend, choking to death on his own blood, already beyond words and his eyes glazing over even as he watched.

The abbot moved towards him, hand raised in a gesture of blessing. 'There is nothing more to be done for him, my son. Pray for his soul when you are safe away. He'll not last the hour out.'

Thomas did not want to believe it. He approached the bed, willing this moment to be part of some hideous dream, from which he would soon awake.

'He has been with me all my life,' he said, in a stunned voice.

'He has been shrived, and is safe in God's hands. You served him well when you brought him to us, and all that is proper will be done for him. Now you must leave him, and us. We've sent word to the ferry at the Lower Lode, and it awaits you.'

Thomas allowed himself to be led away, still gripped in a sense of unreality. It was only when he was actually on the ferry, and moving out across the Severn, that he began to recover himself, realised that Robert Rous and the two archers were still with him.

'John and I used to swim in this river,' he recalled. 'It seems like yesterday, and yet I suppose it's twenty years. We were just boys. Just boys.'

'It looks deep,' Rous answered, for want of something to say.

'It is, and not a little dangerous.' Despenser paused for a moment, his eyes still fixed on the receding tower of the abbey. 'They plucked me out of it more than once. Now I almost wish that they'd left me to drown.'

Elisabeth watched the progress of the ferry from the vantage point of her solar window, saw her son walk his horse ashore, mount up, and ride slowly up the rutted track beyond, until he disappeared into the dark, leafless woods that lined the far shore. Then she knelt down and wept as she had not done since her husband's death, wept herself into a dark and hopeless agony that was somewhere on the other side of tears. She knew in her heart that she would never see Thomas again.

***

Constance watched as her husband said his farewells to his children. It was as well, she thought, that they were both still too young to appreciate that this was not like any previous parting; that they could not hope to see their father again for many years, if ever. The ship that had brought her from Bristol still waited, moored in the deep channel a few yards from the quay, ready to carry him to France. Or perhaps to some distant crusade, further afield, where his presence would not be questioned. Much of his gear was already loaded aboard.

She felt the tears welling up at the back of her eyes, resisted them, and swallowed them down. There would be opportunity for crying when he was gone, ample opportunity. For now she must maintain her poise.

They had had three nights together; less than three days. Time to tell him of the child they had conceived together in the Tower, to give him that small glimmer of hope to carry with him into the chill world. Not nearly time enough to say all that she wanted to say. Now, according to their scouts, Bolingbroke's men were close to Cardiff, no more than an hour or two away. William Beauchamp, Lord Abergavenny, was leading a column of some two hundred mounted men. Beauchamp was Warwick's brother, and the executed Arundel's son-in-law. He had no cause to show them mercy, and nor would he. Thought of resistance was futile. Cardiff was strong enough to hold out for a while, but Harry Boling-broke was capable of marching a national army against them, and blockading the sea approaches with King's ships. Then they would be trapped, starved out. The innocent would suffer uselessly, for there was no hope at all of any relief.

Thomas moved towards her, Bess still gathered protectively under his arm.

'I'd better go,' he said quietly. 'The shipman is concerned about his tide, or some such thing. I dare say that our friends will be here before the next.'

'Shall I go with you to the quay?' Constance asked. She scarcely recognised her own voice.

He shook his head. 'I think not. This is difficult enough as it is, without half of Cardiff watching our parting.'

He kissed her, held her against him as if trying to absorb her into his body. 'I shall carry you with me in my heart,' he said. 'Whatever befalls, the memory of you will lend me courage.'

Constance found that she could not speak; that she could only watch as, very gently, he prised her clutching hands from him, backed slowly away.

'Come,' he said to young Richard, 'I need a squire to lead my horse back from the quay.'

He lifted the delighted boy onto his shoulder, and bore him from the room. She followed as if in a dream, down the stairs to the hall, through the little throng of people gathered there.

The horses were waiting, and with them Hugh Tyldesley, Robert Rous and half a dozen other men, including the two archers Thomas had brought back with him from Cirencester. Despenser lifted his son onto the saddle, and mounted up behind him. He took one last look at Constance, inclined his head to her, and touched his spurs to his horse. Her eyes followed the little procession until it had vanished beneath the tunnel of the gatehouse, and then she stood, still watching the gate, in the vain hope that some forgotten issue would cause Thomas to turn back, that he might come once more into the compass of her eyes, even if only for a few minutes. When Robert Rous returned, leading the horse that bore a very proud Richard Despenser on its back, she gave up her hope, and walked slowly back into the castle, to sit down in the irrelevant splendour of her solar, alone as she had never been in her life until that hour.

***

William Beauchamp had a crabbed face and a long white beard; features that made him look somewhat older than his middling years.

'By the King's appointment, I am Lieutenant of Glamorgan,' he announced. 'My purpose here is to arrest the traitor, Thomas Despenser, and to seize his lands and movables, which are forfeit to the Crown. Therefore, madame, I must trouble you and your women to stay here in this room, while my men search the rest of the castle and make an inventory of all that is within it.'

Constance had not moved from her chair. 'My lord is not here,' she said, her head tilting back slightly. 'As for the rest, I am powerless to prevent it. Do your worst.'

Beauchamp let out a grunt. 'Despenser has kept on running, has he? Well, I dare say we'll run him to earth in the end, and dig him out of whatever hole he has found. A wiser man than his friends who lost their heads at Cirencester.'

She was momentarily bewildered. 'You mean that Surrey and Salisbury are dead? I thought that Lord Berkeley had taken them prisoner.'

'So he had! But at dawn the townsfolk realised how much damage had been done by the fire the rebels started, dragged them out and headed them there and then. Berkeley could do nothing about it. Well, they had their deserts, and your husband would have had the same, if he'd not had the wit to put himself on a fast horse.' He stalked about for a few moments, pausing to finger the hangings, to assess the value of the plate and the candlesticks. Then he turned back to her, clearing his throat. 'As for the rest of the traitors, the rabble were let free, the gentlemen gathered at Oxford for trial. Few have escaped, if any. I dare say they'll all be hanged and drawn. The last I heard was that your brother was one of those who are to judge them. A fitting task for him, do you not think? He should be hangman into the bargain!'

'I have no brother,' she said in a whisper.

Abergavenny went on as if he had not heard her comment. 'I should have mentioned my further commission, madame, which is to take your children into my custody and to convey them to the King, who I do not doubt has plans for their future. Perhaps to place them in households where they'll be bred up as loyal subjects.'

Constance glared at him down her nose. 'If you intend to take *all* my children, you will need to take me,' she said.

He laughed loudly as her meaning dawned on him. 'That's the way matters stand, is it? So Despenser was not too busy with his plottings to get you in whelp? Left you something to remind you of him? You might have been wiser to keep your legs together!'

'Sir, is this the language of a knight?'

He snorted derisively. 'Courtesy is for honourable ladies, not for the wives of traitors. You can make any complaint to the King in person, for you'll be seeing him before long. That's where you're going, along with the rest of Despenser's moveable property. It'll take the rest of the day to settle our business here, but I've no wish to linger. You may pack what you need for yourself and the children, and be ready to leave first thing in the morning. No jewels though. Nothing of value. Those things are forfeit. Anyway, you'll have little need for them in the Minories, or wherever it is the King plans to lodge you. I hope you're suited to a life of contemplation. Hard beds and coarse shifts. Because I imagine that's what's in store for you.'

Constance imagined much the same, though it did not trouble her as much as it might have done. Thomas was safe. That was what mattered. She could endure hardship, as long as she could keep alive the faint hope that he would find the means to return to her. After all, a year earlier Bolingbroke himself had been in no better case. Fortune's wheel had a way of turning.

As for the valuables, there were less of them lying around than Abergavenny might have expected. Some had gone with Thomas. Others she had sent away with Sir John St. John, or with the devastated Agnes Norreys who had retired to Penllyn to mourn her husband in privacy. Others still were secreted around the castle in places where William Beauchamp and his like were not likely to look. She had not wasted her days at Cardiff. The thought brought a distant smile to her face once her opponent was out of the way.

Next day they took ship to Bristol, crammed with horses and possessions into the two small vessels that were the only ones available for hire. Wind and tide were favourable, however, and within ten hours they were nosing their way along the Avon gorge to the quay beneath the city walls.

There were many ships tied up there. One of them, Constance noticed, was remarkably similar in size and painting to the one that had taken Thomas to France. Then, as they drew closer she saw that the name painted on the forward castle was the same. *Katharine of Bristol*. It was the same ship. An impossibility, but there it stood before her, bobbing at its moorings, its sails furled, and its crew very evidently ashore. A chill of fear touched her. Thomas had obviously changed his mind. Landed himself in Bristol. But why? It made no sense at all. They had manors in Devon and Cornwall remote enough for a fugitive to hide, but if that was his choice it would have made more sense to land at some remote cove in the West, not here.

Abergavenny helped her ashore. He was not at all interested in the *Katharine*, did not even spare it a glance. Instead he led her into the shelter of a nearby and relatively respectable alehouse, where they, the children and her women could wait while the necessary unloading took place.

'We'll press on to Bath tonight,' he said. 'It'll be dark well before we get there, but it doesn't matter. It's a good road. You're not afraid of riding in the dark, are you?'

'The children will be hungry,' she objected, not expecting any concession.

'They'll be well fed at Bath Abbey. The monks there are good hosts. Bath today, then Marlborough, then Reading, then London. I know how anxious you must be to see your cousin the King.'

There was no point in arguing. They mounted up, with the light already fading away, and as they did so Constance recognised a face in the crowd of drinkers idling around the entrance of the alehouse yard. It was the shipman who owned the *Katharine*, and he was wearing a fine new cloak. A cloak that belonged to Thomas.

'I need to speak to that man,' she told William Beauchamp.

'What man? This is no time for gossiping! I want to get to Bath, and a soft bed.' Snorting, he slapped her horse into movement, and they rode through the milling crowds into the centre of the city.

In the market place a stake had been planted, ten or twelve feet high, so that it rose well above the people who were busy buying and selling at the stalls. On this stake was a head, presumably that of a malefactor. Not an uncommon sight, but not exactly usual either in such a setting. The head looked fresh, not par-boiled as such examples usually were. Blood had run from it and stained the upper reaches of the stake.

Constance could not take her eyes from it. It occurred to her that it might belong to one of the captured rebels, perhaps to some man she knew. She could at least say a prayer for him, if she but knew his identity.

As they grew closer, it seemed to her that the unfortunate man had a look of Thomas. The same shade of hair. The same cut of the beard. The same...

Abergavenny had gone white. He seized the bridle of her horse, pulled its head around in a sudden and brutal change of direction, heedless of the objec-tions of various trampled plebeians.

'I swear to God, I did not know,' he said, his voice shaking. 'Forgive me, my lady, but this was not my intent. Please believe me. I'd have done anything to spare you such a sight.'

She looked at him without comprehension. Then twisted in the saddle to take another look at the head. 'It is not,' she pronounced stubbornly. 'It is not.'

'Get those children away from here!' Abergavenny was shouting at his men. 'Turn around, go back! Back, I say! Get these scum out of my path!'

Constance felt the blackness closing over her. It merged somehow with the gathering dusk, became a reality stronger than she could fight. Her limbs were no longer under her control, and her horse was somehow sliding away from beneath her. She never knew who it was who caught her as she fell backwards into the dark.

24

King Henry leaned back in his chair, taking in the expressions of his councillors.

'This is much against my conscience,' he said, his voice so low that those at the foot of the table could scarcely make out his words. 'Richard is my cousin, and I swore that I would be a good lord to him.'

Archbishop Arundel hesitated for a moment, and then spoke. 'It has become a matter of necessity.'

'Your Grace, you are about to go to war with Scotland!' Grey de Ruthin always sounded as if he was starting a quarrel, even when making an observation. He was a squat figure, hard as the mountains that circled his Welsh home. 'You cannot leave that man alive in your rear. Who can say what crowd of traitors will rebel next? The Welsh are restless, I can tell you that.'

'The Welsh are always restless,' Edward of York said, offhandedly. 'They never actually *do* anything.'

'There are other traitors still at large besides the Welsh,' Erpingham remarked, in a thunderous grunt. He glared at Edward as if his meaning was not obvious enough.

'There is a fellow living near me,' Grey went on, 'who fancies himself Prince of Wales. One Owain of Glyndyfrdwy.'

'Of where?' Ralph Neville hooted. He experimented with the pronunciation, but could get no closer than 'Glendowerdy'.

'A madman, we may presume?' the Archbishop enquired, with a lofty tilt of his head.

Grey frowned thoughtfully. 'No more mad than the rest of the Welsh. He has a great following among them. Almost as though he were Christ! He traces himself far back, to the native princes. Beyond that, I dare say. Probably to Julius Caesar, and Adam. He's a gentleman of sorts, you understand. As such are counted among those barefooted scrubs. Has quite a bit of property.'

'I really do not see the relevance of this to the point under discussion.'

'The relevance is damn well obvious, Archbishop! Saving your presence. This fellow has already had the gall and impudence to sue me in the King's courts over some lands that have been my family's for generations. He's a cursed *lawyer* I should mention, apart from all else. Well, this *Welsh lawyer* is not satisfied with the outcome of his case, so he's minded to take up other means. He's stirring the

Welsh of my country to revolt, and whom do you think they'll cry up as their rightful liege lord? *Richard* of course! Any half-blind mole can see that! Next door to me lies Cheshire, where every second man believes Richard a saint, and the rest think him the greatest King since the Conquest. Tinder waiting for flame, I tell you. Will it even end there? When this table is covered from one end to the other with reports of disorders across the shires? The King cannot, must not, leave England without first taking this thorn out of his arse. Richard must die. God knows he's already caused the deaths of many men better than himself. I don't intend that he'll cause mine!'

This, for Reginald Grey was a very long speech, and it was followed by an equally lengthy silence, broken only by the scratch of the clerk's pen on parchment as he wrote his rudimentary minutes.

Bolingbroke's eyes were somehow drawn to the moving quill, though he saw it only as an unsatisfactory blur of movement, the detail blurred by his myopia. Then he took in the missing places around the table. Surrey and Salisbury, butchered like hogs in the market place at Cirencester. Exeter, his brother-in-law, run to ground in Essex, summarily executed at Pleshey in the very spot—they said—that the Duke of Gloucester had been arrested. Despenser overcome at sea by men no better than pirates, carried to Bristol, and there beheaded by the mob. Then there were the lesser men. Blount hanged and quartered at Oxford; Richard Maudelyn strung up at Tyburn. Young Alan de Buxhull had somehow managed to get himself acquitted by an Oxford jury, God knew how. The Bishop of Carlisle and the Abbot of Westminster had been consigned to prison, left with nothing beyond their lives. Harry, having seen sufficient heads in baskets, had spared some of the lesser gentlemen, though none would ever hold office or responsibility while he reigned.

He took one hand in the other, stared at the large ruby ring on his right index finger, focusing on its blood-red depths. There were others he now doubted. Lumley's unexpected treason troubled him deeply. Lumley had always been Northumberland's man. Had he really acted without the approval of his patron? That was a mystery. A mystery that would have to be probed… Hotspur was already asking awkward questions about the Mortimer boys. Questions that a loyal man might have thought it better to leave unspoken.

Suddenly he realised that they were all looking at him, expecting him to speak.

'What do you advise, Edward?' he asked his cousin, thinking that the answer might be interesting.

Edward took a deep breath, drew himself up from his usual lolling posture. 'I think there's a great deal in what Grey says,' he offered.

'Do you, by Christ!' Grey exclaimed.

'Yes, I do. But the killing of an anointed King is no small matter.'

The Archbishop lifted his head again. 'The killing of my brother, and of your uncle, the Duke of Gloucester, was no small matter either. You did not object to that!'

'I obeyed my King!'

'You obeyed a dangerous lunatic, a man who still threatens the accord of this land. I agree that no life should be taken lightly. But God understands that that law which covers other men does not bind those who have rule of nations. When a king acts for the common good of his people, not merely for private revenge, he is justified before God.'

Edward shook his head. 'Archbishop, it is not your conscience, or mine, or Grey's that will have to bear this deed. It's easy for us to preach, when we shall still be able to sleep in our beds at night.'

'You speak of sleeping in beds—you!' Thomas Erpingham got out.

Bolingbroke plucked at his beard, became aware of his own gesture, and forced his hand down onto the table. It slapped down rather harder than he had intended. 'Let my cousin speak,' he said. 'Remember also that he *is* my cousin; that he represents my Uncle York.'

That latter point was a claim so large that Edward would not have made it himself.

'Richard has been a sick man for years,' he said quietly. 'Look into his account rolls if you doubt me! His doctors must be as rich as any of us. He no longer has his comforts, and if I know him he'll be as low in spirits as a man can be. Remove him to a less comfortable prison and don't feed him too well. After that I think you can leave him safely to God.'

'Why not go further?' asked Grey, sneering, his head sinking into his fur collar. 'Release him. Give him a title. Let him have his throne again.'

'God knows,' groaned Bolingbroke, 'I wish Richard *were* dead. But not by my hand.'

'You have already shown your enemies too much mercy,' the Archbishop said, 'and reaped a harvest for it. A harvest of sorrow for your people. How long will you draw out their agony? The realm needs peace, and will not have it while Richard lives.'

Harry glanced around them. He could almost hear their breathing as they watched him, waiting for his verdict. The strange thing was that he did not trust a one of them. Today they were voting for Richard's murder. On another occasion they would be just as prepared to vote for his, if it would keep them all established in their power. In some ways he liked Edward best of them. He was a rogue, but at least he was a Plantagenet rogue, not a jumped-up, trouble-seeking border ruffian like Grey or a sanctimonious hypocrite like the Archbishop, a man who would stretch God's word beyond breaking point to serve his ambition.

He stood up slowly, like a very old man. 'So be it,' he pronounced, his voice scarcely audible. He took no joy in the decision. It was Richard or himself. So Richard had to die.

**

Lord Beauchamp of Abergavenny leaned against the wall, his elbow pressing the King's hangings into the stonework.

'Only one woman in a thousand could have kept her child inside her after such a shock,' he said admiringly. 'She didn't even weep much. Or if she did, she didn't let *me* see it, which amounts to the same thing. I let her rest for a day; it was necessary anyway, to arrange some mourning garb for her. Then I had a litter ordered for her. Do you know she walked past it, climbed into her saddle without a hand to aid her, sat there with her back as straight as a lance. Like a queen, I tell you! Like a bloody *knight!'*

He was addressing his much-younger brother-in-law, Thomas Fitzalan, Earl of Arundel. Arundel had something of his late father about him, a grim, very masculine face set above a stocky, powerful frame. Unlike old Arundel though, he was something of a dandy, his darkish hair curled and perfumed, and his houppelande cut very short, displaying powerful legs and an exaggerated, padded bulge.

'Widow of a traitor,' he said shortly.

They both stole a glance at Constance. She was sitting quietly on a cloth-covered bench across the room, awaiting her summons, with her children on either side of her and her three waiting-damosels, her chamberer and the children's nurses standing protectively about her. She was wearing one of her usual gowns that had been somewhat inexpertly dyed black. Here and there traces of the original crimson forced themselves on the discerning eye. The wimple that framed her face gave her the look of a young, handsome nun cast out into the world, unsure and yet determined.

'You talk like a fool, boy!' William Beauchamp hissed. 'That is good breeding stock—would give you sons capable of capturing Jerusalem single-handed! I don't think much of women generally. Most of them are fit only to serve as a man's mattress and to sit around prating with their gossips. That is an exception. A prize worth fighting over. I'd have her myself if I were free to take her. You want to ask the King for her within the week before some other young hound snatches her from your maw.'

'You think he would bestow her?'

'She's his cousin. He'll have to settle a reasonable share of the Despenser properties on her, and her son will inherit the entailed lands at least. What is he? Four? Seventeen years of wardship ahead, say. Taken together that would make a pretty gift for a loyal man, and the King might be glad to see her and the boy in safe hands. You'll have to wait a while of course, with her being left in foal, but there's no harm in speaking a word now, getting the conveyance signed and sealed so to speak.'

Arundel took a breath. 'I don't know,' he said.

'Hesitate too long, and you risk losing her, and her son.'

'I've heard she has a sharp tongue.'

Lord Abergavenny groaned in despair. 'How old are you? Are you a monk? Have you ever *had* a woman? Look at what else she's got, damn you! Her tongue won't harm you. Anyway, treat her right and she won't be using it to scold you, but for something else again.'

'Her husband and her brother helped bring about my father's death,' the young man objected.

'So they did. But you can say the same of the King. Thought of that, have you? No sense in bearing grudges. Not unless there's something to be gained thereby. Anyway, Despenser's dead and rotting. You'll be bulling his wife senseless, breeding out of her and drawing the revenues from her estates. I call that the very best sort of revenge.'

Arundel shrugged. 'She may not even be willing to have me.'

His brother-in-law tutted impatiently. 'At this moment, strictly speaking, she doesn't even own the clothes she has on her back. She's war booty, nothing more. As I told you, the King will have to provide for her, for the shame of it, but there's nothing to stop him attaching conditions, is there? That is a sensible woman, not some greensick girl, and she'll see the way to her own advantage. To be Countess of Arundel is no bad bargain for her in the circumstances.' He paused for thought. 'Not that it would do you any harm to pay your respects, to remind her that you exist. I don't suppose she knows you much from Adam. Go over now, while you've got the chance. But take it gently. Show her the respect you'd allow the Blessed Virgin on Good Friday. This is not the occasion to thrust a hand up her skirts.'

The young Earl gave him a scathing, eloquent glance. 'I am not so stupid, 'Bergavenny, that you need to tell me that.'

He made his way over to Constance, who received his condolences with an automatic graciousness, without really comprehending what he was saying or knowing who he was. She had no inkling of his intent, and felt nothing more than mild relief when he ran out of words and returned to his discussion with Abergavenny. It was as if an irritating fly had stopped buzzing around her head.

Thomas Erpingham emerged from the door leading through to the inner sanctum, his chamberlain's staff in his hand. His eyes rested briefly on Constance before he turned to address Abergavenny.

'The King's ready for you,' he announced, with a blunt absence of ceremony.

Constance stood, and accepted William Beauchamp's proffered hand. She was glad of the support and strengthened by the expression in his eye, which was approving, even admiring.

'There's no cause to be afraid,' she told the children. 'The King is your cousin. Kneel when I do, and don't speak unless he speaks to you first.'

The room she entered was as dark as her heart, the fading light of the afternoon scarcely finding its way in though the tall windows facing the Thames, the fire that blazed in the hearth providing most of the illumination. Bolingbroke was alone, surprisingly alone. He sat on his bed, stroking Math's head with an urgent energy, as if it were the prime purpose of his life to do so. As she made her first curtsey he stood up, and as she began the second he stepped forward, raised her up.

'Cousin, I sorrow to see you so,' he said. 'I wished your husband no ill—hoped that I had given him cause enough to be loyal to me.'

She did not answer. Harry took a deep breath. He had been dreading this interview, ever since the news of Despenser's murder had been brought to him. In some ways, he thought, it was a pity that Constance was not more like his sister, Beth. Beth had been no trouble at all, had accepted the killing of her husband as a minor inconvenience, like a broken fingernail or a snapped lace. Of course, Beth lived for the moment, always had. She did not dwell on things. Constance was made of a different metal altogether.

'Suitable provision will be made for your maintenance,' he went on, 'and you are assured of my protection. Your son's wardship will be granted to you. I can do no more. I only wish that I could.' He stroked young Richard's hair, lifted Bess's chin. 'If the children lack for something, Constance, you have only to ask. Or whatever you need immediately for yourself. Clothes, money—anything. Either come to me, or have someone put a petition in Erpingham's hand. You'll not be refused.'

Constance could find nothing to say; or at least nothing that she could allow to pass her lips. She made another curtsey, a perfect one. That would have to serve as her thanks, for she was not even sure that her voice would function. Her tears were threatening again, and she was forced to concentrate on the task of retaining them. Neither Bolingbroke nor Abergavenny would ever enjoy the privilege of seeing her weep.

***

King Richard's body was brought by slow stages from Pontefract, pausing for a few hours at each town on the way so that the people could file past his coffin and satisfy themselves that he was really dead.

By the time the funeral procession reached London, rumours had begun to spread abroad about the manner of his death. Some alleged he had been starved to death by Sir Thomas Swynford, Constable of Pontefract and eldest son of the Dowager Duchess of Lancaster; others that Richard, despairing after the defeat of his friends, had refused food until he had grown too weak for a change of mind to save him; others still claimed King Harry had sent a knight to Pontefract, one Piers of Exton, to murder his predecessor. No one had ever heard of a Sir Piers of

Exton, but this trivial fact did not seem to spoil anyone's enjoyment of the tale. A speculative Grey Friar, visiting Constance in the hope of a coin or two, went so far to tell her that it was not King Richard's body at all, but that of Maudelyn. The real Richard, he affirmed, had escaped from Pontefract, and was safe across the border in Scotland.

Constance was convinced that Bolingbroke was the callous murderer of their cousin; but she found the notion that Richard had escaped almost equally comforting, and was rather reluctant to acknowledge that the two options were mutually exclusive. She ventured out to St. Paul's to see the body for herself, covering the short distance from the *Old Inne* on foot. Enfolded in a voluminous black cloak over her mourning clothes, her face all but concealed by its hood, she was able to retain her anonymity among the crowds, though her deportment and the presence of two of her father's liveried yeomen at her elbows were clues sufficient for any discerning eye to detect. She swept past the stalls of scriveners, money-changers and relic sellers that occupied a part of the immense nave, and joined the long procession of people slowly filing past the open coffin. For the most part the crowd was made up of ordinary citizens of London, the complete spectrum from aldermen to beggars, but here and there was a face familiar from court. To her surprise Sir John Russell was among them, looking thin and haggard from his long spell in prison, but apparently recovered from his temporary insanity. She did not approach him.

Richard's features were only partially visible, from his eyebrows to his throat; the rest of him sealed in lead and thoroughly concealed beneath a pall of black velvet. The public were kept at a respectful distance by an honour guard of archers, and the coffin lay on the hearse on which it had been drawn from Pontefract, above head height, so that Constance had to crane her neck to see anything of real significance.

She knelt among the pious minority who were there out of more than idle curiosity. The heat of hundreds of blazing candles warmed her face as she wept her prayers for Richard, for Thomas, and for all that was irredeemably lost.

When she returned to the *Old Inne*, she found that guests had arrived in her absence. Hugh Tyldesley and the two archers who had accompanied Thomas from Cirencester. All three had been captured in Bristol, and marched to London in chains, and they had only just been released from the bowels of the Fleet prison. Their beards were overgrown tangles, and what was left of their Despenser liveries hung on them in tatters, covering the spaces between patches of filthy skin. They looked like beggars, and had had grave difficulty in gaining admission to the house, until Tyldesley found the wit to have Mary Russell summoned to vouch for them.

Constance was delighted to see them. 'I'm re-establishing my household,' she said, 'and there'll be a place in it for each of you, if you wish it. I have need of men I can trust.'

Tyldesley and the two archers exchanged glances.

'My lady,' Tyldesley said, 'we are your men, but first we need leave for a week or two. A month at the most. There are debts to be settled. It'd help us if we could have some wages in advance.'

'To settle the debt?'

'It's not that kind of debt,' said Adda, his dark eyes hard.

'To buy clothes and weapons, hire horses, and pay for lodgings on the way,' Tyldesley explained.

'We're going back to Bristol, see,' added the other archer. Constance realised that under the dirt he was little more than a boy. She had a feeling that he might be Adda's son, or perhaps his nephew.

'That's not my lady's concern,' Tyldesley told him. He spoke with authority, but without his usual abruptness, his voice almost gentle as if Madog was a beloved younger brother. 'This is our business, not hers.'

Constance settled herself in her chair. 'It sounds as if it might be my business also,' she remarked.

Tyldesley shook his head. 'No, lady. The less you know about it the better. You might feel obliged to forbid our intent, and I for one would hate to begin my service by disobeying you.'

Constance opened the purse that hung from her cincture, counted out sufficient to make up five pounds, which was equivalent to half Tyldesley's annual retaining fee.

'That's more than ample,' said Tyldesley approvingly, giving each of the Welshmen a few of the smaller coins and putting the rest in his own purse. 'We'll make a start at once.'

'Stay and eat with me,' Constance suggested. 'I'll dine in here, in an hour or so. I keep to this room.'

He shook his head. 'Forgive us, my lady, but we've not the time. I want to be out of London before dark, and there's much to do before that. Much to buy. We've grown used to empty bellies, these last weeks. We can eat on the road.'

When they had gone, Constance examined the contents of her purse. The payment of their expenses had left her very little; she had had to borrow money from Sir Hugh Despenser and the Duchess of York to pay the Chancery fees for her grants, buy a handful of masses for Thomas, and purchase essentials for herself and her little retinue. A certain amount of ready money would arrive soon—Bolingbroke had allowed her the gold Thomas had been carrying—but that apart she would have to raise credit from London merchants to set up her household and keep herself until her rents and feudal dues began to flow again. Sir Hugh would probably be able to advise her as to whom she should approach, though there was no saying when he would visit her again. She did not care to ask her father for advice. The Duke had made it clear that he was coldly furious with her, that he was only allowing her food and shelter because of the obedience he owed the King. He blamed her and Edward equally for Thomas's death, and for the inconvenience that he himself had suffered as a result of the conspiracy. However, Edward had the great advantage of not being lodged in the *Old Inne*. He had found himself more peaceful quarters, attached to the court, and Philippa had discreetly retired to Carisbrooke with the bulk of their household, about as far away from the Duke as she could get without entering another kingdom.

Constance sighed as she contemplated the situation; she did not care to be at odds with her father, but on the other hand she was too proud to plead with him. Her relationship with her mother-in-law was still more chilled. Elisabeth had sent one, dictated letter, a stiffly formal message without a word of sympathy or encouragement. It had informed her that Thomas's body had been buried at Tewkesbury, save for his head, which Elisabeth had petitioned the King to restore. It went on to remind her that the lease of Hanley Castle was now terminated, and Elisabeth had resumed possession. This had been necessary, Elisabeth claimed, because the sheriff's officers, Warwick's men, had presumed to seize the place as a forfeit of treason, which they had no right to do.

A few months earlier the loss of her beloved Hanley would have been a disaster, but in the new scale of things it was a mild annoyance, one of many complex and pressing issues that were facing her as the tangle of Thomas's affairs was unravelled. Some lands were entailed, and thus secure to her son; others unentailed, and so forfeit unless the King regranted them to her; others yet were held in complex trusts, intended by Thomas to serve as a jointure for her, or to support any younger sons that might be born. Then there were Elisabeth's dower lands in Glamorgan, held in trust by Thomas in return for an agreed rental, and now devolving upon her on the same basis. Her head reeled with it all. Sir Hugh Despenser had given her valuable assistance, but Hugh Mortimer had declined to remain in her service, having somehow attached himself to the Prince of Wales, and John St. John, though always willing to turn a coin for himself, was still in Glamorgan, his counsel appearing only in written form, and subject to long delay. She was forced to rely more and more upon her own unsupported judgement.

However, help had come from some surprising quarters. Joanne had been as close as a sister, and Ralph Green, husband to her one-time damosel, Katherine Mallory, and son to the executed Henry, had unexpectedly offered his services, vigorously pursuing the Chancery clerks on her behalf. Lord Abergavenny, not content with apologising for the discourtesy he had shown her at Cardiff, had become positively assiduous, even to the point of carrying her petitions to the King.

After dinner she received another visitor, one who was still more welcome than Tyldesley and the two archers had been. It was Edmund Mortimer.

She remembered that he had come to her before, during her first few days in London, as several others had done, stuttering the conventional words of

consolation and then hastily retiring. This time she hoped he would stay a little longer, perhaps talk to her of Thomas. No one seemed willing to do that; it
was as if they thought the mere mention of him would hurt her. Perhaps
Edmund knew her better.

'I saw you in St. Paul's,' he said. 'The crowd was between us—I couldn't get
near.'

She indicated the bed. 'Please sit down, Edmund. I didn't notice you there,
but I'm very glad to see you now. Will you have some wine?'

He nodded, and sat silently as Mary Russell poured the drink for him, and
placed the goblet in his hands.

'Do you think it really is Richard?' he asked abruptly.

'Yes.' Constance paused, thought about it for a moment. 'Yes, I think it must
be. Bolingbroke would make sure there was no way for him to escape.'

'It turns my stomach to think of it. Death in a fair fight is one thing. Murder
another. Murder by starvation, as they say, worse again. Starvation! Imagine that!'

'I have done.'

He took in her expression. 'Constance, forgive me. I didn't mean to add to
your pain. I shouldn't have spoken of it.'

She shook her head dismissively. 'I hurt so much that no words you could
find would make it worse. It's right that we speak of Richard, right we remember that they shut their anointed King in a dungeon, watched him die by inches.
We must always remember what Bolingbroke is—worse than a murderer. He
has shed more noble blood in the last six months than Richard did in
twenty-two years. I dare say he'll shed more yet, because he's no right to the
throne, and in his heart he knows it.'

'Alianore fears for her sons,' he said grimly.

'I know.'

'Of course. She must have told you about it—when you were at Sonning together.' He paused, evidently ill at ease, looked for somewhere to set down his
wine. 'She sends you her best wishes, by the way.'

Constance scanned his face, sensing his discomfort. 'She's still with the
Queen?' she asked, trying to maintain the momentum of the conversation.

'No. The Queen's household is much reduced now. Alianore's gone to Usk.
She'd have had to leave anyway. Her child will come in another two months or so.'

'I hope to be with her, if it's possible. Though I must stay here until my
affairs are put in order. I have to petition for every little thing, and the Chancery
clerks seem to take pleasure in delay. I'm going to have to borrow some money
to tide me over.'

'I have money,' said Edmund, meeting her gaze. 'My brother gave me a fair
livelihood, and I've never been lavish in my spending. You can have a hundred
pounds tomorrow, if you wish. Two hundred.'

She lowered her eyes. 'I prefer not to be indebted to a friend, Edmund.'

'Who speaks of debt? It would be a gift.'

'Then still less can I accept it.'

'Then I must offer more.' He stood up, paced around uncomfortably, as though in the grip of a bowel spasm. 'I'll not allow you to be forced. You shall have a choice, even if it's a poor one.'

She shook her head in bewilderment. 'I don't know what you're talking about. No one is forcing me to do anything.'

'Then you are *content* to marry Arundel?' Mortimer's expression turned to one of desolation. 'You've agreed? I know he's a great lord, and very rich, but surely, surely you want more than that from a man! At least consider the alternative.'

'Edmund!' she drew him up sharply, astonished by his words. 'I don't know what you've heard, but I've no thought of marrying Arundel, or any other man. How can you even speak of such things to me?'

'I understood it was the King's command; that all your grants were dependent upon it. That's what Lady Charlton said. Alianore's sister-in-law, I mean.'

Constance checked her rising anger, took a breath. This needed thought. Lady Charlton was Arundel's sister, no less. Sister also to Lady Abergavenny. Perhaps that explained Abergavenny's rapid conversion from open enemy to solicitous friend. He might be looking after his family's interests. 'There are no conditions to my grants, Edmund. If there were, I'd not have accepted them. No word has been said to me of this.'

'Perhaps they await their time. I don't know, but Alice Charlton seemed very sure, and I can't believe that one has the wit to invent such a thing. Someone has put it into her head. Arundel himself, it may be, if this is his scheme. After all, what you've been given isn't dower or jointure. It could be taken from you, at the King's pleasure. They could threaten you with that.'

'They can threaten what they will! I am not that easily frightened.'

He took her hand, kissed it with something warmer than reverence. 'If you have need of me...' His voice lowered. 'Let Bolingbroke take back his grants; you'll not lack for anything. My lands are worth a good four hundred marks a year, and you shall have a jointure in every inch of them. I'll make no demands on you. I understand what you have lost. I shall earn your love, if it takes the rest of my life, and in the mean time I shall have the pleasure of caring for you, of living under the same roof and seeing you each day.'

She retrieved her hand, pulling away as gently as she could. 'I cannot be your wife, Edmund. Not on such terms. You deserve better than to be so used.'

25

Thomas was with her again. She could feel his strength as he held her; see his smile. His lips touched hers, and her body responded willingly, longingly. He was pressing down on her, almost on the point of entry... And then she woke. Suddenly snapped into the reality of solitude and pitch darkness. Somewhere outside an owl hooted mockingly, almost as if amused by the deception her dream had worked upon her.

She sat up in bed, rigid with shock, using her hand to stifle something that was half a scream, half an urge to vomit.

It was not her first such dream. If anything they had become more frequent since she had returned to Cardiff, and particularly since Isabelle's birth. They left her body aching with desire and her mind in turmoil, unable to sleep for hours afterwards, if at all. Often they led to a failure of her self-control, to weeping, to screaming, even to blasphemy. She had not only cursed God in the depths of her agony, she had denied His very existence. The very thought of it made her tremble, and lower her head in shame.

Later, when the dawn came, she went at once to hear the early mass in the castle chapel, and immediately afterwards asked her chaplain to hear her confession. Her tale brought a frown of deep concern to the old Franciscan's face.

'It's not your husband who comes to you in these so-called dreams,' he whispered. 'It is a demon.'

'A demon?' Constance trembled under a mixture of horror and disbelief.

'Certainly. These demons are subtle. Like other diabolical creatures, they have no seed of their own, only a cold, infertile mockery of it. So first they lie with a man, tempting him in the form of a beautiful woman, so that they may collect his vital fluid. I was often visited so myself, when I was younger, though it fills me with shame to recall it. Then they pleasure themselves with a woman, taking the appearance of a beloved man. Sometimes even while her husband sleeps innocently beside her, bound by the demon so that he cannot wake. Thus are the devil's children born.'

She felt her gorge rising. She had heard of such children, born hideously deformed, the mark of sin written so unmistakably upon them that they were shut up in monasteries or nunneries, or crawled in gutters, begging for their bread with hideous screams, the outcasts of society. 'I thought it a dream,' she said, her voice little more than a whisper.

The friar's cadaverous features grew yet more solemn. 'Naturally—the demon wished you to think it so. As it wished you to believe it was your lord, so that you would submit to it. The agents of Satan recognise our weaknesses, present themselves to us in pleasing shapes, and not as they truly are, disgusting, revolting creatures. The very sight or scent of which would make you vomit, if not drive you into insanity. You were very right, Daughter, to ask for guidance. Evil is all around us, and our only defence is perpetual vigilance.'

'What must I do?'

'Pray. The saints will aid you; angels guard your bed. Forswear meat for a time. Devote yourself to charitable deeds. Avoid luxury, as far as is fitting for one of your station in life. Deny the claims of the flesh.' He paused, and then went on abruptly. 'That may serve to drive away these devils. If not, then you must consider another way. Not all are granted the grace and blessing of continence. God understands that we are sinful creatures. He does not expect perfection from us, merely that we humbly acknowledge our wickedness and seek to make amends. Sometimes we must choose the lesser of two sins. It is better that you lie with a mortal man than with a creature of Hell.'

'You are telling me to marry again, Father?' Constance was astonished.

'I am telling you to choose the lesser evil. If you cannot be chaste, if you prove unable to subdue your lust by any other means, it is far better to take a man as your lover than to be the whore of demons.' He paused, drew the air through the gaps between his yellow teeth. 'When Lady Abergavenny was here she mentioned to me that her brother intends to ask for your hand in marriage as soon as you have had your year of mourning. Perhaps you should consider that offer, when it is made.'

She flinched from him as if he had become a demon himself. 'How can you suggest such a thing? You, a man of God! How dare you!'

'I dare because it is my duty to protect your soul. Fast and pray, as I have told you, but if you can't accustom yourself to a life of chastity, you are better an honourable wife than a creature of shame.'

Joanna Beauchamp, Lady Abergavenny, had been a most unexpected guest among the women who had gathered at Cardiff to see Isabelle Despenser into the world. Had it not been for Alianore's presence, she would also have been the highest ranking among them, and even more loud and dominant than she had been. She had judged the situation well enough only to make fleeting and oblique references to her brother when speaking to Constance, but it was now obvious that she had made indirect approaches as well. Approaches that had doubtless been sweetened with suitable gifts, fulsome flattery and promises for the future.

Constance felt both weary and irritated. If she could not even trust her own confessor, the chances were the rest of her advisers had been suborned, were only waiting for an appropriate moment to point her in the same direction. Back in her solar she opened her coffer and drew out the letter that Henry Despenser had sent her when he had heard of Thomas's death. In it he had promised to be father, brother and husband to her, as well as uncle, to the limit of his power. But that, indeed, was the rub. Apart from the fact that he was far away in Norwich, his power was limited; he'd been kept in prison for many months, and had troubles of his own in Norfolk, because of his long-standing quarrel with Thomas Erpingham. He was also busy with a new campaign against the Lollards of his diocese. His good wishes were a great comfort, but that was all they could be.

'Tyldesley wants to see you,' Agnes announced abruptly. Somehow she managed to pack the simple statement with venom. She had never forgiven Tyldesley for being where she thought her husband should have been, or Constance for continuing to employ him.

Tyldesley had a formidable roll of documents under his arm. He was delegated to go to Tewkesbury to negotiate with Lady Elisabeth's council, and wanted a final briefing on various unresolved issues.

Constance went through it with him point by point, telling him what he might concede, where he must stand firm, and where she was ready to trust to his discretion. He was not used to such a level of responsibility and nor, for that matter, was Constance herself. It took a long time to agree on everything, but at least she trusted Tyldesley to do his utmost for her. There were few others of whom she could say the same.

'I thought to take Adda and Madog with me,' he said tentatively, when they had settled their strategy. 'The country is restless, and I'll be glad of a couple of sure men for the journey.'

The two archers were enrolled as yeomen of the household now, clad in bright new liveries and showing every sign of being contented with their lot. They and Tyldesley had formed themselves into a little clique, differences in class and nation notwithstanding. The three went everywhere together, even into the brothels of Cardiff when they needed to ease their lusts. An unlikely partnership. Some of the other members of the household had already commented on it, and not with approval. They could not decide whether Tyldesley was demeaning himself or the archers were forgetting their proper place. Neither form of deviation from custom was popular.

'You may take whom you will,' she answered. 'Will you lodge at the abbey?'
'Yes.'
'You'll pray for him?'
'You need not ask, my lady.'
'I'll give you money, to pay the abbot for more masses. I worry—worry, lest his soul be bound to earth in some way. Is it possible, do you think? I see him so often in my dreams, just as he was. I've even—touched him.'

'If he could find a way to be with you, he would,' Tyldesley paused briefly, sucked at his teeth. 'I pray that he's at peace. He was a good lord. A good man. I only wish I could have saved him. Still, at least—'

He broke off, his mouth setting in a firm line. He made a bow, one of his usual ungainly efforts, and began to withdraw.

'At least?' she prompted.

'At least the *Katharine of Bristol* has a new master now. We found that traitor, lady. Adda and Madog and me. He won't betray anyone else. Not where he is now. He's even got a couple of friends to keep him company. Drunken men get very careless, you know. Tend to lose their footing on dark nights, especially near rivers.'

'I see.' She dwelled on the matter for a few moments, shocked by the extent of the delight that was coursing through her veins. Revenge, however inadequate, had its pleasures. 'You've done me a great service, Hugh. I'll not forget it.'

He shook his head. 'I don't want any reward. Nor do the others. It wasn't done for gain. It wasn't even done for you. The truth is, we *enjoyed* it.'

***

The revolt of Owain, Lord of Glyndyfrdwy and Sycharth, had been crushed in less than three weeks. Glyn Dwr, as the Welsh called him, or Glendower, as the English found more comfortable, had taken to the hills. His lands had been forfeited and granted to John Beaufort; his supporters were applying for pardons, and receiving them.

Edward of York, Earl of Rutland, had been appointed Lieutenant of North Wales, and given the task of completing the pacification under the nominal authority of the young Prince. With them at Chester were Harry Hotspur, the prince's governor; Sir Hugh Despenser, who had been appointed to the Prince's council, and, more often than not, Thomas Fitzalan, Earl of Arundel, the principal local landowner, and Reginald, Lord Grey de Ruthin, the principal cause of all the trouble. Edward did not find any one of these companions congenial. Even the Prince had an unfortunate habit of talking about King Richard and thereby raking up issues that his cousin preferred to forget, and of which the others required no reminder.

Of the adults, only Arundel showed him anything better than a cold shoulder. This attempt at friendship puzzled Edward deeply, and he rapidly concluded that the young man had an ulterior motive. The nature of that motive, when it appeared, was only marginally less astonishing than Arundel's apparent confidence that he would think it a desirable development.

Two of Arundel's sisters were wedded to Lord Charlton of Powys and Lord Abergavenny. Charlton's brother was husband to the Countess of March, and had control of Alianore's third of the Mortimer lands. Abergavenny's brother was Warwick, and Warwick's son was married to the daughter and heiress of Lord

Berkeley. Arundel, the Beauchamps, the Charltons and Berkeley, united by these family links, formed a power bloc that dominated the Marches, as well as much of Wales. If Arundel secured Constance and gained effective possession of the Despenser estates, then that domination would be as complete as made no difference. Even as matters stood it was a formidable political grouping, and one that, for various reasons, was almost entirely hostile to Edward of York and unsympathetic to his ambitions. Constance's accession to this confederacy would not be at all to his profit. She was as hostile as any of them, not only refusing to reply to his letters, but actually returning them unopened. It seemed to Edward that she might well agree to accept Arundel, if only as an act of womanish spite. Somehow she had to be reminded of her duty to the House of York, won over to support of his long-term plans.

It was a knotty problem, and one he mused over long and hard. To make matters worse, there was no one at Chester in whom he could confide. Philippa was far away, at Carisbrooke, and she was the only one in whom he had absolute trust.

He began to see a way forward only when a most unexpected letter arrived from his stepmother. It was unexpected because the Duchess had never troubled to write to him before, and the content more unexpected still. It was an invitation to spend the Christmas season at Fotheringhay. Joanne said that she had persuaded her husband to be reconciled with his elder children. Consequently, Constance was also to be invited. Joanne hoped that brother and sister would follow York's example, and agree to make peace with one another.

Edward's mind raced. This was part of the solution, and now he must find the rest of it. At last it came to him. In order to be rid of Bolingbroke, an alternative, credible claimant to the throne was needed. His own claim was too thin, unfortunately, and he had too few friends willing to back it. No, the only practicable alternative to Lancaster was the young Earl of March, Alianore's son. He must build an alliance with the Mortimers.

Alianore had two daughters. The elder, Anne, was almost marriageable. She would make a suitable bride for his brother, Dickon, though it would be a year or two before any such match could be consummated. That might tempt Alianore. As matters stood, Dickon would be Duke of York one day. Edward had long given up hope of children of his own—he'd given many women pleasure, but he'd never managed to make one pregnant. Edward smiled to himself, pleased by his own inventiveness. Constance was as close to Alianore as any sister. She might be persuaded to act as an intermediary, especially if he could lead her to think that it would be to Dickon's advantage. Such an approach would be more likely to succeed than any he might make himself, and if his father or the King found any cause for objection he would be able to say that it was Constance who had made the match, not himself.

He sent a grateful letter of acceptance to the Duchess of York, and wrote at greater length to his wife, outlining his strategy in the vague terms that were safest in a letter, and desiring her to join him so that they might talk of the matter in greater detail. He spent the next few weeks riding around North Wales, handing out pardons and pretending to sympathise with Grey over his burnt villages, stolen cattle and dispossessed tenants. When he returned to Chester, Philippa was already waiting for him. She had been busy making friends with Hotspur and the Prince, both of whom were more than susceptible to female flattery. They were virtually eating out of her hand.

'I thought that the Mortimers were your enemies,' she said, once they were alone together.

'Roger Mortimer *was* my enemy. I've nothing against his son. He's Richard's rightful heir.'

Philippa's eyes hooded for a moment. 'I also thought that you wanted to be King.'

'I did! I do. But it's impossible, Philippa. I lack the power, the support. Surely you see that?'

'Yes,' she mused. 'I suppose, as March is a boy, he'll need a Regent?'

'He's a long way from being crowned yet, my dear.'

'Would it be you?'

'Perhaps. Perhaps Edmund Mortimer. But we must go carefully. You're trying to reap the harvest before we've even ploughed the field.'

Philippa nodded thoughtfully. She sat on the bed and began to unpin her headdress. 'I think Harry Hotspur might be won over to our side,' she suggested. 'He's no friend of Bolingbroke. It shows in little things, even when he talks to someone like me. Was the campaign in Scotland really as badly managed as he says?'

'Do you not read my letters? It was a complete debacle. It's bad enough that we sat at York for weeks on end, waiting for money and supplies to arrive. Cousin Harry surrounds himself with fools, men who have no experience of government. Richard had his faults, but at least he knew how to choose an officer.'

'I'm surprised you've not tried to make Hotspur your friend.'

Her husband snorted. 'He likes the sound of his own voice. Just because he grumbles, it doesn't mean he'll do anything about it.'

'He might. His wife's a Mortimer don't forget. Edmund's sister.'

'That doesn't necessarily mean anything.'

'Of course not necessarily.' Philippa loosened her hair from its coils and began to comb it out. 'On the other hand, it could mean a great deal, if he saw gain in it for himself. It's not a small advantage for a man to have his nephew as King.'

He took the comb from her, began to run it through her hair. He was not particularly efficient in the performance of the task, but it gave them both pleasure 'I've more hope of his uncle, Worcester,' he said. 'Worcester was always Richard's man. I think he still is, in his heart. Of course, if we *could* win Hotspur and his father around, it would make a significant difference. I don't think we can, not yet.'

She arched her back, like a cat rubbing itself against a tree. 'Ned, that's wonderful! I love to feel your hands in my hair. Such a simple thing, but neither of my other husbands would have dreamed of it.'

He plied the comb again. 'Then they lacked imagination.'

'Fitzwalter used me as a man uses a chamber pot. When he felt the urge, and with no more consideration. Golafre seemed happiest when he was hurting me. You, on the other hand, are full of surprises. I never quite know what's coming next.'

'After so many weeks apart? I think you do!'

'There's someone else we need to win over,' she suggested. 'Edmund Mortimer. What's more, I think we may have the proper bait with which to catch him. I mean your sister. I remember, a few years ago, when Golafre and I were at Hanley Castle, I could sense something between them. You could call it friendship, I suppose. Perhaps even more than that.'

Edward was briskly dismissive. 'He's always had a liking for her, but I doubt whether Constance is interested.'

'I think you could be wrong,' Philippa said dryly. 'She's been a widow for the best part of a year. Any woman with blood in her begins to feel it stirring after that length of time. Put her in his company at Christmas, and see what happens. He's an intriguing man, Mortimer.'

'Is he?'

'Oh, not as far as I'm concerned. He's just a boy, Ned, next to you. But I told you what Golafre found him doing at Hanley, didn't I? In the stables, with the goose-girl up against the wall. Constance might like a little of that sort of treatment. My cousin, Thomas, treated her well enough, but I doubt he was one for surprises. Remember, Ned, it will be *Christmas*. Plenty of music and dancing. Plenty to drink. I don't think she'll have the strength to hold him off. After that she'll marry him right enough. She's got that sort of conscience.'

'I wonder if she knows about the goose-girl?'

'I might tell her, one day.' Philippa paused, laughed at the expression she could imagine on Constance's face. 'Not yet, though. We want to make this marriage, don't we? It won't only bring Edmund into the family; it'll make him stronger. As well as keeping her out of Arundel's hands.'

He put the comb down on the bed, turned his attention to the lacings of her gown. 'Yes,' he conceded. 'That's a consideration. Arundel is Bolingbroke's man to the death, and he's powerful enough as it is. Do you really think she'd accept him? Mortimer?'

His wife reached her hand upwards, ran her fingers down the edge of his face. 'It'll not do us any harm to find out,' she said softly.

26

The Duke of York was sitting close to the fire, his hands curled into his fur sleeves as if he was out in the frost-bound fields, not snug and warm in his parlour at Fotheringhay with hot, spiced wine at his hand and a thick blanket of good wool spread over his legs. Constance was shocked to see how much he had aged in a short time. He looked ten years older, not one. She knelt for his blessing, her elder children on either side of her, and felt his fingers quivering as they brushed against her cheek.

'Is this the new child?' he asked, pointing towards the back of the room where Isabelle's nurse stood, holding the baby. The woman curtsied, advanced, and transferred her charge to Constance's arms.

The Duke scrutinised his granddaughter keenly, advanced his finger towards her face.

'Named for your mother?' he asked.

'Yes, Father.'

'Doesn't look much like her.' His eyes turned back to Constance, and suddenly there was something of authority in them again. '*You* didn't either. You still don't. You're mine, like your brother Edward. But there's something of her in you, for all that.'

The words did not have the sound of a compliment. She rose to her feet, trying to find a suitable answer, but the Duke had already turned his attention to her son, smiling at the boy and encouraging him to climb on his knee.

'Thomas was this age, when I first met him,' he said thoughtfully. 'Not so much older when we married him to you. He was the best of my sons, and I did not think to outlive him.'

'Father, I—'

He raised his hand to interrupt her. 'What are you standing there for? Sit down.' He gestured at the chair that faced him across the fireplace. 'We'll not talk any more of Despenser. Not today.'

Constance settled herself, with Isabelle still in her arms, and Bess standing at her side, and waited for the Duke to speak. The room was already growing dark as the December afternoon closed in on them with impatient haste. Bess and Richard were showing subtle signs of restlessness, clear evidence that they were weary from their long journey, more than a week on the road from Cardiff, including a pause at Tewkesbury to visit their father's tomb. They had been roused well before dawn, and now they belonged in bed, especially the boy. Constance longed for nothing more than a bath and bed for herself. She had spent the day in the saddle, she was still half frozen, and almost every bone in her body ached.

'Your cousin has used you generously,' York went on. 'There are many who would have been glad to have this boy's wardship, even at twice the amount you have to pay the Exchequer. Powerful men, who'd appreciate such a gift at the King's hands, and show themselves grateful for it. You should be prudent in your dealings, for your son's sake. He could still be taken from you, and another guardian might be less careful of his interests. Remember that.'

It was a soft-spoken warning, but a warning for all that, and Constance was inclined to resent it. She did not answer, but her back stiffened against the chair and a light came into her eyes that would have daunted a lesser man than her father.

The Duke, of course, was impervious to such subtle hints of rebellion. 'In my opinion,' he said, 'now that you have mourned Despenser for a suitable time, you'd be wise to take another husband. You'd be better for a man's guidance, happier if you confined yourself to those matters that are within the proper sphere of ladies. Accept the world for what it is, Constance—not what you would like it to be.'

'Keep my mouth closed, and my hands in my lap?'

'Spare yourself more pain. No matter what you do, it'll not bring Thomas back. You're dependent on the King's good will, all but living on his charity. It gains you nothing to go about with a sour face, to keep on fighting a war you cannot hope to win.'

'Instead you would have me look for a husband?' She snorted her contempt.

'I would have you reflect on what I've said.' The Duke spoke levelly, his hand resting on his grandson's head. 'You are not a fool, Daughter, though you often talk like one. You're still young, still a handsome woman, and you've lands sufficient to support an earldom. Turn your thoughts to the future, and consider how best to secure yourself, and these children.'

Constance lowered her eyes, focused on Isabelle's small face. 'I've thought of little else, these last months,' she admitted.

'You've already had an offer from young Arundel, I believe.'

She was surprised to find him so well informed. 'Yes.'

'An offer that you've declined?'

'Yes.'

'My advice is that you reconsider. At least negotiate. Find out what jointure he would grant you. It may serve to change your mind.'

She was horrified. 'His father was our enemy. How can you ask me to make such a marriage?'

York stared into the fire. 'Because it would assure your future; that's what matters now, not old quarrels. Arundel is one of the premier peers in the land, and such an offer is not made every day. Nor was it made without the King's approval, *and* mine. Do you imagine that you'll be offered a better opportunity? Make your decision with your head, Constance, not your heart. That's what I ask of you.'

She bit her tongue on the unruly, emotional response that rose in her throat. Having been at odds with the Duke for so long, she did not wish to sour their reconciliation. The silence between them lengthened, but was broken by the beginning of a protest from Isabelle, who was in the uncomfortable process of cutting a tooth.

'I'm wary of putting the children and myself in the power of a man I do not trust,' Constance said over the rising note of the baby's cry. 'Besides, I think him too young for me. He's not yet twenty.'

'He'll grow older,' York grunted.

'I must be sure in my mind before I enter into such a commitment.'

'So you will think on it?'

She nodded briefly, focusing on Isabelle.

'Good!' York did not actually smile, but his features relaxed, as if some part of his pain had been lifted from him. 'I'd give much to see you settled, and happy again. Your brothers can look to themselves, but you—you are vulnerable, my dear. I'll protect you while I can, but I'll not always be here. Consider that when you make your decision, and remember who will sit in my place one day.'

***

The Duchess of York popped another almond into Bess's mouth. It was the fourth in less than four minutes, and Richard Despenser was equally favoured. Constance felt a mild stir of misgiving. Joanne treated children much as she did her spaniels, as receptacles for food and objects for petting. She seemed to have no idea that there might be sensible limits for such spoiling, still less that she was fast approaching that point.

'I'm so glad you're here,' Joanne said. 'I feared you might refuse. Your father has been very ill, you know. He's still too weak to sit a horse, and that leg of his—well, he can scarcely bear to stand on it. I—I thought it proper that he should be reconciled to his children. To you, and to Ned.' She took a breath, put a friendly hand on Constance's arm. 'I know that you've no cause to love your brother. Nor have I, God knows. Even so, I hope you will help me keep the peace. Whatever is done is done. We can perhaps be a united family again, if only for your father's sake.'

They were sitting together on the edge of Joanne's bed, the morning light, diffused by the heraldic glass that filled the windows, spreading over them. It was a room designed for summer, looking out over the River Nene to the south, and rather chill at this time of year, noticeable draughts counteracting the fire that was crackling and roaring in the hearth.

'I expected that Edward would be here,' Constance said. 'I shall not go out of my way to quarrel with him, or with his wife, but I can never forgive him.'

The Duchess nodded. 'I understand. I'm not sure, though, that he *intended* to betray them. He said that he did, of course, but I've thought about it, and it doesn't make sense. I think he'd have kept faith, if your father had not discovered what he was about.'

'I think I know him better than you do, Joanne. I've forgiven him in the past; made peace because I loved him, and each time he has proved false. You should ask your sister about him. Ask Alianore whether his word means anything.'

'Be fair, Constance. That's another matter altogether, and you know it. Men promise the world if it will gain them what they want. No sensible woman believes a word of such talk, and Alianore wasn't a child when she involved herself with him—she knew well what she was about, and how it was likely to end. I don't say that Edward's a saint. Of course he isn't. I just don't think it right that he should bear the whole of the blame. We all had a part in it, one way and another. I encouraged my brother and Salisbury, God rest them. Helped them to conspire together, and meet others of the same mind. How I wish I had not. I meddled without understanding the danger and I'll always have to bear that on my conscience.'

'Edward has no conscience,' Constance said abruptly. She paused, rubbed some warmth into her fingers, and buried them deep within the folds of her gown. 'Even so, as I promised, I'll keep the peace with him as best I can. As a guest under your roof I owe you that courtesy.'

'I dare say we shall all have to bite our tongues. You know what I think of his wife, that odious creature, but I hope I am sufficiently well bred to conceal it. I must admit that she wrote me a most courteous letter from Chester. It was she who suggested I invite Edmund Mortimer to share Christmas with us. She said it would please you. I trust that it does?'

Constance did not answer at once. She had known that Edmund was to be a guest at Fotheringhay, of course, but not that Philippa had arranged for him to be summoned there. She puzzled silently over the mystery, but could find no satisfactory explanation.

'I look forward to seeing Edmund,' she conceded. 'He's a good friend; one of those who helped me after Thomas was killed. It may be that Edward wants to talk to him about the troubles in Wales. The Mortimers own Denbigh, which is close to where the fighting started. Edmund may even know something of this rebel, Owain or whatever he's called. That would make sense.'

It actually made very little sense, and Constance knew it.

Joanne shrugged. 'Well, I'm sure we can make him welcome. We'll lodge him in the Fetterlock, near you and Edward. Sir Hugh Despenser and his lady are at Collyweston. Perhaps we should invite them also? He served with your brother in Wales, so if that's what they're going to talk about they may as well have his opinion as well. I don't know Sybil very well, but we might be glad of her company. She might help to keep Philippa out of our way.'

Constance offered to carry the invitation to Collyweston herself, for the sun was out in full brightness and she was sufficiently recovered from her journey to relish the prospect of exercise. It was no great distance through Rockingham Forest, about ten miles, and Hugh and Sybil Despenser gave her a warm welcome and an overwhelming dinner, evidently glad to be back on good terms with her. They were no less pleased by the opportunity to spend much of Christmas with the Duke and Duchess of York, and cheerfully accepted, Hugh insisting on riding back with his guests so that he might pay his respects to the Duke in person.

The whole party paused during the return journey to cut holly and other greenery with which to decorate the castle, though this was little more than a gesture since many a cartload would be needed to complete the task. Only Agnes Norreys and Hugh Tyldesley did not participate, Agnes sitting stiffly on her horse, complaining of the cold, and Tyldesley standing alert, his sword drawn, because Piers Mohun had warned him that Rockingham was newly plagued with outlaws. Constance was equally irritated by Agnes' lack of festive spirit and Tyldesley's absurd caution. All her experience taught her that outlaws in Rockingham were rare and solitary creatures who never dared come near to Fotheringhay, or anyone belonging to the Duke. She was too busy with her knife to notice that Adda and Madog, though hacking at the holly with a will, had strung their bows, thrust arrows through their belts, ready for instant selection, and had positioned themselves at either end of the group, protecting the flanks just as surely as their leader was guarding the centre.

'Your men do well to take such care,' Sir Hugh told her, when they set off again. 'These woods are full of rogues. Some of my tenants at Collyweston have been attacked, which is one reason why I'm here, and not at Solihull.'

Constance frowned. 'There were never outlaws in Rockingham in King Richard's day,' she said.

'By your leave, Cousin, there were, though not so many, and not so bold. It's a hard time of year, of course, for those without land, with little hired work to be found.'

'They've only to come to Fotheringhay to be fed.'

'Or to Collyweston, or a score of other places I could name. But charity's not enough for some. Besides, they're not all idle labourers, but greater rogues. King Richard's Cheshiremen. Men from broken households with no lord to govern them or keep them in pay. Scum that the present King brought down from the North, and didn't send back.'

She snorted. 'People used to blame King Richard for not upholding the law, but it seems to me that King Harry does no better.'

'Perhaps we were wrong to think he would,' Hugh Despenser sighed. She noticed that his face was weary, as if he had spent many nights without sleep. 'But would we be better placed if the Earl of March were King? Or your brother? I doubt it. I think that all would go on much the same. God forbid that more English blood should be shed in such causes! Enough has already been wasted. Better to admit the world will never be perfect, and concentrate on tending our own small furrows.'

At Fotheringhay it was evident that the Duchess had placed someone to watch out for their arrival, for as they rode in through the gate she was already waiting for them at the head of the flight of stairs leading into the hall. 'Edmund is here!' she announced, as soon as Despenser had been sent on his way to the Duke. She took Constance by the hand, and led her into the depths of her own apartments.

'My face must be red with cold!' Constance protested, putting a hand to it.

'So it is; but he'll not mind. He's only just arrived—been on the road all day. You won't believe the change in him! I scarcely recognised him myself after all this time.'

They were moving at a wholly exceptional speed. Constance only just maintained enough presence of mind to keep the appropriate foot or two behind the Duchess, and the duty page had only barely enough time to throw open the solar door before Joanne walked into it. The room beyond was warmer now, the fire built up into a virtual furnace. A young man sat close to it, making use of Joanne's chair, but it was not Edmund Mortimer.

'You remember my brother,' Joanne said delightedly. 'I told you he had changed!'

The seething excitement that had been flowing through Constance's veins stilled to nothingness in a moment. She moved slowly forward, trying to keep the disappointment from her face as the young giant lifted himself into a standing position, and then twisted himself into a bow.

'Mun,' Constance said, half in recognition, half in greeting.

'He's more than "Mun" now,' Joanne objected. 'He's the Earl of Kent! King Bolingbroke has granted him the title! And the lands to go with it.'

'Most of them,' he corrected. 'I'm still his ward, of course, but I've livelihood enough for my present needs.'

Constance considered him. How old was he? Seventeen perhaps. Surely no more. But Joanne was right. He was changed almost beyond recognition. His body had filled out, his shoulders broad enough to block a door. There was even a wisp of beard, the same gold-brown as his hair. Despite his size he was not gawky, as his brother Surrey had been. There was something of Alianore's grace about him, something of her air of calm.

'I saw you at Cardiff before I sailed to Ireland with King Richard,' he said uncertainly. 'So much has changed since then—and you have suffered a great loss.

My lord your husband was kind enough to befriend me in Ireland. I fought in his company, and he was a brave and honourable knight.'

Constance warmed to him immediately. The mere mention of Thomas was enough. 'You and Joanne have also suffered a great loss. Your brother...'

He shook his head, disclaiming the comparison. 'Joanne feels it more keenly than I do. My brother and I were not close. I regret his death, of course, but he was as much slain by his own ambition as by the people of Cirencester.'

'And you have no ambition?'

'Less than he had. For me it's enough to be Earl of Kent as my father was, and as I am now, by the King's gracious favour.'

She moved a little closer. 'You are generous, are you not? Calling it gracious to allow you what is yours by simple right of inheritance?'

He shrugged. 'I feared worse treatment. I was left in Ireland to act as Lieutenant for King Richard, and stayed there for many months until I was replaced. I had my sister-in-law in my care, and we sailed together for England, but by that time my brother had been killed. We knew nothing of the rebellion, or his death, until the King's officers seized us as soon as we landed at the creek of Liverpool, took all our goods, shut us in prison and treated us like felons. I wrote to my uncle, the Archbishop, and he promised to speak for us, but even so I hoped for little more than my life. The King proved more kind than I expected.'

'Yet not so fond that he wanted you near him at Christmas, ward or not,' Joanne said, baiting him.

'I asked for leave to come here,' Kent answered, turning towards her. 'I thought it too long since I'd set eyes on my favourite sister. Anyway, where else was I to go? Our mother's house is as cheerful as a bishop's gaol in Lent, and Alianore isn't in favour with the King, making so much fuss over those boys of hers. She grumbles as though they were a pair of babies in a dungeon. I've seen them myself, and they're perfectly safe and happy at Windsor—certainly as well placed as I ever was in York's household. Of course they hate their lessons and their tutors, but show me two lads that don't!'

Joanne placed herself on the chair her brother had vacated, motioned Constance to the one opposite. 'Alianore is concerned for tomorrow, not just for today,' she said quietly.

'She's nothing to be concerned about,' Kent said dismissively. 'I don't know what's wrong with her—she never used to stir trouble. She's got her husband and Edmund Mortimer running about after half the lawyers in London, and it won't do them a jot of good. Her boys are as much the King's wards as I am. How can you argue against that? It's the law and custom, and the way it's always been. The way it always will be. All she's achieved is to anger the King. He'd as soon have the devil in his presence chamber as Mortimer and Edward Charlton, and it's all through her folly. If I were Charlton I'd be damned before I'd let my own wife put me in such disfavour. The man must have the spine of a jelly. As for Mortimer, if you ask me, he's after his own ends, and the King knows well what *they* are.'

Constance sat upright. 'Sir Edmund Mortimer is the most honourable man I know,' she pronounced. 'He's doing what he believes to be right; not weighing what will best please Harry Bolingbroke. I admire him for it, and I only wish that others had his courage.'

Kent shrugged. He was not quite sure what he had said to upset her; still less did he know what to do to make amends. 'Well, he won't gain anything by it,' he said, 'save for the King's enmity. Everyone says so.'

'Do they, indeed?'

'We expect Edmund Mortimer here at any time,' Joanne told her brother, the note of warning clear in her voice. 'He grew up in this household, and my lord the Duke is fond of him.'

Kent glanced from one to the other, and back again. 'That was before my time here,' he said lamely. 'I'd forgotten. The Duke might like to warn him, then. You could put in a word, Joanne, and do Mortimer a service.'

***

It was Christmas Eve, and the Yule log had been lit in the fireplace of Fotheringhay's great hall. Massive though the hearth was, it barely held the log, which was nothing less than a substantial tree trunk, cut down earlier in the year and stored away so that it would be fully dry for this ceremony. Carefully tended, some part of it at least must burn for the whole of the holiday, and a small portion would be reserved to act as tinder for the next year's log, a symbol of the eternal cycle of life.

York's troupe of musicians were playing in the gallery, their subtlety of tune already mildly affected by the large cask of perry they had at their disposal, a fearsomely heady brew made from the pears that grew profusely on the Fotheringhay estate. Now they blew a loud fanfare, to announce the arrival of a whole procession of liveried servitors, bearing the traditional frumenty, a sweet mixture of wheat, boiled milk, eggs, honey, and spices. The Duke was served first, then his family, but still the procession continued, doubling back on itself until every single person at table in the vast room had a share in the food. Then the accompanying posset began to arrive, a rich drink made of milk, ale, eggs and nutmeg, so thick that it was easier to take a spoon to it than lift it to the lips. York took the first taste, and a cheer rose from the entire company. Christmas had begun.

'It's good to see so many people happy,' Edmund Mortimer said. He paused to spoon a little of the posset into his mouth, beamed with childlike pleasure at the fulsome flavour.

Constance nodded. No one starved at Fotheringhay, but many of the people in the hall laboured endlessly all through the year to keep body and soul together, their dull lives punctuated and made tolerable by festivals such as this. It was impossible to see the joy they drew from the simple pleasures of food, drink and music, without being a little warmed by it. The chilly void that had once contained her heart stirred a little, responded to the light she could see in Mortimer's eyes. Taking the spoon from her own mouth, she licked her lips clean and smiled at him.

'It's like you to think of other people, Edmund,' she remarked, 'but what of yourself? Are you happy? I hear you have had great trouble for your nephews' sake. That you are by no means the apple of Harry Bolingbroke's eye. Kent was at pains to tell me so. He seems to think you need to be warned.'

'The King's favour, more or less, does not touch my heart. To see your smile; to find you out of mourning, your sorrow eased a little. That means more to me than anything Bolingbroke can bestow.'

Constance took a breath. 'My father has told me it is time that I looked to the future, instead of the past.' She paused, wondering whether it might occur to him that she had brought her coloured gowns with her from Cardiff without first seeking the Duke of York's opinion on the matter, and with an unspoken purpose newly born at the back of her mind. 'My mourning has not truly ended, Edmund. It never will. Outward show is the smallest part of it.'

'I understand that—but I hoped, when I saw you thus...'

He sketched a gesture that took in her dark blue velvet gown, her jewelled headdress and her naked neck and throat, released from the wimple that had confined them for so many months.

'Agnes Norreys thinks me shameless,' she said. It was true. The two of them had quarrelled over the matter, and fiercely, until Constance had offered to release Agnes from her indentures of service. That had silenced Lady Norreys, but not altered her opinion one iota.

He eased himself almost imperceptibly closer to her on the bench. 'I wish you were more so. God knows, Constance, I have wanted you for long enough. Even your father must approve, or he'd not have summoned me here.'

'My father would have me marry Arundel, so as to please Bolingbroke. I've promised him that I'll think about it.'

'And will you?'

'Is it likely?' Her laugh was short and bitter. 'I've done all the thinking I intend to do on that score, and long ago. The last thing that is on my mind is to find a way to please Cousin Harry. I'd sooner *displease* him. I'd like to see *him* lodged in a pit at Pontefract.'

'So would I!' Mortimer said with sudden ferocity. 'I cannot tell you how much it galls me to see him sitting in Richard's place. Even I have more right to the throne than he has, and my nephew March still more. I'm not even suffered to visit the boy. Perhaps Lancaster thinks I'll smuggle him out of Windsor, wrapped in my cloak!'

'It was Edward who had you invited here, not the Duke,' Constance said, returning to the point despite the tempting opportunity to pile further abuse on

Bolingbroke. 'As well he did, or I'd not have troubled to make the journey. I didn't think you such friends, that he should want to have your company for Christmas. I thought perhaps he wanted to talk to you about matters in Wales.'

'Your brother may feel the need to make himself a friend or two. It's sure he has few of them above ground! Well then, for the first time in my life I owe him a debt. I care nothing for his reasons. He has brought me here, and into your company.'

Warily, as though he feared a knife blade in the back of it, he eased his hand beneath the table, and onto her thigh. She felt his controlled strength through the velvet, knew that she ought to resent the liberty, and yet could not. Instead her body relaxed and turned itself a little more towards him, and her hand found his and rested on it, confirming the caress with her consent.

'Ned never does anything without a purpose,' she said, 'and his purpose may not be to your profit. Or mine, for that matter.'

'Then we must think of our own purposes. Not his.'

'We should be cautious, until we know what it is that he wants from you.'

'I think we've been cautious long enough.' His hand moved a fraction, hidden within the folds of her skirts, the tips of his fingers pressing the material gently across the inside of her thigh. 'Do you realise how much I want you?'

'I think I've some idea.' She halted his advances while she still could. 'But this is not the place.'

He took the hint, lifted her hand to his lips in courtly fashion. 'Then the place must be found—and quickly. We know this castle, both of us. There must be some corner in it where we can meet, ourselves alone. I must think on it. I doubt I'll think of anything else until I find an answer.'

'There's always my bed, Edmund.'

'Your bed?'

'Is that not what you have in mind?'

She laughed at the expression on his face. She'd never seen anything quite like it, a complex mixture of disbelief, astonishment and joy.

'Your women—' he objected.

'Oh, you can't have them as well. I want you for myself.'

Her amusement was cut short by the touch of a hand on her shoulder. It was the Duchess of York.

'Philippa and I are going to dance,' she said. 'Will you join us, Constance? Philippa is asking Sybil Despenser to make up a set with us.'

It was virtually impossible to refuse such a request without seeming ungracious, so Constance rose from her place, made a formal curtsey to her stepmother, and walked with her towards the clear space in front of the high table.

'Edmund Mortimer must enjoy posset,' Joanne remarked. 'He looks like a cat that's fallen into the cream.'

Constance silently assessed her tone, wondering how much the Duchess knew, or had guessed. She had been so absorbed with Mortimer it was quite possible that Joanne had been standing behind them long enough to hear her offering herself to him. 'He's very glad to be invited to spend Christmas with us,' she answered, a little guardedly. 'He never knew his own parents, you know—he more or less grew up with Ned and me.'

Joanne nodded. 'Yes, but after what my brother told us the other day, I wonder if I did well to agree to ask him here. I haven't said a word to your father. It would only trouble him, and to no advantage. Perhaps you will warn Mortimer that he is angering the King?'

'I've already done so.'

'Good. I dare say he'll take it better from you, in any case.'

'Edmund will do what he thinks is right.'

'I'm sure he will. That's what makes him dangerous.' Joanne paused for a moment of thought. 'You've had heartbreak enough, Constance. Do you not think so?'

They joined hands with Philippa and Sybil and began the first figure of a slow and stately ronde, Mary Russell and three of Joanne's damosels making up the rest of the set.

Constance had not danced for almost a year, since the previous Christmas at Caversham, and not much in the year before that. Sorely out of practice and conscious of two initial mistakes, she concentrated on her steps, and, gradually finding the rhythm of the dance, began to enjoy herself.

After some time the dance entered another phase. Joanne held out a hand in invitation, and, responding to it, her brother vaulted clear over the table to join them. It was not a particularly wise thing to do, even with the licence of Christmas to stifle etiquette, but he carried it off, his demonstration of physical prowess loudly cheered by the company. He joined the circle between his sister and Constance, a huge grin on his face as he began to lead them at the markedly faster pace dictated by the music.

'I've been watching you,' he told Constance. 'So has half the room. You dance beautifully.'

'Not so well as your sister,' she suggested.

'Better than me at least,' the young giant chortled. 'Joanne says I dance like an ox with a sore arse!'

It was not true, and Constance had to admit it. Allowing for his build, and the amount of wine he had obviously consumed, he danced with a very becoming grace and without any apparent effort. Even though, less limited by his clothing, he was leaping and kicking higher than any of the women. 'I think that is but a sister's way of keeping her younger brother in his place,' she suggested.

'What I need,' said Kent, 'is a long lesson or two. Perhaps you could help me with that, madame.'

'I'm afraid I do not give lessons to boys,' she said, her words blunter than she had intended. The fact was that she was growing heated from the exercise, less in control of herself. Though when she looked at Philippa she saw she was not as winded as some. Her sister-in-law appeared to be on the verge of collapse.

He laughed, showing no sign of offence. 'I believe you said something similar to my cousin, Arundel,' he roared. 'Don't blame you, madame. I wouldn't marry him either. Boring little turd that he is. Takes after our sainted uncle, the Archbishop. Probably more than his *spiritual* son, if the truth were known.'

'*Mun!*' Joanne sounded genuinely shocked. 'You are *drunk!*'

'I am, fair Sister,' the Earl of Kent admitted. 'I'm drunk with your wine, and drunk with the beauty of these ladies, especially your daughter here. A grown-up daughter, more grown-up than you are.'

He seemed to find this hilarious, and he was silenced by his own amusement, not Joanne's stare. The dance continued.

'As for Arundel,' he went on at last, 'why, the insolent rat dares to claim precedence over me. What do you think of that, Joanne? His father never had precedence of ours. I know that for certain sure. The next time he tries to go through a door before me I'll make him regret it, by God.'

'He might make *you* regret it,' said the Duchess crushingly.

Kent laughed again. 'Not he! I could fight him with one hand behind my back.'

Others had begun to join the ring. Edward was among the first to be admitted; then Dickon and Hugh Despenser. Constance looked around for Edmund Mortimer and found, with a mixture of approval and disappointment, that he was inclined to be discreet. Only when a larger, second ring formed around the first did he take to the floor, his dancing clearly more a matter of enthusiasm than technique. It did not matter, because the dance was no longer one of grace and precision, and was rapidly evolving into a breathless, rowdy brawl. It ended only when the unsteady blare of trumpets from the gallery announced the hour. It was time to go in solemn, formal procession to the Chapel for the midnight mass.

***

Constance sat before her glass, and unpinned her headdress. It was, she estimated, very late, perhaps three of the clock. She had begun to think that the celebrations would never end.

The room was lit only by the pair of wax candles burning close to her, and by the fading embers of a charcoal brazier that stood between the window and the bed. Her fingers were chilled enough to make the task of undressing as slow as it was irritating.

She had told her women she would not require attendance tonight. Agnes, Mary Russell and the others were in the adjoining room, and not yet asleep. She could hear them talking still, reliving the pleasures of the evening, laughing

with each other. Though it was unlikely that Agnes was sharing in the enjoyment. Agnes had been made suspicious by the instruction, though she had kept
her mouth closed. Lady Norreys had a very eloquent way of saying nothing.

She lifted the tire from her head, cast it carelessly aside, so that it caught the
edge of the dresser and fell onto the floor, lost in darkness. It seemed to her that
Mortimer was taking his time. Discretion was well enough, but it could be taken
too far. Allowing herself a little frown of impatience, she began to unfasten her
hair from its coils, and then found it caught in her rings, which she had forgotten
to remove in her haste. She plucked them off, dropped them into her coffer. Where
was he? Had she not been plain enough? Did he need a herald, bearing a scroll?
He was probably still where she had last seen him, drinking with Edward.

No sooner had the thought crossed her mind than the latch lifted, drawing
her attention to the door. It opened, slowly and cautiously.

'Constance?' Mortimer's voice was a tentative whisper.

She stood up. 'Come in, Edmund. Bolt the door behind you.' Her voice was
only slightly more assured than his. She picked up the jug of wine on the little
cupboard by the wall. 'Would you like a drink? I began to think that you'd
changed your mind.'

'Have you changed yours?'

'No.' She shook her head. 'No, I do not change so easily.'

'Your brother kept me talking.' In two steps he was next to her, taking the
jug from her hand and setting it down. 'I know you don't change. You're well
named. But in such matters as these, a lady is allowed certain privileges. A
part of me feared you might exercise them.' His arms went about her, and they
stood so in silence for a while, savouring the moment, admiring each other in
the flickering light.

'What had Edward to say that was so interesting it kept you from me?' she
asked teasingly.

The answer came in the form of an exploratory kiss, one that she found so
pleasant that she put her hand to his neck to keep him close. When their lips
met again it was with the bruising ferocity of mutual desire.

'I have this horrid feeling that I am going to wake up,' he said breathlessly,
his hands working their way down from her waist to her buttocks, securing her.
'I've dreamed of this, often enough, but you've never given me cause to hope.
Perhaps we should wait until we can be married. I could bear that, if you promised yourself to me. I love you more than my soul, God help me, and dread the
thought that anyone should think evil of you.'

'Evil to him who evil thinks,' Constance answered. 'I've not made my decision
lightly, nor reached it in the last hour. It may be that we cannot marry, Edmund
Not yet, at any rate. How long shall we wait? How long have you loved me?'

He considered it carefully. 'Years. Long, hopeless years. Since we were both
fourteen. Perhaps even before that.'

'Then I think you have waited long enough, even for the most faithful of knights! Would you have me send you on crusade for seven more years to prove yourself? Ask you to slay a dragon for me?' Shaking her head, she turned her back on him. 'I want you now, Edmund. In my bed. Inside me. Please be so good as to unlace my gown.'

***

'The ground is still pretty hard,' Edmund Mortimer said.

In the dull morning light the line of horses advanced slowly across the expanse of Fotheringhay's great park. Edmund was riding at the extreme left, with Constance next to him, and Hugh Despenser to her right. Beyond them were Philippa, Edward, the Duchess of York, and then her brother, Kent, Sybil Despenser and young Richard of Conisbrough. A few yards in front of Edward a fewterer walked with a leash of greyhounds, a black dog and a fawn bitch both belonging to York, mere saplings little more than twelve months old. The Duke, however reluctantly, had conceded that it was far too cold for him to ride out to see their first serious run.

Constance weighed his comment. 'I think it's just about soft enough not to damage the hounds. The frost was less sharp last night.'

'I found my bed devilish cold. At least compared to the night before.'

'We have to be discreet, Edmund. And I do need some sleep. You exhausted me.'

'Did I?' He was rather obviously pleased by the thought.

She was no less pleased with it herself. Her smile grew as she considered the matter. 'I'm still tingling from head to foot. How about if I came to you tonight? Would you like that?'

'I'm not sure I can wait that long.'

She fixed her eyes on him. Was it her imagination, or was his lip still a little swelled from where she had bitten him in ecstasy? And it was sweet to recall the feel of those lips, first brushing her nipples, and then clamping on them... 'Nor am I,' she admitted, 'but we must do our best.'

He sighed ruefully and changed the subject. 'It must break your father's heart to miss this sport.'

'Yes. He's been very ill, of course. That's why Joanne wanted Ned and me to be here for Christmas. She fears he might not see another.'

'I'm sorry.'

'You've no need to be. Not yet. I think he's a lot stronger than she thinks. But it would have been folly to take him away from the fire on a day like this, when he's still recovering. I hope for the best. I doubt I'll come here again once he's gone.' Her gaze went beyond him, past the border of bare trees, and across the great, dark lake to the castle itself. It was still, somehow, the home of her heart. She might not even see the place again, let alone live in it. Within a few years it would belong to Edward, and Philippa would preside over it as Duchess of

York. 'Thomas and I were happy here, when he first came back from Prussia,' she added, 'and now I've some other good memories of Fotheringhay to bear in my heart.'

She had barely finished speaking when Hugh Despenser's horse started a hare from cover, and she and Mortimer had to spur forward, shouting 'Ho, ho, ho!' to prevent it escaping too swiftly to the flank. The hare turned away from them, diagonally at first, and then in a straight line ahead. The fewterer gave it a good hundred yards of start, and then slipped the greyhounds after it, the riders trotting forward at a sufficient pace to keep the contest in view.

The hare was a large, strong animal that knew its business, changed direction quicker than the eye could follow, and left the young, bemused greyhounds floundering in its wake as it twisted its way about the park. At last it vanished into a ditch, and although the puzzled dogs ran up and down, trying to locate it, it was not seen again. The fewterer set about the task of catching his panting charges, calling them and being ignored. His boy was already bringing up the next couple.

Edward came riding across to where his sister and Mortimer were waiting. 'The fawn looked fast enough,' he observed, 'She ran up well.'

'Yes,' Constance agreed, 'but she needs more work. Those two were both very green.'

'I always like a fawn. What do you say, Edmund? I expect you've got better dogs than these at home.'

Mortimer forced a smile. 'I've a couple of greyhounds I brought back from Ireland. They don't do much but lie by the fire.'

'Constance has a fine park at Caversham. You should take them there. I'm sure she'd be happy to accommodate you. Wouldn't you, my dear?'

'Edmund has reason to know he's welcome to anything that it's in my power to grant him.' She walked her horse forward a step, turning her head away so that her brother would not see the light in her eyes, or the glance of shared amusement she exchanged with Mortimer.

'Good!' Edward positively beamed. 'I've been meaning to talk to you both. I need your help. This is not the place to discuss it, with the coursing scarce begun. But—later?'

'Of course,' said Edmund. 'Somewhere more private, perhaps?'

'I will arrange it,' Edward promised, as he turned away from them.

***

In the middle of the same afternoon they rode out of the castle together, and east through the village, following the road into the fringes of the Forest. The winter sun lit their faces, forcing them to screw up their eyes at times, and the cold was stark enough to ensure that their breath, and that of their horses, appeared as thin clouds of steam.

'The three of us—alone?' Mortimer opened.

Edward smiled at him. 'You and I are both knights. I think we're more than capable of protecting my sister from the cowardly thieves who lurk among the trees. Don't you?'

'Where exactly are we going?' Constance asked. She was suspicious, and the more so since she could not fathom her brother's intentions.

'You shall see. A place where we can talk in comfort, and take our ease in privacy. As Edmund rightly suggested. Shall we canter for a while? The horses will profit from the exercise.'

He seemed to take their assent as granted, and after a little while the canter turned into something approaching a gallop. Constance had just concluded that they were on their way to Collyweston (though it was far too late in the day to make such a journey) when her brother eased his horse's pace and veered off to the left, along a lesser track. After some time the woods thinned a little and the walls of a small manor house became visible. Built in Barnack stone, it almost glowed in the winter sun, a vision of golden ochre amid the gloom of the trees. Edward slowed almost to a halt, as if to take in the sight.

'Knyvet's Place, at Southwick,' Constance said aloud, dredging an old memory. 'Is that where we're going?'

Her brother nodded. 'We're expected.'

'Who lives there these days?'

'No one, for the present. Except a few servants, who've been well paid. It's at our disposal until after Twelfth Night. I had an idea it might prove useful.'

As they rode into the courtyard a man emerged from the shadows to take their horses, and another appeared in the porch, swinging the heavy oak door open to allow them into the small hall beyond. From there a short flight of steps led up to the solar, a sizeable room with shuttered oriel windows at each end, and dominated by a large bed, the walls covered by old but serviceable hangings. A single chair stood by the fire, and next to it a cupboard on which stood a supply of wine, demain bread and spiced wafers, lit by a pair of candles.

Constance allowed her brother to usher her into the chair, pleasantly surprised by the air of cosiness within the room. Edmund perched on the end of the bed, almost within touch of her, and Edward set about serving them with drinks before using one of the burning candles to light two or three more around the hearth. Lastly, he closed the door by which they had entered, and slid home its clumsy bolt.

'Family policy,' he said, 'is best discussed away from prying ears.'

'You said that you wanted our help,' Mortimer prompted. He voice had an edge of impatience. 'What is so secret that you must play these games before you speak of it?'

Edward stood before the fire, draped his arm along the mantelpiece as if he had an affection for it. 'Your brother and I were enemies,' he said, 'but I've never had any quarrel with you, Edmund. I believe we can be good friends. As for you, Constance, I know you think you have a grievance against me, but the truth is that I love you and wish you well.' He raised a hand forestalling their objections. 'We have a common enemy, all three of us. Harry Bolingbroke. He has humiliated me, time and again. Deprived me of lands, titles and offices. Threatened my very life. Because of him, Constance, your husband was killed and you were denied your lawful dower rights, forced to petition for maintenance like a beggar. Edmund's nephew has been kept from his proper inheritance, and is confined to prison. Instead of quarrelling among ourselves, and serving Lancaster's interests, let us begin to amend matters.'

'Fair words,' said Constance bitterly. 'Fair words, as ever. You'll never fight Bolingbroke, Ned. You haven't the courage. You've already proved it.'

He shrugged. 'The work will not be done in a day. It will take time, while we build a faction so strong that our cousin will not be able to resist it. Edmund's nephew is the rightful King. Let's begin with that. I propose to support his claim, and in return I suggest a marriage between our brother, Richard, and Edmund's niece, Anne. As a token of the unity of our families. Since I have no influence over Anne's mother these days, I need you two to act as my emissaries to Alianore, to persuade her that our alliance will be to our common profit. I think it a fair offer. One day Anne will be Duchess of York, as well as sister to the King.'

'What does your father say to this?' Edmund asked.

The shrug returned. 'My father would not approve. But he's a dying man, and fast losing interest in this world. There's no great haste. Dickon is not sixteen yet, and your niece is younger still. They can wait a year or two. All I ask for is a commitment, a betrothal if you like. In return, I shall support your efforts to have the boys transferred to your care. I'll also try to persuade Bolingbroke to restore your dower rights, Constance, to give you the security you need. Remember that Thomas is to be attainted by the next Parliament; it's important that your interests are protected.'

Constance mused on his words. She had effective possession of virtually the whole of the Despenser estates, by one means or another, but her hold on them was tenuous, for her grants were on the basis of the King's grace, and could be resumed at the King's pleasure. The restoration of her dower rights would assure her tenure of at least a third of the lands for life, and she would be in a much stronger position.

'It seems to me,' Edward went on, 'that a further bond between our families could be created by your marriage to each other. I don't believe either of you would find that repellent. If you came to such an agreement, you would be sure of my approval.'

Constance stared at him. She had not, somehow, expected that. 'Is this why you had Edmund invited to Fotheringhay?' she asked. 'So that I could be used to draw him into your schemes?'

'I was not aware that I was holding a knife to either of you. It is a suggestion, nothing more. I hoped it might please you both.'

'Do you wonder that we doubt you?' Mortimer asked, his voice suddenly hard, almost threatening. 'All this sudden good will. Where is your profit? Explain that! Don't pretend all this is for love of us.'

'When your nephew is King, I shall expect a share in the government. Not as great as yours, Edmund. That goes without saying. You shall be Protector and rule all. But I shall be next to you at the table, your loyal, experienced supporter. Your wife's brother. Duke of York and of Aumale, Lord Constable and Admiral of England. With one or two other little things and some small grants of land, of course. The Lancastrian estates in Yorkshire will do for a start. You must admit that that would make a little trouble on your behalf well worth my while.'

He walked to the door, unbolted it. 'I shall leave you here to discuss the matter. You may return on other days if the negotiations prove lengthy. It's a comfortable lodging and you'll not be disturbed.' He glanced briefly at the bed. 'I'll say that we were parted in the Forest, and send men out to search for you. Your own men, Edmund, I shall tell where to look, so that you'll have safe escort back in the dark. I take it they are discreet?'

'Yes. None better.'

Edward's smile was positively avuncular. 'I hope you'll be able to come to an accord. I think I can promise you'll have a good three hours. That should be time enough for a man and a woman who love one another.'

The door closed behind him, and they heard his footsteps descend the stairs. They gazed at each other, the silence broken only by an occasional sharp crack from the burning logs in the fireplace. At last Constance left her place, and moved to sit next to Edmund on the bed.

'We have obviously been less discreet than we thought,' he sighed. 'He knows.'

'Perhaps. Or perhaps he guesses.'

Edmund's glance took in the comforts of the room. 'It was a kindly thought, to arrange this for us. A rare kindness.'

'He is not to be trusted,' she said, her hand reaching out to caress his dark curls, 'and I beg you to be cautious. There is no kindness in him. This is done because he thinks to profit from our love, to rise higher on your shoulders. He would betray you to Bolingbroke as he did Thomas, if he thought it to his advantage.'

'I don't doubt it. But I need him. I need every ally I can muster if my nephew is to have what is his by right, and if you are to be Duchess of Clarence and first lady in the land, as you should be. Your brother may think to use us. We shall use him.'

She looked into his eyes, surprised by the determination in his voice. 'I did not know you had such ambition, Edmund.'

He smiled, and drew her closer. 'Now I have won you, all things are possible,' he said.

27

Caversham stood below the stars, the half moon reflecting from the Thames and casting shadows in the pleasure gardens that ran down to the river from the manor house. At the landing stage the small barge Sir Edmund Mortimer had used to travel upstream from London at Easter edged and dipped with the current, tugging gently at the ropes that had bound it to the bank for the last fourteen days. Its small crew of oarsmen slept on pallets in the hall, their bellies stuffed with food and ale, and their muscles slackening with idleness. As for their master, he lay in bed with the lady of the manor, curled protectively around her so that she was practically sitting on his knees. He also slept, his warm breath stirring her hair against her neck.

It was not the touch of his breath that was keeping Constance awake, nor the weight of his arm, encircling her just beneath her breasts. In truth she could not explain her inability to sleep. Contentment had never caused insomnia before, and content she was, as she had never expected to be again. She slept through the nights, no longer troubled by dreams of Thomas Despenser, or rather of the demon who took his identity. Nor did she dream of Edmund. The solid reality was enough.

Under her own roof she had made no bones about sharing a bed with Mortimer, her only concession to propriety being to stop short of making a public announcement of the fact. Her women could not help but know, of course, though none of them had commented on her behaviour. Whether they were passing on the news to others was another question—she found, to her surprise, that she did not much care whether they were or not. She would marry him as soon as was practicable, but to do so she needed the King's permission. That might not be forthcoming from Bolingbroke, bearing in mind his opinion of Mortimer. If they married without licence she could be stripped of everything she owned, and Edmund might well find himself in the Tower. There was no haste. Not now.

'What if I get you with child?' he asked suddenly.

She started. Not only had he woken, but also he was apparently reading her thoughts. 'Then I shall be a very proud woman,' she answered softly 'I want your child, Edmund. I want as many as you can give me.'

'You will not bear me a bastard,' he said. 'If you even suspect, we'll marry at once, whatever the consequences. Is that agreed?'

'I don't care.'

'Even if I have to hold a knife to your throat, and get my squire to prod the priest with another. What can Bolingbroke do to us? Hang us?'

'He can take all we have, and put us in separate prisons. He could fine us more than we could ever hope to pay. It is just the excuse he needs to ruin you. Better to be satisfied with what we have, for the time being. Matters may have changed in a year or two. Who knows? You may even be in a position to give permission to yourself.'

'Does our sin not trouble you?'

She stirred in his arms. 'There are worse sins. Even my confessor says as much. I'm not as pious as I once was, Edmund. It seems to me that God is a cruel father who beats us whether we obey him or not, so we may as well be beaten for something as for nothing. Thomas and I went all the way to Walsingham a few months before he was killed, and bore ourselves so humbly that we might have been taken for a poor esquire and his wife with ten pounds a year of livelihood. You know how we were rewarded.'

'Yes. But it's not only that. I want everyone to know that you are mine.'

'I *am* yours. I don't know what further proof you need.' She laughed. 'Unless you suppose that I lie naked in bed with every man who asks?'

'As I said, I want *everyone* to know. And I want our children to be honestly born.' He paused, took a breath. 'I've bastards enough already to my name.'

'I suspected you might not be a virgin, Edmund, the first time you had me. So it scarcely surprises me that there are children. How many?'

'Three.' He paused for thought. 'Three that I know about.'

'Well, that's only six little ones between us. Perhaps we can add another six. Twelve children, all happy, all glad to belong to us.' She turned towards him, kissed him. 'Why did you not mention this before?'

'I thought you might not be pleased.'

'You love my children, don't you? Why should I not love yours?'

'Because their mothers live.'

'Their mothers?' She stressed the plural, and laughed again. 'Oh, Edmund, and you have the face to talk about sin! Obviously your conscience hasn't troubled you before. Why should it now?'

As he opened his mouth to answer, there was a thunderous knocking on the door.

'My lady! My lady! Awake!' It was Tyldesley's voice, loud enough to rouse half of Reading.

Constance was astonished, but got out of bed, searched around in the dark for her chamber-robe, and covered herself before opening the door.

'Is the house afire?' she demanded. Tyldesley had Agnes with him, and Mary Russell. Robert Rous was only a little further back.

'Forgive me, lady, but you have guests,' Tyldesley answered.

'*Guests?* What madman comes calling at such an hour? Midnight, is it?'

'More or less. It's Sir Henry Percy, my lady. He's come seeking Sir Edmund.'

'Well, bed him and his followers down somewhere. He can wait until morning, and be grateful he was allowed through the gate, the mannerless dog!'

'He wishes to see Sir Edmund *now*. Insists. Says he's been searching for him for days.'

'I'd better see what he wants,' Edmund called from the bed. 'Hotspur was in Chester when last I heard—I doubt whether he's ridden so far south for no reason.'

He suggested that Constance should go back to bed, but she would not hear of it. She was lady of the house and it was her business to receive guests, even those who lacked the courtesy to arrive at a reasonable hour. She waited until he had pulled on his shirt and his bed-gown, and went down with him to the hall, where Hotspur and his men were waiting. Hotspur himself was pacing restlessly, apparently caring little for the disturbance he had caused to the household.

'I've been scouring all the southern counties for you,' he told Edmund, in something approaching a shout. 'I'd *still* be looking if Rutland hadn't told me where to find you. Have you no sense, man? I thought you were in London.'

'Lady Despenser is here,' Edmund said.

'Hmm,' Hotspur grunted, apparently intending it to serve as an apology. He bowed briefly in Constance's direction. 'Madame. Your servant ever. Edmund, I need your help.'

'My help?'

'I'll not discuss it in front of all these.' His gesture took in his own travel-stained men, and the yawning, half-dressed members of the Despenser household in equal measure. 'Some private place.'

'This is Lady Despenser's house, not mine.' The reminder was terse.

'The parlour,' Constance suggested. She stepped over an empty pallet, led them into the darkened room beyond. 'Fetch candles, someone.'

Tyldesley and one of the yeomen brought a couple each, set them burning on the mantel above the remnants of the fire. Then they withdrew.

'This is not a matter for ladies,' Percy said.

Edmund bristled afresh. 'There are no secrets between Lady Despenser and me. What is told to one is told to both. Besides, Harry, as I have already reminded you, this is her house, and you are a guest in it.'

Constance was already pouring wine for them. 'I am content to leave you to your business,' she said.

'No. I prefer you to stay.'

'Very well,' Hotspur conceded. 'I meant no disrespect, lady. Not the least. It's just that my talk is likely to bore you, and I'd not keep you unnecessarily from your bed.' He accepted his wine from her hand, and then continued briskly. 'Conwy Castle is taken by Welsh rebels. By damnable trickery, and by bloody incompetence on our side. On Good Friday, while the garrison was at mass, would you believe? It's going to be the devil to win back.'

'I dare say the King blames you for the loss?' Edmund hazarded.

'I'm the Justiciar of North Wales. Of course he blames me.' Hotspur shook his head as if trying to clear it. 'He and his Council won't even grant me proper freedom to negotiate. They want the castle taken by force and the rebels hanged. That's not all of it, either. This Owain fellow has emerged from his burrow, wherever that is. He's laying waste to Grey's estates again. Nay, he's gone further this time. Much further. He's raided the King's lands, and Arundel's. All of North Wales is alight, and I haven't even been sent enough money to pay my troops.'

'And what has all this to do with me?'

'You may just like to know that the rebels are leaving the Mortimer lands untouched. The Mortimer lands only.'

Edmund shook his head, puzzled. 'I can't think of any reason why they should.'

'Can't you? I reckon Harry Bolingbroke will be able to supply an answer. It'll be said that you're in league with this Glyn Dwr, or what the hell he's called.'

Edmund set his glass down on the cupboard with such force that the room seemed to shake. 'That's a lie! I couldn't even tell you what Glyn Dwr looks like.'

'I don't doubt it. But these rebels aren't just against Lancaster. They're *for* Mortimer. That's how it looks, anyway, and it puts you in an awkward position. Look, I want you to come back with me to Wales. I've authority over the men of Denbigh in name, but it's still a Mortimer lordship and you're the Earl of March in everything that matters. They'll obey you, whereas they only laugh at me. With your help we'll soon have Conwy back, and the rebels crushed. Then no one will be able to question your loyalty.'

'Do you think I care what the likes of Grey de Ruthin say of me? I don't!'

'You should, because Grey speaks into Bolingbroke's ear. Arundel too. They're not friends of yours, Edmund. For one reason or another.'

'I'm not going to Wales. I've business here.'

'Business?' Hotspur raised an eyebrow.

'I'm in the middle of negotiating two marriages, damn you! And I've my court case at Westminster. Anyway, North Wales is nothing to do with me. You've said it yourself; you're the one who's been given authority over Denbigh. You don't need me to hold your hand.'

'Of course I don't *need* you!' Hotspur snapped. He paced about, the candlelight reflecting in his brown eyes, and casting his stocky shadow on the embroidered hangings behind him, so that he was almost part of the scene of hunters and ladies. 'I was killing Scots before you learned how to keep your shit inside you. But it would be a help to me. A great help. Grey is driving me out of my mind. I need someone who understands the Welsh. Someone who can talk to them as well as fight them.'

'You said you'd been forbidden to negotiate—'

'Bugger what's been forbidden and what hasn't been forbidden!' His hand rose unconsciously to an old scar that lay just beneath his right eye, and stroked it. 'I'm the commander in the field and I can't have my hands tied by a pack of fools in London. Won't, anyway. They can come into Wales themselves and fight if they like, because I'm ready enough to give up. There's neither money nor thanks to be had by serving Bolingbroke. God knows how we ever came to make him King. I only wish we hadn't.'

Edmund sighed. 'I'm sorry, Harry. You've wasted your labour in coming here. I can't do what you ask.'

'Why not?'

'Because I choose not to. For reasons that are my own.'

'One of them lying between this lady's legs,' Hotspur sneered.

Edmund flew at him; clutched at his neck, thrust him bodily against the wall. 'No one insults Lady Despenser in my presence. Apologise, or by the blood of the living Christ, I'll kill you here and now, my sister's husband or not.'

Hotspur shook his head. 'Well, at least we've proved that it's not cowardice that holds you back.' He shrugged, offered them a good-humoured smile. 'I do apologise. As humbly as I may. Though I intended no insult to the lady, Edmund. Only to you.'

Constance went to Mortimer, pressed him back from his brother-in-law. 'You cannot insult one of us, Sir Harry, without insulting the other,' she said starkly.

'So I see.' Hotspur bowed to her, with surprising grace. 'Forgive me. It was my weariness that spoke, not Harry Percy. Edmund, I beg you to reconsider. I've never asked for help in all my life until this hour. Now I ask it of you.'

Mortimer shook his head. 'No. Not now. Not ever.'

***

'What is it that troubles you, Edmund?'

He paused for an instant before answering. 'Nothing troubles me.'

'Was Hotspur right? Is it because of me that you will not go?' The room had grown very dark. Constance wished she could see his eyes, so that she could read what was in them, but all she could see was the dark, vague shape of his body.

'Not in the way that you mean.'

'Then in what way?'

He sat up in bed, his arms around his knees. 'It's hard to explain. I'm not even sure that I can.' He paused again, thinking in the silence. 'Has anyone ever told you what happened when I was born?' he asked.

'No. What has that to do with it?'

'It is said that on that night the horses in my father's stables were found up to their fetlocks in blood. Of course,' he shrugged, 'there could be some natural explanation for it. Perhaps some wild animal got in, and they kicked it to death. Or perhaps it's just a tale that some fool made up, to make my family history more interesting. But, as you may know, "it is said," means more in Wales than it does in England. Some think that it predicts a bloody end for me. Others that I shall cause great bloodshed. There are other prophecies about me among the bards, none of which I truly believe. But sometimes, just sometimes, I have a glimpse of what is coming. Some small part of what is to be. I fear that if I go into Wales I may never come out again. That I shall lose you. Irredeemably. That's why I won't go.'

Constance drew a deep breath. She had never heard of anything like this before, and certainly not from Edmund. 'You can't allow yourself to be governed by such fancies. A man such as Harry Hotspur does not find it easy to ask for help from another. He said as much. He must be desperate for your assistance.'

'That is his misfortune.'

'He's right. You *do* know the Welsh better than most. You even speak the language. If you can help settle this peacefully it would be a good thing for all, Welsh and English alike, and you will put him deep in your debt. Remember, Edmund, that we need *him*. Hotspur has no great love for King Bolingbroke. We might bring him over to our side. If he and his father decided to support your nephew's claim, then we'd be well on our way to success. And it seems we may also have friends among the Welsh. You could put this Owain to the test. See what it is that he truly wants. It may be nothing more than plain justice. Freedom from tyrants like Grey and Arundel. Or he may want to see a Mortimer on the throne.'

'I don't care about any of it. I am not going to risk losing you.'

'There's no question of that. I'll be here, waiting for you to return.'

'It's not any change in you that I fear.'

'Then what?'

His voice grew very quiet. 'Something that threatens us. Something evil.'

She snorted. 'It's called Bolingbroke. That's the only evil I know.'

'I wish it were so. I don't go in fear of mortal men. Or no more than any sane person should.' He sighed. 'There's something else abroad. Something so dreadful that it menaces Bolingbroke no less than us. I told you, I can't explain it. Can't even put it into words. I can only feel it, and I know that I'd sooner fight fifty men with my bare hands than face it.'

'And this demon, this *thing*, whatever it is, lives only in Wales?' She was growing impatient with him, and could not keep the edge out of her voice.

He shook his head. 'No. It's all around us. Something that was released into the world when King Richard was murdered.'

'Then it's here with us in this room, isn't it? In this bed?' She drew him to her, seeking to give him comfort. 'Edmund, this is some childhood terror that's come back to you. Forgotten until Hotspur somehow reminded you of it by speaking of Wales. Why do you not sleep now, and decide what to do in the morning? I promise you; in the light of day these doubts will be gone. You'll laugh to think that they ever entered your head.'

Some of the tension went out of him in response to her touch. He turned towards her, and she pillowed his head on her breasts as though he was a child in need of reassurance.

'You must despise me for a coward,' he said. 'I've never spoken of this to another soul in this world, and yet I burden you with it!'

She stroked his hair. 'Of course I don't despise you!' she said. 'You've bared your soul to me, and I take that as the measure of your love. We all have fears, Edmund, that we don't confide to others. I dare say that even Hotspur has some. There's no cause for your fear. You'll not lose me. I'll fight my way to you through anything that stands between us.'

***

Constance and Alianore walked together through the gardens at the foot of Powys Castle, keeping beneath the shade of the arbours so that their pale complexions would not be damaged by the bright June sunshine. The dull sandstone towers of the castle soared behind them on its mound, and before them the view of open country stretched out for miles to the south, its green shading gradually into the clear cloudless blue of the sky. A few paces behind them were Alianore's sister-in-law, Alice, Lady Powys, and Alianore's elder daughter, Anne. Further back still a whole flock of waiting-women, children and nurses.

Constance drew the warm breeze into her lungs, and focused her eyes on the distance. It was a beautiful scene, one of utter tranquillity, like an illustration in an expensive Book of Hours. The red deer clustered in groups under the spreading trees of the Charltons' park, untroubled by hunters. Lord Charlton and his brother were from home, investigating reports of raids on the western fringes of Powys by Welsh rebels. The disaffection did not extend to the town of Welshpool that lay a little to the north of the castle, at the edge of its protection. The burgesses were as Welsh as Dewi Sant, almost to a man, as the name of their town suggested, and yet their loyalty to the Charltons was beyond question. They were already arrayed in arms, prepared to defend their homes from the enemy, their bows and spears within easy reach as they worked at their crafts or bought and sold.

Constance had been brought to Powys by the need to negotiate with Alianore for the marriage between Dickon and Anne Mortimer. She and Edmund had broached the matter with letters; but there were arguments that could not safely be committed to writing, and time was slipping by, with Edmund still away with Hotspur in the more northern parts of Wales, besieging Conwy and chasing the elusive Glyn Dwr over the hills.

His letters to her during his absence had been irregular and short. That was not surprising in the circumstances, and it gave her some comfort to know that by coming to Powys she had brought herself closer to him. If was even remotely possible that he might ride through the gate one day, for the exigencies of war might well lead him this far south. As if in token of her desire she lightly brushed her fingers against her cincture, a splendour of gold and rubies that Edmund had presented to her on Twelfth Night. It was a continuing marvel to her that he had been able to finance such a gift; certainly he had not done so without sacrifice. She had not dared to wear it at Fotheringhay, for fear of provoking too many questions. At Caversham, for Edmund, she had sometimes worn nothing else…

'Some livelihood for Anne must be assured,' Alianore said, bringing her back to the present.

Constance started. 'She will be Duchess of York,' she pointed out. 'Is that not enough?'

'She may be Duchess of York, one day. But that is not a certainty. What if your brother dies before then? Dickon, I mean. You've said yourself; all he has are grants from the Exchequer, and those for his lifetime only. He hasn't a penny of income from land, nothing with which he could endow Anne. What if your sister-in-law dies? Edward could marry again, father a son. Anne would be left with nothing. Surely you see the difficulty?'

'I do.' Constance linked arms with her friend, bent her head towards her. 'I see your point exactly. But this is no ordinary marriage, Alianore. It's not simply a matter of lands and jointures.'

'Oh, I understand that! You and Edmund and Edward are plotting against the King, and this is some small portion of your plans. Well, your plans may come to nothing, and I have to consider Anne's security. I am all she has in this world.'

'Edmund and I are working for the benefit of all your children. For the advantage of your son March in particular. Once he's King he'll be able to give Anne a hundred manors if he wishes. We need Edward's support to bring that about, and Edward's price is this alliance between our families.'

'Edward's friendship always has a price,' Alianore said.

'Yes. But surely not too grievous a price in this case?'

'There's also the child to be considered.'

'The child?'

'Anne. That's all she is, a child. Twelve years old. She's set eyes on Dickon, but I doubt whether they've ever exchanged a word. I'll not force her to take him, or any other, against her will. I remember too well what that was like.'

'There is no kinder, gentler boy than Dickon in the land. He would never abuse her.'

'I dare say that Roger's sisters would have said the same about *him*.' Alianore sat down abruptly on a turf seat, entwined her fingers in the latticework at the back of it. 'Anne must at least be willing, and she's very young to make such a decision.'

'That is why it's your duty to make the decision for her.' Constance could scarcely keep the impatience out of her voice. It seemed to her that Alianore was simply looking for more obstructions to throw in the way, more excuses for delay. That was the last thing she had expected.

Alice Charlton appeared at her side before Alianore could answer. 'There must be a fire in the town,' she said. 'Look at that smoke.' She pointed to the northwest. In the distance, well beyond the castle walls, a dark column was rising, stark against the cloudless blue. 'Someone has been clumsy in the bakery, I expect.'

Constance hesitated for a moment. 'The fire must have taken hold, by the look of it,' she suggested. 'A burning sack, or even the corner of a roof, would not produce so much smoke.'

'We could ride down there and see for ourselves,' said Alice, who was bored and seeking an excuse for activity. 'Take some men from the castle, and help to fight the flames. We might stop it from spreading any further.'

Alianore rose slowly to her feet, and the three of them stood in silent inaction among the flowers, watching the column grow in size before their eyes and billow out into a cloud that seemed to loom above the castle.

Someone was running down the path towards them, his boots throwing up the gravel as high as his knees. It was one of Charlton's household officers, an elderly man, his cheeks red as beetroot from the exertion.

'My ladies!' he cried. 'Into the castle at once, I beg you! We must raise the bridges and close the gates. The rebels are burning Welshpool, and moving this way through the woods. They number in thousands.'

***

Edmund Mortimer sat his horse at the top of the pass, looked out in every direction, from the bleak scrubland of the hills to the green, wooded country below.

'We seem to have lost them,' he said.

Hotspur nudged his mount forward. 'It'd be more true to say that they've lost us, damn them. God knows where they've gone. Most of them on foot at that.'

'They know this land much better than we do,' Arundel observed. 'It's difficult country, and most of these fellows think no more of walking across the mountain tops than we do of pacing a lady's bedchamber. You can cut off miles that way, and go where horses cannot follow.'

'Humph,' said Sir Hugh Browe through the whiskers of his unruly brown beard. He was an experienced soldier from Cheshire, Arundel's retainer, and most of his contributions came in the form of grunts.

Hotspur's face, framed in his open basinet, glistened with sweat. 'Well, Arundel? You must have some idea of the lie of the land. Where do we go from here? Any ladies' bedchambers in the vicinity?'

The young Earl frowned, conscious that Percy was mocking him. 'I'm not sure where we are, to be truthful,' he admitted.

On the previous morning they had encountered a force of rebels on the slopes of Cader Idris, and, after a brief, fierce fight, scattered them. Hotspur had determined on pursuit, with the mounted portion of their force, and this they had prosecuted with ferocity until darkness had made it impossible to continue. This advanced company amounted to about a hundred mounted men in all, knights, esquires, hobelars and mounted archers. Their infantry, it was to be hoped, was following them as best it could.

'If I'm not much mistaken, we're a few hours from Powys Castle,' Mortimer said. 'It's somewhere over there, to the east. We could go forward slowly, allow the footmen to catch up.'

'They can catch us at Powys,' Hotspur replied, spitting into the parched, coarse grass. 'I dare say your sister can feed us, Arundel? Either that, or we'll have to eat the fucking horses.'

They had left their supply carts with the foot soldiers, and then discovered the difficulty of foraging in Wales. There was water enough, from the streams, but very little else. Edmund moistened his lips with his tongue. The only food he had had in the last twenty-four hours was a small piece of ewe's milk cheese, taken from one of the houses in Dinas Mawddwy. He was one of the more fortunate members of the company.

'Is it agreed then?' Hotspur asked, not really inviting debate on the issue. 'Lead on, Arundel. Your precedence isn't in question here.'

The Earl glared at him, and began the descent, Browe a scowling presence at his side.

'Why do you provoke him?' Edmund asked.

'Do I?'

'You know you do.'

'He's an arrogant young turd. Will that suffice?'

'Not that much younger than I am, Harry.'

Hotspur spat again. 'I'll take my oath, Edmund, that you were more a man at sixteen than he'll be at thirty. Ah, I'm sick of playing nursemaid to that pup and to Bolingbroke's brat. Thank the saints, at least we haven't got that one with us.'

They had left the Prince, Lord Grey and Hugh Despenser to mop up at Conwy, following the castle's surrender. The Tudors of Mon had been pardoned, having first betrayed their own followers, who had not.

'I think you are harsh.'

'Harshness is what boys need, if they're to turn into men—not waiting gentlewomen. The world is a hard place. We have to fight for what we want, kill those who get in our way.' He paused for a moment, his eyes studying the way ahead as if for possible ambushes. 'Look at Bolingbroke. He's your example. He knew what he wanted, and took it. A few broken oaths and the odd murder were neither here nor there. That's what we are going to have to do, Edmund.'

'We?'

'We're going to have to be ruthless. I don't know about you, but I'm weary of fighting Bolingbroke's battles for him at my own charges. This could go on for years, chasing shadows around these hills. I've had enough. I'm going to the

King, to ask for payment, and to let him know that I think we should settle this quarrel by negotiation. I've had a letter from our friend Glyn Dwr.'

Edmund stared at him. 'A letter?' he repeated incredulously. 'Since the battle? How is that possible?'

Hotspur snorted. 'That was no battle, dear brother. That was a minor skirmish. The letter was in my hand before we left Llanwrst, but the truth is I prefer to give a man a beating before I talk terms with him. It concentrates his mind. This is a profitless war. Rooted in misunderstanding. Glyn Dwr sets down that he wants nothing more than his lands—let him have them, I say.'

'Arundel and Grey will never concede so much. Nor Bolingbroke himself, I imagine.'

'Whether he does or not, I am for the North,' Hotspur nudged his horse forward down the slope, keeping a careful eye on the eroded path that stretched out before them. 'The King may find himself another Justiciar of North Wales. It will need to be a man with a deeper purse than mine! I need to consult my father, seek his advice about our future policy, and discover whether the Scots are likely to give us trouble during this next year or two. Since you have no official place here, I suggest that for the present you return to your lovely widow. Or you may care to visit us at Alnwick. Elizabeth will be glad to have sight of her brother.'

'I need to be near London, until I know what is decided about my nephews.'

'Then it sounds like Caversham, and the fair Lady Despenser. Bring her with you to Alnwick afterwards, if you like. Did you know, by the way, that young Arundel sought her hand?'

Edmund found himself resenting the vague air of amusement in Hotspur's voice. 'Yes,' he said quietly, 'I did know that. She refused him.'

'It's one reason the boy will do you an ill turn if he can. Well, it seems to me that the lady has good taste. A countess's coronet would have tempted many. Perhaps she aims higher, eh?'

'In choosing me?'

'Why not? Remember what I said about being ruthless. You've good cause to look for advancement.' He fell silent for a moment, drew air into his lungs. 'You know, I've no great love for Wales. No real interest in what happens here, one way or the other. I don't even like the smell of the country. My heart lies elsewhere. All my family has ever wanted is a free hand in the North. If a King assured us of that, *and kept his word*, we'd follow him to hell. It's something that Bolingbroke doesn't seem to understand. Who knows? Another might.' He laughed, his grey eyes shining. 'You might, Edmund. That's what I mean.'

***

'Will someone quieten that damned woman?'

Lord Charlton's agony provided some excuse for his brusqueness. Stripped of his armour, and of most of the quilted garments that lay beneath, he lay on his bed while Alianore, whose limited surgical skills were the best available, cleaned the large, bloody, open wound in his groin and her woman, Eluned, threaded a needle in preparation for the necessary stitches. Sir Edward Charlton stood by, still fully armed, in case it proved necessary to hold his brother down.

Alice Charlton was weeping uncontrollably, hence her husband's anger with her. Constance, who did not like Alice much, nevertheless felt a guest's obligation to offer consolation. 'Peace, my dear, your husband will be well,' she said gently.

'Not much of a battle was it?' Hotspur said contemptuously. 'You had them on the run even before we arrived. I didn't have to draw my sword.'

'We were fortunate.' Sir Edward said gravely, 'We fell on their rear as they attacked the town and did them great damage, but only because our own people stayed loyal to us.' His glance fell on his brother. 'Even so, we've paid a price.'

'They'll be the same scum we set about yesterday. Or some part of that force, anyway. I dare say we drove them into Powys for you.'

'These have been in Powys for more than a day,' Lord Charlton announced, gritting his teeth against the pain. 'Raiding the outlying settlements. It was Glyn Dwr himself. We almost had him. Tell them, Edward.'

Alianore's husband shrugged. 'With a few more men, and a little luck, we could perhaps have cut off their escape.'

Constance led Alice to the window seat, settled down on it with her, and allowed her to weep on her shoulder. It was a strange chance, she thought, that had brought her here to serve as comforter to Arundel's sister in Arundel's presence. The shutters were open, to allow in such air and light as was available, and on the breeze there still lingered the stench of burning, fainter now, the fires of Welshpool either damped down or dying for lack of fuel. There was damage enough, by all accounts, but most of the town was saved, and the enemy had fled into the hills to the north, leaving many dead on both sides, and not a few wounded, but no prisoners. John Charlton's own wound had been received in the final rout, a Welsh spear thrust up at him as he rode over the man who wielded it, cruel chance directing the point to one of the few gaps in his steel plate protection, piercing the mail and padding that lay beneath, and tearing his flesh abominably.

'It doesn't matter,' said Arundel. 'We can pursue them in the morning. All of us together. Combine our forces.'

'Friend Owain would love that,' Hotspur sneered. 'Follow him into mountains that he can see from his own windows, where he knows every stone, where he can arrange an ambush at every twist in the path? Sound policy, my lord of Arundel. You and your men can take the lead, but don't expect me to dog your heels.'

'The chances are they came here for the same reason that we did,' Edmund Mortimer said. 'To find food. They must be starving by now, very low in spirits after two defeats. As like as not they'll disperse and go home.'

'Humph!' grunted Hugh Browe. 'Always supposing they don't come back to-morrow, stronger than ever, to try again.'

'Let them!' said Hotspur briskly. 'Charlton, were all your cooks killed in the fighting? Edmund has reminded me how hungry I am. For God's love, let us eat. If Browe is right, we'll do better in the morning with full bellies.' He turned to his esquire. 'Hardyng! Get me out of this armour. I'm weary of my own stink.'

Constance rose, and made her way over to Mortimer. 'I'll disarm you my-self,' she said quietly, indicating the way out of the room with her eyes.

'You plan your campaigns well, Edmund, I'll say that for you,' Hotspur laughed. 'Small wonder you advised us to come here for supplies. You must wish that you had such a squire, Arundel. I know that I do!'

The room Constance had been allocated was only a little way off, along a vaulted passage, and it was there that she led him. There, true to her word, she began to remove his armour with her own hands, with some rather grudging and markedly silent assistance from Agnes. Mary Russell was sent off to find Edmund's official squire, and with him such civilian clothes as Edmund had immediately available.

'I don't like to see you doing this,' he said, as she knelt to remove his spurs.

'Why not?'

'Because you are not my servant.'

'We are each the other's servant, Edmund. That's what love means. In any event, I'm glad to have the excuse to be out of that room.'

He grinned. 'It's just Hotspur's way, to speak as he does. He means no harm.'

'I know. Anyway, I'm grateful to him. He's brought you back to me, quite safe. So much for prophecy, and your horses treading in blood!'

'We're not out of Wales yet.' He paused, shrugging. 'Still, we soon shall be. He's as good as told me to go home. I think the fighting is over, that he plans to offer Glyn Dwr a truce.'

She looked up at him, surprised. 'The Charltons will not like that, after the damage done to their town. Nor Arundel, I think.'

'Nor Grey de Ruthin, nor even the Prince himself. Do you think Hotspur cares what they think? What any thinks, save Hotspur? I have a feeling that he'll prove to be a troublesome ally for us.'

'Ally? You have spoken to him?'

Edmund snorted. 'It's more true to say that he has spoken to me. He hopes to see me—advanced.'

Constance took a breath. The combined power of Percy, Mortimer, York and Despenser was formidable indeed, if all the strands could be tied together. It might even be enough. But it was the tying together that was difficult. They were close, but there was so much more to do.

28

'You've fattened the purses of lawyers to no purpose,' Edward of York said. 'There's never profit in such cases. I could have told you that before you began.' He sprawled in his place on the day bed, one foot on the cushions, the other swinging idly in the air. It was a warm summer day at Caversham, the heat oppressive despite open windows and a breath of air that drifted into the house from the river.

Edmund Mortimer shrugged. He stood by the window, looking out down the length of the garden to the swans drifting by on the Thames. 'I didn't expect to succeed in gaining control of my nephews, but I thought I had to make the attempt. For Alianore's sake, as well as my own.'

'And her gratitude is such that she will not even go so far as to accept our proposals for her daughter's marriage.'

Constance looked up from her work. 'She has not refused us, Ned. Merely imposed conditions.'

'Conditions that we can't meet. Not without involving my father, which I don't wish to do. Even if I did, it'd make no difference. He'd not agree to settle lands on Dickon.'

'She has placed Anne in my household. Is that not a gesture of good intent?'

Her brother grunted. 'More likely it's a way of fobbing you off. You forget; I know Alianore all too well. She'll never come to the point today if next month will suffice. Not unless she's pressed. Obviously you didn't press her hard enough.'

'We had other matters to concern us.'

'A raid by a few beggarly Welsh rebels?'

'John Charlton was sorely wounded,' Edmund said. 'They still fear for him, I'm told. In the circumstances we could scarcely force the matter.'

'I don't see why not. It doesn't concern Charlton. It doesn't even concern his brother. It's between Alianore and us. Well, it's too late to do anything now. Cousin Harry has made a decision in your absence. I'm to go to Bordeaux, as Lieutenant of Guienne. It seems that the French are threatening our borders, and I'm to negotiate with them—or make war.'

'You've agreed to go?' Constance was shocked. 'How can you, Ned? With matters as they are, and our father declining with every day?'

He shrugged. 'I've no choice in the matter. I'm commanded, and I've no reasonable cause to refuse. The French are hostile, and the truce could be broken at any time. Even sending Queen Isabelle home has not placated them. They grumble that Bolingbroke has stolen her jewels. Well, knowing him he probably has, but the plain truth is they're itching for any excuse to make war on us. They've suddenly remembered that they were Richard's allies. Ironic, isn't it?'

Edmund shook his head. 'It is when you consider that without French aid Bolingbroke would still be in exile. But this could help our cause. The more the King is stretched by foreign enemies, the weaker he becomes at home. War means taxation, and that means trouble with the Commons, especially as he promised he would govern without it.'

'All that, and the price of corn double what it was last year. Yes, there'll be some discontent; I don't doubt it. But war against France and Scotland could well strengthen Cousin Harry in the end, especially if he wins a victory or two. If you're thinking that we can ally ourselves with the French, Edmund, you should think again. Partly because I'd not trust them the length of this room, but mainly because there's no surer way to turn the country against us. The same goes for the Scots, and for your Welsh friends.'

'My Welsh friends? What do you mean by that?'

'I mean the friends who left the Mortimer lands alone when they burnt all the rest of North Wales. If that's not enough, do you think it's not known at court that you and Hotspur have been negotiating with Glyn Dwr?'

'They know more than I!' Edmund turned his back on the window and stalked across the carpet towards Edward. 'Owain has made it known that he would submit on reasonable terms. I suppose Hotspur may have talked to him in secret, but I've certainly had nothing to do with it, and nor have I sought to join him to our faction.'

'So much the better, in my opinion.' Edward paused, toyed with his rings for a moment. 'Of course, any stick will serve to beat a dog, but for the present this stick is best left alone. Arundel and Grey de Ruthin are hot against the man, and it does not profit us to have them link your name with his.'

'Do they so dare?'

'Not openly. But in the King's privy chamber, who knows? Nothing will satisfy them, short of seeing all the rebels hanged, and they'll have you and Hotspur hanged with them rather than allow Glyn Dwr to have his lands again and a pardon for his faults. I've been watching them, of course, and arguing the point that it makes some sense to pacify Wales by talk rather than fighting. But I can't do either thing from Bordeaux. Perhaps that's why I'm being sent there.'

'I cannot imagine why it is that Grey has such influence,' Constance said. She paused broke off her thread, and turned the work around in her hands. 'Why does Bolingbroke pay heed to him? He must know that Grey's a fool and a rogue, that he's caused most of the trouble in Wales.'

Edward released a brief, snorting laugh. 'He favours him, dear Sister, for the same reason that Cousin Richard favoured John Golafre. He's loyal, reliable and none too nice in his dealings. A King needs many kinds of men in his service; not only those he would choose as friends, or marry to his daughter. Grey has his uses.'

'I'd have no use for him if I were King,' Edmund said.

'Then perhaps you'd not be King for long. Cousin Harry doesn't have your scruples. He'll make use of any weapon that comes to hand. Even me. That's one of the things that makes him a dangerous enemy, one not to be underestimated. We need to be cautious, and wait our moment.'

Constance shook her head. 'Will it ever come?'

'Yes. But not while I am in Bordeaux, and not until we have gathered more support.' He paused, put his hand into his purse, and drew out a small piece of folded parchment that he handed to Edmund. 'I had almost forgot. Look at this. I'd value your opinion of it.'

Mortimer scanned the writing for a few moments. 'A forgery,' he said. 'A forgery or a trick.'

'Look at the seal! Is that not Richard's signet? For if it is not, then I have never seen it.'

Edmund nodded reluctantly. 'It has the look of it,' he agreed. 'But how can this be genuine? We all know Richard is dead.'

He passed the parchment on to Constance, who set her work aside to read it. It was nothing less than a letter from King Richard to his 'trusty and well beloved cousin, Edward, Duke of Aumale', promising his return to England within months, and asking Edward to make ready to rise in arms in his support. She studied the seal most carefully and found, to her unbounded surprise, that it appeared to be genuine.

'Would Richard still have his seal, when prisoner at Pontefract? Surely they would have taken it from him. This is probably some trick of Bolingbroke's, intended to test you.'

'How did you come by it?' Edmund asked. 'The man who carried this took a great risk.'

Edward shrugged. 'I had it from a friar, who was given it by another of his sort, or so he said. Yes, I suspect it's a trick of some sort, though not of the King's. Harry's mind isn't subtle enough, and besides he knows better than anyone that I'm to go to Bordeaux, and would not be here to meet Richard even if Richard came. As a loyal subject I shall have to hand it over to him. It should give him something to think about.'

'There are like to be other such letters,' Constance predicted. As she read the message again it seemed to her that even the signature had a look of authenticity. Was it somehow possible that King Richard lived? She could not bring herself to believe it.

'Dozens of letters, probably,' her brother agreed, 'and they'll cause confusion. Uncertainty among our friends as well as our enemies. We cannot ignore this, because many will look at that seal and believe with all their hearts that Richard is alive. Perhaps we should pretend that we believe it too. As I said before, any stick will serve to beat a dog. Or a Mole.'

***

The King entered Wales with the levies of twenty-two counties, a huge array sufficient to crack a much larger nut than Owain Glyn Dwr of Glyndyfrdwy. Or so Harry Bolingbroke believed, and his advisers did not trouble to disillusion him. He was scarcely over the Severn when the rains began, rains so thick that they were virtually a mist, rains so prolonged and so heavy that they turned every river into a torrent and the roads, such as they were, into swamps. The archers marched with their bow strings stuffed inside their caps for protection against the storms, for wet strings rendered their weapons useless, except perhaps as clubs.

At last they came to the abbey of Strata Florida. It was the largest building for miles, and it offered better shelter from the wind and rain than canvas could hope to do. It also possessed great stocks of food and drink, and animals suitable for slaughter. As the monks were not only Welsh, but also avowed supporters of Glyn Dwr, it could be looted with a good conscience. Matters soon went beyond mere looting, however. Edmund watched with growing disbelief, astonished that Bolingbroke should allow such disorder. No one attempted to keep discipline, and the unrestrained soldiers began to destroy what they could not carry off or put to immediate use. One monk who picked up a billhook to defend himself was promptly seized and beheaded. Casks were staved in, windows deliberately smashed; the monks' gardens trampled, their stores and outhouses put to the torch, the monks themselves driven out into the fields at sword point. The army was turning itself into a disordered rabble, beyond effective control.

Edmund stalked through the chancel of the church, where the horses belonging to the King and the rest of the leadership had been stabled, and along the passage into the abbot's lodgings. Bolingbroke was sprawled on the abbot's chair, drinking the abbot's wine from a gold cup, his feet on the abbot's table. Immediately next to him was his son, the Prince, Hal of Monmouth. The boy's mouth was down turned in its usual sullen expression. When he had first met the Prince, Edmund assumed that Hal did not like him. He discovered later that Hal looked at everyone the same way, without distinction, his large, grey, Bohun eyes staring along the length of his prominent nose. Grouped around them were Bolingbroke's cronies. Grey de Ruthin and the young Earls of Arundel, Stafford and Kent. Richard Beauchamp, newly succeeded to his father's title as Earl of Warwick, was standing by the fire, with the grim-faced Worcester next to him. Apart from headgear they were all more or less fully armed.

'Ah, Mortimer, you are welcome,' Harry said. 'Sit down. The abbot, for a man sworn to poverty, keeps a fine cellar.'

'There's mead too;' remarked Grey, 'though only a Welshman could enjoy that sickly horse-piss. Ale by the gallon. These monks live well.'

'It'd be ungrateful not to make the most of their hospitality,' Arundel added.

'Wouldn't be Christian,' said Mun Holland, emptying his pot at a single swallow. He thrust it into the hand of a white-faced young monk who stood behind him. 'Fetch more, rebel! Be quick about it.'

'Is it Your Grace's wish that the men should raise havoc here?' Edmund asked, trying hard to keep the emotion out of his voice. 'They're running riot. This is, after all, a house of God.'

'A nest of bloody traitors, more like!' snarled Grey. 'It's well for you, Mortimer. You've not had your lands burnt and your people butchered by these Welsh scum. I have! They deserve all they get, and worse.'

The King gestured him to silence. 'Our men have suffered much in this campaign. They deserve to be let off the leash for a while. Grey is right. These monks have sided with our enemies. They must be taught a lesson, by way of example to others.'

'Many of the Welsh are loyal,' Edmund objected. 'This kind of barbarity could rouse the whole country against you. Have you thought of that?'

Bolingbroke's hand hammered the table. 'Sit down, damn you!' He turned to peer at the wide-eyed young monk. 'You! Get him something to drink. Wine. The best, as you've given me.'

Edmund sank onto the bench, unstrapped his sallet and removed it from his head. He took the wine from the monk's hand with a murmured word of thanks, and took a draught of it. It was rich and warming. The abbot obviously had expensive taste in claret.

'Your sympathy for these rebels has not gone unnoticed,' Bolingbroke went on. 'I shall be generous to you, Cousin, and ascribe it to your kind heart. If you were a woman such gentleness might be a virtue. In a man, it has the look of weakness.'

'Weakness? I was always taught it was a knight's duty to protect the Church. Not to ransack monasteries, or behead monks.'

'Perhaps Sir Edmund's counsel would be valuable,' Arundel said. 'He knows Wales better than any of us. Has many friends hereabouts, I believe.'

Edmund turned on him at once. 'What do you imply?'

'That you know Wales well. You do, don't you?'

'I know Wales well enough to wish it was at peace. Do you think that this is the way to pacify the country?'

'You'd prefer to offer them pardons, I suppose?'

'There have been pardons enough, by God!' Grey exploded. 'Glyn Dwr and his rabble are well beyond pardon. Have you any idea, Mortimer, what they've done to my lordship of Ruthin? Of course you haven't, and you don't care. It doesn't touch your purse. Houses burnt. Cattle run off. Tenants driven from their homes. Men maimed, slit open, stabbed in the back. Women raped or carried away. Not just English, either. Welsh too, by their own people. You talk of peace? The peace of the grave is the only peace I'd grant the filth.'

Worcester left the fire, walked to the table, and poured himself a cup of ale. 'If you'd been wiser, Reginald, matters might not have become so serious.' He was the oldest man there, by far the most experienced warrior, and the respect that seniority generated gained him some approximation of silence. He turned to face Bolingbroke. 'Sire, it's no fault of yours that the weather has been so much against you, but the truth is that this campaign has achieved nothing. How long can we continue, this late in the year? Another week at most, in my opinion. The weather can only worsen, and the days are already shortening.'

Harry lifted his head, rubbed his weary eyes. 'What do you suggest?'

'I suggest you cut your losses. Rebellion is fresh hereabouts—offer pardons to those who will accept them. A little leniency may win hearts. Send to Glyn Dwr. Offer terms, and see if he will submit. If he refuses, then you have months to prepare a new campaign, and all spring and summer to fight it in. That's my advice.'

'Go home? With nothing achieved? Is that what you mean?' Grey was horrified and angry. 'We'll be laughing-stocks! Defeated by a Welsh rabble! That's what they'll say of us!'

'We've already done as much as I hoped to do,' Bolingbroke said. 'Would you have us winter in Wales? It's impossible.' He paused, picked up his wine, and set it down again. 'I think there may be something in your advice, Worcester.'

'Sire!' Grey and Arundel protested at the same moment.

He overrode them. 'It commits us to nothing. If I grant Glyn Dwr pardon, it will be on *my* terms, and with the consent of the Council. He will have to compensate you, Grey, and you, Arundel, for the damage done to your lands. Nothing less will serve. If he is stubborn, then I swear on my honour that we shall be back next year, in full force, and that he'll be hunted down and hanged.'

'And which of us is to negotiate with Glyn Dwr?' Arundel asked, his eyes hostile as they rested on Worcester.

'Don't ask it of me!' snorted Grey.

Harry rested his chin on his steepled fingers. 'The only one among us who speaks Welsh,' he said, breaking into one of his rare smiles. 'The obvious choice. My cousin, Sir Edmund Mortimer.'

***

The Duke of York walked with a stick now, and rarely set foot out of doors. He had not stirred from Fotheringhay in many months. Even the transit from one side of the parlour to the other was a task demanding all his strength and courage, a movement made only because it offered him some variety in his pain, temporary relief to his hips and back bought by a more intense agony in his legs. The effort made, he lowered himself onto the window-seat, straightened his back against the wall, and recovered his dignity.

'I was not always so,' he said, as if to himself.

'I know, Father.' Constance moved a little closer to him, awaited his permission to seat herself. She was shocked by the deterioration in him. The previous Christmas he had been recovering from illness, weakened by it. Now he was simply old and, what was worse, clearly weary of living.

'It seems but yesterday that I was your age. I never thought I'd come to this, so weak and useless that I have to be carried to chapel in a litter. I could fight or hunt all day, dance and feast all night, and never have so much as an aching bone. Next morning I'd be ready for more of the same. What a family we were! Your grandfather; your uncles. They used to say that the least of us was a match for any knight in Europe.' He paused to dwell on his words, allowed himself a deprecating snort. 'An exaggeration, perhaps, but not much of one. The world went in fear of us. And where are they now, those brothers? All dead, save me.'

He gestured to the seat opposite him, and Constance settled on the cushions, folding her hands in her lap. The window was open, to allow in the air of the bright, autumn day. Her view faced north, over the lake to the great park beyond. Also visible were the gardens that lay beneath the walls, and on one of the paths Dickon, walking with Anne Mortimer. He was pointing to something in the distance, and Anne was nodding, her eyes following the sweep of his arm. It looked promising. Constance was fond of Anne, a gentle, quiet girl with Edmund's dark colouring and limpid, expressive eyes. She had a feeling that Dickon liked her too, had done so from first sight.

York was still silent, lost in his reverie. She turned her attention back to him.

'Father, I wish you would make some provision for my brother, Dickon,' she said quietly. 'Some small livelihood, a house that he can call his own.'

He blinked at her for a moment, then avoided her eye. 'I think the boy has livelihood enough.'

'His annuity at the Exchequer? You know that can never be the same as a grant of land. It could be taken from him at any time, at the King's whim. It might not be paid at all if the Exchequer is empty. It's neither an inheritance for Dickon's children nor a dower for his wife.'

'What wife?' The Duke sounded impatient. 'The boy's young yet. Not seventeen.'

'By your leave, Father, that makes him almost a man. Some marriage should be purveyed for him.'

'You have someone in mind?'

Her hesitation was momentary before she shook her head in denial.

'I think you do. That Mortimer girl you brought in your train, perhaps?' A hint of suspicion crossed his face. 'What is it that you are about? More mischief?'

'No, sir.'

'Constance, my legs may be weak, but my wits are not yet addled. The King and I wished you to marry Arundel. You defied our wishes, ignored my considered advice. Not with the honourable intent of remaining in a state of widowed chastity, but so that you could give yourself to *Edmund Mortimer*. I used to be proud of you, as proud as any man has ever been of his daughter. What's more, I thought you had pride in yourself. Now I am undeceived. I know what you are—what you have become. I dare say that your lover would be glad to see his niece wedded to Dickon, who is like to be my heir one day. Why should you deny him? You've denied him nothing else.'

She threw her head back so far that her veils rustled as she bruised them against the elaborately painted wall behind her. 'I intend that our cousin, Sir Edmund, shall be my husband.'

'Splendour of God, I should hope that you do!' he exclaimed, his voice a low growl of anger. 'You've little choice in the circumstances. Tell me, did he force you, or were you both drunk?'

'You seem determined to insult me, Father.' Her nose tipped back a little further.

'Do you wonder at it?' He suddenly threw his stick across the room, as if its silver tip had become red-hot in his hand. It clattered against the stone carvings of the fireplace. 'Damn you, girl, what were you thinking about? Marriage to Arundel would have given you security for life, and safeguarded your children. Instead you take it into your head to leap into bed with a fellow who is a pauper by comparison. Cousin of ours or no. A man whom the King dislikes and mistrusts. Of course *that*, I dare say, is a part of the attraction. It seems you've learned nothing, not even from Despenser's death.'

A silence grew between them. Constance lowered her head, found herself watching as her fingers plucked at the azure velvet folds of her skirts, an aimless activity that seemed to have nothing to do with any instruction from her brain. She was aware of her father's breathing, still noisy after the effort involved in hurling the stick, the faint wheeze of congestion in his lungs.

'Edmund is no stranger to this household, sir,' she said at last. 'He grew up in it, if I may remind you, wore your livery for some years. His blood is nobler than that of any Fitzalan who has ever breathed. He *is* our cousin, however small his estate, and descended from King Edward by a line that is senior both to you *and* to Harry Bolingbroke.'

He shrugged, his face sullen. 'I'm past caring, as to your reasons. You've made your choice, and now must live with it, whatever befalls. You should marry

Mortimer at once, before he fills your belly and makes your sin notorious to all. The miracle is that he hasn't done so already, if half what I hear about him is true. Bastards all over the place.' He paused for an instant of consideration. 'You do know about that, I suppose?'

'Yes, Father.' She raised her eyes to meet his. 'I love him, and I shall love his children too.'

'You're a fool, Constance. You know that, don't you? Love may warm a cold bed, but it's a poor defence from the evils of this world. Tell me, are you *never* afraid of what might befall you?'

'I am the granddaughter, daughter and widow of great knights,' she answered quietly. 'I've learned to hide the fears I feel. Above all the dread I have of being left alone in this world.'

He flexed his fingers, trying to overcome the new stiffness in them. 'May God and His saints protect you, child. And may they reward your courage.' He halted abruptly, making a dismissive gesture with his hands as if ashamed of his own words. 'I'm in need of wine, I find. It eases the pain a little, enough to make it—tolerable.' He grimaced, seeming wryly amused. 'I doubt we can ask for more in this world than that our pain be *tolerable*.'

She rose without a word, walked to the dresser and poured wine from the gold jug that stood there into one of the tall crystal goblets that stood next to it. She carried the drink to him, put it in his hand, and watched him as he swallowed it greedily. His first draught left behind little more than a colouring at the bottom of the glass.

'Your brother Dickon will have to wait a while,' he said. 'Let Edward provide for him when I am gone. Either that, or let the boy find an heiress, or a rich widow. Anyone as long as she's not a Mortimer. One of that breed in the family will be trouble enough to bear.'

29

Edmund Mortimer rode warily, his eyes casting about him. Alone, save for his Welsh yeoman who carried his banner, unarmed save for his dagger, uncertain of his exact whereabouts. There was no longer a path or track, not so much a trod worn by sheep, and the ground was growing steeper and rougher all the time as the valley closed in on him. He was uncomfortably aware of the fact that any solitary, skulking archer could make an end of him at will. He could only rely on the good faith of the man he was going to meet, and on the influence of the letters he carried, letters signed by Hotspur and Northumberland, continuing an older correspondence, now authorised by Bolingbroke himself.

Someone was waiting for him at the top of the pass. The man was short, sturdily built and full bearded, his dark hair longer than was fashionable, his clothes of the best broadcloth but cut in a style that would not have looked out of place at old King Edward's court. His low-waisted cote-hardie was of a dull russet colour, matching the autumn leaves, and close to the shade of his tall riding boots. He would have passed unnoticed as a country gentleman in any market town in England. He was on foot, pacing up and down beside a ragged bush. His horse stood a few yards off, its head held by a young boy, the man's only visible companion.

Edmund rode closer, ashamed of an uncomfortable trepidation, as if at last he was coming face to face with the fate he feared in these Welsh hills. 'Lord Owain?' he enquired.

The man bowed his acknowledgment. He was in his middle forties, Edmund guessed, not quite as old as he had expected.

'I am Mortimer,' Edmund said, by way of introduction. He dismounted, thinking it discourteous to keep the advantage of his horse.

'I know you by sight.' The reply was confident, spoken with a strong accent of North Wales and an air of authority. 'Also by reputation.'

'I bear letters for you, sir.'

Glyn Dwr took them from his extended hand, broke the seals and perused them, one by one. He took his time about it, while Edmund stood in silence, aware of the dampness of the air, the snorting of Glyn Dwr's small horse, and the unnatural quietness around them.

'These words are very fair,' Owain said at last, 'but can I trust them?'

'If you doubt it then my word to the contrary would be of little value.' That was said with an asperity Edmund rarely employed.

'I don't doubt *you*, Sir Edmund. Not as to your honour or your good intent. Not in this world. But these are neither the first letters I have had, nor this the first meeting. Harry Hotspur and I spoke together some months ago, and were well agreed, one man with another. Yet I still await some word of grace from your King. Like Hotspur, you may understand my grievances, the grievances of Wales, but your friends Arundel and Grey de Ruthin do not. With all respect, they are greater with Harry Bolingbroke than you are. They have his ear. I dare not put myself into the power of those enemies.'

Edmund thought about retorting that Arundel and Grey were no more his friends than they were Owain's. But then he remembered what he was about, saw that an open admission of division among the English nobility would scarcely strengthen his negotiating position. 'The King has approved this parley,' he answered. 'It may be that there is some chance of a peaceful settlement. Should you not consider it? To save the people of Wales from further suffering?'

Glyn Dwr stared into his eyes. 'You should consider that I did not start this war. It was forced upon me by Grey, and has spread only because of the injustice that bears down on all the men of this land. If I may have an unconditional pardon, for my followers and myself, and my lands restored to me, I'll gladly go back to Glyndyfrdwy, and live as my fathers have lived, in peace. I claim nothing more than the right to be what I was born. Not Grey's serf, nor Arundel's!'

'It is said that you had yourself proclaimed Prince of Wales,' Edmund reminded him. 'Is there truth in that, or is it an invention of Grey's?'

'Do you have dreams, Sir Edmund? Hopes for your future? It was less a dream of mine than a dream of my people. We are made outcasts and slaves in our own land. Do you wonder that some of us resent it? That there are those among us who yearn for a Prince of Welsh blood? So we shoot at the moon, but would settle for less. For justice. If we cannot have that we must fight on, however evil the end may be.' He smiled with sudden, unexpected brilliance. 'Perhaps it will not be so evil. There's a prophecy of Merlin that the Mole will be forced to flee abroad. That a King of Welsh blood will be crowned in London. A Mortimer perhaps? It is no matter of chance your family are the best of the English, descended as you are from Llywelyn Fawr. Other English families share that blood, but only the Mortimers are proud of it.'

'He was a great and noble prince. Why should I not be proud to number him among my ancestors?' Edmund paused, shook his head. 'We are not here to speak of family trees or prophecies, sir, but of an end to your rebellion. The King might be induced to grant the pardon you seek, but he will not do so against the advice of his Council. As you perceive I am not one of his chosen advisers, but merely his subject. I can only report your willingness to come into his peace, to speak for you as far as I am allowed. Beyond that I have no authority to make any promise. In justice to you and yours, I don't wish to raise false hopes. However, the "Prince of Wales" is less likely to be pardoned than the Lord of Glyndyfrdwy.'

Owain shrugged. 'You English set too much store by titles. Call me what you will, I'm still the same man, able to raise up the same number of spears against you. I shall not quibble over a form of words.'

'Your lands and a free pardon. For you and your followers. That will suffice?'

'It will. It must. Though the peace will not last if Grey and his like are not restrained. No matter what the end for us. You may tell King Bolingbroke that. Not as a threat, you understand, but as simple truth.'

Edmund nodded, and prepared to take his leave. He found himself liking the Welshman rather more than he had expected. There was something about him that was rare. A passion, a warmth of the soul that was almost tangible. 'I hope that when we meet again it may be under a roof, one of us the guest of the other, and the land settled in peace.'

The older man extended a hand, grasped Mortimer's firmly in his. 'May it be so! And may Reginald Grey of Ruthin be elsewhere!'

***

Bolingbroke sat among his books in the room he had set aside for them at Eltham. He was an avid collector in his own right, and had inherited scores of precious volumes from his father—who had rarely opened them but thought them a proper thing for a great Duke to possess—and from King Richard, whose tastes, lighter than Harry's, had run to romances, love poetry and lavish illustrations. There were far too many books and manuscripts for the shelves, and he had already ordered an extension. An indulgence, but one he insisted upon.

He had grown up accustomed to limitless wealth, to ordering any luxury he wanted without consideration, to being naturally open-handed. Somehow and suddenly—the circumstances were beyond his understanding—the wealth had simply vanished. Though he had acquired a vast treasure from Richard, and possessed more landed resources than any King in generations, the Exchequer was empty. He had already changed his officers, gone so far as to re-appoint Bishop Stafford as Chancellor for the sake of his experience, but it had made no difference. Fresh letters and petitions arrived every day, and all with the same cry—money! Edward of York, writing from Bordeaux, claimed that the Crown already owed him nearly ten thousand pounds. That was a sum roughly equivalent to the annual revenue of the Duchy of Lancaster. As for the Percys, no amount of coin seemed to satisfy them. They had had cartloads of gold, stacked in barrels, and still they sent tedious petitions that demanded more. It seemed that they scarcely drew a breath without charging it to their sovereign's account.

The thought of them so far disturbed his peace of mind that he set down his book, no longer able to concentrate on the abstractions of morality. Northumberland, Worcester and Hotspur, so arrogant in their power, so assured of their own probity, so burdened by the injustices they imagined had been done to them. They would never be satisfied, whatever he did. They were Richard's men at heart, like so many others who had conveniently forgotten what Richard had been like and why he had grown so unpopular that it had been possible to depose him. Their loyalty was as thin as cheap paper. They and Edmund Mortimer, who shared Hotspur's opinion that Owain Glyn Dwr was a wronged man who deserved a pardon and a royal arm thrown around his shoulders to console his grievances.

Edmund Mortimer had submitted a petition of his own, doubtless thinking that he deserved some reward for his services in Wales. A request for a licence to marry, normally a matter of revenue-raising routine handled by the bureaucracy, and referred to the King only because it had the stink of politics about it, involving two members of his own extended family.

He picked up the document, let it drop through his fingers onto the desk without troubling to read it again. Then he rose, walked across the tiled floor to the small table that stood on the other side of the room. There, among the various discarded manuscripts that he had perused in his hours of leisure, lay the exquisite portrait of Lucia of Milan. Her cousin, the Duke of Milan, had promised her to Frederick of Thuringia now, though Harry's agents in Milan reported that the lady was reluctant.

The portrait that rested next to it was crude by comparison, the work of an indifferent craftsman rather than an Italian master, but Harry was no less drawn to it. The fingers were not realistic, and the mouth was not quite right, but the artist had captured Constance's eyes to perfection, that familiar hint of condescension and disgust in their blue depths. Presumably she did not look at Edmund Mortimer like that. His hands clenched into fists at the thought of it.

The portrait had come to him at the time of the Despenser forfeitures, one of many items removed from Caversham. Somehow he had not got around to returning it, and Constance had never asked for it. Perhaps she had forgotten it existed. It had become one of his minor personal possessions, something he looked at from time to time when the mood took him.

He had been generous to her, his cousin. Treated her as well as if not better than he had his own sister, Elizabeth. Beth, of course, was a fool. The wax was still warm on her patents when she had married herself in secret to her long-term lover, John Cornwall, caring nothing for the fact that he was no fit brother-in-law for the King of England. He had put Cornwall in the Tower for a time, until Beth had worn him down with her tedious pleading. Constance was more cautious than his sister, more devious in her ways, but in the end there was little to choose between them. They both mocked him, held him in contempt, failed to appreciate his kindness. Beth, for reasons of lust, had married a nobody. Constance, for reasons of lust, wanted to marry his enemy.

Mortimer was an enemy, an enemy and a traitor. His blatant sympathy for the Welsh rebels was but the latest indicator of that condition. He wanted his nephew March as King, and eventually he was sure to betray himself, for he was not a subtle man. He was not subtle with the ladies either. A noted whore-monger with a string of bastards. How could Constance defile herself by lying with such a lecher? The very thought of them together sickened Harry, sickened him and filled him with inexplicable anger.

Unconsciously thumbing his beard, he picked up the portrait and held it closer so that he could make out the detail. It really was very poor work. Ignoring the Despenser and York coats of arms it could have represented almost any noble lady. Had it not been for those eyes, those haunting eyes…

She had already been widowed by one traitor; it was no kindness to allow her to repeat the experience. She had to be protected from herself, for her own good. He returned to the desk, picked up Mortimer's petition and tore it across. He would not even dignify it with a refusal.

***

Constance suspected the worst when she saw the grim set of Edmund's face as he rode into the courtyard at Caversham. She greeted him with warmth nevertheless, led him into the parlour and settled him by the fire, had him served with spiced wine and waited patiently to tell his tale in his own time.

'The King will not grant Glyn Dwr his pardon,' he said at last, shaking his head. 'The Council argued among themselves for hours. I wasn't there to hear, of course, but I spoke to Roos afterwards. He said that some agreed, but others would not settle on any terms. I can guess who *they* were! Then there were those who thought that what I had negotiated was too generous, too lenient, that Glyn Dwr ought to be made to pay a fine. They even argued as to how much. But in the end it came to nothing. There was no majority for any motion, no consensus. So it seems matters stay as they are. The fighting goes on, needlessly and to no man's profit. They are already preparing a campaign for the spring, an attack on three fronts. We shall find more abbeys to loot and burn I expect!'

He paused for a moment, took a swallow of the mulled wine, sniffled over the beginnings of a cold. 'I wish I'd never been sent to Glyn Dwr. I *liked* the man; I certainly prefer his company to Grey's, or to Cousin Bolingbroke's for that matter. What must he think of me? That I toyed with him? Deceived him? What else should he believe?'

'The decision was not yours, Edmund. He will understand that.'

'Perhaps. As to the licence for our marriage, Bolingbroke has returned no answer. He's always too busy to speak to me, so I gave up waiting, pleaded family business. No doubt he is still setting the price, calculating how much he can squeeze out of us.'

'We have money enough.'

'Do we?' He paused, buried his nose in the wine for a moment and went on. '*You* may have. I used to have savings, but what the lawyers didn't take was mostly spent on that last campaign in Wales. Now I shall be expected to go to war again in the spring. There may be a promise of wages, but that's all it will be, a promise. Roos tells me there's nothing coming out of the Exchequer at the moment but tally sticks. You have to be one of Bolingbroke's lapdogs to receive coin.'

'I'll pay his price and gladly. I feared he might forbid it altogether; I almost preferred not to ask.'

'He has not given permission yet,' Edmund said grimly; and they sat quietly, watching each other with possessive eyes as the light died around them and only the glow of the parlour fire remained.

Owain Glyn Dwr's answer to Bolingbroke was straightforward. With no hope of peace now he turned in desperation to winter warfare, narrowly failing to capture Harlech Castle in December, burning the town of Ruthin to the ground in January, stealing Grey's cattle, then crowning his efforts by capturing Grey himself and holding him as a prisoner for ransom. In March he devastated the estates of John Trevor, the Bishop of St. Asaph, a man of Welsh blood. In all the north of Wales only the Mortimer lands remained untouched.

That there would be a reaction to all this was never in doubt. Preparations for the projected three pronged assault continued all through the spring, despite delays caused by lack of available funds, and by the deaths of two of the leading Englishmen in the Marches, Sir Hugh Despenser and John, Lord Charlton of Powys. The latter had never really recovered from the wounds he had received earlier in the year, but the death of Hugh Despenser was wholly unexpected. Constance was stunned by the loss, for Hugh had proved himself a reliable friend in the depths of her troubles, when almost everyone else had deserted her. Another link with Thomas was broken.

She was also increasingly concerned about Edmund. He was obviously dreading the day when he would have to return to North Wales, to pursue what he considered an unjust and unnecessary war against people for whom he had more than a little sympathy. At the same time, as the only surviving adult male of the Mortimer family, he could scarcely refuse his duty of leadership. The Mortimer tenants, despite others placed in authority over them by the King, still looked to him for guidance and protection. He was away from Caversham a great deal, attending to the business of his own properties, acting as an arbiter in minor disputes between Mortimer clients, and helping Lady March to manage some of the problems attached to her vast estates, this last task by no means diminished now that Alianore's husband was Lord of Powys in his brother's room. He invariably returned from these duties tired, troubled, and in great need of comfort.

Bolingbroke's betrothal to the Joanna of Navarre, the widowed Duchess of Brittany had been announced, a diplomatic alliance that was intended to put pressure on the increasingly hostile French court. But no licence emerged to authorise Constance's marriage to Edmund. She asked her father to intercede, and York sent a letter to the King that secured a promising response, but still the matter dragged on unresolved, until they found themselves in Lent when no marriage could be concluded anyway.

No sooner was the Easter of 1402 celebrated than a royal sergeant-at-arms arrived, bringing with him an impressive sealed package for Edmund. Their hopes rose until they opened it and found that it was not the licence, nor even a demand for payment in exchange for one, but a peremptory order directing Edmund to go to Herefordshire to take charge of the defence of the county, which was allegedly under dire threat from the rebels.

Constance felt like weeping with frustration, but she controlled herself. 'When will you go?' she asked starkly. She never doubted for a moment that he *would* go. All else apart, much of Herefordshire was Mortimer territory; he could not decline to defend it.

He shrugged. 'In a day or two. There's little to prepare here. A few letters to write, though most can as well be sent from Ludlow, where I shall lodge in the castle and gather my forces.'

A day or two, and after that he might be away for months. Spending his money and risking in his life in the service of a King who despised him, who would not grant him the smallest favour in return. Her blood surged with anger as she considered the injustice of it.

'I'd be safe at Ludlow, would I not?' she asked.

'From Glyn Dwr you would, certainly; it's the strongest of all the Mortimer castles. But not from malicious tongues. You've no cause to be in Herefordshire, except to be with me, and you are not yet my wife.'

'Do you think I care what people say of us? Would you be here now if I did?'

He shook his head. 'I care, Constance. Every time I lie with you I worry in case I get you with child, when I should be hoping that I do. I weary of living so. I can't believe it doesn't trouble you just as much, whatever you may say.'

He was right of course, though she would not allow herself to admit it. During one of his absences she had had what she judged to be an early miscarriage, and in the circumstances that had to be counted as a blessing. Yet in her heart there was nothing that she wanted more than to bear his child, and the loss tore at her, no less because she could not share it with him, knowing that it would add to his troubles.

He saw the sorrow in her face, and raised his fingers to her cheek in a caress of consolation. 'A few months apart,' he said. 'What is that? Spice for the appetite, I say. By the time I return we may have our licence, and if not I shall marry you anyway, openly in church before all Oxfordshire and Berkshire, so that there may be no manner of doubt about it. And after that, if Harry Bolingbroke mislikes it, he may do his will.'

***

Constance walked by the Thames at Caversham, the weight of her clothes making her grateful for the coolness of the river and the shade of the trees along its bank. This part of her garden was a favourite, and she was weary of sitting idly indoors, listening to Agnes Norreys complaining about the summer heat. She had Anne Mortimer and Mary Russell with her, more amiable company than Agnes, as well as her three children. Bess was eight now, and Richard six. It would soon be time to think about finding him a place in a suitable household, so that he might learn the skills of knighthood. It was one of the things she would have to discuss with Edmund when he returned from Wales. As for Isabelle, she was still carried by her nurse, but she was quite capable of toddling when inclined to do so. Isabelle was everyone's favourite, and in great danger of being spoiled, especially by the men. Even Agnes allowed that she was an exceptionally beautiful child. Too much so, Agnes said, for the child's profit.

She settled herself on a turf seat and drew from her sleeve the three letters that had arrived from Fotheringhay that morning, carried by a messenger in the Duke of York's livery. So far she had not had a chance to read them, and now was her opportunity, while Anne, Mary and the nurse kept the children amused. Isabelle seemed happy enough just to be carried to admire the swans, while the others settled upon a game of hide-and-go-seek.

The Duke's letter was brief, mainly concerned with a tale about a priest who had been captured at Ware, in Hertfordshire. This priest had confessed to a plot to restore King Richard, and was making all manner of wild accusations. She detected an oblique warning in York's phrasing, as if he was pointing out the dangers of involvement in such folly. He had written a final line of blessing in his own hand, which had grown very difficult to read. His signature was little more than a scrawl.

Joanne's letter was a little longer, but no more cheering. She had had a visit from her brother Kent, and conveyed his good wishes, but that was the best of it. She was very concerned for York's health, and urged Constance to come to Fotheringhay again as soon as possible, while her father was still there to welcome her. Constance frowned; Joanne had raised this alarm before, and been proved wrong. On the other hand there was always the possibility that her fears were justified this time. Perhaps the journey ought to be made, just in case.

Finally there was a letter from Dickon. It was only when she was about to break the seal that she saw it was not addressed to her, but to Anne. She called the girl across, handed her the letter, and asked, rather pointedly whether it was the first such she had received. Anne admitted that it was not, and went on to add that she had sent several replies.

Constance frowned. 'You are in my care, Anne, and I am responsible for you. You ought not to send or receive letters without my knowledge.'

'I'm sorry, my lady. I meant no harm.'

'I think you may call me "Cousin," don't you?'

'Cousin.'

'Did you think I might forbid it?'

Anne consulted her lap. 'Yes, Cousin.'

'You should both have had more faith in me. If you and Dickon agree with one another, it would please me well. I know your uncle and your mother would not object. You may write to him as often as you like. What's more, you may see him at Fotheringhay before long, or perhaps we can arrange for him to come to Caversham.'

The girl looked up and responded with a shy smile. Constance, as ever, was struck by her resemblance to Edmund. She could as easily have been his daughter as Roger's. Only in her quiet poise was there something that recalled Alianore.

'Dickon is all but certain to be Duke of York one day,' Constance went on, 'so he would be a fit match for you, if it so befell. Of course, you are young yet, and there's no cause for haste. You may like my brother less as you come to know him.'

Anne did not answer; her eyes had caught a movement on the water, a barge coming around the corner from the direction of Windsor. The oarsmen wore the royal livery, and the passengers standing at the rear were a squad of archers. Close behind was another similar vessel, carrying an assortment of men, some of them in full armour, all wearing the King's livery collars.

The oars lifted in unison, and the barges glided silently into place alongside the landing stage at the foot of the garden, the armed men spilling unhurriedly ashore. The leader advanced towards the bench where Constance was sitting, a short, middle-aged gentleman she did not recognise. Her own servants were emerging from the house to greet the visitors, but the archers were moving into position to block the paths.

The gentleman took off his elaborate hat, with its trailing liripipe, and bowed low before her, revealing his straw-coloured hair and the beginning of a bald patch. Clutched in his gloved hand was a writ issued under the Privy Seal.

'Madame, I am Elming Leget of the King's household,' he announced, his voice deep and guttural. 'I very much regret this duty, but I am ordered by the King to remove you from here to the house of the canonesses at Goring, where you are to be confined. Your ladyship stands accused of high treason.'

***

The canonesses were apologetic. They regretted that Constance had to be kept close confined, but that was required by the King's order. There were to be no visitors, and no correspondence. Other than that she might think of herself as their guest. Perhaps take the opportunity for religious devotion, if that so pleased her

Constance's initial anger slowly transmuted itself into bewilderment as the days passed, and her concern grew less for herself and more for her children, her father, and, above all, Edmund. The only sense she could make of the accusation was that it must be part of an attack on him. Perhaps her imprisonment was intended to provoke him into some rash act that might be called treason. Or perhaps he too had been arrested. There was no way of knowing. Mary Russell and Anne Mortimer, the companions she had been allowed, did their best to reassure her, but without much in the way of success.

A fortnight went by before Elming Leget returned to Goring. With the same studied politeness as before, he explained that he was now to convey her to the King, who was at the palace of Kennington in Surrey, a little to the south of London. He did not elaborate on this, indeed proved notably close-mouthed, even in the face of direct and persistent questioning. Having tried both anger and charm in her attempts to shift him, Constance gave up, consoling herself with the thought that she would soon be face-to-face with Bolingbroke, who, King or not, could scarcely deny her an explanation.

Leget seemed content with a steady, ambling pace, with lengthy rest breaks, though whether he was considering the welfare of the ladies in his care or the horses was by no means clear. As a result the journey to Kennington occupied the greater part of three days, Constance growing more impatient by the mile. Her occasional complaints met with an unyielding wall of professional courtesy; Leget would agree to anything that tended to her ease or comfort, but not to any increase in their speed.

It was mid afternoon on the third day before they entered the park at Kennington, and with the trees around them in full leaf, another ten minutes passed before the great house became visible, a place Constance had not visited since King Richard's day. Their path slowly turned from a faint trod to a roadway of grey dust, with much evidence of passing horses. This led to a drawbridge over a shallow moat, and through a gatehouse into a courtyard beyond. Servants hurried forward to attend to the horses, but that apart there was very little sign of life, no great crowds of courtiers or petitioners. Kennington, of course, was intended as a hunting lodge, a place of relaxation, but she had not expected to find it so quiet.

Elming Leget helped her dismount, and as he did so a welcoming party of sorts emerged from the building, a small group of richly-dressed young men led by Mun Holland, Earl of Kent.

'I have been looking for you half the day, madame,' Kent said pleasantly. He bowed low, with his usual surprising grace. 'The King has ordered me to bring you to him without delay—he insists that you should not be kept waiting.'

Constance accepted the guiding hand he offered, placing her own upon it. 'He seemed content enough to let me wait at Goring,' she remarked, the anger in her quiet voice enough to make him raise his eyebrows. 'For what cause I was so imprisoned, God and Bolingbroke know; I do not.'

'There is no cause for you to be afraid,' he assured her.

'Afraid?' She flared up at once. 'Afraid? You mistake your woman, my lord, if you think I fear Harry of Lancaster. I intend to open my mind to him.'

'I pray you do not.' He paused, his face grim. 'I believe he wishes you no ill, Constance. You might do better to listen to what he has to say before you speak.'

The interior of the building was cool, pleasantly so after the heat of the day. Here and there men lounged against the elaborately painted walls, or played dice with one another in corners. Mun led her through the small crowd of idlers, across the hall, and up the broad flight of stairs to the Great Chamber. It was an immense room, scarcely smaller than the hall itself, hung with rich tapestries, including some that displayed King Richard's white hart and sunbursts, too splendid to be thrown away for the sake of imagery. There were two very large window embrasures and a central hearth, empty for the present, but with a louvre set above it for the escape of smoke. A few courtiers and servants stood idly by, including the chamberlain, Sir Thomas Erpingham, who bowed briefly in Constance's direction as if claiming an acquaintance. At the far end of the room was a dais, on which Bolingbroke's throne stood, and above it his cloth-of-estate.

The King, however, was on his feet, addressing himself to three men who knelt before him, heavy chains securing their hands and feet. They were Franciscan friars, their faces dark with stubble, their grey habits smeared with the filth of the dungeon from which they had been dragged. Constance caught Harry's words as he addressed himself to the leading friar, a short, middle-aged man with white-flecked hair and bright brown eyes.

'You, Roger Frisby, are a Doctor of Divinity. Is that not so?'

Frisby nodded. 'It is so, Sire. Also, for my sins, the warden of our house at Leicester.'

His mellow voice filled the room, all the way to the lofted roof, a voice accustomed to preaching.

'Then you should be a wise man. Yet you say that King Richard lives?'

Frisby shook his head. 'I say not that he lives, but *if* he lives, he is the true King of England.'

'He resigned.'

'He resigned while in prison, under duress. That has no validity in law.'

Harry paused. He had become aware of Constance's arrival in the hall, nodded an acknowledgement to her curtsey. Then he mounted the dais and rested his weight on the throne. His voice, when he spoke again, was full of forced patience. 'He resigned with a good will.'

'He would not have resigned if he had been at liberty, and a resignation made in prison is not made freely,' the friar argued, as composed as if they were discussing some abstruse academic point in the quiet of a university library.

Bolingbroke was growing weary of the game. 'He was deposed,' he returned irritably, leaning back in his place.

Frisby snorted. 'When he was King he was taken by force, and put into prison, and despoiled of his realm. And you have usurped the crown.'

Constance, barely able to control herself, let out a grunt of agreement. What a man this insignificant friar was, to speak such plain truth into Bolingbroke's face! How she longed to do the same! Kent, standing in silence next to her, threw her a glance that warned and implored her all at once.

'I was elected to the crown by Parliament,' Harry said brusquely, committing his last reserves of argument and patience.

The little man stood defiant in his chains, his eyes boring relentlessly into his opponent. 'The election counts for nothing, while the true and lawful possessor lives. If he is dead he is dead by your means, and if that is so you have lost all the right and title that you might have had to the crown.'

Bolingbroke had heard enough. He rose from his seat, stepped down from the dais, and seized the stubborn friar by the throat. 'By my head!' he vowed, 'you shall lose yours!' With a contemptuous, effortless push he sent Frisby sprawling on the tiles.

Constance made an instinctive movement forward, but found that somehow Kent had secured a tight grip on the back of her gown. 'Don't be a fool!' he warned, his voice low. 'These friars are traitors, and you and Edmund Mortimer are under suspicion. Will you make matters worse?'

The mention of Edmund's name brought her about. 'Is he here too?' she asked anxiously.

Kent released his hold. 'No. And it's as well for him that he's not. For Blessed Mary's sake, be careful of your words.'

'Lest Cousin Harry uses me as he did that holy man?'

'Holy men should not plot to murder their King.'

The friars were being dragged away by various of the King's servants, without excessive gentleness or ceremony. Roger Frisby was not quite finished though.

'You were ever an enemy of Holy Church!' he hurled at Bolingbroke. 'May you burn in hell for eternity.'

'Amen,' said Constance softly. But then her eyes went back to the King, and she saw from his agonised expression that some part of him was already there. He was visibly shaken, and by something as insubstantial as the friar's curse. It was suggestive, perhaps, of the state of his conscience.

'You lie!' he shouted after Frisby. 'You lie in your teeth!'

The silence that followed was intense, and it seemed to Constance that it lasted fully five minutes. She stood motionless and waited, listening to the sound of Kent's breathing. Eventually Erpingham moved towards Bolingbroke, and bowed formally.

'Sire,' he said, as a prompt. His voice was surprisingly gentle, emerging as it did from so grizzled a warrior. It was almost as if he was bending over his child's cradle.

Harry blinked, as if awakening from a bad dream. 'Will there never be an end to it?' he asked.

'Not until these friars be destroyed,' Erpingham answered, sounding more like his usual aggressive self. Then he quietened again, and went on. 'Your Grace, Lady Despenser is here.'

Bolingbroke seemed to recover his composure. He turned towards her, and advanced, even fashioning a smile of sorts. Constance repeated her curtsey, and waited to be addressed. He looks ill, she thought, ill and bone weary. Much changed since last I saw him. There's even grey in his hair, and he's not yet forty. The crown weighs heavy, Cousin? Not yet heavy enough! May it crush you beneath it, and may I be there to see it! God grant it so!

'Forgive me, Cousin, it was not my intention that you should witness the folly of those men,' he said.

Because you wished to spare my feelings, or because you knew there was truth in the friar's arguments? She did not express her thoughts, merely allowed them to be conveyed by her expression. 'Your Grace is all consideration,' she returned.

'Madame,' Erpingham said abruptly, 'you should know that we have uncovered a treasonous conspiracy against the King's life. These friars were only a small part of it. Many others were accused.'

'Including me, it seems!' Her sniff was eloquent, and her head tilted back. They had dared to call Richard a coward, but *he* had never gone in fear of friars or women.

Harry shrugged. 'I do not doubt your innocence, Constance, but there was no time to sift the evidence. This treason had to be nipped in the bud.' Unexpectedly he offered her his arm. 'This is no place to speak of it, before all. Come!'

In his privy chamber he seated her, and had Kent serve her wine and wafers from the cupboard while he himself explained the reason for her brief imprisonment. A priest, captured at Ware in Hertfordshire had revealed the plot of the Grey Friars, and accused many persons of involvement, including Constance, the Countess of Oxford, and Surrey's widow. All within reach had been arrested, as a pure precaution. Later, under questioning, the priest had admitted that most of those he had implicated were only *expected* to support the rising, and were not part of the conspiracy. He had been executed, and all those falsely accused had been released.

'I had you brought here because I wished to apologise for the injustice done to you,' he said. 'I hope I may make amends. As you know, I am to be married to the Duchess of Brittany. The Duchess will need guidance in our ways and it is my wish that you become the principal lady of her household. I can think of no one better fitted to the task, and it will please me greatly to have you back at court. You have hidden yourself in obscurity for too long; that's perhaps why you've been slandered. We are close in blood, and I wish to honour you.'

As well as keep me where you can have me spied upon, she thought. 'The honour is too great,' she suggested, trying to turn her words into a formula of refusal.

'It is my command, Cousin.' Suddenly the hardness was back in Harry's voice. 'There's no one else of fit rank, since there are good reasons why my sisters cannot live at court. As wives, they have duties to their husbands. You have none.'

'Cousin, you are well aware that it is my intent to be married,' Constance's voice took on its own harshness. 'I shall also be answerable to a husband before the Duchess arrives in England.'

He stared at her wordlessly for a moment, as if on the verge of a seizure. 'Is it possible that you speak of Edmund Mortimer?' he demanded.

'You know right well that I do. We have been waiting these many months for your permission, far longer than is reasonable. You've not even troubled to set a price for the licence.'

'You should thank me, for I have saved you from utter ruin! Were you his wife, you'd be lodged in a far worse place than the nunnery at Goring, and you'd be there for the term of his life. I delayed granting your licence of a purpose, out of concern for your welfare. I feared that Mortimer was false, and now he has proved it beyond any doubt. Has no one has told you what that traitor has done?' Bolingbroke's face was reddening with fury. 'Kent, did you not speak to her of Pilleth?'

Mun shook his head. 'No, Sire. I did not know whether you wished me to do so.'

'Then you must have the tale from me, Constance. This wretch you in your wisdom chose for husband raised an army in Herefordshire, and led it into an ambush. By incompetence or more likely with intent, since no sooner had Glyn Dwr struck than Mortimer's own Welsh archers turned on our loyal men and butchered them! Hundreds died. Hundreds of *Englishmen*.'

Constance stood up, though her shock was such that her feet would scarcely bear her. 'What you say is impossible. A lie. No man in his right mind would do such a thing, and Edmund Mortimer least of all. He has never done a dishonourable deed in his life.'

Bolingbroke snorted his derision. 'I've had the tale from the lips of those who were there with him, men who barely escaped with their lives. Men who crawled wounded into bushes and watched the rebels and their women slitting the throats of those who lay out in the open. Tell the widows and orphans of Herefordshire about Mortimer's bright honour! Will you make a saint of a man who has betrayed us all? Not me alone, or even his country, but his own levies! Men who trusted him and gave their lives! Unfortunately the rebels didn't slit *his* throat. He's Glyn Dwr's prisoner, or claims to be. And he may rot in Wales, for neither I or nor anyone of my allegiance shall offer a penny in ransom. I'll not give gold to my enemies.'

She could scarcely breathe, let alone speak. 'This is your justice? That you will not redeem a man of your own blood, captured while fighting in your cause? Who will be fool enough to fight your next battle for you? Knowing that if he fails he is likely to be a prisoner until he dies!'

He peered back at her, his eyes half closing as they tried to focus on her face. 'Edmund Mortimer is a traitor,' he pronounced. 'His land and goods are forfeit to the Crown, and if he ever comes before me again it will be to hear sentence of death passed upon him. There's no more to be said on the matter, so put him from your mind. There are other men in the world, better than he, and since your judgement is so fallible it may be that I shall choose one for you. It is evident to me that you require proper governance, a firm hand on the bridle to curb your tongue. For the present, Cousin, you may go.'

Constance considered a rejoinder. There would be satisfaction in telling him exactly what she thought of him, but the price for that satisfaction might be high. A return to confinement at Goring perhaps, or even something worse. Better to appear subdued and retain her liberty. Edmund had friends who would rally to his cause. Hotspur and Northumberland for two. Edward almost certainly a third. They could raise a ransom between them and defy Bolingbroke—they were rich and powerful enough. There was work to be done.

Outwardly douce, she curtsied to the very floor, and withdrew from the room without another word. Only the set of her lips and her faintly rising colour told the true tale.

30

The Duke of York had rallied sufficiently to make one last journey. He had wanted to visit King's Langley, where both his late Duchess and King Richard were buried in the Dominican Friary. His intent had been to pray by their tombs, but he was no sooner arrived at the nearby royal hunting lodge, his own birthplace, than he collapsed, and was carried to bed. There he lay, helpless, incapable of coherent speech. It was clear that he would not move again except to be carried in his own funeral procession.

Joanne and Constance stood on one side of the bed, Dickon on the other. They had run out of words, even of prayers. There was nothing to do now but watch. Constance had brought her children with her so that they might see their grandfather for the last time, but he had shown no least sign of recognition, and she had sent them away, tired, tearful and puzzled, to their beds. The long summer evening was tailing off into darkness. Silent yeomen of the household, uniformed in murrey-and-blue broadcloth, lit the candles and withdrew to the background, heads bowed, a motionless guard of honour awaiting orders. York's principal officers knelt at the foot of the bed, clutching their staves of office. Beside them were two of the Duke's chaplains and a local priest, their mouths moving ceaselessly as they brought forth their mumbled orisons.

Constance stole a glance at Dickon, and saw the carefully controlled gravity of his expression. He was barely seventeen, little more than a boy, and about to taste significant responsibility for the first time in his life. In Edward's absence the ordeal of being chief mourner would fall on him, and he would also have to pay off their father's household, settle any outstanding debts, and help Joanne secure her dower provision. All this duty for a father who had never cared for him and a brother who would not trouble to thank him, or even consider that thanks were due. He had not uttered a word of complaint, and was bearing himself in this crisis with a composed dignity that belied his inexperience. She was proud of him, the little brother suddenly grown to manhood.

She had intended to ask him to accompany her to Alnwick, to discuss the matter of Edmund's ransom with Northumberland and Hotspur. That was impossible now—he would be far too busy, and it would not be fair to trouble him with any additional burden. She would have to make her own case with the Percys; a difficulty, because old Northumberland was not apt to take ladies too seriously, and Hotspur was little better, if at all. It was unlikely they would accept that she was speaking for her two brothers as well as herself. She paused in her thoughts. Perhaps it was stretching the truth to pretend she would do so. She assumed that she had Edward's support in this, but assumptions about Edward were always hazardous.

However, there was no telling when Edward and Philippa would be able to return home. Letters might take weeks to reach Bordeaux if there were contrary winds, and even when he received the news Edward would not be able to lay down his responsibilities at a moment's notice. It might easily be Christmas before he was able to set foot in England again. She could not bear to sit idly at Caversham or Cardiff for five or six months while Edmund despaired in his Welsh prison. She had to make some attempt to help him, even if it meant presenting herself to Northumberland in the role of helpless supplicant.

Her straying thoughts returned to her father, and she issued a silent rebuke to herself for considering other matters at such a time. The Duke's breathing seemed to be growing shallower by the minute; occasionally there was an involuntary twitch of the lips, but no comprehensible sound emerged, only grunts. It was strange to think that she would never again hear his familiar voice, or feel the warmth of his smile. They had not always agreed with one another, not by any means, but she had never doubted his unconditional love. Another of the pillars that had supported her life was crumbling, and crumbling fast.

Constance still hoped against hope for some last words from her father, some small, additional memory to retain of him, but she hoped in vain. She watched as his life drained away, down to the final drop, then knelt with Joanne and prayed for his soul as the light gradually returned to the earth. It was the first day of August, a long day that would now seem endless.

***

Northumberland bowed his stiff back over Constance's hand. 'My lady, you do my poor house too much honour,' he said smoothly. 'May I offer you my condolences on the death of my lord your father? He was a better man than most, generous and free from malice. I am a beadsman for his soul.'

She inclined her head. 'You are gracious, my lord. However, I did not spend a fortnight and more on a horse's back to hear your kind words about my father, but to discuss the matter I opened in the letter I sent to your son last month. To which I have had no answer.'

He smiled indulgently. 'You must forgive our neglect, madame, but we have other business to occupy our minds. The small matter of repelling a Scottish army! My son is not here, unfortunately, though we expect him at any hour I hope we may make you comfortable, allow you time to recover from your uncomfortable journey. For the present, allow me to introduce a guest of mine.' He gestured towards a powerfully-built, dark-featured man who rested uneasily on the window-seat. 'The Earl of Douglas, most illustrious of the Scottish lords and knights we took prisoner last week at Homildon—and by far the richest. Douglas, this is the Lady Despenser, sister of the new Duke of York, and cousin of the King.'

The Scot offered her a grim smile. He had his left arm secured in a sling and was bandaged in half a dozen places, most notably across half his face. 'Even with the one eye that's left to me, I can see that England has its compensations,' he said gallantly. 'Forgive me, lady, that I do not rise as I ought. One of your English arrows landed in a place which makes movement uncomfortable.'

'You seem to have many wounds, my lord,' Constance said, surveying him. 'They speak of your courage.'

He uttered a brief laugh. 'A man has no choice but to have courage when he's pierced by a whole quiver of arrows! I never got close enough to strike a blow. I mislike your English way of fighting. In Scotland we prefer the sword or the axe, one man against another until the better prevails.'

Northumberland grunted. 'If you like not our English way of fighting, Douglas, you should not invade our land! We fight to win; not for ceremony or pleasure.'

Douglas licked his lips, evidently enjoying the controversy. 'Your King invaded Scotland two years ago, almost before his arse had warmed his throne! Are we not to repay the compliment? King Richard invaded us too, when I was no more than a wee laddie, and King Edward before him. It's an old tale, with no beginning and no end. We shouldna allow it to come between us and thoughts of our supper.'

The reference to supper was a clear hint, for the afternoon was already well advanced, the meal already under preparation. Constance excused herself, and went with her hostess, Elizabeth Percy, Hotspur's wife, to the chamber that had been made ready for her. It contained a huge bed, and the walls dripped with hunting scenes woven into green silk, but best of all was the bath that stood waiting. There were two weeks of dust and saddle-soreness to soak away, and Constance needed no urging to climb into it while it was still warm. Since there was ample room enough she invited a grateful Mary Russell to share the luxury, and they gleefully soaked themselves while Elizabeth and her ladies stood around them with towels and supplies of fresh clothing.

'You took a great risk, Cousin,' Elizabeth said anxiously. 'Half a dozen men are a scant escort with the Scots over the border.'

Constance had been so anxious to conceal her destination from the King's spies that she had never given a single thought to the Scots. She had stayed at Langley until after her father's month-mind, and then sent her children and almost all her travelling household back to Caversham. With only Mary, Hugh Tyldesley and a handful of yeoman servants to attend her, she had set out on an alleged pilgrimage to St. John's shrine at Beverley, deliberately concealing any hint of their identity under their mourning clothes. The journey to Alnwick had had its interesting moments, with nights spent gnawed by fleas in poverty-stricken convents, obscure manor houses, lonely cottages and disreputable ale-houses. There had been long fasts between simple meals, and endless days on horseback at the mercy of the hired local guides they had needed to steer them through the unknown territory north of York. But more often than not they had shared the company of other travellers for mutual protection and there had never been any hint of physical danger. Reflecting on it, she conceded that she had been complacent. Capture by the Scots would not have been amusing.

'It may be that I was foolhardy,' she admitted, 'but I thought it better that my visit here should not be trumpeted to the world. If we are to find a way to set your brother free from Glyn Dwr's prison, there may be some advantage in secrecy.'

'You've journeyed all this way for Edmund's sake?' Elizabeth seemed utterly astonished. It seemed that she was not one for bold plans and independent actions.

'I'd go much further than Alnwick for Edmund.' Constance paused for a moment, half smiling, awaiting a reaction that did not come. Her hostess seemed merely puzzled. 'Has your husband not told you what Edmund and I are to each other?'

Lady Percy snorted. 'Harry never thinks to mention such things. Besides, he's been busy with the Scots, and as for Edmund I've not had a letter from him in three years. I sometimes think he's forgotten that I'm alive.'

That surprised Constance; but then she remembered that Edmund was closer to Alianore than to either of his sisters, and always had been. He had told her himself that Elizabeth Percy was a virtual stranger to him. She thought she detected a hint of resentment in Elizabeth's voice, and wondered whether this mission might prove to be more complicated than she had supposed.

⁂

Harry Hotspur was home in good time for his supper. Though he had apparently spent all day riding around the county, there was no sign of that in his immaculate appearance. He bowed low over her hand as he raised it to his lips, and she noticed that a rich ring glistened on each one of his fingers, and the gold collar he wore, with its pendant of an enamelled Percy lion, was as good as anything in Bolingbroke's possession.

'My brother Mortimer has lingered too long in Glyn Dwr's prison, to the shame of all England,' he said, without preamble or greeting. His eyes flamed passion as he spoke. 'He shall be freed, and swiftly, with the King's leave or without it. I give you my pledge, lady.'

Constance wondered whether he had been drinking, but his breath carried no fumes to confirm the suspicion. It seemed that he was merely his usual outspoken self. She allowed him to lead her to the table, feeling rather under-dressed in his company in her simple mourning gown of black wool damask, though even that felt luxurious after so many days in travel-stained riding gear.

'Harry,' his father said, interrupting with a smoothness that all but hid his haste, 'such talk is best left until after we have eaten, I think. Lady Despenser is forspent after her long journey, and ought to be allowed some leisure to enjoy her supper.'

This represented a gross exaggeration of Constance's condition, and she was aware that the Earl knew it, and was merely seeking to ensure that his fiery son did not commit them before negotiations had even begun. She was seated at Northumberland's right, with Hotspur at her other hand. Lady Percy and Douglas made up the rest of the company at table, and the first course was digested in ceremonious silence, though Hotspur's restlessness was obvious. The squires and yeomen serving at the table did so with quiet efficiency, their blue and white Percy liveries so starkly clean as to suggest that they were newly issued. They fetched a profusion of dishes, nine for the first course alone, and the glass goblets were kept brimmed with Cyprus wine of the highest quality. However much the king owed the Percys, there was clearly no shortage of money at Alnwick.

Constance tried to think of a neutral topic that would appeal to Hotspur. 'You have other prisoners, apart from Lord Douglas?' she enquired.

He bellowed with laughter. 'More than you can count, madame. Many knights and lords among them.'

'But not here at Alnwick?'

'We have them spread about. Not too many eggs in one basket, if you take my meaning. Besides, not all are such good company as Douglas. Archie,' he went on, raising his voice so that it would carry to the Scot, 'my lady here would like to meet more of your countrymen. I've explained to her that you're the best of them. Certainly the only one I'd choose to have at my table.'

'You forget George Dunbar, Harry,' Douglas returned. 'Your ally, for all that he's a countryman of mine. A wee bird tells me that he claims much of the credit for your victory; that it was by his advice you let your archers finish us, instead of advancing and coming to blows.'

The Earl of Dunbar had switched to the English allegiance, not least because he and Douglas hated one another. He had fought on the same side as the Percys at Homildon, and then ridden off to the King to report the victory.

'Your little bird lies,' Hotspur retorted, rubbing his scar. He forced humour into his voice, but Constance recognised the anger in his eyes. 'My father and I need no Scot to direct us in the ordering of a battle.'

'Perhaps you did no good thing when you sent Dunbar to carry your news to King Bolingbroke?' Douglas suggested. He released an emphatic sigh. 'Dunbar will sing himself the hero of the tale, I've no doubt of that. He and your King are overly close, by all accounts.'

Hotspur fisted the table. 'They should be! They've much in common.'

'Harry,' Northumberland murmured, in quiet warning.

'Dunbar fancies himself rightful King of Scots,' Douglas went on amiably. 'Two kings together in England, and two in Scotland. For we have your King Richard—or one who claims his name.'

'Bolingbroke had Richard starved to death at Pontefract,' Hotspur objected. 'Your man is a fraud.'

'We can't be sure of that,' his father pointed out. 'What of the letters? The letters we've had that bear Richard's signet seal? Douglas, you have met this man. Tell us what you think of him.'

The Scot shrugged. 'He was found on Islay, of all places, in the Western Isles. Some woman said that she recognised him, having seen him in Ireland while he was there, and so he was brought to King Robert. I've seen the man, right enough, but whether he's your King Richard or not I could not swear.'

'I've never even heard of Islay,' Hotspur grunted. 'How could Richard find his way there? Why should he think of doing so? It makes no sense.'

'It makes *some* sense,' Northumberland allowed. 'Richard had dealings with Donald of the Isles; saw him as an ally against Scotland. In desperation, he might have sought refuge in those parts.'

'You're trying to salve your conscience, Father.' Hotspur leaned back in his chair so hard that it shifted beneath him. He sighed with explosive force. 'Face the truth. Richard is dead. We all know it in our hearts, and if we had any room for doubt Bolingbroke has plucked it out by refusing to ransom Edmund Mortimer. He dreads the Mortimer claim to the throne, not Richard's return from the grave.'

'Between us we could surely raise sufficient to bring Edmund home,' Constance suggested. 'I know that my brother York would contribute a sum, and I have money of my own. With your help—'

'I fear it is impossible,' Northumberland said gently.

'Douglas's ransom alone would more than cover it,' Hotspur contradicted. 'Why should it be impossible? We speak of my wife's brother! I will have him free if it costs us all we gained at Homildon and more besides.'

'It's not a matter of money. The King has forbidden it.'

'You go in fear of Bolingbroke? We made him King. We can also *unmake* him! Besides, having saved his kingdom from invasion he owes us a debt, apart from the twenty thousand pounds that are due to us.'

'How shall it profit Edmund Mortimer to come home to a land where he has been declared traitor?' Northumberland shook his head, his long grey hair shaking like a mane. 'Think, Harry! If we buy him back, where will he end? In the Tower at best, if not kneeling for the block. Will you spend our money for that? Will you, madame?'

Constance hesitated, gave herself time to think. 'If Edmund's friends stood behind him, could the King outface them all? I doubt it. He does not sit so secure upon his throne that he can afford to murder another of his cousins. There would have to be a trial, at the least, and for that there would have to be a charge. What charge? It can't be called treason to lose a battle.'

'So you would have us defy the King? Bring his wrath upon our heads? For Edmund Mortimer?'

'I don't go in fear of Bolingbroke!' Hotspur snapped. 'The lady is right. Let's ransom Mortimer, and dare anyone to touch him. He can roost here awhile, out of harm's way. Lancaster would as gladly walk barefoot to Cathay as challenge us in our own country. The very thought would make him soil himself.'

'He is no coward, Harry. Whatever else. No fool either. Shrewd enough to deceive us with his lies at Doncaster.'

Constance was distracted by a sudden stir of activity by the door, which she presumed was the arrival of the second course. One of Northumberland's household officers approached the table, bowed low before his lord.

'My lord, a messenger from the King,' he announced.

The messenger was already over the threshold. Constance knew him at once, Elming Leget, the man who had arrested her at Caversham, and from the quick glance he threw at her saw that the recognition was mutual. All her careful secrecy had been in vain.

Leget came forward, made his reverence to the Earl. 'My lord,' he began, 'the King has received news of your victory, and is greatly pleased thereby. I bear his letter of congratulation to you; also your summons to the Parliament at Westminster. The King expects you to bring the prisoners before it.'

'Perhaps to make a parade with the many he himself captured in Wales,' Hotspur suggested, his tone contemptuous.

'There were few prisoners of note taken in Wales,' Leget answered stiffly. 'Such as fell into the King's hands were executed as traitors, or pardoned, according their merits.'

'You give us news, man! Are we to gather that Glyn Dwr was not among those taken?'

'You, Sir Harry, know as well as any man of the difficulties of making war in Wales. The weather fought against the King, as well as the Welsh. However, many cattle were driven off, and without their animals the rebels will be driven to starvation.'

Northumberland had broken the seal of Bolingbroke's letter, and was scanning the writing, holding it close. 'The King,' he said, with studied calm, 'instructs us not to ransom our prisoners without his leave. They are to be handed over to him. He says that he will give us money in return.'

'Out of the profits of his Welsh wars, no doubt?' Hotspur enquired. He paused, and then broke out into a disbelieving laugh. 'Where will his money come from? Out of the air? Is he not already sufficiently in our debt? The man thinks to make fools of us again!'

'It is his right to claim the prisoners,' the Earl answered solemnly. 'I do not like it, but we cannot justify refusal. Only insist on due payment.'

His furious son rose to his feet. 'He shall not have Douglas!' he roared. 'Never! Not while he leaves Mortimer rotting in a Welsh prison.' He turned on the white-faced Leget. 'Tell him that, little man. Tell him exactly that!'

***

If the Welsh campaign had not been a disaster, it had certainly been a debacle. Lack of funds had forced repeated postponements and inadequate provision for supply, and at the last moment a portion of the men assembled had had to be diverted north, to counter the threat from Scotland. The three armies had at last entered Wales as arranged. One from Hereford under the earls of Stafford, Arundel and Warwick; another from Chester commanded by the Prince; the main force from Shrewsbury led by Bolingbroke himself. No sooner were they over the border than rain deluged on them, even worse weather than that of the previous year. The columns struggled on into the hills, but there was no food and very little sign of life. Defeated by the conditions, not by Glyn Dwr, they withdrew to their bases with hardly a blow struck.

Bolingbroke sensed that people were laughing at him behind his back, comparing his miserable failure to the glorious success of the Percys. It made him the more determined to show that he was master. Northumberland had brought all his prisoners to Parliament. All save one, and that one was the sticking point. The King demanded that Douglas be surrendered, and in return received nothing more than an assurance that Hotspur was on his way, that Hotspur would explain all.

He waited impatiently. Northumberland was outwardly submissive, but there was something in his eye that gave room for doubt. Harry sent for Elming Leget, had him repeat again all that he had heard and seen at Alnwick. Made him confirm that Constance of York had been there, that he had not mistaken some northern lady for her. Puzzled endlessly over the implications.

Westminster was bleak, the river almost black beneath the rain that bounced from its surface. It seemed to Bolingbroke that the weather had followed him from Wales, that it too was mocking him. He had caught a chill, and wanted nothing more than to go to bed with heated bricks and spiced wine. However, a king could not very well discipline an erring noble from his sickbed. It would make him look ridiculous. Instead he sat by the fire, and read a favourite book, candles burning around him so that he had sufficient light. It was mid afternoon, but as dark as night. Eventually his eyes grew weary, and he persuaded Kent to read to him, forcing himself to endure the painful rhythm of a text enunciated without enthusiasm or real understanding.

At last Hotspur arrived, stalking in as if entering the common room of a low-class inn, and making a perfunctory reverence. Behind him was his uncle, Worcester, but there was no sign of the Earl of Douglas.

Harry drew himself up in his chair, forcing his back against it. 'You may bring in your prisoner,' he said coldly. 'Then you may explain why he was not delivered with the others, as I commanded.'

'Douglas is not here,' Hotspur answered. 'Nor will he be. He is my prisoner, not yours.'

'You dare to defy me?' Harry spoke quietly. He could scarcely believe his own ears, preferred to believe that he had misunderstood the other man's meaning.

'Say I hold him as security for the debts you owe us. Pay what is due to my father, my uncle and myself.' The sneer that contorted Hotspur's face left no room for misunderstanding. Worcester grinned in the background, as if enjoying the scene. 'Redeem my brother Mortimer from captivity, as you ought. Then you may have Douglas. Only then.'

'I demand that you surrender Douglas to me at once. On your allegiance. I will go so far as to overlook your present disobedience, and your insolence, if you will give me your word that he shall be delivered to me.'

'I do not take oaths unless I mean to fulfil them,' Hotspur answered. 'Unlike some I could name! In this present Parliament you have agreed to ransom your friend, Grey de Ruthin, the fool who began this trouble in Wales. That being the case, you have no just pretext to leave Mortimer a prisoner.'

'We are not your slaves, Sire,' Worcester put in.

'You are my subjects!'

'And as such have rights, as confirmed by your coronation oath.'

'I will not send gold to my enemies. How dare you ask it of me! How dare you refuse my express command!'

'Shall a man expose himself to danger for your sake, and you refuse to help him in his captivity?' Hotspur demanded. 'You'll send gold to buy back Grey. Or allow it to be sent. God forbid you should part with money of your own!'

'Mortimer was a traitor, who yielded himself by consent to Glyn Dwr.' Harry rose to his feet. 'And you are a traitor too! If you were not you'd have captured Glyn Dwr when you had the chance—you were in secret conference with him more than once. To what end? Not to my profit, I'll swear, or to that of my realm. Rebel and friend of rebels! Traitor!' In fury he struck Hotspur across the face. Drew his dagger on him. Then realised what it was that he had done.

The room was filled with awed silence. Bolingbroke stood open mouthed, his hand still sore from the force of the blow he had struck, his blade all but sliding from his fingers. He watched as the red imprint he had left on Percy's face spread and darken.

Hotspur explored his cheek with the kind of tenderness he would have applied to his wife's breast, almost as if he was making sure that it was still there.

'Struck!' he uttered at last. He exchanged a glance with Kent, and with his uncle, as if seeking confirmation of the event. 'By Christ, that shall be the dearest-bought blow that was ever given in England!'

'This is not the place to quarrel, Harry,' Worcester said, his voice soothing. 'Not the place, and not the time.'

'You are right, Uncle,' Hotspur said abruptly, spinning on his heel and making no attempt at any obeisance. 'Not now, not here; but in the field!'

31

Richard of Coniobrough stood with his back to the fire, mulled wine in hand, his sodden cloak cast aside, and steam rising from the thick woollen houppelande that had failed to protect against the storm. He looked as if he had just been pulled out of the Thames. Anne Mortimer, whom he had brought with him from Fotheringhay, was no less soaked, having been fool enough to ride pillion behind him instead of making use of the carriage Joanne had provided for her journey. She had already been sent away, in Agnes' care, to be stripped and dried and put to bed with a posset.

Constance watched her brother for a little while, stirring in her chair as the draught from the parlour window touched the back of her neck with the chill intensity of a ghost's caressing fingers. His taciturn nature had always been a source of wonder to her.

'The Duchess is well?' she prompted, giving up her hope that he might break the silence.

'Very well.' He paused for a moment, lowering his head as if to inspect his riding boots. 'They say she's to marry Willoughby in the spring.'

'Do they indeed? What does Joanne say?'

He shrugged, and a large raindrop tumbled from his nose, landed somewhere in his wispy, dark-brown stubble. 'She says it's what the King wishes. That she has no option but to accept.'

Constance moved her lands from her lap to the carved arms of her chair. 'He has no right to compel her.'

He shrugged again. 'I don't say that he does. But what choice has she? She's been granted her dower, but there's only Sandal that's a fit place for her to keep a household. The rest of her manors have no decent house, or are leased out. Would you want to live in the wilds of Yorkshire? Or at Fotheringhay, with our sister Philippa ruling over it? I dare say Joanne prefers Willoughby! He's not so ill a man.'

'He's Bolingbroke's lackey. One of the first to rally to him when he landed in England. Now given his reward, a third of the York lands while she lives. I thought better of Joanne than that she would allow herself to be so used.' She stared into the fire, her anger as warm as the reddest coal, for she remembered the King's threat to her at their last meeting, and this of her stepmother struck uncomfortably close to home. Her position was actually weaker than the Duchess's. Lacking the security of dower lands, she was merely a tenant-at-will, however handsome her present income. 'I wish I'd married Edmund while I had the chance. Not even Bolingbroke could ask me to commit bigamy.'

Her brother did not answer, merely continued to drip onto the heraldic floor tiles. In the silence she brooded on Mortimer, wondering where he was, whether he was being well used. There was no saying where Glyn Dwr was holding him. In a cave perhaps, or some hole in the ground. The rebels had no proper base. They'd be dragging him around with them from place to place, like an animal. He'd been a prisoner for almost six months now, and it seemed like an eternity since she had seen him.

Hotspur had sent word to Glyn Dwr, offering to negotiate ransom in despite of the King, but so far there had been no response. She had hoped that Edmund might be home for Christmas, but that seemed unlikely now. The injustice of it rankled, knowing as she did that Grey de Ruthin was at liberty again, much thinner of purse, admittedly, but doubtless as loud and aggressive as ever.

'Still no word from our brother,' Dickon remarked suddenly.

'No.' She answered without being sure of his words, such had been her pre-occupation.

'I suppose I shall have to live where he bids me. In his household, perhaps.'

'Yes. Though you've money of your own, Dickon, and you're a man. That gives you more freedom than I shall ever know.'

'Money?' he grinned sheepishly. 'I've had nothing from the Exchequer these last twelve months and more. The little I had by me is gone. My servants have had most of it, and I'm still in their debt. You're the one with money, Constance. I hoped I might rely on your charity, for it'll be a thin Christmas for me if you turn me away. I've already pawned such jewels as I have. That raised a couple of pounds.'

She stared at him in disbelief. 'You mean that Bolingbroke has not honoured your annuity? Have you reminded him that you're his cousin, and that it's your only livelihood?'

'No one is getting paid, as I understand.'

'Someone must be. He has all the crown revenues, the special taxes, all the Lancaster properties, and half the Bohun lands. He even had the gall to ask for a feudal aid for his daughter's marriage last year! Our Cousin Richard cannot have had anything like his income, and yet he always found your five hundred marks. It's a deliberate insult.'

'Then he's insulting half England. May I stay here?'

She nodded briefly. 'Of course you may. You're my brother, and while I've a roof over my head there'll always be one over yours. That isn't the point.' Her hands went back to her lap, plucked at the sable velvet of her skirts, adjusting their hang to her satisfaction. 'Do you not see? This is Bolingbroke's way of saying that we are *nothing*. He'll not be content until he's made us his slaves, crawling to beg for the scraps from his table.'

His eyes flickered around the room, taking in the rich hangings, the gilt candelabra that stood on the dresser, her sumptuous mourning dress and jewelled cincture. 'You seem to be some way from starvation, Sister,' he remarked dryly.

'I've no security in it, Dickon. It could all be taken from me tomorrow. Father used to protect my interests, but I can't rely on Ned to do the same. You know I can't. My husband is dead, and Edmund lost in Wales. Bolingbroke has already had me locked up in a convent once, on mere suspicion. Or perhaps to amuse himself. Am I really better placed than you are? At least, if all else failed, you could go abroad and sell your sword. I do not have that option.'

He rubbed his chin as if wishing to emphasise his need for a shave. 'Are you ill, Constance? You don't sound like yourself.'

'I've been thinking about these things, since I came home from the North. Our father used to warn me that I was vulnerable, and I begin to see that he was right. I may not show my fear to the world, but that doesn't mean I don't feel it.'

Dickon grimaced. Taking in the fact the room was growing so dark that he could barely make out her face, he selected one of the candles, held its wick in the fire until it caught, and then used it to light the others, one by one. 'I'm sure Ned will do what he can for you,' he said.

Constance remained less than sure. 'You may as well close the shutters, while you're about it,' she suggested. 'It'll be full dark in a hour, and, besides, it'll help to keep out the cold.'

He walked briskly to the window, slammed the first of the internal shutters into place, the candlelight reflecting faintly against its red and gold paintwork. 'Perhaps this will clear by the morning,' he suggested hopefully. 'It's too fierce to last long. I'm glad to be out of it; I'd begun to think we might be drowned, or frozen, up on the ridge. Anne was brave, though. She never murmured.'

'She wouldn't. Anne isn't the complaining kind.'

'The Duchess is very fond of her.'

'We're all fond of her, Dickon.'

He paused, bolted another of the shutters. 'I've been thinking that it's time I had some experience in the field,' he announced. 'Perhaps in Wales, fighting the rebels. Do you think there's any chance that Lord Charlton might find a use for me?'

She raised her head sharply. 'It would not be fitting for you to sign indentures to serve him. Remember, you're the Duke of York's brother and heir, and cousin to the King. Edward Charlton is worthy of respect, but he is not your equal, still less your superior.'

He moved back to her side. 'I don't mean to become his retainer and wear his livery. I thought rather to fight at his side, as a friend, without pay. Surely there could be no objection to that?'

'No,' she conceded. 'You're right to want to prove yourself as a warrior, and Charlton may well be glad of another sword.'

'I might hope to gain his good will. I need a better horse, though.'

'I can lend you the money for that.'

'And some pieces of armour.'

She gave him her hand. 'There's no need to stint yourself. Buy whatever you need, and repay me when you can.'

The rare, delighted smile that crossed his face was repayment enough. He was still finding the words to thank her when Hugh Tyldesley opened the door and stepped inside.

'My lady—' he began.

The intended announcement was cut short as a saturated Harry Hotspur pushed past him. 'There is news from Wales,' he said, in his loud, abrupt voice. He tore off his riding gloves and cloak, threw them backwards in the general direction of his attending squire, who had to stoop to retrieve them from the floor. 'News you must hear—it changes everything.'

'Please sit down, Cousin,' Constance suggested, indicating the chair opposite to her.

Hotspur shook his head. 'I've had sitting enough today, on my horse. Edmund isn't a prisoner any more.'

She leapt to her feet, narrowly resisting the temptation to enfold him in her arms. 'You've ransomed him? He's on his way home.'

'I haven't ransomed him. No one has. He's come to terms with Glyn Dwr. Joined him in his rebellion.'

'*Joined* him? That's unbelievable. The Mortimers have great lands in Wales. Glyn Dwr is as much their enemy as he is Bolingbroke's. The enemy of all things English. It makes no sense. It must be a mistake.'

Hotspur shook his head, cleared his throat by spitting into the fire. He opened his purse and drew from it a piece of folded parchment, which he opened out and put into her hands. It was a letter, and she saw at once that it was in Edmund's own script. It began:

> 'Very dear and well-beloved, I greet you much and make known to you that Owain Glyn Dwr has raised a quarrel of which the object is, if King Richard be alive, to restore him to his crown; and that if not that, my honoured nephew, who is the right heir to the said crown, shall be King of England, and that the said Owain will assert his right in Wales. And I, seeing and considering that the said quarrel is good and reasonable, have consented to join in it, and to aid and maintain it, and by the grace of God to a good end, Amen. I ardently hope, and from my heart, that you will support and enable me to bring this struggle of mine to a successful issue.'

'He has sent this to all his friends in the Marches, and to some who are not his friends,' Hotspur said. 'I would that your brother of York were here, for this gives us much to discuss.'

Constance left the rest of the letter unread, handed it back. 'He's ruined himself,' she said helplessly. 'He can never come back, after this. He's made himself an outlaw.'

'He was that before, and it was Bolingbroke who did the making.' Hotspur paced about as if he could no longer contain his energy. He nodded briefly in Dickon's direction. 'Of course he can come home, and to greater prosperity than before. But not while Bolingbroke lives. Lord Richard, will you and your brother join me in making an end to this so-called King?'

Dickon was out of his depth. 'I cannot speak for my brother,' he mumbled.

'Our brother York has no more cause to love Bolingbroke than any of us,' Constance rejoined, 'but this of Glyn Dwr makes matters difficult. To remove a usurper is one thing; to make common cause with Welsh rebels another. I can scarcely believe that Edmund has been so unwise.'

Hotspur grunted. 'Lady, what choice had he? Even if we'd paid his ransom, he'd never have been safe while Bolingbroke reigned. His only option now is to put another King on the throne, whatever the cost. I intend to help him. With or without the assistance of the House of York!' He threw himself down on the spare chair with a force that made its woodwork creak in protest. Paused for a moment before continuing, his voice softer. 'There's more that I must tell you. It won't please you, but you've the right to know. Edmund has had to commit himself to Owain with more than words. As part of the agreement between them, he has married one of Glyn Dwr's daughters.'

Constance shook her head in disbelief. 'That is impossible,' she got out. 'A lie. He *could* not.'

There was something in Hotspur's eyes that she had never seen before. Pity. 'He had no other way,' he said bluntly. 'Surely you understand that? What had he to bargain with, except himself? See, I have another letter here, intended for you. It will explain all.'

He delved into his purse again, produced a second folded parchment, this with its seal intact. He held it out towards her, and she was vaguely aware of her fingers closing on it, the death warrant of all her hopes. Her eyes swam for a moment, and then she focused on the seal, and saw that it was Edmund's. She stood transfixed, clutching the letter, praying that there was some error, some misunderstanding.

'I think my sister might prefer to read Mortimer's letter in private,' Dickon said. He took a step forward, directed a meaningful glance towards the door.

Hotspur shrugged apologetically. 'Of course.' He rose to his feet, sketched an awkward bow. 'If it's any comfort, my lady, I doubt whether any man captured in war has ever had to pay so grievous a ransom. As for myself, I'd sooner have lost a thousand pounds than brought this news to you. Forgive me.'

'There is nothing to forgive.' Constance scarcely recognised the sound of her own bitter voice. She drew back her arm and hurled the letter to the back of the fire. 'No fault of yours if I was witless enough to believe Edmund Mortimer a man of honour. It seems that I am just another of his many whores.'

'God help the man who names you so in my presence,' Hotspur answered, almost gentle. 'The shame is Bolingbroke's, for leaving Edmund a prisoner, forcing his hand. Remember that always.'

Constance ignored him. 'Tyldesley,' she ordered, 'see that Sir Harry and his men have all that they require for their comfort. Lord Richard also.'

She pushed past them, blindly followed her feet along the hall passage and out into the porch. Out in the courtyard the rain was still teeming onto the cobbles, bouncing off them in splashes that rose a full six inches, and torrents poured from every roof. She watched in bewildered fascination for a moment, then stepped out into the storm, the rain mingling with her tears, rendering them invisible.

The stables were busy. Hotspur's horses and her brother's were being rubbed down, fed, and provided with blankets. No one noticed her arrival, and she had to raise her voice to gain attention. The grooms were surprised to see her there at all, astonished when she told them to saddle her jennet, astounded that she spoke no word of horses for her escort. However, they did as they were told.

'Shall one of us come with you, my lady?' the eldest asked.

She shook her head, scarcely able to speak. 'No one can come with me, Peter. Just lead her to the mounting block. After that I can shift for myself.'

She had brought no cloak to protect herself from the worst of it, and by the time she had settled in the saddle and taken up the reins she was already soaked to the skin. The gates stood open, as they always did during the day, and she rode out through them into the gathering darkness, allowing the horse to take her where it would. It selected the Oxford road, climbing steadily north, away from the river, the same way that she and Thomas had travelled on their pilgrimage to Walsingham.

It seemed a lifetime ago. She had been happy then, prosperous, and secure. Full of hope. Thomas would never have abandoned her, no matter what the alternative. He'd have died first. His love had been complete, no mere matter of words and promises. When she had lost him, she had lost all.

Near the top of the hill she halted, remembering the beautiful view that they had enjoyed on that day together, all the way to the towers of Reading Abbey and beyond. Now all was darkness and driving rain. The abbey bells tolled faintly in the distance, as though struggling to call her back.

She would, she decided, go to Goring. This time of her own free will. The canonesses had been kindly enough. She'd offer herself as a servant, accept whatever lowly tasks she was given. Spend the rest of her time praying for Thomas, her father, and King Richard. It would be easier so, in the end. She might even find contentment in such a life.

She knew the way to Goring, but somehow, for the present, her mind could not focus on it. So she sat her horse alone at the edge of the empty road, while the rain poured down upon her head, and dripped from the heavy branches of the bare, black trees, and she wept her heart out.

***

Constance was with her council at Cardiff. She was faintly conscious of the droning voices of her advisers, but her attention had wandered from the tedium of a routine discussion of her affairs in Oxfordshire. Her receiver there, John Snede, had not been able to satisfy the audit of his accounts, and not for the first time. A substantial sum was missing, and there was little choice but to dismiss Snede and arrange for his prosecution. The talk had moved on from possible alternatives to this course of action, and was concentrating on potential replacements for Snede.

The loss was unfortunate, for it had come at a bad time. She had never realised just how many castles were under her control until she had been forced to garrison them in the face of the mounting threat from Glyn Dwr. Soldiers, now that there was a demand for their services, were not cheap to hire. An archer cost six pence a day in wages alone, so a meagre half dozen, to hold a small castle like her outlying property at Ewyas Lacey, meant an expenditure of over a pound a week. The garrison at Cardiff, which included expensive specialist gunners, cost so much to maintain that she didn't care to think about it. She still had considerable reserves, but her funds were draining fast.

The Mortimer cincture could have bought her many soldiers, but she no longer had it. She had wanted very much to throw it in the Thames, but in the end she had told Tyldesley to take it into Reading, sell it for what it would fetch, and divide the proceeds equally between the monks of Reading and the canonesses of Goring. The sale price had not been as much as she had expected, but each House had sent her a warm letter of appreciation, the abbot even going so far as to deliver it in person and give her his blessing. A minor comfort in the circumstances.

It was Tyldesley who had found her on that awful night, persuaded her back with talk of her children, and a blunt reminder of her duty. He had been furious with her and also, she knew, deeply concerned for her welfare, had used words to her that she had never heard on his lips, before or since. They had not spoken of her folly again, and she had not, despite Agnes' predictions, caught her death of cold. She was not sure when she would return to Caversham. Her memories of the place were still agonisingly raw, and for the present at least she was more comfortable at Cardiff.

'There remains the matter of the King's Ogmore tenants,' John St. John said, breaking into her thoughts. 'The King has again demanded that they be released, ignoring the answer that was made to him. I suggest they are not worth the trouble, that they are better let go.'

Tyldesley poured himself ale from the black leather jack that stood on the table before him. 'The pity is that they weren't hanged straightaway. Your job as sheriff, Sir John. Instead of leaving them lolling about in the gaol. What were you hoping for? Ransom?'

'The Bailiff of Ogmore intervened too swiftly. He was bound to take the matter to higher authority, to the Chancellor of the Duchy at least. He told us so. To have hanged them in such circumstances would have been folly. They're men of some substance. Stradling knows one of them. Even offered to stand surety for the man.'

'I thought we were supposed to be suppressing Welsh rebels, not encouraging them.' Tyldesley took a swig of the ale, scowled at the taste, and wiped his mouth with the back of his hand. 'They *are* Welsh, aren't they?'

'Yes, but not necessarily rebels.'

'Just thieves, you mean?'

'It's plain folly for her ladyship to quarrel with the King over such a trifling matter. It's not even as if the cattle were hers. They were taken from a tenant of my niece, Lady Norreys. The man has even got most of his animals back again.'

Constance spoke for the first time since the beginning of the meeting. 'Can anyone tell me why the King has taken a personal interest in these men?'

No one could.

'They are his tenants,' suggested Thomas Sprotley, drawing the air through the gaps in his teeth. His pockmarked face bore its usual expression of deep solemnity. He was one of the Glamorgan officers, Constable of Kenfig Castle, a remote, sand-blown hold by the sea at the western end of the lordship. The men of Ogmore were his neighbours, or were when he was at Kenfig. Until recently he had treated his office as something of a sinecure.

'Lady Norreys's land is a good way from the boundary with Ogmore. Where were they captured?'

'Close to the boundary, my lady.' That was John St. John again. 'Very close.'

'Which side of it?'

They shuffled uncomfortably. 'Difficult to say,' Sprotley grunted. 'A few yards, one way or the other.'

Ogmore was an anomaly, surrounded by Glamorgan on three sides and by water on the fourth, a small but significant Lancastrian enclave, part of the Duchy. It was a source of endless trouble, with criminals crossing the boundary in both directions to avoid justice in one or other of the jurisdictions. That its lord was now King made matters more complicated still.

'Advise me on the custom of the March,' Constance said. 'My understanding has always been that boundaries can be crossed, in a case of hot pursuit. Is it not so?'

'It is not *quite* so simple as that,' sighed St. John. 'There are exceptions and reservations. In this case such niceties are unimportant. You cannot treat the King as you would another neighbour.'

'If the matter is complicated, and delicate because of the King's interest, we must be careful. Do you agree, Sir John?'

'Of course.'

'So these men stay where they are, while our men of the law consider the matter in more detail, and prepare proper advice.' She thought briefly of her gaol, the fetid vault beneath the Black Tower, and twitched her nose at the mere thought of its stench. 'Whatever befalls, that should be punishment enough.'

'But the King's direct command, my lady—'

'It is contrary to the liberties of Glamorgan. At least, I judge it so. We have a duty to resist such encroachments.' She stood up in her place. 'Enough for today, gentlemen. The decision is made.'

***

'To the right noble and excellent lady, the Dame Le Despenser.

'Madame, I recommend me to you, and understand that you hold certain Welshmen in your prison, tenants of our dread lord the King. It so befell that I was in his Majesty's high presence when he was given to know that you had not released them in accordance with his command, at which he grew so wrath that he was fit to play Herod in a Corpus Christi play. After which many words were spoken that were not to your profit.

'I counsel you therefore, that you release these men, or bring them to his presence as he has commanded, or I fear that matters will go very ill for you.

'Written in haste, and in my own poor hand for default of a clerk, by your loyal friend while he lives...

'Edmund, Earl of Kent.'

Constance paced the length of her solar. Her children watched with undisguised interest, sensing her change of mood, while her women kept their heads low over their various tasks and amusements, having recognised from her expression that the change would not be for the better.

Tyldesley had brought Kent's messenger upstairs to her. She thrust the letter into his hands for him to read.

'This beggars belief,' she said angrily.

He nodded, turned the parchment over in his hands as if he expected to find a postscript. 'I wonder that the King has no greater matters on his mind,' he grunted, 'that he should trouble himself about three Welshmen of no account, thrown into prison for good cause and lucky not to have been hanged.'

'It makes no sense.' Constance halted in her pacing, took the letter back from him. Kent's scrawl was the next thing to illegible, but even at second reading there was no possible doubt as to his meaning. 'I suppose it must be that they are his tenants, and that he holds me in such contempt he will allow no justice to be done against them by me and mine. I will *not* release them. They shall walk in chains to wherever he is to be found. If he insists on setting thieves free, then so be it, and let the fault lie with him. For my part, I shall give plain orders that, once home, they'll be hanged if they as much as set foot on a Glamorgan road again. We'll say that they were rousing the people to join Glyn Dwr.'

Next morning she began her journey eastward, not moving her main household but taking a modest escort of some forty persons, with her son riding at her side, acting as page, and the three Welsh prisoners walking at the rear of the procession, behind a cart, where they could best enjoy the dust.

The court was lodged in and around Reading Abbey, and so Constance found herself back at Caversham after all, and was surprised to find that she was not uncomfortable there, that the shock of Mortimer's betrayal was already fading. It was still her home, still filled with pleasant memories that outweighed the bad.

She was kept waiting for three days, then summoned before the Council, the King evidently having other things to do than hear her arguments. The venue was the abbey chapter house, a vast vaulted room that dwarfed her and the half a dozen counsellors assembled to interrogate her. Edward of York was among those present, but offered no encouragement, indeed did not say a word throughout. She was asked some very awkward questions, and her protests and explanations were swept aside. It was held that the King's tenants had been imprisoned without cause, and their immediate release was ordered.

Constance was outraged. 'Is the world run mad?' she demanded of Agnes Norreys as they walked away from the chapter house. 'Are Welsh thieves to be valued above me, the King's own cousin? Those men *laughed* at me! The Council, I mean, not the thieves. As for my brother York, I know not what to say of him! I've not seen him for more than a year, and yet he didn't aid me with a single word. Just sat there like a block of wood!'

Agnes was far too wise to reply. She had known Constance quarrel with Edward before, only to eat from his hand a month later. She also knew something of Edward's worth.

'We shall go back to Cardiff first thing in the morning,' Constance continued, in the same ringing tones. 'Since Bolingbroke has not deigned to receive me, I see no cause to ask for his leave to go from court.'

The necessary packing was already taking place at Caversham when the Earl of Kent rode into the courtyard, bringing with him a small tail of followers, some in his livery, some in that of the King. It was a chill, winter afternoon, the grass still white with frost, steaming clouds of breath emerging from men and horses alike.

Constance was glad enough to see Mun Holland, because she had not had a chance to thank him for the good intent of his letter.

He shrugged. 'I hope I am your friend, my lady. It was a friend's duty to give a warning in such a case. The King was beside himself. Spoke of taking from you all that you have, of lodging you in the Tower. I had no wish to see that.'

She settled herself on the window-seat, invited him to sit next to her, and had her son pour them wine.

'He's a fine boy,' Mun said, raising his goblet in salute.

'His father was a fine man.'

'Yes.' He pushed the skirt of his heavy, furred houppelande to one side, scratched vigorously at his thigh through his taut blue hose. She could not but note how muscular his legs had grown, and how long and well-shaped they were. 'Constance, you should know that the King has sent me to you. He wishes to remind you that he has appointed you to the Queen's household, and you are expected to go with us to meet her at Winchester. Now that you're here, he desires you to stay with the court.'

She felt the anger burning in her throat again, but bit at her lip, and slowly gained control of herself. 'I do not understand,' she got out. 'The King *hates* me. He will not even uphold my rights against cattle thieves. Why does he want me where he will have me under his eye every single day of our lives?'

She watched as Kent struggled with the proposition. 'I don't know,' he admitted. 'What does it matter? You must see that you've no choice.'

It seemed to Constance that the room was filled with a very special silence, a silence so intense she could hear her own heart and her own breathing. 'I see it perfectly,' she said at last.

32

The bright May morning was full of promise, the fringe of elms and beeches to the East filtering the sun as it warmed the gardens at Easthampstead into life and cleared the dew from the lawns. The chill, cloudless night was over; summer had returned in glory.

Constance sat on the window-seat of the room she had been allocated, her veiling stirred by the mild breeze that entered through the open casement. Though her hands were occupied by the shirt she was mending for her son, her stitching was haphazard, her mind troubled by the latest letters that had arrived from Glamorgan. Sir John St. John reported that he had been driven from his own castle at Fonmon by rebels, and forced to take refuge within the walls of Cardiff. The Norreys manor at Penllyn had been sacked, the Bishop's palace at Llandaff put to the torch, and the Despenser manor of Roath devastated, its valuable cattle driven off. Cardiff itself was now virtually in a state of siege, though it was quite safe, since it could be supplied from the sea. William Stradling, who was not one of her regular correspondents, reported himself and his family on the verge of destruction at St. Donats, and blamed the disaster that was facing them all on John St. John's incompetence. He advised her, in blunt terms, to appeal to the King to send a relieving force to save what was left. Moreover, she ought to appoint a new sheriff of Glamorgan. He suggested that Sir William Stradling might be a suitable choice. In the spirit of public service he would even accept a smaller fee than was customary.

'We had a hard winter in Wales,' Alianore said, breaking the pause in their conversation. 'In Powys the snow was thick on the ground for weeks; even the rivers were solid in places. Not that it stopped the raiding. Nothing does. I don't know how long we can hold on, though our people in Welshpool are loyal enough. Of course your brother Dickon has been a help to us, but even with him and his servants we are very thin on the ground. The fighting's all through the marches now. They say that Abergavenny scarcely dares to open his castle gates.'

'I should be in Glamorgan,' Constance answered, 'not dancing attendance on Bolingbroke's wife. She has no need of me. Prefers her own Bretons. God knows, she has enough of them! She's brought eleven laundresses with her. Eleven! Does she imagine that we never wash our linen?'

'I suppose it's only natural that in a strange land—'

'This is not a strange land; this is England. And she has chosen to be Queen of it.'

Lady March nodded, damped her lips with her tongue, and tried another tack. 'At least no blame can fall on you for anything that may go amiss in Glamorgan. You cannot be accused of complicity with Glyn Dwr, as Edmund was.'

Constance frowned momentarily. 'I suppose I ought to present you to her,' she said. 'Later, perhaps. She's the sort of woman who keeps spaniels and would be afraid of a decent horse. Sits an ambler that a child could manage with one hand. Big eyed and tight-mouthed. Likes presents. The only time you see her smile is when she's given something she thinks worthy of her. Must be costing Bolingbroke a fortune in silk and jewels. He seems to be able to find money for that, if not for paying his just debts to those of his own blood.'

'You know he's heartbroken.'

'Bolingbroke?'

'Edmund—'

'Then his Welsh wife must comfort him!' Constance paused, and snorted her contempt. 'If she can find a heart to mend. I doubt he owns one.'

There was a moment or two of bleak silence before Alianore spoke again. 'I've had letters from him.'

'Letters? He and his friends are burning Powys around you, and he dares to send you letters?'

'You know how matters are in Wales. There are many who fight on one side and have friends and kindred on the other. And men still buy and sell, and meet together in markets, no matter what the King orders to the contrary. Perhaps they ought not, but they do. I dare say that a letter would reach Glyn Dwr himself, if it was put into the right hand. Edmund was always as dear to me as a brother, and he has not changed. He is still Edmund, and he loves you as much as ever he did.'

'That I believe, for he never loved me at all. I had a letter from him myself, which I threw to the back of the fire where it belonged. I've heard enough of his lies, whispered in my ear in naked bed. I've no wish to read more.'

Lady March did not answer, but there was a persuasive look in her eyes. The silence between them lengthened; a large fly found its way in through the casement, buzzed around Alianore's head for a few moments, and then decided to explore the rest of the room. It settled somewhere in the cool darkness above Constance's bed. Constance inserted another stitch, working with exaggerated precision, as though completing a detail on a piece of fine embroidery. Outside a blackbird squabbled in one of the trees. She raised her head to look for it, and then became conscious of another sound, the thud of arrows into a straw target. The butt had been set up on the long sward of grass outside her window, and the lone, practising archer was the Earl of Kent.

'Do you care nothing for him at all?' Alianore asked.

'For Edmund? Why should I? He's another woman's husband.' She snapped off the thread with a force sufficient to turn a charging horse. 'Are you suggesting that I should? Would you have me trailing around Wales after him, pleading for the honour of being his whore? I'd rather see him hanged and gutted!'

'I don't believe you.'

'Then you ought to do.'

'He had no choice. Surely you can see that? Would you prefer that he was still a prisoner? A prisoner without hope, chained in some black hole? Love should not demand such a sacrifice.'

'He could have been ransomed. There was money enough, and Hotspur had all in hand.'

'All except the King's consent. If Edmund had come back to England he'd have exchanged one prison for another. At least, as matters stand, he has his freedom. Do you grudge him that? Out of mere jealousy?'

Constance laid her work aside, and looked out into the garden. Her son, now established as one of the Queen's pages, and wearing Joanna's livery, was running across the grass towards Kent, clutching the arrows he had retrieved. It was evident from his face that he was thoroughly enjoying himself, and she remembered vaguely that Mun had promised to teach him how to shoot. This was presumably part of the first lesson. 'He betrayed my trust, Alianore. I've known him since we were both children, and I used to tell people that he was the most honourable man I'd ever met. I can scarcely believe that I was so far mistaken in my judgement.' She fell silent for a moment. Kent, stripped to his shirt and hose, was loosing arrows with an athletic efficiency that bordered upon contempt, one after the other, scarcely seeming to aim. Then he put his bow aside, set young Richard's bow in the boy's eager hands, and gently guided him into the correct stance.

'Your judgement was not mistaken,' Lady March objected. 'There's no better man above ground than Edmund Mortimer, and I believe you know it in your heart.'

Richard's first arrow had fallen far short. Kent ruffled his hair in familiar, brotherly style, and walked the boy forward, taking ten yards off the range. Richard tried again, and this time his arrow veered wide, vanished into the bushes. Mun's amiable laughter drifted through the window.

'I've no wish to speak of him.' Constance stood up, looped her train over her arm. 'I don't suppose you intend to answer his letters, Alianore, but if you do you may tell him that I've quite recovered my spirits. I'm wealthy, despite all the efforts of his new friends, and have the pick of the men here at court. He need not grieve for me.'

***

Edward of York plumped himself down on the daybed, picked a sugared fig from the gilt tray that lay on the adjacent dresser, bit into it with relish. Bolingbroke sat still in his place in the oriel, the light streaming in through the huge window reflecting from the jewelled binding of his book. 'I was not aware I had invited you to sit, Cousin,' he said evenly.

Edward did not stir so much as a muscle. 'I thought to remind you that you still owe me ten thousand pounds,' he said calmly. 'That is of course a preliminary accounting. The final figure may be half as much again. A small matter to Your Grace, of course, but less trifling to me, since I am not a wealthy man. My wife and I have all our jewels in pawn, and she grows tedious about it. You know how women love their baubles. Besides, we do your court no honour by appearing here like penitents, without so much as a decent ring on our fingers. I'm sure you agree.'

'You will be repaid. You have my promise.'

'Unfortunately I have creditors of my own. Here in England, and in Bordeaux. A man grows thin on a diet of promises, even kingly ones. It doesn't help that my annuities at the Exchequer are in arrears, nor that you have been pleased to take Castle Rising from me, which was my father's, and should have descended to me by lawful inheritance.'

Harry laid his book aside, tried to sit upright on his chair. 'It ought not to have been granted to your father in the first place. By our grandfather King Edward's charter it is parcel of the Duchy of Cornwall in perpetuity, and the rightful property of my eldest son.'

'A convenient doctrine!' Edward reached out to the chessboard that stood next to him, and amused himself by moving one of the pieces, without consideration of either strategy or the rules of the game. 'When I was another King's counsellor, some years ago now, it was always my understanding that no sovereign was bound by the charters of his predecessors. You should be wary, Cousin, of setting too many dangerous precedents.'

'I will find some way to compensate you. What is Castle Rising? A remote hole in Norfolk, at the back of beyond, that's not had five pounds spent on it in fifty years or more, not since our great-grandmother lived there. You shall have better. Grant me a little time. You shall not be the loser thereby.'

Edward tweaked his eyebrows upwards. 'Something on account, perhaps? A rich wardship? Some office of profit?'

'There's nothing that I can give you. Not yet.' Bolingbroke rose wearily to his feet, stepped to the window, and drew the clear morning air into his lungs, peered uncertainly at the colourful figures gathered on the grass about twenty yards away. His blurred vision prevented him from recognising their faces at such a distance, but he was fairly certain that he could identify some of the voices.

'I had no idea that my sister was interested in archery,' Edward chuckled. He had moved to his cousin's side, unnoticed by Bolingbroke, who span on him as if expecting a knife in the back. However, the Duke of York merely leaned a hand on one of the stone mullions, the picture of amiable indolence.

'Your sister is interested in nothing, except causing trouble,' Harry said harshly. Constance's voice was one of those he had recognised; that and her laugh. He screwed up his eyes to see better. Young Kent was one of those in her company. The fool was guiding her grip on the bow, as though he imagined she did not know how to shoot. 'Not long after your father's death, she rode all the way up to Alnwick to persuade the Percys to defy me in the matter of Mortimer's ransom. I suspect it was her interference that turned Harry Hotspur against me. That's the measure of her trouble-making.'

Edward shook his head doubtfully. 'I think you credit her with too much influence.'

'She was at Alnwick, nevertheless. She was recognised by a man of mine who carried letters there.'

'Indeed?'

'Indeed. You'll not persuade me that she made such a journey without some purpose in mind. What could it be, if not to conspire with the Percys?'

His cousin shrugged. 'I doubt whether they heeded her, whatever she said. Northumberland and Hotspur, guided by a woman in matters of policy? Never in this world! Besides, you've soothed them, have you not? Granting them so much of Scotland...'

'All they can conquer,' Bolingbroke muttered. He slapped a closed fist against an open palm. 'I had to give them something, and that grant cost me nothing but the parchment and the clerk's trouble. I thought it might distract them. I think it has, but I can't be sure. The men they have mustered to seize the Scottish marches could as easily be brought south against us, and perhaps make common cause with Mortimer and Glyn Dwr. I cannot afford to keep thousands of men under arms all through the summer, but unless I do there's a chance we'll be taken by surprise, not have time to deal with the threat.' He paused, drew a breath, and went on. 'We may have had our differences, Ned, but we share the same blood, and I can't believe you'd willingly bend the knee to the Percys; nor yet to Edmund Mortimer, whose father neither your father nor mine would have regarded as an equal. Stand with me through this, and you'll not find me ungrateful.'

'To the very limit of my power,' Edward promised, a thin smile tugging at the corner of his lips. 'Alas, as I have explained, I haven't the means to offer much more than my own poor services, and those of such men who will follow me out of devotion, without pay. My father died deep in debt, his widow holds a third of the York lands in dower, and, as I have told you, I have nothing left to pawn.'

'William Stradling tells me that Glamorgan is on the point of being lost to us.' Bolingbroke walked away from the window, crossed the floor of chequered red and white tiles, and sat on the carved chair by his desk. 'Your sister is here at court because I dare not trust her at Cardiff. Her judgement is—uncertain.'

'You mean that she has friends on the other side?' Edward suggested. 'Might even be the link between the Percys, Mortimer and Glyn Dwr?'

'I'd not go so far as that.' Bolingbroke selected one of the quills that his clerk had set out for him, examined its point with an intensity worthy of a better cause. 'However, to be quite plain, she's not a lady whose loyalty I'd care to put to the test. It's for her own good, Ned. I've no wish to see her implicated in treason.'

'Then will you campaign in Glamorgan yourself?'

'No.' Harry absently teased the feather of the quill between his fingers, his expression remote. 'Wales must look to itself this year; we shall be on the defensive, with such forces as the Prince and the marcher lords can muster. That's another problem. Worcester is my son's governor, and commands his forces. I don't trust him and I daren't dismiss him, for fear of what it may provoke. Anyway, I have offered the Percys my support against the Scots, and I'm going up there in force.'

'To support the Percys? Or to fight them?'

'That's as they may choose. At least I'll have an army in the field, and they'll not be able to catch me unaware.'

'I suppose you wish me to come with you?'

'No.' That was decisive. 'No, I've other work for you, if you'll accept it. Glamorgan is too important to be left to its own devices. I want you to go to Cardiff, and do what you can. That's what the situation requires, the presence of a great lord, close to me in blood. I'll ask the Earl of Devon to bring men across the Severn Sea in support of you, and when matters are settled in the North, I'll come to your relief myself. I believe Glyn Dwr may have overreached himself. He's far from home and he's no army in the true sense, just an ignorant rabble of thieves and malcontents who come together from time to time in the hope of profit. Half of them will fall away at the first check. All we have to do is hold on for a little while—then crush them. Will you do this for me? Remember, it will also profit your sister, and her son.'

Edward grinned amiably. 'If you think that the mere name of York will strike terror into these rebels, then of course I will do it. Though, as you are well aware, Harry, there will be limits to what I can do. I don't own a single foot of land in Glamorgan, and my acquaintance with the leading men of the lordship is very slight. Stradling and St. John apart, I'd not know them from Adam.'

'You're my near kinsman and Richard Despenser's uncle. That should be authority enough.'

'His uncle, but not his guardian.' He hesitated, as if giving thought to the matter, then continued. 'If you granted me his wardship that would give me real standing in Glamorgan. What's more the profit from it would reduce your debt to me, and provide me with some funds in my hand that I can put to good use in your service.'

Bolingbroke digested that for a moment. 'I see. You do not care that your sister will be the loser thereby?'

Edward shrugged. 'You've given her lands in her own right that are more than ample to maintain her. She lodges here at court and is fed and sheltered at your expense. I suspect that at this moment she has more ready money at call than the two of us put together.'

Another moment passed. 'You'll leave the boy himself where he is, in the Queen's household?'

The question was as good as agreement. Edward nodded amiably. 'If you so wish.'

Harry met his gaze for a moment. Then he took up his quill again, dipped it into his ink, and began to scribble a reminder for himself to instruct his officers to process the matter. 'I do. On that understanding, the wardship is yours.'

***

The law said that trees and brushwood were to be cut back for at least a hundred yards on either side of the highway, so there would be no shelter for outlaws, but of course no one paid any attention to such strictures. The road from Easthampstead to Windsor ran through the same tunnel of branches it had always done, the canopy of summer leaves providing shading from the brightness of the summer sun and seeming to echo the voices of those who rode beneath its protective cover.

Constance rode a little way behind the gaudily painted carriage that carried Queen Joanna, choosing to make the journey on horseback because it was preferable to being shut up for several hours in an enclosed space with Joanna and her flock of Bretons. There were only a few miles to cover, and nominally they were travelling in an ordered procession. The truth was that the order had broken down before they were out of the park at Easthampstead, with some finding the pace too slow for their inclination and advancing up the column to find friends, or riding off into the fields to start game and trample crops. Others discovered reasons for delay. Alehouses, wells and roadside shrines all provided diversion for some, and here and there a horse went lame, or one of those on foot decided that he had blisters in need of inspection.

Constance had thought herself beyond hurt, but the loss of her son's wardship was a keen blow, one that had devastated her spirits.

'At least,' consoled Lady March, 'you have not been parted from him. You're both in the Queen's household, and may see each other every day. I'm only allowed to see my sons when Bolingbroke pleases.'

That, Constance said to herself, was typical of Alianore's way of thinking, and it completely missed the point. Richard Despenser's proximity was not the main issue—he was at an age when he needed to begin his lengthy training as a knight, and that could not well be accomplished in his mother's household. She recognised that reality and had been considering options for his placement. No, what mattered above all was that she no longer had any say in his future. He could be put in the care of those she despised, taught to value all she hated, and, apart from praying for his welfare, she would not be able to do anything about it. Of course the loss of income and personal influence was also a significant factor, but Alianore had not highlighted that either.

Kent was riding between them, having slipped away from his official station close to the King on some pretext or other. 'I must say I was surprised that York should do such a thing,' he pronounced, trying to look suitably concerned.

'Nothing my brother does surprises me,' Constance said, noting with some approval Mun's fine posture in the saddle, the glowing warmth in his blue eyes, and the floods of golden curls emerging from beneath his hood. No one less like Edmund Mortimer in appearance could be imagined. 'Though I dare say his wife has something to do with it. She's always envied me my children, not being blessed with her own. And Harry Bolingbroke, of course, takes delight in finding new ways to make me suffer.'

'You still have your own lands,' Kent pointed out.

'They're no more assured to me than my son's wardship was. Ned promised to press the King to restore my dower rights, but that's another promise he has broken.'

He fell silent, pondering the implications.

'You should take advice on the matter,' Alianore suggested. Her tone was cheerful. The distant, massive walls of Windsor Castle had come into sight, and within were her boys, whom she had permission to visit. 'Speak to a lawyer or two. There may be something that can be done.'

The road twisted abruptly to the left, opened out into something of a clearing. In it, to the right of the road, a group of men stood by their horses, bowing low as the Queen passed, and then mounting again, ready to join the procession. There were a dozen of them in all, clad in the murrey-and-blue of York, and as Constance took that in she saw the Duke's banner lifted above them as the man carrying it settled into his saddle, and realised that Edward himself was in their company. She immediately fixed her eyes ahead, but found that that was not enough. Her brother rode forward, surrounded by his followers, and obstructed the road. He swept off his furred velvet hat and bowed. 'Good morrow, ladies,' he said amiably. 'Cousin Kent, you're fortunate to have such fair company.'

'We were just talking of you, Edward,' Alianore remarked. Her voice was not as chill as Constance would have liked.

His eyes flicked from her to his sister. 'I hoped to have a word with you both. Kent, the road is narrow. Perhaps you'd be good enough to give place to me, and go forward to the King. He will be wondering where you are.'

'I've nothing to say to you,' Constance said, advancing her horse as far as she could, 'nor do I wish to hear any more of your deceits. Be so good as to clear these fellows from our way. I am not accustomed to having my path blocked by menials.'

Edward gestured, and his liverymen retreated onto the grass. 'I should have thought you might be interested in discussing our brother's future. I wanted you both to know that I have granted him Conisbrough, to him and his heirs, for the rent of a peppercorn. I never go there—Philippa hates the place—but it will make Dickon a home. I shall also retain him, once he comes of age. Give him a hundred pounds a year. With what he has from the King, he should be able to maintain a suitable household until such time as he inherits what is mine.'

'Why should this be of interest to us?' Mun asked. He had moved forward, quietly placing himself between Constance and her brother's men.

'It's not of interest to you, Kent. It's a family matter. I've already asked you to spare us your company.'

Constance was already nudging her horse forward. 'Mun,' she said forcibly, aware of how close his hand was to the hilt of his short sword, 'your sister and I would be grateful for your escort to Windsor. I have nothing to say to the Duke of York. Today, or any other day.'

Edward thought about arguing, but then took in the determination in her eyes, and the rising confidence in Kent's. The procession was backing up behind them, and among the crowd were men wearing Despenser, Charlton and Holland liveries. Not many in total, but enough to make trouble. He had no wish to brawl, so he moved his horse to the side of the road, and let them go on. There would be another occasion, and what he had to say was not for Kent's ears.

33

Despite its stark, whitewashed walls the apartment smelt as if it needed a good scrubbing, or at least the replacement of the filthy rushes that served as floor covering. The windows were small, and glazed with translucent horn to let in the light. On this warm day the casements stood open, looking down on a thirty-foot drop to the cobbles below. It was unfortunate that there was no hint of breeze to clear the fetid air.

The two boys had been playing together with miniature knights that dangled from strings, puppets that with some difficulty could be made to strike at each other with their miniature swords. This had caused debate between them, a squabble so fierce that they did not notice that their mother had entered the room until she coughed to draw attention to herself.

Constance watched as March and his brother scrambled up from the floor and bowed to Alianore, then repeated the gesture in the direction of their sister Anne, Kent, and herself. This formality over the younger boy, Roger, ran to his mother and embraced her. March, clearly more aware of his dignity, seemed to think this display of affection unnecessary.

'As you can see,' Kent said, 'my nephews are perfectly content here. Aren't you, lads?'

She glanced around the room. It was appallingly disordered, with dirty and torn clothes scattered here and there, broken toys piled amid dog-eared school-books, and a stinking chamber-pot that was on the verge of overflowing. 'Have they no servants?'

'Of course we have servants!' March responded, impatient of the question. He was twelve years old, his sulky, turned-down mouth reminding her of his aunt, the late Countess of Arundel, and his dark colouring of his father and of his namesake, Edmund. 'The trouble is, they're all idle rogues and forget that I am the Earl of March and Ulster.'

'They've plenty of fellows to wait on them,' Kent said, raising his voice sharply over his nephew's petulant one. He bent to pick up a wooden sword and gave Roger a playful prod in the ribs with the point of it. 'Besides that they've a tutor to teach them their letters, and all the exercise they need.'

'We were hunting foxes in the park last week,' Roger said. He bounced up and down on the spot, avoiding the thrusts of the toy weapon as best he could. 'Sir Hugh Waterton sent us out with his men. We had crossbows, and dogs to help us.'

Alianore hugged March to her side, despite his obvious reluctance. 'It sounds like good sport.'

'We killed three of them!'

Constance sniffed. Foxes were base vermin, and exterminating them was not a fit task for gentlemen. It was one step up from being told to empty the cesspit. She picked up one of the boys' discarded linen shirts. It was filthy, the right sleeve was ripped for almost the whole of its length, and it looked too small for either of them to wear.

'Does no one wash or mend your clothes?' she demanded.

'Sometimes,' Roger said, looking up at her with eyes that were so like Edmund's they wrung her heart. He shuffled his feet in the rushes, as if scarcely able to contain his energy.

'It's fortunate that I've brought them some new shirts,' Lady March said. 'I had a feeling they might be growing out of their old ones.'

She opened the bundle she had carried with her. A jar filled with sweetmeats was wrapped in protective layers of new clothes. Young March seized the jar at once, removed the lid and plunged his hand inside as though he was on the point of starvation.

'I don't think anyone washes their bodies, let alone what they wear on their backs,' Constance said. She took hold of one of Roger's wrists and investigated his palm, rapidly becoming aware of the smell of stale sweat that hung about him. 'I'd be ashamed if the lowest scullion of mine had such filthy hands. When did you last have a bath, boy?'

'At Christmas, my lady.'

'Waterton lets us swim in the river sometimes,' March said, his mouth crammed with sweetmeats.

'Have you not been taught to wash your hands and faces?'

'No one bothers to bring us hot water. Why should we?' That was sullen.

Kent shrugged, forced a chuckle. He cast the toy sword down on the floor where he had found it. 'A little dirt is of small account at their age. I know it never bothered me.'

'It's a sign of an ill-governed household,' Constance said. Her eyes were drawn back to Roger. He was so like his uncle, Edmund, the resemblance seeming to grow by the minute as she grew more accustomed to his features. Before she could prevent herself she was picturing the children that she and Edmund might have had together, and the pain flooded back over her soul like melting lead. She sat down hard on the boys' bed, and waited in silence for the bitter moment to pass. It was hopeless to dwell on such things. She would never see Edmund again.

Anne noticed the agonised expression on her face. 'Are you ill, Cousin?' she asked, drawing closer.

Kent also had his eye on Constance, and did not wait for her reply, all but lifting her to her feet. 'The heat's stifling in here. Stay with your mother and brothers, Anne. I'll take Lady Despenser out into the fresh air.'

There was a part of Constance that almost resented such treatment, but another that was glad of his strength and his readiness to care for her. She leant against him, allowed him to guide her out into the antechamber. There were beds there for the boys' servants, a leaking cask of ale resting on a stillage and a set of abandoned knucklebones, but of the servants themselves there was no sign. Kent hammered on the far door with almost enough force to put his arm through it and the turnkey opened for them, bowing low as if he anticipated a buffet.

Beyond was a landing at the head of the stairs leading down to the yard. 'Can you manage the stairs?' Kent asked. 'Or shall I carry you?'

Constance shook her head. 'You're very kind, Mun, but I think I can manage well enough.'

'It would be no trouble,' he said. 'I could carry you easily. In truth, I'd enjoy it.'

'Something must be done for those boys,' she murmured, her thoughts still wading through an impenetrable morass of emotion. 'Will you have a word with Waterton about them?'

Kent's face fell for a moment. He would have preferred to carry her for ten miles over rough ground than approach Hugh Waterton on such an errand. Waterton, a dour and blunt-spoken Yorkshire knight who had served Bolingbroke for many years, was well assured of the King's favour. Neither superior rank nor idle threats would impress such a man, nor had he a bribe to offer that Waterton would think worthy of attention.

'I'll do what I can,' he agreed, 'but I don't understand why you are so troubled. Boys need to be toughened, and should not live too softly. It's not good for them.'

'Nor is it good for them to be kept prisoner,' she answered. She began to descend the stairs with him, his arm still supporting her at the waist. 'Remember, Mun, they are your nephews. It's an insult to you that they are not treated with more respect.'

He snorted. 'In my opinion, all March lacks is a good birching, and I've half a mind to supply it myself. He's no manners; addressed you as though you were a laundry woman. He'd better not do so again in my hearing.'

'What do you expect? The boy has no example before him to make him better. He's been shut up for more than three years, either here or at Berkhampstead. What's more, you know why he's been treated so. If we all had what is our own, he'd be sitting in Bolingbroke's place.'

Kent almost missed his footing on the stairs, saved himself by clinging fast to her and reaching out for the wall with his other hand, skinning his knuckles.

'Do not say such things. Certainly not to anyone but me. You do yourself no good by speaking treason, and nor do you help my nephews.'

'It's the simple truth.'

'It's dangerous folly. The King is the King, Constance. I've promised I'll talk to Waterton about the boys, and I shall, because you have asked it of me. Beyond that, I pray you, let matters rest.'

She found herself turned towards him, their mouths so close together that she could feel his breath on her face. Her hand, without conscious instruction, reached out to caress his cheek, testing the feel of the faint, soft stubble with the tips of her fingers. 'You are kind to me, Mun,' she said, 'so kind and patient that I wonder at it. I hope you do not think me ungrateful, for I've shown you little enough kindness in return.'

His grip on her waist grew firmer, as if he thought her in danger of collapse.

'Someone must take care of you,' he said.

Constance considered him. That part of her that could love a man as she had loved Thomas was a casualty of the field of Pilleth, but she was very fond of Mun, and she could not deny his physical attraction. That was what she wanted. To be comforted, protected, cared for. The Earl of Kent could supply all of that, and in full measure. She was weary of fighting alone against the world. Her mouth, seemingly of its own volition, reached up to his, and sealed the unspoken bargain between them.

***

Queen Joanna raised her crossbow and took careful aim at the hart as it emerged from the undergrowth and hurried across the clearing, kicking up dew from the grass. The range was no more than fifty yards, and the animal was presenting his whole side to her. An easy shot. She increased the pressure on the trigger until the string released and the bolt flew away towards its target, singing its way through the air. It struck the hart in the shoulder, pushed it sideways for a moment before it staggered on. A murmur of sympathetic approval rose from the courtiers gathered together in the hunting stand, a temporary structure built from tree branches, the leaves shading the greyhounds and the ladies' pale complexions from the rays of the sun.

The Queen was a small woman, delicately boned, and the crossbow was a little heavy for her. She handed the weapon to Thomas Mowbray, acting as her squire, who at once began to rewind it for her. One of her Breton ladies presented a ewer of water and a bowl so that she could rinse her hands, another a towel, and a third offered a glass of wine. Joanna sipped at the drink, her nose wrinkling at the taste, then took the crossbow back from the bowing Mowbray. He was the son of her husband's late enemy, Norfolk, and a member of her household, a sulky youth bitter with discontent because he had not been allowed to inherit his father's dukedom, only his lesser title of Earl Marshal.

'Perhaps Her Grace should ask Kent to give her lessons in archery,' Edward said, appearing at Constance's side. She was as far away from Joanna as the stretch of etiquette permitted, though nominally supervising the rest of the Queen's women.

One of the few offices Edward retained was that of Master of the Hart Hounds, so his role at the hunting stand was an official one, at least in name. 'Not a single clean kill so far,' he went on, shaking his head. 'It's too hot for greyhounds to do much running. They're already getting tired, chasing after her failures. I'm sure you could shoot better, my dear. Especially after all your recent practice. Where's your bow?'

'I'm in no mood for such work, nor for talking with you,' Constance said. She edged away from him, her boots biting into the soft ground.

He sighed impatiently. 'This grievance of yours. Let me explain. Cousin Harry was determined to take the wardship from you, and I've such debts that I could not afford to refuse it. The boy could have been given to Arundel, or Ralph Neville, or one of Harry's other friends. Would you have preferred that? I thought I acted in the boy's best interests—and your own.'

'Can you even convince yourself, I wonder? You tell so many lies. You must find it difficult to keep a proper account.'

'What I've just said to you is the truth. Nor did I lie about the provision I have made for our brother. I thought you'd at least be pleased by that.'

'Pleased? I'm sure you intend to reap some profit for yourself.'

His hand closed on her forearm before she could escape. 'Remember our private talk at Southwick three Christmases ago. The marriage I wished him to make. The importance of our alliance with the Mortimers. Nothing has changed.'

'Everything has changed!' Her suddenly raised voice drew eyes in their direction and she went on more quietly. 'Since then Edmund Mortimer has abandoned me and you have deprived me of half my livelihood. I don't give a fig for either of you.'

He released her abruptly. 'It seems to me that you prefer Kent's company these days.'

'And why should I not?' She paused, pretending momentary interest in the latest hart to come crashing through the trees, driven out of cover by hounds and beaters. The hunted creature tangled itself for a moment in the briars, then struggled free. It dropped as the Queen's bolt pierced its heart. 'At least Mun cares for me, and helps me when he can. He's the only friend I have here at court.'

'You talk like a green girl.' He kicked at the long, sweet-smelling grass in frustration, the droplets that clung to it damping his brown leather boots. 'What do you suppose he expects in return for his so-called friendship? It's obvious, isn't it? He wants to get beneath your skirts, that's all.'

'You are too apt to judge other men by your own standards,' she said twitching her nose. But she reflected on the feel of Kent's protective arm about her, the taste of his lips on hers, and a pleasurable smile spread slowly over her face, her brother's suggestion not really displeasing her. 'It's not the first time in my life that a man has admired me, Edward, and I scarcely require your advice as to what I must do about it.'

He glanced around them. 'You should remember that he's going north with Cousin Harry. There's more than a chance that he'll not be coming back.' It was a quiet warning, his hand fingering the edge of his beard as he considered the jewels in his rings.

'What are you talking about?' She was puzzled, not so much by his words as by their careful, confidential tone. 'Why should he be more at risk than any other man who goes to war? All they face are a few beggarly Scots.'

He snorted. 'So they imagine, but it isn't so. I've had word from our friend Hotspur. When Harry ventures beyond Trent he'll find the whole of the North risen against him. He'll be overwhelmed by numbers, and I doubt whether the Percys will burden themselves with prisoners. So it might not be wise of you to get too attached to the wretched boy.'

Constance stood in silence, recalling the day at Caversham she kept trying to forget, the day when Hotspur brought her word of Edmund Mortimer's defection. He had spoken then of involving Edward in his conspiracy against Bolingbroke, but she'd not given another thought to it. Now it seemed that the rebellion had gone beyond mere words, and that her brother, for good or ill, was a part of it.

'It could be the end of all our troubles,' he said, turning his hand back and forth as if his wrist needed exercise. 'Fortunately our very dear cousin the King does not require my assistance and has given me authority to resist your Glamorgan rebels. I've sent word to every tenant and retainer I have to muster for that purpose. I hope you'll allow me to gather your men also. You can be sure I shall put them to good use. The stronger I appear, the easier it will be to negotiate a truce with Glyn Dwr.'

'A truce?' she repeated, not sure that she understood him.

'Once March is King, there'll be an end to the war in Wales. Glyn Dwr will be contented, Edmund will be able to come home, and all will be well again.'

She did not answer. Her eyes were on Kent, marching towards them across the field, his long stride eating up the yards, her son all but running to keep up with him. Kent had been out in the tiltyard from first light, practising with his weapons in preparation for what he thought was going to be a minor campaign against the Scots. He'd taken off his armour, and changed into hunting green, but the sweat of exercise still glowed on his face as though he'd been walking through rain.

'It's what we have worked for all these years,' Edward insisted, his mouth close to her ear. 'For the love of God, do not grow faint-hearted now, when we've a fair chance to bury Bolingbroke in a ditch.'

'You may have command of my men,' she said, 'but you must find some way to save Kent's life. He is as much March's uncle as Edmund Mortimer. His nephew loves him dearly and will not thank the man who brings about his death.'

It was a gross exaggeration, but she knew he had not bothered to visit the Mortimer boys, just as he knew that she had. A weak card, but the only one she had to play.

He laughed. 'I am not the god of battles, my dear, to decide whether he lives or dies. The only sure way to save him is to keep him away from the fighting altogether.'

'That's impossible!'

'Is it?' He raised a speculative eyebrow, appraising her. 'Not for you, I think. Persuade him to fall ill, and allow you to nurse him. Offer him something he will value more highly than the chance of gaining a few battle scars.'

She stared at him in disgust. 'I think you are confusing me in your mind with your Duchess. I do not trade my body for advantages.'

'His advantage, fair Sister. His safety.' He shrugged. 'Do as you will. You know better than I what worth you set upon this friendship you brag about. Perhaps he's not worth saving at such a price. Perhaps you should let him take his chance. It is in your hands.'

**

The court moved from Windsor to Kennington, and still Constance pondered on the dilemma Edward had set her, riding pillion behind Kent so that she would have every opportunity to speak to him as and when her mind cleared. This was a new mode of transport for her, and invited some curious glances from various people, including the Queen, but the novelty did not help to solve the puzzle. Kent kept trying to make conversation and was troubled by her virtual silence and obvious abstraction, especially as it was so much at odds with the favour she was showing him by sharing his horse and resting her hands on his waist.

At last they entered the park at Kennington, along the same route she had travelled with Elming Leget the previous summer, beneath the dappled shade of the great trees, and still she could find no answer.

'Mun,' she said, her grip on him tightening so that her fingers pressed into his firm belly. 'I wish you were not going with the King to Scotland, for I shall miss your company. It's the only light I have in my prison.'

'Prison?' He began to laugh, puzzled by her use of the word.

'It's what the Queen's household is to me. In some ways it's worse. The nuns were kind to me when I was shut up at Sonning. Here I'm despised.'

She felt him grow rigid in the saddle. 'If any man has insulted you, you've only to speak his name. I'll make him swallow the length of my sword by way of atonement.'

'No one has insulted me,' she said hurriedly, 'but I am almost alone, especially now that your sister has gone home to Powys. Once you've left me it will be—insufferable.'

'You have your ladies,' he said, 'and the rest of your women. Your son, and at least half a dozen men in your livery. How are you alone?'

'I've a fear that you may not come back to me.'

He took one hand from the reins and covered hers with it. 'I've no choice but to go,' he said. 'It's my duty to the King. You know that well enough. Besides, it's a chance to win knighthood.'

'You could be made a knight tomorrow, for the asking. It's your right by birth and rank.'

'But I don't want it so. I prefer to earn it by my own deeds. To be worthy of the honour.' He paused, his fingers tightening on hers, toying with her rings. 'To be worthy of your regard.'

She sighed, softly kissed the gold curls that covered his neck. 'I don't ask that you prove yourself to me by risking your life. I'd sooner have you safe. In any event, the Scots are no great warriors. The Percys crushed the best of them at Homildon, and with little effort from what I was told. On that one day they took all the nobles and knights worth a ransom. You'll gain scant honour, and less profit.'

'There are profits and profits,' he objected. 'You know I'm still the King's ward, and my marriage is in his gift, not my own. If I distinguish myself in the field, perform some great service, he might agree to reward me by allowing me to make my own choice. Then I could ask you to be my countess.'

She was silent again for a moment, taken aback by the declaration. 'Bolingbroke will never allow it,' she said at last. 'You waste your labour.'

'The King is not as unreasonable as you suppose. I think I might persuade him.' He laughed cheerfully.

Constance frowned at the back of his head, conscious that she had made no progress at all. 'You forget, my lord, that you will have to persuade me first. I've shed sufficient tears in my life, broken my heart enough, without mourning another husband. If I ever marry again, I'll choose a man who sets some value upon his own life and does not go seeking for glory in fruitless wars. A man who loves his hearth and home, and values me above all else.'

He hesitated for a moment, bewildered by the unexpected and inexplicable twist in the conversation. 'This doesn't sound like you,' he said. 'Who has put such thoughts into your head? Some prating priest perhaps?'

'My thoughts are my own. I need no priest to tell me there's a limit to the amount of grief I can bear. What is it that you offer me? Another soul to remember in my prayers? Another tomb to visit? What delight do you imagine a woman finds in that?'

'You are asking me to stay in safety while others fight? To be a coward? Is that truly what you want?'

'What I want seems to be of little consequence,' Constance said, her heart as bleak as a wind-swept mountain in the mid of winter. 'I think you talk of marriage because you hope to gain my lands. I believe you care nothing for me at all.'

Kent was silent for a long time, digesting that. They were approaching the arch of the great gatehouse before he spoke again. 'You may think what you will, lady,' he said grimly. 'I know that you ask for more than I can give.'

***

'Edmund Holland, the Earl of Kent,' Queen Joanna intoned, as if she enjoyed the sound of the words. '*Le Comte de Kent*. My lord of Kent.'

Constance watched her intently, wondering where this was leading. She did not like the expressions on the faces of the other ladies. Their obvious amusement was bordering on insolence.

They were in the Queen's apartments at Kennington, overlooking the gardens. Joanna was seated on her day-bed, the scarlet and blue silk hangings behind her bearing the quartered arms of England and France. Constance occupied the window-seat, her neck warmed by the heat of the sun as it blazed through the open casement, grateful for the refreshing breeze that was blowing through it. The remaining ladies sat on cushions on the floor. Thomas Mowbray, also in attendance, poured wine and prepared to distribute it.

'A boy who is most handsome,' Joanna continued, speaking in French as she always did, being monoglot. Her small, rosebud mouth scarcely opened, and her husky voice reminded Constance of someone struggling to bring up phlegm. 'Do you not agree, madame my Cousin?'

Constance straightened her back, and pressed it against the cushions behind her, her hands clasped together in her lap. 'Yes, madame; I agree.'

'A little young, perhaps, but more than fully grown. I think he is your lover. Is it not so?'

Constance choked with surprise and anger, lifted her eyes to the Queen's face. 'He is not, madame. What makes you imagine such a thing?'

Joanna shrugged, accepting a glass of wine from the kneeling Mowbray. She found English hypocrisy in these matters bewildering. No man would admit to having a mistress, no woman to possessing a lover. Yet the mistresses and lovers existed, of that she had no doubt at all. 'That he admires you is obvious to all.'

'Indeed?' Constance held the Queen's gaze.

'Your brother, York, mentioned something to me while we were at Windsor. Confirmed what we had all begun to suspect. Also, I noticed that you rode pillion behind Kent all the way here. Your custom until now, Cousin, has been to manage your own horse.'

'Customs vary with the seasons, madame. One of the sisters of Kent was married to my father. He is a member of my family.'

'Your uncle by affinity. True?'

'Your Grace is correct.'

'Ah! I understand.' Joanna's hands clapped together. 'So, you ladies and damosels who have been admiring my lord of Kent ever since we came to England need not despair. Madame Despenser is merely his niece—that only! I thought we had more cause to envy you, my dear Cousin. The Duke of York was teasing me, I think. He has a strange sense of humour. Is it not so?'

'Stranger than you imagine, madame.' Constance's own sense of humour was growing rather strained.

'But also most courteous, most charming. And now he is gone to Wales, to fight your barbarians for you at his own cost. You must be proud to have such a brother. You are certainly most fortunate.'

Constance bit her lip for a moment, considering a suitable answer, but none came to mind. Thomas Mowbray went on one knee before her, placed wine in her hand.

'The woman's a bloody fool,' he grunted in English.

'What did you say *Monsieur le Comte-Marshal*?' Joanna asked, made suspicious by his tone as much as anything.

'I apologised, Your Grace.' Mowbray answered, rising swiftly and making a deep bow in her direction. 'I spilled a little wine on my lady's hand.'

'I dare say my lady has had worse things running over her fingers,' the Queen said, raising her eyebrows provocatively.

'It has soaked my sleeve,' Constance protested, seizing the opportunity. 'With your permission, madame, I shall withdraw, and change my gown.'

Joanna considered that for a moment, then gave way. 'Very well. Mowbray shall escort you to your room. And if your gown is ruined by his clumsiness he shall pay for a new one. He's rich enough, from what I hear.'

Constance rose, curtsied, and gave the Earl Marshal her hand, grateful for the excuse to escape for a time.

'It makes me want to vomit, listening to her,' he exploded, as they began to make their way through a series of connected rooms. 'How dare she mock you, and address me as though she thinks me her serf? We should be allies, you and I, against the French bitch.'

'Navarrese.'

'My lady?'

'Her father was King of Navarre, not France. What's more, it's neither courteous nor wise to use such words of her as you did in her presence. You should not presume she has no English at all. I think she has a good deal more than she pretends.'

The Earl Marshal's dark eyebrows drew together. 'I hadn't thought of that. Thank you, Cousin, for your warning.'

She shrugged. 'I don't wonder that you lose your patience. You must find this life even more wearisome than I do.'

'Serving as lackey to a bevy of women?' His grim mouth tweaked at the edges. 'I ought not to boast, my lady, and least of all in your presence, but there are certain compensations. And I keep careful account of the insults, and think often of my father. I shall not always be seventeen, and powerless to avenge myself and him.'

They were both silent for several paces after that, the only sound made by Constance's skirts as they dragged after her along the floor tiles, alternately covering and revealing the white hart badges painted into them as she moved.

'I wish Kent thought as you do,' she sighed. 'He seems to have forgotten his poor brother and his uncle, Exeter. How they died, butchered like cattle in a shambles. King Richard was his uncle too. He never even speaks of him.'

'Perhaps he's less cause to bear grudges than we have,' Mowbray grunted. 'Well, he may come to change his mind. I hear he has debts. Perhaps the King, with his new wife to satisfy, cannot be as generous towards him as he used to be. It's certain he's been in a sour mood since we came to Kennington, like a baited bear with toothache. No man dare look at him twice for fear of provoking a fight.'

Constance felt a pang of guilt, understanding as she did that Mun's dark mood had nothing to do with any lack of funds. She would have to make peace with him, somehow. Then pray for him in his danger, for there was nothing more she could do to protect him.

34

They walked beneath a tunnel-like arbour, fashioned from curved, rustic poles and thickly clad with roses, vines and honeysuckle. The music from the hall drifted out into the gardens on the cool evening air, fading with their every step until it was nothing more than a distant, friendly murmur, like the trickle of an invisible stream heard through summer undergrowth. Constance was conscious of the path of stones below her thin soles, the overwhelming scent of the massed flowers, and Kent's guiding hand, but all else seemed as remote as the music.

'The Queen may wonder where you are,' he suggested.

Constance shrugged. 'I doubt it. I don't much care if she does. We need to talk, and there'll be no time for that in the morning.'

The whole day had been dominated by the noise and bustle of final preparations for the King's march to the North. The crash of weapons and casks of supplies into carts; the clatter of hooves on paving as herds of horses were brought out to be groomed and exercised; the regular braying of trumpets as yet another liveried retinue of armed men arrived to add to the muster. It made the still of evening seem all the more intense by comparison.

'Will you be there to see us go?'

She nodded. 'I shall be with the Queen.'

'When last we talked, we disagreed,' he said pointedly. 'Perhaps it'd be as well not to say too much, lest I offend you again. God knows, it was not my intent.'

She halted, and turned towards him, venturing a smile. 'If you don't want to talk, my lord, you may try something else.'

Kent took a breath, hesitated for a moment, and then seemed all at once to grasp her meaning. His hands went to her waist, securing her as though she were his captive, as though he feared she might take flight. He lowered his head until his lips met hers. The initial kiss was no more than a gentle exploration; but matters soon developed from that, Constance surprised by the extent to which she responded to him, and by the speed of the response. Her hands went about his neck, drew him closer still.

'I do not know where I stand with you,' he said, drawing back to take breath. 'For the present we are thus. But when I spoke of marriage you all but boxed my ears. You said that I cared only for your lands, not for you. It was as if I had insulted you.'

She ran her tongue around her lips, enjoying the taste of him, finding her mouth already a little bruised. 'Mun, I spoke foolishly the other day, but you should not have taken it to heart. Forgive me. Marriage is impossible for us. Even when you're out of the King's wardship you'll still need his consent, which he'll never give. Not unless you can find means to persuade him that I detest you, and would as soon lie in a bed with all the foulest devils of hell. I think you must forget that hope, or pray to St. Jude, the patron of lost causes. I've asked much of him these last three years, but still he does not hear me. Perhaps he wears Bolingbroke's livery.'

'Then what must we do?' he asked impatiently.

'We could walk a little further.'

He grudgingly released her, and they moved on, walking closer to each other now, his arm circling her waist, a confirmation of protection and possession alike. Constance felt her breathing slowly returning to its normal rhythm, the scent of the honeysuckle searing her throat.

Kent opened the small, trellised gate at the end of the path, and they emerged into the herber, an enclosed space as private as any at Kennington. They crossed the newly scythed lawn to the small stone fountain standing at its centre, and stood together gazing into its depths, the chill of the clear water reaching up them, its gentle stirrings loud in their ears.

'The King is in desperate straits for money,' he said, his mouth close to her ear. 'What if I buy the right to make my own marriage? Would you have me as your husband?'

She continued to stare into the water. 'Certainly I will marry no one else. But we waste the little time we have, talking of what cannot be.'

'It *is* possible—' he began.

He was interrupted by the sound of the gate to the herber clicking open, followed by a loud female giggle and Thomas Mowbray's low, persuasive voice answering it. The Earl Marshal's companion was Antonine Dagvar, one of the Queen's damosels, a slim, pretty girl a year or two his elder and presumably one of the compensations he had discovered in his state of servitude. His hand was caressing the underside of the breast nearest to him, Antonine leaning against him as if she could barely stand. They were half way across the lawn before they halted in dismay, suddenly aware that they were not alone.

Constance reclaimed Kent's attention by placing her open hand on his chest. 'The Queen already thinks that we are lovers,' she said. 'Let us leave the matter in no doubt.'

She tilted her head back, inviting a resumption of their kissing. This time Kent was not in the least tentative. His tongue slid into her open mouth, linked with hers, explored the rear of her teeth. He pressed against her as if he had it in mind to absorb her into his body.

At last it ended. They stepped back, gasping for air, and studied each other with a new intensity, as if the moment needed to be etched into the memory.

Mowbray advanced towards them. 'Forgive me,' he said, bowing low. 'I thought the herber would be deserted at this hour.'

There was a gentle light of amusement in his dark eyes. Antonine said nothing, merely swept a deep curtsey and smiled a smile of evident satisfaction.

Constance leaned on Kent's arm. 'We were weary of dancing. Were we not, my lord? The hall was very hot.'

Mun grunted something that was almost a word, his hand resting on the hilt of his dagger as if he was not quite sure whether Mowbray's arrival was a form of subtle insult.

The Earl Marshal shrugged. 'We shall go through to the orchard,' he said, 'leave this place to our betters. Antonine has a great craving for sour English apples. Is it not so, my dear? I do not dare to think what the cause of that may be.'

Antonine seemed to understand about one word in four. She giggled again, pressed herself against her lover, and nudged him forward.

'Will that girl speak ill of you to the Queen?' Kent asked, once the other couple, following their route to the orchard, had vanished behind a yew hedge.

Constance shrugged. 'She can do me no harm. As I told you, the Queen already believes that we are lovers. Let it be so in truth.'

'You love me that much?'

'Yes.' The lie came easier than Constance had supposed it would, and she found herself quite able to hold his gaze as her breathing and pulse slowly returned to normal. She did not love him at all, but she needed him and feared for him in almost equal measure. Perhaps, she persuaded herself, she would learn to love him in time. If only he survived long enough to harvest the fruit.

'Where shall we go?' he asked.

'Where you will.'

Kent broke into a smile, a strange mixture of triumph, delight and disbelief registering on his face. She resisted the temptation to speak again, merely stared into his eyes, occasionally averting her gaze, stroked his soft beard with her fingers, and waited quietly while he considered his options.

The decision was made. Mun lifted her in his arms, without any apparent effort, carried her bodily across the lawn to a turf seat that had been built into a small, rose covered arbour. He laid her gently on the close-shaven grass, and himself rather less gently on top of her, tugging at her skirts and untrussing himself with a clumsy haste that bordered on roughness. Three swift thrusts were enough for his immediate satisfaction, but they lay together, still joined, until he was ready to resume. Constance looked beyond his shoulder to the darkening sky, and took what consolation she could from him, wishing that she were with Edmund Mortimer, not Edmund Holland.

***

There was just enough light in the alcove to continue playing, though the rain was bouncing off the windows and closing down the day. Mun, his cousin Arundel, and the Earl of Stafford had been dicing for some hours, virtually since their arrival at the great castle of Nottingham. The King had gone off to write letters to his Council, and worry about the wages for his soldiers in Wales. The three young noblemen were temporarily unemployed, with nothing to do but drink and gamble.

The pile of coins before Arundel had grown to an impressive height; Stafford, though a little poorer than when he had sat down, was still comfortably placed; Mun was losing heavily.

'We'd better send for candles,' Stafford said. He leaned back in his place, took another sip of wine. 'Either that or call it a day. All the luck seems to be sitting in one place.'

Mun shook his head. 'Play on,' he insisted, signalling for the boy who was attending him to fill his glass. No sooner was this done than he emptied it with a single gulp, and advanced one of his few remaining coins into the centre of the table, matching the other stakes. He picked up the dice and threw them. Two twos and a one stared back at him. He punched the board in frustration, setting dice, cups and coins dancing in terror.

Arundel reached for the dice. 'I think I might beat that,' he said, his rather coarse features easing into a smug grin.

'As I said, you seem to have all the luck,' Stafford snorted. 'I don't know why Mun and I waste our time with you, filling your purse. You're already richer than the pair of us put together.'

Thomas Fitzalan was enjoying himself, and it showed on his face. 'I can't complain,' he brayed. He turned towards Mun. 'Need a loan, Cousin? Or should I throw you some alms?'

Mun shook his head. 'I need nothing from you, Arundel. Perhaps it is luck you're having tonight. Well, there's more than one type of luck, isn't there? There's luck with dice and cards. There's luck in battle. And there's luck with love. Don't have much of that, do you?' He paused to swill more wine down his neck, some of it missing his mouth and running down his pale beard.

'Your throw, Thomas,' Stafford said, with an air of patient formality. He was the eldest of the three, as well as the most responsible.

'Perhaps it's your ugly face,' Mun persisted. 'No matter how many hours you spend with your curling-tongs, Cousin, you still look like a pig with a swollen jaw.' He broke off into mocking laughter.

Arundel placed the dice back on the table with infinite precision. 'I've had more women than you've had griddlecakes,' he sneered.

'Women? I talk of the love of ladies, not the cheap whores you buy. When I speak of love, I mean taking pleasure with women who don't stink of the last three men who rogered them. Women who don't have a queue waiting outside their door.'

'For the love of God,' Stafford protested, 'let it pass, both of you.'

Arundel was too angry to be silenced. He stood up and roared at his cousin. 'Sod you! You're a drunken oaf whose grandfather was nothing but a petty squire made by marriage. The brother of a traitor. You're not fit to sit with gentlemen.'

The glass broke in Mun's massive fist, and he flung its shards across the table, laughing his contempt. 'Perhaps not. But I'll not swap my luck for yours, Cousin. You might be fortunate with dice, but I've had the most beautiful lady at court, one you've only dreamed about. Had her, and left her begging for more. At Kennington. The night before we set out.'

'For the love of God...' Stafford groaned helplessly.

'Your first time was it? That you need boast about it?'

Mun grinned in triumph. 'She belongs to *me* now. I believe you sought her in marriage once, but she heard that you've a cock no bigger than a sparrow's.'

The table went crashing as Arundel walked through it in his urgency to lay hands on his cousin, but Mun, who was not nearly as drunk as he seemed, merely side-stepped and pulled his dagger from its scabbard.

'I've been waiting for this for three years,' he said, his mouth forming into a thin, determined line. 'Draw, you bastard, and I'll show you who's the better man.'

His cousin flew at him, and they crashed down onto a stool, shattering it between them and scattering their servants, while Stafford risked his life by struggling to part them before their blades could do harm. It was a fight without rules or restraint, and, although Mun was the larger and heavier of the two, the cousins were well matched, neither lacking in strength, courage or brutality. Each held off the other's dagger, and twisted and kicked in an attempt to inflict secondary injury. Stafford struggled in vain against their frenzy, trying to force himself between them and receiving nothing but kicks and bites for his trouble. They were quite unaware of the footsteps of an approaching procession of courtiers.

'In the name of Christ! *What is going on here?*' Thomas Erpingham's voice was a deafening roar of fury. He struck the paving with his staff of office. 'Part them!'

His handful of attendant gentlemen pitched into the fray, and, with Stafford's assistance, eventually dragged the furious, gasping cousins apart. Both were bleeding from nose and mouth, and Arundel's left sleeve was cut into velvet rags, exposing the shirt below, a seeping wound turning the fine linen from white to crimson.

Erpingham looked at them with disgust as they still struggled against the restraining hands. 'You pair of young idiots! Call yourselves lords? Earls? How dare you brawl here, like drunken 'prentices? This is the King's household, not some Southwark brothel. What brought this about?'

'A matter of a lady's honour,' Stafford said solemnly, rubbing his leg. It had taken a stray kick and was growing more painful by the minute.

The chamberlain hawked and spat on the floor. 'Silly bastards!' he said dismissively. 'You'll have had fighting enough to sicken you before you're much older, that I promise you. The Percys are up in arms against us.'

He had their full attention now, Mun and Arundel united in declaring his news impossible, Stafford stunned into silence.

Erpingham paused for a moment, his face grim, and went on. 'Dunbar is with the King, and he's brought a copy of their proclamation. They spread the lie that Richard of Bordeaux is still alive, that he's riding with them. They're on their way south to make common cause with Glyn Dwr, declaring the King traitor and usurper. And the rest of us rebels, no doubt. If you want my opinion, the chances are that others will come out for them before too long. Fighting enough, boys, as I said, without quarrels among ourselves to make it worse. I am sent to fetch you to the King, all three of you. He's in such dire straits he thinks he needs your counsel. May the saints protect us all! We'll be on the march before dawn.'

***

The day was baking hot, the old Roman road a long, straight strip of grey dust stretching into the heat haze that blocked the western horizon. It was the drums the children heard first, thudding, repetitive, and persistent. Then a cluster of banners appeared over the hedgerows that bordered the great field, like a magical, mobile forest of colour, and below them the dark shapes of men and horses, indistinct in the distance, the sun glinting on their spear tips and armour. Then the sound of many hooves and feet moving together, a thunder carried on the breeze. Instinct told the children to throw themselves down on the warm grass, to hide among their sheep and watch in awe as the endless column passed them, men in such haste that they looked neither to right or left, but concentrated on placing one foot before the other.

The army was broken into three great divisions. Harry Bolingbroke rode at the head of the second column, with the renegade Scottish earl George Dunbar, Mun and Thomas Erpingham his closest companions. It was Dunbar who had brought the news from the borders, barely escaping capture in the process. The Percys had released their prisoner Douglas, Dunbar's deadly enemy, and Douglas had repaid the compliment by taking their side and marching south with them.

Harry's first thought had been to retire on London, and gather his full strength, but Dunbar had advised against it, pointing out they had a garrison of sorts at Shrewsbury, headed by Hal, the Prince of Wales. They could not, he argued, allow either Shrewsbury or the Prince to fall into enemy hands; it would open England's gates to Glyn Dwr.

The garrison at Shrewsbury had not been paid in months and, according to a letter sent in haste from the Prince to his father, most of the men had deserted with the Earl of Worcester, gone north to Cheshire to join Hotspur. Bolingbroke's clear objective was now to reach his son before Hotspur's army could do so, though it meant forced marches, forty miles in a day. The modest army he had assembled for Scotland was now reinforced by levies from the midland counties, gentlemen and their tenants summoned in haste by the sheriffs. Morale was not high. Harry could see it in the faces of the men he saw slumped at the side of the road, so exhausted that even beatings could not bring them to their feet. He paused each time he came across such a group, spoke encouraging words, assured each man that he was valuable, and that victory was certain.

Yet he knew the task before them was formidable. Hotspur was an inspirational leader, whose men would follow him to hell; Worcester was one of the most experienced soldiers in England, and a fine strategist. Northumberland, the most cautious of the three, was shrewd, a tested warrior and deadly enemy. Douglas was another formidable knight, possessed of great courage. For the most part their followers would be northerners, men who were well used to campaigning and raiding across the Scottish borders, or Cheshiremen, King Richard's most devoted followers, soldiers by trade and inclination.

What could he pit against them? Shire levies for the most part. English country gentlemen and their bumpkin tenants. There was his elite corps of household knights and squires, but of the five earls in his company, only Dunbar, a Scot with hardly any followers of his own, had any significant experience of serious fighting. When Harry looked at Arundel, Kent, Stafford and Warwick, he was struck by their youth. The eldest of them was barely in his twenties, and, though there was not a faint heart among them, they were as green as grass. The Prince, of course, was younger still. Only sixteen. Born in the year of Radcot Bridge. Harry remembered him lying swaddled in Mary de Bohun's arms; it seemed but yesterday.

Bolingbroke knew better than to allow his doubts to show on his face. But he could not drive them from his heart.

***

The race was won by hours. Scarcely was the King's banner set up on the ramparts of Shrewsbury Castle when the rebel army appeared on the Whitchurch road. Hotspur hesitated, and then drew back to a defensive position north of the town, where he made camp at the top of a ridge, looking down on a bean field and an array of ponds and ditches. King Richard had not appeared, and nor was there any sign of Owain Glyn Dwr. Just to be sure, Bolingbroke sent out local men as scurriers on all roads to the west and south, with instructions to hasten back at the first sight of any hostile force.

While his men slept where they had dropped, exhausted from their march, Harry gathered his commanders together around a table in the great chamber of the castle. The young Prince sat next to him, and Dunbar, out of respect for his white hairs and battle experience, at his other hand. Kent and Warwick sat next to the Prince, Arundel and Stafford opposite to them. Beyond them were placed Sir Thomas Erpingham, Lord Saye, and Sir John Stanley, a northerner, the steward of the Prince's household.

The Prince summarised the garrison that was left to him, his youthful voice hard and clear, not a word wasted. Less than a hundred soldiers had remained loyal and most of these were resentful for lack of pay. Some were recovering from wounds collected in skirmishes with the Welsh. He judged there were twenty archers, as many spearmen and about thirty armigers who were fit enough to fight.

'How many did Worcester take with him?' Warwick asked, absently rubbing his hawkish features with the tip of his finger.

'About three hundred,' said the Prince.

'Including nearly all our archers,' Stanley added. He was a grim-faced man with thinning hair and slightly prominent front teeth. He drew a breath through the gaps in the latter. 'The rebels will be plentifully supplied in that respect. As Your Grace is aware, Cheshire is full of fine bowmen, not least the hundreds who served King Richard. Men with a grudge.' He paused, considered, rapped on the table. 'I know the ground they're standing on. If they mean to stay on the defensive, holding that ridge, it'll cost a lot of lives to shift them.'

Dunbar leaned forward in his place. 'At least we know Northumberland is not with them,' he pointed out. 'He must still be somewhere on the road. Harry Hotspur has made a mistake, not waiting for his father to catch up with him. I doubt he or Worcester expected us to stir ourselves so quickly. We must attack before they are reinforced.'

Harry glanced around the table. No one seemed to disagree with the Scot, and Erpingham, Kent and Warwick were all nodding. 'Worcester will have decided their ground,' he said, 'and it will be well chosen, for the man is no fool in matters of war. They are bound to make use of their strength in archers, as they did at Homildon against Douglas and his Scots. But I agree with my lord of Dunbar. If we pause for a day or two it can only be to their advantage. It's not just Northumberland who may join them, but Glyn Dwr, Edmund Mortimer and all the rebels of Wales. Against that, I doubt whether we can hope for any significant reinforcement ourselves. We must engage Hotspur in the morning, as soon as we can marshal our forces into order. We outnumber him, and shall prevail.'

He sounded a lot more confident than he felt, but the others hammered on the table by way of applause and shouted their pledges of allegiance, an encouraging confusion of noise that warmed his heart.

Harry held up his hand for silence. He had decided upon his dispositions before he reached Shrewsbury, and it remained only to announce them. 'Cousin Stafford, I create you Constable of England in Northumberland's room. You shall lead the vanward. Go across the river as soon as you've light to see your hand before your face. Warwick will support you. Dunbar, I may need your advice, and will keep you with me, in the centre. Kent and Saye also.' He took a breath. 'My son, the Prince of Wales, commands the rear battle. He will be guided by Sir Thomas Erpingham, with Arundel and Stanley in support.'

He glanced around the table, saw mixed emotions of delight and disappointment in various eyes. The Prince, gratified beyond measure, attempted to kneel and stammer out his thanks, but was cut off short.

'You command in name, boy,' Bolingbroke grunted, 'but be careful that you heed Sir Thomas's advice. He and Stanley have the experience that you lack. That is all, my lords. It's time for us to seek our beds, and sleep as long as we may. We must be astir again as soon as there is a sign of light in the sky.'

The men stood up, knelt before him one by one to kiss his hand, to wish him a good night, and in some cases to thank him for his trust. Slowly the room emptied of all but the King and his chamberlain.

'I should give much to know where the Duke of York sleeps this night,' Erpingham said quietly.

'Probably at Cardiff. Somewhere in those parts.' Harry leaned back against his chair. He was not only tired, but also troubled by the strange, inexplicable physical weakness that had descended on him several times during the previous year. He knew it would be gone by morning. It had to be. 'We've no hope that he'll arrive in time for the battle.'

'I pray you are right,' the chamberlain sniffed. He paced around, the uneven floorboards creaking in protest beneath his heavy footfall. 'Who can say which side he would join if he did?'

Bolingbroke closed his eyes for a moment. 'I know my cousin of York better than you do, Thomas. He'll not risk his life for the Percys.'

'Sire, you know his sister has had secret dealings with them, quite apart from her past attachment to Edmund Mortimer. She and York may seem at odds, but one thing that life's taught me is that blood is a damned sight thicker than water. I advise that you do not put too much trust in either of that pair. Young Kent might bear some watching too. From what I hear he fancies himself in love with the woman.'

'With Constance of York?'

Erpingham nodded.

'Well,' said Bolingbroke, shrugging off his astonishment, 'if you're right, the boy's a bloody fool; but at least he's a loyal fool.'

'He's a Holland. Another family of treacherous vipers. I think you do well to keep him on a short leash.'

They both fell silent for a moment. The King found himself toying absently with his ruby ring, and drew it from his finger, closing his hand into a fist around its comforting solidity. 'I cannot forgive myself, Thomas. Hotspur gave me fair warning to my face, but I thought I'd placated him. I ought to have known it was not possible. You can't appease a man like that. If the battle goes against us tomorrow, I need you to save my son. Get him off the field and away, at any cost. Arundel and Stanley know this country better than any of us. That's why I've placed them with you. Fall back on London and get him crowned before they find means to crown young March.'

'It will not come to that!' Erpingham protested. His face burned with anger at the thought of it.

Harry shook his head. 'It might,' he said, 'if they are reinforced. Morning may bring us Northumberland. Or Glyn Dwr and his Welsh horde. Even my Cousin York. We shall have to wait and see.'

***

It was Saturday, July 21ˢᵗ 1403, the Vigil of St. Mary Magdelene. The Abbots of Shrewsbury and Haughmond arranged a truce so that there might be an attempt to reach a peaceful settlement. Bolingbroke knew that no such agreement was possible, but the interval gave him time to array his troops into battle order, and so he gave consent and did not grudge the price of his decision, which was to sit meekly in his pavilion while a grave and solemn Worcester pronounced him usurper and murderer, accused him of levying unjust taxes, of pillaging the Church, and of leaving Edmund Mortimer to rot in Wales.

'Even now,' said Harry, when his opponent had at last run out of words, 'to avoid the effusion of blood, I shall forgive all, and seek to redress your just grievances. You have but to dismiss those you have misled into rebellion, and return to your allegiance.'

The armed nobles around him could no longer contain themselves. Their roars of protest might have emerged from a single throat.

The King slapped the arm of his throne. 'I say I will forgive all! Even your abusive words, Worcester. I swear it.'

Thomas Percy laughed in his face. 'You have sworn great oaths before, my lord of Lancaster, and been forsworn. You swore that you would not take Richard's throne. You swore that his life was safe. You swore that you would rule justly. All these solemn pledges you have broken, and many more besides. How may we trust you? How may any man? Let us waste no more time!'

Harry stood up. He had expected no other outcome, and now there was no more cause to be conciliatory. The Prince and the circle of young earls were itching for a fight now, their hot spirits roused by Worcester's insults. 'Then the blood that is shed today is on your head, not mine. We have double your numbers, and we shall give no quarter.'

It was obviously the end of the negotiation. Worcester waited for a moment, casting a contemptuous eye over the king and his followers, then turned on his heel and stalked out of the pavilion. They listened to the fading sound of hoof beats as he and his small band of followers trotted back to their lines.

'Stafford, advance your banner,' Harry said abruptly. 'Begin the attack as soon as your division is ready.'

The ground was difficult. Bolingbroke had recognised that as soon as he had set foot on it and now, mounting his horse, he studied it with frustrated intensity, cursing his myopia that clouded the details. He and his men stood at the bottom of a slope, a slope calculated to slow cavalry to a walk within twenty yards. There were ponds all over the place, ditches, standing crops, and any number of trees and bushes to give the archers cover.

Mun rode up to him, an immense figure on a gigantic brute of a horse. 'I thought there'd be more of them, Sire,' he said. 'Do we support Stafford's attack?'

'If it's successful. It's early in the day to commit our full strength.'

Dunbar had joined them. 'Those bloody ponds are going to hamper the advance,' he pointed out, extending a gauntleted hand in their general direction. 'They'll force our men into close order, make them butts for every archer on that ridge. It'll be hard fighting.'

It was almost, but not quite, a criticism of the King's generalship. Harry breathed in, controlled his impatience. 'Stafford and Warwick will not fail me,' he said, 'and we have no option but to attack.'

They moved forward through the assembled troops to the King's chosen position. Mun's horse was responding to his own frustration, sidling beneath him, occasionally lashing out with hoof or teeth at anyone foolish enough to approach too close. The more he sought to control the animal the more he transmitted his impatience through rein and knee.

Drums thumped and clarions sounded as Stafford went forward at the head of the right wing of the army, mounted knights and gentlemen at the centre of the column, spearmen and archers protecting the flanks. Five thousand men in all, almost a third of Bolingbroke's forces. As they moved to within arrow range they hastened their advance up the slope, but the ponds, as Dunbar had predicted, forced them to close their ranks, pressed them together into a solid mass of men and horses that could scarcely move at all.

The rebels unleashed their arrows all at once, a black cascade that sounded like a flock of startled birds exploding from a wood. Stafford's division pressed on, but many of the men and horses were already down, a new tripping hazard for the rest. A second volley of arrows burst upon them, and a third. Stafford's archers sought to reply, but they were shooting uphill, and jostled in the press. They did little harm.

The fourth rebel volley brought Stafford's banner down, and it did not rise again. The advance halted as if it had walked into a castle wall and, as men started to fall back in confusion and panic, the enemy charged at them. The counter-attack was led by hobelars, lightly-armed horsemen, Percy retainers from the Scottish borders. Behind them the Cheshire Archers, throwing down their bows, ran forward, swords in hand. Stafford's leaderless division did not stand to receive their enemies; they dropped their weapons and routed off the field, those who were not cut down before they could escape.

The right of the field was littered with corpses, with struggling, wounded horses, and with injured men staggering around, or trying to crawl to cover. Warwick dismounted, waved his sword about, and sought to rally what was left of the vanward around his banner. The Beauchamp retainers and a few other remnants formed a line of sorts, only to be pushed back, yard by yard, onto the flank of the King's central division.

'The Prince has engaged,' Dunbar reported calmly.

Bolingbroke did not move a muscle, though his face was grim. Mun ventured a glance to the left, and caught sight of Arundel's banner, then the Prince's, in the middle of a chaos of battle. It was utterly impossible to make any sense of what was going on.

Hotspur's centre was advancing now, the attack announced by a shower of arrows from the rebel archers. The knights around the King closed their visors, and, on Harry's command, dismounted. Static horses presented too easy a target for arrows, and defensive fighting was best done on foot. The animals were sent to the rear, Kent's still kicking and protesting at the indignity.

Mun found Dunbar at his side. Bolingbroke's archers were shooting now, as the enemy came within range, and the rebels broke into a charge, Hotspur's own banner to the fore.

'Guard the King with your life, laddie,' the Scot said, opening his visor again now that the arrow storm had eased, his voice guttural with emotion. 'If he falls, we are all dead men. Stand to his right. I'll protect his left. Don't let the bastards get near him.'

He had hardly finished speaking when the first enemies reached them. Mun's first opponent was a dismounted knight, fully armed, whose heraldry Mun did not recognise. The man came at him with a pole-axe, running through the mud to give added impetus to the blow. There was no time for a consideration of tactics. Using all his brute strength Mun buried his war hammer into the knight's helmet, the spike piercing the solid plate as though it were silk and sending blood and brains gushing out in a stream. The rebel crashed down, dying, but there was another screaming man behind him, and another. There were no niceties of chivalry here, no thought of holding back from a foe who was already engaged. They both rushed at him, while he was still struggling to extract his weapon from his first enemy's head. Bolingbroke lashed out at one with his axe, sending the man reeling, and Mun's squire, pushing forward, held off the other with a desperate swing of his sword, buying the few seconds that Mun needed to recover himself.

Mun had never killed a man before, but there was no time to dwell on it. Nor did he any longer have any awareness of what was going on elsewhere, whether the King's cause was winning or losing. He was caught in a desperate press, with barely enough room to lift his weapon, striking blows and taking them, sometimes sending an enemy falling back, sometimes forced back himself, sometimes all but lifted from his feet. Bolingbroke's cadre of household knights and squires surged forward, seeking to protect their master, but the King was not content with safety, he was advancing, foot by foot, with Mun and Dunbar at the apex of his line.

So it went on. Sometimes the fighting broke off for a time, because the men of both sides were too tired to go on; but they always resumed. Hotspur and Douglas launched attack upon attack upon the Lancastrian centre, their objective the royal banner, their intention to kill Bolingbroke and thereby win the battle.

It was the middle of the afternoon now, seemingly an age since Stafford's division had collapsed in ruin. Mun had killed several men, but he was wounded himself, and could feel blood streaming down his face, taste its salt in his mouth. His strength was failing, and his lips and throat were raw with shouting. The rebels were coming on just as fiercely as ever, driving them back across the ground they had gained, almost breaking the line. The King's standard bearer, Sir Walter Blount, was killed, the standard itself trampled in the mud, barely saved from capture.

Bolingbroke had heeded Dunbar's pleas at last, withdrawn to the rear. It was prudent, but it took some of the heart out of his men, removed all thought of trying to advance up that slope, encouraged them to give ground. Dunbar and Saye were screaming out the order to hold fast, but it was not enough.

'Henry Percy—*king!*' yelled the triumphant rebels. 'Henry Percy—*king!*'

Mun threw himself forward, sliding on some entrails. Douglas was in his path, hacking at Dunbar, and he struck at the Scot's helmet, laid him senseless at Dunbar's feet.

Hotspur was a few yards further on, resting, a smile on his face as he leaned back in the saddle, receiving the acclaim of his followers. Screaming, Mun pushed on towards him, Dunbar with him, but the press was too thick for them to make any progress. They were already being forced back when, before their eyes, Hotspur tumbled sideways from his horse as if hit by an invisible mace. The horse ran off in panic, trampling its way through the press, but Hotspur lay still.

One of the King's archers, shooting from the security of a tree, had found his mark.

'Henry Percy—*dead!*' shouted Mun, at the top of his stentorian voice.

'Henry Percy—*dead!*' gasped Dunbar, so tired that he could barely lift his axe.

'Henry Percy—*dead!*' Bolingbroke's men took up the triumphant cry. Neither they nor their enemies believed it at first, and yet it was true.

Harry Bolingbroke mounted his horse and advanced, clutching his own banner, holding it high. 'Forward!' he shouted. 'Finish them! No quarter! Kill them all, every mother's son!'

Reality was dawning on the rebels. The were retreating now, fighting only when they were forced to it, seeking their horses, looking for a hedge or a cart to hide beneath. Hotspur still lay motionless, the long arrow sticking out from his skull like a miniature standard, and all around him lay walls of dead and dying.

Mun halted when he reached Hotspur's body, taking in the horror around him, and found himself retching uncontrollably. The Prince, Arundel and the left wing were pressing hard on what was left of the rebel army, cutting men down as they fled.

'You have more than won your spurs today,' Bolingbroke said, riding up. He was smiling with relief. 'Dunbar tells me that you saved my life.'

Mun did not answer. Looking back he had little conscious memory of the fighting, beyond naked terror and a desperate striving to stay alive.

The King dismounted, tossing his reins to one of his attendants, and drew his sword. He'd not used it in the fighting, and so its blade was still as bright and perfect as when he had begun.

'Kneel,' he said.

Mun did as he was told, but he could not take his eyes from Hotspur's corpse, nor forget how close they had come to utter ruin. It was the archer, the unknown archer, who deserved knighthood, not he. That man had saved the King, and all of them, and no one would ever know his name.

The flat of the great sword descended on his armoured shoulders, one after the other. He had what he had always wanted, and it no longer mattered to him.

35

Constance sat in the corner of the large oriel window, overlooking the Thames. The sun had passed its zenith, but the brightness of the afternoon still struck sparks of light from the languid waters, highlighted the ripples left by fish rising to the small flies that danced and circled across the surface. On the far bank a man and two women were harvesting the river's fringe of rushes, the man wading in the water with a sickle, his companions tying the rushes into neat bundles and stacking them onto a cart. The man worked in his shirt, and the women's sleeves were rolled back to the elbow, their skirts kilted to the upper thigh so only their shifts covered their legs. All three had bare feet, and every so often they halted to slake their thirst, drinking from the earthenware jar they had brought with them. Their voices drifted across the water, the distance removing the substance of their conversation, merging it with the lows of the cattle beyond them, and the cries and squabbles of the water fowl.

Constance emitted an inaudible sigh. Her heavy clothes and enveloping head-dress made the day seem stifling, despite her inactivity and the light breeze that accepted the invitation of the open window. Her days at Sonning passed sluggish-ly, punctuated only by the small ceremonies that were built around the Queen's routine. She had plenty of time to dwell on her own concerns and misgivings.

Joanna had had enough of silence. She shifted her buttocks an inch or two towards the back of her carved chair, which was a little too large for her slight figure and not nearly as comfortable as it looked, as her feet did not quite touch the floor. 'How unfortunate, my dear cousin,' she said, in her habitual French, 'that your brother arrived too late to take part in the battle. I am sure that he would have been glad to earn his share of the glory.' She folded Bolingbroke's letter and smiled. 'Still, it seems he had the consolation of reaching Shrewsbury in time to see the beheading of milord Worcester. A most fitting end for a false traitor, do you not agree?'

Constance's hands tightened their grip on one another in her lap, but other-wise controlled herself. 'It is a fate usually avoided by those who most deserve it,' she remarked.

They were in the Joanna's great chamber in the riverside palace at Sonning. The Queen had taken up residence there in the aftermath of a summer pil-grimage to Becket's tomb at Canterbury, and intended to remain there in quiet retirement until her husband returned from his campaign. She had no place in government, Harry's Council managing all routine business from their base at Westminster.

Joanna gestured with the letter as a signal for Antonine Dagvar to rise from her cushion and take it from her. 'You are thinking, I suppose, of Worcester's nephew. This so-called Hotspur. Is it not so? Well, he may have escaped the axe, but he will trouble us no more, with his head spiked above the gates of York and his body quartered and nailed up in pieces around the realm.'

'It was not Hotspur I had in mind, madame; though he was a brave man, and a courteous knight. Those who have so misused his dead body bring no glory upon themselves, only shame.'

'Perhaps my lord the King ought to have had this paragon buried with full honour in the Abbey of Westminster?' The Queen sniffed expressively. 'What folly!'

'Hotspur was much admired, Highness, especially in the North,' Mowbray put in. He had been leaning against the plasterwork close to Antonine, but now he advanced, his tall brown leather riding-boots squeaking across the tiles. He sketched a bow of sorts. 'He might have been forgotten more quickly if he'd been given a decent burial.'

'I was not aware that I had invited your opinion on the matter, *Monsieur le Comte-Marshal*. I might set greater value on it if you had fought at Shrewsbury, instead of dallying among my women, far from any danger.'

Mowbray flared up at once. 'I wish I *had* taken part in the battle, madame, more than anything in this world! I might have won back the dukedom of Norfolk, which is mine by right, and which your husband unjustly withholds from me.'

Constance interrupted hurriedly. 'As you know, madame, my cousin was commanded to remain in your household. He had no choice in the matter.'

'He is a foolish boy,' Joanna said, waving a dismissive hand in the young earl's direction, as though he were an annoying dog pestering for attention. 'He ought to confine his attentions to his wife, instead of seeking to seduce innocent maidens of noble birth, like a dishonourable lecher.'

'My wife?' Mowbray repeated explosively. His dark eyes widened, seemed almost to bulge from his reddened face. '*My wife?* Neither her mother, Lady Huntingdon, nor her uncle the King will allow me within a hundred miles of her!'

'I do not wonder at it. I dare say they believe you should grown to manhood first, and learn some manners. Get from my sight, Mowbray! You are not wanted here.'

The Earl Marshal considered a reply, opened his mouth to deliver it, then caught the warning expression in Constance's eye and thought better of it. He made another bow, of ironic depth, and flung out of the room.

'Wretched boy!' Joanna snorted. Her fingers cracked as she twisted her elegant hands together, her sapphire and diamond rings catching the light. 'How much longer must I suffer his presence?'

Constance turned her attention back to the open window. As she looked out she saw that the reed-cutters were resting now, sitting in the long grass below shading trees, passing their jar of ale between them, their faces red with effort and contentment. A sailing barge was tacking its way upstream, its crew of two men and a boy adjusting its canvas to catch what breath of wind was available, its progress almost imperceptible against the current. The vessel would be bringing iron up from London, or sea-coal. Or perhaps wine. As like as not the cargo would be destined for Reading. They would tie up opposite Caversham, below the bridge, and decant the goods into carts, or perhaps venture up the Kennet, to the abbot's quay, if they were willing to pay his tolls.

'And what of Kent?' the Queen asked, breaking into her reverie. 'Not only safe, but made a knight for his valour. Perhaps your heart will soften towards him, now that he has proved himself so much a man?'

Constance's knuckles whitened as her hand closed upon the cushion next to her. 'Of course I am glad to hear of Kent's safety, madame. As for the rest, it will be time enough to talk of it when next I see him. That may not be for many months, if Northumberland holds out in his own country.'

'Ah yes. And young men are so fickle, are they not? So often their devotion is nothing more than a pretence. Or a fleeting fancy.' Joanna paused and turned towards her damosels. 'You should remember that, Antonine. All of you. Especially among these Englishmen.'

***

'John Snede failed to appear before the court, my lady,' Tyldesley reported. 'He has, of course, been outlawed, but that does not bring back any of your money. There can be little doubt that he's been milking your Oxfordshire rents for years. Probably back to your husband's time.'

Constance was suddenly aware that her thoughts had been elsewhere, very far from the peculations of her former receiver for the county of Oxford and his failure to produce his accounts. She glanced around the table at the faces of her small circle of advisers, and wondered how many of the others were filling their purses at her expense or that of her tenants. It was common enough practice, almost a privilege of office, and during her months in the Queen's household she'd had little opportunity to exercise proper supervision. Joanna had conceded her request to be allowed to visit Caversham to see her daughters. The leave had been indefinite, but there had been an implicit understanding that her return was expected within days rather than weeks. She had stretched her absence into more than a full month, and August was almost over. A summons to return might arrive at any moment, and there would be no denying it.

'Nothing much can be expected from Glamorgan this year,' Tyldesley continued. 'Most of your tenants are either in rebellion or put in terror of their lives by
their rebel neighbours. What little can still be collected will have to go towards
paying your officers there, and maintaining the garrisons at Kenfig, Llantrisant
and Caerphilly for which you are still responsible. We've kept them as small as
possible. There's no chance of paying the rent for the lands in Glamorgan that you
lease from the elder Lady Despenser. She will have to wait for her money, like it or
not. And you, my lady, will need to borrow.'

'Borrow? I—'

'To pay wages, for one thing. Your reserves are all but gone. Of course, you
could call in the loan you gave your brother, Lord Richard, for his horse and
equipage. That would give you some cash in hand. It might be enough to pay
off your servants, and you could then break up your household, since you are
living with the Queen. I expect your daughters could be accommodated elsewhere. Perhaps with my lady your sister, the Duchess of York?'

Constance gave him a look of such ferocity it might have shattered the trunk
of an oak. 'No!' she snapped. She paused for thought, went on more gently. 'I am a
princess of the King's blood. It's unthinkable that I should keep no household;
turn off my people as though they were beggars. As for my brother, he has no
means of paying me, and I'll not dream of asking that he should. Borrow what
you must. There's jewellery enough that can be given in pledge.'

The meeting drew to an end, and the men rose, bowed to her and began to
make their way out. She called Tyldesley back. He was still quite young, not
much beyond thirty, and yet his hair, once black and abundant, was thinning at
the edges, its lengths streaked with grey. He looked weary to the bone. She gestured him to the window-seat.

'Is it really so bad, Hugh?'

He shrugged. 'The Michaelmas rents will help, of course. Your English manors will bring in as much as ever they did. Maybe we can even squeeze a little
more out of them, send out a commission to look for reasons to fine some of the
tenants for abuses of your rights. Some fellow will always have cut down wood
that he should not, or enclosed part of the waste land without your licence. But
this war in Wales will swallow all, and more.'

'Perhaps it will end soon.'

He looked at her keenly. 'Perhaps.'

Kent had sent her two letters, the last of them dated from the middle of the
month, at York. It had told her that Northumberland himself had surrendered,
though some of his castles had not, and were awaiting the attention of heavy artillery. There was not a word of Mun coming back to her. As far as she could
gather from his laboured sentences, Bolingbroke was now planning an advance
into Wales before the season grew too late, and had hopes of crushing all remaining resistance.

She chatted with Tyldesley over a cup of wine, discussed the Lancashire heiress he had thoughts of taking to wife and explored whether there was hope of laying Snede by the heels and imprisoning him for debt, but her heart was not in the exercise. She had another matter on her mind that she could not share with him.

When he had gone, she rose from her place and began to pace to-and-fro across the red and cream heraldic floor tiles, measuring the distance between the window and the fireplace while Agnes sat bowed over her work, saying nothing.

At last Constance halted by the window and looked out, though without really seeing anything. She laid a thoughtful hand to her belly and offered a silent prayer of thanks for the current fashion for high-waisted gowns. It would be a long time before the swelling became too large to conceal.

'Wishing will not make it disappear,' Agnes said. 'You will have to do something about it.'

Constance turned so swiftly that she tangled her legs in her skirts and had to steady herself.

'We take care of your linen as well as our own,' Lady Norreys reminded her. 'Do you suppose no one but yourself has noticed that you've missed two fluxes?' She paused, knotting her brow. 'Feverfew might be the answer, if you drink enough of it.'

'You presume too much,' Constance said, but without much fire.

'Nevertheless, it is my duty to advise you.' Agnes plucked nervously at her black woollen gown, but stood her ground like a small, determined soldier defending a breach in a wall. 'I've not served you all these years without caring for you, and for your good name.'

Constance flicked her train over her arm, adjusted its hang with moderate care, and took a brisk step towards the door, her green velvet skirts skimming a note of music from the tiles. 'I do not require advice on my conduct from the daughter of a squire,' she said. Then went down to the garden in search of her daughters. It was a bright, warm afternoon, and most of the younger members of the household were out in the gardens, entertaining themselves in various ways. Bess was involved in a game of closheys with Mary Russell and Anne Mortimer, her face lit with pleasure despite the fact that she was having the worst of the contest. As Constance approached, Anne's ball demolished the king-closhey, sending the rest of the skittles tumbling in a heap. Bess ran across the grass and set about standing them up again, calling on her mother to join in the game. She had Thomas's eyes, grey and rather serious of expression.

There was no sign of Isabelle for the moment, but it could be assumed that she was occupied with her nurse in some other part of the grounds. Constance took the ball that Bess offered and bowled it down the pitch. It missed completely, and everyone laughed, Bess loudest of all.

Constance turned away in mock disgust, and saw that she had an unexpected guest. The Earl Marshal was strolling up the sloping gravel path from the landing stage, with Isabelle Despenser on his shoulder. The little girl was shrieking with delight and plucking at the feather in his hat.

'This beautiful damosel was waiting for me by the river when my barge landed,' Mowbray explained, setting the child down at Constance's feet and sketching a bow. He smiled down at Isabelle and plucked her cheek, but his tone was serious. 'A little too close to the water for safety. I suggest you have the nurse whipped. I might not be there the next time.'

Isabelle clutched at her mother's skirts, as if for stability or reassurance, and looked up with her habitual expression of wide-eyed disarming charm. Constance reached down and caressed the child's gold hair, though well aware that the nurse had almost certainly been deliberately evaded. Isabelle's fearless taste for adventure seemed to grow by the week. Neither of her other children had been so bold at three years of age.

'Thank you, my lord,' she said. 'I shall certainly speak to the nurse; tell her to be more watchful. Though my Isabelle is as slippery as any eel and full of mischief. I sometimes think she should have been a boy.'

'I think she's well enough as she is.' His grin suggested that he was another of Isabelle's many conquests. 'It must be hard for you to be parted from such a poppet.'

'I suppose you have come to escort me back to the Queen? Does she miss my company so much that I can't be spared for a few more days?'

'The King is at Woodstock. The Queen is joining him there, and naturally wishes to have your attendance.' He shrugged. 'The court is moving on to Worcester within the week. From there an attack is to be mounted against the Welsh rebels. Doubtless as successful as all the previous ones have been.'

'I see.'

'Kent is with the King, if that's any consolation to you. You'll have at least a few days with him before he goes off in search of more glory.'

Relief flooded out of every pore in Constance's body. She would see Kent, and all would be well. He would not fail her.

She offered Mowbray her hand, and allowed him to lead her into the shade of the house.

***

'It is a very tiny room,' said Philippa, the Duchess of York. 'Scarcely space enough to turn. I shall speak to York about it, and see what can be done for you. It is not fitting that his sister should be lodged in such a hole.'

Constance advanced towards her visitor, and almost fell over Anne Mortimer, who was kneeling down to the task of unpacking a large coffer. 'I'll have better accommodation at Worcester,' she said. 'There never has been space enough at Woodstock. Thomas and I had to sleep in a pavilion here once, when we were first together at court.'

'Dear Thomas! You must miss him terribly.' Philippa spread herself onto the window-seat, gestured for one of her damosels to come forward to arrange her skirts for her. 'Though, of course, it is a long time ago now, and so much has changed.'

'Yes.'

'You seem a little swollen beneath the eyes, Connie. Have you not been sleeping?'

'I sleep perfectly.'

'Good. I think it must be a family trait. York is exactly the same, his eyes close and he doesn't stir until morning. Even though we are buried in debt and half of England seems to believe him guilty of treason.'

'I wonder that your husband sleeps at all,' Constance said.

Philippa shrugged indifferently. 'Ned has never allowed his responsibilities to trouble him,' she said. 'Heavy though they are. You seem very pale, dear Sister. Not quite yourself. Are you sure you are not unwell? Perhaps you should sit down. As I've told you before, there's no need for any formality between us.'

She gave the cushion next to her a suggestive pat.

'Your Grace is very kind.' Constance's voice contained more than a hint of irony. She remained standing.

Philippa stared out of the window for a moment. 'The men are all out hunting in the park,' she said. 'We'll not see any of them until supper, so there's no particular cause for haste. I know that Ned wishes to speak to you.'

'Does he? I'm well aware that he failed me in Glamorgan. That he used my men for his own purposes, and did not even trouble to pay them.'

'You have not been listening, Connie. There is *no money*. Nothing. Ned says his next step is to pledge his estates in Yorkshire. He doesn't want to, but he has little choice. He certainly can't afford to pay wages to your fellows as well as his own.'

'I'd go to Cardiff myself, if I could.'

'Far too dangerous, my dear. Why, you might be taken prisoner by Edmund Mortimer! There's fresh news of him, you know. It's said that his Welsh wife has given him a son. Swift work, if true. They've not been married a year yet.'

'It's commonplace for a woman to bear her husband's children,' Constance said. 'It's more significant when she does not, and leaves him without heirs of his body. At least Lady Mortimer has not failed in that duty.'

Philippa forced a grim smile. 'I am fortunate to have a husband who places small importance on such matters. He does not need half a score of squalling brats to prove himself a man. He knows what he is, and so do I.'

Constance sat on the bed, rested a hand on Anne's shoulder. 'He is a man,' she said, 'whose heir is his brother.'

***

Constance found it impossible to speak to Kent over supper. Woodstock was so crowded with courtiers that there was no room to accommodate the ladies in the hall. Instead they ate together in the great chamber, on the storey above, with Joanna at one table, alone except for Philippa, who was allowed to sit at one end. Constance herself was senior at the second board, but her companions were Joanna's Bretons, with whom she had very little to discuss. But at last the interminable meal and the desultory conversation that followed were ended, and the Queen led her company downstairs to take part in what was left of the night's entertainment.

The hall was packed, but a herald's clarion announced the arrival of the Queen's procession, and caused a corridor to open through the throng, bounded by ranks of bowing courtiers. Constance looked around for Kent, but could not see him among the crowd of heads and hats. Edward was with the King, his hand resting lightly on the back of the throne, his body stooped as he talked into his cousin's ear. Harry rose to receive his Queen, and Edward knelt to kiss her hand, making some comment that formed her little rosebud mouth into a smile. The formalities were soon over, and space was cleared for a troupe of tumblers, imported from Oxford, to perform their act.

There was nothing exceptional about the acrobatics, though Constance would not have been interested if there had been. From her position on the dais, standing close to Joanna's chair, she continued her search for Mun, while trying to conceal her anxiety about his absence.

After the performers had bowed their way out, various people came forward to pay their respects to the Queen. Warwick was among the first of them and with him, to Constance's surprise, was the Earl of Douglas. Douglas had an ugly scar, not long healed, that ran down from his empty eye-socket to his chin, and he walked with a very serious limp. After he had finished exchanging pleasantries with Joanna he turned to address Constance.

'My lady,' he said, bowing smoothly, 'I regret I have grown no prettier since last we met.'

Constance made the effort to ignore the ruin of his features, and smiled at him. 'At least you are alive, my lord. I thought you might not be.'

The Scot shook his head. 'I am not King Henry's subject, my lady. He could not well cut off *my* head. I was taken alive, after young Kent knocked me senseless on the field. He's a stark fighter, and it consoled me a little to learn that he regards himself as your servant. Though I was very much surprised to hear it. I thought your sympathies might have been elsewhere, after what passed between us at Alnwick.'

She looked towards Joanna, but the Queen was fully occupied dealing with Warwick, Edward and Sir Thomas Erpingham, all of whom were competing for her attention. Douglas's words had not been overheard.

'I have hopes of winning Kent to our cause,' she said.

He shrugged. 'I have no cause, save that of Archie Douglas. That and my duty to my King. I'm a favoured prisoner, my lady, because King Bolingbroke thinks to win me over. Though he cannot and never will. Albeit, were he to hang George Dunbar I might be a wee bit persuaded!'

'So you are held to ransom?'

'Aye, and I think I shall be outwith Scotland for some time.' He shrugged. 'No matter. Even if I have to wait ten years, it'll still be there for me. I regret Hotspur, though. I began to think him none too ill—for an Englishman! For the present I'm better placed than our friend Northumberland. He's kept a close prisoner, locked up at Baginton, wherever that may be. Though I dare say he'll be set free in the end, for what he's worth. They say his heart and spirit are broken.'

If only he had remained loyal to King Richard, Constance thought, his heart and spirit would be intact, and so would mine. But she did not say this to Douglas.

The King's musicians struck up a tune suitable for dancing, and Bolingbroke himself rose to lead a deeply gratified Duchess of York onto the floor. Joanna, presented with several choices, eventually selected Edward as partner. Other couples began to join, forming a circle and processing in slow and stately steps, with much bowing and curtseying and formal gesture.

'I fear I am in no condition to dance, my lady,' Douglas said, with a grunted laugh. 'Since Shrewsbury I've found it hard enough just to stand.'

'It is of no moment,' Constance answered, then noticed that the Earl Marshal was pushing his way towards her. He was dressed in an overwhelming shade of red, his houppelande so short that it barely covered his waist.

'My lady, will you honour me?' he asked.

She apologised to Douglas and allowed the youth to lead her out onto the floor, ignoring the glare of discontent in Antonine's eyes.

'Where is Kent?' she asked, as soon as they had established themselves in the rhythm of the dance.

'In his bed.' Mowbray paused to grin. 'He fell from his horse during the hunt, and was knocked senseless. He's well enough now, I think, but not in any mood for revels.'

Constance's irritation flared. 'Why did you not tell me?'

He shrugged. 'I had no chance, until now.'

It was true enough. 'Take me to him,' she said, more gently.

'Now, Cousin?'

'If you please.'

He hesitated. 'The Queen?'

'The Queen is enjoying herself too much to notice me. I need to see him.'

He nodded his assent, and led her out of the dance, forcing a way for her through the crowds of courtiers, out into the gloomy passage beyond the hall screens. They walked through several interconnected rooms, and climbed a tight spiral staircase that led to one landing and then another. Mowbray selected one of three studded doors, turned the ring, and stood back to allow Constance to go before him.

'We're sharing this with our servants,' he said.

The room was little more than a large cupboard, airless and stinking of male sweat. Kent lay naked beneath the sheets of the only bed, his attendant page squatting on one of the dirty pallets that paved the floor, idly flinging knucklebones for want of anything better to do. The pock-faced boy stood, open-mouthed in astonishment, and Mun sat up in the bed, rubbing his head and smiling with delight.

'Constance!' he said.

She could see from his eyes that all was well, that he wanted her. Joanna had been wrong. He was not fickle in love.

She settled herself on the edge of the bed, and took his hand, noticing the scar from Shrewsbury that marked his forehead.

'Are you not ashamed, my lord?' she asked. 'Lying in bed when you could be dancing with me in the hall?'

He laughed. 'By God, now that you are here, I shall! You, boy! Get me my shirt. Help me dress. This lady has given me all the medicine I need to cure my sore head.'

'Mun, the physician said that you should rest,' Mowbray pointed out.

'It was a fall from a horse I've had. Not the pestilence.'

'Such falls can be dangerous,' Constance said. 'I don't care about dancing. I'm happy to stay here with you. You can tell me how you won your knighthood. Everything.'

Mowbray and the boy left them alone, and Mun began his tale. It was a shorter and less boastful one than she had expected.

'They say I saved the King's life,' he said in conclusion. 'The truth is I don't know whether I did or not. I found all that mattered was to save my own. You were right. There is no glory in such fighting, and I hope that I never see the like again.'

'Lord Douglas told me you struck him down. He called you a stark fighter.'

He snorted. 'Douglas doesn't know how afraid I was.'

'But you conquered your fear. And the King knighted you as you hoped.'

'Yes. On the field. Ten yards from Hotspur's body. He was a brave man, Hotspur. A brave man and a noble knight.' He paused, let out a sigh. 'As for me, I'm to have the Garter next year, and I've been allowed more of my lands. Great rewards. But I asked for still more. I told the King I wanted you, and he agreed to our marriage.'

'He *agreed*?' Constance was hard pressed to believe her ears.

'He said that he would be glad to see you in my care. As soon as I am of age he'll grant me a licence to marry whom I will of his allegiance. A licence that will cost me no more than the fee for the Chancery seal.' He grinned in triumph. 'I told you I could persuade him!'

'But you are not of age yet,' she objected.

'No. He said it was not a thing to be done in haste. That I might change my mind. And of course I shall then have the rest of my lands, be better placed to establish a fit household for you to rule.'

'You are not of age until the January after next.'

He shrugged. 'It will pass. I'll not change my mind, Constance. You are mine now, and no one shall take you from me.'

'I cannot wait so long.'

'There's nothing to fear. The King has pledged me his word, and I have pledged you mine.'

Constance released his hand, stood up, and began to pace around in the limited space available for the purpose.

'You do not understand,' she said. 'The last time we were together you gave me a child.'

He sat up as if someone had stuck a dagger through the mattress. 'A child? But—it was only the once.'

'Once was enough, evidently.'

'You are sure?'

'As sure as a woman can be after two months.'

He beamed, pleased by the evidence of his potency. 'Our son.'

'Your bastard, as matters stand.' She advanced towards him, head high. 'Mun, what will you have me do? Rid myself of it? I cannot! God would not forgive me and nor would I forgive myself. I have sins enough on my conscience.'

'My shirt,' he said, pointing to it. 'Call the boy. He'll not be far from the door.'

She handed him the shirt and summoned the page, who proved to be leaning on the wall outside.

'Go to the Earl Marshal,' Kent told the lad. 'Fetch him back here. Ask him to bring someone else. It doesn't matter whom. Hurry, runt! Before I take my sword-belt to your arse!'

The child scampered off.

'I don't—' Constance began.

'We need witnesses. An irregular marriage is better than none. I'm not having my son born a bastard. Now, help me dress. There's not much time, and my hands are too clumsy to fiddle with laces. That ugly little brat knows better than to linger on my errands so Mowbray will be here before we know it.'

Constance was still tying his points when a puzzled Thomas Mowbray arrived bringing with him an even more puzzled Antonine Dagvar.

'No need to say anything, Tom,' Kent said, before the Earl Marshal could open his mouth. 'No need to say anything, Mistress whoever-you-are. Watch and witness. That's all.'

He took Constance's hand and drew a ring from his index finger. It was engraved with the heraldic lion of the Holland family.

'I take you as my wife,' he said, sliding the ring onto her finger, where it sat uneasily, several sizes too large for its new lodging. 'So help me God and his saints.'

Constance stared at it for a moment, not quite believing and not at all sure that this was a good idea. But it was far too late for doubts.

'I take you, Edmund, as my lord and husband,' she said. 'Until death parts us. May God and his saints witness my vow.'

**

Two days later Constance, one of the many making up Joanna's part of the royal procession, rode into the city of Worcester. The civic authorities had spared no element of an appropriate welcome. The Mayor met the King and Queen at the boundary and made a long speech. The aldermen and guild masters stood bareheaded in their scarlet finery and gold chains until the speech was over, then formed themselves into an escort. The various religious orders of the city chanted their rivalry at one another, and the city gates and the houses within were hung with rich cloths. Musicians played welcoming tunes, wine ran in the conduits and maidens stood on scaffolds to throw flowers down onto the specially swept streets and powdered gold onto the Queen's head. There was even a pageant or two to add to the delay.

The streets were crowded with people, but many stood in silence and showed no sign of rejoicing at the honour done to them. There were many strangers within the walls, driven from their homes by Welsh rebels raiding into Herefordshire. Harry Bolingbroke had the means to enter a city in state, but not to protect his subjects.

Thomas Mowbray nudged his horse closer to Constance. 'There's a rumour,' he said, 'that the King will not enter Wales after all. That he won't be able to raise the funds to pay for his campaign. They say that our next move will be to Gloucester.'

'I dare say we'll hear all manner of lies in Worcester,' Kent said dismissively. He had kept close to Constance almost all the way from Woodstock, as if guarding her. 'The town is bound to be full of Welsh spies and sympathisers.'

'True.' Mowbray's mouth formed into a cynical smile. 'Ride ten miles to the west and you're likely to find a few Welsh arrows as well. They say Herefordshire is all but overrun.'

'But there's no danger here. Do not alarm my lady, Tom.'

'I am not afraid,' she said. 'Glyn Dwr will never dare to venture so far into England.'

The King and Queen and their households were lodged in the Benedictine Monastery attached to the Cathedral, a vast building with ample accommodation for guests. Constance's lodgings gave her a fine view over the Severn, and it occurred to her that she was only a few miles from Hanley Castle, her home for so long. She tried not to think of the place, knowing she would never see it again. It was time to think of the future.

Kent came to visit her when he could escape from attendance on the King, and spent a lot of time talking about his manor of Brockenhurst, in the New Forest, where he thought it would be well to base their household. When she mentioned Caversham, he told her that he did not wish to live on Despenser property. Besides, it was too small for them, and Brockenhurst was far more beautiful, and had a larger park. Brockenhurst it would be. Though, he conceded, they could visit Caversham from time to time if it pleased her.

Constance, remembering that the vows of marriage included a wife's obedience to her husband, gave way. She swallowed her discontent, and told herself she would grow to love Brockenhurst. She would also grow to love Mun himself. Her life was beginning anew, and she had every reason to think herself fortunate.

When Kent was not available to keep her company she walked in the monks' herb garden, or visited the Cathedral. The famous shrine of St. Wulfstan stood in the crypt among a vast collection of lesser relics and, as she knelt before it, she found comfort in her prayers for the first time in many months. Her struggles were over, and soon she would be secure.

She was worshipping at the shrine one afternoon when a voice spoke in her ear.

'Have your prayers been answered?' it asked.

Constance turned and saw that a Franciscan friar had knelt next to her. He drew back his hood, and smiled at her. Even in the uncertain light of the crypt, even with his face clean-shaven instead of bearded, there was no mistaking him. It was Edmund Mortimer.

She shot to her feet. 'What do you do here?' she demanded. 'How dare you speak to me!'

He shrugged. 'I came to see you because you refuse to answer my letters.'

'You must be mad. Be gone before they hang you as you deserve. I have nothing to say to you.'

She made to leave, but he snatched at her wrist.

'I am risking my life,' he said. 'Will you not at least hear me out?'

'No. There is nothing you can say, Edmund, that will amend matters. I hope you burn in hell for the deceit you worked on me.'

'Deceit? What deceit?'

'You know well what deceit, you false, cowardly bastard! You pretended to love me, used me as your whore.'

He shook his head in astonishment. 'There was no deceit,' he said. 'None in this world.' He released her, walked to the shrine, and laid his hand upon it. 'You are the only lady I have ever loved, or ever will love. If I lie, may I indeed burn in hell. But I do not lie.'

She snorted. 'You should save talk of love for your wife. Especially now she has borne you a son.'

'You have heard of that?'

'Of course I have heard! Someone was at pains to tell me of it. I can even tell you his name—Lionel.'

He sighed. 'Catrin is a dear child. But I married her out of necessity, Constance, because there was no other way out of Glyn Dwr's prison. Certainly not because I loved her. How can you imagine such a thing?'

'Perhaps because you have bastards littered through the marches! I believe you would lie with any woman foolish enough to yield.'

'Most men would,' he said, 'but love is more than that. Far more. You know it is so.'

She avoided his eyes. 'You have made your excuses. Now go.'

'I have more to say.'

'Have you? Well, it is too late. You killed my love for you. It is *dead!* I belong to Kent now.'

'Kent? You mean Mun Holland? That boy?'

She laughed in his face. 'Not so much a boy as that, Edmund. He has got me with child, which is more than you could do. I shall be his Countess and fill his house with sons, and have more pleasure with him than ever I did with you. I have an advantage over your Catrin, or whatever she calls herself. I can make comparisons.'

He stood back, as if she had struck him. 'Do you really hate me so much?' he asked.

Her eyes flickered. 'I hate you as much as I used to love you. Perhaps more. Does it matter? I doubt whether we shall ever meet again.'

'I pray that we shall. I need your help, Constance.'

'My help?'

He hesitated. 'It is important, or I'd not ask. Glyn Dwr believes my nephews are in danger. I need you to help me find a way to free them from Windsor Castle.'

'Is that all?' She laughed again. 'You must be mad, or drunk. Which is it?'

He took her hand and raised it to his lips. 'Between us, Constance, we can finish Bolingbroke, place the rightful King on the throne. I do not say it will be easy. I only ask that you think about it. Perhaps there is some way for the boys to escape.'

'It is impossible,' she said. 'Kent would never forgive me if I involved myself in such folly. Why should I risk all that I have for your sake? Or for Glyn Dwr?'

He took a small pewter medal out of his scrip, a crude representation of Mary Magdalene, and placed it in her hand.

'Think on it,' he said. 'Only think. I ask nothing more. Send this to Alianore if you wish to see me again. She will see it safe delivered, for her sons' sakes.'

He pulled the hood back over his head, bowed, and left her, vanishing into the darkness that was formed beyond the light of the forest of votive candles.

Constance considered the pilgrim medal he had left in her hand, and allowed it to slip through her fingers onto the floor. She had no wish to see him again, and so there would be no occasion to send it to Lady March.

She was half way to the stairs before she halted, turned around, and went in search of it.

36

The more Constance thought about Mortimer's approach to her, the more extraordinary it seemed. After a few days she was almost inclined to think it had been some sort of waking dream, and perhaps her brain might have learned to regard it as such had it not been for the medal of St. Mary Magdalene. She wore it about her neck on the same chain as Kent's ring, hidden, clinking together against her skin in the hollow between her breasts. Occasionally, to remind herself of reality, she drew the chain out, held ring and medal together in her palm, and wondered what was to be done.

Mun caught her in the middle of one such reflective moment, taking her hand in his before she could close her fingers around the two objects.

'What's this?' he asked playfully. 'Do you dote on your ring? Or on this?' He studied the medal for what seemed an eternity. 'St. Mary Magdalene,' he grunted, deciphering the crude artistry. 'I didn't know you had a devotion for her. Is she one of your patrons?'

Constance was forced to a hasty improvisation. 'A friar gave it to me. He said that I might pray to her, that she would understand my troubles. That is all.'

Mun snorted in amusement. 'The greater part of these friars are rogues, if not traitors. I dare say you paid for this tawdry trash in gold, and that he's still stuffing his fat guts with wine and capons at your expense.' He released her hand, and slid his arm about her waist. 'My dearest, you should know that your troubles are over. I shall take care of you now. In truth, I'm already pursuing your interests. I've been speaking to my man-of-law about your Despenser dower-rights.'

She allowed him to kiss her and then, their hands linked, to lead her forward, out of the shadows and into the hall. The room was crowded with those Bolingbroke had summoned to Worcester to attend the Great Council. William Beauchamp of Abergavenny was standing near to the entrance, with his brother-in-law, Arundel, but she made the pretence that they had not caught her eye, and swept by without so much as a nod in their direction.

'My brother York long since promised that he would speak to the King about my dower,' she said, her voice hard, 'but of course he broke his word.'

Edward was across the room, one of a little group around the Prince, with Warwick, the Talbot brothers and Sir John Oldcastle. It was clear that he was leading the conversation, his grins and gestures and the relaxed postures of the others suggesting the topic was a light one.

'It is very simple,' Mun went on. 'My fellow will draw up a petition for you to submit to the next Parliament. You have only to sign and set your seal to it, all else will be ordered for you. It's only to be expected that York has not helped you. Once Parliament has granted you your rights, the King will order the various sheriffs to assign your dower, and it's all but certain your brother will lose some of the lands he holds by right of your son's wardship.'

It sounded all too simple to Constance, who knew something of the difficulty of enforcing nominal entitlements, but for the present she found a comfort in allowing herself to be deluded by his cheerful certainty.

'It will make us much more secure,' he continued, their closeness enabling him to speak almost directly into her ear. 'Once our marriage is properly formalised I'll give you a jointure in my lands, and you'll release your Despenser properties to me. They belong to me anyway, strictly speaking, for as long as we are man and wife; but it's better that we should have a formal contract between us. I can probably borrow money against your life-interest in them, and that should be useful. There'll be a great deal of expense, one way or another, and I've not got as much as I should have. I've a great aunt dowered on my lands, as well as my mother and my sister of Surrey, and none of them shows any sign of dying, though Aunt Elizabeth is old enough to be Eve's own daughter. Her *second* husband fought at Poitiers!'

Constance paused to exchange a brief greeting with Lord Charlton, Alianore's husband, but the firm pressure of Kent's hand drew her on before any serious conversation could develop.

'Of course,' he said, 'it would be a great thing if we could win your son's wardship back from York. I can't understand why the King is so generous with him, not when everyone knows that he was hand-in-glove with the Percys. Which reminds me, Constance, I need to mention something else. Douglas and I were talking about you the other day, and he told me that he's met you before.'

She hesitated, taken aback by this unexpected turn in the conversation. 'Douglas?' she repeated.

'He says that he met you at Alnwick. Last year.'

She shrugged. 'There's no secret about it. I was trying to raise a ransom for Edmund Mortimer.'

He took an exasperated breath. 'You never spoke of it to me. You were conspiring with the Percys, and yet you wonder why the King is suspicious of you? I dare say York had something to do with it, didn't he?'

Constance head tilted back a little. 'He was in Guienne. I acted for myself, for my own ends. What dealings my brother had with the Percys I cannot say.'

Kent eyed her for a moment, as if challenging her to flinch under his scrutiny. 'Well,' he sighed, 'it is ended now. Hotspur is dead, and the King secure. You'll not involve yourself in such folly again. I shall see to that.'

'Mun, I—'

'It is ended. Ended forever.'

She considered that for a moment in silence before answering. 'You spoke of my lands, Mun, but they will be worth but little until there is peace in Wales. It's the King, and your cousin Arundel who will not hear of any settlement. A Mortimer king would end the fighting, and there'd be profit from Glamorgan as there used to be in King Richard's time, with rents and dues paid, and no garrisons to maintain. A Mortimer king who would be your nephew.'

He shook his head. 'Do not speak treason in my hearing, Constance. I'll have no part in it, and nor will you, while you belong to me. You should have other matters on your mind. Our child the first among them. You'll only be able to conceal it for so long. You'll need to ask the Queen to give you leave of absence, and find a means to persuade her to agree. Think on that.'

'There is time yet.'

'Either that or we put the ring on your finger, go to the King, and explain all. It might be better so.'

She shook her head. The thought of humiliating herself before Bolingbroke, admitting that premature marriage was necessary to save her from shame, was more than her pride could stomach. And there was something more than that, something she could not quite define. An inexplicable reluctance.

'I will speak to the Queen when the time comes,' she said. 'If you think it good, I shall go to your sister Alianore, at Powys Castle. I know she will care for me, and put the child in her nursery until we can take it back. Alianore loves children, especially babies. She'll not refuse me.'

Kent digested that for a moment. 'Wales? Would that be safe?'

'Charlton's people are very loyal, and the castle is strong. I think I'd be almost as safe there as I am here. What's more, there's little chance of unexpected visitors. With matters as they stand, no one travels in Wales unless they must.'

He nodded slowly, weighing the idea, unable to think of a better one.

Constance gathered she had won her point, and that he was prepared to allow this decision at least to remain in her province. Her eyes left him for a moment, visited Edward again. Her brother was laughing now, his arm draped familiarly around the Prince's shoulder. He had, she reflected, good cause to be pleased with himself. People might suspect what they would, but he was safe in Harry's favour. The King, in a formal pronouncement to the Great Council, had declared him a loyal subject, denying all contrary rumours, and gone on to appoint him Lieutenant of South Wales.

Someone was moving through the crowd towards her, a young man wearing a battle-torn jack-of-plates and filthy riding boots. His lank brown hair and uneven beard looked as if a drunken hedger had trimmed them. It was only slowly, and with some reluctance, that Constance recognised her younger brother. Dickon hesitated, considered joining the group around the Prince and Edward, and thought better of it. Instead he walked up to Constance and Mun, greeting them with a sheepish grin.

'I'm looking for the King,' he said, as if no other explanation was necessary. 'They say he's taking his rest, and not to be disturbed. Rest? Before supper? Is that true, or are they jesting with me?'

Constance cast a disapproving eye over him. 'Have you looked at yourself?' she asked. 'Have you no servant to clean your gear or put a comb through your hair? You cannot enter the King's presence looking like a beggar. You shame us all.'

He shrugged, conscious of her scrutiny and Kent's faintly arched eyebrows. 'I know I could do with a soak in a bath, and a change of clothes,' he admitted. 'I've been on the road for two days. Spent last night in a hay loft.'

'I thought you were still in Powys.'

'I left there months ago. The Prince sent word for me to take my men into Herefordshire, to help the sheriff and the archdeacon defend the county. That's what I've been trying to do all summer, but we're all but beaten into submission. The archdeacon has sent me to beg the King to come to our aid. I bring letters from him.'

She frowned. 'The archdeacon has no business to *send* you anywhere,' she observed. 'Remember you are the King's cousin.'

'The King's penniless cousin,' Dickon said derisively. 'The few men I have left only follow me out of habit; I've nothing to give them. Not a coin. We do well to eat. Archdeacon Kingston feeds us, and he's ruling the shire because there's no one else there with the wit to do it. Is Anne here with you?'

'Yes.' Constance did not elaborate.

'I expect she's forgotten me. I've had no leisure to write letters since I came to Herefordshire. There's been no time for anything but fighting. The rebels press us hard, raiding and burning all over the county, and there's not enough of us to do anything to the purpose. While we're chasing one gang of them back into Wales, another comes in behind us.'

'The King has been ill,' Mun said. 'It's true that he's taken to his bed, to rest. But I think he will want to hear of this. We'll go to Erpingham, see what he advises.'

Constance had no part in this transaction, nor wanted one, so she borrowed Mun's page and had the boy escort her back to her own room, to bring the good news of Dickon's arrival to Anne. But Anne was not there. According to Agnes, the Duchess of York had paid a visit, and insisted on taking the girl with her when she left, for reasons that Agnes had difficulty in explaining. It was not practicable, Lady Norreys pointed out, for the daughter of a mere esquire to deny the second lady in the land. If Lady Anne had made an objection matters might have been different; but Lady Anne had not.

Constance found herself wishing that Agnes's exaggerated respect for rank was more consistent in its application; but saw that there was nothing to be done, and, sliding her feet out of her shoes, settled on her chair to await the time when she would have to prepare herself to attend the Queen to supper. However, Agnes's tidings were not done. There had been another visitor during Constance's brief absence, a royal sergeant-at-arms who had delivered a sealed parchment.

Constance stared at the King's seal for a moment, troubled herself over what might be written within, and then decided that the matter was better put beyond doubt. She forced her way through the sealing tapes, and opened the sheet out on her lap. It was an order to strengthen the garrisons of her castles at Caerphilly and Ewyas Lacey, on pain of forfeiture. These were properties she had on lease from Elisabeth, by an arrangement dating back to well before Thomas's death. The current revenues from them were so low she could not even find the rent that was due, let alone incur more expense on their protection. Caerphilly was so huge it needed a small army to man its walls adequately, not the caretaker and dozen archers that had to suffice. The rebels could take it when they chose, and there was nothing she could do about it except pray. As for forfeiture, that was a mere jest. A king who hesitated to defend an English county because of lack of funds was in no position to take on additional responsibilities in Wales. She laughed aloud at the sheer absurdity of it.

***

The stink was all-pervasive, the reek of burnt thatch mingling with that of blood and scorched flesh. They were barely over the Severn before they caught their first faint whiff of it and it grew in intensity as they advanced, clouds of smoke rising all around them where farms and settlements were ablaze. The Queen and her ladies travelled in the very centre of the armed column, securely protected not only from potential attack but also from the worst of the evidence of war. Here and there were roofless, skeletal buildings by the road, or the body of a slaughtered animal, but no worse sight was visible from the shelter of the Queen's lumbering carriage. But the stench was unavoidable, and lingered in the nostrils even when they were secure behind the walls of Hereford. It seemed to Constance that it had penetrated her clothes, coated her very skin until there was no escape from it.

Bolingbroke visited the Queen's lodgings to reassure his wife that all was well, but his smile was forced and so, Constance sensed, was his conversation. He slumped next to Joanna, addressing her in soft, almost inaudible French, taking her hand as if in need of her reassurance. He was visibly ill and bone-weary, almost drifting off to sleep as he spoke. Joanna, though outwardly composed, was much quieter than usual, her face grey with concern and doubt. Harry had brought several companions with him, including Mun, Dickon and the Earl of Warwick, with the Earl Marshal also present, but it was notable that even these young and vigorous men were taciturn, that they made no serious attempt to converse, flatter the Queen, flirt with the other ladies, or suggest possible entertainments for the company. In normal circumstances Constance would have considered them to be lacking in manners.

'Is it necessary that you go on into Wales?' Joanna asked, breaking the silence.

Harry nodded, forced himself upright. 'Yes.'

'There's a French fleet in Cardigan Bay, madame,' Warwick said uncomfortably. 'Great danger of a landing. They must be opposed.'

'I suppose we should be grateful it's not a *Breton* fleet,' Mowbray said in an undertone, so that only Constance and Mun could hear him. The Bretons had lately raided the coast of Devon and burned Plymouth, to the great embarrassment of the Queen. Since her marriage she had possessed no authority in Brittany, but that did not prevent the English people from attributing some of the blame to her. There were already calls for her Breton attendants to be banished from the realm.

Constance tried not to smile at the Earl Marshal's attempt at humour, but failed.

'Cousin, please share the jest with us,' Joanna said acidly, her dark eyes hard. 'Our men must fight again, so soon after that terrible battle, and yet you are amused?'

'The fault is mine, Your Grace,' Mowbray admitted. 'I did but say that it is fortunate the sea does not quite reach up to Hereford.'

The Queen snorted with disgust, and flapped her hand at him impatiently. 'Imbecile!' she spat out.

Bolingbroke growled with laughter, against all their expectations. 'If it did, it would save us a journey across Wales!' His eyes lit on Mowbray, considering him. 'Well said, boy. There's been gloom enough. Let us have some music. There's no better balm for the soul in times of trouble.'

Joanna gestured to Antonine, who picked up her lute and began to play a gentle French tune, accompanying herself in a song of frustrated love. Warwick knew the words, and joined in the second verse, his singing surprising Constance with its richness and clarity. Then the King himself added his mellow voice to the song, which surprised her less. Harry had always loved his music. An old memory stirred in her mind of listening while he sang in the great chamber at Wansford, with Mary de Bohun accompanying him on her cithar. It was so long ago, before all the trouble had begun. She had been a child and Harry just a benevolent elder cousin, not a hated enemy. So much had been lost since then. They paraded through her thoughts as they did through her dreams. Her father, conscience-torn, living out his last few years with pain in his heart as well as legs; King Richard, her beloved cousin, starving to death by inches in

some hole at Pontefract; John Russell, driven from his wits and never quite recovered; Edmund Mortimer, forced to live in exile, denied to her forever. Above
all there was Thomas. As each year passed she found new reasons to mourn
him, new causes for regret.

Her son was serving wine to the company, making his way around them as
she kept an eye on him, willing him not to slop the drinks, or trip over some in-
considerately extended leg, or, worse of all, forget the proper order of precedence
for the delivery. There was something of Thomas in him that was beyond mere
physical resemblance, the same quiet assurance and stubborn determination. If
he found something difficult, he'd persevere until he succeeded, whether it was
dancing, tilting at the ring with a lance, or a lesson in Latin.

Richard could not remember his father at all. She had questioned him on
that very point, tried to persuade him that he must at least have some recollection of Thomas leaving them behind at Cardiff. The boy had shaken his head
with a firmness that brooked no further discussion. He did not remember, and
refused to pretend otherwise, even for her.

For that, and for all else, Constance blamed Harry Bolingbroke. She lifted
her head and glanced towards him, saw the pleasure on his face as he enjoyed
the singing, and wished with all her heart that he were dead. Harry sensed her
eyes upon him, instinctively returned her gaze, and saw what that gaze contained before she had time to avert it from him.

The song died away, and Antonine paused for a moment and began another
piece of music, a gentle, persuasive melody suitable for a slow dance. No one
stirred. Instead they watched one another in silence over their glasses of wine
as the evening settled upon them. Constance felt Mun move subtly closer to
her, his hand pressing down on her fingers, but in her present mood that produced nothing more than a mild irritation, mixed with a desire to be outside
that stifling room, and very far away.

She rose, advanced to stand before Bolingbroke. 'Cousin Harry, I have something to ask of you,' she said quietly.

The King wondered what it could be, after that intercepted glare. He stiffened his back against his chair, and took a breath. 'Ask then, Constance. You
know how matters stand with us, how little I have to give. But I will not refuse
what is reasonable.'

'You have ordered me to place more men in Ewyas Lacey and Caerphilly,
but I have no means to pay them.'

Harry raised his hand, interrupting her. 'The same order has gone to the
lord of almost every castle in the Marches, for our common defence against
these rebels. I have asked nothing of you that I have not asked of the others.'

'I know it.' She paused, suddenly aware that Joanna's eyes were scrutinising
her. The Queen seem almost ready to speak, but did not. 'However, my case is

different. My lands are not mine to offer in pledge for loans. I cannot even claim a life interest in them.'

'There is nothing more I can do for you.' Bolingbroke seemed to realise how harsh that sounded. He sighed, went on more gently. 'Cousin, if I had the means, I would be more generous. You must manage as best you can.'

Mun had moved up beside her. 'Highness, I did not know my lady intended to speak to you of this. I would have advised her otherwise.'

The King shrugged. 'It is of no force. There is nothing more that I can do.'

'I have a thought,' Constance said, 'but it will need your approval, Sire. I still maintain a household of sorts at Caversham. There is no reason why I cannot move it to Ewyas Lacey. I will do so, if you agree. But I cannot ask my people to live in so wild and dangerous a place unless I myself go with them. You will have to give me leave to quit the Queen's household, at least for a time.'

Harry considered the matter, his hand raised to his beard as an aid to concentration. 'Ewyas Lacey,' he mused. 'A small, remote place, from what I remember of it. I'm surprised you wish to live there.'

'I do not *wish* it. I can think of nothing else that will serve.'

'Perhaps,' Joanna ventured, 'my lady would prefer to live in some private place for some months. Withdrawn from the world, while she contemplates her future marriage. Is it so, my dear cousin?'

Constance did not like the tone in the Queen's voice, and thought it better to say as little as possible in reply. 'Yes, madame.'

'It is hard to think of a place more withdrawn from the world than Ewyas Lacey,' Harry commented, raising his eyebrows. He turned towards Mun. 'Kent. What do you say, since you have an interest in the matter?'

Mun shrugged indifferently. 'For the present, my lady remains her own mistress,' he said. 'I am with you, Sire, to the war in Wales, and shall have little time to be paying court, whether at Ewyas Lacey or Hereford.'

Constance caught the stiffness in his tone, and gathered that in some way she had contrived to offend him. It was unfortunate, but there was nothing to be done.

***

Much later, when she emerged from the Queen's apartments, having supervised Joanna's ceremonial preparation for bed, she found him waiting for her. His hand clamping on her wrist, he drew her into an alcove, a corner of intense darkness.

'You have made a fool of me!' he hissed.

She could scarcely make out his face, but his breath was heavy with wine fumes. 'You are hurting me,' she pointed out, deliberately calm.

He eased his grip a little. 'Why did you not tell me about your change of mind? I thought we were agreed you were going to my sister at Powys Castle. If I had known you wanted to go to Ewyas instead I could have spoken to the King on your behalf. Instead you have made me feel as if I am of no account—nothing. Shamed me before all. Have I treated you so ill that I deserve to be so used? Tell me how I have failed you. Have I beaten you? Forced you? Betrayed you with other women?'

The extent of his anger baffled her. 'I meant no harm,' she said. 'The idea came to me all at once, while we were sitting there. I never dreamed you would object, when it was you who told me that I ought to find a means to leave the Queen's household. You were right in that, and Ewyas Lacey is closer than Powys, and the journey will be easier.'

He was puzzled. 'But Alianore will not be there to care for you.'

'I can move on to Powys later. There's plenty of time, and I'm sure she will not want me under her roof for months on end.' She paused, smiled at him in the darkness, and raised her free hand to his shoulder. 'Forgive me, Mun. I know I ought to have talked to you first, but I thought it right to ask my cousin's permission while there was an opportunity. I see him every day, but there isn't always a chance to speak to him. Since Thomas died, I've grown used to shifting for myself.'

'You've grown too much your own woman,' he said sulkily. 'Cherish your secrets too fondly. Sometimes I wonder if you have any use for me at all, or whether I'm just another lackey you keep waiting upon you. I sometimes think you are closer to Mowbray than you are to me.'

She could not restrain a laugh. 'Mowbray? He's a boy! How can you be jealous of such as him? You are my lord and husband.'

'Yet you do not treat me as such. Do not even trust me.'

'It is not that, Mun. Truly it is not. But we *do* have a secret to keep, and I go in constant fear of betraying it. We are watched, all the time.'

His grip slipped to her waist. 'We are not watched now,' he objected. 'We are alone, and you can talk to me. What is it, Constance? Is it York? Has he been trying to involve you in another of his schemes?'

She shook her head. 'I've hardly spoken to Edward, or Philippa, since I came back to court.'

'Then what is it? Something is troubling your mind, I know. It shows in your manner—your coldness.'

'My coldness?'

'Of late, I'm scarcely allowed to kiss your hand.' The resentment was spilling out of him now, his anger barely under control. 'Do not deny that something is worrying you.'

She snorted. 'Do you wonder at it? When my belly is swelling by the day with your child? When I have no husband I can acknowledge?'

His hand smoothed the belly in question. 'But you do have a husband. And as for the babe, it does not show yet. Who knows of it but us?'

'Do you suppose my women do not know?' She snorted with frustration. In some ways he was still a boy, almost an innocent. 'I think they are loyal to me.

I doubt they will talk. But I cannot be sure. Agnes has never been very good at keeping secrets, and the others are young and easily tricked. The Queen has started to give me strange looks. Sometimes I am sure she has guessed, that at the least she suspects. Women notice small things, Mun, that you might not regard at all. Especially when they have borne their own children, and know the signs. They do not necessarily need to be told when another woman is breeding.'

'And that is what has been troubling you?'

'Do you not think it enough?' She closed her hand on his, halting the caress. 'Have you thought what will be said of me if this becomes known?'

'It will be an evil day for any man who insults you, or speaks ill of you in my hearing,' he said fiercely. 'You may leave that matter to me.'

'It will be no comfort to me that you have killed some other man on my account, deprived some other woman of her husband.' She lowered her head and spoke more quietly. 'Mun, all this has been bearing down on my spirits for weeks. I wanted to speak to you about it, but I feared you would think me a fool, that you would soon weary of hearing me whine about my troubles.'

In the intense darkness, she could not make out his expression, but the pace of his breathing eased, his grip on her changed and gentled, and she knew him satisfied by her explanation. She breathed a little more easily herself, while regretting the deception, or more precisely its cause, the lack of political accord between them. She could not truly confide in him, not while he stubbornly refused to hear a word spoken against Bolingbroke.

His hands and lips were making it clear that he bore her no grudges, and Constance found her body starting to respond to him, even while her mind retained its doubts. They were beyond speech now, and he was tugging at her skirts, lifting them up, pushing her back against the wall. She struggled breathlessly to part her mouth from his, only to find that his strength would not allow it. It was too late to be concerned about any harm they might do to the child, or for any other form of consideration. Mun was in no mood to be denied.

37

Ewyas Lacey stood on high ground, about fifteen miles to the south west of Hereford, the centre of a small marcher lordship that guarded a part of the western flank of the English shire. Beyond the Vale of Ewyas and the isolated Llanthony Priory to the west the Black Mountains soared, and over their peaks lay Bolingbroke's own Lordship of Brecon. Fifteen miles to the south was Abergavenny, where William Beauchamp and his formidable young wife, Joan, Arundel's sister, lived in an almost constant state of siege; beyond that, to the south west, were the valleys of Glamorgan, now largely a nest of rebels. The King and the army had moved westwards through Abergavenny and Brecon, towards Carmarthen, and left behind them a thinly defended land, protected by the garrisons of such castles as were still holding out against Glyn Dwr, and a handful of other troops, most notably the small force led by Richard of Conisbrough and designated to defend Herefordshire.

Dickon, at the King's direction, had added to Constance's security by screening the movement of her household from Hereford to Ewyas Lacey and then remaining with her, using the castle as his forward base. The small and ill-maintained fortress did not in any sense control the main routes into the county from Wales, and so Dickon puzzled over his orders, even though he was not so bold as to question them. He sent out mounted patrols at regular intervals, around a dozen men in each, and tried to do the impossible.

Queen Joanna remained at Hereford, awaiting her husband's return from Wales. She had the men of her household to protect her, of course, as well as the archdeacon, the citizens and their walls. However that did not lift the burden of responsibility from Dickon's eighteen-year-old shoulders, and his detailed knowledge of what little there was standing between Glyn Dwr and Hereford was productive of many sleepless nights.

He tried to discuss some of his concerns with his sister, but found that Constance was preoccupied with other matters and inclined to be impatient with him. It was true there were difficulties involved in settling her household into a castle that had not been used as a family home for more than fifty years, but he sensed there was more to it than that.

There was no one else in whom he could confide except Anne Mortimer, and in a place such as Ewyas Lacey it was difficult to find her alone, and still more difficult to secure a suitable location for private conversation. There were no gardens attached to the castle; if such had ever existed, they had long since been trampled to mud by the resident pigs.

Dickon went out on patrol himself, so that he might ponder the matter in relative quietness. He wore his plated jack rather than his steel armour, because experience had taught him that in this war speed and ease of movement was of greater importance than mere protection, and the lighter its load, the further and faster his horse would travel across the mountains. His expensive pieces of plate lay in barrels, shrouded in their protective grease, much to Constance's disgust. Their brother York had his faults, she said, but he would never ride around the countryside looking like a penniless mercenary, and would certainly not approve of his heir doing so.

To which Dickon answered that as he was fighting for pay, and not receiving any, he *was* a penniless mercenary, so it was not inappropriate for him to be equipped like one. As for their brother, Ned was very far away. Gone with Philippa to London, nominally to prepare for his new duties in Wales. In any event his opinion on the matter could not be tested. Constance had not said much after that, but her way of not saying it had cut him to the bone, and he had been glad to find a reason to leave the castle for a few days.

The country seemed to be at peace, but Dickon had learned from experience that it was wise to be wary, and did not relax his vigilance. Today's peaceful shepherd might prove to be tomorrow's fierce warrior. The people in this part of the country were of low stature, like himself, their faces bronzed by the prevalent wind and rain, their backs bent by the long struggle to scratch a living from their animals, their trees and their small patches of rugged, stone-infested earth. In these borderlands it was difficult for a stranger to detect whether a man deemed himself English or Welsh, because most had the blood of both nations in their veins, and relatives on either side of the border. Nor was name, nationality or language a touchstone of loyalty. An avowed Englishman might take his spear or bow down from the wall and go out with his Welsh neighbours to fight for Glyn Dwr. A proud Welshman might prove staunch for the King. There was no knowing, until the spear was thrust at you or the arrow loosed at your horse.

After three days of uneventful patrol Dickon returned to Ewyas Lacey. It was afternoon, and the late September sunshine lit upon the castle and made it look, from a sufficient distance, almost a thing of beauty. It was only when you came closer that you saw the clear evidence of years of neglect, the weakness of the crumbling walls, the rot in the timbers of the drawbridge and gates, and the tall weeds pushing their way through the uneven, half-buried cobbles of the baileys. In the outer bailey, with the rooting hogs at last confined to their pens at Constance's order, Hugh Tyldesley was drilling some of the men and boys of the household with their weapons, a task that involved much shouting and questioning of parentage.

'Lord Richard,' Tyldesley said in greeting, breaking off from his task, 'we had begun to fear for you.'

Dickon climbed down from his horse, and handed its reins to one of the boys who came running. 'I think the rebels are lying low, with the King in the field. We've ridden in a great circle, almost back to Hereford, and no one has opposed us.' He dismissed his men to their ease, and walked with Tyldesley towards the gate to the inner ward. 'I suppose there's been no trouble here?' he asked.

'Not from the Welsh,' Tyldesley said dryly. He left it there, offered Dickon a faint, secret smile of fellowship.

'My sister is well?'

'My lady came down to the hall yesterday. She settled some dispute between two fools who both claim the same field as their own. Mostly she keeps to her chamber. Lady Norreys and I are managing matters, and not troubling her unless we must. It's easier so for all of us.'

Dickon digested that, took account of what had not been said as well as what had, and sighed. Clearly Constance's temper had not improved during his absence.

Inside the castle he found Anne Mortimer squatting on the stairs, fondling one of the household dogs, a small greyhound bitch that had attached itself to her. Her expression lightened when she caught sight of Dickon, and she stood up to greet him. She was well into her fifteenth year now, and almost as tall as he. She brushed hurriedly at her shabby, workaday gown, as if suddenly aware of its deficiencies.

'Dickon,' she said simply.

He advanced, kissed her hand, and stroked her dog's head. 'I want to talk to you,' he said, drawing her aside and walking with her to one of the window embrasures in the hall. 'Do you know what it is that ails Constance? She will not speak to me of it, but I know there is something, and from what Tyldesley says she's in no better mood than when I left. Why does she choose to live in such a place as this? It is not fit for her, my nieces, or you. I'm not even sure that it's safe.'

'I don't know,' she said, refusing to meet his eye.

He sighed. 'Anne, you must know something. If she hasn't spoken to you, she must have confided in Lady Norreys or Mary Russell. Tell me what it is, so I may do what I can to help her. Do you not trust me? Surely you realise I would never do her harm.'

She stepped up to the raised window-seat, and rested her slight weight on it. The silence between them extended as she consulted the back of her hands. 'I suppose you will discover the truth before long,' she said, sighing. 'Dickon, you must ask her yourself, for I dare not tell you. She would know that I had, and one thing I have learned about Constance is that she does not forgive. Not ever. I could not bear for her to hate me as she does my Uncle Edmund.'

***

Constance was working through her accounts, checking the figures carefully, hoping there were errors in her favour, or at least clear signs of peculation. Here and there a penny was out of place, or a payment was slightly larger than she thought justified, but that was all. She frowned over the task, grateful that her Michaelmas rents were due soon, even though there would be little left to put aside once her most pressing debts were cleared.

Her daughter Bess squeezed onto the seat next to her, and sat there, wordless, until Constance slid her arm about her, and drew her closer.

'What is it, dearest?' she asked.

The child shook her head. Nothing was wrong. All she wanted was the comfort of her mother's affection.

'I suppose you find it tedious here,' Constance said gently. 'I cannot let you ride in the park as you did at Caversham. It's too dangerous. You must stay within the walls, and care for your sister. Play with Isabelle.'

Bess did not answer, just nestled closer, and a contented silence fell over them for a time, until Constance began to trouble herself with thoughts of the future. In a few years it would be time to start looking for a husband for Bess, to provide her with some security for her future. But where was the necessary dowry to come from? It was not reasonable to make Bess wait until her brother came into his inheritance; she needed to be settled long before that.

Dickon's arrival broke the silence. Bess jumped up, curtsied to her uncle, and ran to him, anxious to have his kindly arm about her shoulder. She was not entirely disappointed, but after a few minutes Dickon cut his greeting short.

'Bess, I need private words with your mother,' he said. 'Find your nurse. I think she's in the hall with Isabelle and Anne.'

Constance looked up, minded to say that the child might stay with them, then caught the light in her brother's eye and confirmed the instruction.

'Did you see any sign of the rebels?' she asked, when the door had closed behind Bess. She became aware of the considerable amount of ink on her fingers, rose and went to wash her hands in the bowl of scented water that stood on the dresser.

He shook his head. 'No. But they will be here, one day. Constance, this is no place for you, still less for Bess and Isabelle. It is not safe. The walls look as if a breath of wind could blow them down, and the ditch is clogged. I doubt it's been cleared since our great-grandsire's day. You should go back to Hereford, to the Queen and your son. Leave most of your household here, if you must, but not the women and children, and not yourself.'

She dried her fingers on a linen towel and returned to her seat. 'If this place is safe enough for my servants, it's safe enough for me, and I shall stay, even if Glyn Dwr sets a siege about us. I understand that you and your men may need to leave, that you cannot afford to be trapped here if you're to protect Hereford from attack.'

Dickon's mouth tightened. He detached his short arming sword from his belt, and laid it aside, then threw himself onto the stool next to her chair. 'I want to know what it is that you are keeping from me. There's a reason you have come here, and it's not to defend this desolate hole, or advance Cousin Harry's cause in Wales.'

'You heard the reason. You were in the room when I asked our cousin's permission to live here with my people. I could think of no other way of obeying his order to strengthen this castle. There's no more to it than that.'

'Anne says otherwise.'

'Then Anne should hold her tongue!'

'She has. That's why I'm asking you for an answer.' He waited for her response, and when it was not forthcoming went on. 'Constance, after our mother died, you were the only one who gave me any measure of love or kindness. The best days of my life were when I was with you and Thomas. You've shared your home with me when I had nowhere else to go. You even bought me a horse and armour when I needed them, and have never pressed for repayment of the loan. All this I remember, and always shall. Have faith in me. Whatever troubles you, if there is anything I can do, I will do it, even at peril of my life.'

She avoided his gaze, trying to recall when he had last said so much at one sitting. 'There is nothing you can do that will help,' she said quietly. 'The truth, if you must have it, is I was glad of an excuse to leave the court before my belly became obvious to all. The fewer people that know of my state, the better.'

He blinked owlishly. 'Do I understand you aright?'

'I think you do.'

He hesitated, as if still unsure, until she emphasised the slight swelling by running her fingers across it. 'You and Kent?'

'Yes.'

He fist slammed onto the table, so that account rolls, penknife and ink pot bounced and curtsied with the shock. 'I will kill him!'

She reached out her hand to his, anxious to calm him. 'No, Dickon, you will not. He would kill you if you tried, and that would be no gain to me. Anyway, you've no cause to be concerned about my honour. Mun is my husband.'

He frowned in angry bewilderment. 'How can he be?'

'We've exchanged vows.'

He stood up, snorting. 'By that I suppose you mean you have espoused yourselves in some corner? Without consulting your family? Without the King's leave?

Without banns or a priest? His word against yours if it comes to the test! How could you be such a fool?'

It was a question that Constance had asked more than once of herself, and without securing a satisfactory answer. She nodded solemnly. 'I had little choice, in the circumstances,' she said. 'It was that, or nothing. All can be put right, once he comes of age.'

'It had better be,' Dickon said quietly, 'and I shall let him know it, when next I see him. He ought not to have used you as he has. God help him if he denies you, for it is your word I shall take.'

***

Just one week after this conversation, late in the afternoon of the first Wednesday of October, Kent rode into Ewyas Lacey at the head of a small column of his followers. Utterly taken aback, Constance hurried downstairs to greet him, grateful that her brother was not immediately to hand, having gone out to investigate rumours of a raid on one of the neighbouring settlements.

Mun grinned at her from his saddle, and leapt down to enfold her in his arms, bruising her against the solid steel of his breastplate. 'The campaign is over,' he said, with evident satisfaction. 'There were only a handful of French landed after all, and they fled to the hills with their Welsh friends as soon as we approached. Carmarthen is relieved, and we might have driven deeper into the country save that the King fell ill. But he gave me leave to visit you, for he feared you might be in danger.' He paused for breath, and glanced around him. 'S'truth, what a tumbledown ruin! If I'd known it was so, I'd never have allowed you to come here.'

She eased herself out of his fierce grip, gestured towards the steps rising to up to entrance to the hall. 'It's safe enough,' she said, allowing him to lead her inside.

'Is it?' He laughed. 'I think you must allow that I know more of these matters than you do, my dearest. Glyn Dwr has taken far stronger castles than this by storm, or by trickery.'

She shrugged. 'Well, you are here to protect us now.'

'Only for a week or so, at the most. The King has gone on to Hereford to collect the Queen, and from there they'll move to Gloucester. I've to meet them there by St. Luke's Day. There are other blows to be struck against the rebels.' He paused, considering her. 'Take me up to your chamber. You can help me out of this harness.'

They crossed the hall, and then, Constance leading, made their way up the narrow and twisting stair to the solar. She closed off the alcove containing her bed with the curtains hung for the purpose, and he stood on the rush matting by her window while she began to remove his armour, piece by piece.

'At least we can have a few days together,' he said, reaching to stroke her cheek with his fingers, lifting her chin so that he could study her face. 'The King was truly worried about you, you know. Feared the rebels might have you under siege. Both Brecon and Abergavenny are hard pressed, and neither are far from here.'

'It has been quiet, Mun. We've brought supplies in from Hereford without trouble.'

'So you are not short of wine?' He smiled down at her. 'Will you give me a cup? My mouth's as dry as dust.'

Constance rose from her knees, walked to the dresser, picked up the jug and poured out wine for both of them. She handed his goblet to him, took a sip from her own and, setting it down, resumed her labours.

'It's good to have you performing your wifely duties for me,' he said, pausing to swallow down a large proportion of his wine. 'Perhaps you will order me a bath as well.'

'A bath?'

'Yes. I've been living in armour for almost three weeks and I stink, if you haven't noticed. I think I've also got a few Welsh cattle crawling around and making me itch. I'm sure you don't want them infesting your bed.'

Constance's hand hesitated on the buckle she was unfastening. Somehow she had not anticipated that he would expect to sleep with her, but now she thought about it she realised it was only natural that he should.

She had adequate opportunity for anticipation as he soaked himself clean in her tub, his massive frame seeming even larger now that he was naked. It was a strange fact that she had never seen him so before, for they had retained their clothes during her impregnation at Kennington and his hurried taking of her at Hereford. She found that the view was tending to distract her from his conversation, so that more than once he had cause to repeat himself.

'You could climb in here with me,' he suggested.

She smiled at the thought. 'There isn't room,' she objected lightly.

'I could *make* room.' His response was equally light, and his smile especially persuasive. 'Constance, I really think we should get you away from here. You'd be better with my sister at Powys, as we agreed in the first place. Powys is a stronger castle, and Charlton's tenants are loyal to him. Every time Glyn Dwr has shown his face in their country they've given him a bloody nose. I'd also feel happier about leaving you if I knew that Alianore was taking care of you. Will you go to her? If I ask it of you?'

'Powys is a long way off, across the mountains,' she said. 'It would probably take me a week to get there, and the country between is full of rebels. You've said yourself, you and your men have to go to Gloucester—you haven't time to see me safe there. It's impossible for Dickon and his men to go with me; they have more than enough to do as it is, protecting Herefordshire as best they can. There are my own people, of course, but if I take them with me it will mean that this castle is unguarded. I dare not venture into such country with less than all of them.'

'If necessary we'll ask Glyn Dwr to grant you safe conduct. *Will you go?*'

She hesitated. 'Yes. If you wish it…'

Kent stood up in the tub, shaking himself. 'Good!'

Constance, distracted for a moment, handed him a towel. 'But—will Glyn Dwr agree? To the safe conduct?'

'Why not?' He grinned and climbed out of the tub, drying his shoulders and neck with vigorous strokes of the towel. 'He may be a rebel, he may be Welsh, but he's still a gentleman.'

***

Bolingbroke lay in bed at Hereford, his book laid aside because his eyes were too tired to read by candlelight and his brain too weary to translate the Latin text. The physical weakness that had gripped him at Carmarthen, left him barely strong enough to sit his horse, had eased now. In its aftermath he was both desperately tired and utterly unable to sleep.

He knew too well what would happen if he did. They would gather round the bed and stare at him, grinning, until he woke in a sweat. He would sit up, look into the shadows, and see nothing. Sometimes he would rise, take the sword that rested next to the bed as a defence against traitors, and prod behind the hangings, and always find nothing. But once he had settled down and closed his eyes again they would be back, staring and grinning.

King Richard had been the first to trouble his dreams, and always took precedence, always stood closest to the bed. But of late he had begun to bring half his court with him. Bushey, Greene and Wiltshire, the three Harry had had beheaded at Bristol before he took the crown. Exeter, Surrey and Salisbury, arm in arm. Uncle York with Thomas Despenser, Hotspur with his uncle, Worcester. There were lesser men too, men he had condemned, with faces he remembered but names he did not know or could not recall.

He could no longer resist his tiredness. It overwhelmed him, and he dozed, aware of nothing except the faint spitting and flickering of the candles and then, at last, not even of that. A faint consciousness returned, an awareness of peace. This night, it seemed, Richard and the others were elsewhere. In his dream he muttered a prayer of gratitude, a prayer for the rest of their souls.

A dog's feet padded around the bed. It stretched itself, placed the comforting solidity of its long, sleek head beneath his hand. Harry stroked it, smiling in his sleep.

'Math?'

But old Math was dead, more than twelve months since. He'd not had the heart to keep another in his chamber since. He started awake, and stared at his hand in bewilderment. He was alone, and someone was hammering at his door as if the monastery was on fire.

'Sire!' Erpingham's voice boomed through the timber. 'Sire, it is the Queen!'

Before Harry could do so much as grunt, the door was thrown open. Joanna entered, considered him for a moment as Erpingham shut it behind her, and then turned and slid the bolts home.

'Since you will not come to me, my lord, I have come to you,' she said, advancing towards the bed, shedding her silk chamber-robe as she walked. She wore nothing beneath it, indeed nothing at all except the linen coif on her head and the thin leather shoes on her feet. Now, as Harry sat up and watched, she kicked the shoes off too.

She insinuated her small, slender figure into the bed, slid towards him, and made forceful contact with the bejewelled binding of his carelessly discarded book.

'*Mon Dieu!*' she screamed, snatching at the precious volume and throwing it to the floor in disgust. 'This is what happens when you sleep with your books, and not in my bed!' She rose to her knees and massaged her bruised and mildly lacerated flesh. 'Why, Harry? You have been in Wales for weeks, and now you choose to stay away from me. What is it that I have done?'

Bolingbroke was aware of the scent of her, the tang of rosewater and mint, the warmth of her body. Her breasts, small but perfectly formed, presented themselves at his eye level, bounced slightly as she shifted her position to sit on her heels. His fingers stretched out, traced their way down her side, making her shudder with delight.

'I am tired, Joanna,' he said, pulling his hand away.

'Tired?' She stared at him in bewilderment. 'My lord, how old are you? Six and thirty? Or is it three and sixty? I have bathed for you, demeaned myself by coming here, and you say that you are *tired?*'

'I have been ill, and I've hardly slept this last month. Of course I am tired! Even when I do sleep I have evil dreams that allow me no rest. I thought—I thought it better not to disturb you, to let you lie in your bed in peace.'

Her face fell. 'I do not please you.'

'Of course you do, Joanna! It is not that.'

'I do not please you. Perhaps you would like me better if I were big and blonde.'

The non-sequitur puzzled him. He frowned, and decided to ignore it. 'I need to rest.'

'I need a husband!' Her dark eyes flashed, and her small hand formed into a fist and punched at the heavy hangings behind the bed. 'I spent all my best years married to a cold, cruel man old enough to be my grandfather. The Duke flaunted his whores before me, and yet was jealous and angry if another man smiled at me, or touched my hand. I thought you would be better in every way. They called you the greatest knight in Europe, the most handsome man. Your letters were full of kindness. But now I find that you are colder even than he. *At least the Duke gave me children!*'

'I have given you great lands, madame. I have made you Queen of England.'

'I left my sons in Brittany so that I might come to you. I gave up my powers as Regent. For what? Your people hate me. They spit in the streets when I pass, and beat my Breton servants. It rains all the time here and the houses are full of draughts. What your winters will be like I dare not imagine. All this I could bear, if you were a true husband to me. I do not ask for your love. You may have your women if you wish. But I must at least have a share of you.'

Bolingbroke recognised the abject misery in her eyes, and felt ashamed of himself. 'Joanna,' he said gently, 'if I have hurt you, I beg your forgiveness. It was not my intent.' He reached up to the crucifix that was carved into the bed-head, rested his hand upon it. 'If it is any comfort to you, I swear by this that I have lain with only two women in my life. The mother of my children, and my present Queen.'

She let out a little gasp of disbelief. 'But you were a widower for *eight years.*'

'Even so.' He lowered his hand, placed it around her shoulders. 'I decided long ago,' he said, 'that I should not be like my father. At least not in that regard. You see, I remember the use his enemies made of his dealings with women, how his name was part of the common clack of every market. How they mocked him behind his back. A man is weakened when he allows his actions to be ruled by his own lust. He lies rutting in bed with his whores when he should be attending mass, taking advice from his Council or considering letters and petitions. That was the example my father set me, may God rest his soul.'

'But—'

'You may search my accounts if you will. You'll not find any payments that maintain bastards or discarded mistresses.'

'But I thought...' Joanna's voice tailed off in bewilderment.

'What did you think?' The question was gentle, but his voice left no doubt that he required an answer.

Her eyes focused on some point beyond the circle of candlelight as she considered her words. 'I did but think it strange that you kept your cousin at court for so long; that you delayed her marriage to the young Kent, who loves her so very much, and has served you so well.' Her quiet, sultry voice paused, and then went on more strongly. 'I have seen you look at her, Harry. You do not look at me so.'

He was not sure whether to laugh or be angered. 'Constance hates me, Joanna. Her husband died fighting for King Richard, and she has never forgiven me. Has she never told you of it?'

'No.'

'I could not refuse Kent's request for her, not after Shrewsbury, but I wanted to give him time to think again. He is young. He may yet change his mind.'

'But what if he does not?'

'Then he may have her. Though if he has any sense at all he will keep her close at Brockenhurst, and fill her belly every year. Turn her mind away from what she has lost and cannot regain.' He sighed, and watched as the Queen relaxed her posture and settled down on the bed. Her long silence told him that the subject was exhausted for the moment.

'Will you go back to Wales this year?' she asked at last.

'Not unless there is a disaster. I think we shall go to Windsor. Rest there for a few weeks, perhaps regain my strength.'

He was taken aback when without warning she delved beneath the sheets, clutched his flaccid manhood in her fingers. They lay there looking at each other in silence, each as discomforted as the other by his lack of reaction.

'You must be *very* tired, my lord,' Joanna said with a sigh. She drew her hand away, slapped it down on the top of the coverlet.

'I am more tired than I believed possible,' he replied, squinting at her. 'As I told you, I have not been sleeping as I should.' He paused, chewing his lip, listening to her breathing, and let out a snort. 'Truth is, awake or asleep, I cannot rest. Sometimes, Joanna, I wonder if the Welsh rebels are right in what they say—that I am accursed of God.'

'That is nonsense! Of course you are not!'

He scarcely seemed to hear her. 'Richard was not fit to rule, but when I took his crown from him, I did a fearful thing. There is no greater sin than to usurp a throne from an anointed king. I knew it, and it went against my conscience, but I could see no other way. For my own security or the common profit of England.'

She slid towards him, rested her head on his shoulder and her arm about his belly. 'I think you should sleep now,' she said softly. 'All will seem well again, in the morning.'

'Perhaps I did wrong,' Harry went on, speaking more to himself than to her, 'but it cannot be undone. I have no choice but to go on, and do what must be done to keep this throne. May God have mercy on me. If I fail, I fear my enemies will not spare me or mine.'

38

Snow flurries caressed the red stone walls of Powys Castle, added another feath-
erweight to the white burdens that were weighing down the branches of the surrounding trees, beginning to conceal the few hoof prints that had been added to
the steep approach road that morning. One of Lord Charlton's junior foresters,
leading home a donkey that was heavily burdened with kindling for the castle
fires, lost his footing on the ice and slid beneath the animal's belly, slamming the
back of his head against the rock-hard ground, the rope reins still clutched in his
hands. A rich assortment of Welsh obscenities poured from his mouth.

So absolute was the silence of the afternoon that his cry carried to the castle,
rose to one of the high windows of the great tower. It passed through the translucent horn glazing and the closed, painted shutters behind it, penetrated the defence of a linen head-dress, found its way through thick, coiled braids of gold hair.
Reached the ears of the woman who rested on the cushioned window-seat.

Constance, instinctively alert for danger, raised her head for a moment. Reassured by the renewal of the intense silence around the castle, she returned
her attention to the baby she was suckling, aware of a fierce, protective joy as
the hungry, toothless little mouth tugged on her nipple. Feeding a child at her
breast was a new experience for her, as her Despenser children had all been
farmed out to wet-nurses, in accordance with family tradition and her own
mother's example. Lady March had other ways, and had encouraged her guest
to follow them.

Lord Charlton was reading a letter by the light of the fire, a letter delivered
by a boy who had somehow struggled through the snow from Shrewsbury; a
boy in the livery of the Prince. It was clear from Edward Charlton's face that
there was no tale of joy in its lines.

'The Prince says there will be no campaign in Wales this year,' he said, shaking his head in disbelief. 'There's no hope of money to pay for it, and the most
we can expect to do is hold what we have. This with the French in the field at
Glyn Dwr's side!'

'A few of them,' Alianore said. She was sitting next to Constance, Joan, her
young daughter by Charlton, settled on her knee.

'They may be few for the present, but what if reinforcements land in the summer?' Charlton paced about, his fingers clutching at his hood in frustration. 'What's

to stop them? We've lost almost all of Wales and the marches as it is. How long can we hold out in Powys, when the rebels are all around us and there's no prospect of striking back at them?'

Constance sighed. Matters in Glamorgan were still worse. Even Cardiff had fallen, the castle and town alike looted and burned, Thomas's guns notwithstanding. There was no prospect of any revenue from her lands in Wales until there was a reconquest, and there was no saying when that would be possible.

'The King's previous campaigns have not amounted to much,' she said. 'He's never once brought the rebels to battle, nor made a foot of land more secure to us.'

'Glyn Dwr will soon learn of his intentions, my lady. As like as not he has this news before us! He'll know that for the next year he is safe. His people may plant their crops, breed their cattle, and attend their markets, without any fear that we shall come among them. Meanwhile, our people live in fear of fresh raids, if not invasion, and know that their King cannot defend them and that we, the lords of the march, can scarcely defend ourselves.'

'Then is it not time to come to terms?' Alianore asked.

Her husband snorted, threw himself down on his chair with such force that the wood gave off a loud crack of protest. 'To ask for terms now, with matters as they stand, would be as good as to surrender. Glyn Dwr might demand everything west of the Dyke. The King would never agree to that. Could he keep his throne if he did?'

'So we cannot win the war, and cannot end it?'

There were several minutes of virtual silence as they considered the matter, their eyes focused on the logs burning in the grate, their principal source of light with the shutters closed against the cold.

'Might Glyn Dwr settle for less?' Constance asked. She eased the contented child from her breast, adjusted her clothing, and then rose and settled her daughter into the richly carved cradle Alianore had provided. 'His real quarrel is with Bolingbroke, Grey de Ruthin and Arundel. Not with the rest of us.'

'It has not stopped him ravaging Powys, or Glamorgan, or even the Mortimer lands,' Charlton said. He shrugged. 'There's no saying what's in Owain's mind. The King will not negotiate with him, and I doubt whether he would negotiate with the King. He has no cause to trust us.'

'He could certainly trust you, Charlton. You are an honourable man. I believe he could also trust Lord Berkeley, or William Beauchamp.' She frowned, reluctant to be generous. 'Even Warwick, I think. If you were to approach him, see what terms he would accept…'

'That would be treason, my lady.'

'Would it? I say it is treason to leave matters as they stand. Glyn Dwr and the French have the power to carry war into England itself, and when they do our people will suffer and die and we shall be ruined, spoiled of all that is our own. A king's first duty is to protect his subjects. If he fails in that, then the subjects have the right to take what measures they must. Even to withdraw their allegiance.'

Charlton shook his head. 'I am but one man, madame, and dare not raise my hand against the King. Nor am I of sufficient rank to lead such an enterprise. It's a task for a great lord, perhaps a prince of the blood such as your brother of York.'

'We were talking of men of honour. No one with any sense will trust my brother, and I have never heard it said that Owain Glyn Dwr is a fool.' She settled by the window again, her chin high. 'He is the last man I would involve in such a negotiation, unless I especially wanted Harry Bolingbroke to know every word that was spoken.'

'Do you think that *my* brother would favour such dealings with the Welsh?' Alianore asked pointedly.

'He might,' Constance said, and then hesitated. 'Mun is touched by this—my lands in Wales are worthless to us while this war goes on. But he is not yet of age, nor possessed of all that is his own. He could scarcely take the lead in the matter.'

'Arundel hates the Welsh and will not stomach any talk of peace,' Charlton went on, 'and Warwick, though he is more moderate, and a great lord, is very close to the Prince. I doubt he would keep secrets from him.' He stared into the fire. 'Even if we could find others to support us, even if we persuaded Glyn Dwr to offer reasonable terms, what would it avail us? The chances are that the King and his Council would repudiate any agreement we reached.'

'Perhaps we should do well to consult Edmund,' Alianore suggested. 'Edmund Mortimer, I mean.'

Constance sat upright. 'Do you mean that you have a way to send word to him?'

Alianore smiled. 'You know very well that I do, Constance. You still wear his token around your neck. What did he tell you to do with it?'

'Send it to you, if I had anything to say to him.' Constance contained her irritation. 'I haven't, and I don't want to bring him into it. His head is too full of wild schemes. Do you know that he came to me at Worcester, disguised as a friar?'

'Yes, of course I know that.'

'Then I suppose you know his purpose? To ask me to find a way to free your sons from Windsor Castle! Such folly! As if I have the power to do such a thing!'

'My wife,' Charlton said, 'goes in fear for her sons.'

'It would be better for them to be in Glyn Dwr's hands, rather than Bolingbroke's,' Alianore added. Her eyes lifted from her lap and fixed them on Constance. 'Edmund spoke of this to us, but he asked for your help because he admires and honours you, and knows you can be trusted. There is no one else attached to the court of whom we could say the same. We hoped you might be able to think of a means to free them. Of course, when we discussed it, we did not know you had my brother's child in your belly. I expect that has kept all other matters out of your mind.'

'Edmund Mortimer has been *here?*' Constance stood up, advanced towards them. 'You encouraged him to come to me? Were you both drunk when you thought of it? Only the blessed saints know how he avoided capture at Worcester while he was on that fool's errand. There were hundreds there who might have recognised him. He could easily have been taken, hanged and drawn.'

'When we were at Easthampstead you wished that very fate upon him.' Alianore smiled and exchanged a subtle glance with her husband.

'I think it's time for me to check that a good watch is being kept,' he said, rising from his place. 'In this weather, men have a way of huddling themselves to the fire and neglecting their duties. Excuse me, my ladies, while I see to it.'

When the door had closed behind him, Alianore gestured towards his vacated chair. 'Sit down, my dear. Now Charlton has gone we may speak more freely. As he no doubt perceived.'

'He is a good man,' Constance said, settling herself, turning towards the fire and leaning back.

'Yes. A gentle, generous man who treats me with respect. He was what I needed after Roger March, and we are good friends.' She paused, folding her hands in her lap. 'Edmund Mortimer was well aware of the risk he was running, but he did not care. He wanted to see you, even for a moment, even if it cost him his life. That is the plain truth. He loves you still, loves you as no man, husband or other, has ever loved me. What's more, I believe that your love for him is no less. That you wish with all your heart that child was his, and not my poor brother's.'

'Alianore, we've been friends, almost sisters, for as long as I can remember. Because of that, and because of the kindness you have shown me, I shall forget those words were spoken.'

'The truth is often painful, but it should always be faced. If you hate Edmund Mortimer as much as you pretend you ought to have betrayed him to Bolingbroke. It would have been a supreme proof of loyalty, and you could have claimed almost any reward. Immediate marriage to my brother; your Despenser dower rights; perhaps even a restored earldom for your son. Edmund was in your power, and by allowing him to escape you implicated yourself in his treason. I know you, Constance, and I know that you love him dearly, whether you admit it or not.'

'If ever I loved Mortimer, he killed that love when he broke his promise to me and married Glyn Dwr's daughter.'

'He did that through necessity, as you well know. More often than not, marriage and love are separate matters.'

'Mortimer's love is a matter of words. He "loves" whatever woman he happens to have on the end of his prick. I must have been half mad to let him near me.'

'He loved you for years. Long before he had any hope of gaining you. You must have been aware of it.' Alianore fell silent for a few moments, allowed the hiatus in the conversation to do its work.

Constance stared into the fire, allowed her feet to stretch towards it for warmth. 'It makes no difference now. I belong to your brother, I have borne his child, and I intend to be a faithful wife.'

'Content as such?'

'I dare swear I love Mun as much as you love Charlton. He will make me a good husband.'

'Will he? I doubt whether either of you has made a wise choice. In any event, our cases are different. I'm happy enough to have a man who is better than Roger March. I could have my pick of dozens. It's much harder to find one who is the equal of Thomas Despenser, and I don't see how you will ever be satisfied with one who is his inferior in every way.'

'I have made my bed,' Constance said. 'I shall not scorn to lie in it.'

She fell silent, dwelling on the nights she had spent with Kent at Ewyas Lacey. They had not exactly been unpleasant, for Mun was a vigorous and repetitive lover when given the chance; but he was also somewhat clumsy, and expected little more from her than simple submission. She decided it was better not to make the comparison that Alianore's words had invited.

'If my sons were free,' Alianore said quietly, 'then the world might change. Is there truly nothing that can be done for them?'

Constance, disturbed from her thoughts, hesitated and then shrugged. 'As you know, they are always either at Windsor or Berkhampstead. Both castles are strong, and deep in the heart of England, well beyond Glyn Dwr's reach. When they are moved between the two, they're heavily guarded. It would take an army to snatch them, even assuming their keepers do not have orders to kill them if such an attempt is made. If it is to be done at all, it will have to be done by stealth.'

'If it could be done it would be the end of Harry Bolingbroke. Constance, my son would be King of England! And yours would be Earl of Gloucester. There would be peace in Wales. That for a beginning!'

'Bolingbroke will not yield as easily as that. We'd need thousands of men to fight for your son's cause.'

'Once March is at liberty, and proclaimed King, thousands will rise for him. From the Mortimer lands alone...'

'Even if it is so, they will still need someone to lead them.'

'Glyn Dwr and his French knights will be our allies.'

'Englishmen will not follow such!'

'There is Edmund.'

Constance shook her head. 'Edmund may have the blood, and the name of Mortimer, but we need a leader with land and followers. Indeed, if Bolingbroke is to beaten we need several such. Not a rabble of Welsh and French.'

'What we need,' Alianore said calmly, 'is your brother, York.'

***

In the Great Chamber of Pontefract Castle, Harry Bolingbroke sat beneath his cloth-of-estate and stared balefully at the man who stood before him, Henry Percy, Earl of Northumberland. Northumberland was an old man now, but there was not an ounce of spare fat on his bones, and he stood erect, his piercing blue eyes meeting the King's with an expression in them that bordered on contempt. Parliament had acquitted him of treason and released him. The King had almost immediately summoned him back to court, to discuss the surrender of certain Percy castles that still defied Harry's officers. That had been months ago.

'You were expected long before this, Cousin,' Harry said.

The Earl bowed, very slightly, 'I judged it my duty to remain in the North and maintain the peace,' he said. 'The manner of my son's death, and the treatment of his body, is still remembered by those who loved him.'

'Perhaps you need to be reminded that your son was a traitor! A traitor who died in arms against me, like that other traitor, your brother.'

Northumberland's cheeks reddened slightly, but he controlled himself. 'To many in the North they were martyrs; as your loyal servant, it is those men I have been trying to keep calm, for the common profit of the realm.'

'No doubt it is such men, rebels, who hold Berwick, Jedburgh and Fastcastle against us. Your men, Northumberland. You will order their immediate surrender, on pain of treason and forfeiture of all that is yours or theirs to forfeit.' Harry stood up. He was insufferably hot in his robes, the baking warmth of the June day penetrating the airless room. He descended from his dais, and looked the Earl in the face. 'There will be no further delay, and no debate.'

'I am ready to accede to your demands, Sire.'

Harry took a sharp breath. This swift surrender was not what he had expected. 'Do not think to cozen me.'

'I do not. I am most ready to obey. All I require in return are lands of equivalent value.'

Bolingbroke's frustration broke out, his fist setting a silver wine-jug flying. '*Lands of equivalent value?* Do you, old man, think to bargain with Us? Unless you surrender your castles I will send an army against you, with heavy guns that will blast their walls into rubble. I swear it, by Christ's Holy Blood.'

Northumberland stood squarely before him, not shifting an inch, staring into his eyes as though they were equals, not sovereign and subject. 'I must remind Your Grace that Parliament did not see fit to forfeit my lands. I have rights of property, and I need scarcely add that the last King of England to set aside such rights without lawful authority came to an ill end. Out of courtesy to you I shall accept a fair exchange, since that is your wish. What I will not do is make you a free gift of my castles. Never!'

The King staggered, leaned his weight on the wooden stand from which he had expelled the wine-jug, its uncertain support creaking beneath his hand.

'Get out, before I harm you,' he said breathlessly. 'You and your family have been traitors from the first. I have always known it in my heart. Get out, and never let me see you again.'

The Earl bowed, his fierce, world-weary eyes never leaving Bolingbroke's face. 'I shall await your proposals for the exchange with eager anticipation, Sire,' he said. 'Lands of equivalent value, granted by patent and with the approval of your Council, assured to my grandson after my death. Then you may have my castles. You have my word on it. The word of a Percy.'

***

They rode beneath the dappled shade of the woods, the ground hard beneath the hooves of their horses, the grass bleached with thirst. In the summer beauty of the north country it was possible to forget the losing war in Wales, and the increasingly frequent raids on the southern coasts by French and Breton ships. Here all was quietness and peace, with not so much as a faint breeze to stir the trees. Below them, to the north, the River Aire ran sluggishly between low, reed fringed banks; to their rear, set on high ground, the distant, whitewashed towers of Pontefract Castle emerged through the trees.

'So Bolingbroke has seen fit to pardon Snede, and what the wretch has stolen from me is lost for good.' Constance drew rein, fixed her eyes on the river and the rows of trees that stood beyond it. Apart from a few scrawny, grazing cattle on the far bank, there was no evidence of human activity. 'It is yet another insult.'

Kent sighed. 'I don't suppose it was intended as such. The King is short of money, and pardons have to be paid for.'

'Yes, and in this case with gold that Snede stole from me! Which makes it worse. Mun, I have already reduced my household as far as my honour will allow, and there's little left to pawn. What am I to do? Live like the widow of a petty squire? Sell my horses and go barefoot?'

'At least Parliament has granted your petition for your Despenser dower rights.' He stretched his hand out towards her. 'Constance, we have precious little time to ourselves. If you are not with the Queen, then as often as not I am in attendance on the King. Let us not waste this fair morning by talking of business.'

She recognised the light in his eye, and knew what he had in mind. 'I need you to speak to the King for me,' she said, nudging her horse forward. 'My grant of dower is of no force until he orders the sheriffs to allot my lands. I mean my proper share of the Despenser lands in England; the Welsh lands are not worth a rush, and will not be until we have peace again. I have already sent him a petition by Erpingham's hand, but had no response. If you will not take up the matter with him, then I must do so on my own account.'

'Of course I will speak for you. But the King has many other matters on his mind, and Northumberland has put him in a foul mood. It might be wise to wait until a better time.'

'I am weary of waiting on Bolingbroke's pleasure. I've done it too often, and it has never been to my profit. He's a man of fair words who does not keep his promises. I see nothing unreasonable in my request—a mere prompt for him to order what is mine by right.'

'I have told you I will speak to him. I think you forget—it's to my advantage to do so. The richer you are, the more I shall be pleased.'

'Then it's a pity you cannot find a means to persuade him, to advise him to end the war in Wales. I've heard many men say we cannot beat the rebels, and sooner or later will have to come to terms with Glyn Dwr. My third of Glamorgan would be worth five hundred pounds a year at the least, if I had possession of it.'

'So much?'

'Then there are the lands I have on lease from Despenser's mother—another two hundred.'

He dwelled on that so long and so comprehensively that his horse strayed from its proper line, and he used knee and heel to guide it back alongside her. 'As good as an earldom,' he said, licking his lips at the thought of such an additional income.

'Yes,' she agreed, halting her horse again at the edge of the trees. A faint trod, bounded by abundant cow parsley, ran through the meadows beyond, down to the river. She raised her eyes to the distant, cloudless horizon, the line of the Pennine hills to the west, faintly purple along their peaks.

Mun drew up alongside her, his bulk blocking her view.

'I doubt whether the King will offer terms to Glyn Dwr,' he said. 'Not now that the rebels have brought the French into the war. It seems to me we have no choice but to fight on, to grind them down little by little. They say the Welsh of Anglesey will submit, and Grey de Ruthin says that without Anglesey all Wales must surely starve.'

'If it had not been for Grey de Ruthin the Welsh would not have rebelled in the first place! Bolingbroke should have allowed the fool to rot in Owain's prison. That was his policy for a better man. There is always a choice, Mun.'

Kent did not answer. Instead he dismounted, and tied his horse to a branch of one of the trees. Then he held out his arms invitingly for Constance to join him on the grass. 'Come down, my sweet,' he said. 'Let us not discuss it now.'

***

'They say Parliament will not rest until all Joanna's Bretons are banished from the realm,' Thomas Mowbray said, cramming a juicy slice of apple into his mouth and advancing a pawn. He held onto the piece for a second with his sticky fingers, decided that the move was satisfactory, and released it. 'All of them, from her daughters to her last and most greasy laundress. A good thing too, if you ask me.'

The Queen's damosels, in two sets of four, were dancing in the centre of the great room, to music provided by a group of Joanna's Breton gentlemen. The prospect of imminent banishment did not seem to be troubling either dancers or musicians—all were thoroughly enjoying themselves.

'That will include your Antonine,' Constance pointed out, as she considered her own move. Their board was set up close to an open casement, the afternoon light flooding over it, just a few feet away from the dance. Antonine was one of those on the floor, the most graceful of them all.

'She's not *my* Antonine any more,' the Earl Marshal said with a shrug. His heavy, discontented lips turned downwards. 'Not since I've had my wife. Boling-broke and his bitch of a sister relented on that in the end; saw that I had my rights. Don't really care for her, though, now that I've got her. Bolingbroke's niece, I mean. She shares your name, but the rest of her is too similar to her mother for my liking.'

'Perhaps you will feel differently in a few years, when your wife has given you a few children.'

'Perhaps it will be different when they stop treating me like an idiot. I'm a grown man, my lady, and when I come into my own I mean to show them a thing or two. I have friends, you know.'

'I'm sure you do.'

'I mean important men; men who remember my father and can't wait to see me in my proper place. Sir William Plumpton, for example, and Lord Clifford. They don't talk to me as though I'm some half-witted boy. They know that by right I should be Duke of Norfolk. I'll tell you this too, though I wouldn't tell anyone else. Plumpton says that half Yorkshire would rise against Bolingbroke tomorrow, if they had a leader. You see, you and I are not the only ones who hate him.'

'Hmm,' Constance said, still considering her move. A faint breeze blew in from the west, sufficient to make her veilings lift and brush against her cheeks like an affectionate kiss. 'You should be careful whom you trust.'

She fell silent, suddenly thinking of her daughters, left with Alianore for the time being. Especially she thought of the baby. She had had to put Nell out to nurse in the end, of necessity, so that she herself could return to court. The parting had not been easy, and the only consolation was that she now saw her son every day, for he was still one of the Queen's pages.

For the present Richard Despenser was standing by the Queen's chair, await-ing orders. Fortunately Joanna was fond of the boy, never found serious fault in him, and quite often laid an affectionate arm about his shoulders, or slipped him an unexpected sweetmeat. The Queen obviously missed her own sons, and now she was to lose her daughters as well, and her Breton servants. For the first time since they had met Constance felt a touch of pity for her.

Aware that Mowbray was growing impatient, she made an ill-considered move of her remaining knight, and immediately lost her queen.

He grinned hugely. 'Your mind is not on the game, my lady. Now it's only a matter of time before I finish you.'

She shrugged, toppled her king in surrender. 'I think I should take some air to clear my head. Will you excuse me?'

He rose and bowed in assent, and Constance extracted herself from her place, mumbled some excuse to Joanna, and beckoned Anne Mortimer to follow her. They descended the spiral stair that led out directly into the gardens.

For a time they walked the gravel paths in silence, keeping within the shadows of the arbours as much as possible. There was a small fountain in a paved, central court, where they settled in the shade on a turf seat, and watched the water as it played, content in their quietness until Anne began to ask questions about her favourite subject, Dickon, and Constance responded with some of her recollections and a few of her current concerns. There was a rumour that because of the King's dire financial plight all annuities were to be cancelled, or at least suspended for a year. That would be the ruination of Dickon; he'd be left with no income at all, unless and until the Duke of York kept his promise to retain him once he came of age. Constance made a mental note of the matter, one of many issues to be discussed with her elder brother when the chance arose. Unfortunately he was not immediately available. The last she'd heard of him was that he was visiting Glastonbury, trying to talk the monks into lending him the money he needed to keep his Welsh garrisons from deserting.

The discussion and the quietness alike were broken by the crunch of many feet on the gravel path. The Earl of Northumberland had entered the garden, and, in his normal fashion, he came not alone, but in the company of a dozen friends, retainers and hangers-on, all wearing his livery collar and all talking at the same time, competing for the great man's attention.

Constance looked up, irritated by the disturbance, and as she did so Northumberland, recognising her, halted on the spot, his silver-tipped walking stick loose in his hand. He spoke a quiet word to his entourage, and then advanced alone across the grass towards her, making a stiff bow as he drew close.

'My lady,' he said, 'it is a long time since you visited me at Alnwick. It gives me joy to see you again.'

'Indeed, my lord.' Her suspicions were aroused. Northumberland had not sent her so much as a line of writing from that day until this, and his sudden interest in her was unexpected. She remembered his caution over Mortimer's ransom, the greater caution that had kept him from Shrewsbury. 'Much has changed since then, to the sorrow of us both. Your son was a good friend to me. I have offered many prayers for his soul this last year.'

Northumberland, head low, prodded the ground with his stick, as if testing it for firmness. 'May I sit, my lady? My legs are not as strong as they were.' He settled on the turf seat next to her, his stick between his legs and his hands resting on the top of it. 'My son is a sore loss to us all. The whole of the North loved him, grieves for him, and remembers how he died. How his body was desecrated by the bloody butcher who wears the crown of England.'

'He died fighting a King you made, my lord.' Constance knew he was well aware of the fact, but could not resist pointing it out.

For a moment his eyes blazed with anger and pain. 'Now I intend to *unmake* him,' he said fiercely. 'The North will follow me. On this side of Trent there is only Ralph Neville who would lift a finger for Bolingbroke, and he only because he is frightened of his wife. All I need is a way of sending word to Edmund Mortimer and Glyn Dwr, so that I may meet them and agree a common strategy. If we are united in our purpose, then we shall destroy this devil and set up the rightful King.'

She shrugged. 'Well, Northumberland, I can offer you my prayers. As a woman, and one near penniless, I can do little more to aid your purpose.'

His restless hands gouged the grass with his stick, creating a small trench in the hard soil. 'I well remember why you came to Alnwick. Straight from your father's deathbed, ten days in the saddle, at a guess. Not for the pleasure of seeing my face, or listening to my son's conversation. You made that journey for Mortimer's sake, and I cannot believe you do not have some means to contact him. You have lands in Wales, you have Welsh servants, and you can help me in this.'

Her hand went to the chain about her neck, though she did not delve for Mortimer's token. The silence lengthened as she considered the matter, and a smile grew at the edges of her mouth.

'Yes, my lord,' she said. 'I do believe I can help you.'

39

Edward of York deposited his weight onto the cushioned window-seat next to his Duchess, the force of his landing sufficient to propel her little silver tray of sugared plums onto the floor, his long legs sprawling towards her. Philippa allowed herself a moment of irritation, and briefly considered retrieving the scattered delicacies before deciding that such an untidy movement was beneath the dignity of her rank. Since no underling was currently available, it followed that the plums would have to stay where they were.

'Is there no one else who will lend you the money to pay your men in Wales?' she asked, her brow knotting.

He snorted. 'Not unless I offer still more of my properties as security. I've thought about that, but I don't think it's a very good idea. Too much risk, and not enough reward.'

'Then what will happen, Ned?'

He shrugged. 'Eventually the men will give up waiting for their pay and go home. I can't blame them, since it's what I've done myself. We've lost the war in Wales, that's the truth of it. What's more, Glyn Dwr has signed a treaty with the French.'

'The French and Bretons have been raiding us for ages. What difference will a treaty with Glyn Dwr make to that?'

Edward sighed, stared out through the open casement to the flat lands beyond the River Nene, his eyes locking on a heron that was making its lazy, ungainly way towards its favoured perch in one of the tall trees further down the bank. 'It means that the French are getting bold,' he explained. 'Breaches of the truce by the likes of St. Pol and Orleans are one thing. The French could always say that their King had not authorised the attacks, even that he disapproved of them, that his subjects were running out of control. Open warfare is another matter again. It may be that they'll invade us. Lady Oxford has been arrested for encouraging them to do so. Inviting St. Pol to land an army in Essex.'

'Lady Oxford? That ancient creature? Why should she do such a thing? Is she mad?'

'Perhaps.' He shrugged. 'Perhaps she is just the first to realise that Cousin Harry is finished. Philippa, think about it. *He has lost Wales!* It's almost beyond imagination. How can he hope to survive such a disaster? I have to be sure we are not dragged down with him.'

She reached out a hand towards him, rested it on his forearm. 'I hope you are not going to do anything dangerous,' she said.

'In some ways it's more dangerous to do nothing. If there's to be a change, then I must be part of it. Otherwise I shall have no say in events, and someone may even decide that he likes the look of my lands, and find a reason to be rid of me. I've a lot of enemies, my dear, and precious few friends. I can't even rely on my own family. My sister blames me for all her troubles, from Despenser's death to a broken fingernail, and Dickon is a lot closer to her than he is to me.'

'Constance has always been unreasonable,' Philippa said. 'Unreasonable and ungrateful. I'd not trouble myself about her if I were you.'

His eyes turned to her, and his fingers rose to stroke her heavily powdered and rouged cheek. 'There's more than a suspicion that Bishop Despenser was involved in Lady Oxford's plot. If he was, there's a good chance that Constance also had a hand in it. You know she and the Bishop have always been close.'

'Then they're both likely to find themselves in the Tower, aren't they? It would serve her right if they kept her there for good.'

'You don't see it, do you? Do you think it probable that an addled-witted old woman and a half-lunatic bishop would arrange a French invasion on their own account? The likelihood is there is more to it than that, that what's been discovered is part of a larger scheme.' He hesitated, drew the warm autumn air between his teeth. 'I think I am going to have to have a word with Northumberland, and when last I heard he was living at his castle at Wressel, which is somewhere near York. I'd better seek him there, before he takes himself off to Alnwick, or one of his other places in the far North. After that, perhaps I should also visit the court, to find a way to appease my sister, and discover what she knows about what is happening. I wouldn't be too surprised if she still has some link to Edmund Mortimer, and we'll need Mortimer and his Welsh friends if we're to be rid of the Mole.'

'The Mole!' Philippa laughed, falling back against her cushions. 'It's exactly what Bolingbroke looks like! A big, hairy, ugly mole with screwed-up eyes and red whiskers! Ned, wouldn't it be wonderful to have him caught in a sack?'

'It'd be better to have him hanging from a gallows, with a few rats and voles around him. But we must not run away with ourselves, sweetheart. He's not the man he was; he's grown sickly and idle. But he's no one's fool and he'll not be easy to dislodge from his place. Besides, we've no one to set against him. Except Mortimer, of course, if he can be persuaded to it.'

'Persuaded? Why should he need to be persuaded? What has he to lose?'

'It is a great burden for a man to take upon himself. I'm not sure he has the stomach for it.'

The Duchess snorted. 'He had stomach enough to climb into your sister's bed.'

'If you remember, Pippa, it was we who brought them together, and for a purpose. She would have been the making of him if they'd married, and if Cousin Harry had not sent us out to Bordeaux when he did I'd have seen matters properly concluded. It's a great pity it did not come to pass. We need the Mortimers. I'm a lot less sure they need us.'

Philippa mused on that for a time, her hand resting gently on his. 'Constance loved Edmund Mortimer very much,' she said. 'Almost as much as he loved her. You're right, Ned. She will have some means to contact him, but if she does not trust you she'll scarcely use it on your behalf. Why not say to her that you think she should have her son's wardship? That it's Bolingbroke who will not allow it, and a new king would, with your good will. Even if you have to give it up to her, it's not worth so very much now that the Welsh lands have been ravaged and burnt by the rebels.'

Edward met her gaze and smiled his approval at her. 'That might do very well,' he said. 'It is certainly worth a try.'

***

Constance stood at the edge of the hall at Lichfield, one of the crowd watching while others danced.

'I can no longer bear to be at odds with you,' York said into her ear, his voice covered by the volume of the music.

'Indeed?' She kept her eyes on Mun, who was dancing in a trio with Queen Joanna and Antonine Dagvar. He was his usual vigorous self, smiling and laughing with his partners as he sought to dominate the room with his size, energy and sheer presence. She wondered how she could find the diplomacy to explain to Mun that at times he had a way of making himself look ridiculous.

Edward studied the back of his fingers, his jewelled rings catching the torch-light and sparkling like tiny stars. 'I beg your pardon for the wrongs I have done you, and I swear on my honour that I will do all I can to make amends. Let us be as we were, long ago, before you had any cause to doubt your brother's love.'

The words were so astonishing that she broke her resolution not to look at him. 'I think you mock me.'

'No. Constance, all I ask is that you find it in your heart to trust me.'

She snorted her impatience. 'Trust you? As Hotspur trusted you? As Thomas did?'

He took her hand, raised it to his lips before she could withdraw it. Then he nodded towards the dais, where Harry sat, slumped on his throne, his face pale as death as he watched the dancing through weary, half-open eyes. 'Do you seriously imagine you can bring him down, you and your friends in Wales? You need me. Together, working as one, with our plans well laid, we can finish our dear cousin. Separately, we haven't a chance. Northumberland sees that. You may ask him if you will.'

'You've spoken to Northumberland?'

'I've done a great deal more than that. I visited him in Yorkshire and I rode here in his company. We made something of a detour, by way of Valle Crucis Abbey in the marches of Wales. It was there we met with Glyn Dwr, and Edmund Mortimer.' He paused for a moment, nodding in acknowledgement as Warwick stalked his way past them. 'See, I put myself completely in your hands. You can bear the tale of my doings to Cousin Harry if you so wish.'

She remained silent. After about half a minute, Edward tired of waiting for her answer and went on. 'Mortimer is a fool. The rest of us agreed that he ought to claim the crown for himself, but he will not do so. He insists we must find a way to free March, and crown *him*.'

Constance shook her head, appalled by the risk that Northumberland had decided to take in accepting her brother into their counsels. 'Edmund said as much to me, when last I saw him, even asked me to think of a way for the boys to escape. Alianore has spoken to me of the same thing. I *have* thought about it, and it is impossible.'

'Nothing is impossible, my dear. Together we can find a way. If you will but trust me again?'

He was asking the impossible. She could never trust him, not after so many previous failures to keep faith.

'There is the matter of your son's wardship,' he said quietly. 'It was Bolingbroke who took it from you, not I. I shall see to it that it is restored to you; that you shall pay nothing for it.'

She scanned his face, convinced that he was a liar. 'And my Despenser dower lands?' she asked.

'You shall everything that is yours,' he said. 'I swear it on our mother's soul. Now, tell me about your future husband. Is he with us in this enterprise?'

'I think he may be.' Constance hesitated, turned her eyes back to Kent and watched him lift first Joanna, then Antonine into the air, effortlessly raising their waists above his head and laughing with them as they descended to earth. She felt inexplicably troubled by his energy and high spirits. 'Do not speak of it to him, Ned. Leave him to me.'

'You need not worry. I don't share your taste for his company. But you need to be sure of him, Constance. Sure in every way. I have a feeling you are not.' He rooted in his purse, and drew out Mortimer's token, the pewter medal of Mary Magdalene that Constance had entrusted to Northumberland so that the meeting with Owain could be arranged. He placed it carefully in her hand. 'Edmund was anxious that you should have this again. It may be you will need it.'

***

It was very late. Beyond midnight, Constance suspected. The candles and sconces were burning low and even the musicians were beginning to falter, having worked beyond the point where either gold or wine could refresh them.

She was also beginning to falter, having danced for much of the evening. The gathering of a Great Council brought many additional men to court, but very few additional women, so there had been no shortage of partners. Fortunately the pace had slowed considerably as the evening had drawn on, and her present exercise, with Mun, was little more than a formalised promenade around the hall.

Mun yawned, the edge taken off his formidable energy by his earlier exertions. 'I have spoken to the King about your dower rights,' he said.

Constance had not expected this. She turned her head towards him, waited for him to continue.

'He tells me he can do nothing,' he went on. 'Anything he gives to you he would have to take from your brother York, and he owes York so much that it would be an injustice to deprive him of the revenues.'

Fury flared through her to her fingertips. 'And you are content with that?'

'No.' He hesitated. 'Constance, he *is* the King, and I am still under his guardianship. I cannot press him too hard.'

She maintained her silence for a full minute as they processed across the red and white chequers of the tiled floor. 'I have been speaking to my brother this very evening,' she said. 'He says he would be glad to yield up both my dower lands and my son's wardship, but Bolingbroke will not permit it. So you may measure the value your King sets upon your loyalty and good service, my lord.'

'You take York at his word?' He uttered a sullen approximation of a laugh. 'Why should he be willing to give up such profits when he's been complaining all this year that he's not got two pennies to rub together in his purse?'

'Ned seeks our friendship; he understands what he must offer for it. Can you not see the truth of it? Harry Bolingbroke hates me. Even though parliament has granted my petition, he deliberately withholds my proper settlement from me. As for you, I swear he remembers that you're a Holland, and how your brother and uncle died fighting against him. He has already forgotten how you shed your blood to save his worthless life at Shrewsbury.'

Mun's hand tightened upon her, and he led her from the elongated circle of dancers at so brisk a pace that she could barely keep her feet in contact with the floor.

'I had my rewards for Shrewsbury,' he said, facing down her stare. 'I was knighted on the field, elected to the Garter, granted more of my lands. All that, and the right to marry you for no more price than the Chancery fee for the licence. The King values me highly. Do not dare to say otherwise.'

'He treats you like a boy. Like some low-born hireling!' She watched him carefully, knowing that this was a dangerous path she was taking, that a single blow from him would certainly flatten her even if it did not break a bone. 'You ought to be Duke of Surrey for a beginning, and next in precedence to my brother. Not as a reward, but as of right, by lawful inheritance. I am a princess of the Blood, and the widow of a great lord. Shall I be content as the wife of one who will not protect my interests? Who even lacks the courage to claim what is his own by right of birth?'

They were outside now, in the Bishop's garden, with darkness around them and light drizzle blowing into their faces. 'No one has *ever* accused me of lacking courage,' he said angrily.

Constance took a breath. 'There are many kinds of courage. You have proved yourself in battle, Mun, and in the tilt-yard, and I honour you for that.'

'Do you?'

'Yes.' She paused again, frowning because her foot had stepped into something that was soft and unidentifiable. She hoped it was mud, and not a dog's fault, but it was impossible to see. 'Of course I do. It is just that I weary of watching while Bolingbroke mocks you, and treats you as though you are of no account. You promised me you would protect me and defend my rights. I hold you to that promise.'

'What of your promises?' he asked. 'What of your duties to me? You are my wife, but you do not share my bed. I've not had you since we left Pontefract, and only twice while we were there. You grant it like a privilege, and yet it is my right.'

'I am afraid lest you get me with child again.' She was aware of the quickening of his breath, the strength of the arm that had wound itself around her middle. 'You are very potent, Mun. Remember how easily you gave me our daughter. I do not want another child until I can bear it honourably, under your roof, not hidden away in Wales as though in bastardy.'

'If you loved me you would not be so cold,' he said sulkily. 'Even if you don't love me, it is still my right.'

'A right that a gentleman, a knight, does not enforce against a lady's will. Especially not when she has good cause for refusal.'

He snorted bitterly. 'You were the one who started to talk about our rights and duties. You dare to say the King treats me like a boy, when it is you who does that. You must think I have the wit of a sheep! I'll don't suppose Despenser had to beg your permission before he put you on your back. I'll wager a hundred pounds he had you whenever he wanted, and in whichever way he wanted, whether you liked it or not.'

She shook her head. 'Thomas never forced me.'

To her surprise he released her, and stood back. 'I don't suppose he ever had the need. Well, I won't force you either. I'll find myself a woman who is willing, one who finds me pleasing, not repulsive.'

'Mun, I don't find you repulsive. Do you think I'd ever have allowed you to touch me if I did? Did you not hear my reasons?'

'I've heard your excuses.' He was already stalking away into the enveloping darkness. 'Your body talks louder, madame. It stiffens under my touch, and tells me that I disgust you. So be it. Sleep well in your cold bed.'

'Mun!' She began to hurry after him, and almost immediately sprawled head-long over a low bush. It was a heavy fall, and knocked the breath from her. By the time she had recovered herself, climbed back to her feet, and brushed herself down, he was long gone and she was utterly alone in the dark and increasingly chilly garden.

Cursing her own clumsiness, lifting her skirts for ease of movement and testing every step she took, she slowly picked her way back to the hall.

40

Constance wakened by the noise of activity outside the bed-curtains, sat up and buried her face in her hands, trying to rub away the tiredness as she considered the disaster of the previous evening. She had not slept well, and dreaded the thought of looking at her glass, knowing that she would appear haggard and red-eyed.

The curtains were pulled back by a sudden, swift tug, and Agnes Norreys stood there, with a clean shift over her arm and a halo of light behind her that was far brighter than Constance's eyes could bear.

'It is very late, my lady,' Agnes said, with as much neutrality as her voice could muster. 'The Queen has already sent a boy to enquire after you.'

'How late?'

Lady Norreys shrugged. 'About eight o'clock.'

'You should have woken me long before this.'

'I sent word you were ill. I judged that it must be so, since you are no slugabed.'

Constance worked her way to the side of the bed, and eased her feet out of it, holding out her arms so that Agnes might fit them into the sleeves of the shift. As her head emerged from the garment she found that she could now open her eyes without discomfort, and slowly became aware of what was going on across the room. By the light of the small oriel window that looked out over the Bishop's garden, the gown of last night was spread out between Mary Russell and one of the chamberers, Christina Launder. They were shaking their heads in unison over the ruination that morning had revealed.

'I saw you leave the hall with my lord of Kent,' Agnes said, in the same detached tone as before. Her eyes flicked away towards the gown, which looked as if its wearer had been rolling about in thick mud.

'I fell over, in the garden,' Constance said, feeling that in this case silence was likely to be interpreted to her discredit.

'I should have thought your ladyship at least twenty years too old for such tricks! Will it please you to wash?'

Anne Mortimer had fetched a silver bowl of lukewarm, scented water, and Constance rinsed her hands in it. Then her face, the front of her neck, and the adjoining parts of her shoulders were washed by Agnes, who used a damp cloth, gently applied.

'I thought I heard you cry out in the night,' Lady Norreys said, once Anne had retreated with the water. 'Was I mistaken?'

'Perhaps I dreamed.'

'If so, you dreamed more than once. Did he—did he hurt you?'

'No, Agnes. I've already told you. I fell over in the dark, as any clumsy fool may do. It was no one's fault but my own, and certainly not Kent's. Now, if you please, help me dress. Enough of the day is gone as it is.'

Agnes drew a significant breath. 'I worry about you, you know.'

'Then you have no cause! I am perfectly well and do not require mothering.'

The words were not quite out of her mouth when the chamber door was pushed open, without any warning knock. Before the door stopped moving Queen Joanna came bustling into the room, her long train carried by the young Countess Marshal, with half a dozen of her other women following.

Constance stood up, and made a curtsey, feeling herself at a severe disadvantage in her shift in the presence of so much silk, velvet and jewellery. She rose and waited for Joanna to speak.

The Queen nodded, made a gesture with her hand for Agnes and the others to rise, and began to inspect the chamber with the kind of thoroughness that might have been justified had she planned to take it over for herself.

'I heard you were unwell, Cousin,' she said abruptly. She spoke the words in English, to Constance's great surprise.

'I am better now, madame.'

'Good! I rejoice to hear it!' Her dark eyes considered Constance. 'I see you have your waist again, my dear Cousin. I hope you have not been starving yourself? In my experience, such sacrifices are in vain. Men seem to prefer a certain—plumpness. Do you not find it so?' She sniffed abruptly. 'You have had no other visitors? I thought perhaps you might.'

'None except for Your Grace.'

Joanna's eyes continued their investigation of the room. She seemed to expect to find something of interest in one of the corners, or under the bed. 'Your beloved Kent is nowhere to be found. The King calls for him, but he does not appear. His men have not seen him. In truth, no one has set eyes on him since last night, when I understand he went from the hall in your company, Constance. I thought perhaps he might have something to do with your sudden illness. I even thought he might be here, ministering to your needs.'

Constance's head jerked back. 'You insult me, madame, by making such a presumption.'

'But why?' the Queen shrugged, and settled herself on the only chair. 'Even in England it is surely thought natural for a man to rush to the lady he loves when he hears she is unwell. Is it not so?'

'Kent has no way of knowing how I fare. I've not seen him since last night, when we parted in the garden.'

'The garden?' Joanna had not failed to observe the stained gown, and glanced momentarily in its direction. She allowed herself a brief laugh and a spread of her hands. 'Small wonder you have been indisposed, my Cousin! You will surely have caught a chill from the night air. Or perhaps from the cold ground.'

'I have not seen him since, madame,' Constance said, as close to interrupting the Queen as etiquette permitted, 'and nor do I know where he is.'

'But it is *most* strange, is it not? Are you not worried about him? Your future husband?'

'What could possibly harm him?' Constance, becoming increasingly aware of the contact between the cold floor tiles and her naked feet, took two small steps onto the adjoining rug. 'He's a trained knight and more than capable of looking after himself. I worry about my children, not grown men.'

'Ah, your children! Your son is a charming child—I think he will break hearts when he grows older. But how do your daughters fare? Someone, I forget who, told me that you have left them in Wales. Surely that is not true?'

'They are with Lady March, who is my aunt by marriage. They are quite safe at Powys Castle.'

Joanna shrugged her bewilderment. 'But Lady March's husband is Lord Charlton, is he not? And he has asked the King and the Great Council to agree a truce with the rebels for Powys and Shropshire. So how can it be that this Powys is safe?'

Constance was surprised, and struggled to conceal the fact. She had not thought the Queen to be either interested in or informed about such matters.

'Powys is a very strong castle,' she said hesitantly.

'A very strong castle in a lordship that cannot be defended? And you have three daughters there?'

Constance just checked herself in time. 'Two, madame.'

The Queen smiled innocently. 'What made me think that there were three? Two, of course. At Powys Castle. With Lady March. I have it clear in my mind now.'

***

The Earl of Kent had spent the night in a cheap brothel, because the small town of Lichfield could not sustain an expensive one. Waking with a sore head and a mouth that tasted of stale vomit he discovered a substantial gap in his recollection of the past few hours. The last thing he remembered distinctly was hitting a man, very hard, for no particular reason. The man had stayed down, and the other people in the room, weighing up Kent's size and strength as well as his obvious status, had decided not to make an issue of the matter.

Mun staggered into the Cathedral precincts, checked his purse, and found to his surprise that his expenditure was no more than a drunken man in a stew-house might reasonably expect. The relief at not being robbed was a very small island of consolation in a vast sea of despair. He leaned against one of the stone walls, looked up towards the sky, and realised how late it must be. At that moment one of the Cathedral's great bells began to toll, and when he stopped cursing the noise he realised that it was providing a confirmation of his estimate. It must already be tierce, about nine o'clock. The Great Council would have been in session for a good hour by now, and his absence would be noted. Not because he was required to contribute to the discussions, but because the King expected him to be there. Despite his youth, Mun was one of the senior ranking earls, and his presence added dignity to the proceedings.

He grimaced at the thought of the rebuke he was likely to receive from Bolingbroke at their next meeting. There was no satisfactory excuse for his absence, and he was bound to face a prolonged barrage of awkward questions, followed by expressions of disappointment and a tedious lecture on his conduct.

He struck the wall in frustration and stalked through a passage into the cloisters. Constance had been right. It angered him beyond measure to admit it, but she had. He had proved himself a man by every possible measure, and yet the King still treated him like an insignificant boy. Entitled to sit in the Great Council, but only with the proviso that he kept his tongue still. Fit to risk his life in battle, but not to have his reasonable petitions granted.

Strangely, his realisation that there had been truth in Constance's words did not ease the resentment she had provoked in him. Her outspoken criticism of his dealings with the King, his stewardship of her interests, had landed on him like heavy blows from a mace on unprotected flesh. But her physical rejection of him was worse, her denial of the rights she had granted him when he had taken her under his protection as his wife. It was, he thought, a very poor repayment for his honourable behaviour towards her. Perhaps she thought to control him by the denial; perhaps she intended to continue to do so. The thought renewed his anger. He would not have it so. One way or another, she would have to be taught her place, reminded of the debt she owed him.

He lowered his weight onto one of the stone seats, leaned his back against the wall, and closed his eyes so as to shut out the world. His mind was not so much blank as a busy market place of confused thoughts and troubled emotions. With so much jangling going on it was impossible for him to plan any rational strategy. For the present all he wanted to do was avoid the King and avoid Constance. He dreaded the thought of either of them seeing him in his present dishevelled state. The sight of him would infuriate Bolingbroke and Constance might construe his self-neglect as evidence of frustrated love for her. The cloisters were quiet and the morning relatively warm. He did not actually sleep, but drifted into that state of consciousness that is near neighbour to it, relaxed by the peace, the sound of bird song, and the faint chanting of the clergy in the Cathedral.

But then another sound intruded, the gentle trail of women's gowns along the tiled cloister, and with it the soft tones of female conversation. He kept his eyes closed, and hoped that he would not be observed. He heard them halt, breathed their perfume as they stood close to him, the wanton odour as sickeningly strong as if they had been bathing in it. There were at least three of them, debating in French at so conspiratorial a level that he could only make out the odd word in ten. There was a suppressed, giggling laugh, and the little procession moved on past him.

Yet one of them had not moved on. He sensed her presence even before he heard her gentle footfall, or the rustle of her clothes as she sat next to him on the seat, so close that her flank pressed against him and her breath warmed his cheek.

'Good morrow, my lord,' said the girl, speaking in English. 'Everyone has been searching for you. They thought you might be dead.'

He opened his eyes and saw it was Antonine Dagvar. Last night he had enjoyed dancing with her, and with the Queen. He had some vague memory of it. He said nothing at first, hoping that she would go away, but at length the silence, and her unwavering stare, discomforted him.

'I drank too much,' he said, finding that the most convenient form of explanation. He shrugged. 'I slept it off in a hay loft. At least that's where I found myself. I've no idea how I got there.'

Antonine laughed and stuffed her knuckles into her small mouth, as if he had produced a profound witticism. 'Oh, you Englishmen are all made the same! You guzzle your cups of wine and strong ale as though they were water. It is so foolish. Can you find no better pastime?'

Kent disliked the trend of the conversation, and gave her a scowl that would have put fear into the soul of a lioness. 'I need no advice from you, lady, as to how to spend my leisure hours.'

'You dance so well,' Antonine said, smiling at him and gently laying her hand on his forearm, 'and you are so very strong. If I were *la Dame le Despenser*, you would not be sleeping in any hay loft. Or if you did, you would not be alone in it.'

He read the blatant admiration in her eyes, found it both flattering and irritating at the same time, and did not answer.

'The Queen herself asked her if she knew where you were,' Antonine persisted, fiddling with her veilings and pushing them back behind her shoulders, 'but she said she did not, and that she did not care. My word, but she has the—*sang froid*. How do you say it? The cold blood. Is it the English way for a lady so to conceal her love? I think it must be. She said she worried only for her children, not for you.'

'She said that?'

'Yes.'

Kent felt his heart slink away into a dark corner of his soul, dragging his pride behind it. Not only had Constance no regard or respect for him, she did not even have the courtesy to conceal her feelings from Joanna and the rest of the women. No doubt they all sat around in a circle when he was not there, and had a good laugh together at his expense.

Antonine's hand slid from his arm to his thigh, her fingers tracing his muscles as she shifted her buttocks closer to him. 'We all think she is very cruel to you. But do not despair, my lord. You will find that not all ladies and damosels are cruel.'

Her hand shifted upwards, and her fingers closed gently around him, caressing and investigating at the same time. He was stunned at first, unable to believe what she was doing.

'You filthy French whore!' he roared. 'How dare you?'

'My lord!' Antonine stared at him with her large, dark eyes, pretending to be outraged by his abuse. Then her smile returned, and she leaned forward and pressed her mouth briefly to his, while her bold hand continued the task of untrussing him. '*Je suis Bretonne.*'

***

The lake at Kenilworth, black beneath the grim autumn sky, stirred by a sluggish north wind, was still a thing of beauty. Edward, walking his horse along its banks, idly counting the water fowl and calculating the sport available, found himself wishing that it were his. By comparison the lake at Fotheringhay was a pond for cattle.

'I will know who it is who has begun this slander,' Harry said, his voice petulant. He rode next to his cousin, a good twenty yards ahead of their companions and the sundry hounds and hawks that made up the company.

Edward met his eyes, smiled, and shrugged. 'Impossible to say, Cousin. Save that it must surely have originated with one of your enemies. In the North, perhaps. Though more likely in Wales, I should think.'

'Mortimer!' The King spat the name out as if it were a dog's turd that had found its way into his mouth. 'That traitorous bastard will be behind this, and using his Welsh rogues to spread the lie. Drovers, friars, bards, the scum that crawl over the marches each summer to help with the harvest.'

'Well, be that as it may, the tale is now in the mouths of far greater men, and that's where your danger lies. Of course, some of your friends here are not in the least appalled by it. They think it would be a very good idea.'

'To murder two striplings? Ned, am I so little known that the men of my own household think me a savage? No better than Herod?'

York drew a thoughtful breath through his teeth. 'Those boys are a threat to you. As you must know, there are many who say they are the true heirs of our cousin, King Richard.'

'They are no threat at all! I am the anointed King of England, and anyone who denies my right is a false traitor. What profit should I have from their deaths?'

'They will not always be boys.'

'If harm came to them, it would strengthen Edmund Mortimer's own claim to the throne. It is he, and his father-in-law, Glyn Dwr, who would be advantaged by such a crime. Even my worst enemy must surely see that.'

Edward sighed with a pretence of regret. 'People have a way of believing what pleases them best. I should add that there's another rumour abroad that's almost as damaging. It's well know that March and his brother have the manners of serfs, that they've been taught none of the skills that make a gentleman. Some say they've been kept in their ignorance by your express command.'

Bolingbroke shook his head in bewilderment. 'That is absurd. If the boys are in need of instruction in such matters, then they shall have it. I shall write to Waterton about it.'

'Sir Hugh is your loyal servant,' Edward said. He fell silent for a while, as if giving the matter deep consideration. 'However, I must say that I have always found him rather an uncouth fellow. Most northerners are. If it were a matter of fighting skills, or even of horsemanship, I am sure he'd set them a splendid example. I'm less sure whether he is fit, let us say, to teach an ungainly and graceless boy how to dance or to serve at table. Perhaps that has been the root of the problem.'

'I have never noticed any fault in Sir Hugh's manners,' Harry objected. 'My own children have often been in his charge.'

'Ah, but then they have had the benefit of other influences. Including your own and that of the Queen. A noble, gracious lady can make a great impression on a stripling. I suppose March must be twelve or thirteen by now. At that age a beautiful lady's contempt is often more dreaded than a sound thrashing.'

The King drew his horse to an abrupt halt. The path ahead was uncertain, and his eyes struggled to make out the way forward through the undergrowth. 'You think I should place them in the Queen's household?'

'If half what I've heard of them is true, they're not fit for such service. In time, perhaps, but they need some lessons in courtesy first. They should have had them long ago, Cousin. It will be quite a task to cure them now.'

'It may have escaped your attention, but I have had other business to concern me these last five years besides the education of Roger Mortimer's brats. So have you, I presume, since you have not mentioned the matter until now.'

'These rumours have not come to my ears until now,' Edward said. 'I thought it my duty to mention them to you, rather than allow these things to be said behind your back. I need scarcely tell *you* how dangerous rumours can be if left unchecked.'

The silence between them lengthened. The trees shook their branches in the wind casting off a few more brown and golden leaves to fall around the pair of cousins.

Bolingbroke took a deep breath. 'Ned, I have no time to spare to deal with such trivial issues. As you have given thought to it, what do you advise?'

Edward pretended to hesitate. 'There is one thing that occurs to me, if you will hear it.'

'Yes?'

'Kent is the boys' uncle.'

'You would have me give them into his charge?' Harry snorted his contempt. 'I suppose he could teach them how to drink deeply and make bloody fools of themselves!'

'My sister is soon to be Kent's wife. Send her to Windsor. Let her take charge of the boys.'

Bolingbroke's eyes narrowed with a mixture of suspicion and short-sightedness. 'It would not surprise me if your sister proved to be responsible for spreading these rumours,' he said. 'She's a close friend of Lady March, and at one time had thoughts of marrying Edmund Mortimer. Indeed she would have done, had I not prevented it.'

'That is the very point of my suggestion. Constance is known to be close to the Mortimers. So it follows that if the boys were in her charge no one could possibly imagine you intended to harm them.'

'I'm not sure I should respond in any way to baseless lies.' Harry eased his horse gently into motion, pushing on through the ragged bushes. He frowned over the problem for a minute or two before turning to Edward again. 'Do you suppose Constance would accept appointment as a governess? I rather think she might not.'

'It would only be for a few months, until she is married. Though it might ease matters if you were to allow her son to go with her, and he would also be an excellent companion for the Mortimers. After that, it might indeed be an idea to give custody of the boys to Kent.'

'Hmm,' said the King, without commitment.

Edward followed him deeper into the thicket, sharing a smile with himself, content that he had planted the idea in his cousin's mind. Instead of pursuing the matter further, he began to speculate on what manner of game they might flush out on so unpromising a morning.

***

The list of grievances, written in a fine, clerkly hand, covered a whole sheet of parchment and did not spare any of Bolingbroke's sins. His return from exile without King Richard's leave; his false oath at Doncaster; his deposition of his sovereign, against his vow of allegiance; his execution of nobles and others without trial; the failure to ransom Edmund Mortimer; the brutal treatment of Hotspur's body; sundry injustices done to the church; heavy and unjust taxation; the loss of Wales and the hopeless weakness of English power in Ireland and Guienne. All this not merely mentioned, but elaborated upon.

Constance, seated close to the arched window of her bedchamber, felt her eyes growing weary before she was half way through it, for the writing, however well executed, was exceeding small. She sighed, looked up from it, and met her brother's eyes. Edward was leaning idly against the scarlet and gold wall hangings, watching her reactions as she worked through the manifesto.

'Archbishop Scrope has two or three of his most trusted clerks working on this up in York,' he said. 'Copies will be sent to every man of note in the kingdom, and to every town and abbey of significance. Of course, to produce so many will take months, but I think it's well worth the trouble. The more men we bring out in our support, the more likely we are to succeed.'

'Does our cause require so many words to explain it?' she asked, beginning to roll up the parchment.

He shrugged. 'The Archbishop has a fondness for words. I suppose it befits his cloth. Anyway, there are different words meant for different men. That part about Hotspur, for example, should bring out half the North. The endless grumbles about the wrongs done to the Church mean little to you or me, but they should please the clergy. So on and so forth.'

'That is all very well, but the words will need to be backed by deeds. Your deeds, Ned. I do not see your name written here.'

'None of our names are mentioned, my dear. No need for it at this stage, lest a copy should fall into the wrong hands. I have learned from past mistakes! It will be clear enough who supports our cause when the banners are unfurled.'

'But will there be enough?'

'Northumberland and Bardolph—'

'Bardolph is of small account! I keep more men in my kitchen than he is likely to put in the field!'

'Then there's Thomas Mowbray.'

'Mowbray still has down on his cheeks!'

'But he is also the Earl Marshal, and he hates Cousin Harry. Northumberland and his friends had no trouble winning him to our cause. Then there's the Archbishop, who is much loved by the commons of Yorkshire. He can crown March for us. There's Glyn Dwr and Mortimer, and the French army that will land in Wales next summer.'

'You always used to say that we should not ally ourselves to the French. That it would turn our own people against us.'

'It's a risk, but one we must take,' he said, shrugging. He chuckled dismissively. 'We shall probably have to pay them to go home again, but I suppose we can always pawn Joanna's jewels.'

She watched his expression, but saw nothing there but his customary amused insouciance. 'I am not sure that I wish to be part of this,' she said.

'You already are. I have all but persuaded the King to place the Mortimer boys in your care. If you draw back now, I have no other plan to offer.'

'But I am still not sure that Mun will join us. I am his wife—his future wife. How can I have a part in this if he is opposed to it? It would be disloyal of me. A betrayal.'

He shrugged. 'Then the boys will stay locked up at Windsor, and this rising will fail. We need March, to proclaim him King.'

'Is that really so important?'

'Men need something to rally around, Constance. Something more than these words.' He took the parchment roll from her, and held it high for a moment before tucking it away inside his clothing. 'A great warrior would be better, but March is a handsome boy and the rightful heir. He will have to serve.'

The thought of their potential king made her frown. 'He's an ill-mannered brat. Or he was when last I saw him.'

'Then your first task will be to lesson him. Teach him to bear himself as a prince should.'

'How do you suggest I do that?' she asked, shaking her head as she contemplated the educational process. 'A boy of that age is already all the man he will ever be.'

York shrugged, lifted his weight from the wall, and paced as far as the fire. There was a damp chill in the high vaulted room, and he had begun to feel it. 'That is your business. Do what you must. Have him flogged every day if it's necessary.'

Constance folded her hands in her lap, and tried to appear calm, but her thoughts were racing. She wished she had someone to advise her, but all those she really trusted were either dead or far away. She could not trust Edward. She knew, even as they conspired together, that he would not strap on his armour until he was sure that victory was achieved. If there was success he would share it, but he would never risk the price of failure. Why was it, then, that her heart still wanted to believe in his honesty?

'When we were children,' she said, almost to herself, 'I loved you so much. I was so proud to be your sister.'

He turned his head towards her, eyes half hooded, evidently puzzled by the irrelevance of her comment. 'What are you talking about?' he asked.

'I want you to make me proud of you again. If you are not quite sure that you are ready to see this through to the end, even to death, then let us both withdraw now, and acknowledge Cousin Harry as our rightful sovereign. Not in words, but in our hearts. I would sooner do that than see you fail these men as you failed Thomas.'

He let out a great sigh. 'I told you long ago, I hate Bolingbroke even more than you do. The difference between us is that I have never been fool enough to let him know it. I *am* determined. We shall never have a better opportunity to rid the world of that crooked, half-blind bastard.'

'If you betray us this time, Ned, I shall make it my business to see that you pay the price. Remember always how much I know about you, and how little I have forgotten.'

He made an impatient gesture with his hand, as if brushing away a fly. 'So what of Kent?' he asked. 'Will he join us in this enterprise? And will you play your part if he does not?'

Constance sighed. She had seen very little of Mun of late, and when they had met it had usually been under the Queen's watchful eye. He seemed always to be in attendance on the King, or when he was not he was away on the King's errands, sometimes for weeks at a time. There had been little chance to discuss politics; nor did he encourage such discussions.

'I need time,' she said. 'I need to talk to him. To persuade him.'

'I should have thought you had more than ample arguments to persuade the likes of that fool,' York grunted. 'You owe him nothing, Constance. He should think himself honoured that you ever deigned to glance at him.'

She shook her head. 'I have promised myself to him and I owe him my loyalty.'

'There are other loyalties. Have you forgotten them?'

Constance stared at him, as much angered by his reference to the past as by his hectoring tone. 'Unlike you, I have never forgotten them.'

A knock on the door interrupted her. Richard Despenser, bright in the Queen's scarlet livery, entered the room and made a reverence, first to his uncle, and then to Constance.

'My faith, lad,' York exclaimed, 'you look more like your father with every day!'

'My lady Mother,' said the boy, 'the Queen's Highness asks you to attend her. She is in her bedchamber. She wants you to come at once.'

Constance rose from her place, smoothing down her skirts as she did so. 'Did the Queen say what she required of me?' she asked.

'No, Mother.' Richard rubbed his ear thoughtfully where it smarted from recent contact with the back of Joanna's hand. 'Her Grace is angry, though. Very angry.'

Edward's eyebrows rose in an elegant arch of surprise. 'I think you had better go to Her Grace, fair Sister,' he said. 'It may be she has lost a treasured ring, or something of that importance. You can tell me later what you have decided to do in the matter of our friends.'

Constance nodded her assent, and then, with Agnes and Mary attending her, followed her son down the short flight of stairs to the Queen's apartment.

In the outermost chamber the usual guard of Breton gentlemen had forsaken their dicing and card playing, and were standing in one corner, their faces grim and their feet shuffling. Though they were slow to notice Constance's arrival, they made their bows to her, and one of them opened the door to the next room for her, pushing it back with what she thought was an exaggerated caution.

In the presence chamber Mowbray's wife and nine of the Queen's damosels were gathered together in a similar bewildered knot, though unlike the men they were all talking at once. A stool stood on its side, and Antonine's lute lay shattered in pieces against the wall. From the bedchamber beyond came the sound of Joanna's raised voice, followed by screaming and pleas for mercy.

'In God's name, what is happening here?' Constance demanded.

The Countess Marshal turned towards her, an expression of relief on her face. She reached out and rested her hand on Constance's arm. 'The Queen is crazed with anger,' she said quietly. 'None of us has ever seen her so.'

The Breton damosels shook their heads in unison, and there was some spreading of hands. 'The Queen is beating Antonine,' said Marie Sante, the eldest of them. 'Perhaps killing her, I think.'

Constance did not answer, but stepped forward decisively and entered the bedchamber. It was her clear duty to calm Joanna if she could, since it was obvious that no other member of the Queen's household would dare to do so.

Joanna had paused in her tirade of abuse. Her head turned towards Constance as the door opened, her chest still heaving with anger and her eyes as hard as black diamonds. Constance made her curtsey, and as she rose saw that Antonine was kneeling at the foot of the Queen's bed, her cheeks streaming with tears and reddened by the repeated blows of Joanna's hands. There was a streak of blood around her mouth where one of the Queen's rings had caught her.

'Ah, my dear Cousin, you are here at last!' Joanna said explosively, having recovered some of her breath. 'You are the senior among my ladies, are you not? In age, rank, and certainly in experience! Is it not your business to supervise the maidens of my household? To advise and guide them? To prevent them from becoming whores?'

Constance took a moment for consideration. 'I think not, madame,' she answered. 'They are not my servants, but yours. They should look to you for example.'

'I am the Queen of England! Have I time to keep an eye on all of them for every minute of every day? I say it is your business, madame, and you have failed in your duty. To me, and to this wretched girl. Now I must make a marriage for the slut, and quickly, before the scandal is known to all. Do you understand me? She is *enceinte*.'

Antonine sat back on her heels and continued her silent weeping, her head low. Constance looked towards her, feeling sorry for the girl. Antonine had always been lively and amusing company, and her music had relieved many a tedious hour.

'It is unfortunate,' she said, forcing herself to remain calm and hoping that her soft words would soothe Joanna's fury. 'However, if the father is such as she may marry, I do not see that there is any real difficulty.'

The Queen snorted a bitter laugh. 'He is *not* such as she may marry. He is a great lord, a very great lord.' She advanced on Antonine in a flurry of skirts, and landed another vicious slap on the girl's head. 'Speak, whore! Repeat the name of your child's father. My Lady Despenser ought to know the extent of her negligence.'

Antonine howled.

'Speak!' the Queen repeated, backhanding her. 'Repeat what you told me. Or I'll do more than slap you. I'll have you stripped naked and the skin taken off your back! I'll have you carrying a taper through the streets, barefoot in your shift! Speak!'

'Madame, the girl is terrified,' Constance said, as sharply as etiquette permitted. She had an idea that she knew the name of the father, that it would be the Earl Marshal. Perhaps, his wife not withstanding, he and Antonine had renewed their mutual affection.

'She *ought* to be terrified!' Joanna's eyes turned on her, narrow pools of darkness. 'She will be more than terrified before I have finished with her.'

'My lord of Kent,' Antonine sniffled, almost inaudibly. 'My lord of Kent.'

'My lord of Kent,' repeated the Queen, her voice contemptuously mimicing Antonine's whimpering. 'Did you hear that?

Constance was momentarily stunned by the allegation, to the extent that she considered whether this might be some elaborate joke, concocted by Joanna's extraordinary sense of humour. Then reality broke over her, and she stepped forward and took the girl by the neck of her gown, shaking her back and forth and landing a resounding slap of her own across her cheek. 'Liar!' she snapped. 'How dare you tell such lies? The Earl of Kent would not even look at you.'

'He did much more than look,' Antonine said. She raised her eyes, flooded with tears and yet strangely triumphant. 'It is his child I bear. He told me how cold you are. How little you love him. He wishes he had never set eyes on you. It is me he loves now. Me!'

Constance pushed down on the damosel, forcing her back onto the floor, kicking at her legs. 'No! You lie in your teeth!'

'Foolish little girl!' Joanna snorted. 'Do you truly suppose that a great English lord has any love for the likes of you? A dowerless nobody! I warned all of you about these Englishmen; that they have the blood of ice and the treachery of the devil. He has merely been saving himself the price of a prostitute. Get up and get out! Go to your confessor, and ask for penance for your wickedness. I hope he tells you to walk barefoot to Rome, but I don't suppose he will. Get out!'

Antonine evaded Constance's clutching hand, scrambled to her feet, and all but ran from the room, glad to escape from the furies. After the door had closed behind her, there was a period of silence as Joanna and Constance struggled to regain their composure and their breath.

The Queen seated herself on her large, painted chair, arranged her skirts and looked up at Constance with black, angry eyes.

'I blame you for this,' she said. 'You should have kept an eye on that child, and you should have kept Kent occupied yourself, instead of playing your cruel games with him. He adores you—though God and his saints know why—and you should have found ways to content him, to keep him from preying on ignorant young virgins of gentle birth.'

Constance was already infuriated, and Joanna's accusation made matters worse. The guard slipped from her tongue. 'It is no fault of mine, madame, if that girl is no more than a common whore, and your household no better than a stew. An ignorant virgin? I doubt she's been that since she was eleven! I dare say that *she* preyed on *him*.'

'Silence!' Joanna's voice was far from its usual low, caressing pitch. 'I shall see to it that he is sent from court immediately. I shall see to it that you are *both* sent from court. You may rusticate together in the country, wallow with the pigs and peasants in your English mud.'

Constance could barely contain herself. 'I can think of worse company, madame,' she said abruptly. 'Have I your leave?'

The Queen's hand moved in a weary gesture of dismissal. 'You have. What's more, you need not trouble yourself to attend me again.'

'I thank Your Grace for that reward,' Constance answered, making her curtsey and dodging the crystal goblet that Joanna hurled at her.

Elaborate French curses followed her all the way out of the room. In the presence chamber a devastated Antonine was crouched by her ruined lute, comforted in her agony by two of her closest colleagues. The remainder of the damosels merely looked on with a mixture of detached interest and amusement, calculating their own advancement in the pecking order.

Richard Despenser was standing by the door, trying to make himself as unobtrusive as possible. His mother went to him, and slid her comforting arm around his shoulders.

'Go and find your Uncle York,' she said. 'Tell him that I shall be glad to do as he asks. Tell him I now know where my loyalty lies.'

41

Constance stepped into the little church of Pilleth and was immediately aware of the lingering stench of charred timbers and of the soot that coated the wall paintings and emphasised their crude antiquity. The optimistic parishioners had already replaced the thatched roof, but that only added to a grim darkness that was relieved only by the yellow-grey light of the winter sun forcing its way through unglazed windows little better than loopholes, and the flames of two small candles. These burnt in front of the church's principal adornment, a crudely-painted and roughly-hewn wooden statue of the Virgin and Child.

The floor was of beaten earth, trod and kneed into solidity by generations of worshippers too poverty-stricken to finance tiling. She advanced cautiously, spread her cloak before the image, and knelt on the cloth to spare her skirts from the dirt that she confidently expected the darkness to conceal. Prayers slid from her tongue with automatic ease, and the familiarity of the words reassured and comforted her, reduced her feelings of uncertainty and unease.

Agnes Norreys, and one or two of the other serious-minded members of her retinue, followed her into the church and knelt in silence behind her; the majority, however, merely waited with the horses, or busied themselves by keeping her children amused, playing games with them among the anonymous humps of the churchyard. The children's laughter drifted into the building, reminding her of the world that lay outside, and of the loyalties and debts that constrained her. Her father's cognizance, the falcon enclosed within the fetterlock, came into her mind. As the falcon was confined, so was she, within the tight grip of duty and custom.

She saw from the corner of her eye that the parish priest had added himself to their company, no doubt investigating the invasion of his territory by her meinie. He did not disturb her devotions, but as soon as she completed them and rose to her feet he waddled across to her, his thickset, ruddy face beaming with delight.

'My lady, you are welcome,' he cried. 'We rarely see your kind in this humble church. Not at all since the wars began.' His fleshy, callused hand rose in a gesture that encompassed the whole building. 'As you can see, we have suffered great damage. All that was worth stealing was taken at the time of the battle, and the church set alight. Rebuilding has been a slow process. The people here are very poor; the land barely supports them, and they struggle to pay their rents and feudal dues. They have little left to give to God.'

Constance knew what was expected of her. She drew a small gold coin from her purse and pressed it into his hand. She judged it a cheap price to pay for his blessing and his departure, not being in the mood for the unctuous discourse of a country priest.

'Ever since the battle we have been troubled by the rebels and the King's men alike,' he went. 'Hardly a month goes by without some band of men descending on us, stealing our animals and trampling the few crops we are able to plant. I fear many children in this parish will go hungry this winter.'

She eyed his corpulence and suspected he would not lack for a meal, or a cup of ale, even if all the local children died of starvation. She had met priests of this kind before, who took their tithes, threatened defaulters with excommunication, and offered little in return except an occasional celebration of the mass. As like as not he knew less Latin than she did herself. However, another coin followed the first, and his hand motioned in a solemn but rather clumsy gesture of blessing.

'You will say a mass for my late husband,' she said, not as a request, but as an instruction. 'His name was Thomas, and he was by far the best man I have ever known.'

'Of course.' The priest studied the coin for a moment, as if checking the inscription, and then tucked it away in his scrip, where it clinked musically against several neighbours. He hesitated for a moment. 'Was he—your husband—killed in the battle here?'

She shook her head. 'No. It was my life that ended on that day, though I have only just come to understand it. Since then I have wandered, like a lost soul without purpose. Only now do I know what I must do.'

The priest stared at her, his literal and unsophisticated mind not beginning to comprehend her meaning. She realised that he thought he was dealing with a lunatic, and smiled reassurance at him.

'Where were they buried?' she asked. 'The men from the battle?'

'A little way along the hillside,' said the priest, crossing himself as he thought of it. 'All together, Welsh and English alike. We of the village buried them ourselves, what was left of them. You cannot fail to the see the mound.'

Constance thanked him, and went outside, walking towards the edge of the churchyard. She glanced around in the dull afternoon light until she recognised the shape of the mass grave, a little to the west, a little further up the slopes of the hill of Brynglas. The wind, blowing into her face with sudden venom, billowed her skirts against her legs, halting her in her tracks and causing her to pull the hood of her cloak over her simple head-dress of fine linen.

Tyldesley stepped towards her, picking his way through the long grass, the clash of his armour warning her of his approach. 'It will be full dark in a few hours, my lady,' he observed. 'I don't know this country, and I'll be glad to be out of it.'

'We must wait a little while yet. Our friends will not fail us.'

A momentary twitch passed over his rather grim and very unshaven face. 'I hope they do not, my lady, but I think you have too many uncertain friends.'

There was a warning shout from the tower of the church, where the archer Madog, whose eyes were the keenest in the company, had positioned himself. Constance and Tyldesley lifted their heads and saw that he was pointing westward, along the line of the track they themselves had followed only an hour earlier.

'How many?' Tyldesley called.

'Six. Mounted men, moving no faster than a walk.'

'I told you they would not fail us,' Constance said quietly, so that only Tyldesley heard her.

It was all she could do to stand still, to wait patiently with Tyldesley at the edge of the churchyard for what seemed like an hour, until Mortimer's banner emerged from the bare branches of the trees, and beneath it, riding an undistinguished bay palfrey, a figure she recognised at first sight to be Mortimer himself. As he drew closer, she saw that he wore no single piece of armour, that he was dressed in green broadcloth as though he were a prosperous squire on a hunting expedition. Closer still, advancing up the rising track to the church; she was able to make out his features, to watch his mouth widening into a smile.

He dismounted, tied her horse to a bush, and strode towards her, his feet dislodging the stones of the path in their haste. Still she did not move. Instead she watched as he bowed low before her, became aware of her hand reaching out to meet his, felt the touch of his lips on her fingers.

'Your message found me at Harlech,' he said, without preamble. 'I feared I might not be here in time. That you might already be half way to Windsor. I thank God and his saints I am not too late to see you.'

'You should thank St. Mary Magdalene in particular,' she said, raising her voice a little against the wind and feeling the first drops of the rain it carried with it hitting her face.

He smiled, drew from his purse the little medal she had used to certify her message to him, and handed it back to her. 'I do thank her,' he said, 'and I thank you for what I understand you intend to do.'

'I have yet to find the means,' she answered, 'but I shall, once the boys are in my care.' She found that she had regained the use of her legs. 'Edmund, shall we walk together? There is much to discuss. Perhaps it is better that others do not hear.'

'Walk?' he repeated. 'Walk where?'

Constance laid her hand on his arm. 'Where you will. Perhaps to that mound, where the men from the battle are buried. We could say a prayer for them.'

They traversed up the slope, Constance glad of his support when she discovered that the way was steeper than she had expected, and that there were great tracts of slippery mud hidden among the long, coarse grass, making it difficult to keep the thin, smooth soles of her riding boots in firm contact with the hill side. At last they found themselves following a thin trod that rose gently in the direction they required, and it was possible to stride out with greater confidence.

'So here they lie,' Mortimer said when they reached the edge of the mound. He sighed, his face grim, and fell to his knees to pray for the souls of the fallen. She followed his example without a word, feeling the ground soft and spongy beneath her, and conscious of the intense silence of the place. The wind had dropped somewhat, and the splashes of rain on her face were becoming heavier and more intensive.

'I have not been here since that day,' Edmund said at last, standing up. He offered his hand again, helping her to her feet.

'I wanted to see the place. The place where you were lost to me.'

He had not released her hand. 'I've fought the battle many times in my mind,' he said, his eyes surveying the landscape. 'You can see how the ground lies. That's a marsh at the foot of this slope, and there was little choice but to follow the track above it, narrow though it is. Owain's men were up here, about where we are standing now, shooting their arrows at us. We could not go back. My own men blocked the way. So what could we do but charge uphill, and try to scatter the archers? Of course, *then*, the rest of them came over that ridge.' He pointed up the slope. 'Hundreds. Thousands it seemed at the time. Then most of my own Welshmen turned upon us, and we had enemies on every side.'

Constance tried to imagine it, her eyes running from the marsh, to the church, to the top of Brynglas, and back to his face.

'I told you,' he said, looking into her eyes, 'what I feared if I returned to Wales. That I should lose you. So it proved, and though I have torn my hair out thinking about it, I cannot see how it could have been avoided, not once I decided to advance this way. I suppose I might have run away, right at the start, but then I should have been a coward, without honour, and you would have despised me.' He hesitated for a moment. 'Perhaps God wished to punish me for my sins. Perhaps, in His eyes, I did not deserve you. Or perhaps it was that I was fighting in an unjust cause. For had I triumphed it would have been to Bolingbroke's great advantage. There were many who came flocking to join Owain in the aftermath of that day.'

'You need not have lost me. I did not care that you were a prisoner. I'd have waited all my life, if you had but kept faith.' She shook her head. 'Edmund, I loved you so much, and had such complete trust in you. When I heard that you had married Glyn Dwr's daughter, I think the shock drove me from my reason. Yet how can I reproach you, when I have been still more foolish? Kent showed me some small kindness, and I was grateful. So I gave myself to him. Hoping to hurt you and satisfy my own lust at the same time. I have never stopped regretting it, and now I realise that the love he pretended for me was a deceit, that he sought me for my lands and the hope of gaining my son's wardship for himself. I am too ashamed of my folly ever to condemn yours. Well, I have my punishment and penance. I am bound for life to a man I have learned to detest, and must submit myself to him, and bear such children as he may give me. I suppose it is no more than my just deserts.'

'Do not speak of it!' His face had reddened with anger. 'It shall not be so. When you bring my nephews into Wales, you shall stay safe at Harlech, under my protection and that of Glyn Dwr himself. If Kent sides with Bolingbroke, he shall not survive the fighting, I promise you.'

She shook her head. 'Once I have delivered the boys to you, I must turn back. Face whatever must be faced. Kent is my husband. It is sin enough that I am deceiving him, but to desert him would be worse.'

'Constance, you must know that they will call it treason, your part in what we intend. At the best Bolingbroke will imprison you. He might even have you burnt.' His left arm found its way about her waist, drew her a little closer. 'I will not allow you to take such a risk. You'll be safe at Harlech.'

Constance allowed them both the comfort of pretence for a few moments, even went so far as to put her arm about him. 'You have a wife,' she said at last, 'and we have no right to injure her. We could not fail to do so, you and I, if we lived under the same roof, and that would be a great sin. It is better that we keep apart.'

She watched his expression as he considered her words, the light of hope that grew in his eyes.

'You have forgiven me?' he asked.

'For a time I deceived myself. I thought I no longer loved you. I was mistaken.'

He laughed with delight. 'Then all is well!'

'No it is not, Edmund.' She stood back from him, as far as his grip would allow. 'There is Kent and there is Catrin. That is her name, isn't it? Like it or not, we belong to them, not to each other. I shall not stop loving you, but I cannot be an adulteress. My mother was such, and because of it my father doubted in his heart that my brother Richard was his. I'll not inflict that on a child of mine, even though I want you more than I dare tell you.'

She pulled herself from his grip and took a step away from him, down the hill side, glad of the rain that drove into her face and helped to conceal her tears. Though she had rehearsed her arguments a dozen times, and made her firm decision long before reaching Powys, she had not been prepared for the effect that his presence would have on her. Her calculations had not allowed for the feelings provoked by his arm about her waist, or the mere sound of his voice filling her with desire for him.

'We could say we were precontracted,' he suggested. 'A dispensation would free us both.'

She shook her head, and took another careful step down the slope, conscious of its steepness and the wetness of the grass. 'It would be a lie. We never said the words.'

'We said them in our hearts. We intended marriage. Would you have lain with me if it had been otherwise?'

'Yes! I would have lain with you on any terms. I was half-mad, and thought only of our love, not of the sin. I cannot lie, Edmund, not to God.'

'We can buy our freedom from the Pope,' he said, taking one great step towards her, enfolding her with his arm and drawing her back to him. 'Once his seal is set upon the document, that will settle the matter. I will swear on the Gospels that we took an oath to each other before we bedded.'

'But we did not.'

He grinned. 'But it would be my word against yours. And in such cases, where there are no other witnesses, the man's word is accepted. That is the canon law. You would not have to perjure yourself, Constance. I'd take the sin upon myself, and think it a cheap price to pay to lie in bed with my belly next to yours.'

She shook herself free of him. 'No. I will not speak of it. You have a wife and children.'

'A wife who was forced on me as the price of my freedom.'

'And the children? Were *they* forced on you? What is their crime that you should wish to make bastards of them? I thought you had bastards enough.'

She began to descend the slope, with more speed than was wise, lost her footing and slid helplessly, on heels, thighs and buttocks, until her grasping hand caught the branches of a hawthorn bush and was torn by its prickles. Edmund scrambled after her, sliding and slipping himself, but with rather more control of his feet. He lifted her by her armpits and waist, enquired after her injuries.

'I am well enough,' she said, examining her damaged hand and lifting its wounds to her mouth. She paused, tasting her own blood and drawing out a broken thorn. 'I am well, but you are not the man I knew. I think he must have died here, with the rest of them.'

He looked into her eyes, their faces close together. 'I am the same man, except that I love you even more than I did. When last we met, your brother York told me he thought me too nice in my dealings. He was right. It is not a world for idle dreamers. We must take what we want, or be trampled.'

'That is Bolingbroke's way,' she said, working very hard to persuade herself that she did not want him to kiss her, and failing with distinction.

'Yes; and Bolingbroke is King of England. He made himself so, and did not care what lies he told, what oaths he broke. We can profit from his example.'

His lips closed on hers, and Constance relished the experience for rather longer than her conscience though proper before she gently and reluctantly pulled back from him.

'Then what need have you of your nephews?' she asked, still moderately breathless. 'Why do you not take the crown for yourself, as Edward and Glyn Dwr both said you should?'

He shrugged. 'Because it is my nephew's right, and we stand on what is right. Besides, I believe the Mortimer tenants are more likely to rise for Roger's son than for me, and we need those men if we are to fight Bolingbroke.'

What of Catrin's rights? Constance thought. What of your children's rights?

'Once my nephew is King,' he said, 'once I am Regent of England, the Pope will dance to my tune. It will be as I have said.'

Constance dared not let him kiss her again. She eluded his grip and stood back, the rain hurtling into her face, the wind dragging at her cloak as if it were a sail.

'I shall send you word when I have a means to take the boys from Windsor,' she said, bringing him back to a consideration of their present business. 'You must meet us in the marches, as near to England as you dare. With many men, in case we are pursued. Where would you have me bring them? Worcester?'

He considered the matter for a few moments. 'Tewkesbury,' he determined. 'You know the country thereabouts, which is an advantage, and I promise I shall meet you on the west bank of the Severn, with five hundred picked men. The best of Owain's archers and spears. You have only to bring the boys to the ferry, and you will be safe. Though I'll not rest until you and they are secure within the walls of Harlech.'

Constance nodded; but she decided at once that she would not cross the Severn, that she would place March and his brother on the ferry and then turn back. She knew she must never meet Edmund Mortimer again.

She allowed him to embrace her one last time, drew out the last moment of pleasure as they kissed again. Then went down the hillside with him, back to their waiting retinues. And stood in the rain , watching, until he was no longer visible among the trees that lined the road to the west, until she was sure that he would not turn back, that he had ridden out of her life forever.

***

The chill of winter had fallen on the land, and a bitter north wind shook the dark, leafless trees and tore across the frosted grass of Windsor park. Constance eased her horse to a halt, and watched the clouds of white steam emerging from its mouth as she waited for the Mortimer boys to catch up with her. Her son and Anne Mortimer, who had kept pace with her, shared in the silent contemplation.

March and his brother, their expressions set in solemn concentration, rode up to them at a cautious pace, clinging to their ponies as if expecting to slide off at any moment. They were followed by their inevitable escort, half a dozen of Sir Hugh Waterton's garrison.

Constance took a deep breath, controlling her patience. At least the boys were more presentable than when she had taken over their care. They wore new Despenser liveries that had been adjusted to fit them and which were kept brushed by the new and efficient servant she had assigned to them; their hair had been trimmed into an approximation of neatness by the same man; she herself checked each day that they washed at appropriate intervals and paid due attention to the cleaning of their fingernails and teeth. However they still required a great deal of refinement, and this matter of their riding was a good example. They filled their saddles like two sacks of oats.

'We're *very* tired, my lady,' complained young Roger. He had a running nose, which he proceeded to wipe on his sleeve.

'Tired and cold,' added March, with a hint of his accustomed sulkiness.

'You are tired and cold because you have not had enough exercise,' Constance said briskly. 'Straighten your backs! I've seen churls with better posture riding their oxen back home from the fields! What fool was it that taught you to ride?'

'We don't ride much,' said March. 'Usually, when we move to another place, we go pillion behind Waterton's men.'

'From now on you will ride every day, for at least two hours, whatever the weather. Every single day, until you can gallop from here to the castle with your hands on your heads. Is that understood?'

The boys nodded, their eyes lighting with a quiet, grudging pleasure, as if this was one change that they welcomed. They'd not much cared for her other innovations; the relentless scrubbing and tidying of themselves and their accommodation; the order and discipline she had introduced to their routine; the abrupt dismissal of the servants and tutors who had tolerated their former idleness and boorish manners. Nor had March much liked being laid out flat by Richard Despenser's fist in retaliation for an injudicious remark made about Richard's mother. The difference in their ages had proved to be more than balanced by the toughening Richard had received through living with other boys in the Queen's household.

Sir Hugh Waterton was less pleased by Constance's proposal, which she broached to him as soon as she returned to the castle. He rose somewhat reluctantly from his document-strewn desk.

'My men have more to do each day than ride around the park,' he said gruffly. He took a step towards her, brushed one of his account rolls onto the floor with his trailing sleeve, and grunted a curse over the accident. He was stockily-built, with a ragged forked beard that was turning white at the edges, and the accent of his native Yorkshire.

'Sir Hugh, your men need not stir themselves from their pots of ale,' Constance replied, without any effort of diplomacy. 'I have servants of my own more than capable of seeing that the boys come to no harm.'

The knight grunted, and took another step forward. The advance was not to his advantage, as she was the taller of them by half a head, and he found himself having to lift his head to meet her gaze. 'My lady, the King may have appointed you to teach the Mortimer brats to carve at table, and dance, and mumble poetry, and all such manner of things. However, as long as I remain Constable of Windsor, their security will be my responsibility, and they'll not set foot outside the walls unless my men are there to protect them. I know where my duty lies.'

'I should have thought it your duty to see that they were taught to ride long before this.' Constance paused, and drew a breath. 'I believe, Sir Hugh, that you resent my presence here and seek to thwart me in every possible way. You do not even trust me with the keys to the boys' bedchamber, though if they were to fall ill in the night I might need to attend them.'

'Their servant sleeps in their chamber. Let *him* attend them.' Waterton ran his eyes over her furred cloak and the rich mulberry gown that lay beneath. 'Any road, I don't see you cleaning up puke, my lady, or mopping their brows, even if there were need for it. That key stays with me, where I know it is safe. If necessary, one of your men can summon me.'

'May I remind you that the King has placed me in charge of the boys? By what right do you deny me access to them, at any hour?'

She thought the rising note of anger in her voice and the implied threat of appeal to Bolingbroke might intimidate him. It did not.

'If the King orders me to do differently, then I shall,' he said abruptly. 'Now, my lady, if you'll forgive me, I've much business to occupy me.'

Constance saw there was no purpose in arguing with the man, so she left him and made her way to her own apartments. A surprise awaited her there. The Earl of Kent stood warming himself against her fire, having arrived during her temporary absence; Agnes Norreys had seen to his comforts, and he had a cup of spiced wine clutched in his hand. He reached and set it down on the mantelpiece, then took a hesitant step towards her.

'My lord,' she said, by way of acknowledgement.

'I am newly returned from Brockenhurst,' he said, making a deep bow in response to her formal curtsey. 'I hope I find you well, my lady.'

'Yes.'

'I have the licence for our marriage.' He drew the document from his close-cut, green velvet sleeve, the parchment crackling with friction against the rich cloth. He studied it for a moment, then held it out to her, showing her the King's seal.

'So I see.'

'My uncle the Archbishop says we must send to Rome for a dispensation to marry anew, and do penance. It's no great difficulty. A matter of a few coins. I shall arrange it.'

'As you please.'

The silence between them was prolonged. The winter afternoon was already shading towards premature dusk, and the room was darkening by the instant. Constance's eyes were drawn beyond Kent, to the flickering red glow of the fire as its logs crackled and sparked. She shed her cloak, handed it to Anne Mortimer for disposal, and settled on her chair, rubbing the life back into her cold hands.

Mun turned towards her, and she heard his sharp intake of breath as he struggled for words. 'I have seen our daughter,' he said. 'She has grown since I brought you from Powys.'

'It is the nature of children, my lord. To grow.'

Mary Russell poured her a glass of wine and placed it in her hand. Constance raised it slowly, allowed her mouth to linger in its warm ruby depths. The wine was Malvoisie of the first quality, part of an unexpected Christmas gift from Bolingbroke himself. She was aware of Mun watching her, the stark discomfort on his face as he towered over her.

'Antonine Dagvar has been married to one of the Queen's Breton squires,' he said, keeping a cautious eye on her as he formed the words. 'Not that I was there to see it, of course, but Mowbray sent me news. I am under orders to avoid the court, until Candlemas.'

'So you come here? To me?'

'I hoped you might have forgiven me by now.' He shrugged, and ventured a smile. 'You know, there really is no reason for us to be at odds. Antonine was never a threat to you. It's not as if I cared for the whore, or intended to keep her.'

'I never supposed you did.'

'It is you I love.'

Constance doubted he knew the meaning of the word, but conceded to herself, if not to him, that he might possibly think he did.

'Christmas at Brockenhurst was very tedious,' he went on. 'I have missed you more than a little. Do I not have a right to your company?'

She nodded, but offered no other encouragement. Nevertheless, his face brightened as if she had thrown herself into his arms.

'The Mortimer boys,' he said, taking the opportunity to shift tack. 'It was shrewd to have the King put you in charge of them. I hear they might be placed in our household, and that will be profitable, one way or another. Are they behaving themselves? Showing you a proper respect? If not, tell me, and I'll give them a good thrashing before I leave here.'

Constance presumed that the offer was another attempt to placate her. 'There is no need of that,' she said. 'Even if there were, it might not be wise to beat a boy who may one day be your king.'

He snorted. 'Boys need beating as flowers need water. It never did me any harm.' He paused, suddenly considering what she had said. 'King?' he repeated. 'March? I doubt whether it will come to that.'

They supped with Hugh Waterton, and his plump, agreeable wife Kate. Mun dominated the conversation, growing louder and more affable with each new cup of wine. He did not seem to be concerned by Constance's modest contribution to the talk, indeed seemed to regard it as entirely proper that she should not have too much to say for herself.

While they still lingered over the wafers and spiced wine that ended the meal, Constance's yeoman, Richard Milton, entered the room, carrying the coveted key as a token that the boys had been locked up for the night. He handed it to Waterton, who placed it next to his plate, as though he thought to use it as a second knife. Constance's eyes focused covertly on the key, and her mind was so occupied with considering ways and means by which she might take possession of it that at first she did not notice the weight of Kent's hand on her thigh, or even its initial exploratory movements. She had already decided that the Mortimers must escape under cover of darkness, if there was to be any hope of success. For that to be attempted, the key must be secured. But how? Waterton was already slipping it into his purse. The chances were that he would keep it close at hand, even he did not sleep with it under his pillow.

Constance retired to her bed, and brooded over the matter until a scratch at the door announced Mun's arrival. She had expected no less, and watched in resignation as his large, dark shape shed its chamber-robe and climbed in next to her. It was, she admitted to herself, his right as her husband, and, anyway, she was too weary for an argument. He kissed her and toyed with her breasts for a little while, then climbed between her legs and took her without the least ceremony, clawing at her buttocks as he grasped them in his passion. It was soon over, and he was far too pleased with himself to question her lack of participation in the act. He muttered something about the pleasant healing of lovers' quarrels, and went off to sleep.

Constance turned from him, and curled herself into as small a space as possible, trying not to think of Edmund Mortimer. She felt no hatred for Mun, and saw little point in indulging in self-pity. She had made her choice, and now must live with it, in accordance with the dictates of her conscience. She took her lower lip between her teeth and forced herself to focus on the arrangements for the boys' escape, and in particular the problem presented by that key. Her mind struggled for an answer until weariness defeated her, and she slept.

When she woke it was almost light again, and Mun's muscular arm was secure about her waist, his hand caressing her belly even as he continued to snore. He was cheerful over breakfast, almost to the point of singing, and insisted on taking the Mortimers and Richard Despenser out into the tilt-yard. He sparred with them for the rest of the morning, using about a quarter of his strength in their mock fights and tolerating March's incompetence with a patience that both surprised Constance and touched her conscience. He was equally kind to her daughters, and made no distinction between the Despenser sisters and his own child. All received hugs, kisses and presents from him, and he was not above crawling on the floor to join in their games. He might be awkward in his ways, thoughtless and maladroit, but that there was good in him she had to acknowledge.

They had a few more days together, during which time he even managed to stir her to physical pleasure on a couple of occasions, a development that added both to her confusion and her underlying feeling of guilt. Still cheerful, he rode off, speaking of the need to consult his uncle the Archbishop about the financing of their dispensation, and of his intention to pursue once more the question of her Despenser dower rights with the King. Constance was glad to see him ride out through the gates of Windsor. She spent the rest of the day fasting, with many hours on her knees in the chapel, but found that the process left her as confused and guilty as ever.

**

The Duke of York arrived at Windsor half way through the afternoon of the Monday after Candlemas. He brought with him a modest portion of his household, perhaps a hundred men and boys in his livery, together with his Duchess and her extensive tail of ladies and serving-women.

He told Waterton that he was on his way to Kennington, to join the court, with the intent of going on from there to attend the Great Council the King had summoned to meet at Westminster on St. David's Day, the first of March. He was, however, in no haste, and intended to spend some time with his beloved sister.

By this time Philippa was already ensconced in Constance's apartments, fingering the bed-curtains for quality, counting the jewels that Constance's ladies and damosels wore in their livery collars, and summoning the Mortimer boys so that she might inspect behind their ears for dirt.

Constance, who had previously deluded herself into believing there was nothing Edward's wife could do or say that would surprise her, discovered that she had once more underestimated the Duchess. Philippa, settled in her chair with the air of one who owned the castle, if not all England, beckoned Anne Mortimer to her, spoke amiably to her, and took her by the hand, guiding her to stand next to her.

'I think it high time that Anne was married to our brother, Dickon,' she said briskly, turning her eyes upon Constance as if daring her to disagree. 'I do not know what you and York have been about, allowing the matter to drift for so long.'

Constance drew a breath. 'It is simple enough. They have nothing to live on, and Anne's mother will not consent until they do.'

Philippa waved her hand as if striking at a lazy fly. 'Lady March ought to be grateful for the service we are about to do her. Our efforts will make her son King of England, while she sits at home in safety. Dickon is heir to the dukedom. Is that not livelihood enough?'

Anne was beaming and nodding her head all at the same time, and she and the Duchess exchanged conspiratorial smiles.

'Dickon is not here,' Constance objected.

'Oh, but he is!' the Duchess said. She held out her hands to receive the small spaniel one of her women passed to her, and paused to fondle the dog, ruffling its ears. 'We brought him with us from Fotheringhay. The matter should be settled.'

'I forbid it,' Constance said. 'The girl is in my charge, and I am answerable to her mother for her welfare. Nothing shall be done without Alianore's consent.'

Philippa was trying to make the little dog dance on her lap. Her firm grip on its front paws caused it to squeal with discomfort. 'I'm sure Lady March will not object,' she said, not taking her eyes from the animal. 'In any event, it is my lord the Duke's wish that they be married. You know very well, Connie, that the alliance is essential to us. We must have some link to the Mortimers, and since you failed to marry for the profit of your family it follows that Dickon must.'

'It would be better done after Anne's brother becomes King. So great a marriage ought not to be celebrated in a corner, but openly, so no one can question it. It will set the seal on our triumph over Bolingbroke.'

In her anxiety to counter Philippa's proposals, Constance quite forgot that the Earl of March and his brother were still close at hand and very far from deaf. March's sullen mouth dropped open for a moment. Then he closed it, and stepped forward.

'What is it you say?' he asked. 'How am I to be King?'

'That is not your concern, boy,' Philippa said, in her most crushing voice.

However, the cat was no means to be returned to the bag. Constance eventually realised that she had no choice but to explain what was intended, while adding that the time was not yet ripe and swearing both the youngsters to secrecy. This process took a great deal of time, and was not helped by the Duchess's occasional haughty interjections or by Anne's increasing impatience with her brothers' questions and objections that seemed to her to stand in the way of her long-desired marriage.

March straightened himself up to his full height and shuffled his feet for a moment, scuffling his shoes as he considered his options. 'If I am to be King,' he said to Constance, 'why do you not curtsey to me? Why does the Duchess of York sit in my presence? Where is York himself? He should be here, on his knees, pledging his allegiance.'

'You are not King yet!' Philippa answered from her chair. 'Ungrateful brat!'

Constance resisted the temptation to box his ears, considering whether he really was the most obnoxious youth she had ever met, or merely a leading contender for the title. He reminded her very much of his aunt, Lady Arundel, although the comparison was not really fair because, whatever else she had lacked, Philippa Arundel had not been short of either courage or intelligence.

'You are a very long way from being King,' she said. 'Many will have to give their lives to make you so, and you will have to learn to bear yourself more like a knight. More like a man. Once you have earned your crown, then you will have my reverence, and my sister of York's.'

March's expression grew even more surly, if that were possible. 'If I am the King, then I am the King. I don't have to *earn* anything.'

'Is this the fellow?' Edward demanded, as he strode into the room. 'God's grace, but he looks a puny brat! Like a maid, except he's too ugly to be one!'

'He is certainly insolent,' Philippa said, her eyes hard. 'He seems to expect us all to fall on our knees before him.'

York laughed. 'Boy, you will never be King of England unless we and others make you so. Remember that.' He continued his visual inspection of March, as though assessing a recruit, and finished by tweaking the boy's nose. 'I'm not sure we should. Cousin Bolingbroke has his faults, but at least he looks like a king. Even if only when he sits away from the light!'

'Edward!' Constance objected.

'Yes, my dear, I know. We are too far committed to change now. God help us. A piglet in ermine would look more kingly.'

Young Roger Mortimer dissolved into laughter, while his elder brother's colour deepened to purple. His gobbling outrage was only silenced when York slapped him viciously across the mouth.

Edward shook his head, as if regretting the necessity for the blow. 'Hold your tongue, boy, and do exactly as my sister tells you. It's your only hope.'

42

The locksmith Tyldesley brought up from the town was a young, thin faced fellow with an untidy tangle of pale yellow hair.

'If you will give me the key, my lady,' he said, 'I can have it copied for you in an hour or two.'

Constance leaned back in her chair, shaking her head. 'The key is only in my possession for a short time each day. It must be copied quickly, without anyone knowing you have done it.'

The young man's hand visited his beard and his feet shuffled. 'My lady...' he began hesitantly, and then halted. 'I'm not sure that I understand you.'

She reached across the table in front of her, opened the purse that lay half open upon it, and drew out a gold coin, a noble, which she placed between them. 'Perhaps this will aid your understanding,' she suggested.

The light streamed into the room through the frost-whitened glazing of its great window, and warmed the gold into a hint of life. The locksmith stared at the coin in an agony of contemplation. It was as much, or more, as he could hope to earn in two weeks of normal business. For a few hours of work it represented very good pay indeed. Enough to have the front of his shop painted anew, and perhaps to buy his wife the thick winter cloak she coveted. 'If I had the key for a Paternoster-while, I could make an impression in wax,' he said. 'With that, I could make a copy. It would take longer...'

Constance pushed the coin nearer to his hand. 'I'm not interested in the secrets of your mystery, only in the key I need.' She gestured towards the coin. 'Two of these. One now, one when I have the key. Is that a fair price?'

'More than fair.' He hesitated. 'My lady, it is far too much.'

'The price of your work is only a part of it. There is also the price of your silence.'

She held his gaze, watched as comprehension appeared in the locksmith's eyes, the understanding of the risk he was taking. He swallowed, nodded, and she pushed the coin towards him. He hesitated, just for a moment, then picked it up, stared at it, and slipped it into his purse.

Tyldesley led him out, and Constance reached for a piece of parchment and began to write a letter to Edmund Mortimer. She had her date chosen now, Valentine's Eve, when the moon would be full, giving enough light to make it possible to ride through the night, to gain the essential start on those who would pursue when her escape was known. A couple of days would see them at Tewkesbury, the boys on the ferry, herself in sanctuary at the abbey. Her son and Anne would go with the Mortimers. Her daughters and the rest of her women, headed by Agnes, would remain at Windsor, and the men of her household, once they had escorted her to ferry, might go where they would, either into Wales with Edmund, to fight for their rightful King, into sanctuary with her, or to their own homes if they preferred the path of safety.

The quill had grown fragile, and broke under the pressure of her hand, leaving an untidy blot in the middle of the salutation. She cursed softly, took up her penknife and began the task of cutting another pen to shape, finding that her fingers had grown inexplicably awkward. She had to take a breath, and concentrate on the work in order to make progress. While she was so distracted, her brother Dickon walked into the room, with all his usual lack of presence. Though the Duke and Duchess had left Windsor that morning, he had remained behind to spend a few more days in Anne's company.

'Constance, what is it that you are about?' he asked bluntly.

She threw down knife and half-formed pen in frustration. 'I should have thought that might be obvious, even to you.'

'I don't mean that.' He paused, seated himself on the bench opposite to her, and studied her handiwork with a critical eye before reaching for it and the knife. Two decisive cuts, and he had the job finished for her. 'I want to know why it is that you don't wish me to marry Anne. I never thought the day would come when our sister Philippa would wish us well, while you stood in our way.'

'You have nothing to live on, Dickon,' she pointed out. 'How can Anne's mother be expected to agree to a contract of marriage when you have no means of providing for a wife? Even if your annuity at the Exchequer were paid regularly, as it ought to be, it makes no provision for a widow. She, and any children she bears you, could be left destitute. Our brother York must order some proper livelihood for you, before you can think of marriage.'

'He has promised that he will.'

She treated him to a thin, cynical smile across the width of the table. 'You should know what Ned's promises are worth. As I do. He must not promise, he must grant, and give you real possession. It is the least that Alianore March will expect for her daughter.'

'Anne and I do not care about lands or money!'

'Then you are both very foolish. Without lands you'll never have independence. You'll be at Ned's beck and call, or the King's, for the rest of your life. A hired servant. Is that what you want?'

'I want Anne.'

'You shall have her. In a few months, if all goes well, her brother will be King of England, and able to make a proper settlement on her. You and she need only be patient. I wish that I were so well placed.'

Constance found herself unaccountably studying her hands, and folded them in her lap in an attempt to relax her mind. She adjusted her posture on the hard, wooden seat, throwing back her shoulders and her head and looking directly into Dickon's eyes.

'You tell me not to trust Ned's promises,' he said, 'and yet you must know that all depends on him. Your very life is in his hands. By this time tomorrow he will be presenting himself to the King. How can you be sure he will not fail you?'

She took a breath. 'I cannot. But if he does, I shall make sure that he never fails anyone again.'

***

The duplicate key was in her hands. Though it had already been tested in the lock, time and again, the uncertainty remained, as chill as the winter night.

Constance had settled her daughters to sleep, and watched over them for a time, aware that many months might pass before she saw them again. Bess had shed a few tears, and needed to be comforted, but she was peaceful now, her favourite cloth doll in the crook of her arm, while Isabelle, who took partings with a placid indifference, lay curled next to her in the bed, her long fair hair emerging from her linen cap. The baby Alianore slept separately, nestled beneath the blankets of her own small bed, her chubby face pouting its contentment.

Agnes Norreys emerged from the darkness, her solemn features dimly lit by the candle she had clutched in her hand.

'I do not know how you can bear to leave them,' she observed, her voice harsh in the still silence.

'Because it is my duty, Agnes,' Constance said. 'I have no other choice.'

She pushed past an unconvinced Lady Norreys, and out into the adjoining room. Anne Mortimer, who had been sitting by the remains of the fire, rose from her place, took up Constance's cloak from the press on which it had been lying, and helped her into it.

They emerged onto the landing where Tyldesley and Robert Rous were waiting, seated restlessly over a candle-lit game of dice, which they abandoned at once, pausing only to scoop up their stakes. Richard Despenser was with them, his eyes bright with excitement.

'All is quiet, my lady,' Tyldesley said. 'Our men have secured the gates. It needed no more than a little good fellowship, a few gallons of ale and a pinch or two of poppy-juice. The watchmen are sleeping soundly, and will do so until they are relieved. It gives us until dawn.' He touched the hilt of his sword, unconsciously reassuring himself that it was in place. 'Even so, I'll be glad to be away from here.'

Constance nodded. There was a sizeable community living within the castle walls, to say nothing of the people in the town outside its gates. The guards on duty at the gates might not trouble them, but it would be all too easy to wake someone, to provoke sufficient curiosity to raise the alarm.

The key to the boys' room worked perfectly, as if to make a mockery of her misgivings. March and his brother had been prepared by their servant, Richard Milton, and were waiting impatiently for the adventure to begin, stamping their feet at protest against the cold.

'You're very tardy, my lady,' March sniffed, carefully wiping his nose on his trailing sleeve. 'We've been standing around for hours. Your man made us get up far too early. He's a dolt! A dolt and a peasant. If I'm to be king, I ought to have gentlemen to wait on me. *Knights!*'

Constance governed her impatience, and drew him towards her with her arm instead of boxing his ears, as she was tempted to do. 'There's no time to speak of that now. Hurry! Tyldesley will take you on his pillion, and Milton will take Roger. You must keep as quiet as you can. Set an example, Eddie, for your brother and my son will look to you to lead them. You are the eldest.'

'The eldest, *and* their rightful King?'

'Yes.' Constance made the concession with grim determination and gritted teeth, as a price to be paid for progress.

The boy's teeth glinted in the darkness for a moment as he broke into a rare smile of satisfaction. 'Then it is fitting I should have a horse of my own,' he objected, 'and not ride pillion like a maid.'

'It would indeed be fitting,' Constance agreed with faultless amiability. 'However, until you can manage your horse above a canter without falling off every dozen yards, you must be content with the pillion. This is not a gentle procession through the streets, my lord of March. We shall be riding for our lives, galloping through the dark. A horse of your own? You'd break your neck before we were even clear of Windsor.'

Little Roger laughed into his sleeve. 'It is true, Eddie. You would fall off!'

March's mood was not helped by this contribution from his brother, but at least he was content to sulk in silence, and follow where he was led. They descended to the courtyard, where the other male members of Constance's household were gathered around the horses.

The moon provided light enough for them to see their way to the first of the gates, a black tunnel leading out into the lower ward. As Constance mounted, she felt the first chill flakes of snow brushing lightly against her cheeks, and drew the hood of her cloak lower across her face. She was vaguely surprised, having thought it too cold for snow, but there was no time to dwell on the matter. She gestured towards the gate, and they walked their horses forward. Despite their caution, the noise of the hooves seemed to raise thunderous echoes from the stones, but no one stirred within the castle, no sentry yelled a challenge, no alarm bell rang. The road to Wales lay open before them.

***

The King was still lingering over breakfast when Waterton's messenger brought the news to him. Bolingbroke did not waste time in asking supplementary questions, or in raging aimlessly. Instead he gave peremptory orders for his horse to be saddled, and for every man at Kennington to follow him to Windsor. He rode at the head of them all, galloping through the snow with such reckless regard for his safety that only the most skilled and best-mounted horsemen among his household knights and squires were able to keep within a furlong of him.

When the journey began it was barely light, and he did not draw rein until it was almost noon, and he was within the bounds of Windsor park. He eased his horse to a walk, and allowed some of his exhausted followers to catch up with him, to form some semblance of a procession. His immediate fury driven out of him by his long, fast ride, he began to think. Constance had the best part of twelve hours start on him. Even if he and his men were provided with fresh horses, and made an immediate start, there was no hope of catching her before she was over the Severn and into Wales.

Hugh Waterton was waiting for him in the courtyard, shamefaced, shuffling his feet like a guilty schoolboy. Stuttering, he began to explain, but Harry gestured him to silence.

'Hugh, there is no need. Have you sent men after them?'

Waterton nodded hurriedly. 'Almost the whole garrison. I also raised the hue-and-cry in the town. I doubt that they have more than a couple of hours start on the first of my men, and this snow means there will be tracks to follow.'

Bolingbroke dismounted, passed the reins to one of the boys who had come running forward to serve him. More of his followers were making their way through the gates now, the enormous courtyard slowly filling with them. 'There will be no need to follow hoof prints in the snow,' he said. 'There's only one road they're likely to take. Through Abingdon and Burford, and on to Glamorgan. Where else is she taking them but to Wales? To Glyn Dwr. To Edmund Mortimer!'

He spat the last name out as if it were a stray lump of vomit. The flood of energy that had brought him in such haste from Kennington drained away as rapidly and as inexplicably as it had arrived. Weary to the bone, he led the way into the castle, drawing his gloves from his hands as he walked, careless of the chill air that numbed his fingers.

He had Constance's women brought before him, and questioned them closely, though to little effect, since they knew little that was not already obvious. Agnes said nothing at all, but only smiled at him, even when he stormed at her and threatened her with the penalties of treason. At last he gave up, summoned a clerk and dictated a hurried, brief note to his Council at Westminster, informing them of the new conspiracy and ordering them to close the ports, because he feared that Constance might have sent a messenger to the French.

Food and drink was placed before him, but he scarcely deigned to touch it. In his present mood it seemed to him that it might be poisoned; besides, he had no appetite. He rose from the table, studying the white, fearful faces around him, the eyes that lowered rather than meet his gaze. Men bowed before him, knelt on the tiles, as he crossed the room, but what was in their minds he could not tell. With every step a part of him expected a blade between his ribs. He all but braced himself to receive it.

'Where is the Earl of Kent?' he demanded.

Many glances were exchanged, but no answer was forthcoming.

Harry's half-brother, John Beaufort, was the first to speak. 'I have not seen him this day, Sire,' he said with solemn formality. 'He may still be at Kennington, I suppose.'

'Or it may be he has gone to his woman!' Bolingbroke flinched at the thought of it. Kent had saved his life at Shrewsbury, at no small risk to his own. Was it possible that Constance had turned him into a traitor? More than possible, it seemed. 'Give orders for his arrest!'

Even as he spoke, Kent appeared at the threshold of the room. Mun had woken late and sore-headed, and his hurried ride from Kennington in pursuit of the King had reddened his unshaven face. He advanced slowly, a path opening through the crowd as men recognised him and drew back in respect for his rank and his physical presence.

'I am here, Your Grace,' he said, going onto one knee before Bolingbroke. 'Whatever has happened, I had no part in it.'

Harry could feel himself trembling, and was unsure of the cause, whether it was anger or mere weakness that had set him shaking. There was a chair by the fire. Taking his eyes from Kent, who still knelt motionless as a rock, he walked towards it while his feet would still obey him, and sat down.

'Leave us!' he said abruptly, his voice explosive in the prevailing silence of the great vaulted room. John Beaufort and Waterton protested, but he over-rode them. 'Face-to-face, with a weapon in my hand, I do not fear Kent or any other man that lives. Let him do his worst if he will.'

They trooped out of the room, leaving Mun still kneeling, his red-shot eyes fixed hopefully on Bolingbroke's face.

The King jerked a hand in his general direction. 'Get to your feet, boy. I suppose I should have expected nothing better. Blood shows in the end, and you are Holland. Your brother and your uncle were false traitors to me, so what else should you be?'

Kent rose to his feet, and took a step forward, his left hand resting uneasily on the hilt of his dagger. 'I have told Your Grace; I had no part in this. If it were otherwise, I'd be half way to Wales by now.'

'You must at the least have known what was intended. Why did you not speak?'

'I swear I did not know. On my honour.'

'Constance is your intended wife, and the boys are your nephews. Not long ago you were here at Windsor, in their company. My cousin is scarcely close-mouthed. She has a way of speaking her mind. You expect me to believe that she did not speak to you of her plans?'

'Sire, she said nothing.' Kent's bewilderment was slowly turning to anger, and to a sense of outrage that he should have to justify himself. 'Why should you not believe me? Have I ever proved disloyal? Have I not shed my blood in your cause?'

Bolingbroke snorted. 'If you are not a traitor, then my cousin has shown that she holds you in contempt, and proved you are not man enough to rule her. If you are not a traitor, you will be the laughing-stock of my court.'

'I will strangle the bitch when next I see her!'

'My lord of Kent, you speak of a lady of our blood,' Bolingbroke said, with dreadful formality. He straightened himself in his chair, forcing himself to sit upright even though his every muscle longed to slouch at ease. He watched as Mun's eyes narrowed in confusion, watched as the young man's lips first hinted at a reply and then formed into a still line. 'Lady Despenser is guilty of high treason, beyond doubt. Guilty of conspiracy with my rebels in Wales, and thus with my adversary of France, who has made himself Glyn Dwr's ally against us. She will be tried, found guilty, and burnt at the stake, in accordance with the law.'

Kent remained silent for a moment, and then shrugged. 'It is no more than she deserves,' he said abruptly. 'Let her burn!'

Harry considered his rings, holding his hands clasped close to his lowered head. 'It is fortunate that I delayed your marriage to her,' he murmured. 'If she were your wife, you could scarcely escape a share in her guilt.'

Mun avoided his gaze, seemed to be casting around the room in search of reassurance in the walls. 'Sire, it was her lands I wanted. You know how my creditors press me, how little I have to live upon, the great charges I have incurred fighting in your wars.'

'Yes, all this we know.' Bolingbroke took a deep breath, as if he had just emerged from swimming underwater. 'There are other ladies with sufficient dowries to repay your debts. I will search for one that even you are capable of managing.' He fell silent. Even as he visualised Constance in her shift, chained to a stake, the flames licking around her feet, he knew that he could never bring himself to order such a sentence. The very thought of it tore at his heart, almost made him want to retch. 'Foolish woman!' he said quietly, speaking more to himself than to Kent. 'When she was widowed, I gave more to her than to my own sister. I even granted her the wardship of her son, and control of all the Despenser lands. God knows that I have never wished her anything but good. Why could she not see it? Why?'

***

Constance was within an hour of safety. They had passed the scattered village of Cheltenham, and she was convinced that only the prevailing chill mist was concealing a distant view of the tower of Tewkesbury Abbey. The mist and the surrounding trees, for they were deep within a wood, the brittle, naked branches reaching down to caress them as they rode cautiously along the narrow, frozen track.

She was weary of the bitter cold, of the reek of the snow that had permeated the edges of her hood, and of the persistent icy drips of water that fell from the trees into her face. There had been no sleep since Windsor, save for inadvertent dozes in the saddle, little rest and less food. March had long since stopped complaining about the journey. Exhausted, he and his brother clung to Tyldesley and Milton, their heads leaning into the men's backs, their eyes closed. Richard Despenser was no less weary, but he was managing his own horse, focused on the task of ensuring that it took its next step. His head was bowed, and every so often he let out a racking cough that echoed through the intense silence of the wood. Anne Mortimer was fading fast. She was clinging to her saddle with grim determination, but one of the men had her mare on a leading rein now, because Anne no longer had the strength to guide it.

There was a shadowy movement ahead of them, so slight that at first Constance dismissed it as a trick of the light, and then persuaded herself that it might be a deer.

It was an armed man on a horse. She hesitated, considering the possibility that Edmund and the Welsh escort had crossed the Severn to meet her. Another horseman emerged from the trees, and then another. She shook her head, struggling to believe the truth of what her eyes were telling her. The men were not Welsh. They wore Bolingbroke's own livery.

She forced her horse's head around even as Tyldesley shouted a warning. The wood was suddenly filled with enemies, closing on them from every side; men who rode in confident silence, advancing slowly, weapons in their hands. There was no way to escape.

***

The barge drifted easily down river with the tide, the oarsmen working by the light of blazing torches that cast golden reflections on the black water. A faint heat from the torches drifted into the canvas tunnel at the stern, not sufficient to take the edge from the bitter chill of the night but serving as a reminder of the luxury of fire and shelter.

Constance sat between Hugh and Kate Waterton on the cushioned bench beneath the canopy. Kate had helped her into a change of clothes at Windsor, but neither she nor her husband had had much to say to her during the journey, their demeanour as icy as the weather. It was understandable, of course, and a part of her was glad of their silence. It had helped her to compose herself for the forthcoming ordeal. She was bone weary, having scarcely slept in days, but she still bore her head high.

Her son, the Mortimer boys and Anne were back at Windsor and, though she was concerned for their welfare, she doubted they were in any immediate danger. She was much more worried about the fate of the men of her household. Some had been sorely wounded in their desperate and futile attempt to cut a way through. All were prisoners, in peril of their lives for her sake.

The dark, vast irregular shape of Westminster crouched on the left bank, its windows shuttered against the winter night so that only the lighted lanterns on its landing stage provided a visible evidence of occupation. The barge steered by the beacon provided, the crew lifting their oars from the water as they approached the stone stairs that led into the palace, the vessel swiftly losing way and coming alongside the quay with only a small suggestion of a jolt. It was no sooner secured to the bank than the abbey bells began to toll for compline.

'My lady,' said Hugh Waterton, a slight gesture of his hand extending his words into an invitation to go ashore.

Constance rose from her place, feeling the boat move unsteadily beneath her, and climbed out onto the wet and slippery stairs. For the first time in her life, no man made any attempt to aid her in this process, and she almost lost her footing in dark, the shock of it awakening her like cold water splashed in the face. She steadied herself, and walked through the open doors and up a broad flight of stairs, the two Watertons following her closely.

She was left standing in a gloomy anteroom for what seemed like an hour while various people wandered to and fro, some pausing to stare at her as if she had developed a second head, but no one troubling to speak. Her strength was failing her, and when Hugh Waterton touched her arm she realised that she had practically fallen asleep on her feet. The great door to the council chamber stood open, and he guided her through it, almost propelling her.

It was a cavernous, vaulted room, lit by so many candles and blazing torches that her eyes narrowed defensively against the brightness. Above her head, the dark blue ceiling, painted with silver stars, seemed almost a continuation of the night sky. A long table stretched across the room, blocking her path, and behind it, settled in their oak chairs, the men to whom she must answer, their faces only half visible to her because of the light from the three candelabra that stood before them. The central chair, raised on its small dais, stood empty. Bolingbroke was not present. The intense silence was prolonged sufficiently for her to assume that they were waiting for him. Then it proved that they were not.

'You must explain to us by what right you removed your charges, March and his brother, from Windsor Castle.' The voice emerging from the shadows belonged to her cousin, Henry Beaufort, Bishop of Winchester. He was Lord Chancellor now, in Bishop Stafford's room, appointed despite the fact that he and his brother the King were on very prickly terms with one another and always had been. He sat next to the empty throne.

'For their protection,' Constance said. The words seemed to emerge from her mouth of their own volition, before she could consider them. She heard Hugh Waterton choking with indignation and closed her teeth on her tongue.

'Protection? From whom?' It was Thomas Erpingham who spoke. She knew him by his Norfolk burr, even though his face was quite invisible to her.

This time she considered her answer, and found there was none that was either safe or sensible. The silence lengthened, and their impatience seemed to growl at her.

'Cousin, you must speak,' the Bishop said. 'You must tell us who it was who led you into this folly. This treason. It is obvious to us that you did not act alone. As you hope for mercy, you must speak.'

Constance did not answer. She felt herself swaying on her feet, and pinched herself in an effort to regain control of her limbs.

'Give me leave, and I swear I shall make her speak,' Kent roared. She heard the noise of his chair scraping back as he rose to his feet, turned in his direction and found that she could recognise his face. Until that moment she had not realised that he was sitting among her judges. 'Give me but a little time, and you will have the names of those who misled her. Those we cannot already guess.'

'Kent, you have the manners of a bully in a Southwark stew,' Edward of York yawned. Constance realised that he was sitting on the opposite side of the throne to Beaufort. His hands spread out before him, the candlelight reflecting on his ruby ring as he moved. 'It is an unknightly deed to threaten a lady with violence, especially when there is no need for it. My sister's actions are very easily explained. Her mind has been troubled for many years. You all know the cause. She blames the King for her husband's death, and in her lunacy she will have thought this a way to avenge herself on him.'

'She is no more lunatic than you or I,' Mun returned. He hammered his fist down on the great table, creating a thunderous echo. 'Her silence suits you well, York, of that I have no doubt. It might be that the full tale of her doings would have some small mention of you!'

Edward laughed dismissively. 'More likely of you, her promised husband, the uncle of the Mortimer boys.'

'The King does not question my loyalty!'

'Do you say that he questions mine?' York's voice was suddenly cold with the arrogance of insulted rank. 'You forget your place, boy. Wipe your mother's milk from your mouth and learn some wisdom before you give any more advice at the King's council table.'

Bishop Beaufort was growing impatient with this skirmishing and tutted an interjection. 'My lords, cousins, let me remind you we are not here to quarrel among ourselves, but to question a prisoner.'

Edward yawned again, with still greater emphasis. 'What will be gained by such questioning? I have no doubt that my sister has conspired with the Welsh rebels, and with Edmund Mortimer, who was once her lover. But those taken with her, as I understand it, were her own men. Why should anyone suppose that others were involved? What evidence is there of it? There have been no stirrings, no gatherings of armed men. No one has made any attempt on the King's life, or sought to seize the Tower. Erpingham, tell us of your friend in Norfolk, the Bishop of Norwich? Has he risen in revolt?'

'No,' answered the knight, almost with regret. 'He busies himself looking for heretics to burn, and claims to find one behind each bush, but he has not shown any sign of lifting a finger against the King.'

'If any man were to be taken into her confidence, or likely to join this hare-brained scheme, it would be Bishop Despenser! Yet he is sitting on his hands in Norfolk.' York spread his hands apologetically. 'As I have said, my sister has been troubled in her mind for years, and of late we have grown more and more concerned for her welfare.'

'We?' The word broke sharply from Kent.

'We of her immediate family; my Duchess and myself; the King.'

Constance took an uncertain step forward, not at all sure what Edward was attempting to achieve, other than to establish distance from involvement in their conspiracy. His old trick, holding back just far enough to be sure of attaching himself to the winning side.

'No doubt, my lord Duke, that was why you lately visited Lady Despenser at Windsor.' It was Hugh Waterton who spoke, and Constance, who had almost forgotten his presence, turned towards him and saw the contempt and suspicion on his face. He at least was not deceived by Edward's words.

'Of course I visited her!' Edward snapped back. 'I am her brother, and the King asked me to keep an eye on her. As for you, Waterton, you should remember that you have a case to answer yourself. Were it not for your incompetence this would never have happened.'

'I do not see that this is bringing us any nearer to the bottom of this conspiracy,' Bishop Beaufort said wearily. 'I suppose you are not accusing Sir Hugh of being a part of it?'

'No, I do not, but he seems close to accusing *me*, and I demand an apology for the insult. I am not answerable to a petty knight from the arse end of Yorkshire. I warned the King that my sister had something of this sort in mind. If it was obvious to me, it should have been obvious to Waterton, who saw her every day.'

Constance jerked out of her near stupor. 'You warned the King?' she repeated forcefully. 'You betrayed me? Is that why I was caught?'

Her brother flinched from what he saw in her eyes, but answered boldly. 'Of course I warned the King. It was my duty as a loyal subject to tell him that you were contemplating treason.'

It seemed to Constance that her blood had turned to ice, and in that process woken her from a deep slumber. She drew herself erect, and spoke what was in her heart. 'Did you also tell him that I did your bidding? That it was you who asked me to take those boys to Wales? Did you tell him of your meeting with Glyn Dwr? Of your intent to murder him, and make young March king in his place?'

There was an intense silence for a moment, as if she had put them all under a spell. Then they all jumped up from the table and began to shout at once, even those who had not so far spoken a word, even the clerks at the end of the board. York was shouting louder than anyone, but he could not make himself heard. He tried to push his way around the table to reach her, but others were just as determined to stop him. Erpingham stood yelling into his face, pushing against his chest, and Kent was doing his utmost to climb over the abandoned chairs to join the confrontation.

'It is all a lie!' Edward yelled as the noise eased a little. 'I told you—she is mad; mad as a March hare. How much more proof do you need?'

'You are the liar, my dear Brother,' Constance answered, advancing another step. 'What's more, I begin to think that if either of us is mad it is you. You must know that I can prove your falseness, that you have been a traitor a dozen times over. Half of it is common knowledge, but I can speak of the other half, the half that is neither suspected nor pardoned.'

He snorted contemptuously. 'And who do you suppose will believe you? What worth has the unsupported word of a crazed woman, against mine? Where is your proof? Where are your witnesses?' He turned from her to his fellow members of the Council. 'Can you not see what she is about? She hates me! Has done ever since I led the King's vanguard against her traitorous husband and his friends. She blames me for his death, and would do anything, tell any lie, to revenge herself on me.'

Constance tried to put it to the test. She began to tell them all she could of the conspiracy, then realised that there was a limit to what she could say without involving Northumberland, Mowbray and the Archbishop of York. Without the fullest details, without the mention of names, she could scarcely expect them to believe her.

'It is indeed my word against my brother's,' she admitted, breaking from the tale. 'If I were a man there would be a simple way to prove the truth. The way of battle. As it is…'

'As it is you had better put an end to your false allegations. It is obvious to all here that you are a foul liar, as well as a traitress and a whore.'

'As it is, I ask for a champion to prove the truth of what I have said. I defy the Duke of York and challenge him to trial by combat.'

She was astonished by her own calm, aware as she was that if her champion failed it would mean her own death by fire. Then again, she faced that anyway, and she was sure that her champion would be Mun. Kent was more than capable of defeating Edward in the lists, and it was a far better end than her brother deserved.

She turned towards Mun, only to find that he had slumped back into his seat, and was avoiding her eye. 'I demand a champion,' she repeated, watching as a slow smile began to spread across Edward's face.

There was a movement behind her as one of the King's squires stepped forward to throw down his glove for her. He was a small, dark haired youth whose name she did not know.

York stepped around the table. 'Mr. Maidstone, you'll not live long enough to claim your exquisite reward,' he said, bending to pick up the gage.

'Let it lie!'

Edward froze as he recognised Bolingbroke's voice, and the peremptory note in it. Those who had just resumed their seats leapt up again, this time in silence, waiting to see what would happen next.

The King advanced from the shadows, into the centre of the room, his shoulders bowed as if by a weight. His eyes ran over them, one by one, until they settled on Constance. She curtsied, and almost collapsed with the effort, her legs all but failing her.

'Get my cousin a stool,' Harry ordered. 'Can none of you see she is at the end of her strength?'

'Sire,' Edward protested, 'my sister deserves no consideration. She is a false liar, as I shall prove. When you have heard—'

'I *have* heard.' Bolingbroke's eyes were hard now. He made his way to his chair, and settled into it, gesturing abruptly for the rest of the company to sit. Maidstone had brought up a stool for Constance and she eased herself onto it, uncertain as to whether she would have the strength to rise again if that was required. It took her some time to process Harry's words, to understand that he must have been standing in the gloom at the back of the room for some time, that he had heard all or most of what had been said.

Edward was the only one of them still standing. 'Your Grace, forgive me if I seemed to lose my temper, but I have been falsely accused of treason. This is no light matter.'

'You have certainly been accused.' Bolingbroke's voice was clipped, and as chill as ice.

'Not for the first time,' Erpingham ventured, half under his breath.

'You told the Council that you warned me of your sister's intentions,' Harry said, revealing just how long he had been waiting. 'That is a plain lie. You gave me no such warning.'

Constance stared at her brother, and saw the growing panic in his eyes. He had told one lie too many. The irony of it was that without his pretence of betraying her, she would never have accused him.

'Your Grace is mistaken.' Edward said, still trying to wriggle out of the trap he had dug for himself.

'I am not. What's more, it was you who advised me to give the March children into Lady Despenser's care. Do not dare to deny it!'

'I do not. But surely, Cousin, you do not suppose I had this folly in mind when I made the suggestion?'

The silence was intense as Bolingbroke took his time to consider the question. 'It needs no combat to prove the truth of this,' he said at last. 'Your sister has many faults, but she has never pretended to be anything but my enemy. I prefer the word of an honest enemy to that of a false friend.' He turned to Erpingham. 'Arrest the Duke of York! Have him taken to the Tower.'

Edward kept on protesting his innocence, but he was propelled towards the door by half a dozen willing pairs of hands. His shouted complaints of injustice faded into the distance as he was marched away.

***

Constance rose from the window-seat on which she had been resting, took the eight graceful and unhurried steps that carried her past the foot of her bed to the equivalent window-seat at the other side of the room. She turned, lowered herself onto it, and picked up the piece of mending-work she had discarded half an hour earlier. Apart from the bed and the window-seats the polygonal room contained a fireplace, a small stand with a washing bowl and ewer and, next to her, a curtained portal leading to a garderobe. There was very little else, and the small windows gave a very restricted view, the lake in one direction and the walls of the keep in the other.

The days seemed endless. It was more than three weeks now since the Constable of Kenilworth, John Ashford, had invited her to take supper at his table, and almost as long since Mistress Ashford had climbed the spiral stair to her room for an hour or two of gossip as they sat together over their needlework. Since the King's court had established itself at Kenilworth she had been close confined. Ashford's chaplain occasionally visited to say a low mass for her, or to treat her to a few platitudes, but he was notably deaf and his conversation was limited, while the girl who tended to her linen and fetched her food was too much in awe and haste to provide more than fleeting companionship.

She had been more than eight months at Kenilworth, and before that a month in the Tower. The time in the Tower had been worst. Various members of the Council had visited her to elicit further details of the conspiracy, and she had had to play a dangerous game of bargaining with them, admitting as little as possible in the face of threats against the lives of her men. Eventually, satisfied with the extent of her confession, they had promised pardons to her followers. The young locksmith had been the only one to be denied mercy. They had cut off his hands, and then his head, and they had made her watch. His face was an addition to the ones that already haunted her dreams.

Throughout the summer small pieces of news had filtered to her through the Ashfords. There had been two defeats of Glyn Dwr's supporters in south east Wales in small but decisive battles. Then Archbishop Scrope and the Earl Marshal had risen in revolt in Yorkshire, but prematurely. Northumberland had failed to join them in time, and they had been taken by treachery and subsequently executed at Bolingbroke's orders. Northumberland, saved by distance, had escaped to exile in Scotland.

Though Constance was horrified by the Archbishop's death, and judged that the King would burn in hell for it, it was Mowbray for whom she said her prayers, remembering with sorrow the bitter, discontented youth who had been a friend to her when she had needed an ally against Joanna.

Towards the end of August the Franco-Welsh army had advanced as far as the outskirts of Worcester, too strong for Bolingbroke to attack and yet not strong enough to feel confident of attacking him until they received reinforcement from English rebels, reinforcement that never arrived. There had been a few fights to the death between individuals, but the French knights had not prospered in these combats. At last Glyn Dwr and his allies had retreated into Wales, forced away by lack of supplies. King Harry had survived his greatest crisis, though only just. It was said that his health had grown much worse since Scrope's execution, that he was bedridden for weeks at a time.

Of Edward she had heard nothing, save that he was imprisoned at Pevensey on the Sussex coast, in the same castle as the Mortimer boys. Philippa was shut up in the York family manor of Fasterne in Wiltshire. Their lands, like hers, were forfeited. There was no word of Edmund Mortimer, or of Kent, and nor could she discover anything about the whereabouts or welfare of her children, though the Ashfords assured her that there was no cause for her to be concerned.

She was considering whether to continue with her stitching or undertake a renewed count of the floor tiles when her ears caught the sound of the door being unlocked. This was unexpected, supper being at least three hours away, so she watched the door with interest to see who would appear. The newcomer proved to be a small woman wearing a plain black gown, her oval, kindly face framed by a linen hood and wimple. Constance recognised her at once, though she had not set eyes on her since Harry's coronation. Mun's mother, Alice, the Dowager Countess of Kent, had lived in virtual retirement since her husband's death, more than eight years ago now, and she was the very last person Constance had expected to see.

Alice Kent's lined face broke into a gentle smile. 'Well, my dear, your affairs are in a pretty muddle it seems. I do not know what your father would say, were he here today. How are you?'

Constance rose, curtsied in welcome, and gestured her guest to a seat on the bed. 'I would be content enough, if I knew how my children fared. Have you any news of them, my lady? Any at all?'

'Your son is here, with the Queen, in her household as before. He seems to be a favourite, so I don't think you need have any fears for him. The girls are well cared for. I have visited them, and they are perfectly safe and happy. All three of them.'

'And Mun?'

'You humiliated him, Constance; made him look like the worst kind of fool. You're old enough to be aware that no man relishes such treatment. Mun least of all. He has not forgiven you, and nor will he while he lives.'

The silence that followed was an awkward one. 'I hope he will,' Constance said at last. 'I wish I might have the chance to speak to him, to explain. Is he here at Kenilworth?'

'He is, but I must tell you he has no wish to see you. Whatever you might say to him would make no difference.' Lady Kent paused, and folded her hands in her lap. 'Why? What made you do such a thing?'

Constance, who had been studying her fingers, lifted her eyes to meet those of the elder woman. 'Need you ask me, my lady? You lost a son because Harry Bolingbroke stole the crown, just as I lost a husband.'

Lady Kent sighed. 'You forget I had no more cause to love King Richard. He killed my brother Arundel, and for no reason but spite sent my other brother the Archbishop into exile. We cannot build our lives on hatred, Constance. We must make the best of what we have, we women especially. I wish I could understand you. You had my son, who adored you, and through your folly you have lost him, and all else besides.'

'He is still my husband, whatever he thinks of me. Perhaps in time he will begin to understand.'

'Your husband?' Alice's eyebrows flicked upwards for a moment, and she extended a sympathetic hand towards Constance. 'My dear girl, I know that was intended, but now it can never be.'

'We took vows together.'

'Mun denies it.'

'Before witnesses.'

'What witnesses?'

Constance opened her mouth to speak, and realised that one of them, Thomas Mowbray, had been silenced forever. The other, Antonine, was scarcely likely to support her, and scarcely likely to be credited even if she did. 'Your daughter, Lady March, knows the truth. I stayed with her when I lay in with Mun's child.'

Alice's face twisted with sorrow. 'Have you not been told? Alianore died this summer, in child-bed.'

'Alianore? Alianore is dead? She cannot be!'

'She bled to death. It was God's will—nothing could save her.'

Constance was stunned into silence. Alianore had been a frustrating friend at times, but a dear friend nonetheless. This new loss, piled on so many others, was too much to bear. She felt the first tear sliding from her eye and down her cheek, the precursor of many she would shed for Lady March.

'My dear,' said Alice, 'the pain will pass. Nor is there any cause for shame. You are not the first to make a mistake with a man. It is in our sinful nature. I know it is hard for you to believe, but I was young once. There were many who admired me, and a few I favoured. Your father among them.'

'My father?' Constance could scarcely credit her ears.

'Yes. Do you find it so hard to believe? He was a very handsome man in those days, and he was always kind and gentle. You know that my lord was his friend, and you must remember how often we were at Fotheringhay. There was a short time when your father and I were as close as a man and woman can be. You were young of course, six or seven, or thereabouts. You would not have realised that we were lovers, though I think your mother knew. Edmund was godfather to my son, but the truth was that he was rather more than that.'

Constance felt a cold chill running down the length of her backbone. She could scarcely breathe, let alone talk. 'Do I understand you aright?'

'My son Kent is your brother, almost certainly. That is what I shall swear to a church court if you demand him for your husband.'

'I do not believe you. You lie!'

Alice shook her head. 'I ought to have spoken long before this. It has sat on my conscience ever since he first told me that he intended to wed you. I hoped against hope that he would change his mind.'

'But what of Joanne? Your daughter! You let her marry my father!'

'Why not? She was not of his getting, and I knew that he would make her a good and gentle husband. Such men are rare prizes.'

Constance scarcely knew which horror to consider first. She tried to speak, but found there were no words, and settled back in silence, aware of the tears pricking at her eyes, and of an immense emptiness within her, so bleak, so devoid of comfort, that she wanted to howl like an anguished animal.

Alice shared her silence for a long time, watching her with her kindly blue-grey eyes. 'I think it may be for the better, my poor child. Mun is no husband for you—he would make your life a living hell. Let him go. There are, after all, many advantages to widowhood.' She paused again for a moment. 'The King has arranged a marriage for him, to the Lady Lucia of Milan. She has a great dowry, and he will be able to pay off his debts. I shall see to it that he makes proper provision for your daughter.'

***

John Ashford walked before Constance down the steep spiral stair, continually looking back to ensure that all was well with her. When they reached the landing at the foot, he bowed low and offered her his arm, and they walked together down the broad steps that opened into a corner of the great hall. Ashford was a small, plump man in his forties, amiable enough as jailers went, but somewhat lacking in conversation. When he did speak, it was with a certain care and circumspection.

'The King, my lady, is much changed since last you saw him. Unwell. I say this so that you are prepared.'

Constance nodded, expecting him to go on, but he did not. They emerged into the hall and found the vast room crowded, many men and a sprinkling of women gathered together in groups, their various conversations combining into a blurred noise that almost drowned out the music that was being played in the minstrel's gallery. She was surprised by the extent to which she had become unused to crowds and to the normal bustle of the court. As one or two glances turned in her direction she grew conscious of her shabby gown and insignificant headdress, reacting to her discomfort by throwing back her head and returning the stares with the best pretence of confidence she could contrive.

Ashford led her right through the crowd and up the stairs at the far end, into the King's apartments. There was a series of interconnecting rooms, each less populated than the last, until a final door opened into a darkened chamber, a lodging lit only by its blazing fire and a pair of candles. Heavy curtains excluded what there was left of the afternoon light.

'Thank you, Ashford,' said a voice she recognised as Bolingbroke's. She saw that he was leaning back against his large, carved chair, a blanket covering his lap and a book sitting unread in his lap.

'Sire?' Ashford seemed puzzled.

'You may leave us. Your duty is done.'

Constance remembered to curtsey, and as she rose from the obeisance she heard the door shut behind her escort. She and Harry were alone.

'Come closer, Cousin,' he said. 'You will see that I am a treat for your eyes.'

She advanced hesitantly, a step at a time.

'Look at me!' he commanded, and she gasped as she obeyed and saw that his face and hands were a mass of ugly pustules and red blotches. He extended one hand towards her, evidently expecting her to put her lips to it. Struggling to conceal her revulsion, she sank into another curtsey, and did so.

'You are a brave woman,' he said, with an admiring guffaw. 'Do you not fear I might have leprosy?'

She stood before him, returning his gaze. 'My life is not precious enough for me to care,' she said.

Harry snorted. 'It isn't leprosy, but half my court believes otherwise, and more than half the people.' He paused, steepling his hands before him. 'So, what is your reason to be weary of life? You are not like me. My flesh is become little more than a prison for my soul. I was a warrior, and now I sometimes lack the strength to lift the food to my mouth. You are as you were. My eyes may be weak, but they see enough to assure me of that.'

Constance did not answer. After a moment he gestured her to sit on the cushioned stool that stood close to his desk. She noticed the portrait of Lucia of Milan standing among his papers, and wondered who the young woman depicted might be, but did not choose to ask.

'I have released your brother from prison and restored his lands,' he said quietly. 'I grew tired of reading petitions from his wife. Besides, the Prince has a use for him in Wales. Or so he says. I dare say that they are already conspiring together, seeking my death or my abdication. Ned has found a new candidate for my throne. One more credible than that Mortimer brat.' He considered her for a moment, and then looked away to the fire. 'I should have had his head cut off, of course, but I could scarcely do that without having you burnt. I found I could not do that, whatever your deserts.'

'I suppose I should thank you for that mercy. A mercy you did not extend to others.' She thought grimly of the locksmith, the Archbishop, and young Mowbray, and shook her head.

'You are my cousin,' he grunted, if that explained it.

'So was that boy, Mowbray.'

He smiled, shaking his head. 'Constance, no one but you would state that truth at such a time as this. I think that is why I have always admired you. In a world of liars and flatterers, your insolence warms my heart.' He paused. 'I have something to ask of you. Do you not think you have fought me long enough? Glyn Dwr is finished now. He will hold on for a few more years, but his end is as inevitable as the sunset. Northumberland is an old, broken man, begging his bread from the Scots. Your brother York is Hal's man now—he knows that March will never be king. Can you go on fighting me alone?'

She shook her head. 'No. You have won, Cousin, and I acknowledge it.'

'Won?' His hands gestured towards the dark corners of the room. 'Behold my kingdom! I live in one sick room or another, hiding from my people lest my face frightens them. Oh, I may be better next week, or next month, but I know I shall return to this, and one day there will be no recovery. I think you have no cause to envy me.'

'It was hatred I felt, not envy. But as I have been persuaded, we cannot live by hate. I can never forget, and I shall never believe that you were right to take the throne. Yet I must stop hating, and try to forgive, before my soul is consumed and I am condemned to a hell more terrible than this one in which I live.' She met his gaze, and almost felt pity for his evident suffering. 'I shall be quite content if you will give me my children, and some means by which to keep them and myself. I shall even pray for your soul, if I chance to outlive you.'

He nodded. 'Erpingham has your belongings in his care. I shall order him to restore them. As for your lands, you may have those too, after the Queen has had the benefit of the Easter rents. I promised her a year's revenue from them. Where will you choose to live? We have won back Glamorgan, you know, though I dare say there is much to build anew.'

'Caversham, I think.'

'Caversham? A peaceful place.'

Constance nodded. It was a home of memories, and she still had sufficient hope to think she might find peace there. She had no other surviving ambition.

'Perhaps I shall visit you, one day,' he said.

They both knew that he would not, that the suggestion he might was mere politeness. As she stood and curtsied, and made her way from the room, Harry realised that it was probable he would never see her again at all, for she had no cause now to come to court, and every reason to avoid it.

After a while he rang his hand bell, and one of his gentleman hurried in to attend him. Harry pointed to the portrait of Lucia on his desk. 'Wrap that in cloth, and give it to the Earl of Kent,' he told the man. 'Say it is my gift.'

Once he was alone again, he rose uncertainly to his feet, and eased himself across the room to another portrait that lay face down on one of the window seats. This one he would not gift away. He would keep it close to him until he died; though even to that last day he would not admit, even to himself or to God, why it mattered to him.

THE END

Historical Notes and "what happened next"

Although *Within the Fetterlock* is a work of fiction, and should not be regarded as a text book, it is largely based upon historical fact, or at least upon my interpretation of it, which is of course not quite the same thing. The politics of Richard II's reign are exceptionally complex. Professional historians still struggle to disentangle the issues, so I do not presume to suppose that I have answered all the questions in this account.

However, some of the most bizarre episodes in the novel are those that are not invented. For example, Richard II really was warned to beware of toads and later saw Bolingbroke wearing a garment decorated with toads; Arundel's body was exhumed in the macabre manner described; John Russell's life was saved by his apparent insanity—from which he soon recovered; the greyhound Math's desertion to Bolingbroke is described by two independent chroniclers.

I have generally followed the known chronology of events, the main exceptions of which I am conscious being a slight change in the time and place of Bolingbroke's initial accusation of Mowbray, and Erpingham's presence at Shrewsbury. The itineraries of Richard II and Henry IV are known, and so those scenes taking place at the royal court are invariably placed where the court was at the time. The movements of other characters, including Constance, are more difficult to track, though I have tried to use such information as is available.

There is no historical evidence for the relationship described between Alianore, Countess of March and Edward of York, or that between Constance and Edmund Mortimer. On the other hand Constance put herself to enormous risk to rescue Alianore's children, and her objective was undoubtedly to take them to Edmund in Wales. It seemed to me that the destiny of the York and Mortimer families was already inextricably linked, and I wanted to explain this in human terms.

Edmund Mortimer starved to death during the siege of Harlech Castle, which fell to the King's forces in February 1409. His wife and children were captured and taken to the Tower, along with Glyn Dwr's wife and various other members of his family. Catrin and all but one of her children are known to have died there. The fate of the remaining child (possibly the only son, Lionel) is unknown but is unlikely to have been prosperous. Glyn Dwr's rising had passed its zenith by this time, and gradually faded away as most of his former supporters deserted him and sought pardons from the Crown. Following his accession Henry V offered pardon to Owain himself, but Glyn Dwr never submitted and his eventual fate and resting place remain unknown. Only one of his sons, Maredudd, survived the war.

The nature of Constance's relationship with Edmund, Earl of Kent, is far from clear. Though he was a Holland, he appears to have been thoroughly loyal to Henry IV, and it seems unlikely that he would have approved of Constance's conspiracy. Kent was killed during a raid on France in 1408, when a crossbow bolt entered his open visor. In the 1430s his daughter by Constance, Alianore, the wife of Lord Audley, claimed that her parents had been married, but this was rejected by Parliament on petition of Kent's heirs, though the verdict of the spiritual courts on the matter (if any) is not known.

As for Constance's other children, her son, Richard, died in 1412 or 1413, having been briefly married to Eleanor Neville, later Countess of Northumberland. Elizabeth (Bess) died young, probably about 1407. It was therefore Isabelle, Thomas's posthumous daughter, who inherited the Despenser estates. She married Lord Abergavenny's son, Richard Beauchamp, in 1411, and widowed, took as her second husband, his cousin and namesake Richard Beauchamp, Earl of Warwick, in 1423. (The same Richard Beauchamp you met in chapter 3 of this book.) She died in 1439. Isabelle's daughter, Anne, Countess of Warwick, was the mother of Anne and Isabel Neville, respectively the wives of King Richard III and his brother George, Duke of Clarence.

Richard of Conisbrough, Constance's younger brother, married Anne Mortimer at some time before 1408, and was made Earl of Cambridge by Henry V. He was executed for his part in the mysterious Southampton Plot of 1415, but his son became the 3rd Duke of York, and, as his mother's heir, inherited the Mortimer lands following the death of Anne's brother, the Earl of March, in 1425. The 3rd Duke's sons ruled as Edward IV and Richard III from 1461–1485.

Edward, second Duke of York, survived long enough to be one of the few Englishmen killed at Agincourt in 1415. He was incredibly fortunate to end his career so honourably, having been accused of high treason on a number of separate occasions. His book, *The Master of Game,* was reprinted in 1904, and is not only full of information about medieval hunting, but reveals something of his personal charm. His bones lie in an Elizabethan tomb at Fotheringhay. His widow Philippa, much his elder, lived until 1431 and lies in Westminster Abbey.

Joanne, Duchess of York, acquired a total of four husbands before her death in 1435. One of them, Lord Scrope, died with her step-son, Richard of Conisbrough, because of his part in the conspiracy against Henry V.

King Henry IV, although not continually incapacitated, suffered bad health for the rest of his life. The exact nature of his illness is still debated, but many of his subjects believed him to be a leper. He died in 1413, in the Jerusalem Chamber of Westminster Abbey, thus fulfilling the prophecy about Jerusalem. His wife Joanna of Navarre survived him by many years, despite a long period of imprisonment following an accusation of witchcraft.

Constance herself, having outlived almost everyone who mattered to her, including both her brothers, died in November 1416, probably at Caversham. She left no will, and it may be that her end was sudden. She was buried in the Choir of Reading Abbey. The abbey was dissolved by Henry VIII, and her tomb was lost.

There is nothing left of Fotheringhay Castle now but earthworks and a few stones, while still less survives of Hanley Castle. The medieval Caversham manor is also long gone, though the BBC World Service broadcasts from what was once Constance's deer park. Cardiff Castle is so changed that Constance would scarcely recognise it. Happily Tewkesbury Abbey survives, and with it the chantries of Isabelle Despenser, and her grandparents, Elisabeth and Edward. The burial places there of Thomas Despenser and his son are marked by simple brass plaques.

Glossary

Affinity	Loosely, those who looked to a lord for leadership and protection. His household, retainers, tenants and general hangers-on.
Armiger	Man entitled to use his own 'coat of arms'.
Austringer	Man employed to train and look after hawks.
Baselard	Long knife, or short sword. Often worn with civilian clothing.
Cognizance	Badge worn (particularly by servants or retainers) to signify attachment to or support for a particular lord. Such badges were also used by the lords themselves as a personal device, for example as a decoration for their property.
Coney	Adult rabbit.
Damosel	(Damsel). Unmarried woman or girl of gentle or noble rank.
Destrier	Horse used for mounted combat—heavy (though not a carthorse!) and extremely valuable.
Dinner	Meal taken at midday, or the late morning.
Douce	Sweet, submissive.
Dower	Settlement of property made upon a widow, traditionally (but not always) a third of her late husband's estate. Retained for the life of the widow, with reversion to her husband's next heir. Sometimes also used as a synonym for 'dowry'.
Entail	Legal settlement which kept land in a family (often with preference for male heirs) and made alienation difficult if not impossible. Usually entailed land was protected from forfeiture for treason.
Esquire	See Squire.
Hobelar	Lightly armed horseman.
Houppelande	Type of gown worn (in different versions) by both genders.
Jennet	Small horse, ridden particularly by ladies.
Jointure	Estate held in common by husband and wife, retained by the survivor for life, and (usually) reverting to the husband's heir.

Livery	Distinctive clothing, etc., worn as an outward sign of attachment to a lord (or guild in the case of merchants); those in a lord's service normally received food, wages, etc., as part of their contract, and the word was inclusive of these and the uniform provided. The word is sometimes also used for the food and drink allocated to an individual.
Lollard	Follower of John Wycliffe. The term 'Lollard' covers a range of opinions broadly hostile to the Catholic Church of the period and, in some cases, to the social order. Used as a term of abuse roughly equivalent to 'Red' in 1950's America.
Malvoisie	A kind of Malmsey wine imported from Crete.
Marcher Lordship	Feudal palatinate in Wales or the adjoining parts of England. The private owner of such a lordship had extensive powers within its boundaries, including most of those, for example rights of justice, which would be exercised by the King in an English county. The royal estates in Wales (the Principality) were effectively Marcher Lordships owned by the Crown, but Wales (as understood today) was not a single political entity.
Mark	Two thirds of a pound (Thirteen shillings and fourpence). An accounting term, not a coin.
Money	It is difficult to give exact comparisons, because the relative value of many items has significantly changed. For example, compared to present values, medieval beer and bread were very cheap, and medieval silk extortionately expensive. It is perhaps useful to say that there were 240 pennies in a pound, and a wage of six pence a day for a skilled worker was relatively generous. A common retaining fee for a knight was £20 per annum. In Constance's era an annual income of 1000 marks—just under £667—was considered to be the minimum endowment for an earldom, and £1000 for a dukedom.
Palfrey	Horse used for riding.
Pattens	Wooden overshoes worn out of doors to protect thin leather soles.
Pavise	Free standing shield used to protect archers.
Pleasance	Pleasure garden or park.
Rere-supper	A late or additional supper—supper itself normally being taken about five o'clock.

Retainer	Man 'retained' by another to follow him in war, attend him to prestigious events and/or to support his causes. Not necessarily a servant in the strict sense. Often more akin to a mercenary.
Sea-Coal	Coal brought by sea to London (and other places.)
Serf	The lowest level of feudal tenant, bound to the lord's land but possessed of customary rights as well as duties. By this period many (if not most) feudal dues had been commuted to money rents and payments. (It should be noted that some serfs were much more prosperous than others. Holdings could range from cottage and garden to the equivalent of a very substantial farm.)
Squire	Young man training to be a knight and attending on a knight or man of armigerious rank unwilling or unable to take on the (expensive) burdens of knighthood.
Stew	Bath house. The public stews were usually brothels and the term was used accordingly.
Tire	Headdress.
Villein	Alternative name for 'serf'.

Printed in the United States
91129LV00004B/1-21/A

9 780972 209113